The Extraordinary Adventures of a Russian Scientist (Volume 2)

also by Brian Stableford:
The New Faust at the Tragicomique
The Shadow of Frankenstein
Sherlock Holmes and the Vampires of Eternity
The Stones of Camelot
The Wayward Muse

also translated and introduced by Brian Stableford:
News from the Moon – The Germans on Venus (*anthologies*)
by Félix Bodin: The Novel of the Future
by Charles Derennes: The People of the Pole
by Paul Féval: Anne of the Isles and Other Legends of Brittany – The Black Coats: 'Salem Street – The Black Coats: The Invisible Weapon – The Black Coats: The Parisian Jungle – The Black Coats: The Companions of the Treasure – John Devil – Knightshade – Revenants – Vampire City – The Vampire Countess – The Wandering Jew's Daughter
by Paul Féval, fils: Felifax, the Tiger-Man
by Octave Joncquel & Théo Varlet: The Martian Epic
by Jean de La Hire: The Nyctalope vs. Lucifer – The Nyctalope on Mars – Enter the Nyctalope
by Gustave Le Rouge: The Vampires of Mars
by Jules Lermina: Panic in Paris
by Marie Nizet: Captain Vampire
by Henri de Parville: An Inhabitant of the Planet Mars
by Gaston de Pawlowski: Journey to the Land of the 4th Dimension
by Pierre-Alexis Ponson du Terrail: The Vampire and the Devil's Son
by Albert Robida: The Clock of the Centuries
by Villiers de l'Isle-Adam: The Scaffold and Other Cruel Tales – The Vampire Soul and Other Sardonic Tales

The Extraordinary Adventures of a Russian Scientist (Volume 2)

by

Georges Le Faure & Henri de Graffigny

translated, annotated and introduced by

Brian Stableford

A Black Coat Press Book

English adaptation, introduction and afterword Copyright © 2009 by Brian Stableford.

Cover illustration Copyright © 2009 by Jean-Pierre Normand.

ISBN 978-1-934543-82-5. First Printing September 2009. Published by Black Coat Press, an imprint of Hollywood Comics.com, LLC, P.O. Box 17270, Encino, CA 91416. All rights reserved. Except for review purposes, no part of this book may be reproduced or transmitted in any form or by any means, electronic or mechanical, including photocopying, recording, or by any information storage and retrieval system, without permission in writing from the publisher. The stories and characters depicted in this novel are entirely fictional. Printed in the United States of America.

The story so far

Gontran de Flammermont, a French diplomat attached to the embassy in St. Petersburg in 1880, falls in love with Selena, the daughter of the astronomer Mikhail Ossipoff, and goes to the scientist's house to ask for her hand in marriage. When Selena tells her father that a Monsieur de Flammermont is coming, Ossipoff, distracted by the fact that he has just discovered a new an unprecedentedly powerful explosive, initially jumps to the conclusion that the man in question must be the famous French astronomer of that name, and is so delighted with the prospect of her marrying a fellow scientist that she feels obliged to pass of her would-be fiancé as a relative of his namesake, with similar interests. In fact, Gontran has no interest in science, but he goes along with the pretence because he wants to marry Selena.

With Selena's help, Gontran bluffs his way through the initial interview with Ossipoff, but his difficulties increase when the astronomer whisks him away to Pulkova Observatory in order to observe the Moon. In order to illustrate his passion, Gontran declares that he would go to the ends of the universe, if necessary, to have Selena as his bride. When they come back from the observatory, however, Ossipoff is arrested as a suspected nihilist. He has been denounced by one of his colleagues, Fedor Sharp, who is avid to get his hands on Ossipoff's new discovery—which he, like Ossipoff, wants to use to effect a journey to the Moon, by means of a cannon like the one described by Jules Verne in *From the Earth to the Moon.*

Ossipoff is exiled to Siberia, where he is pressed into service as a bookkeeper in a mine. Meanwhile, Gontran recruits the aid of his old school-friend, the scientific genius Alcide Fricoulet, in order to mount a rescue attempt. Selena grows impatient while waiting for Fricoulet to complete the new type of aeroplane with whose the rescue is to be carried out, and sets of for Siberia alone, thus having to be rescued along with her father when Gontran and Fricoulet finally make the journey. Selena then extracts a promise from Fricoulet that he will help to support Gontran's imposture for as long as necessary.

Caught in a violent storm as it heads for Paris, Fricoulet's aeroplane eventually crashes near Nice Observatory. There, Ossipoff learns that Sharp has sold his plans to a joint stock company organized by the American millionaire Jonathan Farenheit, who has made his fortune in the pork-fat business. Farenheit's plans are well-advanced, but Gontran naively suggests that Ossipoff might still be able to reach the Moon first by making use of the volcano Cotopaxi as a natural cannon, if Fricoulet can built a shell to carry him there.

Fricoulet cannot take the project seriously, but agrees to build the shell with money provided by Ossipoff, who was lucky enough to be given a hoard of precious gems by a fellow convict prior to his escape. Fricoulet continues as

Gontran's tutor in his masquerade as a scientist, and Ossipofff is fooled to the extent of believing that Gontran is the inventive genius while Fricoulet is merely a conceited engineer who keeps trying to steal his friend's thunder. When Gontran sets off to reconnoiter Cotopaxi, Fricoulet expects him to send back a message regretting that the project is impossible, but instead receives a summons to bring the shell.

While *en route* to Cotopaxi, Fricoulet and Ossipoff witness the blast-off of the rival shell, and find Farenheit in great distress, having been cheated by Sharp, who has stolen the missile and set off to claim the glory of being the first man on the Moon for himself, in company with one of his assistants, Voriguin. The volcano is adapted to serve as a cannon while a predicted eruption is in preparation, and Ossipoff eventually sets off in pursuit, in company with Gontran—who is being held to his reckless promise—Selena, Fricoulet, and Farenheit. They catch up with Sharp, whose own shell has been becalmed in a "neutral zone" where the gravity of the Earth and the Moon cancel one another out—a circumstance that already bought Sharp and Voriguin to the point of planning to murder one another, in order to stretch their supplies a little further.

The near-collision of the two shells permits their mutual gravitational attraction to drag Sharp's out of the neutral zone, and both fall on the Moon. Ossipoff and his companions fall on the side invisible from the Earth, which has a localized atmosphere; there they make contact with the Selenites, giant humanoids whose civilization is much older than the human one. With a Selenite named Telinga as their tutor and guide, Ossipoff's party make a tour of the far side of the Moon in relative comfort, but they have to make an excursion to the airless near side in order to obtain a supply of an element unknown on Earth, which is attracted to light and which ought be able to lift their shell from the lunar surface and allow it to be navigated sunwards to make a landfall on Venus.

Ossipoff's party runs into trouble in the stormy zone between the far side an the near side, but they succeed in gathering supplies of the necessary element with the aid of "respirols"—crude space-suits—and also find Sharp's shell, which has crashed in such a fashion that it was impossible for its occupants to get out. They find that Sharp is still alive, although comatose, having kept himself alive by killing and cannibalizing Voriguin. They take him back to their lunar base, but when he wakes up during their temporary absence, he immediately makes for the shell that has been carefully fitted out for its voyage to Venus. When the shell's owners attempt to prevent him from stealing it he kidnaps Selena and inflicts a near-fatal injury on Farenheit by means of a grenade.

All the humans seem doomed by virtue of the theft of their supplies, but Ossipoff succeeds in synthesizing food from chemical elements available on the Moon. Telinga then reveals that the Selenites have long been in desultory communication with the inhabitants of Venus, by means of electromagnetic signals, and that they once built a spacecraft capable of utilizing the same waves as a means of propulsion, although the scheme was abandoned. The spacecraft in question is taken out of mothballs and refitted to enable Ossipoff, Gontran, Fricoulet and Farenheit to set off in pursuit of Sharp. Again, in spite of terrible difficulties experienced during the voyage—which force them to abandon the selenium sphere that serves as their spacecraft's propulsion unit in collaboration with the waves beamed from the Moon—they contrive to reach their goal, splashing down in the vast Venusian ocean only a few days after Sharp's arrival there.

Although Venusian civilization lags some way behind its Earthly equivalent, the planet's near-human inhabitants have found it necessary to invent primitive submarines, and one of these picks up the shipwrecked Terrans. They are taken to land, where they eventually obtain an audience with a king to whose palace a mysterious object recently arrived from space has been taken. Unfortunately, it turns out to be the selenium sphere formerly attached to their own craft rather than Sharp's shell, and they are forced to improvise a means of making use of it again in order to pursue Sharp further sunwards.

Again, the interplanetary voyagers run into trouble when the propulsive waves transmitted from Venus are interrupted, and they seem likely to fall into the Sun, but they manage to reach Mercury, a primitive world devoid of humanoid inhabitants. They find Selena there, abandoned by Sharp lest her weight inconvenience the progress of his shell, but the scoundrel has already set off again and they have no means of following him. Indeed, it seems that they might all die imminently when they discover a comet hurtling toward them—but the comet strikes the planet at such an acute angle that it merely carried away the portion of its surface on which the Terrans and their seemingly-useless craft are stranded (rather like the Earth-striking comet in Verne's *Hector Servadac*). Although the comet's native environment will not support life, the captured fraction of Mercury's surface retains its own component of breathable atmosphere.

Gontran falls out with Ossipoff after recklessly making reference to the planet Vulcan, which Ossipoff believes to be non-existent in spite of numerous reported sightings in the wake of its predicted existence by Urbain Le Verrier, on the same basis that he employed to anticipate the existence and calculate the position of Uranus. Gontran then sets out to find the planet, and appears to do so—but it turns out that what he has actually seen is Sharp's shell, which then crashes on the cometary surface. With the aid of respirols, Fricoulet and Gontran rescue Sharp, and agree to let him live if he will support Gontran's cause by falsely confirming the existence of Vulcan. Gontran, who has been trying to maintain his pretence by cribbing from one of his namesake's books, needs all the support he can get, as most of what he reads and much of what Fricoulet tells him conspicuously fails to stick.

As the comet carries the celestial voyagers away from the Sun towards its aphelion in the vicinity of Saturn's orbit, Ossipoff looks forward to a long sojourn there and a chance to observe the planets beyond Earth's orbit. Fricoulet, however, formulates a plan to use the selenium sphere as a balloon to make a relatively short journey between the comet and Earth as it crosses that orbit. That plan does not work out, but is cleverly reformulated as the comet approaches the orbit of Mars.

Farenheit, who still harbors murderous intentions toward Sharp, falls out with him yet again over a huge piece of diamond found on the comet, with which the millionaire hopes to recover his losses but which Sharp judges too heavy to be transported in the makeshift balloon's gondola. When the time comes to take off, however, Farenheit takes the diamond and saves the necessary weight by stranding Sharp on the comet. Even so, the descent to Mars goes awry and the balloon is forced to land on Phobos instead. There, a further accident results in it being carried aloft again, with only Fricoulet aboard.

Stranded on Phobos with limited supplies of air, Ossipoff, Farenheit, Selena and Gontran seem yet again to be doomed, but they are rescued in the nick of time by a Martian vessel commandeered by Fricoulet, who has contrived to reach the planet's surface. Fricoulet explains to his companions that Martian civilization is not only older than Earth's, but far more advanced technologically, scientific discovery having been its primary motive force for a long time. This leads Ossipoff to look forward to their arrival there with keen anticipation—an anticipation that the reader will doubtless share…

Chapter XXXIV
The Warrior Planet

"On landing on this new world, the first impression received by our mind is not very different from the impression that the spectacles of nature impose upon us. We find ourselves transported to a world strangely analogous to ours. The edges of its seas receive, as they do here, the eternal plaint of the waves that break and die on the shore—for there, as here, the breath of the wind wrinkles the face of the waters and gives birth to waves that follow one another and fall back. If the sky is pure and the atmosphere calm, the mirror of the waters reflects, as it does here, the dazzling Sun and the luminous sky.

"The European villager who, cast up by the wave of emigration on the shores of Australia, wakes up one fine day in the midst of an unknown country where the soil, the trees, the animals, the seasons and the courses of the Sun and the Moon are very different in appearance from what he has previously seen in his native land, is no less surprised and lost than we are on arriving in the planet Mars. To be transported from the Earth to Mars is simply to change latitude."[1]

Thus, with regard to the planet on which our voyagers were landing, the celebrated propagator of astronomical science expresses himself—and Gontran, analyzing his own sensations, could not help recognizing how concordant they were with the thoughts contained in the passage from *Les Continents célestes* reproduced above.

It was night when a sign from the Martian who appeared to be the captain of the vessel invited them to come out of the gondola, and the entire landscape surrounding the Terrans was immersed in profound darkness. Here and there, however, thicker shadows stood out, confused but intriguing by virtue of their mass or their height. Our voyagers' eyes strained in vain to pierce the obscurity. The only thing of which they were truly conscious was a sheet of water that extended to their feet, making soft sounds like those of the minuscule waves of our Mediterranean impelled by a spring breeze. In the water, as in a burnished silver mirror, the sky was reflected, with its myriad sparkling stars. One might have thought it a silken cloth sprinkled with gold.

Instinctively, our friends looked up.

"But the sky hasn't changed!" Gontran exclaimed. "There are the same stars, the same constellations...that one sees from the Paris Observatory."

Ossipoff turned to him enthusiastically, retorting: "The same stars, perhaps...but the same planets?" By the tone in which these few words were pronounced, the young Comte scented an ambush, and prudently uttered a little dry

---

[1] This quotation is an abridged version of the first paragraph of Chapter II of *Les Terres du ciel*, pp.20-21.

cough to attract Fricoulet's attention—but the engineer was much too busy studying the maneuvering of the balloon to think about his friend, so the latter's embarrassment increased.

With his nose in the air and his gaze fixed on the starry vault, Gontran slowly pivoted on his heels, summoning to his aid all the gods with whom mythology had been pleased to populate the sidereal immensity. The gods were doubtless asleep, though, for no inspiration came to the unfortunate ex-diplomat. Suddenly, though, a voice as light as a breath whispered behind him: "Over there, on your right...Jupiter, then Saturn...and then on the other side...the Earth."

Meanwhile, astonished by the incomprehensible silence, Ossipoff uttered a "Well?" replete with suspicion.

As if gripped by a dream, Flammermont shivered. He passed his hand over his forehead, redirected his gaze to the old man and said, in a vibrant voice: "Excuse me, Monsieur...but the sight of my native planet evoked memories that took entire possession of my mind."

"Only memories?" asked Selena.

"Naughty!" he replied, taking her hand and kissing it affectionately. "Not only memories, but hopes too...since it's there alone that our happiness will become complete..."

Ossipoff coughed lightly, for he was always rather embarrassed when Gontran made allusion to his problematic marriage to Selena. Then, to change the subject, he pointed toward the brilliant star. "In truth," he said, "would one not swear that one were looking at Venus? It's the same soft light...the same situation..."

"We probably play the same role for Mars?"

"If, by that, you mean that the Earth is the Martian evening star, you're right."

"Evening?" said Jonathan Farenheit. "Do you think that star you're admiring is an evening star?" And, without waiting for a reply, he held up his chronometer. "It's 1:30 p.m. in New York," he said, after a momentary pause.

"6 p.m. in St. Petersburg," added Selena

"5 p.m. in Paris," said Gontran, in his turn.

"With the result that it's 4 a.m. in the morning here," concluded Mikhail Ossipoff. "You're right, Mr. Farenheit."

"Isn't that the Earth, then?" stammered Gontran.

"What's problematic about that? Isn't Venus both an evening and morning star for us? It precedes the dawn and follows the dusk...it depends..."

"Yes," Gontran repeated, mechanically. "It depends..."

"Depends on what?" Farenheit asked him.

The young Comte found himself suddenly embarrassed, all the more so because Mikhail Ossipoff was staring at him. Instinctively, he leaned backwards to put his ear within rang of Selena's lips. Then, straightening up, he replied: "It depends on the seasons, of course, my dear Mr. Farenheit. We've been leading such a singular life for so long that I scarcely know what month it is."

"It's May," replied Ossipoff. "May 8. Yesterday, the Earth was at its greatest occidental elongation, 37 degrees and 37 minutes, and it will remain the morning star until October."

Oof! thought Flammermont, uttering a slight sigh. *That's the Q.E.D. of the problem. This oral exam is interminable.*

Fricoulet arrived at that moment. "My friends," he said, "we'll get under way, if you're ready."

"Where to?" the Terrans immediately asked, with one voice.

"To the City of Light, as the planet's capital is called."

"And is your City of Light far from here?" asked Farenheit, already alarmed by the prospect of making use of his legs.

"If I've understood Aotaha's summary explanations..." Fricoulet began.

Gontran interrupted him. "Who's Aotaha?" he asked.

"A very friendly and learned Martian whose acquaintance I have made, and who seems to fulfill the role, on this planet, of Grand-Master of the University."

Flammermont could not help emitting a short burst of mocking laughter. "If you've understood, you say; do these people talk, then, as one does on the Boulevard Montparnasse?"

"Pooh!" said the engineer, with a moue of disdain. "It's a long time since the Martians left syntax and everything connected with it behind; time being, for them, the most precious thing in the world, they've sought a linguistic system permitting the expression of thought as rapidly as it springs to mind."

"A sort of stenographic language?"

"Precisely; the five vowels serve as the basis for this very simple system, in such a way that, according to the tone in which they are pronounced, they express some thought or another."[2]

"But that gives them a very restricted vocabulary," Mademoiselle Ossipoff objected. "Remember that the voice only has two and a half octaves—which gives, by its division into semitones, a total of 30 different sounds. These people would only have very imperfect means to express their thoughts."

The engineer smiled. "You can't be unaware, Mademoiselle," he replied, "that it's vibration that forms sounds; thus, the deepest note of the human voice corresponds to 160 vibrations, while the most elevated is 2048. Well, in going from 160 to 2048, the sound is modified by each added vibration, which gives 1888 different sounds. You see that the Martian language is richer than you think."

---

[2] The reader might wonder how "Aotaha" and the other Martian names subsequently recorded in the text are derived from this system; Fricoulet is however, rather economical with his explanations.

"What you say is quite accurate," Flammermont riposted. "Unfortunately, the human ear is unable to grasp such subtle nuances."

"The human ear, agreed—but these people's ears are subject, from birth, to an education that even permits them, after a certain number of years, to achieve a truly marvelous perception. Young Martians are taught to distinguish the vibrations that compose a sound just as we learn to discover the subtle beauties contained in a text by Virgil, Homer or any other ancient author."

"But we have grammars, dictionaries and a whole host of instruments..."

"Just as they do..." The engineer took a rather singular apparatus out of his coat; it resembled a helmet ornamented on each side by who appendages similar to the funnels of hunting-horns. "This," he said, "is what infants of the most tender age carry; these shell-like items, made of a metal that has the property of vibrating with extreme facility, are fitted over the ears and transmit the vibrations stored within them to the eardrums. As the child grows, the size of the shells diminishes, to disappear entirely when education is complete."

With an easily-imaginable curiosity, the Terrans studied the bizarre instrument, which each of them tried out in turn.

"Myself," said Gontran, rather ironically, "I find that it distorts speech."

"Because we don't make use, as these people do, of monosyllables to render our thoughts; the vibrations of each of our speech-acts are confused with one another."

"Ending up as an incomprehensible cacophony," said Farenheit.

"And you already understand what they're saying?" asked Selena, ready to fall at the engineer's feet in admiration.

"Oh!" the latter replied. "You have too high an opinion of my intelligence—which is to say that the excellent Aotaha, with a patience beyond all praise, has enabled me to make use with him a sort of pidgin, by pronouncing certain monosyllables and then showing my the object to which he is referring. I only know the ABC of the Martian language; as for the theory I've just outlined, I deduced it from what I could understand of Aotaha's language."

"Well, old chap," said Flammermont, "from this day forward I nominate you as my private interpreter...for I've never had a liking for vocalization exercises, having always had a tin ear."

"To get back to your City of Light," said the American, "you were saying..."

"That the city is located at the extremity of the continent Kepler, on the 195th degree of longitude."

The American uttered a dull groan. "That's all very well—but first, where are we?"

"Not far from the Lake of the Sun, on the continent that Schiaparelli baptized with the name Thaumasia."

"Which is to say," added Ossipoff, "on the 90th degree of longitude. We have, therefore, about 105 degrees to travel...which is 6800 kilometers."

"I'll never do that on foot," Farenheit complained.

"Who said anything about that?" asked Fricoulet. "We have a vehicle ready, and if you'd care to follow me..."

Marching on the engineer's heels, the Terrans moved back toward the place where the national balloon had set them down. To their great surprise, they saw the gondola in which they had made the crossing from Phobos to Mars standing on rails of some sort. The enormous cylinder that had surmounted it had disappeared, however, along with the propeller and the rudder. As it now was, it had the exact appearance of a gigantic shell—or, rather, a monumental Lebel rifle bullet.[3] Its tip was directed toward a metallic mass about ten meters high and as many wide, which had suddenly extended from the ground to an extent of 30 or 40 meters.

"Devil take me!" said Farenheit, who had approached the monstrous apparatus and was examining it closely. "It's highly reminiscent of the breech of a cannon."

As he finished these words, a sort of electric bell rang and the object that the American had just compared to the breech of a cannon opened up, displaying a profound cavity sparkling with light. Taken by surprise at first, the Terrans took a step backwards.

"What's that?" murmured Selena, in a fearful voice.

"Nothing very frightening, Mademoiselle," replied the engineer.

"What, then?"

"I've told you about the inestimable value that time has in the Martians' eyes. You'll not be astonished to learn, therefore, that all their efforts tend to shorten distances—which is to say, to travel the said distances as rapidly as possible."

"Don't their wings enable them to do that?" objected Farenheit.

"Just so—but because their muscular force isn't much greater than ours, relatively speaking, they can't accomplish much more in flying long distances than we Terrans could by walking. They have therefore been obliged to invent systems of locomotion...and this is one of them, which will transport us to the City of Light."

"That doesn't explain..." said Selena.

"Listen," said Fricoulet. "You know the pneumatic system that transports dispatches enclosed in little vessels resembling rifle bullets through a network of underground tubes? What you see here is a system of locomotion based on the same principle..."

---

[3] The Lebel Model 1886 rifle, introduced in that year, had a distinctive "boat-tailed" bullet. The narrative voice is probably entitled to make the comparison for the benefit of its 1889 readers, even though the scene is set in 1884.

Mademoiselle Selena's slightly anxious face cleared as if by magic; without waiting any longer, she leapt on to the platform of the gondola with a single bound and disappeared inside.

Less than two minutes had elapsed since Fricoulet, who was bringing up the rear, had rejoined his companions, when a dull noise was audible outside.

"That's the doors of the tube closing again," the engineer replied, to the mute interrogation in Selena's eyes.

For a few moments, a profound silence reigned in the cabin; each of them, absorbed in personal reflections, was silent.

Farenheit was the first to speak. "One thing that astonishes me, my dear Monsieur Ossipoff," he said, "is that this world, which the Creator has endowed with two satellites, should be worse lit by night than the Earth, which has but one."

"One thing that astonishes me more," retorted the old scientist, with a smile full of condescension, "is your astonishment. Two reasons, in fact, prevent Mars from receiving a very bright light from its satellites. The first is the distance that separates Mars from the Sun, which appears to the planet only in the form of a circle 21 millimeters in diameter, whereas its disk, seen from Earth, is between 31 and 32 millimeters...an appreciable difference, you'll agree."

"I agree to that, but you'll also agree that the difference might be counterbalanced by the proximity of the satellites to the planet they ought to illuminate. While the Moon orbits the Earth at 90,000 leagues, Phobos traces its orbit at 6000 kilometers and Deimos at 20,000...that's also appreciable."

Ossipoff nodded his head. "Undoubtedly!" he said. "But you're forgetting one thing, which is that, even at 6000 kilometers, the disk of Phobos is no larger than seven minutes, and that of Deimos only two minutes; that of the Moon is 31—which is to say, three and 15 times larger..."

"And in conclusion from these figures," Fricoulet said, in his turn, "do you know how much difference of light-intensity those differences of distance give? As the light received from the Sun varies according to the position of Mars, the result is that the brightness of Deimos is between 1/400 and 1/675 of our moonlight and that of Phobos between 1/45 and 1/67. Is that clear?"

"Clearer than the light of the Martian satellites," Farenheit replied, laughing, "but if they don't serve as illumination, what are they useful for?"

"Regulating clocks and longitudes with remarkable precision, thanks to the rapidity of their rotation," Gontran replied, half in jest and half seriously.

Fricoulet wagged a finger at him. "That's not yours," he whispered in his ear.

"Not mine!" relied the young Comte, almost offended.

"You memorized *Les Continents célestes* with such great ardor that you've ended up appropriating its contents and, without being conscious of it, offering us the theories of your illustrious namesake as your own..."

"That's quite possible," muttered Flammermont.

"Now then!" cried the American, suddenly. "Will we be leaving soon?" He consulted his chronometer and added: "It's nearly 20 minutes since we got in, and we haven't budged."

"There's every chance that we've arrived," replied Fricoulet, seeing the door open and Aotaha beckoning to him from the threshold.

There was a rapid and animated dialogue between the Terran and the Martian, mingled with expressive gestures on the part of the latter and curt monosyllables pronounced with bizarre intonations on the part of the former.

Afterwards, the engineer came back to his companions. "I guessed right," he said. "We've arrived."

"Arrived where?" asked Gontran. "At the City of Light?"

"No, we've only traveled 400 kilometers and we're on the shore of the Lake of the Sun."

"Or Terby Sea," Ossipoff rectified.

The America's amazement was profound. "But that's magical," he stammered. "We didn't experience any shock on departure or arrival...even better, we heard neither the rolling of wheels or the friction of the vehicle's walls against those of the tube."

"There's a very simple explanation for that," replied the engineer, smiling. "First, the vehicle has no wheels; second, its walls have no point of contact with those of the tube in which it circulates."

"That's a fairy tale!" exclaimed Flammermont, involuntarily. "You want us to believe that our vehicle is suspended in the middle of the tube without touching it at any point?"

"I don't want you to believe it—I affirm it."

"What about the wind?" added Flammermont. "What do you do about that? If things were as you say, the compressed air propelling the vehicle would pass into empty space and there'd be a considerable loss of force."

The engineer shrugged his shoulders and replied: "Your argument lacks common sense; even so, when I have a minute to spare, I'll refute it. For the moment, we have to disembark."

As he spoke, he went to stand underneath the aperture pierced in the cabin's ceiling and, with a slight thrust of his feet, leapt outside. At that moment, the Sun appeared over the horizon, and its golden darts split the somber mantle of the night, causing a liquid immensity whose surface was rippled by a slight breeze to sparkle before the Terrans' marveling eyes.

"The Lake of the Sun!" exclaimed Mikhail Ossipoff, in a ringing voice. With his elbows on the rampart, he sank into ecstatic contemplation.

Meanwhile, with a curiosity not exempt from suspicion, his companions examined a host of individuals similar to Aotaha, who were surrounding the vehicle, pressing together, jostling one another and pointing at the strange beings gathered on the footbridge, with forceful gestures and exclamations.

"Great God!" moaned Selena. "Just as long as they don't come any closer."

"Don't be afraid, Mademoiselle," said Fricoulet. "Curiosity alone impels them."

"It's singular," Gontran murmured, "that the extreme civilization you claim for this advanced Martian race doesn't render them more beautiful than they are."

"And why do you expect this world to be different from our own? To take but one example, compare our ancestors, the ancient Frankish warriors, with the coxcombs that we are."

"So you say," Gontran retorted, jokingly. "Speak for yourself."

"Assuredly," said Selena, "I don't find Monsieur de Flammermont to be as much of a coxcomb as you might think..."

The engineer shrugged his shoulders casually. "Just put a heap of weapons into his arms, and chain-mail from the Middle Ages on his torso, and you'll see how freely and easily he carries himself."

"What are you getting at?" asked Flammermont, in a bittersweet voice, not very pleased at being subjected to ridicule in the presence of his fiancée.

"I'm trying to make you understand that the more a race advances in civilization, the more it atrophies...the brain monopolizes vigor, to the detriment of the rest of the body."

At that moment, Ossipoff released a cry of terror. A host of those strange creatures had suddenly risen from the ground, spiraling in the air above and around the group formed by the Terrans. One might have taken them for a flock of immense birds, whose wings beat the air almost silently.

At a gesture from Aotaha, all that ceased, as if by magic. Folding their wings, their curiosity doubtless satisfied, the Martians drew away.

"Our guide is signaling to us to follow him," said Fricoulet, touching Ossipoff on the shoulder.

The latter raised his head and saw Aotaha—who, deploying his wings, flew rapidly down to the ground.

"Follow him!" muttered the old scientist, his mind still full of the dreams he had been entertaining. "That's easy to say—but how?"

"By the same route!" retorted Gontran. Tensing his leg, the young man jumped over the side and landed lightly beside the Martian. One by one, his companions did likewise.

Moored to the shore, a singularly-shaped boat was bobbing. It attracted the attention of the Terrans, especially Fricoulet, who ran to it in a few strides. "Hey!" he exclaimed, summoning his companions with cries and forceful gestures. "Hey! It's Raoul Pictet's apparatus!"

"What do you mean by that?" asked Ossipoff.

"I mean an apparatus equipped at the rear, like this one, with a vast plane surface forming a keel, permitting the boat to glide over the surface like a sleigh over ice."

"A boat on skates, then!" said Gontran.

"Very nearly."

"And what results from that?" asked Farenheit.

"Considerable speed—something like 40 or 50 knots."

"That's prodigious."

"I don't know whether it's prodigious," Gontran said, in his turn, "but it's a very graceful navigation apparatus, at any rate."

And he was certainly right; the bow, highly elevated above the waves, was curved in the fashion of the gondolas plying the Venetian lagoons; the rounded stern rested on the vast triangular platform spread out over the liquid sheet like a gigantic peacock's tail. On the poop and along a third of its length stood a cockpit pieced by portholes, and a floor had been built on to that cockpit at prow level, forming a second deck—which was itself covered by a light roof designed to protect the passengers from the ardor of the Sun. In the posterior section of this deck, enclosed by the boat itself and partly resting on the cabin on the lower floor, was a launch, which a simple spring could dispatch into the water in a matter of seconds.

Once the Terrans had taken their places aboard this strange vessel, Aotaha gave a signal. Driven by a propeller set beneath the launch in the middle of the platform, the boat drew away from the shore. As Fricoulet had explained, it skimmed the crests of the waves like a seabird, with incredible velocity, without any pitching. In less than an hour, the coast disappeared over the horizon.

"At this rate," murmured Ossipoff, who had unfolded one of Schiaparelli's maps, "we'll have crossed the entire width of the ocean before nightfall."

"Do you know that the width in question is 600 kilometers?" Flammermont asked.

"If you'll take the trouble to make the calculation," the old scientist retorted, "you'll see that I'm not exaggerating."

All day they glided over the waves without any incident breaking the monotony of the voyage. Ossipoff, whose eyes never quit the map, declared that they must be approaching the equator, not far from Schiaparelli's Nodus Gordii.

The Sun, almost at its zenith, directed its rays vertically, and the heat was fearsome. Suddenly, there seemed to be an extraordinary animation aboard. The Martian crew, grouped on the deck, were arguing enthusiastically and pointing into the distance as a point invisible to the Terrans, but which the Martians, with their acuity of vision, could make out clearly.

"An accident, no doubt," grumbled Farenheit. "You'll find that we'll be obliged to continue the journey on foot."

"We'd have to begin by continuing it by swimming," Gontran retorted.

"I don't know," Ossipoff murmured, shaking his head, "but all that fuss doesn't augur anything good."

Fricoulet, who had gone to find Aotaha at the very first moment, came back with a grave expression, seemingly annoyed. On catching sight of him,

Gontran exclaimed, jokingly: "Here he is, his misfortunes written on his brow/He has the face and the manner of the first to fall."[4]

"Given that my misfortunes are yours too," complained the engineer, "I think it's ungracious of you to mock."

"Really? What's happened?"

"We can't go any further."

There was a general exclamation. "No further!" said Ossipoff. "Now then, what sort of joke is this?"

"It's not a joke—the canal is closed."

"The canal!" cried Farenheit. "What canal are you talking about?"

"The one we're on, of course."

"This is a canal?" exclaimed the American, indicating with a sweep of his hand the sheet of water that extended as far as the eye could see in every direction."

"Yes, a canal…a simple canal 500 kilometers long."

Farenheit stood still, his eyes wide and his mouth wide open, so profound was his amazement.

Gontran, no less astonished, hid his amazement beneath an apparent indifference. "Admit, my dear Mr. Farenheit," said the engineer, clapping the American on the shoulder amicably, that Suez and Panama are child's play by comparison with this canal."

"But you can't persuade me that this ocean—for I persist in giving it that name—was hollowed out by the hand of man!"

"It's necessary, though, that I make you believe it, since it's the truth. Besides, you'll be able to convince yourself with your own eyes before long. They're in the process of hollowing out one at right angles to it, and that's why we can't go on."

Ossipoff had abandoned his companions and gone up to the bridge in order to be the first to establish, with his own eyes, the truth about the famous Martian canals—one of the largest question marks posed by the scientists of the entire world.

For an hour, the old man waited, his chest constricted, his heart beating rapidly and his eyes obstinately staring into space.

Finally, in the far distance, a vague line appeared, which gradually became distinct, grew, lengthened, and finished up barring the uniformly blue horizon, with a slight tint of yellow ocher. It was the eastern bank of the canal, where the boat was not long delayed in landing.

"Well?" asked Farenheit. "What are we going to do now?"

---

[4] Gontran is quoting from Jean-François Regnard's comedy *Le joueur* [The Gambler] (1696); the dialogue in which it features was often reprinted in collections of homilies, thus becoming familiar to many readers who never saw the play.

"We're going to continue the journey," Gontran replied.

"Like these folk, no doubt," said the American, ironically, pointing to the Martians, who were taking flight on every side.

"Certainly not—*pedibus cum jambis*," riposted the young Comte, who was greatly amused by Farenheit's reluctance to make use of his natural means of locomotion.

Ossipoff intervened. "Before anything else," he said, "I want to see the works of the canal that's being dug at present."

"Another detour that will delay us," grumbled the American.

Without reacting to this manifestation of bad temper, the Terrans set off walking, under the guidance of Aotaha, who fluttered alongside them. Suddenly, they perceived a veritable swarm of living beings tearing formidable masses of earth from the ground, which they were loading on to balloons similar to the one that had searched for the Terrans on Phobos. Enormous machines were running silently, each activated by some sort of thermoelectric pile that transformed solar radiation into electrical energy. As far as the eye could see, they perceived the same swarm, occupied in digging a trench several kilometers wide across the Martian continent.

"A strange notion, to cut their planet up like this," muttered Farenheit.

Meanwhile, Fricoulet was listening in amazement—which grew with every passing second—to the explanations that Aotaha gave him in his laconic language.

"It appears that they're carrying out this gigantic task in anticipation of an imminent war," the engineer said, responding to the American's explanation.

"A war?" cried Ossipoff. "A war, did you way? That scourge, which I considered as the fatal consequence of the state of barbarism into which we are plunged! That terrible, hideous, abominable scourge exists in these lands—which, I thought, had reached the summit of progress and civilization!" And the old man, prey to a strange discouragement, let his head fall into his hands.

In his capacity as an engineer, Fricoulet was prodigiously interested by the works that were being carried out in front of him—before his eyes, so to speak. Suddenly, a question crossed his mind, which he formulated immediately.

"What do you do with all the displaced earth?" he asked the Martian.

"You see those balloons," replied Aotaha. "As soon as they are loaded they depart for Phobos. Phobos was once one of the asteroids that exist between Mars and Jupiter; it was a rock measuring no more than half a league in diameter. When it was captured by our attraction, we thought of utilizing it by establishing a dump there for the waste generated by the digging of the canals."

"Something like a rubbish-tip for the dirt and refuse of a great city," murmured Gontran, for whom his friend had translated the Martian's reply. "But if they go on like that indefinitely, the entire planet will end up being transported to its satellite."

Fricoulet laughed. "Fortunately," he said, "the apogee of these great works has passed."

"How do you know?" asked Flammermont, skeptically.

"Schiaparelli found out for me," the engineer replied. "His studies, during the last conjunction on Mars, revealed to him that the number of canals remained stationary and that..."

His sentence was cut short by an exclamation from Ossipoff. "I deeply regret," the old man said, rubbing his hands together, "that Fedor Sharp is not here. When I think that one day, at the Institute of Sciences, he bored us for several hours in order to prove to us that the Martian canals were nothing but a sort of land-register of collective farms on a globe 'that has attained the era of harmony'!" He paused, rubbing his hands energetically, and added. "What a long face he would have if he knew the bellicose purpose of these works, so peaceful in nature—according to him!" Then, after a second pause, gripped once again by humanitarian ideas, he murmured, bitterly: "So they still make war on Mars!"

Fricoulet, to whom Aotaha had just furnished a long explanation, turned to the old man. "It's not, as you might think, a residuum of barbarism," he told him, "but a fatal, inevitable product of civilization exaggerated to the degree that it has attained on this world."

"That's a paradox, or I don't know one," said Gontran.

"I share Monsieur de Flammermont's opinion," said Farenheit, in his turn.

"Before pronouncing judgment," said Ossipoff, sententiously, "it's necessary to know the facts."

Then, repeating what their guide had said, the engineer explained that war, on the world of Mars, was necessary and indispensable, made by common agreement between the populations of the planet. Several centuries before, at a conference held by delegates of all the Martian nations, the abolition of war had been decided; an international tribunal had been appointed, charged with judging, as a last resort, all the differences that might arise in future between fraternal populations. For a long succession of centuries, the decisions of this tribunal having legal force, the world of Mars lived in unalterable peace and devoted all its efforts to the perfection of arts and sciences, especially sciences, which were solely capable of permitting humanity to reveal the secrets of nature.

Unfortunately, thanks to the progress accomplished in all things, medicine became so powerful that all diseases—all the scourges that had once inflicted terrible but necessary ravages upon the planet—became impotent. There was no need even to combat them; they were prevented. That led to a terrible excess of population. The continents, which began by being too small to nourish all their inhabitants, ended up having an insufficient surface even to contain them. Maritime cities and aerial agglomerations were created; artificial aliments were invented by extracting the nutritive principles indispensable to the renewal of Martian strength from air, water and minerals. Soon, all these expedients became insufficient, and the disasters once produced by war were nothing compared to those that famine engendered.

Then, as had happened several centuries previously, all the nations of the Martian globe sent delegates to a conference in the City of Light; they decided unanimously to re-establish war. As people had been habituated for a long time to consider one another as brothers, however, and, on the other hand, civilization had expelled from the souls of sovereigns all the sentiments that had formerly caused some to take up arms against others, the conference decided to regulate war. It was, in consequence, established that, four times a century, two nations designated in advance by an international assembly would pit themselves against one another, in such a way as to bring the Martian population back to a figure in rapport with the continental surface.[5]

"That's why," Fricoulet said, concluding his story, "every 50 years, after having fixed the number of victims by means a census, the two nations designated by lot are put into a closed field designated for that purpose, and slaughter one another for the good of humankind."

"That's horrible!" said Selena.

"I don't agree with you," the engineer replied. "In these humanitarian wars there are neither victors nor vanquished; the lure of glory doesn't enter into it at all, but only the desire to live—and once the number of victims is achieved, they live in peace, cultivating the arts and sciences until the conference decision brings them face to face again."

"At least, in that fashion," Gontran said in his turn, "those who fight die without ulterior motives, without fear of leaving their home and family at the mercy of a pitiless conqueror."

"Very true," muttered Farenheit, "except that I don't see what the story has to do with the canal."

"The canal is quite simply designed to transport the combatants designated by the supreme tribunal to the battlefield."

A gleam appeared in Flammermont's eye. "So there's going to be a war here quite soon?" he said.

"Next month, according to what our guide told me."

"We'll be here, eh, Mr. Farenheit!" cried the young Comte.

---

[5] The modern reader might think it strange that the highly advanced Martians never thought of birth-control as a humane alternative to mass slaughter (just as modern readers are sometimes surprised that Thomas Robert Malthus, who originated the argument extrapolated here, never mentioned it). The fact is that in both Protestant England in the 1790s and Catholic France in the 1880s, birth control—though widely practiced in both nations—was literally unmentionable in print, especially in a book intended to be read by children as well as adults. Insane and absurd mass murder, by contrast, was perfectly acceptable.

"By God!" growled the American clenching his fists. "It reminds me of the Civil War!"

While talking, the Terrans had started walking in the direction of Holion, an important city where, their guide said, they would find a means of locomotion to transport them to the City of Light.

"Do you see?" Ossipoff suddenly said to Gontran, showing him the map he was holding. "The canal that brought us this far was the Oreus. A few degrees further to the left is the Pyriphlegeton, and we'll cut across the equator in order to descend towards the land of Amazonia."

"I don't know whether we'll cut across the equator," Farenheit muttered between clenched teeth, "but I do know we're cutting across fields and that my legs are exhausted."

They were crossing an immense field, which was not verdant but the color of rust. There were occasional clumps of small trees with orange flowers, bearing clusters of pink or scarlet fruits. The plants that covered the ground with a soft carpet were all red, and their large leaves spread out in marvelously graceful plumes.

"Hey!" Fricoulet murmured in Gontran's ear, as he pointed at this singular vegetation. "Do you understand now why the Martian atmosphere seems red to terrestrial astronomers?" Then, turning to the American, who was whining incessantly, he said: "What's the matter, my dear Mr. Farenheit?"

"I...I...need a road. My feet can't do any more."

Fricoulet laughed. "A road!" he said. "We could, I think, travel all over Mars without finding a single one, given that, for people traveling by water and by air, the ground has no utility from the viewpoint of locomotion."

"I declare," said the American, stopping on the edge of a wide ditch that had to be crossed in a single bound, "that I'm stopping here, even if I have to sleep under the stars."

Ossipoff looked at Selena, who, although she was not complaining, was giving evidence of great fatigue. "Ask the guide," he said to Fricoulet, "whether it would be inconvenient for us to spend the night here. We'll resume the march tomorrow morning."

Aotaha, for whom the engineer translated the old man's question, uttered a few guttural sounds, then deployed his wings and flew off into the sky, which dusk was already darkening.

"Now then!" said Farenheit. "Is he abandoning us?"

"No, he's going to enquire about a means of locomotion, and will return at dawn." As he spoke, the engineer took out the flask of nutritive liquid with which he was equipped—cautious man that he was—and passed it to Selena. "The honor is yours, Mademoiselle," he said.

Chapter XXXV
The truth about the series 4, 7, 10, etc.

The first rays of sunlight were already gilding the high Martian clouds when the voyagers woke up. Some ten meters above their heads, a strange apparatus was suspended, motionless, as if it were attached to the ground by an invisible tether. It was a sort of mast that appeared to be about 15 meters high, and which bore, on its upper section, a helical rotor with eight blades, each of which was at least as large as the sail of a windmill. Above that, on the same prolongation, but around an axle concentric with the first, were two small superimposed helices with only four vanes, turning in the opposite direction to the larger one.

50 centimeters lower down, the two axles went into a sleeve on which metallic arcs were fixed, sustaining a kind of folded tent. Further down, supported by hoops, were ten seats somewhat similar to those of bicycles, with the difference that they were equipped with backs. Finally, the bottom section of the apparatus terminated in two cylinders, doubtless containing the motors operating the rotors, and also activating a horizontally-placed drive-shaft, at each extremity of which was fixed a little paddle-wheel serving as a propeller.

"Either I'm very much mistaken, or that's a helicopter!" cried Fricoulet, who had been looking up for some time studying the machine attentively.

"Helicopter!" murmured Gontran. "I knew that...hang on..." After a pause, elevating his voice in order to be heard by Ossipoff, he said: "Why, of course! It's Ponton d'Amécourt's apparatus."

The old scientist turned round. "You mean Philips' apparatus."

"I beg your pardon," replied the young Comte. "I said Ponton d'Amécourt; I even recall that I was able to see his model...in some museum or other...it was made of aluminum."

"So you've only seen the model," Ossipoff riposted. "Personally, I've seen the apparatus itself. I remember having witnessed the trial of a steam helicopter whose inventor was named Philips; it was in 1845, in Varsovia."

"Come on," declare Fricoulet. "I'll put you in agreement. I've also seen an apparatus very similar to this one, but it was due neither to the inventive genius of Ponton d'Amécourt nor that of Philips; the inventor was the Italian Forlanini." So saying, the engineer flexed his legs, reached the apparatus with a single jump, and took his place there. "A charming country!" he said, leaning over his seat. "Lower the stairways and ladders!"

Gontran and Ossipoff joined him immediately, and were soon followed by Selena, to whom the Martian had gallantly offered a hand, and who had been effortlessly transported to her seat by the guide, with his wings deployed.

That left Farenheit, who considered the strange vehicle suspiciously, his feet nailed to the ground.

"Well?" Flammermont shouted to him. "Aren't you coming up?"

"Those perches are only good for monkeys or parrots," retorted the American.

The young Comte frowned. "So you say, Mr. Farenheit," he muttered. "It seems to me that you're scarcely polite. Besides, do you think that the United States would be more dishonored by your presence than France and Russia are by ours?"

"Anyway," added Fricoulet, "each of us is free to choose the mode of locomotion that suits him. We've chosen the air…you prefer dry land. You're free to do so—but I advise you to stretch your legs if you want to arrive in the City of Light at the same time as us." With that, he made a sign to Aotaha, who pressed a lever to put the helicopter in motion. "If you lose your way," the engineer shouted, jokingly, to the Yankee, "ask the first policeman you meet…"

This sally provoked a general burst of laughter, which was lost in the air as the apparatus rose up rapidly. They were already three of 400 meters from the ground when they saw Farenheit brace himself, launch himself like an arrow, and attempt to rejoin his companions with a single prodigious leap.

"The poor fellow!" said Selena, putting her hands together. "He'll never get this far!"

Scarcely had she uttered this exclamation than the Martian pressed a switch that immobilized the apparatus, while he opened his own wings and took a header—as the vulgar expression has it—into the etheric element. A few seconds later, he was beside the American, whose leg-muscles had been insufficiently powerful to take him all the way to the helicopter, and who was slowly falling back to the ground, shouting and desperately waving his arms and legs. Aotaha seized him by one of his side-whiskers and, steering his flight toward the apparatus, soon rejoined it, dragging Farenheit—who seemed to be floating in mid-air like a blow-up doll—in his wake.

"By God!" the American complained, taking his place on a seat between Fricoulet and Ossipoff. "I thought you were going to abandon me…"

"I don't know," riposted the engineer, "how awkward perches like ours appear to you to be, but I must tell you sincerely that, as seen from a height, even though you were on firm ground, you gave a paltry impression of American dignity."

Farenheit muttered a few words whose meaning Fricoulet could not catch, then abruptly turned his back on the engineer and addressed his left-hand neighbor. "How long will we have to spend on this machine?" he asked.

Ossipoff transmitted this question to Fricoulet, who translated it for the Martian. The latter, after a few seconds of reflection, replied: "If the wind continues to be favorable, we shall arrive at about midnight."

The old man unrolled his map and measured the distances carefully. *Damn!* he thought. *We won't be wasting any time, for we still have more than 500 leagues to cover.*

"What I don't understand," said Gontran to Fricoulet, "is why we couldn't arrange matters so as to come directly from Phobos to the destination of our journey. By landing where we did, we've been forced to undertake a journey of 1800 leagues—quite gratuitously, it seems to me."

The engineer darted a sideways glance at Ossipoff; the old man was so absorbed in studying the map that he had not heard a single word of his future son-in-law's observation. Prudently lowering his voice nevertheless, he replied: "If you think about it for a moment, you'll immediately realize that it was impossible, by virtue of the motion of Phobos around the planet, to land anywhere else."

"Ah!" said Gontran, with an intonation that made it easy to understand that the engineer's words were only vaguely meaningful to the young Comte.

"During our journey, Mars has rotated on its axis, with the result that the objective had drawn away. To arrive directly at the City of Light, it would have been necessary to calculate the rapidity of rotation of the planet and the speed of our balloon, and to direct our course 300 or 400 kilometers in advance of the place we wanted to reach."

Gontran shrugged. "Pooh!" he said. "I knew that—it's the ABC of the manual of the prefect hunter; when you aim at a partridge, it's necessary to aim at the head to hit the wing or the leg."

"It's the same thing. Now, the most urgent thing was to save you, wasn't it? Not to mention that, by means of this voyage made as a bird flies, you can take account of the areography."

"Oh," Flammermont replied, "*Les Continents célestes* suffices for me..." Pointing at the immense panorama that was unrolling beneath the vehicle with vertiginous rapidity, he said: "It's always the same; the countryside is depressingly uniform."

"Exactly like the Moon," said Farenhheit, in his turn. "Except that there were volcanoes there, and here there are canals."

"That animal is never content," muttered the engineer.

"By God!" riposted the American, "Try to see things from my point of view. What am I doing here? Nothing—absolutely nothing. Don't you think that, instead of dragging my gaiters through the celestial worlds in your company, I'd be much better off in New York?"

"What would you be doing in New York, then?" demanded Fricoulet. "Do you think that the United States are marching any less straight along the path of progress because one of their citizens is missing?"

"No, of course not—but my shareholders will say to one another, at their general meeting in June, that they don't see me at my post. Then again, the Eccentric Club's elections take place in July...where will I be in July? Oh, by God! By God!" And the American fell silent, his fists clenched and his lips taut with impotent wrath.

"Monsieur Fricoulet," said Selena, who was sitting with her elbows on the back of her seat, observing with intense curiosity the landscape extended at their feet, "Are all these 'canals,' as you call these seas that criss-cross the planet in all directions, known to terrestrial astronomers?"

The engineer smiled enigmatically. "Your question, Mademoiselle," he replied, "proves that you don't know our scientists very well. Yes, all these canals are known, catalogued, baptized...they even have the advantage over a great many Christians of having been baptized several times over."

"Why is that?"

"For the very simple reason that fate has dictated that the same canal has been discovered at the same time by astronomers of different nationalities, who have hastened to give it a name in accord either with their own personal or national pride, or with their own imagination."

"How does one get one's bearings, in that case?" the young woman asked, ingenuously.

"One doesn't get one's bearings, Mademoiselle," replied the American, with comical gravity.

"Mr. Farenheit goes too far," Fricoulet declared, "but it's certain that the hastiness of certain astronomers to baptize their discoveries has rendered sidereal maps confusing to the *vulgum pecus*."

Throughout the day the helicopter flew from north to south, following a line almost strictly parallel to that track of the Oreus, sometimes passing over red-glowing fields enameled here and there with grayish patches that Aotaha declared to be towns and villages, sometimes above silvery threads glittering in the sunlight, which extended away to the right and the left and were nothing but canals intersecting with the Oreus at right-angles.

The principal characteristic of the countryside, as Fricoulet noted in his observational log, was a depressingly monotonous flatness—not the slightest mountain, or anything more than the smallest hill, emerged from the waves that bathed it. When Selena expressed astonishment, the engineer explained this lack of relief in the topography by the erosion resulting from the friction of the Martian surface against the molecules composing the ambient atmosphere.

About 6 p.m., as the Sun was about to disappear over the horizon, the voyagers perceived beneath them, extending as far as the eye could see, an immense liquid sheet from which the last rays of the day star were reflected.

"That's the Trivium Charontis," declared Ossipoff, who was following the progress of the apparatus on his map. "It's a sort of lake, or rather Mediterranean, into which several canals discovered by Schiaparelli flow, including the Oreus, the Laestrygonians, the Cerberus, the Styx, the Hades, the Erebus..."

In a matter of seconds, the helicopter was flying over the ocean, and the continental coast vanished from the Terrans' sight. Suddenly, without any transition—as occurs in our equatorial regions—night succeeded day, and our voyagers found themselves enveloped by a vague darkness into which the surface of the planet melted, becoming confused and indecisive.

The Sun had just disappeared beneath the horizon after having reddened the atmosphere for a few seconds with its final rays; immediately, though, at the precise point where it had just sunk into space, a star rose, shining with a soft clarity that cast a strange melancholy over the seascape.

"The Moon!" exclaimed Gontran.

Ossipoff started so violently that he would have fallen off his seat if Fricoulet had not grabbed him by the arm.

"What did you say?" the old man exclaimed, in a strangled voice.

This attitude amazed his future son-in-law and made him indignant, but a kick dispatched by the engineer by way of advertisement warned the young man about the heresy he had just committed. "Yes," he said, with marvelous self-assurance, "the Moon of Mars—or rather one of its moons...isn't that the role that Phobos plays?"

Ossipoff inclined his head affirmatively.

"Quite right," he murmured. "I thought..."

"What did you think?" asked Flammermont, affecting a slightly haughty stiffness.

"Nothing, nothing," the scientist hastened to reply. "The expression you used made me think...but it was a mistake..."

Fricoulet laughed covertly, so amusing was the worthy scientist's embarrassment. Fortunately, an exclamation from Farenheit put an end to the difficult situation. "Another moon!" he cried, pointing to the east.

"Well," said Gontran, "what's surprising about that? It's Deimos."

"But that moon there isn't moving in the same direction as the other one."

"As you can see."

"They're going to meet, in that case."

"It's bound to happen sometimes."

"What will happen then?"

"An eclipse, quite simply," replied Fricoulet. "Partial or total, according to the positions of the two satellites in the sky. That's another originality of this world...and you'll admit that it's worth the journey."

For three hours the apparatus streaked through the sky beneath the gentle clarity of Phobos and Deimos—which did not afford the Terrans the spectacle of an eclipse that evening.

Finally, in the distance, piercing the light mist that floated above the surface of the ground, a spray of light became visible to the voyagers. In a few moments, they were floating 800 meters above the City of Light, the intellectual capital of Mars.

Viewed from that height, the spectacle was magical, reminding each of the Terrans of the capital of his own fatherland. Gontran and Fricoulet declared that they recognized the Opera quarter, sparkling with its many lights and its extraordinary animation. For Selena and her father, it was the Nevsky Prospect whose shining image extended at their feet. As for Farenheit, he proclaimed immediately that New York, with its rectilinear avenues and brilliant lighting, must certainly have that appearance from the gondola of a balloon. What gave the City of Light a strange and fantastic aspect, however, was not so much the numerous lights that carved the very carcass of the city out of the shadows of the night, with its streets and its monuments, but more especially the many sparks streaking through the air in every direction, like myriads of will-o'-the-wisps dancing over the surface of the ground.

"Uh oh!" said Flammermont, in a bantering tone. "The Martians are going in search of their pleasures."

"Or to work!" Farenheit put in.

"The night isn't usually the time that one chooses to go to work," the young Comte replied.

"Business!!!" the American replied, sententiously. He turned to Fricoulet. "Didn't you tell me, only yesterday, that these folk, even more than us, conform to the motto *Time is money*?"

"Certainly—but I didn't tell you that they dedicate the time that is so precious to them to business affairs."

Farenheit opened his eyes wide. "With what, in that case, do they employ their time?"

"I told you—the Martians, endowed by nature with a considerable amount of curiosity, dedicate their lives to satisfying that curiosity. To them, everything is a problem...and every time they succeed in solving one—however petty it might be—they're convinced that they've taken another step toward absolute perfection...so all their efforts are directed toward science, the only key that can open the doors of eternal mystery to them."

"Then you're convinced that all these individuals aren't in search of pleasure?" said Gontran.

"And you believe that they're not attending to their affairs?" Farenheit added.

The engineer smiled and shook his head. "You're both right with regard to the expressions themselves, but you're wrong in the sense that you mean them. By affairs, I, personally, mean the employment of time. Well, when one employs one's time following one's tastes and aptitudes, doesn't one experience true pleasure?"

At that moment, Aotaha uttered a guttural exclamation, extending his hand toward a sparkling aggregation of light in the very heart of the city.

"What's that?" asked the engineer.

The Martian's reply provoked a sharp surprise in him.

"What's the matter?" asked Ossipoff.

"If I've understood correctly, that illuminated monument is both a kind of Institute and a Governmental Palace."

"What!" said Gontran. "Politics and science lodge under the same roof?"

"For the simple reason that they're one and the same thing...or, rather, that the former is absorbed by the latter. In a world as advanced and civilized as this one, the special Earthly tribe known as 'politicians' must have disappeared a long time ago. It must certainly have existed, but in an epoch that is, so to speak, prehistoric—perhaps corresponding to our present."

"Ah, the happy nations!" Flammermont sighed, satirically.

"Happy because they're practical; and then again, it's another consequence of their *Time is money*. Time in their eyes, is too valuable to be wasted in politics. Besides, among us, politics always conceals personal interests, and these people have minds too deep and hearts too large for any similar pettiness to find a place therein."

"Ah!" cried Gontran. "If my love for Selena did not make me desire ardently to return to Earth—since only there will I find the municipal sash indispensable to my happiness—I'd pitch my tent here...for a country in which no one talks politics, especially one in which politics does not even exist, is Paradise!"

During this conversation, the apparatus had quit the heights at which it had been flying and descended gradually to 100 meters above the city. Aotaha pronounced a few monosyllables, which Fricoulet presumably understood, for he got up and took the Martian's place as the latter deployed his wings and left the machine.

"Where is he going?" the Terrans asked.

"He's going to notify the authorities of our arrival," the engineer replied. "He'll come back shortly."

Soon, indeed, a sound of wings cleaving space was heard, and Aotaha rejoined them. Without saying a word, he seized the control lever and the helicopter headed for the monument described by Fricoulet as "the Institute." Once there, the large upper rotor came to a stop; sustained only by the two smaller ones, the apparatus fell vertically, like the bob of a plumb-line.

Then the voyagers passed through a sparkling zone—so sparkling that they closed their eyes against the pain; without being immediately capable of figuring out why, they heard an indescribable tumult of noise.

Suddenly, a slight shock made them jump on their seats and they opened their eyes tentatively. The apparatus, now immobile, was suspended by its large rotor from the vault of a vast hall—a transparent vault, for the starry skies were visible through it, although it simultaneously mirrored the many lights sparkling everywhere. Beneath them, a restless and gesticulating crowd was looking at them in astonishment, emitting brief interjections amid a precipitate fluttering of wings.

"Damn!" said Fricoulet. "We seem to be having a certain effect."

"Yes," riposted the American, sarcastically. "The effect of a theater chandelier."

"My word, that's true!" said Gontran in his turn. "It's only regrettable that we aren't incandescent. We resemble a cluster of Jablochkoff lamps!"[6]

Mikhail Ossipoff swelled with pride, convinced that this whole multitude had gathered to acclaim him and his companions. "This is what glory is," he whispered in Flamermont's ear.

The latter shrugged his shoulders imperceptibly. "Don't be under any illusion, my dear Monsieur," he replied. "If what Fricoulet had told us about these people is accurate, we can't be anything more than little children to them...compared with thinkers who have extracted such a large fraction of nature's secrets, we've scarcely reached the scientific alphabet."

"Look who's talking, my dear Gontran," said the engineer, "and you're all the more correct because they aren't waiting for us; all these people are scientific delegates from different districts of the equator, who have come to hear interesting communications regarding the impending war."

Aotaha touched Fricoulet with his finger to impose silence on him; then he launched himself on to a tall column topped by a sort of platform, where he folded his wings again. Once there, he pronounced a few guttural sounds, which appeared to make a profound impression on the assembly, and then rejoined the voyagers.

"What did he say?" asked Selena.

"He's playing Barnum, introducing us to the Martians just as some deformed monster or inhabitant of an unknown country is presented to the public in the circuses of Paris. From his viewpoint, at any rate, we're perfectly ugly and we represent a very backward species of Universal intelligence."

"But what did he say at the end, which appeared to excite the hilarity of the audience?"

"He made an allusion to our inferior limbs—thanks to which, he said, we're so disgracefully late. He declared that many canals would be hollowed out on the surface of their world before we grow wings."

"Wings...wings!" growled Farenheit. "Do they consider wings to be the summit of perfection, then? They seem reminiscent to me of enormous birds."

The American's indignation amused the voyagers greatly; they burst out laughing. Their hilarity was drowned out by the unimaginable racket that greeted the appearance on the column that served as a pulpit of a Martian whose ponderous flight and entirely white down gave him the appearance of an old man. Fricoulet, told by his guide that this was, indeed, one of he oldest and most renowned scientists of the Equator, got ready to listen attentively.

---

[6] Paul Jablochkoff (1847-1894) invented an early electric arc-lamp in 1876, which was usually known by the slightly derisive nickname "Jablochkoff's Candle."

Soon, his companions saw him smile pityingly. "Parbleu!" he murmured. "That's a rather ridiculous idea—which, in any case, ought not to be too lethal: cannon loaded with air."

"Indeed," said Gontran, "as an engine of war, that seems to me rather Platonic."

"More Platonic, to be sure, than fine 24 inch field-pieces loaded with good 500-pound cannonballs," Farenheit muttered.

Fricoulet put a hand on his arm. "In fact, no," he replied. "They'd be even less lethal than the air-cannons about which that individual is talking."

"Why's that?"

"Because, by reason of their lack of weight, your good 500-pound cannonballs would never come down and would fly forever into the sky…unless a portion of the combatants had taken a position on Deimos or Phobos, and then…"

The Terrans' attention was drawn back to the orator, whose speech seemed to be having an effect one the audience diametrically opposed to the one he had expected. He gesticulated in vain, holding up a glass tube nearly 50 centimeters long by 20 centimeters in diameter. In vain, too, he uttered exclamations that, on occasion, attained the intensity of veritable screeches; the efficacy of the system he was proposing seemed less than proven. Then he suddenly aimed his tube at the part of the room where the opposition was most heated and, without saying a word, directed a flaming jet into the tube. This demonstration was conclusive; all those who happened to be in that direction were knocked down, collapsing like cardboard monkeys.

For a few moments, there was indescribable confusion: a concert of cries, groans and fearful flutterings; in the sudden chaos of individuals, families dispersed, became muddled up and confounded, trying to sort themselves out—and as soon as the husbands found their wives, the fathers their children and the children their mothers, their wings opened up and they fled through the open bay windows with which the hall was dotted.

The other audience-members, convinced by this striking example, gave voice to a slight clicking of tongues by way of applause, then slowly withdrew. Then darkness fell, and the Terrans, overcome by fatigue, fell profoundly asleep aboard their apparatus.

Fricoulet was the first to wake up. Already, the sunlight had penetrated every part of the immense hall, which Farenheit alone filled with the sound of his snoring. As soon as he opened his eyes, the engineer thought of investigating the neighborhood in which he found himself, so he ran to one of the openings through which he had seen the crowd of Martians fly on the previous evening. He uttered a cry of surprise that woke his companions and brought them running to his side.

"But it's Venice!" exclaimed Selena.

Instead of being solid, the streets were, indeed, liquid; the houses were reflected in the water.

"How do they get about?" asked Farenheit.

"As one does in Venice, of course!" riposted Gontran. "They go by boat."

"That's hardly necessary...their wings suffice."

"That's true; I always forget that these folk have the ability to fly—but that must modify their architecture strangely."

"No need for staircases, in fact."

Flammermont folded his arms in a comic gesture. "Ah, the lucky people!" he sighed.

"What's so lucky about that?"

"That they're unfamiliar with one of the worst scourges invented by our civilization: the concierge! Because the houses have no doors, there's no need for anyone to guard them. The tenants go in and out, and receive guests, without being obliged to pass before the eyes of that Argus/Cerberus hybrid. Oh, the lucky people!"

Fricoulet—who, although he liked his friend, never neglected an opportunity to torment him, murmured in his ear: "Unfortuntely, if the Martians don't know the concierge's sash, they're equally ignorant of the mayor's tricolor version..."

The young Comte's smiling face darkened immediately.

Aotaha arrived at that moment.

"A world as advanced in progress and civilization as this one must possess marvelous telescopic instruments?"

These words, pronounced by Ossipoff, were addressed to Fricoulet. "Undoubtedly," the latter replied—and he immediately transmitted the old man's reflection to the Martian.

Aotaha pointed to the enormous column at the top of which the Martian inventor had experimented with his air-cannon the previous evening, and the Terrans noticed, to their great amazement, that this column—which was 24 meters long and measured almost three meters in diameter—was nothing but a gigantic equatorial. Ossipoff uttered a cry of joy and admiration; in one bound, he was next to the instrument.

"What do you expect to see in light like this?" asked Fricoulet.

"I want to resolve one of the most interesting problems of modern astronomy," the old man replied. "From here, with an equatorial this powerful, one ought to be able to penetrate the veil that envelops the minor planets." Rubbing his hands together raptly, he added: "Eh, Gontran? The minor planets?"

The young man searched Fricoulet's face; the later laughed covertly.

"Ah yes, the minor planets," Gontran repeated. "What a magnificent treat!" And again he implored the engineer for help.

While Ossipoff maneuvered the equatorial to aim it in the desired direction, Fricoulet leaned toward the Comte. "Minor planet observation is impossible at this moment," he whispered.

Gontran immediately repeated: "But, my dear Monsieur, you can't devote yourself to any study of that subject at present."

The scientist straightened up. "And why not?" he asked.

Gontran looked at Fricoulet; the engineer directed his attention to the Sun, whose gilded rays were irradiating the sky.

"Simply because it's daylight," replied the young man, affecting a slightly mocking tone.

Ossipoff slapped his forehead. "My word, that's true!" he said. "There are moments, I swear, when I don't have my wits about me." Then he added: "Well, I'll wait for nightfall. There'll be no shortage of objects to observe, thank God!" And, with a cheerfulness all the more ineffable because he had not enjoyed it for such a long time, he stuck his eye to the ocular lens of the equatorial.

When he saw the old man depart into space in the wake of his line of sight, Gontran drew Fricoulet aside. "Tell me about the minor planets, please," he said. "What are they?" Taking is head in his hands he groaned: "My brain will never be strong enough to withstand all the work I'm making it do."

"Is all this changing it?" the engineer joked.

"Too much…"

"Well then, renounce your marriage plans, and become the Gontran of yore again."

The young Comte made a forceful gesture. "Never! I prefer to swallow the planets, small and giant, after having devoured the medium-sized ones—even if I have to die of indigestion!"

"In that case," said Fricoulet, laughing, "get your stomach ready…the astronomic crammer is about to start…."

"I'm listening—speak."

The engineer took his inevitable notebook from his pocket, gave it to his friend, and said: "Write down the following numbers: 0, 3, 6, 12, 24, 48, 96."

"I've done that—now what?"

"Now, what do you notice?"

The young man's eyes widened at this question, and his tongue became mute.

Selena, who had just joined them and was looking over his shoulder, murmured: "That each number is double the one preceding it—is that it, Monsieur Fricoulet?"

"Mademoiselle," replied the engineer, "I have rarely seen a person of your sex endowed with an observational sensitivity as intense as yours."

The young woman blushed. "It's not very difficult," she stammered, "and if Monsieur Gontran cared to take the trouble to pay attention…"

"Now," said Fricoulet," to each of those numbers add 4."

Gontran started. "But this isn't astronomy," he aid. "It's one of those petty party games to which bourgeois families devote the kind of soirées they call 'social evenings,' and in which..."

A formidable yawn interrupted him. "Come on," said Fricoulet. "Have you added 4?"

"Yes—there, it's done. Now I have 4, 7, 10, 16, 28, 52, 100."

"That's very good. Now, do you know what each of those numbers represents, approximately?"

"You're asking preposterous questions. These numbers might represent any number of things...it depends what one's talking about..."

"I don't know that we're talking, at this moment, about anything other than astronomy. Well, since you don't know, I'll tell you. Each of those numbers represents the mean distance of a planet from the Sun. Write this: Mercury 3.9, Venus 7.2, Earth 10, Mars 15, Jupiter 52, Saturn 95."

"Indeed," Gontran observed, "they're almost identical..."

"But in comparing the new numbers with the first, you don't notice anything?"

The young man was silent for a few moments. "My word, no," he said. "I don't notice anything."

"What about the number 28?"

"Yes, that's right! It doesn't correspond to any planet."

"It's precisely that lacuna that Kepler pointed out in his *Harmonies of the World* and the existence of which Titius and Bode later confirmed. Besides, when Herschel discovered Uranus in 1781, it was located at the distance that continues the series, 196..."[7]

Flammermont listened to his friend speaking without appearing to understand much of his explanation. "Then," he said, "the number 28..."

---

[7] Johannes Kepler (as he signed such Latin texts as *Harmonies Mundi,* first published in 1619) spent a great deal of time searching for mathematical order in the layout of the Solar System, in the course of which he discovered that the planetary orbits are elliptical rather than circular, thus solving some of the mathematical difficulties associated with the Copernican model. His attempt to explain the distances of the various planetary orbits from the Sun by reference to Plato's set of "perfect solids" was less successful, and is generally regarded by modern astronomers as a mystical wild-goose chase, but it was carried on by other seekers of arcane order, including Johann Daniel Titius (1729-1796), who came up with the arithmetical sequence cited here, long known as "Bode's Law," after its subsequent popularizer, Johann Elert Bode (1747-1826). Fricoulet refrains from pointing out that Neptune's eventual discovery was an embarrassment to those convinced that the Titius-Bode sequence had some as-yet-undiscovered significance, because its mean orbital distance does not fit the sequence.

"Is one which represents the distance at which, between Mars and Jupiter, there ought to be another world, which has thus far escaped human observation..."

"That's odd," murmured Flammermont. "I haven't seen anything similar in *Les Continents célestes*."

"Your memory is at fault. There's the question of the minor planets."

"Indeed—I've seen a chapter bearing that title...but it didn't seem very important and I passed on to Jupiter."

"Well, you were wrong...for it's precisely these minor planets that represent the number 28."

"The minor planets!" repeated the young man. "How many are there, then?"

Fricoulet pushed out his lips in a dubious moue. "Pooh!" he said. "Something like 234, I think...but more are being discovered every day."

Gontran started in fright. "You don't imagine," he complained, "that I'm going to stuff the names of 234 planets into my head?"

"It's not just their names; there's also their fundamental data—which is to say, their diameter, surface area, density, and the orbits they describe around the Sun, with their aphelia, perihelia, etc..."

"And there's an etcetera!" groaned Gontran. "No, as you can see, I'm going mad!" And he held the borrowed notebook out to Fricoulet.

"However," the engineer persisted, "prudence demands that you don't allow yourself to be taken by surprise by the questions that Monsieur Ossipoff will surely not neglect to ask you this evening."

Gontran assumed an air of resignation. "Go on, then, executioner," he murmured. "Murder me with your 234 planets...even if each of them is only as large as the Earth, you'll have enough to crush me."

"What!" replied the engineer. "See how right I was to insist! You've just committed a formidable heresy. According to the general theory of the planetary system, the total mass of these 234 planets can't be more than a third of the terrestrial mass..."

"Why is that?"

"To reply would delay me needlessly. It's sufficient for you to know that it is...later, when I have a moment, I'll explain..."

"Explain to me, then, why this sidereal zone was considered for such a long time to be deserted."

"Because of the infinite smallness of these asteroids, of which the most important are 500 kilometers in diameter at the most, and which appear to us as stars of the 11th magnitude. On the other hand, you must have noticed that there's a much greater chance of finding something that is known to exist than one for which one must grope without any precise indication or certainty."

"That's true."

"Well, on the day when number 28 was declared by Titius to have no celestial representation, an association of 24 astronomers was formed to search space and find the world that evaded human curiosity in this fashion."

"And did they find it?"

"Themselves, nothing at all—but an astronomer in Palermo, who was observing the smaller stars of Taurus, discovered by chance, precisely at that distance of 28, a new world that he baptized with the name of Ceres."

"By chance!" exclaimed Gontran. "Was it really worth the trouble of constituting a society of 24 scientists?"

"Many great discoveries of which humankind is proud are due to chance, my dear Gontran," said Mikhail Ossipoff, who had come to rejoin his companions.

The young Comte shivered and leaned toward Fricoulet. "Above all, don't abandon me," he whispered in his ear,

"In any case," the old man went on, "although the first was discovered fortuitously, it wasn't the same for the following ones, which were all the result of relentless study and resolute research."

"There are astronomers," Fricoulet said, in his turn, "who have, so to speak, made a specialty of minor planets. Palisa has discovered 40 of them; Peters—one of your compatriots, Mr. Farenheit—has discovered 34; we owe 14 to Prosper Henry of the Observatory of Paris, and another 14 to a German painter, Goldschmidt..."[8]

The engineer would have continued in that vein for longer if Ossipoff—convinced, as ever, that the young man was making a boastful display of superficial science—had not cut him off with an impatient gesture. "Since this is the subject of conversation," he said, addressing Gontran, "I'd be grateful if you'd give me your opinion."

"My opinion about what?" asked Flammermont, silently adding: *Here it comes.*

"Your opinion on the formation of the planets, of course," said the old man.

Gontran was momentarily cornered by his ignorance; nervously, he tugged his moustache, while um-ing and ah-ing in a revealing manner, and his desperate gaze was settling on Selena when he saw the young woman take out her watch and drop it.

Ossipoff exclaimed in surprise and leapt forward—but the young woman beat him to it and, gathering up the pieces, showed them to Flammermont with a

---

[8] The last two figures in this sequence, referring to the discoveries credited to the two brothers Prosper Henry (1849-1903) and Paul Henry (1848-1905) and to Hermann Goldschmidt (1802-1866) remain the same today, but Johann Palisa (1848-1925) eventually totted up the record total of 122 asteroids discovered, while Christian Peters (1813-1890) eventually scored 48.

singular smile. This gesture lit up a sudden inspiration in his brain. "Of course!" he said, with assurance. "All these minor planets can only be the fragments of a world that must have broken up, for some reason still unknown—but which science will discover."

Ossipoff shook his head. "Yes," he said, "I know that opinion has fervent supporters—but it's not mine."

"And why is that?" asked the unfortunate Gontran, still with assurance.

"Because a zone as extensive as that occupied by the minor planets is absolutely unnecessary to a single world of a mass equal to scarcely a third of the mass of the Earth." And he looked at the young Comte, waiting to see what he would say to refute this argument.

It was Fricoulet who replied, before the old man could stop him. "What you just said would be logical if that fragmentation had not been successive and if Jupiter were not there to explain how the orbits of the fragments became so widely dispersed." Seeing Ossipoff stamp his foot impatiently, he hastened to add: "I don't have any ideas of my own on the subject—I'm only repeating, word for word, what Gontran said to me just now…"

The old man's irritation was appeased; nevertheless, he replied in a slightly dry tone: "All opinions are free; for myself, on the contrary, I consider that, far from being the fragments of a planet, these asteroids are the constitutive elements of one, detached from the solar equator by the powerful attraction of Jupiter and prevented by that same attraction from ever uniting to form a whole."

Gontran shook his head in a knowing fashion.

"That theory is at least as plausible as yours," said Ossipoff, in a slightly bitter tone.

"Undoubtedly…undoubtedly…."

Fricoulet, who had noticed how his interventions irritated the old man and took a mischievous pleasure in exasperating him, asked in a naïve tone: "How do you explain in your theory, the particularity that the orbits of these minor planets all intersect at one point? Isn't that a proof supporting ours? As you know, a law of mechanics specifies…"

Ossipoff looked daggers at him. "Ah!" he said. "You're very glad to have learned that a little while ago, in order to parade it now."

Fricoulet frowned slightly.

"Alcide!" murmured Gontran, in a prayerful tone.

"Monsieur Alcide!" implored Selena, who dreaded that the engineer, exasperated by the old man's acerbic manner of speaking, might let slip some imprudent comment.

Fricoulet, however, having already collected himself, made a sign with his hand to tell them to have no fear.

"On the other hand," Ossipoff continued, this time addressing himself directly to Flammermont, "the largest of these worlds are spherical: Ceres, Pallas, Juno, Hebe, Psyche, Calliope…"

Yet again, Fricoulet intervened. "What about Camilla, Sylvia, Zelia, Lumen and Gallia?" he asked. "What do you think of their form?"

The old scientist smiled scornfully. "My dear Monsieur," he retorted, "when one butts into a conversation, one must at least know something. Now, you imagine that you possess astronomical knowledge, because Monsieur de Flammermont has told you a few things from time to time; unfortunately, that layer of scientific varnish cracks of its own accord. With respect to the bodies that you've just named, Gontran has perhaps neglected to tell you—or, more plausibly, you have neglected to remember—that they are so small that they only appear as luminous dots in the most powerful telescopes."

"It's exactly that on which we base our claim," Fricoulet declared, striking a pose of comic importance, "that these worlds are little splinters of polyhedral form—fragments of a destroyed world."

Ossipoff burst out laughing. "If that's your reasoning," he muttered, "all discussion between us is futile."

To create a diversion, Selena said: "If these worlds are so tiny, there's very little chance of their being inhabited."

Gontran, to whose memory the philosophical theory of his illustrious namesake suddenly returned, replied with an authority that impressed Ossipoff: "And why is that, my dear Selena? What basis do you have for proclaiming that these worlds uninhabited? Their exiguity—but I don't see how that can prevent them from taking part in the concert of universal life. Have we not proofs even on Earth that I might cite? Was not Greece, that territorially-trivial land, the torch of Antiquity for many centuries?"

"Except that," Fricoulet objected, mischievously, "the gravitational conditions on Greek terrain are very different from those on the surfaces of these globules in which you appear to be enormously interested—I don't know why."

"Nothing proves that humankind can't be colossal; on the contrary, everything encourages us to think so—the stature of inhabitants being in inverse proportion to he intensity of gravity." Satisfied with this formula, which had just germinated in his head, Gontran leaned toward Selena with a gracious smile on his lips.

"Do you realize where you end up with such reasoning?" Ossipoff said, then. "With inhabitants who are larger than the worlds on which they're summoned to live!"

Gontran shivered, and looked at the engineer, who signaled to him that the old man was right.

Fortunately, a group of Martians had just landed in the observatory, soon followed by another, and then yet another, setting up a sequence that soon formed a long queue similar to the human ribbons that extend every evening from the doors of our theaters. One odd thing, which Selena was the first to notice, was that children were in the great majority.

"Doubtless there's a matinée performance by some conjurer or circus troupe," said Flammermont, jokingly.

"The best means of finding out what's going on," proposed Fricoulet, "is to follow these people. Given that we're on a world in which curiosity is the motive for all actions, they can't begrudge our being curious."

This opinion was judged sound, and the Terrans joined the queue without delay.

After a wait that was not long—the Martians bringing an unusual rapidity to all their actions—our voyagers arrived at a doorway, whose threshold they crossed in the wake of those preceding them. They immediately found themselves enveloped by dense shadows—so dense that they were not only unable to distinguish what sort of place they were in, but even whether they were alone or not.

Suddenly, without their having moved, it seemed to them that they were being transported through space, beneath the celestial dome strewn with a myriad of stars, among which sparkled the easily-recognizable constellations and planets.

Then, one of these worlds—which had appeared until then as a luminous point—increased in size, racing toward the spectators with a vertiginous rapidity, to be transformed, as if by some miracle, into an enormous sphere that soon filled the entire sky. Now, the Terrans—mute with amazement, with their chests constricted by a singular anguish—were able to distinguish, as powerfully as they could have done with a powerful telescope, the bizarre topography of this unknown world. It was an inextricable confusion of land and ocean: of lands that seems to be ardent furnaces and oceans that seemed to be agitated by waves of liquid fire. There were also dark holes, as well as volcanic craters and peaks sparkling like the summits of snowy mountains; greenish clouds arrayed in parallel bands at the equator formed a sort of screen over that region.

Gontran felt someone jog his elbow and a voice—Ossipoff's—murmured in his ear: "I no longer know where I am, my dear friend. What about you? No celestial map mentions such a planet. What do you think?"

His last sentence ended with an exclamation of simultaneous surprise and fright. Just as it seemed to the Terrans that the colossal sphere, still advancing toward them, was about to crush them with its mass, it burst, like those beautiful multicolored rockets bursting in mid-air that usually conclude firework displays—except that, instead of dissolving like the infinitesimal debris of rockets and becoming invisible, the fragments of this world, driven away by a force interior to the sphere, fled in every direction into darkened space. Soon, there remained nothing but a bright small sun, which slowly continued its march into infinity.

Then the stars appeared to fall back into darkness; everything disappeared and the shadow thickened around the Terrans again.

"By God!" complained Farenheit. "That's a very interesting trick, which would be a great success in New York."

"Pooh!" replied the skeptical Fricoulet. "It's nothing but the magic lantern complicated by phantasmagoria and melting views. Gontran was right just now to say that the Martians were going to a matinée performance; one might think that this was a conjurer's tent."

"But what was that supposed to show?" asked Ossipoff.

"Planet number 28, no doubt," Fricoulet replied.

"You're mad."

While talking, the Terrans had retraced their steps; on re-entering the observatory, they found Aotaha.

As might be imagined, Fricoulet's first impulse was to ask him for an explanation. Having listened to the Martian's brief and rapid speech, the engineer turned to his companions. "My dear Gontran," he said, "they're right to say: 'to innocents, full hands.' "

"What do you mean by that?"

"Quite simply that what we have just seen is confirmation of your theory of the minor planets."

Ossipoff started violently. "How do you know?"

"Because Aotaha has just told me."

"How does he know?"

Fricoulet's only reply to that question was a shrug of his shoulders. To Gontran, he said: "Thousands of years ago the Martians discovered a means of recording light, just as we have found, in the phonograph, a means of recording sound. The gripping spectacle that we have just witnessed was photographed from Nature, and the break-up of that planet appeared to us as it appeared, centuries ago, for the Martians."

"That's incredible!" muttered Farenheit.

"These living images, so to speak, serve for the education of the young. That explains why the crowd that we followed was almost exclusively composed of children."

Ossipoff, very thoughtful and somewhat humiliated, said nothing.

"Monsieur Fricoulet," said Selena, "you know so many things—explain to me how such a result could be achieved."

"My word, Mademoiselle, with regard to the Martian system, I can't answer you, not having studied it; as to what master-conjurer did, it's quite simple: by rapidly drawing away from a screen extended between the spectator and the optical apparatus, the illusion is created of the approach of the apparition, by the opening of a second lantern which lights up gradually as the first goes out, the projection of the subject in view is changed."

"It's what they call *dissolving views*," said Farenheit.

"Or *melting views*," added Gontran.[9]

"Monsieur Fricoulet, I'd like to ask you something else."

"Go on, Mademoiselle."

"These people have photographed a planet that no longer exists; perhaps they're sufficiently interested in the Earth to have created images of it by similar means."

The engineer turned to Aotaha and translated the young woman's question. The Martian inclined his head slightly and signaled to the voyagers to follow him.

As before, the Terrans stopped in a dark room; then, suddenly, a veil was removed, revealing the immensity of the heavens, in the depths of which a slender crescent appeared, shining with a soft and feeble light. Gradually, this crescent grew, extending it two immense horns over the entire horizon; then its dimensions became such that the horns themselves disappeared, and only a part of the planet was framed by the view.

"By God!" muttered Farenheit. "But that's London we can see there...look, there's the Thames on the left...and all those chimneys...all the masts of the ships..."

"It's very odd," said Fricoulet, in his turn. "One would think that we were floating in a balloon a few kilometers above the ground."

An emotional exclamation burst forth almost immediately. "France! France! Oh, how fast it's going! It's Paris that's emerging from the mist...Paris!" A formidable sigh escaped Gontran's breast; along with the vision of the city of his birth, the young Comte had just seen unroll before his eyes the silhouettes of all those he had left behind there—relatives, friends and comrades—and he wondered whether he would ever see them again.

"Parbleu!" sniggered Fricoulet. "I bet you're looking for the Rue d'Anjou."

"Why the Rue d'Anjou?"

"Isn't that where the town hall of the eighth arrondissement is? The most fashionable arrondissement in Paris?"

Flamermont squeezed his friend's arm forcefully. "Shut up," he said. "Your jokes are ill-timed."

---

[9] The trick of substituting one lantern-slide by another by means of two projectors, as Fricoulet describes—exploiting the persistence of vision to give the impression of a transformation—was a popular device in the years before the invention of cinema, which made much more striking substitutions possible. Although de Graffigny and Le Faure were writing only few years before the invention of cinema, it is not surprising that Fricoulet could not describe "the Martian system" in more detail, and the anticipation of such cinematic effects as the zoom—which have now become perfectly familiar but were then hard to imagine—is striking even in the absence of a hypothetical mechanism.

Successively, the panorama of Central Europe passed before the eyes of the mute and marveling Terrans: Switzerland exhibited its glaciers, ravines and snowy peaks, Germany its old ruined towns and its mysterious forests, Italy its gilded countryside and blue coasts. Then the white immensities of Russia appeared, the gilded cupolas of Moscow, the icy Neva in St. Petersburg, the minarets of Constantinople…then there were the Siberian steppes, the jungles of India, the Chinese paddy-fields and the cities of the Celestial Empire, with their bizarrely-carved monuments…then another expanse of water, which appeared to extend as far as the eye could see but whose limit nevertheless appeared in a few minutes.

Then a formidable "By God!" suddenly burst forth—it was Farenheit, testifying to his joy at seeing New York and its harbor swarming with steamers. "Ah!" he said, sighing deeply. "Haven't the Martians—these people of progress and civilizations—got some means of sending me back to Fifth Avenue?"

"They've just done it," Selena replied. "Hasn't their visual ray transported you to your native city?"

"Look, but don't touch," Flammermont added, jokingly.

"It's the torture of Tantalus," Fricoulet concluded.

Chapter XXXVI
Cannon fire and lightning strikes

"Exactly how long," Farenheit suddenly demanded, "do you propose to drag me in your wake like this, Monsieur Ossipoff?"

At this bluntly-posed question, the old man closed the notebook in which he was scribbling figures, raised his head and stared at the American. "My dear Mr. Farenheit," he replied, after a brief pause, "you're asking me for information that it's rather difficult to give you."

"By God!" exclaimed Farenheit. "Who can give it to me, if not you?"

"Me, of course!" said Fricoulet.

The American ran to the engineer. "Oh, you!" he said. "I know full well that you're a true scientist."

"Me, no," replied the young man, modestly, "but he is." And he pointed at Gontran, who was chatting to Selena a short distance away.

Farenheit nodded his head admiringly. "Oh, Monsieur de Flammermont!" he murmured. "I formed an estimation of him a long time ago...what's his opinion, then?"

"His opinion is that it's necessary not to think of returning to Earth before having extended our voyage to the limits of the Solar System."

"Which is to say?"

"As far as Neptune, 1,100,000,000 leagues from the Sun."

The American's eyes widened and his expression became fearful. "1,100,000,000 leagues," he stammered, waving his large skeletal arms in the air, despairingly. "But do we even have a means of getting there?"

Ossipoff replied, with imperturbable calm: "The means is nothing...it's the time that we might not have."

Farenheit's fear increased. "What does he mean?" he whispered in the engineer's ear.

"He simply means that we'll need, at the lowest estimate, about 50 years for that little excursion."

"But we'll be dead!" he moaned.

"You, perhaps...Monsieur Ossipoff will, for sure. As for the two lovers and me, we'll doubtless still be in this world, but I wonder whether the few years we'll have left to live will be worth the trouble of coming back."

"Coming back?" exclaimed Ossipoff. "You have a means of coming back?"

"Me, no...but Gontran..."

"What do you mean?"

"Quite simply Comet Halley, which will reach its aphelion beyond Neptune 50 years from now, and which, in resuming the route to its perihelion, might be able to collect us and bring us back toward Mercury. Once there, we'll follow in the reverse direction the itinerary that we followed to get there…then, from the Moon to the Earth is a mere bagatelle…"

Ossipoff laughed.

"Isn't that correct?" asked Fricoulet.

"Perfectly correct—except that you've forgotten one detail…oh, a very tiny detail, which is that if it takes you 50 years to reach Neptune, it will take you a little longer to return to the Moon. That gives you 100 years, in round numbers…now, even if you give proof of a longevity rare among Terrans, you'll only return to your native land to be buried there. Is it really worth the trouble?"

Fricoulet shrugged. "Certainly not, and if it were only up to me, take it from me that I wouldn't worry much about returning…but won't it be necessary to give those two children, before dying, the supreme satisfaction of marrying one another? Just between ourselves, doesn't an engagement of nearly 100 years deserve a marriage *in extremis*? Don't you think so, Monsieur Ossipoff?"

The scientist understood the reproach contained in these words and lowered his head.

As for Farenheit, he was in a state of stupor difficulty to describe. With his chin resting on his breastbone, his eyes wide open and staring straight ahead, his lips pursed and his arms slumped alongside his body, as if exhausted, he was quite dumbfounded. Finally, shaking his head in a superb gesture of defiance, he muttered: "That's all right. I'll think of one."

"You'll think of what, my poor Mr. Farenheit?" asked Fricoulet, with a hint of mockery.

"Of a means of getting back to Fifth Avenue," the American replied, furiously. And he headed for the door of the observatory.

Meanwhile, there was a noise of wing-beats in the air and Aotaha, landing near the Terrans, addressed a few rapid monosyllables to Fricoulet.

"My friends," the engineer said to his companions, "our guide informs me that if we want to witness the great Martian hecatomb that he mentioned to us, it's necessary to leave now."

"What!" exclaimed Selena, whose soft-voiced conversation with Gontran was interrupted by this news. "So soon!"

"Remember, Mademoiselle," Fricoulet replied, "that the place where we're going is 90 degrees west of the City of Light."

"And what means of locomotion are we going to employ?" asked Ossipoff, who had risen to his feet at the first words, ready to depart.

The Martian presumably guessed what the old man had said, for he extended his wings to indicate the air.

"He can't suppose that we're going to fly," muttered Farenheit.

No one paid any heed to this remark, especially as Gontran said, very seriously, to Ossipoff: "Aren't you afraid to take Mademoiselle Selena with us? What if she were to suffer some accident?"

The old man frowned anxiously. "I had the same thought as you, my dear boy," he replied, "but what can we do? I know Selena; she'll never consent to remain here alone...and I'm reluctant to separate from her myself."

"Me too," Flammermont added. After a momentary pause he murmured: "If propriety weren't opposed to it, I'd gladly offer to stay here with her."

"That wouldn't be entirely unpleasant for you, my lad," sniggered Fricoulet. "Unfortunately, propriety demands..."

"Alcide," Flammmermont said, "you're my friend..."

The engineer shrugged. "You've never doubted it, I assume!" he said.

"Me, doubt your friendship? Oh, Alcide!"

"You don't doubt it, and yet you're asking me to prove it."

"That's true."

"But illogical. Anyway, go on!"

"Would you look after Selena?"

The engineer made every effort to conceal the grimace provoked by that demand.

"You're not enthusiastic," said Gontran.

"Indeed! In any other circumstances, I'd be at your disposal—but to come to Mars and not to witness the impending combat...not to see the effect that the air-cannon will produce...that's hard!"

Gontran turned his back on him, muttering dryly: "Thanks all the same, old chap." He remained pensive, his eyes on the ground, seeking inspiration. Suddenly, he uttered a joyful exclamation. "I've got it!" he said. He turned to Farenheit. "Mr. Farenheit," he said, pressing the American's hand. "I have a great favor to ask you."

"Go on," said Farenheit, astonished by the grave intonation with which the young man had pronounced these words.

"Would you keep an eye on my fiancée? It's a mission of trust with which I'm charging you. Will you agree?"

"By God! Monsieur de Flammermont, you flatter me enormously. While I'm alive, I swear to you that nothing will happen to Mademoiselle Selena." Then, leaning closer to Gontran, he added: "But I will say this, Monsieur de Flammermont: it's your fiancée that I'm watching over, not the daughter of that old wretch." And he pointed at Ossipoff.

"What has he done to you?"

"What has he done to me!" the American moaned. And, in a few words, he told the young Comte about the conversation that had just taken place between him, Fricoulet and the old scientist.

Momentarily overwhelmed by the prospect of the marriage *in extremis* conceded to him by Fricoulet, Gontran soon recovered his self-possession. Providence, which had saved him several times already since the beginning of this astonishing voyage, would come to his aid again, in this circumstance. He shook the American's hand warmly and said to him: "Have no fear, Mr. Farenheit, it would be truly diabolical if the two of us couldn't find a means of getting back to our native planet before the era predicted by those gentlemen."

Meanwhile, Fricoulet was conversing with Aotaha, translating what the Martian said for Ossipoff as they went along. It was, quite naturally, about the war that was about to start; Aotaha declared that he had absolute confidence in the machine tried out a few days before at the Institute.

"But what about your adversaries?" asked the engineer. "Do you know whether they, too, have a means, not of achieving victory—that's not the point—but of conserving life?"

"No one knows," replied the Martian. "They certainly have a weapon, but its secret is well guarded. For every one of us, it's a question of life or death; the destruction is necessary, indispensable—everyone agrees in recognizing that—but the individual instinct of self-preservation impels everyone to desire to come back to enjoy life amid his own people in preference to his adversary. It is, in consequence, the most intelligent who survive, and that is justice."

With that, he beckoned to the voyagers to follow him outside.

In front of the Observatory, an odd-looking apparatus was floating a few feet above the ground; it was a sort of mechanical bird with a narrow body and vast concave wings. Ossipoff and his companions installed themselves in the aisle formed by the body of the bird and a motor activated by the Martian immediately imparted a gentle and uniform movement to the wings, thanks to which the apparatus was soon soaring at a prodigious height.

The City of Light now appeared only as an aggregation of stone cubes emerging from glaucous waves. Aotaha had set a course south-westwards, and the shore of Huygens continent was already visible on the horizon.

For two days, they flew in this manner, heading at top speed for the site of the gigantic and pacific duel they intended to witness.

Although they were flying at a great height, the voyagers were able to observe an extraordinary animation on the planet's surface. The canals, which connected the seas, were streaked with innumerable vessels packed with Martians heading in the same direction as our friends. The sky was similarly striped by the rapid flight of immense aeronefs that were arriving from all points of the horizon, like a gigantic swarm of bees returning to their hive.

"But in the final analysis," Gontran whispered in Fricoulet's ear, "what's the purpose all these immense canals? Their length is one thing, but it's their width I can't explain."

"It's a simple system of irrigation," the engineer replied. "The water essential to the Martians is canalized and intelligently divided again throughout all their continents, in order to bring them fecundity and life."

"But why, instead of contenting themselves with a single canal, do they arrange them in pairs almost everywhere?"

"That's a matter that I haven't yet elucidated. Undoubtedly, though, there's a reason of security for that measure. I wouldn't be surprised if, in each of these pairs of canals, one were devoted to the outward journey and the other to the return—but that's merely a hypothesis."

Like two-track railways, Gontran thought.

Finally, they arrived at the goal of their journey. If Mihkail Ossipoff could be believed, they were now below the equator, on the 270th degree of longitude, on the continent baptized by Schiaparelli with the name of Libya, only a few degrees from Syrtis Major, more commonly known by the name of the Hourglass Sea.

"To the north," said the scientist, addressing Gontran, "Libya is bordered by a sea named after your illustrious namesake."

The young man pretended to cast an expert eye over the map. "I confess, my dear Monsieur Ossipoff," he said, in a natural tone, "that I no longer know where I am."

"That doesn't surprise me, given that I too…"

"Are we lost, then?" asked Selena, smiling. "With you here, Father, that seems to me to be impossible."

"This planet, you see," he murmured, "is more treacherous than one might expect—it's a veritable chameleon. Here, where seas extended a few years previously, one perceives continents. The latter, on the contrary, have given way to liquid expanses; the snows have melted to form lakes, the canals double up, disappear and form again."[10]

"It's a veritable set of Chinese boxes," added Flammermont, importantly.

"In consequence," said Fricoulet, in a slightly mocking tone, "we don't know where we are."

Ossipoff seemed to reflect. "Hang on, though," he said, after a moment, "to get here, we've followed two canals, one of them Cerberus, the other Hephaestus. From that I conclude that the expanse of water I see there, on our right, must be Schiaparelli's Lacus Moeris; others call it the Hand Gulf."

Gontran clicked his tongue impatiently. "It's a vile habit that you terrestrial astronomers of giving 36 names to the same celestial locality. It makes it hard to remember…not to mention to mention that it can't make scientific discussion any easier."

---

[10] The alleged "treacherousness" of the Martian surface, as observed by 19thentury astronomers, was actually evidence of their tendency to improvise too much detail in what they "saw" through their various instruments. In seeking a physical explanation for that treacherousness, the authors add a further dimension of reckless imagination to an image of the red planet that is already error-strewn—but not as reckless as the elaboration that Percival Lowell and his followers were to add as they carried forward the myth of the Martian canals in the 1890s.

"What do you expect?" Ossipoff retorted. "Every nation has a more or less considerable number of celebrities of every sort to honor; that's why the names of illustrious men are attached to continents, lakes and mountains discovered in the Heavens."

"We raise statues to them, ourselves," declared Fricoulet, in a serious manner.

"A singular idea," muttered Farenheit.

"It's the only manner we have of honoring our celebrities," the engineer retorted. "There are so many of them that the supply of celestial objects for naming is no longer sufficient."

They had disembarked on the edge of a canal forming the line of demarcation of two armies. On each side, extending as far as the eye could see, was a formidable host, from which singular sounds rose up into the air. At every moment, rapid flights of aeronefs appeared, streaking through the sky, transporting bodies of troops to various points of the battlefield to take up their battle stations.

Strictly speaking, these were not combatants facing up to one another, for the masses were unarmed. Science had, in fact, brought engines of destruction to such perfection that not only had hand-to-hand fighting been rendered impossible, but battle could only take place at distances too great for any individually-held weapon to have the slightest effect. In the hands of their commanders, these masses were simply gigantic pawns on a gigantic chessboard, which they could maneuver at their whim.

"Mr. Farenheit," said Gontran, "We're going to split up. You've promised to watch over my fiancée...this is the moment to keep your promise."

"At your orders, Monsieur de Flammermont," the American replied. "What do I have to do?"

"Climb back into the apparatus that brought us here and await the outcome of the impending battle at an altitude of 2000 meters."

Farenheit scratched his head anxiously. "It's just," he said, "that I don't know how to maneuver that machine."

"Don't worry about that detail," Fricoulet replied. "Aotaha will set the motor and you have only to allow yourself to be taken up; the apparatus will stop at the desired height."

"But how will we get down."

"Our guide will come to get you."

"Don't forget us up there," said Farenheit, taking his place beside Selena, whose father was just giving her a hug.

"Don't be afraid—we won't let you die of hunger," retorted the engineer, jokingly.

One last kiss for her father and one last squeeze of the hand for Gontran, and Selena gave the signal to depart personally. "Above all, don't expose yourselves to any danger," she shouted to her friends as the apparatus left the ground.

So rapid was the aeronef's flight that their answer did not reach the young woman.

Not without emotion, Gontran followed the rising apparatus with his eyes as it diminished visibly.

"Don't worry—they'll be watching these people's revels as if from the height of a balcony." So saying, the engineer drew his friend along in Ossipoff's footsteps. The latter, accompanied by their guide, was already moving through the foremost ranks of the inhabitants of the Equator.

"By the way," the young Comte murmured in the engineer's ear on seeing 100 gigantic glass tubes arranged along the edge of the canal, aimed at the enemy, "you must explain how that device works...the other evening, at the Institute, I pretended to understand, because of Ossipoff, but frankly..."

"My poor friend, to give you a good grasp of the mechanism I'd have to explain a law of physics that you don't know, and that would take us too far astray. Suffice it to say that the combustion of pure hydrogen produces a series of detonations, which set layers of air in motion, forming a sort of artificial hurricane, of a power you can hardly imagine."

As he finished these words, a formidable roar started up a few paces away; then there was an uninterrupted series of thunderclaps all along the line, which burst with incredible intensity. "Oh!" said Gontran. "The action's starting, I think." With the aid of his marine binoculars, he looked at the other side of the canal.

Enormous holes were hollowed out in the profound masses which, immobile a moment before, now seemed to recoil. "Hey!" exclaimed Gontran. "A fine invention, those glass cannons."

Suddenly, thick smoke emerged from the enemy's midst, forming a thick cloud 300 meters up in the air, which glided over the heads of the Equatorials. Looking up with wide eyes, with his mouth open, Flammermont watched this atmospheric transformation. "Do you see that?" he asked Fricoulet, in amazement.

"Pooh!" said the engineer. "It's a cloud."

"A cloud...but it rose up over there and it's heading for us, as if sent by them."

"Well, don't we make artificial clouds on Earth to preserve the surface of the ground from frost?"

"Bah!" murmured Gontran. "I didn't know that."

The other shrugged his shoulders disdainfully. "There are many things you don't know."

"Assuredly—for example, the purpose for which those people formed that cloud. Should we be afraid of being frozen?"

The engineer did not have time to reply; a dazzling flash of lightning suddenly sprang forth from the flank of the cloud and stuck the ground; at the same time, a formidable thunderclap shook the atmospheric layers. A sudden clamor broke out behind the two young men, who turned round and saw immense gaps in the ranks of their friends, which the lightning had just hollowed out.

They were still dumbstruck when they heard Ossipoff, who had rejoined them, murmur: "No doubt that's the terrible engine, the secret of which our adversaries kept until the last moment."

He was not mistaken. From that moment on, the struggle for existence was joined, obstinately and persistently, equally murderous on either side. Hundreds of hydrogen cannon spat out artificial hurricanes, with terrible roars, which swept away profound masses in the course of their trajectory—and in response, fulgurant lightning-bolts illuminated the shadows projected by the thick clouds extended above the Equatorials, without any discontinuity. Entire companies fell, struck down at a single stroke. Above the sound of the thunder and the roar of the cannons rose the intense, horrible and heart-rending howls of the wounded, the cries of the dying and the enraged clamors of the survivors.

Suddenly, in spite of the uproar, Gontran's attention was caught by a sort of crackling that seemed to be coming from under the ground; he looked down at his feet and saw something reminiscent of myriads of will-o'-the-wisps on the surface of the ground. "Hey! There's something curious!" he said to Fricoulet.

The latter went very pale. "Damn it!" he growled. "We're in a tight spot."

"What's happening, then?"

"The electrical tension of the ground and the clouds has reached its maximum, and the shock of recoil will occur within minutes."

"And then?"

"Then, the violence of the shock will be such that everything within an area of several square kilometers will be annihilated."

"That prospect isn't very cheerful, you know. Are you quite sure you're not mistaken?"

"Listen, and judge for yourself. That cloud formed by our enemies is still harboring a great deal of electricity; for its part, the ground, electrified by influx, also contains an enormous quantity of fluid, with which we ourselves are saturated to the most infinitesimal part of our being. Now, these two electrical changes—that of the cloud and that of the ground—tend to reconstitute themselves; if that recombination takes place, the cloud will discharge all its fluid at a single stroke and will condense as water, while the ground will revert instantaneously to its neutral state."

"In that case, we've nothing to fear but a powerful deluge—but we've seen many others!"

"You're ignoring the abrupt passage from the electrical to the neutral state, equivalent to a clap of thunder—and, whether or not we find ourselves in the path of the spark, we'll be done for, because we can't withstand the shock."

Gontran's face expressed genuine anxiety. "You see," he said. "We'd have done better to get into a balloon, like Selena and Farenheit."

“Regret is futile,” riposted Fricoulet. Stamping his foot in rage, he groaned: “Oh, if only the electricity the cloud contains could be discharged harmlessly!”

“A lightning-conductor would suffice,” Gontran declared.

“You haven’t got one on you, I suppose,” muttered the engineer.

“I find your humor ill-timed,” said Ossipoff, prey to a profound anxiety. Then, seeing Flammermont jump into an unoccupied helicopter, he cried: “Are you mad? What are you doing?”

“Simply making a lightning-conductor.”

“A lightning-conductor!” repeated Mikhail Ossipoff, looking at Fricoulet.

The latter had guessed his friend’s plan, though. “Wait for me!” he shouted, running toward him—but it was too late; the rotor was already in motion and the apparatus rose up vertically, straight toward the stormy cloud, unrolling behind it a long metallic cable that served to attach it to the ground.

At that moment, the fight reached its climax and a relative silence hung over the battlefield; the dull roar of the Equatorials’ cannons was the only sound to be heard; the voice of the thunder had ceased in an atmosphere that was suddenly calm. The enemy ranks allowed themselves to be swept away by the hurricane, impassive and without riposte, their eyes fixed on the cloud that would, in their expectation, annihilate the Equatorials.

Suddenly, a formidable cry of rage rose up from the other side of the canal; the enemy had just perceived Gontran’s helicopter, and the audacious Terran’s plan was clearly apparent. Immediately, the sky was filled with a whirlwind of winged beings, who hurled themselves toward Flammermont—but the latter, anticipating their move, accelerated the motor; just as they were about to reach him, the apparatus flew like an arrow into the cloud and disappeared from his enemies’ view.

Immediately, a long trail of fire ran along the cable, all the way to the ground, which was discharged of its dangerous surplus of electricity, while the terrible cloudy machine was reduced to black shreds, borne away by the wind. As if by magic, the sky cleared, while the suddenly-condensed vapors were transformed into an abundant rain, which inundated the Equatorials.

Up above, the Sun poured down its warm rays.

In less than five minutes, Gontran’s apparatus landed.

“Oh, my boy—my dear boy!” stammered Ossipoff, clasping the young man in his arms.

After this quasi-paternal hug, Flammermont had to submit to a no less amicable one from Fricoulet, who murmured in his ear: “So you know the theory of the lightning-conductor?”

“Didn’t I have to learn Franklin’s theory for my *bachot*?[11] You know—the story of the kite.”

---

[11] *Bachot* is a slang term for the *baccalauréat* that French high school students take by way of graduation.

The engineer unclasped his arms, grumbling in a disappointed tone: "And I thought you'd finally decided to get your teeth into the sciences!"

The young Comte shrugged his shoulders. "What does it matter," he said, "since I've just saved the fatherland with my ignorance?" Striking a comical pose, he added: "I demand to be awarded the honors of the Panthéon!"

Meanwhile, the whirlwinds launched by the Equatorials continued their ravages in the enemy masses—who, now disarmed, received death with the impassivity of despair. They were seen to oscillate in the mighty gusts of wind and then fall down, packed like fields of wheat crushed by a storm.

"It will not be much longer now," declared Aotaha.

"Perhaps you might go in search of our friends," suggested Gontran, who was eager to see his fiancée again.

As he pronounced these words he looked up and uttered a cry of joy; the apparatus containing Selena and Farenheit was descending rapidly from the height at which it had been soaring for several hours. It could now be distinguished perfectly, like a gigantic bird with a slender body and huge wings gently beating the air. Floating behind it like a plumed tail was a long streamer, undulating in the breeze.

"Of course!" exclaimed Fricoulet. "Mr. Farenheit has hoisted the American flag—I recognize his starry waistband."

The apparatus descended a few meters more, and Selena appeared over the edge, waving a handkerchief to inform her friends that she had seen them. Farenheit also became visible, standing up in the apparatus, waving his arms in the air in telegraphic gestures, doubtless as a sign of victory.

Fricoulet suddenly looked round for Aotaha, but the Martian had disappeared. The engineer frowned. "That's annoying," he muttered.

"What's annoying?" asked Gontran.

"I would have expected that Aotaha would go to fetch them, as we agreed."

"But it's unnecessary now, since they're here. Mr. Farenheit probably mastered the mechanism."

"Undoubtedly, undoubtedly...but misfortunes happen so quickly..."

"What misfortune do you fear? Even if the machine were to break down, the gravity is so weak that they'd fall like feathers."

At that moment, Fricoulet began waving his cap desperately. "Stop! Stop!" he cried, with all the force of his lungs—but the roar of the artificial hurricanes drowned out his voice, and Farenheit continued the descent.

"You've gone mad!" exclaimed Gontran, seizing his friend's arm. "You can see perfectly well that it's going marvelously."

"Yes," said Ossipoff, in his turn, paralyzing the engineer's other arm. "Let them land peacefully...all your telegraphing might disturb Mr. Farenheit in his maneuver."

Friculet looked at them both pityingly. "You're asking me if I'm mad," he replied, "but I've no need to ask whether you are—I affirm it. Don't you see that they're coming down in front of the lines, and that..."

He did not have time to finish. Perhaps the American, pressed by Selena, had activated the descent voluntarily; perhaps, as Ossipoff had just said, he had been disturbed by Fricoulet's signals...at any rate, the apparatus fell. Its wings were immobile, but they formed a parachute.

"Run!" cried Gontran. "We'll catch them in our arms."

"Run!" repeated Ossipoff.

The two of them were already racing forward when they came to a standstill, as if their feet had been suddenly nailed to the ground, and a frightful scream escaped their anguish-contracted throats. Having come within 50 meters of the battlefield, the helicopter had just been seized by a mighty current of air and it disappeared from the Terrans' view in less than a second, like a large sea-bird carried away by a tempest.

"Selena! Selena!" cried Flammermont, desperately.

"My child! My poor child!" sobbed the old man, wringing his hands.

"Come on," muttered Fricoulet. "I prophesied doom, but what the hell? They didn't want to believe me."

Aotaha, who had witnessed this unexpected event from some way off, sped towards them as fast as his wings could carry him and exchanged a few rapid words with the engineer.

Immediately, the latter took his notebook from his pocket and, with marvelous self-composure, scribbled a few figures on a blank page. Then he tapped Gontran lightly on the arm. "Why torture yourself this way?" he said. "All's not lost yet. Mr. Farenheit's not an imbecile—he's a calm and courageous man; as for Selena, you know that she's not lacking in energy."

Flammermont shook his head. "Yes," he stammered, "I know all that...but what can they do against a tempest? Master it?"

"No—but after all, if my calculations are correct, that tempest isn't blowing at more than 200 kilometers a minute, and I estimate that, after covering 700 or 800 kilometers, it ought to peter out."

"So what?"

"So, we have only to march in that direction until we reach the 800th kilometer, and there's a good chance we'll find them."

"Only *a good chance*," complained Flammermont, dejectedly. Then, as if Fricoulet's words had restored courage to his heart anyway, he raised his head and said: "Let's go!"

"Depart like this, on foot, without a guide! You're mad!"

"What, then?"

"We're going to go to a nearby town, where Aotaha will procure a means of rapid locomotion, which will permit us to fly off in search of your fiancée."

So saying, the engineer took both Ossipoff and Gontran by the arm and, almost carrying them, he followed the guide.

Chapter XXXVII
The Snowy Isle

With Aotaha flying and the Terrans bounding, the little troop arrived at their journey's objective in less than an hour. On the shore of an ocean—in what Mikhail Ossipoff declared to be the cul-de-sac formed by the extremity of the Hourglass Sea, in the very center of Libya—stood a strange town. It was a graceful confusion of towers measuring no less than 100 meters in height; quaintly-shaped turrets topped them off, themselves surmounted by very long metallic spires, whose tips seemed to be lost in the clouds. The parts that appeared to form the living quarters were pierced with numerous bay windows, through which the winged population circulated like a swarm of bees buzzing around their hive.

An extraordinary animation seemed to reign in the town, through which the Terrans passed at speed, following their guide; that animation was so great that the voyagers excited scarcely any curiosity from the people they encountered.

"The news of the victory has probably got them all excited," murmured Gontran—who, despite his anxiety regarding Selena, had, as the saying has it, not enough eyes to look around him.

"They're presumably on their way to sing a *Te Deum* in some cathedral," replied Fricoulet.

The further they went, the more compact the crowds they met became, and the denser the winged battalions streaking through the air became. "That's really it...that's really it," murmured the engineer while striding along. "I'm not mistaken." And this conviction increased when he and his companions emerged into a vast plaza, on the far side of which was a monument in the same form as the town's dwellings, but taller by a third. "It's doubtless their Notre-Dame," he said to Gontran.

The plaza was swarming, and the facades of the houses, their turrets and even their lightning-conductors were covered with Martians, all of whose faces were turned toward the monument, to which Aotaha slowly drew nearer.

"Tell me," murmured the engineer, "doesn't it seem to you, as it does to me, that these people don't seem as delighted as the circumstances demand?"

"They seem anxious, in fact."

"One would think they were waiting for someone or something," said Ossipoff, in his turn.

"Perhaps the official proclamation of victory," added Fricoulet. He leaned toward Aotaha, who was ahead of him; the latter turned round and replied briefly, raising his hand toward the sky, then continued on his way. Only then did the Terrans notice the threatening quality of the sky. Beneath the leaden grey dome that the skies rounded our above their heads, black clouds were descending rapidly toward the ground, as if they wanted to crush it, and the atmosphere, charged with electricity, had become stifling.

Fricoulet's face, also darkening, betrayed a certain anxiety.

"What's the matter?" asked Flammermont.

"I fear that it will be necessary to delay our departure...."

The young Comte uttered a furious exclamation. "No, damn it!" he declared. "For what reason?"

"Because the battle that we just witnessed has disturbed the atmospheric layers so profoundly that a meteorological cataclysm is imminent."

"What difference does that make to us?"

"The difference that Aotaha will refuse to go with us."

"We'll do without a guide."

"That's impossible."

Gontran stamped his foot violently. "Impossible!" he groaned. "It's me you're saying that word to...it's you who's pronouncing it!"

"Certainly—how do you expect to find your own way across this unknown world?"

Flammermont laughed sardonically. "Unknown! The world of Mars! Come on—I thought, on the contrary, that Mars was the best-known of the planets."

"The best-known, I won't dispute, telescopically speaking—but from there to knowing it sufficiently well to go for a walk, cane in hand, without Joanne or any other guide—stop there!"[12]

"You're speaking for yourself, no doubt," complained the young Comte, "but I'm quite certain that Monsieur Ossipoff...what use is being an astronomer if he doesn't know any more than me?" He took the old man by the arm, and said: "Fricoulet claims that a cataclysm is impending, and that Aotaha will refuse to serve as our guide."

A profound anguish was painted on Ossipoff's face.

"That won't prevent us from going in search of Selena, will it?" the young man continued.

"Without a guide!" cried the old scientist, involuntarily.

"Don't you have Schiaparelli's map?"

Ossipoff shook his head. "Don't you remember what I said to you a little while ago? Mars is the most treacherous of all the planets; to launch ourselves in search of the unfortunates without a guide would be to run to almost certain death—and without any chance of success."

"Doomed, then!" Gontran lamented. "She's doomed!"

"No," said the engineer. "We'll get her back, your Selena—but give us time for reflection, damn it! Anyway, the scientists deliberating in there might declare that their terror was vain and their prognostications absolutely false."

---

[12] The geographer Adolphe Joanne (1813-1881) was the author of a great many travel guides employed in 19th century France.

At the word "scientists," Mikhail Ossipoff had pricked up his ears. "Tell me," he said, taking Fricoulet by the sleeve, "is there any means of witnessing this deliberation?"

They had arrived at that moment, in spite of the crowd packing the plaza, at the foot of the monument that seemed to be the objective of Aotaha's efforts. The engineer communicated the old man's question to the Martian.

Without replying, Aotaha seized Fricoulet by his hair, which he wore long, and, thus burdened, rose up vertically with a thrust of his wings to the summit of the edifice. It was surrounded by a sort of circular balcony, on which he deposited the bewildered engineer. He did the same for Gontran and Ossipoff; in less than five minutes, the three Terrans found themselves reunited in a hall where some 30 Martians, with their eyes glued to optical instruments, were staring into space.

Suddenly, a black dot appeared on the horizon, which grew rapidly and soon took on the form of a winged being, who landed in the midst of them. "The entire atmosphere of Mars is in turmoil," he declared. "The atmospheric condensation caused by the battle in the Libyan plains is producing considerable perturbations everywhere."

As he concluded these words, another Martian appeared, coming from the opposite direction. "The ice at the southern pole is melting and dispersing," declared the new messenger.

A third arrived then, who said: "A violent whirlwind has formed over the Southern Ocean, produced by the double phenomenon of the suction and repression of air between cold regions to hot ones."

He had scarcely concluded before a fourth messenger entered, furled his wings, and, in a voice even ore vibrant than the first, pronounced words that, on their translation by Aotaha, made Gontran shudder dolorously. "The waters of the Ocean are astir and, under the combined impulsion of the tide produced by the attraction of the two satellites, the Sun and the cyclone, they're beginning to invade the continent."

Fricoulet rubbed his hands together with an attitude of great satisfaction. "There we go!" he said. "The plot thickens!"

A groan uttered beside him, however, attracted his attention to Flammermont. "Damn!" he said, clapping his friend on the shoulder amicably. "What's up with you? You seem distinctly out of sorts."

In a desolate voice, the young Comte murmured: "Selena! Must I only get her back to lose her all over again?"

"It's the story of happiness. You touch it with the end of your finger, you think you've grasped it, and then: *bang!*—it flies away from you." He added, between clenched teeth: "With the difference, however, that Selena doesn't represent happiness." At that moment, he darted a glance outside. Like a flock of immense crows, the black clouds were descending upon the ground, enveloping the entire town in an obscurity that was, so to speak, more complete and more terrifying.

"It's strange," Ossipoff murmured, "how nervous I am."

"That's not surprising, in the midst of this atmosphere saturated with electricity," Fricoulet replied.

"A good storm would soothe us," the old man went on.

"Unfortunately, a storm in impossible here—those numerous lightning-conductors by which the dwellings are surmounted are neutralizing the electricity of these mists and drowning the fluid in the damp ground."

Rain began to fall in large drops, and was soon transformed into a veritable cataract pouring torrents of water down on the town, with a sonorous drumming sound.

"So we can't think of leaving here?" Fricoulet asked his guide.

"We must wait."

"Wait for what?"

The Martian extended his wing toward the west. A dull and indistinct rumble was coming from the depths of the horizon, borne on the wings of a powerful wind. It was like the distant voice of the sea when a tempest lifts it up and hurls it against the cliffs. Leaning forward, with anxious eyes and cocked ears, the Terrans listened.

"What's that?" stammered Gontran.

"The sea...the sea that has broken its dikes...it's invaded the continents and is running towards us."

The Terrans shivered. "But that's a flood!" they cried, in unison.

The Martian inclined his head affirmatively.

"And we're just going to wait, meekly, without doing anything to stop the waters?" stammered Flammermont.

Ossipoff's emption had lasted no longer than a few seconds; he recovered almost all his serenity almost immediately, and Fricoulet heard him murmur, in a satisfied fashion: "My word—I'm having better luck than I had any right to expect; I'm going to have the key to mysterious transformations about which other astronomers remain confused: a sea dries up, a continent is transformed into an ocean...that's certainly not an everyday spectacle." He seized Gontran's hands and said to him in a vibrant voice: "We're going to catch the Chameleon's secrets, eh?"

"Eh?" cried the young man. "Never mind your Chameleon—have you no heart? Have you no thought for Selena, then?"

"No heart—me!" exclaimed the scientist. "No thought of my daughter! Are you mad?"

"You certainly seem to be far more preoccupied with the flood than the fate of your child."

"Eh? Selena will be found, I'm convinced of it—while the opportunity to study the Martian perturbations and their causes will never arise again." With these words, unable to resist the ardent curiosity that was devouring him, he went out on to the balcony circling the edifice. The rumbling that had attracted his attention a few moments before had increased in intensity and now filled the air entirely; without seeing them, it was possible to divine the presence of the immense, powerful and terrifying waves far away, beyond the horizon, galloping like a stampeding herd of bison, destroying everything in their path as they advanced.

Suddenly, the thick screen of cloud that masked the landscape parted. Through the torrents of water that striped the ethereal plan, the old man perceived, still indistinct in the distance but thickening rapidly, a white line spread across the entire width of the horizon. That line soon swelled, and swelled further, and took on form—and the foamy waves appeared, running with lightning rapidity, leaping up beneath the brutal lash of the wind. "The sea! The sea!" he cried, extending his arms in a gesture of terrified admiration. Clinging to the balcony, risking being torn away and carried aloft by the furious breath of the cyclone at any moment, he waited for the terrible element.

Inside, the Martians were debating the matter, calmly and impassively. One might have thought that the frightful scourge was not about to fall upon them—and yet, the howling of the waves was terrifying, and before the powerful breath of the tempest, the monument was vibrating from top to bottom.

"We've been accustomed to these cataclysms for a long time," Aotaha replied to Fricoulet, who was interrogating him. "It's not rare to see one of our continents suddenly and completely invaded by the waters; besides, we take every precaution to avid overly troublesome complications. As you have been able to observe, all our habitations rest on watertight components, which permit them to float to the surface when an inundation occurs."

"I understand," replied the engineer. "And these phenomena doubtless occur on a regular basis?"

"No. These sorts of gigantic tides—for, strictly speaking, that is what these floods are—only occur in the wake of exceptional circumstances; it happens that today, the condensation of the atmosphere caused by the abrupt discharge of stormy clouds coincided with the maximum attraction of the Sun and out satellites. That is why it is probable that the waters, this time..."

The Martian did not finish his sentence; the first waves had just reached the town and his words were lost in the frightful racket of the furious elements. A violent shock shook the edifice, which oscillated on its base like a ship whose hull has been suddenly struck by waves. It seemed momentarily that it would fall sideways, so powerful was the pressure of the wind; then it straightened again, recovered its aplomb; then it leaned in the other direction, and came back yet again to a vertical position.

It seemed to the Terrans that they were aboard a ship in the open sea, perched on the summit of a mast; the wind was howling around their ears, and the damp spindrift and savage clamor of the waves reached out to them.

Ossipoff had tried to remain at his observation-post, but the waves, as if irritated by the sight of this pygmy, who seemed to be defying them, rose up toward him in a titanic swell, soaking him to the bones with their icy foam. He came back to join his companions. "What a sublime spectacle!" he exclaimed, putting his hands together in an admiring gesture.

"Sublime! Sublime!" muttered Fricoulet, pulling a face. "It seems to me that the sublime extends as far as horror."

"It's all the more beautiful for that!" riposted the old man.

"Provided that the tower can withstand it!" murmured the engineer. He had not finished this remark when terrible screams—cries of fright and cries for help—resounded outside, rising above the howling of the tempest and the noise of the waves. At the same time, strange detonations were heard, soon followed by sinister cracking sounds that made the tower itself shudder.

"*Parbleu!*" said the engineer. "What I feared is happening!"

"What did you fear?" asked Gontran.

"The moorings that attach the habitations to the ground, making them resemble ships at anchor, are beginning to break."

"And then?"

"Then the town will break up," Fricoulet replied, placidly.

"But we're doomed!" cried the young Comte.

The engineer shrugged his shoulders. "Why? This tower might well perform the office of a transatlantic liner and bring us safely to port."

"Safely to port? Where?"

"Wherever it pleases the tempest to take us!"

All through the night and the next day the situation remained the same. The entire town was carried away by the cyclone toward the south-west. In the place where the cultivated regions of Libya had existed a few days before, a muddy ocean now extended its tumultuous waters as far as the eye could see. Fricoulet estimated that a surface of 400,000 square kilometers—the dimensions of the whole of Europe—had been submerged.

Aotaha declared that the Newton Ocean must have run dry and that the Flammarion Sea had certainly diminished in depth.

While Fricoulet wondered how this strange odyssey would end, and Gontran thought about Selena, Mikhail Ossipoff continued his studies of the unknown world on whose surface he was sailing in such a bizarre fashion.

Yes, he thought, *this is certainly what the telescope showed me when I examined it from the Observatory at Pulkova; no important asperities, the ground eroded by the rotation, scarcely more elevated than the average level of the waters, thus permitting the slightest external cause to produce enormous differences of sea-level, considerable floods that change the planet's appearance completely...* Rubbing his hands together with enthusiastic satisfaction, he murmured: "Ah, my brothers, my colleagues, how many of you would gladly take my place?"

During the 36 hours they had been floating in this manner they must have traveled a considerable distance, which even the Martians could not measure. Had they always been heading in the same direction? Had they deviated at a considerable angle, or even retraced their steps? Fricoulet asked such questions, but his friend Aotaha was unable to answer them. In every direction, as far the eye could see, there were waves, more waves and yet more waves. Above their heads was the leaden grey sky, streaked by rain, in which thick black clouds raced like a herd of wild horses at the gallop.

"It's enough to make one despair of ever arriving," murmured Fricoulet.

"Arriving where?" asked Gontran.

"Wherever we're going to stop, of course."

As evening approached, however, a calm seemed to be developing. The wind was blowing less violently, lifting the waves less furiously; the tower was not pitching as much, and the sky, swept clear of the clouds that were darkening it, permitted the last fires of the setting Sun to play on the liquid surface on which our friends were floating.

Suddenly, Gontran, who was scanning the horizon, uttered a cry: "Land! Land ahoy!"

His companions ran to confirm the news. Scarcely ten kilometers away, lying on the waves like a great cetacean, a low-lying body of land appeared. In the distant interior, crowned by a thin mist, stood a sharp and sparkling mountain peak.

Turing to Ossipoff, Fricoulet laughed sardonically. "What do you say, Monsieur Astronomer, who claims that Mars is as round as a billiard-ball? It seems to me that you haven't examined it thoroughly—or, at least, that you don't know all its nooks and crannies..."

"Why is that?"

"Because, damn it, it seems to me that that's a mountain, which seems quite tall—and even that the mountain in question is covered in ice."

The old man slapped his forehead, as if an idea had suddenly come to mind. Without replying to the engineer, he took out his map, consulted it, and exclaimed in a vibrant voice: "Would you like me to tell you where we are?"

"Do you need to ask?"

"Very well! We're at 33 degrees of longitude and 26 degrees south latitude."

"Which is to say?"

"Almost in the middle of the Kepler Ocean."

"On what do you base that?" asked Fricoulet, incredulously.

"On that island—which is none other than the Snowy Isle."

"But we're going to land on it," said Gontran. "The wind seems to be pushing us toward it."

Fricoulet released a small sigh of satisfaction. “So much the better. That will permit me to stretch my legs a little—I’m beginning to seize up.”

Flammermont leaned toward his friend. “Do you think that the weather is clearing up?”

The engineer looked up and examined the sky attentively, then shook his head. “Hmm!” he replied. “This seems to me only to be an intermission; I wouldn’t be at all surprised if the tempest soon began again, with new vigor.”

Gontran made a forceful gesture. “Whatever happens,” he declared, “I warn you that if I set foot on that island, I’ll only leave it to start searching for Serena.”

Fricoulet became pensive at the sound of that name. “Eh?” he murmured, as if talking to himself. “It’s not impossible.”

Gontran shivered, and took his friend’s hands, seized by a presentiment. “You’re thinking about Selena aren’t you?” he said.

“That’s true,” the engineer replied.

“To what were you referring in saying that it wasn’t impossible?”

“Nothing, I swear,” said the other, embarrassed—and he added: “An idea of mine…but which it’s useless to communicate to you. Why give you false hope?”

“Oh, I beg you,” Flammermont insisted, “answer me…tell me your idea.”

Fricoulet seemed very annoyed, and hesitated momentarily, then eventually said: “The Snowy Isle is 800 kilometers away from the location of the battle. Now, that’s precisely the distance, you’ll remember, that I calculated that the tempest might have carried the aeronef.”

For a few moments, Gontran remained mute and immobile, so great was his shock. Suddenly, he launched himself upon the engineer and hugged him, crying: “Alcide! Alcide! You’re the best of friends.”

“But you’re choking me!” exclaimed the engineer, disengaging himself from that amicable embrace. “You see,” he added, “it was a mistake to tell you that…you’ve been carried away by a problematic hope…and if I’m mistaken….”

Gontran’s features became tragic. “If you’re mistaken,” he groaned, “I’ll kill myself.”

At that moment, a shock powerful enough to make them lose their balance threw them rudely together; then all oscillation ceased. The base of the tower had just touched the bottom. Aotaha put his finger on Fricoulet’s shoulder to attract his attention to the direction of the island. Half a kilometer away, scarcely emerging from the muddy surface of the waters, a low and devastated coast appeared, on which the fleecy waves were breaking into yellowish spray.

Fricoulet uttered an exclamation and grabbed Gontran’s arm. “Look!” he said, in a strangled voice. “Look!”

Flamermont strained his eyes in vain; he could not see anything.

"Now then!" complained the engineer. "Am I seeing things? I don't think I'm mistaken, though."

"Nor me," stammered the young Comte. "Tell me...tell me...you can see that you're getting on my nerves..."

With his hand over his eyes, like a shade, Fricoulet was still gazing. "Damn it!" he said. "I'd put my hand in the fire to swear that that's Mr. Farenheit's famous waistband that I can see over there, floating in the air."

He had not finished speaking when an exclamation from Mikhail Ossipoff made him turn around. Gontran was no longer there, but the engineer saw the old man, who was leaning over the edge, looking down with a distraught expression.

"Gontran! Gontran!" stammered Fricoulet, in alarm.

But the young man was already no more than a dot in mid-air; a few seconds later, he reached the liquid surface, into which he disappeared, sending up sprays of foam all around. He soon reappeared, swimming toward the shore with all his strength. Ossipoff turned to look at Fricoulet. "The poor fellow!" he murmured, putting his hands together. "What's he doing?"

"He's simply doing what we're going to do—he's heading for dry land, which, no doubt, will offer him more security than this town on which we've been sailing for 48 hours." So saying, he put his leg over the balustrade and prepared to dive head-first in his turn.

The old man hesitated. "Look!" said the engineer, showing him long winged columns striping the sky. "These good Martians are setting us an example..."

"But I can't swim," Ossipoff replied.

Fricoulet shrugged his shoulders. "A minor detail," he said. "Give me your hand and jump boldly."

The old man hesitated.

"I swear that I'll get you ashore, dead or alive."

This declaration appeared to make a deep impression on the old scientist. The engineer noticed that and added, jokingly: "I'll make every effort, of course to take you alive rather than dead."

"Very kind of you," Ossipoff muttered, peevishly.

"It's not just for you that I'll do it," the other said, sardonically. "It's also for your daughter, to whom it would cause too much grief."

"The old man shook his head dolorously. "Alas, my poor Selena..." he murmured.

Fricoulet pointed toward the land. "But your Selena's there!" he exclaimed.

Ossipoff grabbed his hand. "There!" he said, in a strangled voice. "You've seen her!"

"Her, no—but I'll bet my head that I've seen Mr. Farenheit's starry girdle. Now, if the American is saved, your daughter must be alive…otherwise, I think I can affirm that he would have died with her…"

Ossipoff's physiognomy was suddenly transfigured. "Let's go," he said, simply.

Fricoulet gasped him strongly by the arm, and they both jumped.

Meanwhile, Flammermont was swimming vigorously. His body was scarcely immersed and, strictly speaking, he was gliding over the surface of the water with inconceivable rapidity. All around him, borne by a current created by a rather rough northerly wind, was debris of every sort: uprooted plants, broken tree-branches, Martian corpses, and even enormous ice-floes, doubtless torn from the polar ice-caps. The swimmer was nearly crushed 20 times over by these bobbing and rolling masses, to which he paid scarcely any heed, for they came at him with prodigious speed.

Finally, he uttered a cry of triumph and joy. His feet had just touched the ground and, scarcely 100 meters away on the shore, Farenheit and Selena were standing, motionless and anguished, scanning the liquid immensity that surrounded them, wondering whether the corpses of their friends might pass before their very eyes.

"Selena! Selena!" called Gontran, in a voice stifled by emotion and happiness.

"My God! My God!" said the young woman. "That's Monsieur de Flammermont's voice!"

"By God!" growled the American. "I think you're right." And both of them, without even thinking about what they were doing, headed in the direction from which the young Comte's calls seemed to have come.

Suddenly, without transition, the Sun, dying on the horizon, set fire to the liquid plane with its last rays, and darkness fell, enveloping the sky and the entire landscape with its veils of shadow, pricked by the stars like a multitude of golden pinheads. The waves seemed blacker still, then, with a little spark illuminated at the crest of each one by reflected starlight.

"My God!" cried Selena, clinging to Farenheit's arm. "I can't hear any more…"

"Not hearing anything is a detail," the American replied. "The most terrible thing is that we can't see anything, and that Monsieur de Flammermont might pass us by without our even suspecting it." They had both stopped, already knee-deep in water.

"We have to turn back," said Farenheit. "In this darkness, there's a risk that we won't be able to get back to the hospitable land on which we took refuge—not to mention that we have no chance of finding our friends."

"No, no," the young woman relied, forcefully. "Let's go on…I sear to you that it really was Monsieur de Flammermont's voice whose echo reached my ears just now." And she added, in a profound tone: "The heart can't be mistaken, you see, Mr. Farenheit."

The American uttered a little groan. "The heart, perhaps not," he retorted, "but the ear…but even so…." With these words, he clamped the young woman's hand to his arm and resumed his forward march.

Suddenly, to the east, Phobos appeared, illuminating the immense of turbulent liquid plain with a soft light, like that of a lamp.

"There! There!" cried Selena, pointing at an ice-floe passing 20 meters away.

Farenheit had no sooner steered his eyes in that direction than he muttered a forceful: "By God!" Abandoning his companion, he hurled himself in the direction indicated by the young woman. In a few strides he had reached the floe, which was drifting away, and he came back rapidly, holding Flammermont's body in his arms, stiff and inanimate.

"Dead!" moaned Selena.

"No, Miss, don't worry…his heart's still beating, so there's still hope—but let's get back to shore as quickly as possible."

Followed by the young woman, Farenheit returned to the island, taking gigantic strides. As he deposited his burden on the shore it moved, then uttered a groan, and finally raised itself up on an elbow, stammering in a faint voice: "Where am I?"

"Heavens! He's alive! He can speak! Oh, God be praised!"

On hearing Selena's voice, the young man got to his feet. Seeing the young woman, he held out his arms to her, crying: "Ah, God is good—since he permits me to see you again before dying!"

"Dying!" exclaimed a shadow that emerged from the water at that moment, joyfully. "Who's talking about dying?" It was Fricoulet, who had arrived just in time to hear his friend's despairing exclamation. He was followed by the worthy Monsieur Ossipoff, who—sometimes wading, as best he could, and sometimes dragged by the engineer—had succeeded in getting ashore.

The old man hurled himself upon Selena and hugged her to his breast for a long time. Then, turning to the American, who was watching this tender effusion impassively, he shook his hand energetically. "Mr. Farenheit," he said, in a vibrant voice, "for as long as I live and until I die…"

"No need for such profusion, Monsieur Ossipoff," replied Farenheit. "But if you think you owe me a little gratitude, you can pay me back by getting me back to my native land as soon as possible."

The old man groaned, but made no reply.

Gontran, to whom Fricoulet had just given a draught of the cordial that he always carried about his person, leaned toward the American. "Mr. Farenheit," he whispered in his ear, "you've saved my fiancée's life and you've just saved mine. I'll take responsibility for discharging Monsieur Ossipoff's debt at the same time as my own."

The engineer, who had overheard, said, in the same tone: "You appear to be making reckless promises, my friend."

"And why's that?"

"Because events might not allow you to keep your promise."

"I shall do everything, at least, that is in my power...by why that sinister prognosis?"

As if to answer this question, a frightful din suddenly resounded in the north, filling the air. The clouds tore apart, and the very sky seemed to open up—and an intense, terrifying light set the horizon on fire, throwing bloody reflections over the surface of the water.

"What's that?" cried Farenheit, in alarm.

"It's the curtain lifting on the final act of the drama," Fricoulet replied, sardonically.

A savage howling suddenly burst forth; it was the wind, unleashed again, swelling the waters beneath its formidable breath, which lifted up in gigantic mountains only to hollow out in unsoundable abysms.

"Flat on the ground!" cried the engineer, immediately hurling himself face-down on the ground to set his companions an example. "Quickly, everyone—fall flat!"

They imitated him, understanding that in that position they provided less purchase for the hurricane—whose gigantic wing brushed them, without the power to snatch them from the ground on which they were, so to speak, encrusted.

Selena had seized Gontran's hand immediately. The latter clasped his arm forcefully around the young woman's waist and murmured in her ear: "Oh, my dear heart, if we must die, at least death won't separate us."

"Gontran!" she stammered, happy in spite of the death that threatened them. "Gontran, my last thought will be of my father and you."

He squeezed her hand in a passionate grip; then they both fell silent, almost driven crazy by the roar of the tempest and the howling of the waves.

Suddenly, a kilometer away from the island, like the shadow of a gigantic phantom drowned in the sinister obscurity of the night, the Martian town sped away with vertiginous rapidity, carried by the hurricane. For the second time, lightning split the sky, and by its livid light the Terrans were able to perceive the towers, turrets and spires dancing atop the waves like corks, colliding with one another, their pinnacles overlapping like the masts of an immense squadron of ships, buffeted by the tempestuous wind.

Then everything became dark again, and the fantastic apparition melted away, disappearing as if by magic into the sinister mists.

The hurricane seemed to have reached its full intensity now; an immense mass of cloud, as black as ink, covered the sky from horizon to horizon, extending over the horrors of the cataclysm like a funereal shroud—and in that frightful obscurity, they heard the unleashed winds battling against the enraged waves breaking on the shore, covering the semi-conscious Terrans with spray.

Suddenly, they were snatched out of their torpor by a fearful shock; it seemed that the entire island had quivered, shaken to its deepest foundations. Then there was a second shock, more violent and more terrible, and the ground vibrated.

Involuntarily, the Terrans sat up, convinced that an underground quake was about to swallow them up in some crevasse, and the fear of death gripped them. Gontran, raising himself up on one knee, clutched the head of the unconscious Selena to his breast. Farenheit, clinging to Fricoulet, groaned "By God!" over and over again, without interruption, enraged at dying before being able to present his accounts to his shareholders. Even though his mind was a trifle distressed, Mikhail Ossipoff was trying nevertheless to determine the cause of this unchaining of the elements.

As for Fricoulet, in whose eyes life had only ever had a relative value, he had but one regret: that it was pitch dark. Since suffering a horrible nightmare in early childhood, he had maintained the habit of sleeping with a nightlight, and he did not care to surrender himself to eternal sleep without being able to see clearly. *Bah!* he thought. *When one can't do otherwise, it's necessary to take the weather as it comes.* Scarcely had this philosophical reflection been formulated in the engineer's mind than a third shock was felt, even more powerful than the first two, which tore the Snowy Isle from its age-old base.

Like an immense raft, it was borne away in the midst of the torment, toward the South Pole.

Chapter XXXVIII
The Castaways of Mars

The night that Ossipoff and his companions spent clinging to the wreckage of the island, which carried them along with it through the demented waters was frightful and terrifying. Soaked by the waves and lashed by the wind that howled through the air, the unfortunates felt the fragile ground that served as their raft trembling beneath them. The acuity of their eyes was multiplied tenfold by fear; even so, they could not succeed in piercing the thick gloom that enveloped them like a black shroud. Thy were conscious, however, that the waves eating away at the Snowy Isle were attacking it with range, like carnivorous monsters attacking a cadaver, from which each bite tore another shred. They expected to see their fragile raft break apart and crumble at any moment, delivering them into the gulf.

Suddenly, Farenheit—who had contrived to drag himself to a cleft in the rock, in which he had wedged himself, felt someone place a hand on his arm. He made an abrupt fearful movement; the nerves of that phlegmatic, imperturbable man who could not be moved by anything, had been so over-excited by the strange adventure in which he had become involved that the touch terrified him. "Who's there?" he grunted, in a strangled voice.

"It's me, my dear Mr. Farenheit!" someone exclaimed in his ear.

"Who's *me*?" howled the American, who did not recognize the voice of the man who had spoken to him.

"Me, Fricoulet, damn it! Who did you think it was?"

"I don't know, I tell you," replied Farenheit, whose teeth were chattering in spite of the efforts he as making to master his unconscious terror. "I don't know anything." He added: "I'm very glad that you're not dead, my dear Monsieur Fricoulet." His hand search in the darkness for the engineer's, and squeezed it forcefully.

"Thank you for the kind sentiment that motivated those words," replied the young engineer. "I'd like to think that it applies equally to our companions."

"Are they alive too?" exclaimed the American.

"All as alive as me. I beg your pardon, but have you conserved your chronometer in the midst of this debacle?"

Farenheit patted himself anxiously; that chronometer was a marvelous instrument indicating, along with the hours and the seconds, the day of the week and the month, the seasons and the phases of the Moon. He had bought it at the beginning of his pork-fat business, with the first profits it had realized, and he had paid no less than $450 for it. The engineer's question had given him a perfectly natural moment of panic, for he was fond of the chronometer, from which he had never been separated for many years, and which he was accustomed to consider a sort of fetish. He uttered a sigh of satisfaction, therefore, when he felt it in its place, in his coat pocket. "Yes," he replied, "I still have it—but how can that be of interest to you?"

"You'll understand. Would you please make it chime?"

The Amrican took the instrument from his pocket, put it very close to his ear and pressed the switch activating its chime. There was a single feeble ring.

"That's the quarter-hour," he said.

"Quarter past what?" Fricoulet complained.

"That's right—I'm so distracted that I wasn't thinking about the hour." He pressed another switch. This time, the chronometer sounded three scarcely-discernible strokes.

"3 a.m.," said the American.

"3:15 a.m.," murmured Fricoulet, as if talking to himself. "Another two hours to wait."

"To wait for what?"

"Daylight, of course." And the engineer added, in a tone full of satisfaction: "In two hours, we'll be able to see clearly."[13]

"So what?" grumbled Farenheit. "Whether it's light or dark, the situation won't change."

"The sunlight will certainly have no influence on the catastrophe that's turning the planet upside down...however, as it's unimaginable that things can continue in this vein for long, perhaps it will provide a means of getting some information."

"What information?"

"You're asking too much," said the engineer, impatiently. "How do I know? Even if the light of day had no other consequence than to let us see one another, it seems to me that that would be an appreciable result...we'd feel less isolated." With these words, whose sharp tone aggravated the American perceptibly, Fricoulet crawled back to the spot he had occupied before, next to Flammermont. "Gontran!" he said.

"What is it?" demanded the Comte, in a bleak voice.

"It'll be light in two hours."

"What do I care?" the other replied, in the same tone.

"You too, then!" grumbled the engineer. "Day and night are all the same to you? You don't care about the advantages we might obtain from the sunlight?"

"Do you think the sunlight can get us out of this?" Gontran retorted, bitterly.

---

[13] The reader might wonder how it comes about that Farenheit's chronometer seems to be in phase with Martian days that are slightly, but significantly, longer than Earthly ones. The authors also seem to begin wondering about it shortly, when further a time-check is made that seems to be blatantly inconsistent with this one.

"Who knows? Perhaps."

Flanmermont shrugged his shoulders, although the darkness hid the gesture from Fricoulet. Afterwards, he fell back into despairing silence. He held Selena's head clasped to his bosom. Fear had caused the unfortunate young woman to fall into a comatose state so complete and so absolute that Gontran would have believed her dead had he not felt a feeble heartbeat beneath his fingertips. For long hours, she had neither made any movement nor pronounced a word.

As for Ossipoff, Flammermont and Fricoulet had heard him talking to himself all night long. What was the old man saying? Neither the engineer nor his friend spoke Russian, and it was in his native language that the astronomer was expressing himself.

The torrential rain that had begun to fall at the commencement of the tempest had, however, stopped some time ago. The wind, no longer howling in as sinister a fashion as before, had diminished in violence, and the gentler waves were no longer crashing voraciously upon the islet that served as the castaways' refuge. Fricoulet observed, by contrast, a swaying movement comparable to the rocking of a boat, the cause of which he could not explain. Assuming that the Snowy Isle, torn from the foundations that formerly linked it to the bed of the Ocean, was now adrift, its surface area was such that, although it was gliding over the surface of the waters, they should not have had any influence on its center of gravity. In any case, the engineer did not linger long over the question, reserving it for elucidation when it was light.

The two hours that still separated the Terrans from the sunrise seemed as long as two centuries to them—and yet, save for Fricoulet, none of them hoped that the light of day might bring about some amelioration of their situation.

Finally, like the lifting of a gauze veil, the thick fog that enveloped them dissipated, and the darkness of night gave way to the wan and indecisive light of dawn. Then, in the distance—very far away—a pale pink line appeared on the horizon and, with surprising rapidity, the orient caught fire beneath the rays of a sparkling Sun. A profound sigh escaped our friends' bosoms. As if by magic, Selena seemed to come back to life on perceiving the radiant star that she and her companions had despaired of ever seeing again.

Above their heads, the sky extended its blue cupola, pure and untainted, pricked by a myriad of stars fading away in the sunlight. All around them, as far as they could see, an immense sea displayed its liquid expanse, suddenly flat and mirror-smooth. The wind scarcely continued to blow, lightly rippling its surface.

Gazing around the ground that carried then, Fricoulet then obtained an explanation for the swaying of the surface of the Snowy Isle that he had previously found inexplicable. In a single night, it had been almost entirely devoured by the waves bent on its destruction. The immense peak several kilometers high, covered with eternal snows, which had dominated it and had earned it the name with which terrestrial astronomers had baptized it, had sunk into the ocean. The ragged shores of the isle, worn away and crumbled into fragments, had been reduced to such an extent that the engineer and his companions were now transported by an islet only a few 100 square meters in area. Alone among his companions, Fricoulet had conserved enough self-composure to make this observation, which he kept to himself, judging that his friends were depressed enough already, and that there as no point in augmenting their despair.

Farenheit, meanwhile, had emerged from his listlessness and, going over to the old scientist, asking him in a voice vibrant with ill-contained anger: "Well, Monsieur Ossipoff, it'll soon be six months since you dragged us in your wake, with the hope of getting us into an inextricable situation.[14] This time you must be well satisfied—for I'm damned if I know how you can get us out of this one."

The old man contented himself with shrugging his shoulders and made no reply.

"If you were only able tell us where we are," muttered the American, "but in view of the questioning glances that you're darting in very direction, it's easy to guess that you're as ignorant as we are on that score."

"There's a distinct shortage of reference-points," said Gontran, with a sardonic laugh.

"Pooh! It's not knowing where we are that interests me, but where we're going."

Fricoulet addressed the American then, saying: "Mr. Farenheit, if, perhaps, it will soothe your chagrin to know which Martian country it is in which fate has condemned you to terminate an existence so far devoted to the animal-fat trade, then be satisfied; at this moment, we must be in the middle of the Kepler Ocean, called the Erythrean Sea by Schiaparelli, and—see how precise I am—in the place designated by them as the region of Pyrrhus."

Selena, who had recovered her courage and good humor along with the Sun's rays, emerged from the silence in which she had so far been confined. "Monsieur Fricoulet," she asked, "would you be so very kind as to resolve a question for me that I have been asking myself fruitlessly for a quarter of an hour?"

"Go on, Mademoiselle. If it's in my power to answer, I'll answer; otherwise, I'll have to send you to my friend Gontran for enlightenment."

Flammermont, who was standing beside Ossipoff, shook his head sadly—but the old man was busy releasing the marine telescope that was slung over his shoulder in order to clean it, and he was too absorbed by this task to think of listening to what was being said around him.

"Monsieur Fricoulet," said Selena, "The ground on which we're standing at this moment is of the same composition as terrestrial ground, isn't it?"

---

[14] The reference to "six months" is puzzling; the text clearly states that the voyagers left Earth in March 1882, and also that they hitched a ride on Tuttle's Comet in 1884—but six months does seem closer to the time actually taken up by their intervening adventures than two years.

"Absolutely, Mademoiselle—at least, that's how it seems to me at first sight."

"It would be impossible, however, on our native planet, to make a square of earth or a block of stone float on the surface of the water."

"Indeed."

"How is it, then, that this fragment of an island can serve us as a raft?"

"It follows, Mademoiselle from the fact that on the world where we are, the mean density of materials is a third less than that of terrestrial materials, and that the gravity is three times weaker. It is therefore presumably that the islet carrying us has a density slightly inferior to that of this ocean...perhaps a density equal to that of ice."

At that moment, the young woman's face contracted painfully; then she put her hands to her bosom in a dolorous gesture and became very pale.

"What's the matter, my dear Selena?" cried Gontran, putting out his arms to support her.

"I don't know," she stammered, "but I feel...an intolerable pain there. Perhaps it's hunger."

Scarcely had Mademoiselle Ossipoff pronounced these words than Farenheit uttered a formidable oath. "By God!" he complained. "That's it—that's definitely it. It's been a quarter of an hour since I said anything; I've been experiencing an inexpressible, incomprehensible illness...I'm hungry." And he looked around avidly, like a starving wild beast.

Fricoulet frowned. "My poor Mr. Farenheit," he said, "your appetite is ill-timed, for the larder is empty...or very nearly..."

"Or very nearly," repeated the American, drawing nearer.

The engineer took a small bottle from his pocket. "My friends," he said, "in here there are 12 doses of the nutritive liquid that my foresight led me to bring."

Farenheit made as if to take possession of the bottle.

Gontran threw himself into his path, menacingly. "Mademoiselle Selena first," he declared.

"So be it," retorted the American. "But hurry up, for I'm about to faint."

As Flammermont reached for the precious bottle, the engineer said: "One more moment. Let's be clear that there's no point in further disputes between us. To stay healthy, we each need two doses a day. The phial one contains 12. That will limit our alimentation to 24 hours."

"Very well calculated," growled Gontran, "but hurry up, please..."

"I propose, in consequence, that we content ourselves with one dose only for today..."

"What will that achieve?" groaned Farenheit. "It'll only serve to prolong our agony."

"In that case," the engineer suggested, sardonically, "abandon your share to the others now, renounce any chance of salvation that might present itself to us within 48 hours, decide to die right away and leave us in peace."

This speech, both logical and forceful, but hardly diplomatic, produced a salutary effect on the American. "But reducing us to one dose a day for 48 hours," he said, in a softer voice, "only uses up ten doses, and you said just now that the bottle contains 12. What are you going to do with the other two?"

"Sorry," Fricoulet went on, as he held out the bottle to Gontran. "I wasn't planning on reducing Mademoiselle Selena's ration. Having a weaker constitution, she's less able than we are to suffer privations that we're obliged to impose on ourselves."

Flammermont thanked the engineer for that kind thought with a grateful glance. Then, having poured Mademoiselle Ossipoff's ration into a cup, he made her drink it, with considerable difficulty. The young woman was literally dying of hunger and her pain was so intense that her clenched teeth refused to let the liquid pass. Eventually, he succeeded, and Selena's pale face gradually recovered its color.

As for Farenheit, his stomach cramps were such that he precipitated himself toward Fricoulet with the simple aim of getting hold of the precious bottle—but the engineer, who had little confidence in the famished American's delicacy, and feared that he might swallow all his companions' nourishment in a single draught, pushed him away, saying: "Let's take it gently, my dear Mr. Farenheit. I've read in accounts of voyages that unfortunates dying of hunger have died by virtue of having absorbed the nourishment their saviors gave them too gluttonously. Beware of indigestion."

Farenheit shrugged his shoulders mightily and seized the cup that the engineer held out to him. Its contents disappeared briskly down his throat.

For a few seconds he remained motionless, seemingly enjoying the agreeable sensations produced by the absorption of the regenerative liquid, but a sudden grimace twisted his features. His face became apoplectic, his eyes rolled desperately in their orbits, and the veins in his neck stood out under the pressure of blood. What Fricoulet had feared had happened; the American's voracity had produced, not indigestion but poor digestion.

"Walk a little, Mr. Farenheit," the engineer said to him. "It will do you good."

Gontran took Fricoulet to one side. "What shall we do now?" he asked. "Just now you mentioned favorable circumstances that might present themselves in 48 hours...do you really think we might get out of this?"

Before replying, the engineer put his finger to his mouth and stuck it is all the way. Having dampened it thus, he raised it above his head. "Still from the north," he murmured. And his face expressed a profound satisfaction

"What are you doing?" Gontran asked.

"Seeing which way the wind's coming from."

"And that's what seemed to give you such tangible pleasure?"

"Indeed. I've established that the wind hasn't changed and is still blowing from the north."

"So?"

"So the current that's carrying us is still heading in the same direction, and it seems to me that we're bound to end up landing somewhere."

"Perfectly logical reasoning...only you're forgetting that, if we haven't encountered some hospitable land within 48 hours, we'll be dead of hunger..."

Fricoulet rummaged in his pockets, took out his inevitable notebook, opened it and traced a few hasty calculations on one of its pages. Them putting his hand on his friend's shoulder, he smiled and said: "Don't worry. We shan't be dining with Pluto just yet."

Flammermont seized his hands. "Are you certain of that?"

"Unless some unforeseen circumstance bars our route."

"What route?"

"The one to the continent of Secchi—which, as you know, is in the southern hemisphere of Mars, and whose shores are bordered by the Kepler Ocean."

"The ocean we're on!" exclaimed Gontran.

"The very same. Now, supposing that the current is drawing us along at 300 meters a minute, that makes 18 kilometers an hour."

"Well?"

"Well, don't you know that from the Snowy Isle to Secchi, or Schiaparelli's Noachis, across the Kepler Ocean, is 900 kilometers? Let's assume that, in consequence of the flood, a certain portion of the latter region has disappeared—let's say, if you wish, 1800 kilometers. You can clearly see that we might well be saved within 48 hours..."

"For that, it's necessary that the speed of the current doesn't decrease, and that our islet doesn't suffer any damage."

"What damage?" said Fricoulet, looking at Flammermont curiously. "What do you mean?" He struck the ground with his heel and added: "We're not, like vulgar castaways, on a raft made of plants and cords, which the waves might break up, but on a mass of earth and rock."

At that moment, Farenheit came back toward them, having taken a constitutional stroll around the island fragment that carried them.

"Well, Mr. Farenheit," said the engineer, "how do you feel?"

"Better...much better," the American replied. He continued walking, saying: "I'll go round again...then I'll be completely better."

He had already taken several strides when he stopped and turned round, on hearing Fricoulet call to him.

"What time is it, Mr. Farenheit?" asked the latter.

The American took out his chronometer. "Four o'clock," he replied.

The engineer started. "Four o'clock!" he cried. "4 a.m. or p.m.?"

"A.m...I think..."

Fricoulet seemed pensive. Then, raising the head that he had allowed to fall on his chest, he asked: "When did you last reset your chronometer?"

"In the City of Light. I wound it and set the hour."

"That's fine, Mr. Farenheit—thank you."

The American drew away and the two young men remained alone, facing one another, Fricoulet thoughtful and Gontran looking at him curiously.

Finally, Gontran heard the engineer murmur, as if talking to himself: "City of Light...270 degrees of longitude...4 a.m...hmm...hmm..."

Fricoulet raised his eyes to look at the Sun momentarily. Already high above the horizon, it was sending down a rain of fiery rays upon the resplendent waters. Then the engineer looked at the islet. Suddenly, he said to Gontran: "Don't move."

The other froze, and Fricoulet looked at him attentively. "That's it," he muttered. "The shadows, which have diminished since this morning, are now stationary. There wouldn't be anything astonishing that, given the region we're in. It's mid-day...or very nearly..." He grabbed Flammermont's hand and exclaimed: "Do you understand, eh? Do you understand?"

The young Comte shook his head and, darting a wary glance at Ossipoff, replied in a low voice: "Not a word."

"It's quite simple, though... Mr. Farenheit's chronometer indicates that it's 4 a.m. in the City of Light, and in this region, the Sun indicates that it's mid-day. There is, therefore a difference of eight hours between this region and the City of Light...that's about 120 degrees of longitude." He interrupted himself abruptly, and asked: "By the way, didn't Ossipoff entrust a map of Mars to you before setting off?"

"It's quite possible. I don't remember."

"Search your pockets—perhaps you slipped it into one at the moment of the debacle."

The young Comte followed this advice and did, indeed, pull a folded piece of paper out of his jacket. It was damp, in a pitiful state.

"Bah!" said the engineer, in reply to his friend's sorrowful expression. "Even as it is, it can render us good service." He unfolded the map with great care, laid it out on the ground and knelt down. He ran his finger over the indications it contained, which were a trifle confused and blurred by the water.

"You see," he said to Gontran, who had knelt down beside him, "that it's impossible to suppose that the current has drawn us westward of the City of Light."

"No, I don't see that."

"What! Haven't I just said that we're about 120 degrees of longitude away from the 270th degree? And don't you see that the map of Mars has no trace of any ocean at that distance?"

"Ah! Yes…I see that—but permit me to tell you that it proves nothing, for we might perfectly well be sailing, at this moment, on the lands traced here by Schiaparelli and inundated since."

Fricoulet reflected for a moment. Then replied: "If your reasoning, the logic of which I recognize, were correct in this instance, we would already have landed somewhere in the time that we've been drifting. Besides, the violence of the current leads me to suppose that the liquid mass transporting us is very deep—a depth inadmissible if we were merely floating on a submerged continent. I therefore resume my reasoning: we can't be west of the 270th degree, so we must be east of it. As for the latitude, the height of the Sun above the horizon at mid-day gives me that…unfortunately, I don't have a sextant."

"A sextant? What's that?"

"An instrument for measuring the height of the Sun."

While speaking, he pivoted on his heels, evidently looking for something to replace the instrument he lacked. Suddenly, he saw Ossipoff, who was lying on his back studying stars that were invisible to his companions in the blue sky, but which his telescope doubtless permitted him to perceive.

The engineer went over to him. "I beg your pardon, Monsieur Ossipoff," he said, in a very friendly tone, "but would you lend me your telescope for a few moments?"

"What for?" grumbled the old man, furious at being disturbed in his studies.

"Monsieur Flammermont needs it to use instead of a sextant." In reply to the interrogative gaze that the old man fixed upon him, he added: "He wants to measure the height of the Sun, in order to calculate the latitude."

Ossipoff's face cleared, as it did every time he was able to observe the scientific qualifications of his future son-in-law. "That's all right," he said, handing Fricoulet the requested instrument.

The engineer returned to the young Comte, saying to him loudly enough for the old man to hear: "Here's what you need."

Gontran took the instrument mechanically. "What do you expect me to do with this?" he asked, in a low voice.

"Measure the Sun," replied Fricoulet, in the same tone.

"How do I do that?"

"Simply aim at the Sun with your telescope, and the angle between the instrument and the horizontal will give you the Sun's height."

Meekly, the young Comte aimed the instrument at the day star, while Fricoulet made the necessary measurements, without seeming to do anything. Eventually, he murmured in Gontran's ear: "The height of the Sun is 65 degrees."

"So we're on the 65th degree of latitude," said Gontran.

The engineer started. "Fool," he said. "Do you want to be strangled by the worthy Monsieur Ossipoff?"

Flammermont stared at his friend in such bewilderment that the latter could not help smiling.

"This is our exact situation," he said. "20 degrees of south latitude and 30 degrees of west longitude, taking the meridian of the City of Light as a reference point. If you want to communicate these results to Monsieur Ossipoff, they will certainly give him pleasure, and will allow you to show off your scientific knowledge at the same time."

Gontran greeted his friend's mockery with a shrug of the shoulders; even so, he was about to go over the old man when he had second thoughts and asked: "What if he takes it into his head to ask me what I think of the situation?"

"You'll tell him that the wind's blowing from the north and that the Sun seems to indicate that we're drifting south-eastwards."

"Then I can say, boldly, that we'll land on the territory of Noachis you mentioned just now?"

"Absolutely—barring unforeseen accidents."

"And you have every reason to add that, Monsieur Fricoulet," declared Farenheit, who had arrived behind the young men."

They both turned with a single movement, and uttered a cry of surprise. The American's face expressed a violent emotion; his lips were trembling and beneath his thick, bushy eyebrows his eyes were shining with a strange gleam.

"What's the matter, Mr. Farenheit?" said Flammermont. "And what do you mean by what you just said?"

"I mean that, if things continue as they are, we'll soon have nothing to plant our feet on to carry us to that Promised Land."

Fricoulet looked at the Amrican in a manner suggesting that he was beginning to have serious doubt about his mental equilibrium.

As for Gontran, he said: "What do you mean, if things continue as they are? What are you talking about?"

"About the island we're on, which is shrinking."

The Comte's eyes widened. He looked at Farenheit for a moment, then leaned toward Fricoulet. "I think the poor fellow's going mad," he murmured.

"That's my opinion too," the engineer replied, in the same tone. Addressing the Amerian, he said. "The Snowy Isle's shrinking, then?"

"One might think that it's melting."

"That might be so, if we were on an iceberg—but stones, rocks and earth don't melt."

"No—but it wears away."

"And on what do you base your statement?"

"Just now, when I was gripped by the singular malaise that you advised me to combat with a hygienic walk, I walked until I had made a complete circuit of the island."

"We know that—we saw you."

"But what you don't know is that I counted my steps while walking."

"That's proof of a meticulous mind," joked Flammermont. "And how many steps did it take you to complete a circuit of the Snowy Isle?"

"520, plus two of my feet, the heel of one being placed at the toe of the other."

"So what?"

"As you have also seen, I made a second circuit; out of curiosity, I counted, like the first time, and..."

"You counted fewer strides?"

"No, I counted the same number—520."

"What's worrying you, then?"

"It's my two feet that were lacking."

Fricoulet burst out laughing. "In truth!" he cried, "that must really have set your head reeling. "You took longer strides on the second circuit than the first, that's all.

Farenheit shook his head gravely. "Monsieur Fricoulet," he said, "before starting out in the suet trade, I was a surveyor in the Far West. I was one of those who measured the greater part of the lands in the New World presently occupied by the emigrants that the Old World sends us every year. That tells you that my legs have, for a long time, measured out a distance that doesn't vary by an inch: 95 centimeters from one heel to the other. I'd bet my head on it."

"I don't say anything different, Monsieur Farenheit," the engineer riposted, "and far be it from me to think of denying the constant length of your strides—but there might perfectly well be an error in your estimation, given that the difference consists solely of two feet."

The American pointed to his legs. "Do you know, Monsieur," he said, in a dignified manner, "that each of my feet measures no less than 37 centimeters—which, putting them end-to-end—gives a length of 74 centimeters. Well, never—never, you understand, in my career as a surveyor—have I made an error so considerable. Thus, given that I cannot admit that I'm mistaken, it's the surface that has diminished."

Gontran shrugged his shoulders. "That's quite logical, as reasoning," he said, "but it's your infallibility I can't admit."

Farenheit became red with anger. "Check my calculation," he said. "Decide for yourself. As for me, I have a clear conscience." With these words, he turned on his heel and resumed walking."

Behind him, following exactly in his steps, came Gontran and then Fricoulet. All three of them made a circuit of the islet in single file, striving to be as regular as possible in their strides, which they counted in low voices.

Once they arrived back at their point of departure they stopped, and the American cried triumphantly: "What did I tell you? I count no more than 518; that's two strides and two feet less than the previous circuit."

"Personally, I counted 525," said Flammermont.

"Ah!" said the engineer, displaying his short legs. "Large as my natural compass is, for myself, I was unable to take less than 570 strides."

Fricoulet took out his notebook and inscribe the figures furnished by himself and his two companions on a blank page; then he said: "Now, let's begin again."

And the departed, but in the opposite directions, Gontran having affirmed that it would provide further proof, like checking a bill by adding it up in reverse. The further the two friends went on that second walk, the longer their faces became; their features expressed a profound disquiet.

Finally, when they were back where they started, they looked at one another, and Gontran exclaimed: "You, too, eh? You observed a diminution."

Fricoulet replied with an affirmative nod of the head. "Yes, he said, "a perceptible diminution. Instead of the 570 strides that the first circuit gave me, I only found 559...and I'm certain that they were as long as the others."

"As for me," Gontran replied, "I only counted 518."

The three men looked at one another silently for some time. Their faces were grave and the deep wrinkles streaking their foreheads testified to the horrible anguish gripping their hearts. The islet's surface was diminishing hour by hour; constantly battered by the waves, shaken and loosened by the horrible shocks of the tempest, the ground was gradually crumbling away, and it was necessary to anticipate a moment when the Snowy Isle would no longer present sufficient surface area to continue to play its role as a life-raft, thanks to which the Terrans had escaped the cataclysm.

"What can we do?" murmured Gontran, instinctively, his eyes moving toward Selena, to envelop her in a tender gaze.

"Nothing," Fricoulet replied. "Against what's happening, we're powerless. Let's wait, and hope that the rapidity of the current will compensate for the crumbling away of the islet."

"But it seems to me that the stronger the current is, the more violently it will eat away the shore."

"That's quite true," the engineer replied, "So let's hope for nothing and wait. Above all, though, not a word of this to the old man or the young woman. There's no need to alarm them in advance. There'll be time to warn them when the peril is imminent."

Gontran and Farenheit indicated their agreement on this point by nodding their heads; then they all drew apart to devote themselves to their reflections in peace, according to their temperament. Fricoulet calculated; Farenheit raged; Gontran lamented.

The entire day passed in this way without anything troubling the desperate monotony of that strange journey: no living being in the air or the water, no sail on the horizon, no vestige of land that might offer hope to the unfortunate castaways. The region seemed completely deserted, and when the Sun set in the west that evening, the raft seemed motionless, fixed at the center of an infinite liquid circumference.

Fricoulet, meanwhile, estimated that they had covered 50 leagues in a south-eastern direction—but a further walk around the islet also demonstrated to him that the number of strides had decreased by nearly 100 *Damn!* he thought. *This is worrying. If it continues at the same rate, we won't get through tomorrow without catastrophe.* And he added, philosophically: *But after all, what good does it do to worry? If it's written up there that I won't see the Boulevard Montparnasse again, and that I'll end my days at the bottom of a Martian ocean...whatever I might say or do, my destiny will be fulfilled.* And on this fine thought, he went to lie down beside Gontran and Farenheit—who, exhausted by fatigue, were already snoring, careless of the peril that menaced them. Was it not wise of them, in any case, to put into practice the proverb according to which "he who sleeps, eats"? The penury of their larder made it their duty to seek to forget their hunger pangs in sleep.

They were woken up by a sudden shout from Ossipoff. "Land! Land!"

In the blink of an eye they were on their feet and running to the old man, who was standing still, with his telescope aimed at the horizon. Dawn was breaking, and through the light mist floating on the surface of the water, they saw a blurred grey line barring the distant horizon.

"Saved! We're saved!" howled Farenheit, throwing himself into Fricoulet's arms.

The latter, scarcely conscious of the American's formidable grip, pushed him away rudely, saying in a bad-tempered tone: "You seem to be selling the bearskin before having shot the bear, my dear Mr. Fareneheit. The country you see out there, which can only be the continent of Noachis, is still 40 kilometers away."

"And before we've reached it," continued Gontran, who had just arrived after conducting a new survey, "the islet will be reduced to its simplest expression."

"How many strides?" asked Fricoulet.

"124," the young Comte replied.

"And it's only 5 a.m.," murmured the engineer, in a dejected tone.

They absorbed a dose of the liquid nutriment—the last—and then stood still, frozen in mute contemplation of the land toward which they were drifting, with desperate slowness.

By mid-day, they had covered 20 kilometers and already, with the aid of Ossipoff's telescope, they could vaguely make out the low and jagged coast of the much-desired continent.

"It seems to me that we're progressing more rapidly," said Farenheit.

"Proof that our islet's surface is diminishing," the engineer replied. In fact, the Terrans were now gathered on a rocky platform that measured no more than ten meters long by four meters wide.

"Isn't there any means of accelerating our progress?" Flammermont asked. "A sail, for example."

"And with what would you like to fabricate a sail?" asked Fricoulet.

"With our clothing, our underwear..."

"It would be necessary to join everything together; even then, the ground that's carrying us is still too heavy to be able to obey the impulsion of the wind."

Farenheit stamped his foot furiously. "What, then?" he groaned. "Must we die, without making any attempt to save ourselves?" And he waved his clenched fist at the land that represented life, and which it seemed to him to be impossible to reach.

Fricoulet suddenly touched his forehead with his finger and whispered to Gontran and Farenheit: "I've got an idea."

They huddled around him. "An idea! An idea that might save us?" they asked.

"That might save us," the engineer repeated, with assurance.

"What?"

"Let me think it over...wait, and when the moment comes, I'll tell you my plan."

Three more hours passed, during which the American measured the islet ten times over. "You know that it's still shrinking," he said to Fricoulet, on his return.

The latter shrugged, and calmly replied: "That's good, let it shrink."

Finally, at about five o'clock in the afternoon, the Terrans ended up tightly bunched, elbow to elbow, on a sort of promontory of grey rock measuring two square meters at the most. Then Fricoulet decided to speak. "My friends," he said, "I've thought of a means that, while giving our raft a greater speed, will also lighten it."

Farenheit opened his eyes wide and Gontran exclaimed: "Are you thinking of equipping our islet with some motor you've invented?"

"Precisely."

"What is it?" The young Comte put the tip of his index finger to his friend's forehead.

The engineer shook his head, laughing. "Don't worry," he said. "I'm not mad."

"In that case, explain yourself. Of what does this motor consist?"

"Of our arms and legs."

"You're out of your mind!"

"No. Mr. Farenheit, as we've been able to observe on many occasions, is an outstanding swimmer. Without having any pretension to emulate Lord Byron, the century's strongest swimmer, I can acquit myself with honor. So, if Mr. Farenheit sees no objection, he and I will get into the water, and we'll both push the islet."

"But that's crazy!" cried all the Terrans, in chorus.

"Craziness that decreases the weight of the raft by 50%—which, by itself, will increase the raft's speed in the same proportion, not counting the speed that we'll be able to impart to it..."

The voyagers looked at one another, not knowing what to think. Seeing their indecision, Fricoulet cried: "Let's try it anyway...the attempt won't pose us any risk; as for Mr. Farenheit, I think that he's as keen as I am to take a bath."

The American looked down sadly at his clothes, which the whole of the previous day and night had scarcely sufficed to dry out. "Let's go, then," he muttered, finally. "If you think that it might be of some help..."

As he finished these words, there was a noise behind them. Turning round, they observed that a section of the islet, gradually undermined by the waves, had just fallen into the water. At the same time, the ground seemed to sink beneath the liquid surface, and the voyagers found that they were ankle-deep in the water. Selena uttered a cry of fright. Gontran hastened to reassure her and took her in his arms—but the abrupt movement he made caused the wreckage to sway so much that it nearly capsized.

"Well?" Fricoulet demanded, mockingly. "It's time, I think, to throw out the ballast. Let's go, Mr. Farenheit..."

With these words, he raised his arms above his head, put his hands together, and dived head-first into the ocean. There was a splash of silvery foam; then, almost immediately, the engineer's head reappeared at the surface. "Well?" he asked. "Does it seem any lighter?"

"Our feet are almost dry," Ossipoff observed.

Farenheit was still hesitating, alternating his gaze between his clothes and the liquid sheet in which he had to immerse himself. Fricoulet had already gone to the rear of the islet, and, swimming with one arm, he pushed it with the other. The American became ashamed of his hesitation then; while muttering a bad-tempered curse between his teeth, he imitated the engineer and threw himself into the water.

"Hurrah!" cried Gontran. "We've risen up by two feet."

"Of course!" Fricoulet riposted, gaily. "The full extent of Mr. Farenheit's 37 centimeter feet!"

They progressed in his fashion for three hours. The two swimmers took turns to rest, one floating on his back and letting the other drag him in his wake, while the other made use of his "natural motors," as the engineer called his arms and legs.

Fortunately, the night was clear, although the light clouds floating in the sky hindered the perception of the stars. Phobos had not yet appeared over the horizon; only Deimos was illuminating Mars. Lost in the mist only a few kilometers away, the land of Noachis was vaguely discernible. Now, though, the wreck no longer seemed to be moving forward; Fricoulet and his companion were exhausted by fatigue and dying of hunger. It was all that they could do to struggle against a current into which they had drifted, and which was drawing them westwards.

"I think we're doomed," the engineer murmured in the American's ear.

"Doomed," muttered the other. "Doomed, when land is in sight—so close! It's sinking to port, by God!" Then, he suddenly uttered a groan and stammered: "Help me, Monsieur Fricoulet! I think I'm fainting."

Before the engineer could grab his arm to sustain him, though, the American's head had disappeared.

"Damn!" muttered Fricoulet. "What's he doing, rolling up his eyes that way, without a word of warning?"

He was getting ready to dive when a voice cried out, vibrant with joy, from on the other side of the islet—the front. "Saved! We're saved!" The voice was the American's. "There's a foothold here," he continued. "Come and see."

With a few strokes, the engineer rejoined his companion, and saw that he was standing up, chest-deep in the water. Gently, he let himself subside, and was surprised to find solid ground beneath his feet. As he was shorter than the American, though, the water came up to his neck. "Victory! Victory!" he cried. To Gontran and Ossipoff, he said: "If you believe me, you can do as we're doing and get into the water—that is, I think, the best means of arriving on firm ground as soon as possible."

A lively discussion ensued between the old scientist and his daughter. Selena wanted to imitate her companions and quit the wreck along with them. "I'm ashamed," she said, "to increase the fatigue of these brave friends any further. I'm not made of sugar, and I certainly won't melt if I follow your example."

Ossipoff did not want to hear that, and demanded that the young woman remain on the islet.

"My God, Monsieur Ossipoff," Fricoulet said, then, "we're losing precious time here. Personally, I think Mademoiselle is right, not because of the surfeit of fatigue that dragging this block of earth would cause us, but because it would slow us down."

"You see, Father dear—I was right!" said the young woman.

"Possibly," grumbled the old man, "but I don't want you to get in the water, even if I have to pull the wreck by myself."

"Eh!" exclaimed Fricoulet. "My dear Monsieur, who mentioned Mademoiselle Selena getting into the water?"

"I don't understand, then?"

"Give me your overcoat."

Although he did not understand, Ossipoff meekly took off his coat.

Then the engineer shouted: You, Mr. Farenheit, get hold of this overcoat here, and you, Gontran, grip it there. Now, doesn't that form a comfortable hammock in which Mademoiselle Selena can sit comfortably?"

In spite of her reluctance to increase her companions' fatigue, the young woman was obliged to take her place on the improvised stretcher and the little caravan set off, preceded by Fricoulet, who prudently sounded the terrain. Ossipoff followed, ready to take the place of whichever of the stretcher-bearers tired first.

They advanced thus, at speed, for half an hour, while the level of the water steadily decreased. Suddenly, Fricoulet cried out and stopped. The others, thinking there had been an accident, came to join him at a run. Some distance away in mid-air, slightly obscured by the night-mists, they saw a multitude of shining stars whose light illuminated the ground.

"It's as if the entire Milky Way had detached itself from the sky and fallen on to Mars," said Gontran, laughing.

"Don't you think it gives the same impression as the approach to a large terrestrial city?" said Fricoulet in his turn. "Wouldn't one swear, on seeing that from a few 100 meters away, that it was the nocturnal panorama of Paris, with its thousands of gas-jets, whose reflection turns the sky red for several leagues around?"

"With the difference," said Ossipoff, "that the reflection is from the sky downwards."

"Let's go! Move on!" the engineer went on. "I don't know why, but a presentiment tells me that this great light will be for us what the charcoal-burner's light was for Petit Poucet when he suddenly perceived it in the forest."

Chapter XXXIX
How Gontran's genius saved the situation again

The Terrans had set off again, treading sensuously on the Martian soil on which they had despaired of ever setting foot again for so may long hours. They had forgotten their fatigued limbs, their hunger-racked stomachs and their anguished headaches. They felt revived, and were breathing in the fresh night air voluptuously. Taking the enigmatic light, whose intensity increased as they moved forward, as a sort of beacon by which to steer their course, they were following the edge of a liquid expanse that cut into the land like a narrow bay or the estuary of a river.

"Do you really think that it might be a city?" Gontran whispered in his friend's ear. "Insipid as the means of alimentation on this planet may be, I need to restore myself...the hunger pangs are beginning again."

"What do you want me to say, old chap?" replied the engineer. "On that subject, I'm as ignorant as you are, and I'm reduced to hypotheses."

Suddenly, Selena, shouted: "Look! A falling star!"

They all raised their heads and did indeed perceive a luminous point streaking across the dark sky like a ray of flame. The point appeared to have become detached from the brilliant agglomeration that Flammermont had taken at first for the Milky Way, In addition, it seemed to be heading toward the Terrans.

On hearing his daughter's exclamation, Ossipoff shrugged his shoulders. "A falling star!" he muttered. "My poor darling, you wouldn't have had the time to point it out before it had disappeared!"

"And not only hasn't it disappeared, but it's becoming brighter and brighter," Farenheit declared.

"Doesn't it seem to you that a dark mass is perceptible, moving in the wake of that luminous point?" asked Gontran.

Fricoulet clapped his hands joyfully. "Bravo!" he cried. "That star is nothing other than a Martian's electric lamp!"

"May you be correct, Monsieur Fricoulet," said Selena—who, like her companions, could not wait to be able to rest after such long fatigue.

As she spoke, a whistling sound became audible, similar to the sound of wings cleaving space. Almost immediately, a body set down close to the voyagers. As Fricoulet had predicted, it was, in fact, a Martian, who directed the light of the minuscule but powerful lantern attached to his forehead toward them. When he had considered them attentively, he uttered a few guttural sounds.

The engineer—who, it will be remembered, had served as his companions' interpreter thus far—advanced toward the native and exchanged a few rapid monosyllables with him. The Martian then resumed his flight and disappeared like an arrow into the night.

Gontran uttered a disappointed exclamation. "Oh well," he said. "He's going, just like that—what about us?"

"Be calm," said Fricoulet. "He's coming back with a vehicle, which I believe, given our situation, will be most welcome..."

"And the lights...?" asked Ossipoff.

"Are those of an aerial city, to which we're going."

"An aerial city!" Gontran repeated. "In this accursed country, things get more and more spectacular, as at Nicolet's."[15]

"You don't know how this city was constructed?" Ossipoff asked.

"I confess to you, Monsieur," the engineer replied, "that I didn't have time for ask for explanations on that subject...all the more so because, for the moment, it doesn't interest me much."

"As long as we find sufficient sustenance there and can sleep safely, the rest's not important," Farenheit declared.

The old scientist looked at him sideways. "Savage!" he muttered, between his teeth.

Hunger presumably multiplied the American's acoustic faculties tenfold, for the epithet reached his ears and he was about to reply in a fashion that Ossipoff surely would not have found agreeable when the darkness above their heads suddenly lit up brightly. Almost immediately, descending though the air as lightly as a bird, an apparatus similar in every respect to the one that had transported our voyagers to the City of Light touched down.

Scarcely had they taken their places than the helicopter took off at incredible speed and sliced through the air, to stop after a few minutes on a vast platform sparkling with lights, around which habitations of a type identical those the voyagers had already encountered on the planet rose up on invisible foundations.

Once they had disembarked, their guide led them into a vast building, in which he gave them bottles of nutritive liquid and showed them a heap of quilts extended on the ground. Then he wished them goodnight and retired.

Which of them was most astonished when they woke up? It was Fricoulet, on seeing Aotaha, who was standing beside his bed looking down at him and smiling. He came to his feet with a single bound, delighted to see the brave Martian who had been so helpful to him and his companions during their sojourn on the planet. Immediately, he engaged him in conversation.

He learned then that the City of Light, drawn by the great equatorial current and after having crossed the Erythrean Sea, had run aground two days be-

---

[15] Jean-Baptiste Nicolet (1728-1796) was a theatrical director who eventually founded his own Théâtre de Nicolet, which became famous for increasingly spectacular productions, leading to the popular use of the saying that Gontran quotes here: "*C'est de plus fort en plus fort comme chez Nicolet.*"

fore in the place where the Terrans, carried by the same current, had landed the night before.

The inhabitants of Toouh, the aerial city, warned by telegraphic means of the cataclysm that had occurred in the wake of the battle on the Libyan plain, and informed of the route followed by the City of Light, torn away from its foundations, had put at the disposal of its compatriots the motors necessary to tow them and their dwellings back to the location they had formerly occupied in the equatorial region.

"But what about you?" Fricoulet asked, when Aotaha had finished telling his story. "How is it that you're still here?"

"I was preparing to go in search of you," the Martian replied, simply.

Having thanked him warmly for this good intention, Fricoulet asked for explanations regarding the singular place in which he and his friends now found themselves, and the Martian placidly furnished all the information necessary to satisfy the Terran's curiosity.

This land of Noachis being, more than all the other countries of the planet, subject to formidable floods capable of lasting for several years, the inhabitants had thought of utilizing the astonishing progress realized by science to protect them from this terrible scourge. A second reason prevented them from embedding the foundations of their houses in the ground itself: the pestilential miasmas given off by the marshy terrain of the immense island. They had, therefore, suspended their city in the air by the simplest possible means; immense metallic compartments, filed with a gas lighter than air, played the role of balloons and served as foundations for the houses. As for the materials employed in its construction, they were almost all composed of pure cellulose, rendered as hard as steel by special treatment, while remaining very thin and waterproof.[16]

The gas that filled the compartments was produced by the reaction of chemical substances upon one another; by means of cables attaching the aerial city to firm ground equipped with internal metallic wires, electricity produced on the ground was transmitted to the dwellings to provide the light, heat and motive force indispensable to everyday needs.

The Terrans, to whom the marveling Fricoulet passed on the Martian's explanation of these admirable achievements, were dumbstruck with amazement. Even Farenheit, who listened without overmuch understanding, was stupefied by so much ingenuity. Deep down, although he let nothing show, his national pride was slightly dented; the Americans seemed very small and rather backward to him by comparison with these people—so he promised himself that if Provi-

---

[16] Cellulose had been isolated and its basic chemical formula determined by Anselme Payen in 1838, but the more important precedent for this passage is the development therefrom of the first artificial polymer, celluloid, in 1870, which opened up the possibility of further developments in organic industrial chemistry.

dence allowed him to set foot in the United States again, he would never say a word about the planet Mars to those who asked him to tell the story of his extraordinary voyages. *That*, he thought, *would surely be the best way of getting myself blackballed in the presidential election of the Eccentric Club.*

At that moment, Aotaha pointed to a singular machine moored to the aerial pontoon on which the dwelling in which the Terrans were stood.

"What's that?" asked Fricoulet.

"The vehicle that will transport us to the equatorial regions."

"That!" exclaimed Gontran, for whom the engineer had just translated the Martian's reply.

The young Comte's stupefied and slightly scornful was explained by the vehicle's bizarre form. It was a sort of metallic cigar about 30 meters long, coming to a point at each extremity and appearing to have a diameter between four and five meters at its widest point. From each of its flanks jutted a sort of horizontal mast, also metallic, serving to support vast sheets of canvas and terminating in a double helix. Fore and aft of the vehicle were propellers activated by invisible motors.

Fricoulet approached this vehicle and examined it with considerable interest. "A singular machine, eh!" he said to Gontran.

"If I had not already tested the extraordinary civilization of these folk," Flammermont replied, "I'd hesitate to climb into it, on my word of honor."

Ossipoff, his daughter and Farenheit had already embarked; the engineer did likewise and the young Comte followed his friend, grumbling all the while. Some kind of electric bell rang then; the moorings were cast off, and the propellers started up.

After rising into the air, as straight as an arrow, the aerial boat flew horizontally for a short while; then, at a given signal, the two masts inclined backwards, presenting a vast surface of inclined planes to the air.

"Oh, of course!" cried Fricoulet. "It's simply a kind of aeroplane with several superimposed wings."

Ossipoff shook Flammermont's hand energetically.

"Eh? What's up, my dear Monsieur?" the young man asked, surprised by this attention.

"This vehicle reminds me of my escape from Ekaterinburg," the old man replied. He added: "Aren't you proud, my dear boy, of the resemblance between that ingenious aeroplane—to which I owe my liberty and perhaps my life—and that of the Martians, the most civilized and most learned people in the Universe?"

Gontran shrugged his shoulders insouciantly. "My God!" he replied. "Not as proud as all that, Monsieur Ossipoff, I assure you."

The old scientist enveloped him with a tender gaze. "What modesty," he murmured.

Beneath them, the clouds were flying by with a vertiginous rapidity, allowing the sight through their gaps of the uniformly flat soil of Mars, with its canals mirroring the sunlight, seemingly forming a sparkling metal net around the planet. At times, dark dots of unequal dimension appeared; these were villages, towns and cities, but the height at which the apparatus was flying prevented them from being distinguished very clearly. Only Ossipoff could make out details, thanks to the American's binoculars, which he monopolized, and to which his eyes remained glued throughout the journey.

When the Sun set, they arrived at an aerial city similar in all respects to Toouh, which Ossipoff declared to be situated between the middle of the land of Secchi, called Hellas by Schiaparelli.

At daybreak they got under way again; for several hours they followed the course of the Alphea canal, then flew over the Newton Ocean, and reached the equator at noon exactly. They set an eastward course then, and the Terrans found themselves over Libya—but from the Hourglass Sea to Lake Moeris the waters had invaded the continent, and for long hours, the voyagers' eyes could see nothing but a liquid sheet, sparkling in the sunlight like an immense steel mirror, extending all the way to the horizon.

Meanwhile the speed of the aerial ship had increased, and Fricoulet calculated that they were traveling a no less than 200 kilometers an hour—the speed of an earthly tempest. Despite the prodigious displacement of air produced by that vertiginous course, however, neither he not Gontran wanted to leave the upper deck of the apparatus, which permitted them to perceive, a few 100 meters below them, the 14 canals observed by Schiaparelli between the 200th and 250th degrees of longitude. Successively, the engineer named them for his friend—who, leaning over the rampart with his head in his hands, made incredible efforts to persuade his memory to retain the strange names: Lethe, Amenthes, Aethiops, Fainestos, Cyclops, Hephaestus, Galaxias, Cerberus.

Having reached the last-named, the ship change course, following the path of the canal in the air as far as the Trivium Charontis. Then, abruptly, a distant spray of lights illuminated the darkness; it was the City of Light.

"Well, Mr. Farenheit," said Fricoulet, on disembarking, "do you know how much distance we've covered since yesterday?"

The American shook is head negatively.

"2500 kilometers, no more and no less. In 48 hours, that's quite smart. That leaves your famous railroad far behind, don't you think?"

Farenheit replied with a grunt; every time he was obliged to concede an inferiority of the United States, his national pride was sharply wounded.

Several days had elapsed since the Terrans' return to the City of Light. Ossipoff had plunged into a sequence of astronomical studies, facilitated by the marvelous optical instruments collected in the Martian observatory. Fricoulet made a close study of the works of the indigenes, taking notes every day, recording—with increasing surprise—the progress realized on the planet by the mechanical arts. Selena and Gontran, left to themselves, spent entire hours talking about the future, building Castles in Spain to lodge their love—and in that occupation, the hours seemed to fly by with vertiginous rapidity; night fell when they had not yet said a quarter of the things that they had wanted to say when they got up. When one is in love, conversation is nothing but a continual recommencement.

Jonathan Farenheit was the only one who did not know how to employ his days and, for want of other occupations, spent his time cursing Mars and planetary explorers. The return to Fifth Avenue for which he had been hoping for such a long time was becoming more and more problematic, and a frightful fury took hold of him at the thought that, since August 31—the day of the twice-yearly liquidation—the shareholders in the Lunar diamond company would have considered him a thief. If looks were guns, Mikhail Ossipoff would have been long dead, for every time the American encountered the scientist, his hatred sprang forth from his eyes. Fortunately for the old man, though, the human gaze is harmless, and Ossipoff continued his studies peacefully.

There remained Fricoulet and Gontran, with whom Farenheit had reached an understanding regarding a collective return to Earth, but the former spent almost all his time going up hill and down dale in search of some strange scientific application and it was not easy to lay a hand on him; besides, from the astronomical viewpoint, the American only had limited confidence in the engineer. That left no one but Flammermont on whom Farenheit could count; he was a veritable scientist, and had had the incomparable advantage over his other companions of having a direct interest in returning to his native planet—but with him too, it was not easy to have a secret conversation; he hardly ever left Mademoiselle Ossipoff's side, and if he did draw slightly apart she immediately ran to take his arm in order to resume their interrupted duet, which was always the same and always full of charm for them.

One evening, however, when Selena, having been brusquely summoned by Ossipoff, left Gontran alone, the American—who was waiting in ambush—fell on his prey. "Monsieur de Flammermont," he said, in a low voice. "I have something to say to you."

Surprised by Farenheit's tragic tone, the young man exclaimed: "Go on, my dear Mr. Farenheit—what's it about?"

"Not so loud, I beg you, Monsieur de Flammermont," said the other, putting his hand on the young Comte's arm, "and let's take ourselves away, if you please; no one must hear what I have to tell you."

"You're making me veritably anxious, you know," Gontran said—but meekly followed his companion.

The latter finally stopped and, looking the young man straight in the eye, asked—in the same tragic tone that Don Diègue adopted to ask Rodrigue[17] whether he had courage—"Monsieur le Comte de Flammermont, what value does your word have when you give it?"

Gontran looked at the American in amazement. "Are you serious?" he asked, doubting that he had heard correctly.

"Do I look as if I'm joking?" Farenheit replied.

The young Comte frowned. "It's just," he said, slowly, "that your question, in itself, constitutes a grave insult."

"Don't read more into it than I meant to imply," the American retorted, "and give me a straight answer..."

"If we were on Earth," growled Flammermont, "I'd only answer by sending two friends to see you..."

"Charged with demanding reparation or retraction, no? Fortunately, we're not on Earth, for the means of which you speak has never served to elucidate any question."

"Well then, at least tell me what you're getting at?"

"I want to know, quite simply, whether you recall a certain statement you made, in a fit of gratitude, when, believing that your fiancée was lost forever, you found her safe and sound on the Snowy Isle, thanks to me."

"I remember, Mr. Farenheit, that you rendered me the greatest service that a man can render another, and that my gratitude is eternal."

"I know, I know," said Farenheit, "but we sons of the New World are practical men, and as you promised me that your gratitude would be translated into something other than words..."

"Me!" said the young man, in surprise.

"'Mr. Farenheit,' you said to me, 'You've saved the life of my fiancée and you've just saved mine; I'll take responsibility for settling Monsieur Ossipoff's debt of gratitude along with my own...' Do you recall those words?"

Gontran took the American's hand and shook it energetically. "Do I recall them?" he cried. "They're engraved on my heart."

"Do you also remember that I replied: 'If you think me deserving of a little gratitude, you can settle your debt by returning me, as soon as possible, to my native land'?"

Flammermont's face fell, as he anticipated what was coming, and he remained silent.

"To which," Farenheit continued, "You replied: 'I'll do everything I can.' "

---

[17] The reference is to Pierre Corneille's famous tragedy *Le Cid* (1636), based on the Spanish legend of El Cid—the epic movie starring Charlton Heston as Rodrigo owes as much to the play as the legend, so modern cinemagoers will understand the reference well enough.

The young man moved his head up and down several times. "Yes…yes…I remember now."

The American uttered a profound sigh. At the same time, his features relaxed and expressed a keen satisfaction. "In that case," he said, "When do you expect to fulfill your promise?"

Gontran shivered. "My promise…my promise…" he stammered. "My promise consists of doing everything I can."

Farenheit slapped him on the shoulder amicably. "In that case," he said, with an amiable smile, "I shall soon be setting foot on the soil of the United States—for the moment a scientist like you…"

"Permit me…" the young man tried to say.

"The moment a scientist like you becomes determined to succeed," Farenheit completed, "he succeeds." Clicking his fingers with an attitude of sovereign scorn, he added: "Besides, if I remember correctly what I heard Monsieur Ossipoff say, the distance between Mars and Earth is only 15,000,000 leagues, and for men like us…"

"I beg your pardon," said Gontran, "but it was two months ago that the distance between the two planets was only 15,000,000 leagues. Since then, each of them has moved on in its orbit, and now…it's a big stride that one would have to take to pass from one to the other."

This argument had suddenly presented itself to the young man's mind as a means of getting out of the difficult situation in which Farenheit had just put him, and he considered the American's visibly-elongated face with great satisfaction.

"Then there's nothing we can do?" groaned the other.

"For the moment, not a great deal," Flammermont replied, shaking his head.

"Do you know that I'm afraid of going mad!" howled Farenheit, shaking his companion's arms as if to break them. Then, suddenly leaning toward him and looking at him furiously, he said: "Do you know something? I'm beginning to believe that you too are nothing but a fake scientist—like your friend Fricoulet." And he added, with a sigh of regret: "Oh, if only Fedor Sharp were here!"

Gontran shivered, and looked at him in amazement.

"He was a scientist—a true scientist," Farenheit murmured. "Besides, to be appointed permanent secretary of the St. Petersburg Academy of Sciences, it's necessary not to be a cretin…like that wretch Ossipoff, who has never had any entitlement."

"Except to your resentment," said Flammermont, jokingly.

"Oh, that!" roared the American. "I'll strangle him some day."

"Are you taking about me?" asked a cheerful voice behind the two conversationalists.

They turned and saw Fricoulet, who had disappeared two days before in company with his friend Aotaha to visit the factory in which a new model of aerial vehicle was being constructed, in which electricity played a surprising role.

The engineer repeated his question. Farenheit replied, in a surly tone: "I don't have anything against you—you're not the cause of me being so far from my native land today."

"I can even tell you," Fricoulet said, "that if it had been up to me, you'd have stayed on Cotopaxi."

Farenheit looked at him interrogatively.

"Yes," the engineer went on, "on the very morning of our departure, I went to find Monsieur Ossipoff and I urged him strongly not to give you a place in our shell. I fear that the excess weight would cause difficulties. He dismissed my fears as puerile...and you came along."

"Oh, I wish to Heaven he'd listened to you!" cried the American. "I wouldn't be here now, downcast, so far from my native land."

Fricoulet shrugged his shoulders to indicate that he could do nothing, and was about to go back to his bunk when the sky, which was darkened by the veil of night, was suddenly streaked by a luminous rocket. It vanished almost as rapidly as it had appeared.

"A shooting star!" the engineer exclaimed—and, as Selena came running toward them, he said to her, jokingly: "Make a wish, Mademoiselle."

"A wish?" she repeated, in surprise.

"Don't Russian young women, like French young women, have the charming superstition that invites them to make a wish when a shooting star lights up the sky? It's claimed that the wish soon comes true."

Selena smiled and replied: "No, Monsieur Fricoulet, we don't do that in Russia—but have I not been French at heart for some time?"

"Make a wish, quickly," said Gontran.

"It's already made," she replied.

"Without indiscretion," the young man said, "may I know what it was?"

The young woman wagged her finger at him. "Can't you guess?" she said,

"Monsieur Fricoulet," said Farenheit to the engineer, "have you heard it said that wishes made in similar circumstances by men will come true?"

"I confess, my dear Mr. Farenheit, that I have no information on that subject...but for very little cost, you can always try." After a pause, he added: "I have no need to ask you..."

"Certainly not. I say it out loud: I wish to return to the United States as soon as possible."

As he finished this statement, the darkness was suddenly striped by a veritable rain of fire, incessantly dying and being reborn, which lasted several seconds.

"Well," said Fricoulet, "on Earth, today must be November 24." He took an old calendar from his pocket, which he had carried in his wallet. After consulting it, he murmured: "Yes, it is indeed." He turned to the American. "My dear Mr. Farenheit," he said, "your wish is granted."

Farenheit looked at the engineer incredulously. "You're mocking me," he murmured.

"Not at all." Extending his hand toward a new luminous streak that was just crossing the sky, he said: "Sit astride one of those shooting stars, and you have every chance of seeing the United States again."

The American shrugged his shoulders. "I think about serious things," he complained, "and you talk to me about absurdities."

"Not as absurd as that," Friculet replied. "Don't you know that a scientist compatriot of yours, Simon Newcomb,[18] has calculated that no less than 46,000,000 shooting stars fall on the Earth every year?"

"46,000,000!" repeated the engineer's companions, veritably astounded by the figure.

"To prove to you that it's no exaggeration, know that in 1833 an astronomer in Boston observed a rain of stars and compared them to half the number of snowflakes that one sees in the air during a normal fall of snow. In a quarter of an hour, even though he limited his observation to a tenth of the horizon, he counted no less than 600—which, for the whole of the visible hemisphere, gives a total of 8660; which is 34,640 stars per hour. The phenomenon lasted more than seven hours, so 240,000 stars were displayed in Boston."[19]

"But Monsieur Fricoulet," said Selena, "does anyone know exactly what a shooting star is?"

"To begin with, it was thought that they were gaseous entities, some sort of nebula, but we have been led to conclude that, in order to have the force to penetrate our atmosphere, they must be solid bodies."

---

[18] Simon Newcomb (1835-1909) was a notable American popularizer of astronomy. Graffigny was probably familiar with the *Popular Astronomy* he published in 1878, but could not have known that he would go on to publish a scientific romance of his own, *His Wisdom the Defender* (1900).

[19] The great Leonid shower of November 12-13, 1833 was a sensational event, which initiated the serious study of such showers and had a considerable effect on numerous religious men in search of signs of the impending end of the world. The comparison with snowflakes seems to have been very widely quoted at the time and afterwards, but might have originated in an account by Agnes Clerke, whose count produced an estimate of a total fall of 240,000 meteors. Fricoulet's inference regarding the date is mistaken; although November 24 is just about within the range of the shower's annual appearance, the mean date is November 17. The comet whose debris produces it, nowadays known as Tempel-Tuttle, has a period of 33 years—which presumably gives rise to Fricoulet's subsequent comments about "floods" in the "asteroidal river."

"By God!" exclaimed the American. "And you believe that 46,000,000 solid bodies might fall on the Earth in this fashion without causing any damage?"

"Permit me to ask you, Mr. Farenheit, what happens to a swarm of gnats through which a cannonball passes?"

Farenheit contented himself with a shrug of the shoulders.

"There would be no fear, would there, of the cannonball being damaged? By the same token, if an elephant were to amuse itself by trampling an ant-hill, it's certainly not for the pachyderm's life that you'd fear. Well, those two comparisons are the best response I could make to what you've just said."

"However," said Gontran, "without wishing, like Mr. Farenheit, to take things to extremes, the Earth's encounter with a shooting star must result in a collision of some sort."

"When I speak of the Earth I mean the Earth and its atmosphere. Now, when a star penetrates our atmosphere, its velocity is such that its motion is transformed into heat; it bursts into flames—volatilizes, so to speak—and only arrives at the surface in the form of dust."

"How can one know, then," asked Selena, "that the shooting stars are solid bodies? For you told me just now that they were solid bodies."

"And I'm not taking that back, Mademoiselle, because it's the truth—but the phenomenon of inflammation and volatilization occurs only in respect of minuscule asteroids. Those, on the other had, whose weight varies from a few hectograms to thousands of kilos, are resistant. Under the influence of the heat, however, their surface melts and is covered by a layer of glaze, and because that same heat slows their progress, they only arrive on Earth with an insignificant velocity."

"But that must end up augmenting the volume of our native planet," observed Selena.

"Oh, by very little—and, above all, very slowly. Consider that, giving all these asteroids a mean dimension of about one cubic millimeter, our annual 46,000,000 stars represent 146 cubic meters and 8760 kilos. In a sequence of 100 centuries, that increase in volume would be 1,460,000 cubic meters—which, spread over the surface of our globe, which measures no less than 510,000 square kilometers, would only form a layer one centimeter thick. You can see that it's hardly worth talking about." He fell silent, and watched the luminous streaks that had begun striping the somber mantle of night again.

Gontran, who was standing beside him, whispered in his ear: "Why did you strike your forehead just now and exclaim that it must be November 24 on Earth?"

"Because of that shower of stars..."

"Does it happen on fixed dates, then?"

"Of course! Haven't you ever noticed that?"

"I must confess that I haven't. Until I met Mademoiselle Ossipoff, my attention was entirely devoted to diplomacy and the European harmony..."

"Which interested you more than the harmony of the spheres; I understand that. For the moment, though, bless the fact that Ossipoff's studies are keeping him glued to his telescope. Otherwise, you can be certain that he would already have given you an oral exam."

"Instead of making that little speech," said Gontran, peevishly, "you'd have done better to give me a few explanations."

"Well, briefly, this is it. Until recently, a planetary origin was attributed to shooting stars—that is to say, it was supposed that they formed rings around the Sun with a velocity almost equal to that of the Earth and following near-circular orbits. Quite recently, though, Schiaparelli, struck by the analogy between their velocity and that of comets, came to suspect that, like the latter, they must move parabolically and, consequently, belong to a celestial system foreign to our Solar System. In addition…"

Gontran, who was listening to his friend with profound attention, interrupted him abruptly. "If I understand you correctly," he said, "they'd be a sort of comet whose nucleus, instead of being formed of a single large body, like those of Halley's comet, Bilela's comet and others, would be composed of an aggregation of infinite numbers of corpuscles, separate from one another but circulating through space in convoy?"

Fricoulet nodded his head. "You've got it," he said. "Schiaparelli's theory establishes that this agglomeration of corpuscles forms an uninterrupted chain, which follows a parabolic course in a plane at right angles to that in which the Earth moves…"

"But then," said Gontran, whose face suddenly expressed an extreme agitation, "a moment comes when the Earth goes through that chain?"

"Perfectly logical; it forms a sort of corpuscular river, so considerable that the Earth, although intersecting it at a right angle, takes four or five days to get through it."

Flammermont uttered a cry of joy that brought Farenheit and Selena—who, seeing the young man chatting in low voices, had moved away to one side—running back. "Oh, my dear Selena," said the young Comte, taking the young woman's hands in his, "the wish that you made just now might well come true."

"What do you mean?" exclaimed Mademoiselle Ossipoff, staring at her fiancé curiously.

"I mean that the Earth will probably see us again sooner than we thought."

The American could find no other means to make his joy manifest than throwing his cap in the air. "Hurrah!" he cried. "Hurrah for the Comte de Flammermont!"

Selena looked at Fricoulet to ask him whether he knew what his friend was talking about, but the young engineer, shaking his head, put his index finger to his forehead to indicate that he was beginning to have serious doubts about Gontran's sanity.

The latter perceived the engineer's gesture and smiled in an indefinable manner. "No," he said, "I'm not crazy. But before I tell you the plan that just formed suddenly in my mind, I need to work out my ideas more fully, and that's how I'll spend the night." And with that, he wished Mademoiselle Ossipoff goodnight, shook Farenheit's hand and retired to the apartment he shared with Fricoulet.

Chapter XL
In which Fricoulet remembers that he is a machine-builder

All night long, the engineer heard Gontran moving restlessly on his bed, as men obsessed with a particular idea do. Finally, at dawn, seeing his friend sitting up on his elbow in a pensive manner, staring vaguely, he asked: "What are you thinking about?"

As if emerging from a dream, Flammermont shivered, passed his hand across his forehead and replied: "I'm thinking about leaving Mars and returning to Earth."

"Ah! Yesterday's idea has taken hold of you again?"

"It never let go of me."

"So it's serious?"

"As serious as anything could be."

"Are you going to give Ossipoff the slip?"

Gontran started. "Do you think I should?" he asked. "Won't I have need of him there—to give his consent?"

"But he'll never consent to abandon his celestial circumnavigation!"

"To avoid any discussion or recrimination, then, let's not tell him. We'll assure him that it's a matter of continuing the planetary voyage in progress, and, once in sight of Earth..." Gontran completed his sentence with a gesture clearly signifying that, when that moment came, he would not worry overmuch about the old scientist's wrath.

"But he'll use that betrayal on your part to refuse you his consent."

"Bah! You're enough of a friend to take that treason to your own account."

Fricoulet shook his friend's hand, satirically. "Thank you for thinking of me," he replied. Then, affecting a seriousness that was far from his thoughts, he said: "Do you really have a means of getting us away from here?"

"Yes, a marvelous and yet simple means. I'm astonished that an intelligent fellow like you hasn't thought of it."

"One can't think of everything," the engineer relied, with a little smile. "Let's hear your means."

Gontran assumed an earnest attitude. "Before replying, I'd like you to add a few explanations to those you gave me yesterday on the subject of the great current of asteroids that circulates in space, and which the Earth intersects, as you said, at certain determined times."

"Go on."

"It's these 'determined times' that I can't reconcile with 'the uninterrupted chain' circulating through space. Is it necessary to understand that there are temporary breaks in that chain?"

"Not at all; I explained badly. The river of asteroids runs without interruption, but at certain times, like a real river, it has formidable floods; it was of those that I spoke yesterday in saying that our planet takes more than five days to pass from one shore to the other."

"And what's the periodicity of these floods?"

"33 years!"

Flammermont shivered. "Yes," said Fricoulet. "Every 33 years, in the month of November, there's a gigantic tide of stars..."

Gontran's face expressed a profound disappointment.

"What's the matter?" asked the engineer, surprised by the sudden change in his friend's physiognomy.

"I...those 33 years destroy my plan."

"Because?"

"Because it's that tide that I counted on using to regain the Earth...and now it's necessary to wait for the next one."

"Pardon me," said Fricoulet, but the phenomenon that occurs on Earth in the month of November only happens here later; the rain of stars that we saw yesterday is only the advance guard of the great tide that will invade Mars imminently."

Gontran threw his arms around his friend's neck. "Oh, my dear Alcide," he said, "you've saved my life."

After disengaging himself from this cordial embrace, the engineer went on: "You know that you haven't told me anything yet, and I wouldn't be sorry to be acquainted with this marvelous plan, thanks to which I stand a chance of eventually seeing my dear Boulevard Montparnasse." While saying this, he fixed Gontran with his little grey eyes, lit up by a slightly mocking gleam.

"My dear friend," said Flammermont, then, "I read *Les Continents célestes* very attentively last night, and I found there, extensively detailed, the information you gave me in brief yesterday. One thing in particular caused me extreme pleasure: the declaration of a certain Norman Lockyer, a terrestrial astronomer whose has been much occupied with meteoric stones: 'In the plane in which the ring of the twentieth of November asteroids moves, the void of space has disappeared and is replaced by a meteoric plenum.' "[20]

---

[20] Norman Lockyer (1830-1920) was most notable for his observations of the Sun and for founding the journal *Nature*. This quote is atypical of his work, and its meaning is slightly confused because it deliberately (and rather flippantly) echoes the Classical dispute as to whether space ought to be regarded as a void or a plenum—put crudely, empty or full. Greek atomic theory required a void in which the atoms could move, but anti-atomists like Aristotle, who thought that "nature abhors a vacuum"—i.e., that the concept of a void was in some way essentially repugnant—preferred to think of space as an elementary fabric: the aether. 19th century scientists were in two minds; modern atomic theory had

"Yes," said Fricoulet, nodding his head approvingly. "The density of the ring is more than 1000 times greater than that of intersidereal space—I know that. So what?"

Gontran raised his arms above is head and waved them desperately. "So what?" he cried. "Don't you understand that we have a river at our disposal—a veritable river—and that it will be sufficient for us to abandon ourselves to its current..."

"You're forgetting one thing, and that's that the current flows from Earth to Mars, nor returning until it has passed Saturn, Uranus and other places..."

"Very well," said the young Comte, not in the least disconcerted, "we'll go upstream...it will take a little longer, that's all."

"Are you serious?"

"All of this is exceedingly serious. What's impossible about it? What prevents anyone from sailing in space? It's the void, isn't it? The absolute void. Well, here's a route in which the density, you say, is 1000 times greater than that of space. Hazard dictates that this route passes via Earth, where we want to go..." He suspended the sentence and looked hard at Fricoulet, awaiting his response.

"All right," said the engineer, after a rather long pause, "I'll grant you the practicality of the route...in principle—but you don't, I suppose, intend to set off along it as a tourist, with your walking-stick in hand and a knapsack on your back?"

"We'll need a vehicle, of course...but that's up to you."

"Me!" exclaimed Fricoulet, rolling his eyes.

"Of course!" Flammermont replied, calmly. "That's not my business...I'm an inventor, which requires genius, not an engineer, which requires specialized studies."

Poor Fricoulet was literally astounded by his friend's aplomb. "What!" he murmured. "You want me to construct..."

"What's impossible about it? Didn't you construct the shell that carried us to the Moon? Wasn't the selenium sphere, thanks to which we landed on Mercury, your doing, as well as the metallic balloon that brought us here? Your alarm just goes to prove your extreme modesty; personally, I have no doubt that, by racking your brains, you'll find something..."

---

made void theory fashionable again, but the wave theory of light seemed to require a "luminiferous ether." Lockyer knew—although the text takes his remark far too literally, perhaps for purely literary purposes—that the stream of particles left behind to the comet responsible for the Leonid shower, which the Earth intercepts at the relevant point of its orbit every year, was extremely tenuous, and could not possibly be likened to a "river" capable of carrying a solid object as an actual river carries a boat.

"Word of honor," cried the engineer, "it takes an ignorant fool to have no doubt!"

"And to give confidence to scientists," Gontran riposted.

"You fool!" said Fricoulet. "Don't you know that the army of asteroids whose advance guard we perceived last night will march past Mars in three weeks' time?"

"All the more reason to work double shifts and not waste time. I'll leave you to your calculations." And, turning on his heel, he went to join Selena, from whom Farenheit was trying hard to extract the details of her fiancé's plan. The young woman had assured him forcefully that she knew nothing about it, but the American persisted nevertheless in questioning her.

"Ah, my dear heart!" said Gontran, squeezing his fiancée's hand, "I think we'll achieve happiness at last."

"Is it possible?" she murmured, fixing him with a gaze steeped in affection.

"What if I were to tell you," he replied, "that we'll be leaving here in a fortnight?"

A surge of blood reddened Farenheit's face. "And when do you think I'll be in New York?" he asked.

Flammermont appeared to reflect, and eventually replied: "A month after our departure."

"But what about my father?" Selena asked, timidly.

"Oh," said Gontran, in an exceedingly casual tone, "we'll make your father think that we're heading for Jupiter, Saturn and company, while actually turning our back on them. He'll console himself for not having seen the Giant Planets in contemplating the happiness of his children."

As soon as Flammermont had left him, Fricoulet took out his notebook and set about blackening it with figures and sketches for nearly half a day. After beginning his calculations and plans 20 times over, he went to find the obliging Aotaha, with whom he had a conversation that lasted until nightfall.

The next day, at dawn, there was a further conversation between the engineer and the Martian, whose consequence was a plan of construction for a sort of ship designed to transport Fricoulet and his traveling companions along the asteroidal river.

Following Aotaha's advice, the young engineer had adopted a helix as a propeller and had chosen electricity as a motive force, its applications being commonplace on the surface of the planet Mars. The helix, however, was not designed to act directly upon the cosmic corpuscles—which is to say, to use them as a point of purchase, like a helical propeller in a real ship. In Fricoulet's apparatus, it acted solely as an intermediary—which is to say that it aspired the asteroids through one tube of narrow diameter and expelled them at the rear through a large aperture. The external form he adopted was that of a cylinder five meters in diameter and six meters long. This cylinder was traversed internally, along its length, by a concentric pipe a meter and a half in diameter and three times as long, in which a triple-threaded Archimedean screw played the role of a propulsive helix. At the anterior extremity, this tube terminated in a conical trunk; the other extremity affected the funnel-shape of a locomotive chimney.

The voyagers' accommodation was to be formed by the annular space separating the interior pipe from the larger cylinder, which formed the vessel's hull. This space was divided vertically into two equal parts by a horizontal partition taking the place of a floor, and also longitudinally, by another partition equipped with a door; in this manner, the apparatus was made up of four cabins, arranged in two superimposed pairs. One of those in the upper section was to serve as a ward-room—which is to say, a common room; the other, divided into two parts, was for Ossipoff and his daughter. One of those in the lower section would be shared by Farenheit and Gontran, the other would serve simultaneously as a kitchen, engine-room, store-room, larder, etc. Fricoulet intended to make himself a little niche next to the engine, in order to monitor it at close range.

Once this plan had been thoroughly examined and discussed by Fricoulet and Aotaha, the latter took responsibility for putting it into practice, and the young engineer had the leisure to marvel at his ease at the wonders of Martian industry.

It had been decided that the entire apparatus would be made of metal. The exterior cylinder, initially constructed of wood, was molded in sand following the metallurgical procedures in use on Earth; then, when the mold was completed and the 'soul' set in place, the cylinder was founded in a single piece.[21] While the metal cooled, another crew of Martians fabricated the median pipe designed to serve as the envelope of the screw, by means of an immense electrically-power lathe. As for the helix, it was constructed by embedding thin metal stalks, connected to one another by metal plates, in a helical groove traced on the drive-shaft. Meanwhile, the cooled cylinder was taken out of the mold and turned. Then they went on to the assembly.

More than nine days were employed in these various operations, which, given the three days devoted to preparatory study, only left three days of respite before the arrival in the region of Mars of the great army of asteroids with which the Terrans' departure would coincide.

Three days! Fricoulet calculated that it would require at least that long to bolt the floor and partition walls—but that primitive method was not the one in use among the Martians, and the young engineer was as surprised as he was joyful when he was able to observe the speedier method employed by the planet's

---

[21] This method of spaceship construction is reproduced faithfully in Octave Jonquel & Théo Varlet's *The Martian Epic* (Black Coat Press, ISBN 978-1-934543-41-2), where the resultant shells are then painted with a phototrophic element identical to the one featured in Volume One of the present work.

inhabitants to fit the pieces together. As soon as they had been turned, the pieces to be joined were placed in contact, brought to white heat by an enormously powerful electric blow-lamp and welded, without the help of any solder. In only a few hours, the different parts of the apparatus were set in place.

More than two days remained for the installation of the electric motor, and that was quite sufficient. Then, the apparatus was transported into one of the great halls of the City of Light's Observatory. It was from there that the bold voyagers would launch themselves again upon the conquest of space, in the presence of the planet's scientific elite, gathered for the occasion.

By unanimous agreement, Ossipoff had been left in absolute ignorance of his companions' project; they feared resistance on his part, based on his incomplete scientific observations, and that the departure would be abruptly interrupted. By telling him only at the last moment, they had the advantage, firstly, of avoiding a protracted struggle, and secondly, of exciting the old savant by dazzling his eyes with the prospect of Jupiter, Saturn, Uranus and Neptune, and a unique opportunity to visit them. He was, as ever, absorbed in his telescopic studies when Gontran touched his shoulder, obliging him to leave his instrument and look at him.

"Well, my dear Monsieur," said the young man. "Have you made good progress and do you think your observations will soon be finished?"

Ossipoff shook his head despairingly. "It's veritably alarming, my dear friend," he replied. "The further I go, the more aware I become of the gigantic task that I've undertaken."

There was a pause, after which Flammermont said: "Do you realize that if things go on that way, we might be stuck here indefinitely?"

"Do you find it uncomfortable here?" the old man asked, surprised.

"No...but life is a little monotonous...and then..."

"And then?"

"It was agreed that we would only stop on each planet long enough to get our breath back...and I wouldn't be displeased to go and see what's happening on Jupiter. You haven't forgotten that from here to Jupiter we have a respectable number of leagues to travel."

The old scientist raised his arms in the air. "Jupiter!" he cried, with a glint in his eyes. "The giant of worlds. Oh, to see it! To contemplate it! To study the skeleton of that monster at close range!" But the glint in his eye went out, and he murmured, sadly: "Unfortunately, that's a dream, and Mars will surely be our last stop on the great voyage we've undertaken."

"Our last stop!" exclaimed Flammermont. "Are you joking, Monsieur Ossipoff? You've promised us that we'll visit the entire Solar System; it's necessary to keep your promise. To see Jupiter! But that's our dream too: Mademoiselle Selena's, Fricoulet's, and even Farenheit's..." And he added: "You can't avoid your engagements like this..."

"But how can I keep them? You said yourself just now that millions and millions of leagues separate us from Jupiter! How can we cross such a frightful distance?"

"In that case, let's return to Earth," Gontran suggested.

The old scientist shivered, and replied in a curt tone: "For that, there's no urgency. We can take all the time we like to think about that."

The young Comte concealed the smile that rose involuntarily to his lips and replied: "I was joking, my dear Monsieur Ossipoff. My motto, as you know, has been, since I set off on this great voyage: 'Onwards, ever onwards.' Well, faithful to that motto, I came to tell you today, Monsieur Ossipoff, that we are not stranded here. Onwards!"

The young man had pronounced these words in a vibrant voice, which seemed to make a profound impression on Ossipoff. His lips quivered in a nervous tremor, and his gaze attached itself to Gontran curiously.

The latter added: "Do you know what day it is on the terrestrial calendar, Monsieur Ossipoff?"

The old man shook his head.

"St. Michael's Day," Gontran told him. "Which is to say, Monsieur Ossipoff, that it's your feast-day."[22]

"My word, that's true," murmured the scientist. "It's my feast-day. Absorbed in these interesting studies, I'd completely forgotten." Then, after a moment's astonishment, he asked: "Why tell me that?"

"Because, if you have forgotten, we have remembered...to celebrate it for you..."

An expression of contentment spread over the old man's face. "That's nice," he said. And he shook the young man's hand cordially.

"Can you guess," Gontran said, in a mysterious tone, "What we've got you?"

"There are several of you, then?"

"For the gift in question, it was necessary to club together; Mademoiselle Selena remembered that your feast-day was today."

"Dear child," murmured the old man, affectionately.

"Farenheit declared that it was necessary to celebrate it."

"He's a good man, deep down, that American, although violent."

"As for me I found the gift that it was necessary to give you."

A further handshake thanked the young man for his words.

"As for Fricoulet," Gontran concluded, "he helped me."

"Pooh! Helped do what?"

"To make you the gift in question."

---

[22] St. Michael's Day is September 29—which does not fit in with Fricoulet's observation that it was November 24 on Earth a few days ago.

The old man shook his head in a manner that demonstrated the scant esteem in which he held Fricoulet's help. Then he asked: "And what is this gift?"

"Jupiter!"

Ossipoff stepped backwards, staring at his future son-in-law with some slight anxiety. "What did you say?" he exclaimed.

"I said: Jupiter."

"You're offering me Jupiter as a gift?"

"Yes—Jupiter itself...*et ipse*, as my tutor at the Lycée Henri IV would say."

"You've lost your mind," retorted the old man, whose anxiety had increased.

As Gontran was about to reply, a flock of Martians came into the observatory, amid a deafening noise of fluttering wings. They were carrying the apparatus, under Fricoulet's direction.

Ossipoff examined the singular instrument with amazement in his eyes.

"What's that?" he murmured.

"The vehicle that will transport us to Jupiter."

"Is that possible?" stammered Ossipoff. "By what means?"

"By means of the parabolic current of asteroids that forms a natural river on which we shall sail..."

The old man uttered an indeterminable exclamation and, precipitating himself upon Flammermont, seized in his arms and hugged him for a long time. "Oh, my boy, my dear boy!" he stammered, emotionally. "There are those whose bronze statues stand in public squares who are less deserving of that honor than you."

While the young Comte gave the old scientist a detailed tour of the apparatus, Farenheit expressed his profound amazement at the lightness of the apparatus to Fricoulet. "But it's constructed entirely out of metal?" he observed.

"Entirely."

"If I'm not mistaken, there's at least 1000 kilos of cast iron there?"

Fricoulet laughed. "Scarcely 600—on Earth. Here, by virtue of the law of gravity, those 600 kilos are reduced to only two."

The American made a circuit of the apparatus, unable to convince himself that the engineer was telling the truth.

"So what is the metal whose weight is so feeble?"

"Lithium."

"Lithium," repeated the American. "I don't know that one."

"There are many other things that you don't know," Fricoulet replied, lightly. Then, suddenly, he burst out laughing.

"What's up with you?" asked Farenheit, dryly, thinking that the other was mocking him.

"I'm thinking about your block of diamond that I was obliged to throw overboard like a vulgar sack of ballast during my abrupt departure from Phobos, and whose loss has caused you such despair."

"And that's what's making you laugh?" growled the American. "It's really nothing to..."

"When you know why I'm laughing, you'll share my hilarity—I'm certain of it."

"In that case, hurry up and tell me."

"You thought you were taking back a fortune, didn't you, with your fragment of crystallized carbon?"

"Of course! About a million."

Fricoulet's lips protruded in a disdainful moue. "Pooh!" he said. "A million—not much!"

"It's a lot better than going back as poverty-stricken as Job."

The engineer indicated the apparatus with a nod of his head. "Do you know," he said, "how much that's worth?"

"That has no other value than that of the metal."

"What price, do you think?"

"Eh? How should I know? I've never been in the scrap business—I only know about animal fats."

Still laughing, Fricoulet persisted: "Go on, in your opinion, what value might it have?"

Farenheit reflected for a few moments. "I think," he said, "that it'd be an overestimate to rate a kilo at...at..." Scratching the end of his nose, he hesitated to pronounce a figure.

"All right," exclaimed the engineer, "let's say 77,000 francs..."

The America started violently. "77,000 francs!" he repeated. "Per kilo!"

"Yes, per kilo...that's the price of lithium in Europe."

"But in that case, there's a gigantic fortune there!"

"Yes—nearly 46,000,000 francs."

Farenheit could not believe his ears. "Are you sure of what you're saying?" he asked.

"You'll see when we arrive," replied the engineer, greatly amused by his companion's bewilderment.

The American made another circuit of the apparatus, enveloping it with an affectionate gaze with the sensuousness of a miser, with his hand on the shiny polished metal. Suddenly, a shadow of anxiety passed over his forehead. "Do you know," he said, stopping in front of Fricoulet, "what's better than being a scientist?"

"What's that?"

"The veritable fortune that you'll be taking back to France, of course."

"I'll wager that you haven't made a single deal in animal fats as profitable as that in your entire life," joked the engineer.

"46,000,000 francs!" repeated the American, in a regretful tone.

Fricoulet thought he understood the sentiment that was saddening his companion, and he clapped him on the shoulder amicably, saying: "Even split into five parts, the *Eclair* [23]—that's what I've baptized the apparatus—still represents a tidy sum for each of us."

"Into five parts!" Farenheit exclaimed. "What? You'd be generous enough to..."

"There's no generosity on my part, but simple justice. There are five of us here who have shared a good deal of bad luck, and might yet share more. Shouldn't we share the good?"

The American fell upon the engineer's hands. "But 46,000,000 francs, divided by five, makes each part more than 9,000,000 francs," he said, in a vibrant voice.

"You calculate marvelously, my dear Mr. Farenheit," Fricoulet declared—and, releasing himself from his companion's grip, he headed for Ossipoff, who was coming out of the *Eclair*, followed by Gontran and Selena.

"Well," said the engineer, "are you satisfied, Monsieur Ossipoff?"

The old man looked at his future son-in-law, his expression full of pride. "Admit," he said to Fricoulet, "that this is one of the most admirably-organized brains of our epoch. This apparatus is a pure masterpiece." Then, suddenly remembering a question he had forgotten to ask, he said: "For how long, my dear boy, can this motor function?"

Gontran, who had heard perfectly well, but who was incapable of answering the question, made a show of increasing the animation of his conversation with Selena.

Fricoulet understood his fiend's embarrassment, and immediately said: "The motor can function for six months without interruption. There are also six months' worth of respirable air and food-supplies in the stores."

The old man's face was radiant. "How long before we depart?" he asked.

Fricoulet turned to Farenheit. "What time has your chronometer, Mr. Farenheit?" he asked.

"11:45 a.m."

"Monsieur Ossipoff," the engineer said then, "We have another quarter of an hour to remain—the departure is set for noon exactly."

For some time the air had been lined in every direction with Martians—who, informed of the strange voyagers' departure, were coming from every part of the Equatorial region. The Great Hall of the Observatory was already full of notable scientists gathered in conference and the wing-beats of the impatient crowd were audible outside. At a signal from Aotaha, the cupola of the Observatory separated into two parts and drew back to ether side, thus forming a large bay through which the *Eclair* could take off.

---

[23] Thunderbolt.

"11:55 a.m., Monsieur Fricoulet," said Farenheit, who still had his chronometer in his hand.

"It's time to embark, my friends," said the engineer, turning to his companions.

The apparatus was standing up vertically, its conical extremity pointed toward the sky, so that the walls separating the cabins served as floors.

"Are we set?" asked Fricoulet, after darting a rapid glance around to ensure that everything was ready.

"All right!" replied Farenheit, in a vibrant voice. And he added, without thinking of Ossipoff, who could hear him: "*En route* for the United States!"

Chapter XLI
How Jonathan Farenheit lost his mind

With the aid of a sextant, Fricoulet measured the exact height of the Sun, while Gontran and Ossipoff hastened to close the manhole by means of which the voyagers had entered the apparatus.

Suddenly, the engineer murmured: "Noon!" At the same time, a little silver bell rang in the silence; it was Farenheit's chronometer chiming the hour. "We're going!" said Fricoulet, simply. He pressed a switch; a crackling sound immediately became audible, followed almost immediately by a slight vibration, which shook the interior walls of the cylinder—and the engineer added: "We've gone."

"Joker!" exclaimed the American, hurrying to one of the portholes. Immediately, though, he uttered a resounding "By God!" which drew the others to his side.

They had gone—and the *Eclair* did marvelous justice to the name with which it had been baptized. Already, in only a few seconds, it had transported its passengers several 1000 meters above the Martian surface, which extended beneath them like an immense geographical map.

The canals, whose waters reflected the Sun's rays, formed a kind of sparkling network with which the entire plant was enveloped, and the oceans were like gigantic burnished silver mirrors, which projected the intense light descending from the Sun, then at its zenith, as far as the voyagers. With every passing second, the *Eclair* continued its rapid progress, like an arrow launched by a monstrous bow, flying though the air and carrying the voyagers ever higher.

Farenheit, whose enthusiasms did not last long and whose churlish character always found material for recrimination, suddenly said: "Do you know, my dear Monsieur Fricoulet, that the apparatus's vertical position is not at all comfortable. Humans are not built for walking on walls like flies. Floors are not made for dogs..."

"Bah!" Gontran replied. "All that's just a matter of principle—for I'd like to know what difference you find between the walls and the floor, at this moment? A square box, perfectly identical in all its faces, has neither top nor bottom..."

"In any case, Mr. Farenheit," said Fricoulet, "it's only a matter of time. At the speed the *Eclair* is going, we'll be able to resume the horizontal position that is so dear to you within ten hours."

"Within ten hours!" repeated Ossipoff, frowning slightly.

"Alcide is right, my dear Monsieur," Gontran said, in a detached tone. "It will certainly not take us any longer to reach the great asteroidal current of which we intend to make use in order to return...to reach, I mean...the other worlds toward which our curiosity is drawing us."

He had pronounced these words with such imperturbable seriousness that the American allowed himself to be taken in. Taking the engineer to one side he muttered in his ear in a threatening tone: "By God, Monsieur Fricoulet! It was agreed that we'd attempt to get back to Earth, and here's Monsieur de Flammermont talking about continuing this accursed voyage! Who's fooling whom here?"

Fricoulet slapped him amicably on the shoulder and replied in a mocking tone: "What does it matter, as long as it's not you?" And he emphasized his statement with a glance in the old scientist's direction.

This reply cheered Farenheit up, and he uttered a little mocking snigger, quickly followed by a "Poor chap!" full of commiseration. "And tell me, my dear Monsieur Alicide"—when he was in a good mood, the American willingly called the engineer by his first name—"do you know at what speed we're going to navigate the celestial river toward which we're presently heading?"

"That's a question it's impossible for me to answer, at least for the moment, my dear Mr. Farenheit," the engineer replied. "Our speed will depend on the velocity of the aerial river itself. I've told you that we'll be going upstream, and you'll easily understand that the greater its velocity is, the slower our progress will be, since part of our force will be employed in fighting the current, which will tend to carry us in a direction opposite to the one in which we want to go."

The American nodded his head approvingly. "I understand," he said. "But one more question...is the force you've just mentioned certain to be sufficient in quantity to make the voyage? That helix that's driving us forward—what's the motor that makes it turn? And will that motor be able to turn until we get there?"

Fricoulet laughed. "Your question contains several," he said. "Even so, I'll attempt to answer them. You've noticed, I suppose—or, at the very least, you've had the same opportunity as me to notice—that the Martians have attained an intellectual level far superior to that which we have reached ourselves. They've perfected to a high degree the means we have of utilizing the almost infinite power of natural forces. More than that, they've extracted the secrets of forces of whose existence we know, while remaining ignorant of their intimate nature: light, sound, electricity, winds and currents, for example..."

Allowing himself to be carried away by a subject that was so familiar to him, Fricoulet was threatening to go on at length and enter into details that were making the American yawn in advance. "But with particular regard to the vehicle that's transporting us," the latter said, to cut short the explanations that he anticipated. "What method have you applied?"

"The principle of electricity."

Farenheit seemed astonished. "I've inspected the *Eclair* in detail," he murmured, "and haven't seen any machines or batteries..."

Fricoulet smiled. "That's because the Martians, being expeditious in all things," he replied, "instead of fabricating the fluid, are content to collect natural electricity, always active in nature, and store it in reservoirs of a sort, from which they take it at will, according to their needs."[24]

The American shook his head. "I haven't seen any such reservoir here," he said.

"Electricity is furnished to us by a sort of battery of accumulators...that's the only name I can give to the apparatus; except, instead of lead plates plunged into acidic solutions, they resemble cartridges that are dissolved by a molecular effect."

"But that's solidified electricity."

"Of a sort...which permits us to dispose a formidable quantity of fluid in a very small volume. Anyway, if you care to follow me, you can watch the apparatus functioning with your own eyes."

"Follow you!" laughed the American. "That's easy to say—but the door's in the ceiling, and to get to it..."

"To get to it," retorted the engineer, "you have only to imitate me."

So saying, he tensed his legs slightly and without apparent effort, rose up as far as the door, which he opened, and through which he disappeared. "The perennial effect of weight diminishing the further one draws away from a center of attraction," he shouted, putting his head through the opening and laughing at the sight of the American's dazed expression.

The latter, having recovered from his surprise, imitated the engineer—and, after a few minutes, they both found themselves in a special compartment of the *Eclair*, standing in front of a row of tubes established in a case, which the engineer declared to be full of electricity. On exiting from the case, all the currents produced were measured and regulated in order to be directed from there by ordinary conductors to a motor driving the helix by means of transmission levers. This motor, as ultimately economical of power as of volume and simplicity, was also a transformer, for it multiplied the power of the electricity in the manner of a Ruhmkorff induction coil,[25] while utilizing that electricity by means of the attraction of artificial magnets of great power—electromagnets, to be exact—operating on items disposed for that purpose.

The American listened silently to all the explanations the engineer gave him. "Do you know," he said, when Fricoulet had finished, "that there's a fortune to be made from a system as simple and as powerful...? By God! If we get

---

[24] A similar imaginary process had been employed by Jules Verne to power the *Nautilus* in *Vingt mille lieues sous les mers* (1870).

[25] Heinrich Ruhmkorff (1803-1877) patented his induction coil in 1851; in 1858 Napoléon III awarded it a 56,000 franc prize as the most important electrical innovation ever. The device had been invented in 1836 by Nicholas Callan, who got no reward.

back in time for the Great Exposition in Philadelphia,[26] the Devil may take me if we don't win the gold medal with that!" Calculating in advance the considerable sums that the exploitation of the new model motor might bring in, the American rubbed his hands.

"Well, Mr. Farenheit," Fricoulet said to him, "Are you still annoyed to have attempted this little aerial peregrination?"

"I'll tell you when I'm back in my home on Fifth Avenue," Farenheit replied. "For I still fear some accident, you see, that will postpone the moment that I set foot in free America..."

"I'd like to believe, this time, that your fears are in vain, my dear Mr. Farenheit, and that within a month you'll be able to devote yourself to the delights of the suet trade and the honors of the Eccentric Club!"

"May the Lord hear you!" the American replied, gravely, raising his cap.

They went back to the large room where their companions were. Ossipoff, installed at one of the portholes, was using a telescope to examine the surface of Mars, which was diminishing with astonishing rapidity. In a corner, to one side, Gontran and Selena were sitting side by side and hand in hand, chatting in low voices.

Fricoulet, with a pair of binoculars in hand, went to station himself at a vacant porthole. Meanwhile, in order to pass the time, Farenheit drafted a contract between him and the engineer for the exploitation of the famous motor.

The hours flew by rapidly in this fashion, from the voyagers' viewpoint, and the American suddenly noticed that time had moved on, his head having become heavy with drowsiness and his eyes swollen. "By God!" he muttered, with a sonorous yawn. "Isn't it nearly bedtime?"

"To go to bed," Gontran retorted, "we need to be able to string up the hammocks, and while we're in a vertical position..."

"A little patience, damn it!" said Fricoulet. "We're getting there..." And he pointed to an intensely black space lined with many fiery streaks.

"That's the famous ring, is it?" Gontran asked him, whispering in his ear.

"What do you think it is?" the engineer replied in the same tone. "What time do you have, Mr. Farenheit?" he asked the American.

"11:55 a.m., Monsieur Fricoulet."

"That's good. In five minutes you'll be able to talk to your pillow."

"Have we reached the river of asteroids already?" asked Mademoiselle Ossipoff.

"Yes, Mademoiselle...but I'm waiting until we've gone further into it to let us go with the current and resume our normal position." He hurried into the engine-room and waited, his hand on a lever. "What time?" he shouted to Farenheit again.

---

[26] As the Great Centennial Exposition in Philadelphia had taken place in 1876, this hope seems as fragile as all Farenheit's other aspirations.

"Midnight!"

Fricoulet stopped the propeller and the *Eclair*, abandoned to the sole force of the meteoric current, at right angles to which it found itself, slowly swung around, like a boat set across a river, which the current replaces in line with the water. The frightful distance that now separated the Terrans' vehicle from Mars nullified all weight, to the extent that the *Eclair* had become a new world in space and not an inert apparatus, as the shell had been as it emerged from Cotopaxi. In a few minutes, the reorientation was complete and the motor started up again. The *Eclair* was flying with the current.

"Damn it!" murmured Gontran in the engineer's ear. "What have you just done?"

"You can see perfectly well, I think."

"It's precisely because I can see that I'm asking whether you're insane?"

"Why that question?"

The young Comte led his friend to the rear of the boat and showed him, through the porthole, a luminous star whose light irradiated space. "What's that?" he said.

"What a question! It's the Sun."

"Very good—and that little scarcely-perceptible point of light like a stain on the solar disk. What's that?"

"The Earth."

"Better and better—and in which direction are we going, pray?"

Fricoulet extended his arm toward the front of the boat. "In that direction," he replied.

"Which is to say that, instead of heading toward the Earth, as was agreed, we're heading away from it. Am I right to ask whether you know what you're doing?"

Fricoulet shrugged his shoulders and, looking at his friend with an expression full of commiseration, jeered: "And here's a chap who claims to have been born to diplomacy!"

"Answer me—you can mock me later."

"Do you think," asked the engineer, "that Monsieur Ossipoff is so absorbed by the contemplation of celestial things that he can't take account of the direction in which we're headed? And do you think that, wishing to go to Jupiter, he wouldn't perceive that we were not taking that route?"

"So?"

"So, I set a course for Jupiter—but at the same time, I set the motor at minimum velocity, in order not to go too far in the wrong direction. As soon as the honesty and credulity of the old man—whose trust we're abusing outrageously—are plunged into the solace of sleep, I'll turn around, set the motor working flat out, and we'll hurtle toward our native planet. Tomorrow, when your future father-in-law wakes up and notices the change of direction, it'll be too late to retrace our steps..."

Privately, the engineer added: *If, after such a trick, Ossipoff persists in wanting to give his daughter's hand to Gontran, the Devil may crunch my bones.*

Flammermont shook his friend's hand energetically. "Indeed," he said, "that's what they call diplomacy."

"But that's not all," Fricoulet said. "You'll see." Leaving the little corner in which they had been whispering so mysteriously for several minutes, the engineer approached the other voyagers. "My friends," he said, "we shall, if you wish, establish a system of watches. We all need rest and now that we're well on our way, we can get a few hours sleep without danger. Stretch out your hammocks, therefore; as for me, I'll take the first watch."

"Why you rather than me?" asked Ossipoff.

"Because I need to study the motor, to see whether it's working properly, and to note its expenditure of force." So saying, he addressed a knowing wink to Gontran.

"May I take the watch after yours?" asked the young Comte.

"Agreed—number two to you. Number three will be Mr. Farenheit's. As for Monsieur Ossipoff, he'll take the first morning watch." With that, the engineer retired to his machinery, while Gontran and Farenheit went to their respective hammocks, after wishing Ossipoff and his daughter goodnight.

The American had no sooner laid his head on his pillow than he was sound asleep, as his sonorous snoring, reminiscent of the bellows of a forge, testified.

Was it that snoring or anxiety that prevented the young Comte from imitating his companion? Either way, he could not close his eyes. In the end, weary of turning over on his mattress like a carp in a frying-pan, and furious at seeing sleep flee so obstinately, Flammermont got up quietly and went silently to the engine-room. *Since I can't sleep*, he thought, *I'd do better to take my watch straight away, so Fricoulet can go to bed; he'll undoubtedly have more luck than me.* He opened the door, but the engineer, bent over a piece of paper that he was blackening with figures, was so absorbed in his calculations that he did not hear his friend come in. Gontran went over to him and, without saying a word, put his hand on his shoulder.

Fricoulet shuddered and, raising his head, showed the young Comte his face, which was darkened by a veil of anxiety. "Oh, it's you!" he said, in a strange tone.

"Yes, it's me...no way to sleep...so I've come to relieve you. But what's the matter? That creased forehead...those frowning eyebrows....what's happening?"

The engineer shrugged his shoulders furiously. "What's happening," he grunted, between his teeth, "is that the river in which we're immersed is flowing in a direction directly opposite to the one in which we want to go. Instead of going toward the Earth, it's coming from it."

"You're not telling me anything new. I know that as well as you do—but that was anticipated. It was agreed that we'd go upstream."

"Except that we didn't anticipate that the velocity of the current would be equal to our own velocity."

"Which means?"

"Which means that, for more than an hour since the *Eclair* was brought around, it's been as motionless as a stone. It's not going backwards, it's true, but it hasn't advanced by a millimeter."

"I thought that your motor could impart a considerable velocity to our boat."

"Indeed—42,570 meters per second," the engineer retorted, bitterly. "That's no small matter, I imagine."

"What, then, is the velocity of the corpuscles that surround us?"

"It's equal to the velocity of the translation of the Earth, multiplied by the square root of two."

"Why?" asked Gontran, who had only retained very vague memories of the course in cosmography he had taken at the Lycée Henri IV.

"Why? Why?" said the engineer, impatiently. "To explain would take too long. Suffice it to say that the Earth's orbital velocity is 29-1/2 kilometers per second, that the square root of two is 1.414, and that the two numbers, multiplied by one another, give a total of 42,570 meters per second. Do you understand now?"

The young Comte waved his arms in the air despairingly. "Oh," he said, "why isn't this accursed current flowing in the opposite direction?"

"It would scarcely take a fortnight to get back to Earth."

"You said a month."

"Yes, by abandoning us to the current like a block of wood, but by adding our own speed to that of the aerial river in which we find ourselves, the duration of the voyage would be reduced by half." Then, showing his friend the calculations in the middle of which he had just been interrupted, he said to him: "I've just measured our progress since we left Mars—we haven't covered more than 1200 leagues...100 leagues an hour! Do you know how long it will take us, at that rate, to reach the Earth? A little more than 1000 years."

A tremendous weight suddenly descended upon the unfortunate Gontran's head. He could not have been more depressed. "1000 years!" he repeated. "1000 years! I'll never live long enough to marry Selena!"

"It's hardly probable," Fricoulet said, sardonically. "Such longevity is unknown in our day, and Methuselah himself only lived for a few more than 700 years."

"We're doomed, then."

"Who knows? Perhaps there's a means of saving the situation."

Flammermont threw himself on his friend's hand. "Oh, find that means, Alcide," he begged, "I entreat you."

"Not right now, alas. I'm falling asleep and my eyes and fluttering so much that everything's dancing before me. Tomorrow, my sight will be clearer, and so will my thoughts."

"But what will happen between now and tomorrow?"

"Absolutely nothing. The force of the current being exactly neutralized by our own force, the *Eclair* will remain as motionless as if it were at anchor."

While speaking, the engineer darted one last glance at the motor, and securely fastened the lever that was connected to the tiller. Then, wishing his friend goodnight, he retired to the little niche fitted into a corner of the engine-room.

Flammermont too was forced to return to his hammock, where sleep finally decided to visit him, in spite of the terrible preoccupations to which Fricoulet's revelation had just given birth in his mind.

Penetrating through the portholes, the Sun's rays were already filling the engine-room with bright light when the engineer woke up with a start.

"Damn!" he said, rubbing his eyes, which were still swollen with sleep. "That's strange—I could have sworn I just heard laughter." And he remained there, propped up on his elbow, bewildered by that abrupt awakening—while, indeed, a burst of mocking laughter resounded behind him.

He turned and saw Mikhail Ossipoff standing at the head of his bunk, with his arms folded across his chest, considering him with a mocking expression.

"Good day, Monsieur Ossipoff," he said. "It's late, eh?"

"About 9 a.m."

With one bound, Fricoulet was out of his bunk, murmuring: "I'm truly ashamed to be so late rising."

"It's something else of which you ought to be ashamed, Monsieur Fricoulet," the old man replied, sarcastically.

"And what's that, pray?" asked the young man.

"Your unqualified stupidity."

The engineer looked at Ossipoff interrogatively.

"Could you describe otherwise," asked the scientist, "the action of a pilot who steers the boat confided to him in a direction diametrically opposite to the one in which he is supposed to be going?"

Fricoulet made an alarmed gesture. "What do you mean?" he murmured, while having a presentiment as to what the old man's reply would be.

"It was agreed yesterday evening, was it not, that I should take the fourth watch? Which is to say that I was to wake up at 6 a.m. Now you know, do you not, that when one goes to sleep with a firm determination to wake up at a set hour, it's very rare that sleep does not abandon you at exactly that time? That's what happened to me. It was about 5:30 a.m. when I got out of my bunk...and I was surprised, on passing through our friends' cabin, to find both of them snoring, fast asleep. As for you, you were sleeping no less profoundly than them..."

"Human endurance has its limits," said Fricoulet, by way of excuse.

Ossipoff shrugged his shoulders and went on: "That was of no great importance, though, and I headed for the machine...but then, do you know what I found?"

The engineer did not reply, but he looked at the old man anxiously.

"I found," Ossipoff went on, triumphantly, "that the prow of our apparatus was pointing toward the Earth. Ah, for a pilot, Monsieur Fricoulet, you're some pilot!" He sniggered.

"What have you done, then?" asked the engineer, in a tremulous voice.

"You ask that! What you would have done in my place if you had found such a complete error. I've changed our direction, diametrically. I've set the motor to full power; in a few hours, we'll have regained all the time that your negligence lost us. At this moment, we're more than 1,000,000 leagues from Mars."

Fricoulet folded his arms across his chest and looked at the old man, with an expression that was half-furious and half-mocking. "Well," he said, "good for you."

These words plunged Ossipoff into a profound bewilderment. "What do you mean by that?" he asked.

Scarcely had he pronounced those words than Fricoulet had regretted them, but it was too late. Without answering the old man's question, the engineer exclaimed: "Then you're taking us to Jupiter!"

"Certainly—and from there to Saturn, to Uranus, to Neptune..."

"It's madness—it will take us years to each the furthest planets in the Solar System."

"Years? Why? We're traveling at a little over 85,000 meters a second—76,620 leagues an hour, to be exact, or 1,850,000 leagues a day. In two months, we'll be on Jupiter, and we'll reach Saturn in five."

As he finished speaking, Farenheit appeared on the threshold of the engine-room. He was very pale and his cheeks were quivering with anger. "Monsieur Ossipoff," he said, in a voice in which barely-contained anger was discernible, "I'd like to know whether what I've just heard is a joke?"

"A joke? Why?"

"Because I've as much use for Saturn and Jupiter as a fish for an apple!" he cried. "Because I intend to get back to Fifth Avenue as soon as possible...and because your diabolical planets are not on the way." So saying, he had come forward to stand in front of the old man threateningly, with his fists convulsively clenched.

"My dear Mr. Farenheit," Ossipoff replied, quite calmly, "I'm truly upset by what's happening, but what you ask is quite impossible."

The American turned to Fricoulet. "You've deceived me, then?" he growled, furiously.

The engineer shrugged his shoulders. "How could I foresee," he replied, "that the *Eclair*'s velocity would be equal to that of the accursed current?"

"One does not make a promise when one is not sure that one can keep it," Farenheit replied.

"Eh? I've promised you nothing, myself," cried the engineer, who was becoming irritated by Farenheit's obstinacy. "Talk to Gontran..."

The latter, attracted by the sound of voices, came into the engine-room. "Was that my name?" he asked.

"Ah, there you are!" howled Farenheit, hurling himself toward him. "Did you or did you not promise to return me to Earth?"

The young Comte, amazed, stood there for a moment without answering. Then, with a glance, he directed the American's attention to Ossipoff—but Farenheit cried: "What good is all this mystery? He knows everything now. We can speak in front of him."

The old man's eyebrows furrowed. "There was a conspiracy, then?" he said, looking around him in an inquisitorial fashion.

Gontran bowed his head. "We wanted to make you happy in spite of yourself," he murmured. "You shouldn't hold it against us."

"My happiness lies in satisfying my scientific curiosity."

"You're a bad father," Gontran replied. "You don't love your daughter...you're coldly sacrificing her to your scientific egotism."

"Which is to say that she was your accomplice in this business—that she behaved like a bad daughter. She has her whole life ahead of her in which to be happy; only a few years remain to me—I'm condemned to die soon."

Fricoulet, who never abandoned his mania for jokes, even in serious situations, added: "And custom grants those condemned to death anything they ask for...except life, of course."

Selena ran in, her face flooded with tears, and threw her arms around the old man's neck, murmuring: "Forgive me, Father...but I love him so much!"

"Do you love him more than me, then?" replied Ossipoff, into whose heart a sentiment of paternal jealousy had suddenly slid.

Farenheit, however, did not think that Gontran had settled his account. "You told me you were a man of honor!" he complained. "This is, I think, the moment to prove it. You promised to take me back to Earth—take me back there, and then go to the Devil, if that suits you."

"My dear Mr. Farenheit," the young Comte replied, "I did, it's true, make you that promise—but I made it a trifle lightly."

"By God! A man of your worth doesn't commit himself lightly—I call upon you to keep your promise."

"I'm not refusing," Flammermont replied, "but I'm asking you for a delay."

The American breathed in, and asked, in a dissatisfied manner: "How long a delay?"

"Between 1000 and 1200 years."

Scarcely had Gontran pronounced these words than Farenheit, uttering a terrible roar, threw himself toward him with his hands wide open, ready for strangulation. Suddenly, though, he stopped short and fixed his immeasurably widened eyes on the young man. Then his wild facial expression disappeared, to give way to a foolish one.

"By God!" he said, while his mouth broadened into a loud outburst of laughter. "Jupiter...Saturn...they're beautiful planets...new worlds, where there must be lots to do from the industrial and commercial viewpoint. What do you think, my dear Gontran?" And he came forward, extending his hand to Flammermont, who did not understand the abrupt about-turn at all.

Fricoulet put his finger to his forehead, to indicate that, in his opinion, the American's mental equilibrium had been suddenly disturbed. "You can certainly count him as one of your victims," he murmured in Ossipoff's ear.

"Why is that?" demanded the old man.

"Because it's surely madness that has disturbed his mind."

As he finished these words, Farenheit uttered a strident scream and, putting his hands to his forehead, recoiled to the partition wall, giving every indication of profound terror. At the same time, his bloodshot eyes seemed to want to pop out of his head. Whitish foam flecked his lips, and all the muscles of his face were afflicted by convulsive tremors. Finally he collapsed on the floor, where he remained outstretched, unconscious.

"Quickly," Fricolet said to Gontran. "Get hold of him—I'll take the feet, you take the shoulders—and lock him in his cabin. Who knows whether this might not be a case of furious madness?"

Chapter XLII
Through Zone 28

Since the scene recounted in the previous chapter, existence on board had been subject to a complete transformation. Everyone kept to himself, only speaking to his companions in cases of extreme necessity, eager to fall back into mutism as quickly as possible and return to his solitude. The frustration of Farenheit's supreme attempt to return to Earth had delivered a terrible blow to the voyagers, who—without knowing exactly why—blamed one another reciprocally for that frustration, imputable to fate alone.

Without having had the opportunity to communicate their sentiments to one another, however, there was a commonality of ideas between them regarding Ossipoff. The old scientist was for them "the mangy wretch that is the source of all our woe"[27]—so he lived even more apart than his other companions, in a sort of quarantine that was rigorously-observed, except by Selena, who spent a few minutes with him now and again. Between the father and the daughter, however, there was no conversation—not even a banal exchange of greetings—merely an indifferent kiss deposited by the old man on his daughter's forehead. Then, without paying any heed to her presence, he went back to work.

Since his departure from Mars, the old man had been trying to organize the observations he had made since the day he set foot in the crater of Cotopaxi, and expected to employ the two months of captivity imposed by the voyage to Jupiter in bringing that heavy task to completion. Deep down, he was perfectly well aware of the odious role he was playing; he understood very well the hatred he had inspired in his companions, forgiving himself even so for the reproaches contained in Selena's resigned attitude and desolate gaze.

Yes, driven by the irresistible wind of scientific folly, he was running to his doom, dragging in his wake the daughter he adored, and three men for whom he had no other sentiments than those of sympathy—but his incommensurable love of science, his ever-insatiate curiosity regarding the unknown, had desiccated his heart and expelled from his mind all other ideas than those having to do with the immense infinity that he had resolved to travel from one end to the

---

[27] The original version of the quoted phrase is from one of La Fontaine's verse fables, "Les Animaux malades de la peste" [The Plague-stricken Animals], in which a court of animals tries to figure out whose sin has brought down the wrath of God upon them in the form of a plague. The lion and the fox confess sins of predation, but are too powerful for the court to punish, so the burden of the court's wrath falls upon a donkey, which confesses to having eaten grass from the grounds of a monastery and is then made a scapegoat, condemned with the insult in question.

other. He therefore opposed a serene brow and an imperturbable calm to Gontran's furious glances, Fricoulet's sarcastic smiles and Farenheit's menacing howls.

The last named had been declared by Fricoulet to have attained a perfectly characterized state of mental alienation. For a long time already, the American had not calmed down; he had been living in an uninterrupted state of overexcitement, and the final collapse of his hopes had struck him a blow so terrible that a cerebral lesion had ensued. In the interests of all the travelers, including his own, it had been unanimously decided to lock Farenheit in his cabin, where he never ceased to vociferate the most terrible threats against his companions, especially against Ossipoff.

Gontran was even sullen with Selena, who could do nothing about it—poor thing! But human nature is made in such a fashion that when desperation takes possession of us, the creatures dearest to you become indifferent, even odious, and egotism, with its sharp claw, transforms all our sentiments. Certainly, to have done as he had done—to renounce his career, depreciate his fortune, abandon his family and his fatherland—in order to engage in such improbably adventures as those into which he had followed Selena, Flammermont must have veritably and profoundly adored the young woman, and that adoration had resisted all the disappointments that he had suffered for so many months. This time, however, things surpassed all measure; it was no longer in weeks or months that the delay in his marriage was to be measured; he had to reckon in years! And how many years? A minimum of 30? But in 30 years, Gontran would be 57 and Selena close to 48![28] 105 years between them! More than a century! In truth, that was a grotesque prospect—not to mention that there were 99% chance that their affection would not endure such a long education.

The prudence of parents restricts as much as possible the period during which a fiancé pays court to his fiancée; in studying too long, one ends up perceiving mutual faults; one notices that the pretty face, so fresh, owes something to the produce of Veloutine Fay,[29] and that a corset from that celebrated manufacturer might be making a contribution to the slimness of the figure—just as, on the other hand, one observes that the scalp is perceptible through the hair, an indication of imminent baldness, and that the wrinkles in the corners of the eyes, invisible a first, betray a precocious fatigue. The moral is the same: Mademoiselle is a coquette, Monsieur a gambler; Mademoiselle is a shrew, Monsieur gets

---

[28] This sentence implies that Gontran is now 27, while Selena is 18—but we were told that Gontran was 25 or 26 when the story began and Selena 16 or 17, both of which imply that only one or two years has passed, while the dates given in the text record (albeit somewhat unreliably) a lapse of at least three years.

[29] Veloutine Fay [approximately translatable as "magical flannelette"] was the name of a fashionable Parisian boutique in the Rue de la Paix, whose principal stocks-in-trade included cosmetics and corsets.

carried away, etc., etc. If a few weeks suffice to strike a blow at a love-affair, what can remain of an affection, however profound it might be, after 30 years? That is what Flammermont asked himself straight away. Then again, there was that devil of a century with which they would be blessed when they arrived on Earth; it was true that it would be shared between them, but it was no less ridiculous for that, and ridicule kills—even love.

Selena whose heart did not reason, perceived the change that had overtaken her fiancé—a change that was further emphasized with every passing day and whose cause she could not determine. This time, Gontran's attitude was no longer the same; it was not sadness, but a sort of indifference, or detachment. The poor child had too much dignity to demand an explanation or to voice a complaint, but when she was alone, she wept; her eyelids were constantly swollen and reddened now.

Alone among the company, Fricoulet maintained his unalterable good humor. In addition to the strong dose of philosophy that convinced him of the futility of raging against Fate, he did not have the same reasons as Farenheit or Gontran for cursing the course of events. Nothing summoned him back to Earth; unlike the America he had no shareholders to whom he had to render accounts, and unlike Gontran, he had no happiness for which he was in haste to appeal to the blessings of a mayor and a priest. Besides, his landlord, a grumpy and miserly man and a stickler in the matter of rent, would have sold the meager property he had left in the Boulevard Montparnasse a long time ago.

The engineer's heart was a trifle anguished at the thought of his beautiful instruments and his dear books being dispersed to the four corners of Paris, by order of the court, but what could he do about it? It was, therefore, preferable to take things as they came and not to blow his brains out.

In addition to the uncertainty as to where he would lay his head—the hospitalities of the night rarely made him smile—there was another reason for the scant enthusiasm that Fricoulet experienced at the prospect of returning to Earth. Instructed by his celestial peregrinations, when the young engineer compared his native planet to the worlds that he had visited, he saw that it occupied a very low rank in the scale of astral civilizations, and almost blushed on its behalf when he thought about the humankinds of Venus and Mars. So, far from cursing Mikhail Ossipoff, that Christopher Columbus of the Heavenly Earths, who had associated him, in spite of himself, with the realization of his sublime chimera, the engineer was, on the contrary, grateful to be taken away from the depressing spectacles that he had witnessed on Earth, where the struggle for existence drives the strong to triumph over the weak, where injustice is victorious, most of the time, over equity, where money is everything, where virtue counts for little, and where, above all, mechanical science is still in its infancy....

Fricoulet contented himself with thinking in this way, however; nothing in the world would have made him communicate these sentiments to his traveling companions. From the viewpoint of principle, he thought that they had reason to feel aggrieved by Ossipoff, and that the latter, paternally speaking, was a frightful egotist. Even so, he attempted, as conscientiously as possible, to play the conciliatory role he had adopted. Thus far, he had obtained no result, but that did not prevent him from conserving the hope of bring the members of the little colony back to the harmony of better days.

Such had been the reciprocal attitudes of the voyagers since the famous day when they had been obliged to bow to the terrible authority that bore them toward Saturn instead of bringing them back to their native planet, as they had hoped.

For almost two weeks since they had left Mars, the *Eclair* continued its rapid progress through space; its propeller functioned without respite, under the impulse of the electricity stored in the accumulators. At first, the perpetual light in the midst of which they sailed had made the voyagers uncomfortable and disturbed all their habits—but Fricoulet, who had taken possession of Farenheit's chronometer, had taken responsibility for regulating time in accordance with it. Every 12 hours, he closed the portholes through which the external light came, lit the lamps and crossed off one more day on the old calendar contained in his wallet. By virtue of that, the Terrans had an exact notion of time and were able to regulate their occupations.

One morning, as the engineer was taking his watch, replacing Gontran—who had just lain down in his hammock—the door of the retreat in which Ossipoff had shut himself up with his papers and instruments opened abruptly and the old man appeared on the threshold. His right hand was brandishing the eyepiece of a telescope while his left was feverishly gripping a micrometer.

"What has made you so joyful, my dear Monsieur?" asked Fricoulet. "Have you, perhaps, discovered some new star?"

The old man's face was, indeed, radiant, and his eyes were shining with a singular brightness. "We're moving into the zone of the minor planets," he replied, in a voice slightly choked by emotion.

"Already!" said the engineer, initially surprised by this news. "Are you quite certain of that?"

The old scientists tapped the telescope. "This isn't mistaken," he replied. "Then again, if you only cared to calculate the number of kilometers traveled since our departure from Mars, it would be easy for you to establish that we must have reached the distance of 28 specified by Titius and Bode's law."

"I believe you, Monsieur Ossipoff, I believe you," said Fricoulet, having no wish to get involved in a discussion of that subject, which was of little importance to him. Seeing that the old man was ready to continue his route in the direction of the cabins, he asked him: "But where are you going?"

"To find Monsieur de Flammermont. Although his attitude to me is not entirely that which I have the right to expect, I cannot leave him in ignorance of an important scientific fact that must be of great interest to him."

"It's merely that Monsieur de Flammermont has only just gone to bed," Fricoulet said. "Today has, it appears, been extremely tiring for him, and as he lay down in his hammock a little while ago, he begged me to let him rest for as long as possible."

"An event of this nature, however," retorted Ossipoff, with a hint of bad temper, "certainly warrants waking him up."

"I would agree with you on that point, my dear Monsieur" Fricoulet replied, "if we didn't have plenty of time before us to study these little worlds at leisure. Remember that the zone in which the minor planets orbit measures no less than 67,000,000 leagues in width, and that we'll cut across 234 planetary orbits. Thus, you can let Gontran rest entirely at his ease, without any scruple, since he'll have a whole month to savor this astronomical feast."

The old man was about to jibe at the irony that the young engineer's last words contained, but the latter immediately set out to calm him. "What made you realize," he asked, "that we have penetrated into this famous zone? Have you perceived one of these worldlets?"

"No, it was calculation alone that led me to the conclusion that we had just crossed the orbit of the first of the minor planets, Medusa."

"You haven't seen it?"

"No—doubtless it's still too distant.

Fricoulet's face expressed the profoundest amazement. "In that case," he said, "what did you want to show Monsieur de Flammermont?"

"Nothing—I wanted to give him that news and, at the same time, invite him to observe space with me."

The engineer suppressed a mocking smile, with some difficulty, and replied: "That would doubtless have been a meager feast for him…at least wait until you have something visible to show him." Privately, he added: *That way, dear Gontran will have time to go over his* Continents célestes.

Slightly disconcerted, Ossipoff had turned on his heel to go back into his den when the engineer called him back.

"Tell me," he said, with the utmost seriousness, "do you intend to land on every one of the 234 planets that we'll encounter *en route*."

Ossipoff examined the engineer attentively, wondering whether he might be the victim of a joke; then he replied in a sullen voice: "Telescopes aren't made for dogs, I suppose, and, if you have no objection, we'll content ourselves with examining these little worlds from a distance."

"For my part, I have no objection to that," replied Fricoulet. "It's your business, and Monsieur de Flammermont's." He had added these words in an earnest tone that brought an approving nod of the head from Ossipoff—and with that, the old man retired to his lair.

"If I'm not mistaken," Fricoulet murmured, with a smile, "there's a difficult situation in preparation for dear Gontran." He rubbed his hands together, thinking that this might provide the long-anticipated occasion that would finally ruin a marriage that would, in his opinion, make his friend unhappy. Then he reflected that, after all, a marriage postponed for 30 years had every chance of never taking place, so he decided that it would be more appropriate on his part not to oppose Gontran in his matrimonial plans and to appear, on the contrary, to be smoothing his path to the altar.

He waited for a few hours, and when it seemed to him that Flammermont had had enough rest, he went into the cabin, went to the hammock and put his hand on the sleeper's shoulder.

The latter lazily opened his eyes, closed them again, opened them for a second time, stretched out his limbs, yawned twice and said: "Oh, it's you! You cut me off in the middle of a very pleasant dream."

"What was it?" asked Fricoulet.

"It was my wedding day and the Mayor of the eighth arrondissement was making a very nice little speech to Selena and me. He even called us 'the fiancés of space.' He was about to conclude when you interrupted him..." He propped himself up on his elbow. "Anyway," he said, "why did you wake me up?"

"After the dream, the reality," the engineer replied, gravely.

The young Comte started in his hammock. "You're frightening me," he stammered. "What are you talking about?"

"The minor planets."

Gontran burst out laughing. "Is this some bad joke?"

Fricoulet shook his head. "It's not a joke...I'm speaking quite seriously." And, with comic gravity, he cried "Wretch! While you were sleeping peacefully, the asteroidal wave that is carrying us has penetrated into Zone 28! We've already crossed the orbit of Medusa."

"Well, what do you want me to do about it?" Flammermont asked, placidly.

Fricoulet raised his arms toward the ceiling. "And the worthy Ossipoff wanted to come and wake you up several hours ago, to tell you the good news."

"I'd be very grateful," groaned the young Comte, "if he'd leave me in peace, with his stars, his planets, his suns and all the rest. I care as little, now, for astronomy as *that*!" And he clicked his thumbnail noisily against his teeth.

"Aren't you forgetting, you fool, that Selena is at stake!" Fricoulet exclaimed.

"Oh, Selena!" murmured Gontran, shaking his head. "30 years from now, she'll be nearly dead...and so will I."

The engineer took his friend's hand. "You shouldn't talk like that," he said. "30 years, in this instance, is only a maximum...and the hazards are so great."

"What do you mean?"

"That it would be prudent for you to be on your guard, as they say, and not to compromise the good opinion Monsieur Ossipoff has on you by getting carried away."

"What must I do, then?"

"Play your role conscientiously, and bluff—for the subject of the Minor Planets is one of his enthusiasms..."

"How do you expect me to be enthusiastic about something I know nothing about?"

"I suggest you go back to *Les Continents célestes*,"

Gontran gave vent to a long and sonorous yawn. "That's good," he said. "I'll take a look...later."

"On the contrary—immediately. Ossipoff might descend upon you at any moment."

"But it's cold!"

"The Minor Planets will warm you up."

Gontran seemed dejected.

"My God!" exclaimed Fricoulet, "do you recall the conversation we had on this subject at the Observatory in the City of Light? In 1801, in Palermo, Piazzi discovered the first minor plant, which he called Ceres. In 1802, an astronomer in Bremen, Olbers,[30] discovered the second, Pallas—then several years later, the fourth, Vesta. The third, Juno, had been found in the interim by one named Harding.[31] Afterwards, 38 years passed without anyone paying much heed to zone 28, when, suddenly, the appetite for research was renewed, and 234 of them were discovered."

Flammermont was listening attentively. "I think," he said, eventually, "that I'd better get *Les Continents célestes*. You're telling me that too briefly..."

"That's also my opinion," said the engineer.

The young Comte uttered an enormous sigh, fetched out the precious work hidden under the mattress of his hammock and, having riffled through it, opened it at the chapter on the Minor Planets.

"Go away," he said to Fricoulet, in the voice of a victim. "Close the door, and if Ossipoff asks you about me, tell him I'm still asleep."

Since the moment when the *Eclair* had crossed Medusa's orbit, the voyage had continued without encumbrance, offering the Terrans nothing to break the desperate monotony of the passing hours but the observation of the daily diminution of the solar disk.

On Mars, the voyagers had already been able to remark a substantial difference between the heat and light received by that planet and that received on Earth; at that time they had come straight from the Sun, in the vicinity of which they had had to support a colossal temperature, surpassing that of boiling water, and they had seen that heat and light decrease progressively in proportion to the disk of the star itself.

---

[30] Heinrich Olbers (1758-1840).

[31] Karl Harding (1765-1834).

When the comet carrying them had passed its perihelion, the solar diameter measured more than a degree—one degree 44 minutes, to be exact; when the crossed Earth's orbit, that same diameter measured no more than 32 minutes; on Mars, it had diminished further, dropping to 21 minutes. Now, in the center of the asteroid swarm, it measure no more than 15 minutes in width, and was declining further every day.

According to Ossipoff's calculations, the apparatus had traveled 216,000,000 kilometers across the stellar immensity in a month, and its distance from the Sun was about 100,000,000 leagues. They were now traveling through the region crossed by the greatest number of minor planetary orbits, and the old scientist estimated that within four weeks they would reach the orbit of Jupiter. They would then be 198,000,000 leagues from the central star.

Scarcely a day passed without Ossipoff's vigilant eye catching sight of some new star, on the subject of which it was necessary for Gontran to submit to interrogation—to which he replied victoriously. Fricoulet knew the order in which the minor planets would present themselves, and the young Comte studied his lesson in advance in *Les Continents célestes*.

After Medua they had encountered Flora, Ariadne, Harmonia, Melpomene, Victoria, Zelia, Urania, Athor, Baucis and Iris.[32]

"Tomorrow," Gontran said, one evening, "we shall doubtless see Barbara."

He had said this in such a singular tone that Mademoiselle Ossipoff could not help asking: "And what is so remarkable about the planet that you should inform us of it in that manner? Presumably, it's more important than those we've been permitted to see thus far."

Flammermont shook his head. "It's one of the smallest in the system," he said, "measuring no more than 50 kilometers in diameter, but it has the originality of having been discovered on purpose."

"On purpose!" exclaimed the young woman, smiling.

"Yes, Mademoiselle. Generally, when a fiancé pays court, he offers flowers to the choice of his heart as an emblem of his affection. The American astronomer Peters thought that too banal. In spite of being 78 years old, he had fallen

---

[32] It is, of course, unlikely in the extreme that all these minor planets would simultaneously occupy points in their very long orbits from which the might be observed from a vessel cutting across their orbits, but the narrative virtually ignores such niceties, with respect to all the objects in the Solar System—as did most early scientific romances and science fiction stories. The lists included in the text are adapted from a very useful table provided by Flammarion in *Les Terres du ciel*, which lists every single known minor planet along with its mean distance from the Sun, its physical characteristics and the name of its discoverer, along with the relevant date.

in love with the daughter of the famous optician Merz,[33] and to prove to her how different his love was from that of other men, he searched for two years for a sufficiently brilliant unknown star worthy of being offered to his beloved. That star he baptized with her name, Barbara."

"That's a delicate touch," murmured the young woman.

"I regret, believe me," Gontran replied, "not having discovered anything yet—but for a godmother such as you, that would be too small a star; a sun would be required..."

After Barbara, it was nearly a week before they encountered another asteroid; then the *Eclair* arrived in a richly populated region. It passed scarcely 100 leagues from Aethra, which appeared to the voyagers to be merely an irregularly-formed rock, measuring scarcely 30 kilometers at its greatest diameter, surrounded by a thin atmosphere. Then they saw Eve, Maia, Proserpine, Lumen, Frigga, Clotho and Juno; the last two planets seemed to be sailing in convoy and Ossipoff declared that, by virtue of the small mass of these bodies, gravity was so scarcely perceptible at heir surface that material erupting from a volcano on Clotho could quite easily fall back on Juno. Successively, they caught sight of Ianthe, Brunhilda, Rodope, Felicity, Eunice, Pompeia and Dynamene.

One night, the little colony had a bad fright. The *Eclair* almost collided in passing with the planet Lamberta and, if Fricoulet had not had the presence of mind to change the apparatus' course with a violent thrust of the tiller, the Terrans would have been done for. A few days later, they were able to observe that Ceres and Pallas, the first two minor planets to be discovered, were true worlds, spherical in form and surrounded by an atmosphere, just like Laetitia and Bellona, which they sighted a few days later.

They had left behind the confused orbits of Isabella, Eudora, Antigone, Aglaea, Calliope, Scylla, Psyche, Vindobona, Clytemnestra, Hesperia, Palles and Europa when Gontran—who was, as he jokingly put it, preparing the next day's lesson—said to Fricoulet: "You know, in a few hours we'll be in sight of two planets that have no baptismal names; I can only find them catalogued as two serial numbers, 222 and 223. Is that an error or an omission?"

The engineer laughed. "My dear chap," he replied, "if you have savings to invest in land, and the slightest desire to be a landowner, those two planets are for sale."

"You're joking."

"It's not a joke, it's the exact truth. So, taking your example from the American astronomer you mentioned the other day, you'd be able to offer those

[33] The most famous "optician"—i.e., maker of optical instruments—named Merz was Georg (1793-1867), but he cannot be the one in question; in his later years, he worked in collaboration with his son Sigmund, but the chronology makes it more likely that the father in question was one of Sigmund's nephews, who subsequently took over the family business: Jakob or Matthias.

two planets to your fiancée, instead of buying her a little house with a courtyard and a garden."

"Explain what you mean?"

"Quite simply that, to make a living from the stars, the astronomer Palisa—the discoverer of the two planets in question, who is nevertheless a practical man—has fixed at a price of 1250 francs the honor and pleasure of taking those two stars to the baptismal font. If your heart tells you..."

Finally, after 48 days of travel, the last planet in the group, Hilda, was left behind. The 67,000,000-league-wide zone in which the worldlets orbited had been traversed, and the *Eclair* was now 90,000,000 leagues from Mars—which had disappeared into infinity some time before. 46,000,000 leagues still remained to travel before reaching the orbit of Jupiter; according to Fricoulet, that represented 25 days of journey time.

Chapter XLIII
Jonathan Farenheit gets up to his old tricks

"Gontran! Hey, Gontran!"

For five minutes, Fricoulet had been shaking his friend, who was lying in his hammock, fast asleep. "He still won't wake up…the animal!" grumbled the engineer. "So much the worse for him!" He took the sleeper in his arms, lifted him from the bunk and planted him on his feet.

"Eh? What? What's happening?" complained Flammermont, opening his eyes, which were still vague and full of sleep. Then, perceiving Fricoulet, who was looking at him and laughing, he stammered: "Oh, it's you, Alcide. What are you doing here?"

"As you can see, I've come to wake you up."

"It's my turn already?" murmured the young Comte, regretfully.

"Midnight's just sounded. It's your watch."

Gontran shrugged his shoulders. "Watch…watch…" he muttered. "Really, what's the point of breaking our nights up like this, to the detriment of our health, and without any advantage to our security…which isn't at risk?"

"Is that what you believe?" retorted the engineer.

"Of course! In the nearly two months that our voyage has lasted, which isn't far from 60 nights, has there been any incident, however trivial, that legitimates our sentry duty?"

Fricoulet seized his friend's hand. "Fool! At this moment, our sentry duty is more useful than ever. Remember that we're no more than 1,500,000 leagues from Jupiter, and that the slightest false maneuver or mechanical breakdown might hurl us into the giant like a bat into a wall."

"At 1,500,000 leagues? You're exaggerating. If you think that Jupiter can exercise the slightest attraction on us…"

Fricoulet uttered a little laugh replete with mockery. "Gontran, my friend," he said, "You're neglecting your *vade mecum*, and you're shouldn't. *Les Continents célestes* has what you need."

Flammermont shook his head dispiritedly. "What good is there," he murmured in my racking my brains with all that stuff? While I still had some hope of realizing the dream of happiness that I'd conceived, I could consent to play the comedy, but now that I have the prospect of a 30 year delay before being able to marry Selena…for it will take 30 years to get back to Earth by following the course of this river that's carrying us along, won't it?"

"Yes, 30 years, give or take a few months," replied the engineer. Then, involuntarily moved by his friend's depression, he put a hand on his shoulder. "My God, old chap, is this you that I see so discouraged? A truly strong man never loses hope. Who knows? Some opportunity might present itself…"

A brief glint appeared in the Comte's eye. "Do you really think that there might be some means of cutting this excursion short?" he said.

The engineer pushed out his lips. "When one is navigating the unknown, as we are," he replied, "one never knows...so I advise you, if you still want Selena, to reopen *Les Continents célestes* and to read, attentively, what it says about Jupiter."

"To get back to what I was saying just now," said Flammermont, "you think that 1,500,000 leagues..."

"Ah!" Fricoulet retorted. "Ossipoff will smell a rat if he hears talk of that sort. Fool—don't you recall the fundamental axiom which says that the attraction exercised by a body is directly proportional to its mass? Now, Jupiter and the Earth are in the same proportion as an orange and a pea. If a giant were to knead together a considerable number of Earths, it would require no less than 1230 of them to equal the volume of that formidable world. As for weight, 800 Earths placed in the pan of a titanic balance would scarcely equilibrate the Jovian mass. Remember that its diameter is more than 11 times that or our native planet; it attains 141,800 kilometers, and the circumference at the equator is no less than 111,000 leagues."[34]

"You just said 'at the equator,' " Flammermont objected. "Isn't the circumference the same everywhere?"

Not exactly. The vertical axis that passes through Jupiter's poles is 8000 kilometers shorter than the horizontal diameter, which corresponds to a flattening of 1.17."

"That's odd. Is it known why that flattening occurs?"

"Quite simply from the rapidity with which Jupiter turns on its axis; you know that the duration of that rotation is nine hours, 55 minutes, 45 seconds—with the effect that the days and nights are less than five hours. That rotational velocity is such that a point on the equator is moving at 12 kilometers a second—24 times as fast as a point on the Earth's equator. In consequence, the centrifugal force developed reduces weight at the equator by a twelfth; an object that weighs 12 kilograms at the poles weighs no more than 11 at the equator..."

"Well," said Gontran, insouciantly, "if we have to fall, let's try to do it on the equator—the shock won't be as rude."

The engineer shrugged his shoulders pityingly. "My poor Gontran," he murmured, "you don't know anything about anything."

"Possibly—but I recall perfectly that the density of the materials comprising Jupiter is a quarter of that of terrestrial materials, so..."

"So," said Fricoulet, sardonically, "weight there is reduced, no? That's what you mean? Well, you're completely wrong. On Jupiter, the gravity is two

---

[34] None of these figures correspond exactly with those given in modern reference books, although the only one seriously in error (perhaps by virtue of a misprint) is the mass, which is actually 317.89 times that of Earth.

and a half times greater than on Earth. A terrestrial kilogram weighs 2.5 kilos grams there...with the effect that, instead of 75 kilos, you'd weigh more than 180, and a dropped stone falls 12 meters in the first second, rather than 4.90 as on Earth." To complete his friend's bewilderment, he added, in a perfectly natural tone: "Given that, if you multiply our total weight, which would be 6000 kilos on Jupiter, by the height of our fall, you'll arrive at a jolly total of 46,000 meters per second as the velocity with which we'd encounter the surface of Jupiter. If that encounter, effected in similar circumstances, is agreeable to you, you have only to return to your hammock and resume the sleep that I have so untowardly, in your view, interrupted. As for me, I'm exhausted. I'm going to bed."

And with these words, Fricoulet turned on his heel to go to Farenheit's bunk, which he had adopted since the American had been living in isolation.

The scarcely-seductive prospect that the engineer's last words had evoked in Gontran's eyes woke him up entirely, simultaneously chasing away any inclination to laziness. He went to the engine-room and sat down, with his hand on the lever controlling the rudder and his gaze fixed on the batteries of accumulators. "Damn it!" he murmured, jokingly. "A fall from a height of 1,500,000 leagues...we'd be reduced to dust, or vapor, before getting to the bottom..."

At that moment, a slight grating sound became audible behind him. He turned round and uttered a cry of surprise on seeing Farenheit emerge cautiously from the cabin in which he had been imprisoned.

"You!" Gontran exclaimed, getting to his feet.

Seeing that he was discovered, the American came toward the young man, and the light of the lantern, falling directly upon him, illuminated a pale and emaciated face, in which the eyes, shining with a feverish glare, were wildly gleaming points. The bridge of the nose, as thin as a knife-blade, curved over a mouth with discolored lips. His hair and beard and grown prodigiously and were almost entirely white. His step was hesitant and his movements jerky.

Damn! thought Gontran. *Captivity hasn't done him any good—but how the Devil did he get out of there? That idiot Fricoulet must have forgotten to lock the door.*

While the young Comte was indulging in this mental monologue, the American had stopped two paces away from him, with his arms folded across his chest and his half-closed eyelids filtering a malevolent gaze, studying him and shaking his head. Finally, as if he had read Gontran's thoughts, he said, in a hoarse voice: "Yes, Monsieur de Flammermont, it's me. It surprises you to see me at liberty...but with patience, one can do anything. For the month and more that I've been locked up in there, like a vicious animal in its cage, I've had but one goal: to recover my liberty and avenge myself. Freedom I have—as for vengeance, I'll have that shortly..."

Solitude hasn't calmed him down, Gontran thought. *He's still in the grip of the same madness that has taken possession of him for five weeks. Let's try to bring him round with gentleness.* Aloud, in a tone full of affability, he said: "Avenge yourself, my dear Mr. Farenheit? But on whom?"

"On all of you, wretches that you are, who made a fool of me for months, and for whom I've long served as a plaything!"

The young man understood that it would be dangerous to get into a discussion on that subject. It would be better to humor the American, hoping by that means to take him meekly back to the cabin that served as his padded cell.

"Indeed!" he said, lowering his voice mysteriously. "You're right. Yes, you were fooled—and me too. That Ossipoff is certainly a great joker, and many a man has been guillotined on Earth who merited it less than him—but what do you expect? For the moment, there's nothing we can do...except wait patiently for the hour of vengeance." And he added: "Look at me! Don't I have as much reason as you to complain? Isn't the role of eternal suitor to which I'm condemned just as maddening? Well, that doesn't prevent me conserving my self-composure and hiding my rage with smiles. Do as I do..."

It seemed to the young man that this little speech produced a salutary effect. Farenheit's contracted features relaxed; his eyes lost their wild stare and the taut lips almost smiled. "Listen," he said, when the young man had finished speaking. "It's doubtless God who kept you awake tonight, during your watch. If I'd found you asleep, like last night, you'd have been done for."

"Like last night!" Gontran exclaimed.

"I told you just now that, since my captivity began, all my strength of mind has been concentrated on a single idea: to get out of my prison. Now, when an American wants something, it's rare for him not to succeed in getting it. I wanted my liberty, and I have it. For five nights I've waited for the moment when Monsieur Fricoulet cedes his place to you...then, when I see you sound asleep, I slip out of my cabin..."

"And what do you do then?" asked the young man, who was beginning to think that, for a madman, Farenheit was marvelously rational.

"I work on my vengeance," replied the American, whose lips twisted into an evil smile.

"Your vengeance!" Gontran repeated. "But you're mad."

"Yes," growled the Amercian, "I'm mad...but not the way you mean. I'm mad with rage—for, not content with dragging me along with you in this adventure, which becomes more insane every day, you've shut me up like a vicious beast. Well, listen to this: you're all doomed. The boat is mined. With the powder I extracted from my revolver cartridges, I've made up a charge and disposed in such a fashion that when it explodes, it'll blow the *Eclair* and everyone it contains into little pieces."

"But you're one of them too," Flammermont replied, unable to convince himself that Farenheit was serious.

"Isn't dying thus, quickly and soon, many times better than languishing for years? I've carefully weighed the pros and cons, you see...and the course I've settled on is the more reasonable."

"Do you realize that, by acting thus, you'll damage the interests of your shareholders?"

"What do you mean?"

"According to Fricoulet, this boat represents a considerable fortune, of which one share is yours. You'd be increasing the deficit inflicted on your company's funds by that rogue Sharp."

The American shook his head. "In 30 years," he replied, "I'll be dead and, in consequence, beyond any possibility of making use of that fortune. No, my resolution is sound, and I'll put it into execution, unless..."

Gontran looked at him inquiringly.

"Just now, I told you that Providence was doubtless watching over you, since it prevented you from going to sleep tonight, as on previous nights."

"To permit me to oppose your odious project!" muttered the young man. "For, in order to set off a charge it's necessary to set fire to it—and while I live, you won't succeed in doing that..." He took a step toward Farenheit, threateningly.

"Have no fear," said the latter. "My precautions are taken, and well taken. Even if you knock me down, tie me up and lock me up, the *Eclair* will explode, if I wish...but listen to me...I consider you to be a superior man, who surpasses that wretch Ossipoff and that puny engineer in intelligence by a vast margin...and you're resourceful..."

"In truth, my dear Mr. Farenheit, you flatter me..."

"Not at all. Although I've spent the greater part of my life in the suet trade, I can judge a man's true worth as well as anyone else. Tell me—where are we, at this moment?"

"In the vicinity of the planet Jupiter."

"That's no answer...I don't know anything about Jupiter...tell me, how far are we from the Earth?"

"More than 150,000,000 leagues.

"And when we've passed this...Jupiter...where do you propose to go?"

"There's talk of going as far as Saturn—about 1,200,000,000 kilometers..."

The American folded his arms across his chest and, in a voice vibrant with barely-constrained rage, said: "Monsieur de Flammermont, do you persist in refusing to fulfill your promises? Do you persist in denying the possibility of returning to Earth? Do you persist in continuing to play the ridiculous role you're playing?"

"Mr. Farenheit," the young man replied, "the impossible has been attempted; I did all I could...my conscience is clear."

"That's your final word?"

"I have nothing more to say to you."

"Very well…I know what I have to do."

And before Gontran could stop him, the American went to the partition wall and put his finger on a switch that controlled the wires of the rudder. Immediately, a spark sprang forth, which ran along the floor like a will-o'-the-wisp. Only then did Flammermont notice an unobtrusive fuse snaking across the floor, which seemed to end at the motor.

"Fool!" cried the young man. He ran toward the fuse to extinguish it. With a mighty leap, however, the American hurled himself upon him, clasped him in his arms—with a strength multiplied tenfold by rage—threw him to the floor and immobilized him.

"Help! Help!" Gontran howled. "Fricoulet! Fricoulet!"

Farenheit put his large hand over his mouth to stifle his cries, simultaneously crushing his chest beneath his knees—but the young man's appeals had been heard in the meantime. There was a commotion in the boat's interior, in the midst of which the voices of Ossipoff, Fricoulet and Selena mingled fearful questions and brief responses. At the same time, a noise of footsteps resounded.

"By God!" growled Farenheit. "Will they have time to get here before everything is finished!" With his ears pricked, he kept his ardent eyes fixed on the burning fuse.

The steps of the iron staircase leading to the engine-room creaked under a clatter of feet.

"They're here! They're here!" roared the American despairingly—but just as the door opened, the flame reached the motor. A dull explosion was heard and a jet of flame shot up to the ceiling. At the same time, Farenheit and Gontran were projected forward, in the midst of a hail of debris torn up by the force of the explosion.

Flammermont was the first to come round, thanks to the cares that his companions lavished on him. In a few words, he told them what had happened, and they immediately hastened to transport the unconscious American back to his cell, in which he was carefully imprisoned, leaving Providence to watch over him and bring him back to life. They had other things to do, for the moment, than occupy themselves with that criminal maniac; it was necessary, before anything else, to see to the *Eclair*.

After a minute examination of the apparatus, in its entirety, they established that, in spite of the formidable shock that had shaken its frame, the *Eclair*'s hull had not suffered any damage. As for the engine-room, the damage that the ignition of the cartridge had caused was less serious than Fricoulet had feared at first. The cartridge having been placed under the base of the motor itself, it had been uprooted; several piston-rods had twisted and two accumulator batteries had been put out of action. Fortunately, the lithium walls had resisted the shock, as had the partition walls—and that was the most important thing, for all the air in the vehicle would have escaped through the slightest crack, and the voyagers would have been irredeemably doomed.

"Well, Monsieur?" demanded Ossipoff of Fricoulet, when the latter had concluded his inspection.

"Well, Monsieur Ossipoff, there's ten hours work here—after that, it won't show any more."

"Ten hours work!" cried the old scientist. "If I understand you correctly, that means ten hours during which we'll have ceased moving forward."

"Not at all—we'll continue following the current."

"Yes, but our vehicle won't have any power of its own."

"Of course, since the motor won't be functioning."

A profound creased appeared in the old man's forehead, and he ran out of the room.

"Where's he going?" asked Gontran, on hearing him race up the staircase.

Fricoulet shrugged his shoulders, which signified that he knew no more than his friend. "Let's see," he added, looking around. "Where shall we begin?"

As he was thinking, Ossipoff came back in, frowning under the influence of a grave anxiety.

"What's the matter, Father?" asked Selena.

"The situation is terrible."

"No more terrible than five minutes ago," said Fricoulet.

"Most assuredly—five minutes ago, I didn't know what I know now."

"And what do you know?"

"That Jupiter, from which we're no more than 1,200,000 leagues distant, is acting upon us and attracting us!"

"We'll have to wait," murmured Gontran. "What will the consequence of that be?"

"If we haven't got the propeller working within two hours, the planet's attractive force will exceed the violence of the current of asteroids that's sustaining us, extracting us from the river that's carrying us. Once we're in the void, we'll fall on Jupiter, at the surface of which a very simple calculation reveals that we'll arrive in 22 hours and 32 minutes."

"Oh well," said Selena. "What's so terrible about that, Father dear? After the Moon, Venus, Mercury and Mars, isn't it quite natural that we should visit Jupiter?"

"Mademoiselle is right," the engineer said, in his turn. If we're making the journey, we might as well complete it—neglecting to study Jupiter, in the circumstances in which we find ourselves, would be like traveling through Italy and neglecting to visit Rome."

Ossipoff clicked his tongue impatiently.

"My dear Monsieur Fricoulet," he replied, "you might have a certain competence in mechanics, but, for God's sake, I entreat you to abstain from talking about things you know nothing about. Astronomical questions are beyond your compass—and yet, strangely enough, you have a mania for talking about them."

Astonished by this abuse, the engineer looked the old man squarely in the face. "Would it be indiscreet, my dear Monsieur," he said, "to ask why you're speaking to me in that fashion?"

Ossipoff folded his arms. "You speak as if it were a very simple thing to visit Jupiter. Do you even know whether Jupiter is habitable and whether we could live on its surface?"

"Oh, I can't form any opinion on that," replied the engineer, with feigned modesty. "Whatever you say, I don't pose as a scientist and I have every faith in your knowledge of such matters." So saying, he bent over the motor, the damaged parts of which he examined carefully.

Gontran, addressing Ossipoff, exclaimed: "But why shouldn't Jupiter be habitable! Isn't the basis of any atmosphere water vapor? And hasn't it been established that there are clouds—clouds 60 kilometers thick—on the planet's surface? That seems to indicate a dense atmosphere!"

"Too dense, in fact," replied the old man. "For, if you assume, as is logical, that the atmosphere in question is composed of the same elements as the terrestrial atmosphere—at the density that has at ten kilometers above sea-level—the simplest of calculations will prove to you that the air, at the surface of Jupiter, must be 10,000,000,000 times greater than the density of platinum."

"Which is absurd," declared Fricoulet.

"It's therefore necessary to suppose that the atmosphere has an entirely different composition," said Gontran, in his turn.

"Unless one assumes," the engineer continued, "a very high temperature, permitting such an atmosphere to retain its gaseous state." He had pronounced these words without appearing to attach the slightest importance to them—but Ossipoff started and looked at him curiously.

Where did you learn that?" the scientist asked.

"While chatting to Gontran last night."

The old man turned to the young one, but Selena evidently guessed that her father was about to ask her fiancé some potentially-embarrassing question, for she asked: "But where would Jupiter get such heat from? Not from the Sun, surely, since it's five times further away from it than the Earth. Didn't you tell me, Father, that because the surface of the Sun seen from Jupiter is 27 times smaller, the intensity of the heat and light the planet receives is reduced to one part in 36,000,000 of the intensity of the heat and light received by Earth?"

As he listened to his daughter speak, the old man's face became radiant. "Ah, daughter, daughter," he murmured, affectionately, "you're the joy and pride of my old age." He kissed her on both cheeks—then, carried away by his temperament, which drove him to speak compulsively about the science he loved more than anything else, he added in a professorial tone: "No, Jupiter can't receive its heat from the Sun...otherwise, it would be necessary to admit that whether or not that giant world has an atmosphere would depend on its distance from the Sun. Remember, in fact, that its orbit is so eccentric that it's 20,000,000 leagues further away from the Sun at its aphelion than at its perihelion, when its distance is 183,000,000 leagues."

"Damn!" murmured Gontran. "To complete and orbit like that must require years of a prodigious length."

"What was that you said?" the old man asked, abruptly, Gontran's words having reached his ears, although indistinctly.

The young man did not reply immediately—with the result that Fricoulet had time to start speaking. "Gontran told me," the engineer said, "that it's the difference in the distances of Jupiter from the Sun that cause true seasons on Jupiter—which, it appears, takes no less than 11 years, 10 months and 17 days long to complete its orbit."

Mutely, Ossipoff nodded his head in approval; nevertheless, his expression remained a trifle suspicious, and he was getting ready to pursue his investigation further when Selena, addressing the engineer, prevented him from doing so.

"Didn't you just say *true* seasons, Monsieur Fricoulet?"

"Yes, Mademoiselle, you heard me correctly."

"Are there two sorts of seasons on Jupiter, then?"

"No, there's only one sort—the one I meant—for Jupiter has an axis perpendicular to the ecliptic, with the result that it completes its orbit in a vertical position instead of being inclined, like the Earth. If, instead of describing an ellipse about the Sun, Jupiter described a perfect circle, it would have no trace of any seasons, and the planet would enjoy a perpetual spring. Unfortunately, there's that difference of 20,000,000 between the distance at perihelion and aphelion, which destroys the harmony resulting from the position of the planet itself."

While the scientist was speaking, Fricoulet had stopped working, but Gontran, who understood how dangerous his silence was, appeared to be concentrating all his efforts and all his attention on one of the piston-rods that the engineer had given him to repair. Ossipoff, however, had gone to a porthole and was looking space with a serious expression and his brows furrowed. Abruptly, he abandoned his observation-post, left the engine-room and was heard rapidly climbing the staircase leading to the cabin in which he had installed all his instruments. As soon as he had gone, Flammermont abandoned his task and released a profound sigh.

"Oof!" he said. "Another hurdle crossed…I was in mortal terror."

"I advised you to look at *Le Continents célestes* again," Fricoulet replied.

"How could I? With that brute Farenheit…" He moved closer to the engineer and said, in a calm voice; "Now that we're alone, give me a few details, so that I won't put my foot in it the first time I'm asked a question."

"Details about what?"

"Jupiter, of course."

"But you already know nearly all that there is to know; one couldn't demand any more of you if you'd passed your *bachot*."

"You think so?"

"Riffle through your namesake's book if you doubt me."

"What about the satellites?" murmured Serena, smiling.

Fricoulet slapped his forehead. "That's right!" he exclaimed. "This devil of a motor's made me lose my head. Yes, there are the satellites."

Gontran folded his arms in mock-indignation. "What!" he cried. "Jupiter has satellites and you didn't tell me! Presumably they're so minuscule that one can consider them as negligible."

The engineer raised his arms in the air. "Negligible! Worlds that have diameters of 3800, 3400, 5800 and 4400 kilometers! But what does that mean to you, damn it! Think that the largest is twice the size of Mercury, a true planet. If Ossipoff heard you talk like that...in truth, ignorance is a beautiful thing!"

"Come on, come on," said Gontran, impatiently. "Instead of insulting me like that, you'd do better to give me a few details about these interesting worlds. First of all, what are they called? If they're as important as you say, it can't have been difficult to find godfathers to take them to the baptismal font..."

"First we have Io, 107,500 leagues from the planet's center; then Europa, at 170,700; then Ganymede, at 270,000; and finally Callisto, at 478,500. You'll know all their essential details when you know that they rotate around their planet, respectively, in one terrestrial day and 18 hours, three days and three hours, seven days and three hours, and 16 days and 16 hours, and that their density and surface gravity are very similar to those of Mars. We also know that these satellites appear to rotate on their axes in such a way that they don't always present the same face to the planet, as the satellites of Earth and Mars do. As for their physical make-up and their geography, we still don't know anything."

"So much the better!" said Gontran.

"Why so much the better?"

"Because it's one less effort of memory for me—no mountains, no craters and no canals, then?"

"No, none at all."

"Oh, what charming satellites!"

Selena and Fricoulet were still laughing at Gontran's contentment when Ossipoff appeared. "We've left the middle of the current," he said. "We're moving sideways."

"What do you expect?" retorted the engineer. Instead of spending your time with your eye glued to your telescope, you'd be better employed getting hold of a pair of pliers and helping us."

Without reacting to the slightly peevish tone in which these words had been pronounced, the old man joined his companions and all three of them worked incessantly for hours, nailing, screwing and smoothing. Finally, when the shipboard chronometer marked midday, with the transmission re-established, the motor repaired and the accumulators recharged, Fricoulet declared that they could now try to move forward.

As Ossipoff had anticipated, however, it was then too late. Under the influence of Jovian attraction, the vehicle had traveled more than 100,000 leagues; it had left the current of cosmic corpuscles that had drawn it along until that time and was falling through the void in a straight line toward the planet whose immense disk extended to the horizon.

"Monsieur Fricoulet," said the old man, then, "have you any idea of the speed at which our impact with Jupiter will take place?"

"My God, Monsieur Ossipoff," the engineer replied, with astonishing calmness, "it will be something like 29,000 meters a second. I don't think I'm much mistaken, if I'm mistaken at all."

"Indeed, we're falling at a rate of 27,650 leagues per hour."

Gontran and Selena made fearful gestures.

For his part, Fricoulet shrugged his shoulders slightly with superb indifference. "Bah!" he said. "From the point where we are, a few 1000 leagues more or less…"

"I think," the old man stammered, bowing his head, "that we're doomed…" He drew his daughter to him and hugged her to his bosom. "My poor child," he said. He offered his hand to Gontran and said: "Can you forgive me?"

"Just a minute!" said Fricoulet, whose face had cleared to display an enigmatic smile. "Monsieur Ossipoff, serve your emotion for later—and you, Gontran, save your forgiveness until our doom is inevitable." All three of them looked at him in amazement. "I have an idea," he added, "that this time, once again, we'll get ourselves out of it."

Chapter XLIV
Through the Jovian atmosphere

Ossipoff had gone back to his telescope and resumed his astronomical observations. While there was no immediate danger, the old man thought it futile to let anguish lose him time that he might employ in satisfying the ardent curiosity that was devouring him. Fricoulet had said that they might be saved; that was, for him, the main thing. As for the means that might be employed, he left it entirely to up Flammermont to examine, discuss and verify their worth.

For the moment, Gontran was standing beside Selena, and both of them were watching the engineer with anxious curiosity as he added up his figures.

Finally, Fricoulet lifted up his pencil, shut his notebook and uttered an "oof!" of satisfaction.

"Well?" the young couple asked, with one voice.

"Well, everything might be all right—at least, there's room for hope." And, while making that encouraging reply, the engineer rubbed his hands together vigorously.

"Would it be indiscreet to ask for some explanation?" said Gontran.

"Not indiscreet—but you wouldn't understand."

"Because I'm so stupid...." riposted the young Comte, bitterly.

"I didn't say that. Far from it. It isn't everyone who could sustain a role as difficult as yours for months on end, damn it—but when one doesn't have the knowledge..."

"Tell us all the same," suggested Selena, with a little smile. "Between the two of us, we'll understand...or, at least, we'll try as hard as we can to do so."

Fricoulet shook his head, to indicate how limited his confidence was. He got up, though, went to a porthole and summoned the young couple to join him. "Look," he said, pointing to the enormous disk of Jupiter, which appeared in the distance, radiant in the somber immensity of the heavens. "We are, at this moment, about 600,000 leagues from the planet on which we're going to arrive, in the fashion of an aerolith weighing 10,000 pounds, with a final speed of 30,000 meters a second."

Selena put her hands together in a fearful gesture.

Gontran uttered an "Oh!" that testified to a certain emotion, then stammered: "And that's what you hope to save us from?"

The engineer slapped his forehead, reopened his notebook, checked his calculations, altered a few figures, and said with a mocking smile: "I made an error; our speed will be either greater or less than 30,000 meters a second."

"Greater!" exclaimed Gontran. "But we won't even reach Jupiter. We'll be volatilized in advance."

"Quite correct…unless we succeed in reducing the velocity of our fall to its minimum."

Gontran raised his arms toward the ceiling. "Resist the powerful attraction of such a giant!" he cried. "But that's madness."

"Tell us your plan anyway, Monsieur Fricoulet," said Selena.

"This is what it amounts to—but first, it's necessary for you to know that Jupiter travels in its orbit with a velocity of 12,600 meters per second, and rotates on its axis in such a fashion that a point on its equator travels an almost equal distance in the same time. It follows that, at midnight, a point situated on its equator facing the Sun is displaced with a velocity of 12,600 plus 12,500—which is 25,100—meters per second, while the point situated at a diametrically opposite position, is only moving at a rate of 12,600 minus 12,500 meters per second—which is to say that it's almost stationary."

Fricoulet paused, looking at his listeners as if to ask them whether they were following his reasoning. They both nodded their heads affirmatively. Then the engineer went on: "In the former case, that velocity of 25,000 kilometers per second has to be added to that of the moving object carrying us, with the result that we'd touch down on Jovian soil with a velocity of 53,250 meters per second."

Selena uttered a cry of fright.

"With the result," Fricoulet continued, "that we'd not only be reduced to dust, but volatilized, as in a simple shooting star in which a similar motion is transformed into heat. In the second case, on the contrary, we would only have to consider our own velocity, and not that of Jupiter, which would be no more than 100 meters per second—to the extent that moving the machine backwards, at he moment of our arrival in the thick Jovian atmosphere, we might nullify, or very nearly, our own speed, and reach the ground that's attracting us without a shock."[35]

With a spontaneous movement, Selena's hands seized Fricoulet's and squeezed them forcefully. "Ah, my friend!" she said, "you've saved us yet again!"

Gontran did not say anything, but a certain movement of his head betrayed a preoccupation further emphasized by a frown.

"What's up?" asked the engineer. "You don't seem entirely convinced."

"To be frank," replied the Comte, "I confess that I'm not."

"Bah! Why not?"

"Because your reasoning is based on the rapidity of Jupiter's rotation, and that's a point on which it seems to me to be impossible to be sure."

Fricoulet shrugged his shoulders. "Ah, the ignorant!" he muttered. "All more incredulous than one another!" He took Gontran by the arm and obliged

---

[35] This argument is, of course, utterly specious.

him to put his face to the porthole. "Do you see that white stain," he said, "that can be made out on the planet's disk?"

"Perfectly—I'd already noticed it a little while ago—except that I observe that it has changed its place. It's moved from the edge of the disk toward the center."

"Well, my dear friend, it's by studying the progress of that stain that astronomers have been able to determine the planet's speed of rotation."

Flammermont uttered a little mocking laugh, then folded his arms. "In that case," he said, bitterly, "my fears are well-founded, and I congratulate the terrestrial astronomers on the accuracy of their work, if that's the way they operate."

"I declare," said the engineer, "that I don't understand a word you're saying."

"That stain," replied Gontran, "is part of Jupiter's atmosphere, is it not? Now, atmosphere implies wind...consequently, as the speed of the wind cannot be regulated like that of a train or an omnibus, it seems to me that one must be reduced, as regards the duration of Jupiter's rotation, to simple conjectures, since one has nothing before one's eyes but cloudy masses going more or less rapidly, according to whether they are driven by a west wind or an east wind..."

The engineer had listened to the young Comte de Flammermont speak with the utmost seriousness. When the latter had finished, he replied: "In principle, your reasoning isn't lacking in justice, but where you're mistaken is in attributing such carelessness to the scientific community. Astronomers know better than anyone else that they mustn't be deceived by appearances, and they've taken account of the phenomena you mention. It wasn't easy to determine the exact duration of the Jovian day, and that study, begun in the 17th century, was only concluded a few years ago."

"The 17th century!" exclaimed Gontran.

"Yes, old chap it was in 1665 that, for the first time, Dominique Cassini[36] thought of trying to ascertain the duration of the Jovian day. His initial observations gave him a period of nine hours, 56 minutes and a few seconds. Having recommenced his studies in 1691 and 1692, always taking as a basis one of the characteristic stains of the Jovian disk, he found it to be no more than nine hours 50 minutes, which is a difference of six minutes—an enormous difference that he could not explain."

Flammermont shrugged his shoulders. "Six minutes!" he said, sarcastically. "In truth, that was worth the trouble of putting poor Cassini in distress."

"For more than 100 years, Jupiter was somewhat neglected. Then, in 1773, Jacques de Sylvabelle[37] began a series of observations that he continued for sev-

---

[36] The Italian astronomer Giovanni Domenico Cassini (1625-1712) began styling himself Jean-Dominique when he was appointed director of the Paris Observatory in 1671.

[37] Guillaume de Saint-Jacques de Sylvabelle (died 1801).

eral months, and which led him to the figure of nine hours, 56 minutes. In 1778, Herschel found a period varying from nine hours 50 to nine hours 54 minutes. In 1785, Schröter of Lilienthal opted for a period of nine hours 55."

"So all these people did nothing but quibble over a difference of a few seconds?" said Gontran.

"It is necessary to believe, old chap, that those few seconds were, from the viewpoint of astronomy, extremely important, since celebrated scientists like Beer and Mädler, Airy of Greenwich, Julius Schmidt, Hough[38] and many others, devoted long study to the question."

"And did they finish up with a result that satisfied them all?"

"They finished up by concluding that Cassini had been right and that the equator of the immense Jovian planet makes a complete rotation in nine hours, 54 minutes and 30 seconds, and the poles around nine hours 56 minutes."

The unfortunate Gontran's aversion for everything that smacked of science was such that Fricoulet's explanations bored him considerably, however important they might be. "In that case," he said, when the engineer had finished, "let's hope that this litany of astronomers was not mistaken in declaring that Cassini was right, since that's the datum on which you've based our problematic survival." While speaking, he had moved closer to a porthole, his gaze invincibly drawn toward the giant world where death might await them him and his companions—but he suddenly uttered a cry of alarm and took a step backwards.

"What is it?" asked Fricoulet, joining him.

"Instead of falling toward Jupiter, we're drawing away!"

"That's a fine joke."

"The disk is smaller now that it was a little while ago."

The engineer shrugged his shoulders imperceptibly, looked through the porthole and burst out laughing.

"That's not Jupiter!" he declared. "My poor friend, that's only Callisto, the planet's outermost satellite."

"Then that's where we're going to fall..."

"Pooh! If we've deviated from a vertical line in the course of our fall, so be it...perhaps Callisto's attraction is great enough for that...but don't worry, we'll pass more than 20,000 leagues from the satellite."

Gontran made an incredulous moue.

"Here," said the engineer, to convince him. "Would you like me to tell you how long it will be before we land on Jovian soil?" He adjusted the figures in his notebook. "Given that Callisto traces its orbit 478,500 leagues from the mathematical center of Jupiter, whose radius is 17,750 leagues, I can establish, consequently, that we're presently 460,750 leagues from the planet's surface—which is to say that our fall, whose velocity is increasing with every second, will end in 12 hours or thereabouts."

---

[38] George Washington Hough (1836-1909).

The engineer's confidence greatly impressed Selena.

"Couldn't you also tell us, my dear Monsieur Fricoulet," she said, "at what point on the planetary surface we'll land?"

Gontran, thinking that it was a joke started to laugh, but the engineer replied with imperturbable seriousness: "A little while ago, I would have given you an answer and would have been mistaken, for I wouldn't have taken account of the perturbations to which the four Jovian satellites will subject us. At present, I shall ask to reserve my response until a few calculations have informed me on that subject. In any case, if the circumstances in which our descent is taking place allow it, I'll do everything I can to ensure that the point on contact between our vehicle and Jupiter takes place on the 45th north parallel. Then..."

Meanwhile, Callisto had increased enormously in size and its disk, violently illuminated by the solar rays, filled a large part of the horizon.

To pass the time, Flammermont had picked up a telescope and was examining the satellite. Suddenly, he uttered a slight exclamation of surprise. "That's quite bizarre!" he said, when Fricoulet interrogated him. "Darkness just fell, abruptly, for no more than a second; the disk melted into the blackness of space, only to reappear again as bright as before." While speaking, his eye had not quit the lens, and a further exclamation advertised the observation of a new phenomenon. "It's starting again," he said, "but not as violently. It resembles fluctuations in the brightness of electric light. Is the cause of this bizarrerie known?"

Fricoulet shrugged his shoulders. "On that subject, as on many others," he replied, "one is lost in conjecture. Not only does Callisto sometimes appear absolutely black when it passes in front of the planet, but it sometimes seems to lose its spherical form to present a polyhedral shape."[39]

"A chameleon world," Gontran murmured.

"To give you an idea of the abruptness of these inexplicable transformations, on December 30, 1871 the English astronomer Burton, who had already noticed on one or two occasions that Callisto was sometimes dark and bordered to the south by a bright crescent, found it to be perfectly circular; by contrast, on April 8, 1872 he found it elongated in the direction of Jupiter's bands, and sharper on the eastern side than the west; furthermore, it was completely black. Erck[40] noticed the same thing on the fourth of February 1872; he perceived Cal-

---

[39] The observed alternation in Callisto's color results from the fact that the hemisphere perpetually facing Jupiter and the opposite hemisphere really are different in color, but the reported differences in shape were an optical illusion deriving from small bright patches on the surface.

[40] Wentworth Erck (1827-1890). I have not been able to obtain any more detailed identification of the "W. Roberts" who was observing Callisto on the same day; the initial might be misprinted in Flammarion's *Les Terres du ciel*, from which the reference is appropriated, but it is unlikely that the person indi-

listo elongated in the direction of the Jovian bands and dark grey in color, while its shadow was round and black; on March 26, 1873, the world was very dark, but brighter than its shadow, and presented a polyhedral form."

"And how are these transformations explained?" asked Selena.

"They aren't explained, Mademoiselle; people have been content to observe them."

"Which is infinitely more comfortable," Gontran sniggered.

"On that same March 26, 1873," the engineer continued, another astronomer, W. Roberts, who was also examining the Jovian satellite but from another observatory, was struck by its darkness and its form. He drew it too; it was not exactly the same shape as the one seen by the previous observer, but corresponded in the important fact that the eastern edge of Callisto was sharper than the western edge. I can also..."

The engineer broke off abruptly; without any transition, the most profound darkness had just enveloped the vehicle—which, until then, had been flying through irradiated space.

"Damn!" muttered Gontran. "Something else has broken!"

The engineer groped his way to the commentator and the electric lighting came on immediately. On seeing the disconcerted expressions of Flammermont and Selena, Fricoulet burst out laughing.

"Instead of mocking us," grumbled the young Comte, "You'd do better to explain..."

"That we have, quite simply, passed into the cone of shadow that Callisto projects 500,000 leagues behind it, opposite to the Sun."

"A 500,000 league shadow!"

"Yes—it must have that dimension in order for terrestrial astronomers to be able to perceive its projection on the disk of Jupiter itself."

"As I was unaware of that detail..." murmured Gontran.

"How long will it take us to go through the shadow?" asked Mademoiselle Ossipoff.

"About ten minutes."

When that interval had elapsed, the *Eclair* flew into the light again. Gontran observed that Callisto was diminishing rapidly in volume while Jupiter's disk was increasing formidably.

"There—Ganymede!" said Fricoulet, suddenly—and his extended arm pointed out a shining point in space to his companions.

"Ganymede" murmured Flammermont, scratching his forehead with a preoccupied finger. "Ganymede...there's a name I know..."

"Of course! It's that of Jupiter's the third satellite."

---

cated is the English amateur astronomer Isaac Roberts, whose observations date from a later period.

"That scarcely-perceptible point out there—all the way out there! The Devil may devour me if it resembles a satellite."

"It's precisely because it is out there—all the way out there—that it's scarcely distinguishable. That doesn't prevent Ganymede from being almost as large as Mars and having more than double the volume of Mercury."

"But in that case," Selena observed, "the world ought to be inhabited."

"Why should it not, Mademoiselle? The Moon is, and these worlds that you have before your eyes are far better equipped than the terrestrial satellite to accommodate life."

"Who can know that?" asked Gontran, skeptically.

"I'm only quoting the opinion of your famous namesake."

"In any case," said Mademoiselle Ossipoff, the inhabitants of these satellites, assuming that they exist, must enjoy a magical spectacle. For them, Jupiter must be a star far more magnificent than the Sun is for us Terrans."

"In that, your suppositions are absolutely justified," replied Fricoulet. "Remember than the planet presents a disk whose grandeur is 35,000 times greater than that of the Sun, which appears to the inhabitants of these satellites to be 1400 times more enormous than the latter appears to Terrans. In addition to its veritably gigantic dimensions, however, Jupiter offers a truly magical multiplicity of bright colors, from orange and red to violet and purple, not to mention the rapid variation of its appearance due to its rotational movement." He turned to Gontran. "The word *chameleon* applies much more accurately to Jupiter than its satellite, don't you think?"

The young Comte did not reply—for the very good reason that he was asleep.

"Ah, Mademoiselle," the engineer murmured, comically, "I fear that your friend will never get his teeth into astronomical matters."

Selena smiled in a fashion seemed to indicate that she was not unduly worried about that; then she sat down by a porthole, though which she stared curiously into space, while Fricoulet resumed his calculations.

"Hey, Gontran!"

The young man started and looked around him with the alarmed gaze of an abruptly-awakened sleeper. He seemed very surprised to see his traveling companions grouped around him. He sat up abruptly, ashamed of allowing himself be overtaken by fatigue, and said: "What's happening?"

"The critical moment is imminent," Fricoulet replied, with a hint of mockery in his voice, "and my conscience wouldn't allow me to let you pass without transition from sleep to death."

Flammermont raised his eyebrows prodigiously. "To death!" he stammered. "But I thought you'd found a means..."

“Certainly—but as no one’s infallible, it’s necessary to be ready for anything. Anyway, I’d prefer you to die standing up—if you do have to die—in order to be able to shake your friends’ hands.”

“You’re joking, aren’t you?” aid the young Comte.

“Oh, yes…at least, I hope so. I have only to switch the current back on and the propeller will begin to operate at top speed…better than that, I’ve already chosen the point where we’ll land, and, if my new calculations are correct, I think that we’ll touch down with a velocity of scarcely 1000 meters a second.”

Gontran stifled a formidable yawn with his hand. “Have I been sleeping as long as that, then?” the murmured, in a low voice.

“Fricoulet simply said: “Look.”

Space was dark; Europa and Ganymede, in quadrature, only emitted a feeble light, and beneath the vehicle the immense disk of Jupiter filled the entire horizon, hollowed out like a vast funnel, ready to engulf the voyagers.

“I think,” said Ossipoff, who was studying the planet with his telescope, “that this is the moment.” The old man had pronounced these words in a grave and solemn voice. Turning to the young Comte, he added: “Don’t you agree, Monsieur de Flammermont?”

The latter looked at Fricoulet, who nodded his head imperceptibly. “I think exactly the same as you, Monsieur Ossipoff,” he replied. As he completed this sentence, the engineer pushed the stem of the commutator; immediately, a violent trepidation shook he apparatus, proving that the propeller was working at top speed.

“Do you think we’re already in the Jovian atmosphere?” asked Fricoulet.

“We’re going into it at this very moment,” the old man replied, “and if you ask me, we should take our precautions.”

The hammocks were set up side by side, by courtesy of Fricoulet and Gontran, and each voyager, stretched out in his own, waited, silent and motionless, for the shock of impact to occur.

“Monsieur Ossipoff,” Fricoulet suddenly said, “How long do you think the fall should last?”

“About 20 minutes.”

“Do you realize that it’s now half an hour since we penetrated Jupiter’s atmosphere?”

“Are you certain of that?” said the old scientist, brusquely.

“My eye hasn’t left my chronometer…we should have arrived ten minutes ago.”

“Or volatilized,” murmured Selena.

“I think we’re on our way to volatilization, though,” observed Gontran. “It’s stiflingly hot in here. I’ll wager that the thermometer marks at least 60 degrees.”

“Less than that,” Fricouler replied.

“It reminds me of the temperature to which we were subjected in the vicinity of the Sun,” said Selena, in her turn.

“I tell you, Mademoiselle,” said the engineer, “that you and Gontran are exaggerating considerably. It’s warm…even very warm…but between this and the heat of the solar zone…anyway, we’ll go with clean consciences…” Before anyone could stop him, he had leapt out of his hammock.

“Imprudent!” cried Osipoff. “If the impact took place…”

"Without heeding the old man, the engineer ran to the thermometer. “What did I tell you?” he cried, triumphantly. “Only 40 degrees!”

“Only!” complained Gontran. “You don’t think that’s enough?”

Fricoulet threw himself down the steps that led to the engine-room. The motor was working perfectly and the helix was spinning at top speed. He went back up to the common room, darted a glance through one of the portholes and exclaimed, dully: “We’ve arrived!”

His companions got up immediately.

“Where?” demanded Selena. “On a mountain? In a river?”

“But we would have felt a shock,” said Gontran.

“Then again,” said Ossipoff, “we haven’t stopped, since the motor’s still functioning.”

“I assure you that we’re immobile in the vertical dimension.”

The voyagers glued their faces to the portholes, but they were enveloped in a fog so thick that it was impossible to distinguish anything. The instruments that Fricoulet had consulted offered the only indications of the fashion in which the vehicle was behaving. The *Eclair* was no longer falling; it was moving forward with a surprising rapidity, as if, instead of weighing thousands of kilograms, it were filled with gas and possessed the lightness of a balloon. It was veritably floating in the atmosphere.

Ossipoff stood motionless in front of his porthole, with his eyebrows contracted and his lips pursed in an anxious moue, looking out with persistent attention. As for Gontran and Selena, they waited hand-in-hand. For what? The final catastrophe that their ignorance made them dread.

“Ah! That’s very good!” Fricoulet suddenly cried.

Everyone turned and fixed the engineer with mutely interrogative stares.

“Would you like me to explain this inexplicable phenomenon?” he said. “Well, as you already know, Jupiter’s atmosphere has a prodigious density—so prodigious that our vehicle, despite its weight, is presently playing the role of a veritable aerostat.” He turned to Gontran, and asked: “Haven’t you ever performed the experiment of throwing a cork weighed with a nail into a bowl of water?”

“No,” Flammermont replied. “I confess, in all sincerity, that I’ve never performed that experiment.”

“That’s a pity, since you’d have understood immediately what has happened to us. The cork, thus weighted, descends until it reaches a depth that equilibrates its weight; then it stops and floats. It's the same for the *Eclair*, which is navigating in a zone of density equal to its own."

"So?"

"So, it will be impossible for us ever to reach the surface of Jupiter."

Ossipoff stamped his heel violently on the floor. "What can we do, then?" He went to Gontran, took him by the hands and said, in an imploring voice: "My dear friend, you need to find a way of allowing us to land..."

"My poor Monsieur Ossipoff," the young man replied, "in the face of the laws of nature, the genius of man is impotent."

The old man let himself fall into a chair. With his face in his hands, he seemed prey to a profound despair.

"Well said," whispered Fricoulet in his friend's ear. "It's true, for one thing—and scarcely compromising besides."

At that moment, an abrupt change occurred outside the vehicle. The heavy veil of cloud around the *Eclair* was suddenly torn away, beneath the force of a titanic breeze, which carried the floss over the horizon. Only a few kilometers away, the Jovian surface appeared, in all its horror and all its terrible splendor. It was like an immense ocean of molten iron, sending fiery light and stiflingly hot vapors into space. At intervals, pressure produced in the very heart of the planet caused the waves to swell up and climb up, rising into the atmosphere in mighty jets, to fall back in a rain of sparks. Then, as if breathed out by the crater of some invisible volcano, black spirals twisted, after the fashion of immense volcanic plumes, to condense in liquid streaks, which no sooner rose into the air, volatilized by the heat, than they fell back in torrents of water, beneath which the burning metallic ocean boiled violently for several seconds.

The Terrans were watching this titanic battle of natural forces, mute with amazement and admiration, when, all of a sudden, clouds surged over the horizon like a huge herd of galloping horses, filling the air again—and gathered together, becoming confused as they welded themselves to one another, extending like an impenetrable curtain over the grandiose genesis of that world in formation.

The *Eclair*, well-equilibrated until then, was seized by a vertiginous whirlwind; pirouetting like a child's top around its vertical axis, it was dragged away by the storm-wind.

"A tempest!" said Fricoulet, with imperturbable calm. His voice was lost amid the racket of the unleashed elements. As impassive as he had been on the platform of his aeroplane, the young engineer followed the progress of the cataclysm through a porthole, with one eye on the compass and his hands on the levers controlling the motor and the rudder.

Ossipoff looked out and made notes. Gontran and Selena at next to one another, silently.

Taking advantage of a moment of calm, Fricoulet put in a few words: "We're making nearly 10,000 leagues an hour. In 20 minutes, we'll be in darkness."

"What can we do?" asked the Comte.

"Nothing; one can't fight a hurricane 1100 times faster than the most violent terrestrial cyclone. We can only comply, and think ourselves fortunate not to have to fear an encounter with some mountain, against which we would break like glass."

At that moment, Ossipoff left his telescope and said to Flammermont: "I recall that one of your compatriots, the French astronomer Trouvelot, witnessed an upheaval similar to this in 1856. From the equator to the poles, Jupiter was prey to a general revolution; the bands and patches that are perceptible on its disk from Earth moved from east to west, covering the entire diameter within an hour, while the equatorial band, whose existence is constant, extended southwards to twice its original width. By analyzing these rapid movements, Trouvelot arrived at the scarcely credible result that the clouds borne by the storm-wind were traveling with a velocity of 178,000 kilometers per hour."

"Hello!" said Gontran. "What's happening now?"

Darkness had fallen abruptly; that was what had prompted the young Comte's surprised exclamation.

"It's nothing," Fricoulet replied. "We've just entered the disk's dark side."

The spectacle that the Terrans had been watching for several hours, while carried by the vertiginous course of their vehicle, then became veritably marvelous, and simultaneously terrifying.

In the mist of the darkness, the ruddy light of the continents in formation split the clouds, and volcanoes with immense craters became visible, vomiting incandescent rivers, oceans of boiling water and geysers with burning jets, and plumed with bloody vapors. At intervals, lightning-flashes streaked the darkness over an extent of several 1000 kilometers; then, everything fell back into an even more frightful darkness, in the midst of which the uninterrupted din of the warring elements resounded. Sometimes, deafening and lugubrious, thunder burst forth.

Inside the apparatus, the heat had increased further, and the voyagers had been obliged to take off all their garments one by one, conserving only what was strictly necessary. The thermometer marked 58 degrees Centigrade, and Fricoulet declared that it would not hold there. In the reflection of the fires that shot their bloody flames through the fiery atmosphere, the lithium walls were terribly hot, and a thick vapor filled the cabin in which the Terrans were gathered.

Selena, lying in her hammock, seemed to be unconscious; sitting at her bedside, the exhausted Gontran, with his eyes bloodshot, his throat dry and his lungs on fire, held her hand to give her courage. Ossipoff, whose love for science made him forget physical suffering as well as moral pains, continued his telescopic studies, and the engineer watched over the progress of the apparatus.

Suddenly, a horrible scream of suffering rang out. It was Farenheit—who, forgotten in the cabin that served as his prison, was in the process of roasting like a mere leg of mutton. They were all, however, too preoccupied with themselves to think of going to help the unfortunate American, who continued howling all night.

Finally, they saw daylight again, after having gone three-quarters of the way around Jupiter—about 25,000 leagues—in two hours. The voyagers greeted the Sun's reappearance with a cheer, as if the rays of the central star might have been able to bring a remedy to their situation.

The thermometer stood at 70 degrees.

Ossipoff, also vanquished, had abandoned his instruments. Having dragged himself as far as his hammock, he was lying on his burning mattress. Fricoulet, his face on fire, the veins in his neck inflated to bursting-point, his breathing hoarse and is eyes veiled with blood, was only holding the tiller with a shaking hand. As for Selena and Gontran, they were not giving any sign of life.

In a few minutes, the thermometer had climbed further, and marked 80 degrees. A few degrees more, and they would be dead.

The human organism is known to be able to resist temperatures that seem excessive; many people can endure with impunity the heat of an ordinary furnace—which is to say, more than 100 degrees—and history records factual accounts of several supposedly incombustible men taking their places in an oven and staying there until the meat set beside them was completely cooked. To those of our readers who find it surprising that Ossipoff and his companions were able to adjust themselves to the great variety of temperatures they encountered, from the outskirts of the Sun to nearly 200,000 leagues from that star, we make the observation that life on Earth furnishes continual examples of that organic elasticity. Thus, in Africa, the maximum temperature observed are 55 degrees above the melting-point of ice; in Siberia, the greatest cold measured is 60 degrees below zero—and yet, many individuals submit to these enormous variations of climate and temperature. That explains why, despite the proximity of Jupiter, Ossipoff and his companions had not yet perished. Their position was, however, becoming critical, and the engineer anticipated a moment when the interior of the apparatus would reach the temperature of boiling water…and even surpass it.

Suddenly, as rapid as a lightning-flash, a thought crossed his mind. He threw himself upon the levers of the machine, on which he pressed down with all his strength. "The Devil with it!" he murmured, at the same time. "To die one way or another…"

An intense vibration shook the entire framework of the apparatus; the internal walls creaked; the floor groaned. It seemed that everything was about to burst apart. An energetic impulse seemed to be generated.

Several minutes passed, during which, leaning over the thermometer, the anguished engineer watched the progress of the mercury in the glass tube. Soon, he uttered a cry of joy. The mercury was descending. "Victory! Victory! We're saved!"

These words brought Ossipof and Gontran out of the prostration into which they had fallen.

"Saved!!!" the old man articulated, turning an astonished gaze toward the engineer.

"Yes, saved!" repeated Fricoulet. "We're drawing away from Jupiter.

At these words, the scientist shook off his torpor entirely and ran toward the young man. "We're drawing away from Jupiter!" he muttered.

"We're already out of its atmosphere."

Ossipoff raised his arms toward the ceiling. "Without trying to land there?"

"We'd have arrived there completely charred."

"But there would at least have been a means of completing our studies..."

Fricoulet shrugged his shoulders. "A few minutes more," he said, sardonically, "And you'd have had no need of the *Eclair* to bear you away from Jupiter—your soul would have taken flight alone."

The old man seemed crushed.

It was Gontran's turn to interrogate his friend. "Did you say just now that we're out of the Jovian atmosphere?"

"Effectively."

"But we can't sail through space, and we'll inevitably fall back."

"Not at all! I've primed our vehicle with an initial velocity that, in one single bound, will enable us to rejoin the cosmic current and continue our voyage."

Flammermont looked at the engineer incredulously.

"If you don't believe me," Fricoulet said, "look at the thermometer."

The mercury had, indeed, dropped to 45 degrees.

"If that's not enough for you," the engineer went on, "take a look outside."

The planet's disk was visibly diminishing.

"Hurrah for Fricoulet!" cried Gontran, throwing himself upon his friend's hands.

"Pooh!" said the latter, modestly. "I can't take much credit for this salvation—and if your head hadn't been full of the danger your fiancée was in, you'd certainly have thought of it yourself."

"Of what?"

"Don't you know as well as me," the engineer replied, "that heat diminishes the internal resistance of primary and secondary piles, thus increasing, to a notable degree, the electrical output? The memory of that physical law sudden came to mind, and I thought of utilizing that mortal heat to multiply our motive force tenfold. I risked blowing up the apparatus, it's true, but death was there, lying in wait for us—then again, I preferred to give the *Eclair* the greatest possible speed and, taking as a point of support the atmosphere of the planet itself, I steered straight for the asteroidal current, escaping Jupiter's attraction at a tangent."

Gontran considered his friend with sincere admiration.
"That's marvelous!" he stammered.
"No, it's simply physics."

Chapter XLV
In which, thanks to Selena, Gontran is able to increase his astronomical knowledge

A month had gone by since Fricoulet's ingenuity had once again saved the cosmic explorers. Borne by the asteroidal current, the *Eclair* had recovered its initial velocity of 1,800,000 leagues per day.

Far behind—very far behind—the Sun was visible, the diameter of its disk diminishing more and more evidently, absorbing the Earth, Venus and Mercury within its radiation. Mars could still be distinguished with the naked eye, like a first magnitude star, oscillating between the right and the left of the solar disk, alternately playing the role of morning and evening star. Ahead, already above the horizon, Saturn had appeared, a pale blue moon with a silver aureole—and in the darkness of infinity, sparkling like diamonds in a velvet-lined casket, shone Orion, Ursa Major, Pegasus, Andromeda, Ursa Minor and Gemini.

The appearance of that sky, similar to what she had seen from Earth, made no small contribution to Mademoiselle Ossipoff's continuing astonishment. "But we're nearly 250,000,000 leagues from Pulkova Observatory now," she said to Fricoulet, one day.

"Which proves to you, Mademoiselle," the young engineer replied, "That where infinity is concerned, distance counts for no more than time does with respect to eternity."

"A nice phrase!" said Gontran, with a little mocking laugh.

"I make no claim on its paternity," replied Fricoulet, laughing. "I found it in *Les Continents célestes*—which, just between the two of us, you seem to me to be neglecting somewhat."

Flammermont shrugged his shoulders bad-temperedly. "Don't talk to me about *Les Continents!*" he muttered.

"What do you have against them?"

"That they caused a frightful scene between myself and Monsieur Ossipoff."

"Yesterday evening, wasn't it?" said the engineer. "I heard you—the conversation seemed lively."

"It wasn't a conversation—it was an argument."

Fricoulet shrugged his shoulders. "Still regarding our return, no?"

"Wrong! It was about Jupiter."

The engineer looked at his friend in amazement.

"Yes," Gontran went on. "I was standing my watch, quite peacefully, without a care, when I suddenly saw Ossipoff appear in the doorway of the engine-room."

"*It was during the horror of a dark night*," quoted Fricoulet, mockingly.[41]

"If you interrupt me all the time," Gontran complained "I'll never get to the end of the story. So, I saw Ossipoff appear; he had a rolled-up piece of paper in is hand, and his face bore all the traces of evident satisfaction."

"What was the roll of paper?" asked the engineer. "A marriage contract, I'll wager."

Flammermont stamped his foot impatiently. "You're getting tiresome, Alcide," he declared. "What Monsieur Ossipoff brought me were his notes on the planet Jupiter...you can see that from here!"

"What did he want you to do with them?"

"He wanted me to give him my opinion."

"Well, you had only to approve."

"That's what I would have done, if he'd begun by giving me his opinion. Unfortunately, he started out by asking mine…"

"Aieee! That was dangerous!"

"Of course! I set off on a false track; to give him pleasure and flatter his national pride, I told him that I agreed entirely with the opinion given on Jupiter by Monsieur Bredichin, the director of Moscow Observatory.[42] According to Monsieur Bredichin, the planet is already solidified; there is, close to the equator, a very elevated solid zone, but not surpassing the height of the atmosphere, and the crust of the southern hemisphere transmits more heat into the atmosphere than that of the northern hemisphere. That state of things exercises a great influence on the direction of currents of air and vapor passing from one hemisphere to the other. As for the Red Spot, it's nothing but the planetary surface itself, seen through a foggy atmosphere, traced by an ascendant current of hot air…"

"You have a prodigious memory," declared Fricoulet. "Well, what did he reply to that?"

"He flew into a frightful temper, declaring that Bredichin was an ass, that I was little better, and that the truth—as Monsieur Hough, director of the University of Dearborn in Chicago had proclaimed—was that the Jovian surface is covered by a semi-incandescent liquid mass; that the bands, the Red Spot and other dark patches are composed of relatively cool matter; that the white polar caps are opening in the semi-fluid crust; that the equatorial white patches are clouds in suspension within the atmosphere; and that…in brief, he crushed me, for half an hour, beneath an avalanche of arguments—irrefutable proofs, according to him."

"And what did you say?"

---

[41] Fricoulet is quoting from Jean Racine's tragedy *Athalie* (1691)

[42] Theodor Bredichin (1831-1904); the authors did not know when they wrote this passage that Bredichin would be appointed director of Mikhail Ossipoff's beloved Pulkova Observatory in 1890.

"Me? I paraphrased the theories of the director of the Moscow Observatory, augmenting them with my personal observations—but he maintained that only he and Hough were right."

Fricoulet shrugged. "It's unfortunate," he said, "that I didn't participate in this discussion, for I'd have been able to claim, with Russell, the director of Sydney Observatory,[43] that, despite its cloudy zones and Red Spot, Jupiter is a planet analogous to Earth—which, seen from afar in space, must offer the same appearance as Jupiter, with bright zones and atmospheric voids of varying darkness."

Selena, who had not said anything thus far, asked: "How is it that you can't reach an agreement, after having approached the planet so closely? Didn't you see anything, then?"

"To tell you the truth, my dear Selena," Gontran replied, "I saw nothing but fire..." Addressing Fricoulet, he added: "However, I believe that the theory you've just proposed can be discounted. It's impossible, in fact, that our native planet should offer to someone examining it from an altitude of a few kilometers, the fantastic spectacle to which we were witness."

"Do you think," replied Fricoulet, "that an observer who had flown over Central America at the moment of our departure from Cotopaxi would not have seen something similar?"

"I agree with you, but it's scarcely probable that Jupiter has, thus far, given birth to beings bold enough to do what we've done."

"To begin with," said Selena, "Jupiter isn't inhabited."

"That's not the opinion of the Austrian astronomer Littrow," said Fricoulet.

"He believes in the habitability of Jupiter?" cried the young woman.

"Not only does he believe it, but he has calculated some profound differences that must exist between their life and ours, in consequence of the rapid succession of days and nights. According to him, the Jovians must possess a singular mental and physical elasticity. 'How few of us,' he said, 'would be satisfied if the nights only lasted five hours and we were obliged to wake up so rapidly. Gourmets, in particular, would be very embarrassed here if they were obliged to eat three or four meals in the space of five hours. And how loudly would our women—who demand almost nearly twice the length of a Jovian night to get dressed—complain about nights so short, and balls even shorter? On the other hand, though, official astronomers in that world's observatories must be delighted—if the Jovian atmosphere very permits them to work—for they would never get tired!' "

"And you believe that?" asked Mademoiselle Ossipoff, naively.

"No, Mademoiselle," the young engineer hastened to reply, laughing. "And Littrow himself, if he were alive today, would no longer write it—for astronom-

[43] Henry Chamberlain Russell (1836-1907).

ical science has made progress since then, and we now know many things that were unknown a few years ago."

"Which did not prevent Victorien Sardou from describing the inhabitants of Jupiter!" riposted Gontran.

"The author of *Patrie* has not only depicted Jovian humanity," said Fricoulet, with imperturbable seriousness, "but has etched a view of the planet, with its inhabitants and animals, in nine hours, despite not knowing how to draw."

Selena looked hard at the engineer, doubting that he was talking seriously.

"That's what it takes to be a medium," the latter added.[44]

There was a pause; then Gontran exclaimed: "In any case, whether or not the planet itself is inhabited, its satellites must be populated! Globes as large as Mars and Mercury..."

"Their size is not a sufficient reason," Fricoulet replied, "and you have to pay attention to the enormous difference of situation that exists between the planets you cite and the four Jovian satellites. Remember that the latter are ten times as distant from the Sun as Mercury is."

"I've caught you out in a flagrant contradiction!" riposted Flammermont. "Didn't you tell me, recently, that there's an undeniable analogy between the distances and relative volumes of Jupiter and its four satellites on the one hand, and the four inner planets and the Sun? You also told me—and I'm not dreaming—that Jupiter is the true Sun of its four satellites, which receive a supplement of heat from it not to be disdained, given the heat sent to them by the Sun."

"I certainly did tell you all that," the engineer replied, "but, in saying that, I was only revealing the theories of the majority of scientists. It's indubitable that Jupiter is much more useful to its satellites than they can be useful to it, by virtue of the scant light they send it. Besides, the conjunctions of three of the worlds, taking place in the cone of shadow that Jupiter projects behind it, are entirely lost to it. Furthermore, as the moons rotate in the equatorial plane, the polar regions—which have the greatest need of light—never see them. Beyond the 80th parallels north and south, those satellites are never seen to rise or set."

---

[44] The dramatist Victorien Sardou (1838-1908) was at the height of his hard-won fame when this passage was written, but had earlier combined his playwriting with enthusiastic participation in Allan Kardec's investigations of "Spiritism"—the French rival to American Spiritualism. Sardou met Camille Flammarion in Kardec's circle, and Flammarion might have had some influence on his experiments with automatic writing and automatic drawing—when he began to "receive" messages from Jupiter dictated to him by the spirits of the composers Wolfgang Amadeus Mozart and Bernard Palissy, who were now supposedly resident there in the city of Julnius. The etchings to which Fricoulet refers, depicting life on Jupiter, were made in the early 1860s. The historical drama *Patrie* (1869) is unconnected with these Jovian fantasies.

Gontran shrugged his shoulders. "What can be seen, then?" he sniggered, "Nothing." And he added, in a complaining tone: "It was hardly worth Galileo giving himself so much trouble for discovering worlds that are useless."

"Pardon me," Fricoulet elide laughing, "but at least they're of use to their inhabitants."

Selena had got up and had taken a box out of a drawer; she brought it to the two young men in a mysterious manner. "I'll show you something interesting," she said. She undid the string that sealed the box and took out a sheet of parchment, which she carefully unfolded. A photographic print then appeared, old and yellowed. She carefully picked it up in her fingertips.

"What's that?" asked Gontran.

"That," replied the young woman, deliberately emphasizing the syllable, too disdainfully pronounced, in her opinion, by the count, "is part of my father's little collection. It's in this carton that I put all the things he holds dear—dearer than his life, perhaps—before leaving the little house in St. Petersburg."

"But more precisely," said Flammermont, "what does it represent?"

"It looks like a telescope," Fricoulet said, "albeit a primitive telescope."

The young woman smiled. "My father bought this print very dearly, from an Englishman who was visiting the Venice museum at the same time as him, and who, at the request of the curators, photographed all the objects worthy of attention with an apparatus of microscopic dimensions."

"And this," Gontran repeated, not taking the trouble to hide is surprise, "represents something worthy of attention?"

"My God!" replied the young woman, in a tone of affected indifference. "It seems that it's the first telescope that Galileo used, and which he fabricated himself."

Flammermont nodded his head knowingly. "In that case," he murmured, with imperturbable seriousness, "I understand that the print has a considerable interest in your father's eyes."

"I don't know how the Englishman who served as his traveling companion got hold of it...but it appears that he succeeded in scraping off a little piece of the telescope with his pen-knife and that he put it in a locket suspended from his watch-chain."

The two young men opened their eyes wide.

"He was mad, that Englishman..."

"No, simply an astronomer who had made the journey from London to Venice with the sole purpose of seeing Galileo's telescope. My father offered him relatively considerable sums for a share of the piece of lead that he had removed, but he would never consent."

"A piece of lead, did you say?" exclaimed Gontran. "So it was a telescope made of lead?"

"Yes," said Fricoulet. "It was a lead tube, the end of which was fitted with a plano-convex lens and a plano-concave lens. It was rudimentary, but it must be remembered that Galileo fabricated the instrument on mere hearsay, relating to an invention made by a Belgian that had the effect of bringing objects nearer."[45]

"But how did he arrive at that result."

"He supposed that the apparent nearness must result from the magnification caused by the refraction of the image through the lens." As he examined the photographic print that he had taken from Selena's hands, approvingly, Fricoulet added: "To think that it was with this crude instrument that the great scientist made the majority of his celestial discoveries!"

"Everything in the sky was still to be discovered, of course," Gontran remarked, a trifle churlishly. Leaning over the proof, he continued: "What's that date I can see there in the corner, written in ink: January 7, 1610?"

"It's the date on which, thanks to that rudimentary telescope, Galileo saw the satellites of Jupiter for the first time."

"What!" Gontran murmured. "The satellites of Jupiter date from that era?" Seeing Fricoulet smile, he went on: "I mean, I thought their discovery was more recent."

"No—on January 7, 1610 Galileo noticed two tiny stars to the left of Jupiter and one to the right. At first, he thought that they were simply fixed stars, but the next day, the three stars had moved to the right. The day after that, he could only see two, both to the left. Finally, on the 13—which is to say, six days after his first observation—Galileo was able to see all four satellites. From that moment on, his studies made rapid progress, and soon afterwards, the movements of the Jovian satellites had been determined and their orbits calculated. What do you think of that, eh!"

"I think quite simply," Flammermont replied, "that if Galileo had not done what you say...he would not be Galileo."

Fricoulet shrugged his shoulders. "And if he had only done that!" he exclaimed. Then, tapping the box in which Selena had re-sealed the precious relic with his hand, he went on: "To think that, thanks to that bit of lead, astronomical science took a giant step so suddenly and so rapidly...for, in that same year, after having discovered the satellites of Jupiter, Galileo also discovered the rings of Saturn."

Selena smiled. "I believe you're mistaken, Monsieur Fricoulet," she said, softly.

---

[45] The invention of the telescope is shrouded in mystery, probably because its utility in identifying ships at a distance was a vital strategic accessory in a time of frequent naval warfare and enthusiastic exploration. The allegation that lenses could be combined to make objects seem nearer had been made by Roger Bacon in the 13th century, but the suppression of his writings on suspicion of unorthodoxy had meant that they had to be rediscovered in the 16th century. By the time the hearsay reached Galileo, the news was probably quite old.

Fricoulet looked at the young woman in surprise. "What?" he said. "Wasn't it in the summer of that same year of 1610 that Galileo…?"

Mademoiselle Ossipoff stopped him with a hand gesture. "Excuse me," she said, "if I take the liberty of interrupting you, but I'm speaking in the interests of my happiness."

"My God, Mademoiselle!" replied Fricoulet, increasingly bewildered. "I'd be very grateful if you'd tell me what connection there might be between Saturn and your happiness."

"It's quite simple. My happiness is entirely dependent on Monsieur de Flammermont's lips. If my father were even to harbor suspicions about my fiancé's scientific knowledge, my dream would be destroyed. It's therefore important that dear Gontran hears nothing that might lead him to error—and it seems to me that you are, in fact, mistaken when you attribute the discovery of Saturn's rings to Galileo."

Fricoulet started. "What!" he exclaimed.

"You understand," Selena went on, still smiling with her usual calmness, "that I have heard my father talking about Saturn on many occasions. On his return from Italy, he even gave a lecture on Galileo and his discoveries—I was the one who organized his notes for that lecture, and it was necessary for me to serve as an audience for my father before he decided to speak in public…for he's as timid as he's knowledgeable…"

"Mademoiselle," Fricoulet replied, respectfully, "all this is very well, but…"

"You no longer remember this, then?" And Mademoiselle Ossipoff put a piece of paper on the table and rapidly the following line on it:

Smaismrmilmepoetaleumibunugttaviras.

She handed to the piece of paper to the engineer, who exclaimed: "You're right—or, at least, it's me who explained badly. I simply meant to say that Galileo was the first to discover that Saturn was not an ordinary and isolated planet, as it had previously been believed to be."

"In that case, we're in agreement," murmured the young woman.

Meanwhile, Gontran had also cast his eyes over the paper. "What's this gibberish?" he asked. "It looks like a puzzle."

"It's that too—Galileo was secretive by nature and when he didn't have a perfectly clear explanation of a scientific phenomenon, he made a note of it in such a fashion that no one could make use of his preliminary work to follow in his footsteps."

"That doesn't tell me what this chaos of letters signifies," said Flammermont.

"In the mind of their author, it signified that the planet appeared to him to have a luminous appendage to either side; that's why he described it by means of the name 'tricorps.' After trying for a very long time to discover the secret hidden by that enigma, Kepler thought he had found it and assembled the mixed-up letters in the following manner: *Salve umbistineum geminatum Martia Proles*—which means 'Salute the Gemini who are the progeny of Mars'—and he announced to the world that Galileo had discovered two satellites of Mars. The Florentine astronomer immediately contradicted this false news and gave the alphabetical chaos its true form: *altissimum planetam tergeminum observavi*, which translates as 'I have observed that the most elevated planet is a set of three.' "

"Which is false," declared Gontran. "I'm astonished that a great scientist like Galileo..."

"My dear chap," replied the engineer, "you mustn't accuse people without knowing all the facts. Now, you doubtless know that, by virtue of the movements of Saturn and the Earth, the rings present themselves to us edgewise every 15 years and become invisible. That's what happened in 1612, when Galileo suddenly saw his two stars disappear. He searched in vain for an explanation, became discouraged, and gave up on the problem."

"He had only to suppose," Gontran joked, "that Saturn, faithful to mythological tradition, had swallowed his children." After a pause, he added: "So you were leading me to error just now, by claiming that Galileo was the discoverer of Saturn's rings."

"I've admitted that," the engineer replied, dryly. "You don't contest, I suppose, that *errare humanum est*?"

"In short, who was the true discoverer?"

"It was Huygens who published the truth of the mysteries of Saturn in 1659—but, doubtless thinking that Galileo had been too obvious in his mode of publication, he adopted this..."

And on the piece of paper that already contained Galileo's anagram, Fricoulet traced the following bizarre assembly of letters:

aaaaaa, ccccc, d, eeeee, g. h, iiiiiii, mm, nnnnnnnnn, oooo, pp, q, rr, s. tttt, uuuuu.

Gontran's eyes widened in alarm. "And that means?" he stammered.

"*Annulo cingitur, tenui, plano, nusquam cohoerente ad eclipticam inclinato*...do you get it?"

Flammarion sniggered. "I haven't forgotten Molière to the extent of being unable to understand his Latin! Your gibberish simply signifies: 'It is surrounded by a light ring, not adhering to the star at any point, and inclined to the ecliptic.' "[46]

"My dear Gontran," Selena said then, "would you permit me to give you some advice?"

"Go on," said the young man, hurriedly.

---

[46] The anecdote regarding this sequence of ciphers is reproduced from *Les Terres du ciel,* pp.669-671.

"You ought to acquaint yourself with the subject a little, in order to be able to sustain, successfully, a conversation with my father that might fall upon the topic of Saturn at any moment."

Flammermont looked at his fiancée with a piteous expression. "Do you think there's any use in doing that?" he stammered.

"It's more than useful, it's indispensable."

The young Comte could not suppress a formidable yawn.

Fricoulet burst out laughing, and said to Mademoiselle Ossipoff: "You're driving poor Gontran mad, with all these planets and all these satellites."

"Not to mention," Selena's fiancé riposted, "that my *vade mecum, Les Continents célestes*, goes on at length about the subject on which, at any moment, your father might decide to give me an oral exam. And then..." He made a gesture, which signified that then, the dream of happiness would be destroyed.

The young woman remained pensive for a moment; then a smile strayed across her lips and she said: "Wait a moment."

As light as a bird, she went out of the engine-room and climbed the steps that led to the upper cabins. She came back after five minutes holding a slender scroll of paper in her hand, which she gave to Flammermont, saying: "Here's your brief."

"What's this?" asked the young man, untying the faded and crumpled blue ribbon securing the pieces of paper. Scarcely had he cast his eyes upon it than he exclaimed: "Your handwriting!" Immediately, he read the lines written at the head of the first page:

LECTURE GIVEN BY MIKHAIL OSSIPOFF
ON THE SYSTEM OF SATURN
February 15, 1878.

"Yes," said Selena, "It's the famous lecture I mentioned just now, which my father gave on his return from Italy. Their Imperial Highnesses, the Grand Dukes, were in the audience. It was on that very occasion that my father was decorated with the Order of the Red Eagle." After a pause, she added: "You'll find everything you need to know in there, for my father only had me write out the principal points that would serve him as reference-points for his scientific and philosophical developments....in less than 20 minutes, you'll be able to read and re-read these few pages well enough to assimilate their contents."

Meekly, Flammermont went to sit down in a corner of the engine-room; then he opened up the document and began to read.

Ossipoff began with a historical resumé; he established that Saturn must have been one of the last of the five planets known to the ancients to be discovered, because its brightness was inferior to that of Venus, Jupiter and Mars—Mercury came later. He then passed on to a review of the role played by the star among the different peoples of antiquity, according to their religion. He repeated the opinion of the astronomer Burton, according to which Saturn's ring was known to the ancients because an image had been found in the ruins of Nineveh of the Assyrian god Nisroch—Saturn—enveloped by a ring. Gontran skipped over all that rapidly, in order to reach what was of immediate interest to him.

Saturn, said the Russian scientist's notes, *with its multiple rings and eight moons rotating around it with various periods, constitutes a veritable universe. The planet moves around the Sun following an orbit 720,000,000 leagues in diameter and 2,215,000,000 in circumference—which is to say, almost ten times as long as the terrestrial orbit. In traveling this immense distance, Saturn, only covering 9500 meters a second, takes 29 terrestrial years and 67 days. As for the orbit itself, its eccentricity is such that Saturn is more than 40,000,000 leagues closer to the Sun at its perihelion than at its aphelion.*

From the Observatory at Pulkova, Ossipoff went on, *I have measured the arc subtended by Saturn, and that arc varies according to the planet's distance between 15 and 20 seconds—which permit me to attribute to Saturn a diameter six times longer than that of the Earth, or 30,000 leagues. Saturn therefore has a volume almost equal to that of Jupiter; its equatorial circumference is 100,000 leagues, which implies a surface 86 times greater and a volume 780 times greater than the surface area and volume of Earth. While the equatorial diameter in 30,500 leagues, however, the vertical axis only measures 27,450, so that the planet is even more flattened at the poles than Jupiter, and it has been possible to establish, with regard to the polar flattening, the following proportions: Earth 1/280; Jupiter 1/15; Saturn: 1/10.*

From the preceding, it follows that the physical conditions on the surface of Saturn are totally different from those on Earth; they are closer to those on Jupiter. Thus, not only is gravity there weaker than on our planet, but that gravity varies from pole to equator by virtue of the centrifugal force developed by the rapid rotational movement, in such proportions that, if the planet only turned twice as rapidly, objects would no longer weigh anything in the equatorial regions.

Gontran paused in his reading and said to Fricoulet: "There's something I don't understand." And he repeated the preceding paragraph.

"You must have seen," the other relied, "that there is a large difference between the equatorial and polar diameters?"

"Yes—something like 3000 leagues."

"Well, that's what produces that difference in weight. Add to that the contrary attraction of the ring, which contributes to a further reduction in weight. Anyway, if you want proof..." He took Gontran by the arm, led him to the telescope aimed at the Saturnian disk, and said: "Do you see those cloudy bands, analogous to Jupiter's, cutting the disk parallel to the equator?"

"Yes," the Comte replied, "after a few seconds of observation."

"Now, do you see, along the equator itself, one band a little more distinct and a little darker?" In response to an affirmative grunt from Flammermont, the engineer added: "That's proof of the considerable attraction exerted on the planet by the ring, for it's supposed, strongly, that the band in question is nothing but a cushion, an enormous swell of cloud. There must be prodigious atmospheric and marine tides on that strange world."

"But I've just seen that the rotation of Saturn is extremely rapid—how do they know that?"

"Doesn't Ossipoff talk about it?"

"He simply puts, underlined in red crayon: *duration of rotation 10 hours 16 minutes*—that's all."

"The same method was used for Saturn as for other planets: following an atmospheric patch from one edge of the diameter to the other. The duration of 10 hours 16 minutes was established in 1793 by Herschel, and confirmed more recently, in 1877, by Hall in Washington."

"But if there are Saturnians," observed Flammermont, "they must have a considerable number of saints of both sexes."

"Why?"

"With a calendar like theirs—25,215 days per year."

"That's true," said Fricoulet, smiling.

"Well, are you making progress?" Selena asked.

"Not very quickly," Gontran replied. "If what I were reading weren't inscribed in your charming handwriting, I think I'd go to sleep."

"Where are you up to?" asked the young woman.

"The seasons."

He was about to resume reading when the engineer aid: "You can skip the pages related to that if you can remember this: the axis of rotation is inclined to the orbital plane by 64 degrees 18 minutes, which gives Saturn an obliquity to the ecliptic of 25 degrees 42 minutes, very nearly the same as Earth's. Saturnian seasons and Earthly seasons thus resemble one another with respect to the zonal divisions. As for their duration, that's a different matter. On Saturn, spring, summer, autumn and winter each last seven years; each pole and each side of the ring remain sunless for 14 years and eight months!"

"Well," said Flammermont, "those are latitudes I wouldn't care to live in."

"Because?"

"Because I need my warmth, and..."

The engineer smiled. "It's not the Sun perceived by the inhabitants of the Saturnian equator that must tan their skin. Being 90 times less extensive in surface area, it must send Saturn 90 times less heat."

"Their teeth must chatter, then."

"No, for it's necessary to suppose that the planet, whose enormous volume must have slowed down its cooling, draws all the heat it needs from itself."

"That's a supposition drawn from your fertile imagination," said Flammermont, sardonically.

"No, it's a logical deduction from recognized scientific facts."

"And these scientific facts are…?"

"The indubitably-established existence of water vapor in the Saturnian atmosphere."

"Well, how does that prove that there's a tolerable temperature there?"

"Do you think that, if Saturn only received solar heat, water would be able to exist there other than in its solid state as ice? The more water vapor, the more clouds, consequently, the more meteorological variations observed on Saturn—similar to those observed on Jupiter, but less intense."

"And is there water vapor in the ring too?" asked Selena.

"Thus far, the spectroscope has revealed no trace of it, which leads to the supposition that the ring has no atmosphere—or, at least, one so thin that it makes no impression on terrestrial instruments."

"Which won't prevent Ossipoff," grumbled the young Comte, "from proposing that we take a stroll around the rings—and, if necessary, imposing one on us, should the whim take him." And he returned to his corner to resume his interrupted reading.

Chapter XLVI
En route for Saturn

18,000,000 leagues remained to travel before arriving at Saturn—whose disk, at present, measured no less than four degrees and was growing by the hour, its pale blue face standing out against the velvet obscurity of the celestial vault. There were still ten days of navigation left, and Gontran amused himself, like a child, by checking off every 1000 leagues they covered on a sort of horary that he had fabricated, each mark bringing him that much closer to the moment when it would be possible for him to get out of his lithium cage and stretch his legs a little.

"I seem to be hardening," he said, jokingly, to Fricoulet. "I'm beginning to fear that I might no longer be able to make use of my legs. Think of it—five months of captivity! You don't need much more to lose the use of your arms and legs."

"You're joking, I take it?"

"No, I'm talking seriously. Don't you think so?"

"I think that history proves to us that individuals, after having spent years rather than months in the Bastille, the Châtelet or any other delightful place of a similar nature, come out as active as they went in."

Flammermont slapped his chest. "What about my lungs?" he said. "Do you think that it will do them any harm to breathe a little natural air, since they've been nourishing themselves for so long on adulterated air?"

Fricoulet frowned comically. "Eh?" he replied. "You're making me yawn with your adulterated air! You're forgetting that I'm the fabricator of the air in question. Anyway, after five months of absorbing it, you appear to me to be bearing up marvelously."

The young Comte nodded his head. "Yes," he said, "the body is fine…it's this that's sick." And he placed his finger on the left side of his breast.

"The heart!" mocked the engineer.

Gontran released a formidable sigh. "It's a long—a damnably long—engagement."

"My dear chap," the engineer replied, gravely, there are nations in which engagements last for years…"

"But it's for years that Selena and I will be engaged, and I don't belong to the nations of which you speak—so I'm enduring the torture of Tantalus." He took the engineer's hand and shook it energetically. "Come on," he said, in a desolate tone, "put yourself in my place. Do you think that it would be pleasant to live side by side with a young woman as adorable as Mademoiselle Ossipoff, whose hand was promised to you, who was to be your wife one day, and not even have the right to kiss her on the forehead?" He suddenly became animated.

"Oh, no!" he said, angrily, "I've had enough of that sort of existence! It must end, or else…"

Fricoulet shrugged his shoulders philosophically. "My dear chap," he replied, "it's not me you should be telling, it's Monsieur Ossipoff."

"I know that! But, come on—can't you, who know so many things, find a way of cutting this voyage short? Of allowing me a glimpse of the conclusion to which I aspire so ardently, with the briefest possible term?"

"My dear chap," repeated the engineer, "I'm not a sorcerer and can only do what the feeble scientific knowledge I've acquired permits. We're at an impasse; either we stop on Saturn to renew our provisions—that is to say, to see what use we might be able to make of the physical forces existing on that world's surface—or we pass it by and continue our voyage. In the former case, we lose time, but have stronger probabilities of finding a means of satisfying our lungs and our stomachs. In the latter case, we lessen the duration of the voyage, to be sure, but death—certain death, by asphyxia—will then await us."

The engineer then brought Gontran up to date with the situation. As concerned food, there remained a provision of liquid nitrogen and Martian liquids sufficient to nourish and water the five voyagers for five more months. The materials for the manufacture of respirable air were in great enough quantity to permit them not to envisage the likelihood of asphyxia for a similar period. What they would lack, however, before much longer, was electricity. The accumulators were working incessantly; for some time they had been reliant on them not only for the force necessary to activate the propeller, but also for light and heat. The latter was indispensable to compensate for the lowering of the temperature; at the distance they were from the Sun, the radiation they received brought them no more than a soft light reminiscent of soft moonlight; as for heat, there was none to speak of—to the extent that the accumulators, overtaxed, contained no more than a fortnight's supply of fluid, assuming that unforeseen circumstances did not oblige the voyagers to make further demands on them.

"You, see, old chap," said Fricoulet, having finished his explanation, "the situation is quite clear. Either we stop to re-provision, and God knows when we'll get back, or continue onwards, and every league will bring us closer to famine and asphyxia."

"Oh, it's a headache!" muttered Gontran. And he added: "As far as I'm concerned, I'd prefer to continue the voyage without stopping."

"Without stopping!" repeated an angry voice from behind the two young men.

They turned round; Ossipoff was there, with his arms folded, looking at them indignantly.

"So," he said, "we adopted a grandiose ambition: to travel the celestial immensity. That ambition we have fulfilled, in part—and we should stop, having come so far! Now, then, Monsieur de Flammeront, are you certain that you're in your right mind? You'd renounce the heartfelt pleasure of all the marvels that a visit to the strange world of Saturn promises us? Remember that everything you have seen so far is nothing by comparison with what the future promises us."

"Heartfelt pleasure!" retorted Gontran. "No, Monsieur Ossipoff—you're mistaken if you think that I'm abandoning the marvelous dreams that have haunted me. There is, however, another dream, anterior to those, whose realization is my life's goal..."

Guessing that the young man was about to talk about his marriage, Ossipoff cut him off. "Besides, Monsieur Fricoulet must have demonstrated to you that a stop on Saturn is indispensable to the continuation of our voyage."

Gontran, irritated at being unable to complete his sentence, shrugged his shoulders lightly. "Seriously, Monsieur Ossipoff," he cried, "Do you expect to find everything that you need on Saturn?"

"Do you doubt it?"

"Yes, I doubt it—and it seems to me to be imprudent to speculate about probabilities as hazardous as those."

"Really! Well, listen to me—I assure you that the universe of Saturn is inhabited, and inhabited by a race that is probably much better formed and much more intelligent than ours. It's in that superior sphere that true happiness much exist."

"That's not a reason why the elements indispensable to us should exist there. It's not true happiness that we aspire to—it's electricity and breathable air."

These words seemed sufficient to choke Ossipoff—who threw his arms in the air in a gesture of indignant stupefaction. The he leaned toward Fricoulet and murmured in his ear: "The poor boy's lost his mind."

"Why do you think so?" the engineer replied, loudly. "I find, on the contrary, that he's reasoning quite clearly—as for me, I won't hide the fact that I am, indeed, curious to know whether the Saturnians measure up to the portrait you've painted of them—if they are, in reality, as superior to the Martians as the Martians are superior to the greater part of terrestrial humankind."

"If you believe Monsieur Ossipoff," said Flammermont, irreverently, "the celestial universe it's just like *chez* Nicolet—always better and better!"

"You tell me," the engineer continued, "that the Saturnians' world is very old; that's quite true, since the epoch of its creation is lost in the night of time—an epoch in which our own planet, Jupiter and Mars, did not yet exist. It remains to find out how we'll manage to communicate with these extra-human philosophers."

Ossipoff shook his head, in a confident manner. "What happened to us on the Moon, Venus and Mars ought to have given you hope for the manner in which we'll cope with these new circumstances," he replied.

Gontran arched his eyebrows in alarm. "But remember how long it took us to find the keys to the Selenite, Venusian and Martian languages. Do you intend to prolong our sojourn indefinitely?"

"No. The road we've traveled since the Sun is nothing in comparison with the distance that remains to be traveled to accomplish our interplanetary voyage in its entirety. Remember that, after Saturn, we must visit the final worlds of our Solar System: Uranus, Neptune and Babinet's trans-Neptunian planet.[47] We need to make haste..."

"If we wish to die en route," Fricoulet finished, with an ironic smile. As the old man turned on him abruptly, with an interrogative stare, he calmly asked: "Have you thought about this, my dear Monsieur Ossipoff? By driving our apparatus with all the speed of which it's capable, and utilizing the cosmic current that serves us as a point of support, we can obtain a velocity of 81,000 meters per second, which is 72,000 leagues per hour or, in round numbers, 1,800,000 leagues per day. Now, I'm telling you nothing new in saying to you that, while Saturn orbits with a mean distance of 355,000,000 leagues from the Sun, Uranus is 700,000,000 leagues away, Neptune 1,100,000,000 and the trans-Neptunian planet 1,850,000,000 leagues from the center of the Solar System..."

"So what? So what?" muttered the old man. "You don't, I suppose, intend to give Monsieur de Flammermont and me a course in astronomy!"

"God forbid!" riposted Fricoulet, with imperturbable seriousness. "Except that you scientists live continually in the clouds, wrapped up in theory, without worrying about the means to bring things about in the world—and that's why I, a humble machine-builder, who knows nothing about the stars, but to whom these down-to-earth questions are familiar, am permitting myself to draw your attention to certain details."

Ossipoff was showing unequivocal signs of impatience. "Get to the point!" he said

"If, therefore," the engineer continued, "we have spent 166 days, or five and a half months, in getting from Mars to Saturn, it's easy to calculate and take account of the fact that, to reach Uranus, by reason of that planet's astronomical situation, we'll require 300 days—which is to say, six entire months. Neptune remains, at which we shall arrive in a further 318 days, or seven further months. As for the trans-Neptunian planet, I won't mention that, for the good reason that its situation is absolutely unknown."

Gontran seemed positively overwhelmed.

"To sum up," Fricoulet continued, "and to recapitulate that entire voyage, we took 20 months to visit the inner planets and reach Mars; it's five months that we've been shut up in this vehicle to reach the region of Saturn; that makes

---

[47] When Urbain Le Verrier first published calculations attempting to establish the position of a trans-Uranian planet, they were challenged by Jacques Babinet (1794-1872), who alleged that the hypothetical planet must be considerably further from the Sun. When Neptune was discovered, Babinet continued to argue that there must be a trans-Neptunian planet in the orbit he had identified, which he called Hyperion.

a little more than two years since we left Earth.[48] Well, frankly, Monsieur Ossipoff, do you think it will be possible to live for 18 more months cloistered in these metal walls, especially if you think that in 18 months, we'll be more a billion leagues from Earth, and that it will be necessary for us to resign ourselves to a similar existence for 611 days—a year and eight months—in order to get back to our native planet?"[49]

"That's a total of five years and more!" groaned Gontran.

Ossipoff shrugged his shoulders and looked at his future son-in-law pityingly. "In truth," he aid, "is it really you that I see in such a downcast state—you, my collaborator from the beginning; you, who will share with me the glory of his marvelous voyage! Five years!" He folded his arms and said, in a vibrant voice: "What's that, in comparison with what we've already seen, and all that we shall yet see? How many scientists would envy our situation and would overlook the slight inconveniences that it involves, to have the ineffable joy of lifting, as we are doing, the mysterious veil that hides from terrestrial view and comprehension the impenetrable secrets of celestial worlds and humankinds?"

The old man became increasingly animated as he spoke. "Shall I give you an example? Look at Sharp, who went as far as theft, betrayal and crime in order to attempt and pursue this voyage! And here are you, bewailing your fate—you, who have the chance of being one of the first and only human beings to undertake this prodigious voyage from planet to planet."

"Well," riposted Flammermont, "if I had encountered an officer of the civil estate on only one of these planets, or even a consul of my nationality, who was able to marry me to your daughter, you would, by contrast, see me laughing, and I would be the first to welcome the voyage's indefinite protraction. A honeymoon can never last too long...but a voyage of betrothal...it's too much, I tell you, Monsieur Ossipoff. It's too much. Then again, have you thought that on our

---

[48] This statement is inconsistent with the dates earlier cited regarding the return of Tuttle' Comet, which implied that two years had elapsed since the launch from Cotopaxi long before the travelers reached Mars; it is also inconsistent with the ages attributed to the characters in Chapter XLII, but in the opposite direction.

[49] Fricoulet's suggestion that it might be possible to return to Earth in 611 days is inconsistent with the previous assumption that such a journey might require the better part of 30 years—that being the orbital period of the "dissociated comet"—or with the correction made to that figure when the *Eclair*'s own velocity has been added into the equation. The relationship between the distances to be covered and the previously-cited velocity of the vehicle do not support the figures cited in the previous paragraph with respect to the potential duration of the journey, which appear to have been manufactured for the sake of potential narrative convenience.

return to Earth, Mademoiselle Ossipoff, whom I hoped to marry as a young woman, will have coiffed Saint Catherine.[50] Well, I ask you, is that funny?"

The old man had bowed his head, as if crushed by the logic of this speech.

"My God!" said Fricoulet, it has to be admitted that my friend Gontran is not entirely wrong. If it were only me—even though, as you often repeat, I'm not a scientist initiated into the beauties of astronomy—I wouldn't complain. I'm curious by nature, and it seems to me that the pleasure of visiting all these worlds and clearing up with my own eyes all the mistakes that scientists and philosophers have made in writing about their subject is not too dearly purchased by a few months of seclusion. Besides, personally, I'm alone; I have no parents who will weep for me, nor a fiancée who sighs for me, nor a career that calls me back, and I'm in no hurry to return to that miserable planet on which I was born, where I lived in poverty for 20 years, and where the first visiting-card I receive on my return will be that of my landlord, transformed into a legal document demanding 15 months unpaid and overdue rent."

"Good for you," murmured Ossipoff. "That's straight talking!"

"Unfortunately," continued the engineer, "I'm not alone—or rather, my dear Monsieur Ossipoff, we're not alone, and we don't have the right to impose our existence on our traveling companions. Gontran and Farenheit have their reasons—reasons that are, in sum, quite plausible—for wanting to return home as soon as possible...and so far as I'm concerned, I declare to you frankly that my conscience would not be tranquil if, as leader of the expedition, I had reduced one of my companions to madness and the other to despair, by virtue of my obstinacy."

Fricoulet had pronounced these last words in a firm voice. Flammeront took his hand and shook it vigorously. "Good for you!" he said, in his turn. "That's straight talking!"

Ossipoff stamped his foot impatiently and cried: "And what's the point of all this fine talk? To what conclusion does your fine reasoning lead? Are you proposing to take Monsieur de Flammermont and the American back to Earth before we've completed our voyage?" He marched back and forth across the engine-room, taking long strides, prey to a profound perplexity. It was obvious that a violent combat was raging within him. Suddenly he stopped short and, looking at Gontran angrily, said: "Monsieur de Flammermont, "I won't hide from you how disappointed I am by your attitude and your language; your only excuse, in my eyes, is the passion to which you are obedient." And he added, in a dull voice: "Fatal passion!"

Gontran raised his eyebrows prodigiously. "What? Are you reproaching me for the affection that I have for your daughter?"

---

[50] The phrase "coiffé Sainte-Catherine" was conventionally used in 19th century France to describe women who were still unmarried at the ripe old age of 25.

"God forbid!" the old man retorted, sharply. "But in me, you see, there are two distinct beings: the father, who approves of the choice he has made of a son-in-law like you, and the scientist, who deplores having enlisted a collaborator in whom the sacred fire is fading day by day—a collaborator who is transforming himself into an obstacle...a collaborator..."

Flammermont cut him off with a forceful hand gesture. "A collaborator," he continued, with a pained expression, "of whose services you seem to me to be too forgetful. In the final analysis, it's thanks to me that you're here, my dear Monsieur. Without me—without my prodigiously fecund imagination—you'd never have found the means of replacing the system of locomotion that the rascally Sharp had stolen from you, to take you from the Earth to the Moon. And who was able to adapt the Selenite apparatus in order to reach Venus? Me. It's thanks to me, again, that we were able to launch ourselves from Venus in the direction of Mercury, and, yet again, thanks to me that we reached the Mercurian planet. Must I remind you that, without me—the first to think of utilizing our selenium sphere—you'd still be on Tuttle's Comet? And that, finally, if you're presently navigating the cosmic river that took you into the atmosphere of Jupiter and is taking you to Saturn, it's because I found, in my brain, the means of locomotion that we've been using for more than five months?" Having said all that in one go, Gontran, although out of breath, still had the strength to add: "Decidedly, you're nothing but an ingrate."

Under this accusation—which, deep down, he knew that he deserved—the old man winced as if he had been suddenly stung by the lash of a whip. "Very well," he replied. "You're mistaken—no, I'm not an ingrate, and the proof is that, in consideration of all the services that you've listed, I'll resign myself to not landing on Saturn or any of its satellites. I'll content myself with studying it as we pass by, and, after having seen Neptune, I make a solemn promise to turn around and come back at maximum velocity."

Moved by this sacrifice, whose full extent he sensed, Flammermont precipitated himself toward the old man's hands. "You're a good man!" he murmured.

"But not very serious," said Fricoulet. "You admitted yourself, just now, that it's indispensable to land on Saturn to renew our supplies, and now you've just said the opposite. As for me, I declare that I can no longer take responsibility for operating the boat if I'm not provided with the electricity the motor needs."

"What are you trying to say?" asked Ossipoff, not without bitterness.

"That your plan, while inspired by natural goodwill, is nevertheless insufficient."

"So what do you conclude?"

"I conclude that it's necessary to land on Saturn to renew our stores of electricity, breathable air, food—liquid or solid, as you please—and then resume the route to our terrestrial homeland directly..."

As the engineer was speaking, Ossipoff's face reddened under the influence of violent anger. His lips were trembling and blanched, and there was a fiery gleam in his eyes. He marched straight up to Fricoulet, with his fists clenched as if he wanted to hit him.

"Stop my interplanetary voyage mid-way!" he exclaimed, hoarsely. "See my entire life's hope close to realization, and renounce it myself! Break off my sublime dream in mid-flight to return to a grotesque worldlet that I despise! You're mad, Monsieur Fricoulet—yes, mad! Ask me anything you like—ask for me life—but such a renunciation...! Never. Rather kill me!"

"And you accuse me of madness!" riposted the engineer. "Isn't it rather you who warrants that accusation? The light and heat of the Sun will decease incessantly, and we'll soon be subject to the temperature of space itself—which is to say, something like 130 or 140 degrees below zero. To continue this exploration is to hasten to confront a death as certain as it is frightful. I know that your scientist's soul is brave enough to support anything, so it's to your father's heart that I appeal, and I ask you whether you're cruel enough to watch your daughter expire in terrible agony that you yourself have provoked?"

Ossipoff did not reply. He had hidden his face in his hands. From certain convulsive movements they could deduce that he was weeping.

Fricoulet went on: "Furthermore, you know full well that the cosmic river on which we are sailing does not extend as far as Neptune. Its aphelion only corresponds with the orbit of Uranus, and we would lose its support long before you had attained the goal at which you're aiming. That's another consideration—entirely material, this time—that is worth no less than moral considerations."

Ossipoff remained silent. The engineer shot Gontran a glance that said: "We have him!"

The young Comte thanked his friend with a glance for the severe blow that he had just struck.

Suddenly, the old man cried out, showing the two young men his face, streaked by the tears he had shed but animated by an indomitable will. "You're right, Messieurs," he said, "so I won't dispute your arguments—but I don't believe that I'm wrong. Don't ask me what my belief is based on; I can't tell you. It's a matter of presentiment." And as he saw Gontran shrug his shoulders, while he caught sight of a mocking smile on Fricoulet's lips, he added: "Presentiments! Yes, I, a man of the exact sciences, believe in presentiments! Oh, you can mock, you can call me mad—nothing will shake my resolution. I'm committed to pushing forward, always and in spite of everything." With these words, he turned on his heel and left the engine-room, slamming the door behind him.

Once they were alone, Gontran and Fricoulet looked at one another silently for a moment, literally astounded.

"Well?" said the former.

"Well?" repeated the latter.

"I think he's treating us rather too off-handedly."

"He has absolutely no consideration for us."

"He's entitled to his opinion," the Comte de Flammermont muttered, "but as I consider that my skin has the same weight in the balance-pan as his, we don't need his permission to do what reason commands us to do..."

"If I weren't restraining myself," added Fricoulet, "I'd lock him up with that madman Farenheit." And he added: "What have we decided, then?"

"What we decided to begin with—to land on Saturn, and then set a course for Earth."

"I'll go to the Devil if I can't find a means of exploiting the natural resources that must exist on Saturn as on other worlds—and once re-provisioned..."

Gontran seemed pensive.

"What are you thinking?" asked the engineer.

"At this moment, I'm wondering whether Saturn's atmosphere has the same chemical composition as Earth's atmosphere. I confess that it would be very painful for me to be obliged to put on one of our accursed respirols in order to come and go on that planet."

Fricoulet raised his arms in the air, in a gesture of complete ignorance. "I can't inform you on that subject," he said, "until we get there. All that I can say is that I strongly suspect that the ringed world will have plenty of surprises in store for us."

"The fact is," Flammermont added, "that with a similar density and an atmosphere as thick as that of Jupiter, we're going so see a lot more grey..." He shrugged his shoulders. "Finally," he murmured, in a philosophical tone, "by the grace of God!"

It was on this note that the conversation ended. Fricoulet went back to his motor and Gontran returned to his hammock, where he began urgently riffling through *Les Continents célestes*, trying to read between the lines what the celebrated astronomer, his namesake, thought about the new world on which the necessity of the situation constrained them to land.

Several days had passed since the regrettable scene what we reported above. Saturn—which was, so to speak, growing visibly—now presented an enormous disk. Gontran, having measured it with a micrometer, found that its diameter was twice that which the lunar disk offered to Terran gazes.

Although the role of scientist imposed on him by circumstances weighed heavily upon him, and had entirely dispossessed him of any penchant he might have had for astronomer, he could not, in spite of all his preoccupations and frustrations, be entirely disinterested in the celestial marvels surrounding him—and among all these marvels, Saturn, about which he had just read surprising details in the *Continents*, intrigued him greatly.

It was now possible for him to make out, with sufficient clarity, the rings surrounding the planet, and he continually interrogated Fricoulet about them. The latter having told him, one day, that the rings presented their faces in turn to the rays of the Sun, the young Comte asked him, in bewilderment: "What do you mean by that? I confess that I don't really understand."

"It's quite simple, though. The Saturnian year is equal to 29 Earthly years; the result of that is that each face of the ring is plunged into darkness for 14 years and six months."

Selena, who was busy sewing, put in: "These rings aren't transparent, are they, Monsieur Fricoulet?"

"No, Mademoiselle. Supposedly—for the scientific world only has vague information on this subject—the rings are formed by an infinity of corpuscles, barely separated from one another and, by virtue of their distance, seemingly forming a compact mass in the eyes of the planet's inhabitants." The engineer added, with a smile: "Is that very interesting to you, Mademoiselle?"

"Oh, only in one respect. Given that the rings are compact, they must intercept the light of the countries located beneath them."

"You're quite right. Not only do they prevent the solar rays from reaching those countries, but they also project a shadow so deep that those countries are plunged in darkness."

"It must be a night of fixed duration," said Gontran, reflectively.

"That depends on the latitude, for the shadow projected on the planet gets larger as the latitude becomes more elevated. Thus, the Saturnian countries whose latitude corresponds to that of Madrid are subject to a total eclipse of the Sun that lasts more than seven years, while those whose latitude corresponds to Paris are only subject to it for five years. At the equator, the eclipse is not as long and is only renewed every 15 years. Every night, though, there are eclipses of the moons by one another and by the rings, with the effect that these strange lands remain plunged in a profound darkness of which it is impossible for us Terrans to have the least notion."

To pass the time, Flammermont had undertaken to make an in-depth study of the eight Saturnian satellites, which were shining with a gentle and mysterious clarity in the dark depths of the sky. Fricoulet, whom the young Comte had enlisted to his project, smiled imperceptibly, watching his preparations for observation with a skeptical smile. While Gontran had taken down the telescope he needed from the upper room to the engine-room, set up the telescope in the embrasure of one of the portholes, brought a chair, and set a pen and paper on a table with which to record his impressions, the engineer said to him, jeeringly: "You're getting ahead of yourself!"

"What do you mean?"

"That you always act without thinking. It will need someone cleverer than you to succeed in clarifying anything of the impenetrable mystery that surrounds these worlds."

"If they're as large as you claim, they'll have to allow themselves to be caught in the objective lens, whether they like it or not, in profile or full face."

Fricoulet shrugged his shoulders. "My poor friend," he said, "you talk like a birdbrain. It's not the first time that something like this has come up, and I've always given you the same explanation. The visibility of a body depends less on its dimension than on the brightness with which its face is illuminated. Now, the Saturnian satellites only receive, over an equal surface area, a ninetieth part of the solar light received by our Moon. The result is that all the satellites put together, as close as possible to full and all above the same horizon, wouldn't receive 100th part of the lunar light."

Gontran made a face. "Indeed," he murmured. "To make out anything at all, one would need the eyes of a lynx."

"Or to supplement acuity of vision with depth of knowledge."

"Everyone had his trade, my dear chap," Gontran muttered. "You're a scientist, I'm a diplomat. Permit me to believe—without any conceit, moreover—that if circumstances had presented themselves to you as they have presented themselves to me, you might not have played your character as easily as I've played mine."

"Of course I would," retorted the engineer, "with a prompter like me!" He added, in a tone of mock-inspiration: "Then again, love is a divine master, thanks to which one rapidly acquires omniscience!"

Gontran was still standing up beside the telescope, which he was considering indecisively. "You ought to have told me all that," he said, "before I set everything up. Monsieur Ossipoff has seen me, and questioned me about my intentions."

"Did you tell him that you wanted to study Saturn's rings?"

"And he rubbed his hands," Gontran added, "saying: 'Good idea—I'll come down later to see how you're getting on.' "

Fricoulet tapped his foot impatiently. "You're always the same," he complained. "You don't know how to swim, you launch yourself blindly into a river you don't know, and when you lose your footing paddling, I have to leave firm ground and throw myself into the water to pull you out…"

Gontran shook his hands vigorously. "Dear friend," he said.

"Yes, yes…I know," said the engineer, shaking his head. Then, abruptly, he pushed Flammermont aside and said: "Go on—go back to your hammock. In the meantime, I'll observe in your place."

"What if Ossipoff comes?"

"I'll tell him that you've asked me to make a few unimportant preliminary studies."

Gontran pulled a face. "If it's all the same to you," he said, "I'd prefer to remain here."

"As you please."

While the young Comte went to lie down in a corner drowsily, with his eyelids lowered but his ears pricked, in order not to be taken by surprise by the old scientist, Fricoulet set about playing his role as lifeguard conscientiously. From time to time he abandoned the telescope's ocular lens, jotted a few notes on the paper, and silently resumed his post, without pronouncing a syllable.

From time to time, too, Gontran asked: "Well?"

"It's progressing," the engineer replied, laconically.

Bed-time arrived, however, and Fricoulet made no move to go to his hammock.

"Tell me," asked Flamermont. "Do you have any intention of going to bed?"

"None. I need to finish my observations of the second moon. I still have two hours to wait."

"Two hours!" murmured Gontran, with a huge yawn.

"You're under no obligation to wait—on the contrary; since I'm working on your behalf, the least you can do is sleep on mine."

The young Comte got up. "Where have you got to?" he asked.

"I've already observed, in a general fashion, that the Saturnian satellites, like the Jovian ones, are animated by a rapid rotational movement about their planet and present their successive phases in a short time. As I told you just now, I've finished studying the motion of Mimas..."

"Mimas?" Gontran repeated, with profound astonishment. "What's that?"

"The moon nearest to Saturn. Do you know how long it takes to pass from the state of the thinnest crescent to that of a half-moon? No? Well, it takes five and a half hours." He added: "You were wrong to cede your place to me. Nothing is as curious as following that transformation, as visible as the progress of the hands of a wall-clock."

"Bah! That's not my vocation."

"It is now, since you've abandoned diplomacy," the engineer replied, laughing.

"Abandoned...abandoned..." muttered Flammermont. "That's not the right expression...I asked for a leave of absence...."

"Do you expect ever to don the embroidered jacket of an ambassador again?"

The young Comte shook his head. "Who can boast of knowing the future?" he murmured. Then, changing his tone, he said: "You're not going to bed, then?"

"No, not yet—in two hours..."

"Why two hours?"

"Because, if my calculations are correct, I'll have finished my study of the second moon, which should arrived at quadrature in eight hours..."

"Three hours longer than the first."

"Because it's further away from the planet, its motion is less rapid—do you understand?"

"Yes, I understand—but do you intend to study Saturn's eight satellites in succession?"

"No—the first two will serve as the basis for establishing a proportion between the distance and rapidity of the other six, that's all..."

"Well, I'll leave you to it," said Gontran. "Until tomorrow..."

"Until tomorrow," the engineer replied, returning to his telescope.

On awakening, Flammermont found a carefully-rolled up piece of paper stuck in the mesh of his hammock, over which he hastened to cast his eyes.

He shrugged his shoulders, laughing. "Damned Fricoulet!" he murmured.

This is what the young Comte had read:

Results of Monsieur de Flammermont's astronomical studies on the satellites of Saturn.

These satellites, numbering eight, arrive at full moon respectively in 5, 8, 22, 32 and 53 hours, and 8, 11 and 40 terrestrial days. Eclipses are not as frequent as in the Jupiter system, however, for the equator of Saturn is inclined to its orbit so as to form an angle of 27 degrees; it follows that at the solstices, the Sun appears to draw away from the equator, to which the movement of the satellites—save for the eighth—is confined, and that the moons draw away from the cone of shadow projected by their planet instead of penetrating into it and being eclipsed by it.

If there is a Saturnian humankind, the movement of the satellites must give rise in its perception to eight different kinds of months, varying between 11 hours and 79 days—that is to say, from approximately one Saturnian day to 167. The latter must surely be the one most commonly employed as a division of time, for the Saturnian year, which is made up of 25,217 days, would comprise no less than 154 months of that length.

Fricoulet had added:

N.B. Don't forget that the satellites turn around the planet in the same fashion as the Moon—which is to say, always presenting the same face.

Second N.B. If Monsieur de Flammermont happens to observe, one day, the sudden disappearance of Saturnian satellites, he should not manifest any astonishment, especially in the presence of Monsieur Ossipoffl in consequence of the position occupied in the sky by our vehicle, the satellites will have been eclipsed in perspective.

Third N.B. Will Monsieur de Flammermont please tear up the present note, after having digested its contents.

Needless to say, Gontran, after having followed his friend's recommendations point for point, transcribed the above note in his own handwriting—and that further increased, if possible, the scientific esteem in which Ossipoff held his future son-in-law.

Meanwhile, the *Eclair* impassively continued its journey through space, devouring millions of leagues with a vertiginous rapidity, tearing the mysterious veil that masked the marvelous universe for which they were heading from Terran eyes as the hours passed.

One evening, when they were little more than 2,000,000 leagues from Saturn, Frcoulet, with his eye to the telescope, was amusing himself by watching the corpuscles composing the asteroidal current in which the *Eclair* was sailing fall through the Saturnian atmosphere—where they burst into flames, according to the law that transforms movement into heat. The rain of shooting stars on that gigantic moon, whose pale blue disk was hardly distinguished from the velvety black of space, was a marvelous effect.

Suddenly, the engineer uttered an exclamation of surprise that brought his companions running. Even Ossipoff abandoned his observatory and raced down the stairway that led to the engine-room, excitedly stammering: "What's happening?" As he entered, he saw that Fricoulet's face was upset; thinking that something was wrong he launched himself toward him, saying: "Speak, please! What do you see?"

"The dark face of the ring just appeared to me lit up by phosphorescence," the engineer replied. "One might have thought there was a vast fire."

The old scientist stamped his heel on the floor, furiously. "In truth, my poor Monsieur Fricoulet," he said, "it's obvious that, despite your scientific pretensions, you don't understand the first thing about the beautiful science of astronomy, or you'd find nothing extraordinary in a phenomenon so simple, and wouldn't stand there gawping at aeroliths streaking the Saturnian atmosphere." Shrugging his shoulders scornfully, he added: "The phosphorescence you thought you'd discovered was seen a long time ago."

The engineer permitted himself a skeptical laugh. "Really?" he said. "And can you tell me the name of the astronomer to whom the finding is due?"

"Isn't it the opinion of the author of *Les Continents célestes*?" Gontran put in, timidly.

"Precisely," replied the old man. "It's your celebrated namesake to whom I was referring."

"I beg your pardon," said the engineer, "but the author of *Les Continents célestes* is not as affirmative as you claim…and whatever you might say, I'm convinced that I'm the first to have perceived this phosphorescence with my own eyes."

"Of course," muttered the old man, "if my telescope had been directed that way, I would have perceived it as the same time as you."

"Agreed—so, I shall not draw any pride therefrom, but merely the conclusion that the heat reigning on the surface of Saturn is simply due to the ring. Exposed to the solar heat for 15 consecutive years, and even though its constituent particles rotate on their axes, it must warm up significantly and transmit a path of that stored heat to the nearby planet."

"Possibly, possibly," muttered the old scientist. "What good is it to prognosticate, anyway, when we shall see when we get there?" With these words, pronounced in an irritated tone, he left the engine-room.

Chapter XLVII
In which our heroes overshoot Saturn

The distance that separated the *Eclair* from the Saturnian planet was diminishing every day. Even Gontran, gripped by the majesty of the spectacle that was offered to his eyes, stood motionless at a telescope for entire days. Ossipoff could not contain his admiration, which betrayed itself by abrupt exclamations emitted in a curt voice in the midst of the silence. For the sake of prudence and attempting to avoid dangerous questions, Flammermont had installed himself as far away as possible from the old scientist, on the far side of the room, beside his friend Fricoulet, on whose aid he counted to get him out of any embarrassment.

Meanwhile, the hours ran by. Ossipoff, absorbed in his contemplation, seemed to have forgotten the presence of his companions when, suddenly pushing his telescope away, he got up and threw his arms in the air in a gesture of profound satisfaction.

"Of course!" he cried. "I was sure of it!"

Gontran felt his heart sink, and lowered his head. Fricoulet, by contrast, raised his head and asked: "What were you sure of, Monsieur Ossipoff?"

The latter glanced at the engineer scornfully and addressed Flammermont, saying: "My dear Gontran, have you made an exact determination of the constitution of the rings?"

"They seem to me to be gaseous," the young Comte replied, with a certain hesitation in his voice.

Ossipoff shuddered, and his eyebrows acquired a significant frown while he produced two words in an aggressive tone: "Why gaseous?"

"Because the last ring permits perception of the planet's disk."

"First of all, what do you mean by *the last ring*?"

Gontran darted an imploring glance at Fricoulet, who came to the rescue. "The last ring," he said, "is the innermost ring—the one closest to the planet, which was discovered by the American astronomer Bond in 1850."

"I'm sorry to correct you on the last point," Ossipoff replied, dryly, "but the innermost ring of Saturn, simultaneously dark and transparent, was discovered by a German astronomer, Galle of Berlin, in 1838."[51]

---

[51] Johann Galle—the astronomer who first sighted Neptune after Le Verrier's calculative "discovery"—was indeed the first person to record the existence of Saturn's "C ring" in 1838, but he was then in a junior position and no one took any notice until the more prestigiously-placed George Phillips Bond (1825-1865) made a second sighting, after which Galle—who had acquired higher status in the meantime—was able to assert his priority.

"That's possible," said Fricoulet, annoyed by the old man's eagerness to catch him out in an error.

"What? That's possible…I tell you that it's so."

The engineer shrugged his shoulders. "Pardon me, but we're not here to take a course in astronomical history. Whether the ring was discovered in 1850 or 1838 has no effect on its transparency."

Ossipoff uttered a mocking laugh. "Well, know that you're in error," he said. "Since its discovery, the ring has changed its appearance; instead of being entirely transparent, as in 1850, it only appears so now in its inner half."

"Perhaps the first observers were mistaken," Gontran objected.

Ossipoff started. "Why suppose that," he said, "when all observers record surprising changes in the Saturnian system. Don't you recall the analysis made in 1852 by Otto Struve,[52] according to which the inner edge of the rings appeared to be gradually approaching the plant, while their total width was increasing…"

"Tell me, Monsieur Ossipoff," Gontran said, "would there be anything impossible in our witnessing, one of these days, the dislocation of the rings and their fall upon the planet?"

The old man pulled a face. "One of these days! What does that mean?"

"It's just an expression…it's certain that such a spectacle could only be seen by our descendants."

"Assuming that our worldlet still exists at that time," muttered Ossipoff, with his habitual pessimism. Then he changed his tone. "But returning to our point of departure," he said, "you suppose that the rings are gaseous?"

"I suppose…yes—which is to say that it seems to me, because of the transparency of the last…"

"And it's precisely because the last alone is transparent that you cannot attribute that transparency to a gaseous state, for the others are certainly made of the same matter as that one, and they're opaque."

"Do you think they're liquid, then?" murmured Flammermont.

"You're forgetting that movement is transformed into heat and that, if the movement were diminishing, the rings wouldn't take long to fall on the planet."

Selena—who, until now, had taken no part in the discussion, asked: "But why go so far? Isn't it natural to suppose that the rings have the same constitution as the planet itself—which is to say, solid."

Ossipoff immediately burst out laughing. "What!" he cried. "Is it you who's talking thus—you, whom I brought up in the middle of my laboratory, surrounded by my books and my instruments, who have heard me treat all these questions 20, 500 or 100 times over? Have you lost your memory?"

---

[52] The reference is to a report on recent observations of the outer planets by Otto Wilhelm Struve (1819-1905), published in the *Memoirs* of the St. Petersburg Academy of Sciences.

Selena bowed her head in shame. The old man continued. "But if the rings were solid, unfortunate child, the constant variations in the attraction of the planet, combined with that of the eight satellites, would have broken them up long ago, pulverized them and hurled them to he four corners of space—and would have impeded their formation in the first place. No, the rings are elastic—or they wouldn't be there."

"Well," Fricoulet complained, "unless they're supposed to be made of rubber, I don't see how..."

The old man shrugged his shoulders. "You don't see how!" he replied. "That proves that nature has not endowed you with a strong dose of observation and reflection. What if the rings were composed of an infinite number of distinct particles, rotating around the planet at different speeds, according to their respective distances? Do you see how?"

"Yes, I see how the rings might have enough elasticity to adapt themselves to the exigencies of the various attractions that solicit them—but I don't see how one of the rings might permit the perception of the planet's disk, while the others are opposed to it."

Ossipoff smiled pityingly. "For one very simple reason: that the two outer rings are composed of particles in great enough number for the particles, squeezed together, to prevent any transparency."[53]

"You have an answer for everything, Monsieur Ossipoff," Fricoulet declared, "and I declare myself satisfied."

"If I've understood properly," Selena said, "the rings are comparable, in their composition, to the asteroidal current in which we're sailing?"

"Absolutely."

"Except," said the young woman, "That our agglomeration of molecules is always moving, while the rings..."

Ossipoff started, and put out his hand. "Not another word!" he cried. "You're about to pronounce an enormity!" As Selena looked at him in amazement, he added: "What! Unfortunate girl, how do you imagine the rings would maintain their equilibrium if they were immobile? It's only because they're rotating, and rotating even more rapidly than the planet itself, that all these asteroids of which the rings are formed can successfully overcome Saturn's attraction."

"Now," said Gontran, "the Saturnian globe turns on its axis in 10 hours 16 minutes..."

"The inner ring," the old man continued, "thus makes a complete rotation in a period that varies between 5 hours 57 minutes and 7 hours 11 minutes. The

---

[53] The thesis that Ossipoff is quoting here had been advanced by James Clerk Maxwell in 1859, but was still unproven when the present text was published; spectroscopic studies provided what was generally considered to be satisfactory confirmatory evidence it in 1895.

rotation of the central ring is effected between 7 hours 11 minutes and 11 hours 9 minutes, and that of the outer ring between 11 hours 36 minutes and 12 hours 5 minutes."

Selena, who had bowed her head, suddenly raised it again, asking: "But where did these rings originate?"

"From the planet itself; they escaped from the Saturnian equator as its satellites did...and, strictly speaking, they provide us with an image of the formation of worlds."

"Then how does it come about," Selena asked, "that these corpuscles have conserved their annular form instead of condensing into globes like the satellites?"

"Because the eight satellites, formed in advance of them, continually alter the equilibrium of the corpuscles by virtue of their rotation, thus opposing any continuing process of aggregation."

Ossipoff fell silent momentarily, waiting for some sign of approval from Gontran, but the young Comte, deliberately fleeing this field of discussion, had resumed his position at his telescope and appeared to be absorbed in contemplation. Seeing that, the old man went back to his own telescope and resumed his studies.

Flammrmont then leaned toward Fricoulet's ear. "It's still agreed, isn't it, that we'll stop on Saturn?" he whispered.

"We'll be treading on Saturnian ground within 48 hours," the engineer replied.

"Tell me, then—do you think there's a chance we'll encounter some sort of humankind on that world?"

"My dear friend," the engineer replied, "my principles, in matters of general philosophy, lead me to believe that all creation has taken place with but one end: life. To suppose that the celestial Universe is populated by stars that are as many worlds, and that these worlds are deserted, is as distant from my mind as the *Eclair* is presently distant from our native planet."

"You believe in a Saturnian humankind, then?"

"Yes, certainly—but don't presume from my reply that we'll find ourselves face to face with beings similar to Terrans. The constitution of Saturn is so different from that of Earth that the beings to which this marvelous planet has given birth—in the animal kingdom or the vegetable kingdom—ought not to have any point of resemblance to us. Personally, I consider the light specific gravity of Saturnian substances and the density of the atmosphere to be two primordial causes for the vital organization taking place in extraterrestrial conditions; that's why I don't think it's possible for the human mind to imagine the forms in which life will be manifest there."

"It might be the case, then," Gontran observed, "that we'll find ourselves in the presence of a specimen of Saturnian humankind without realizing it."

"That supposition is absolutely logical. Assume, for a moment, that the law ruling this plant is instability, that its surface has nothing fixed—being liquid, while the planet itself is merely skeletal—and that all manifestations of life are gelatinous..."

"That supposition is in the realm of pure fantasy," Gontran replied.

"Not as much as you think, my dear friend. Consider, in fact, that not only are the gravitational conditions on this strange world very different from those on Earth, but that they vary from latitude to latitude."

"I've read certain details about Saturnians and their mode of existence in *Les Continents célestes*."

Fricoulet smiled. "Ah!" he said. "I remember: the Saturnians are beings with transparent bodies, through which one can see life circulating; they don't sense the weight of matter and they fly, without the benefit of air, in the bosom of a nutrient atmosphere that frees them from the grossness of terrestrial alimentation and its gross consequences."[54]

"O poetry!" Flammermont cried, jokingly. "Doesn't the author also suppose that he Saturnians, existing in a quasi-angelic state, enjoy a longevity similar in some respects to that of Methuselah, are born with innate scientific knowledge and spend their time studying the mysteries of worlds and the Heavens?"

"You have an excellent memory," the engineer retorted, then suddenly added: "Do you believe in metempsychosis?"

"That depends what you understand by it."

"I understand it as the existence on a new world of a being that has already existed on another planet."

"Well?"

"Well, I imagine that, if the Creator is just, he must send to Saturn the souls of all humans infatuated with astronomy..." He burst out laughing. "Can you imagine Monsieur Ossipoff, equipped with a pair of angel's wings and armed with a telescope?"

"Not to mention that down there, one must enjoy a magical panorama. *Les Continents célestes* contains details that would make your mouth water."

Fricoulet shook his head. "Ha ha!" he said. "I don't know whether the suppositions of your celebrated namesake are correct in their entirety, as regards the

---

[54] Camille Flammarion was fascinated by the notion of a way of life that combined breathing and alimentation, and disposed of such embarrassments as excretion and evacuation; the possibility is raised in *Lumen* and crops up in several subsequent texts featuring images of extraterrestrial life, including the best-selling *Uranie* (1889), which might well have appeared while the authors were in the process of composing the final draft of the present volume of their text. The central theme of *Uranie* is the kind of metempsychosis that Fricoulet is quick to introduce into the conversation.

celestial spectacle to which the Saturnians are witness, but I know that I'd gladly undergo metempsychosis to see only half of it."

The young Comte looked at his friend, doubtful that he was speaking seriously.

"Yes, yes," said the engineer, "I mean what I say." Then he changed his tone. "Ignorant as you are, wretch, remember that during summers down there, the ring appears in the form of a gigantic rainbow whose summit is at the meridian and whose extremities rest on the horizon at points equally distant from the meridian."

"It must resemble a gigantic suspension bridge," said Flammermont.

"Yes—something like the bridge built by the engineer Eiffel over the Douro, except that the Saturnian bridge, instead of having a span of 166 meters, like the Portuguese bridge, measures several 100 kilometers. Furthermore, instead of being made of iron, it appears to be made of silver, since it offers to Saturnian eyes a tint fairly similar to that of the lunar face."

Flammermont licked his lips like a gourmet. "And to think that it's thanks to us that Monsieur Ossipoff will enjoy such a spectacle; after having seen that, he'll be able to console himself for not visiting Uranus and Neptune."

The engineer clicked his tongue. "We don't yet know," he murmured, "whether we can enable him to see that marvelous spectacle."

Gontran looked at his friend in amazement. "But it's agreed that we're landing on Saturn," he objected.

"Everything depends on the location where our descent takes place."

"What does it matter?"

"It matters so much that if, instead of landing on the equator, we land in the region of one or other pole—about the 63rd degree of north or south latitude, for example—it's goodnight suspension bridge!"

"Bah—why's that?"

"Because it's only at the equator that the rings appear thus, similar to a gigantic bow with its highest point at the zenith, curving down to the east and the west, progressively diminishing in width according to the laws of perspective. If you leave the equator to go toward either pole, you emerge from the plane of the rings, whose summit sinks progressively toward the horizon until it reaches the same level and disappears from the sky entirely. Do you understand?"

"Marvelously. It's as simple as can be—but then, those Saturnian who inhabit the polar regions, and whom nature has not endowed with a taste for travel, are ignorant of the very existence of this marvel?"

"Exactly—and they therefore know less about their own planet than we do, situated 1,000,000 leagues from Saturn."

The conversation ended there. Fricoulet resumed his telescopic observations and Gontran went to lie in is hammock, where he now spent the greater part of his time.

When he woke up, a few hours later, he saw the engineer standing beside him. Surprised, he jumped out of bed—but, to his great surprise, he fell heavily on to the floor. His astonishment was so great that he remained in the position in which he found himself without even thinking about getting up.

"Are you injured?" asked Fricoulet.

"No," he stammered, "but I feel as heavy as lead, and that fall...where did that come from?"

"It's simply that while you were asleep we've penetrated Saturn's zone of attraction. The giant planet's power is making itself felt on the cosmic river in which we're sailing, and on the lump of metal that's carrying us. That's why the weight that was nullified on our departure from Jupiter has suddenly returned, as strongly as on the Earth's surface."

"Ah!" said Gontran, still stunned by his fall. "We've penetrated into Saturn's zone of attraction?"

"Yes," replied the engineer, phlegmatically. "It's because of that that I woke you up. We're probably going to impact the Saturnian surface with a velocity of 14 kilometers a second."

"What did you say?" exclaimed Gontran, shivering.

"I said 14 kilometers a second."

These words struck the young Comte like a whiplash. He flinched, and considered his friend with visible anxiety. "I hope that you have some means of attenuating the shock," he said.

The engineer could not help laughing at Flammermont's fearful manner. "You're forgetting that we can put the machine in reverse," he replied, "and, in consequence, slow our fall down until it becomes insensible." He added: "One more day, and we'll be breathing the pure air of the Saturnian countryside."

"Liquid countryside, according to you," Gontran retorted, "But that's not important. As soon as it became the end-point of our journey, I decided to find it perfectly charming."

Fricoulet put a hand on his arm. "Speak more softly," he murmured in the other's ear. "If poor Ossipoff were to hear you..."

"That's true—but didn't you wake me up because you had need of me?"

"Indeed; it has become indispensable, in view of our proximity to the planet, to keep a close watch on the functioning of the apparatus."

"You want me to stand a watch, then?"

"You've just been resting, damn it! While I make no secret of the fact that I feel very tired."

Having pronounced these words, the engineer headed straight for the hammock that his friend had just quit, while the latter went out of the cabin and into the engine-room. Once installed beside the motor, he put his eye to the lookout telescope, took the machine's commutators in one hand, and began keeping attentive watch on the whitish steam in the bosom of which the *Eclair* had been sailing for so many months.

In front of the apparatus, circulating through dark space like a gigantic lava flow, the river cut across the orbit of Saturn in the distance, to bury itself thereafter in the black depths of infinity. Having nothing better to do, and to keep himself awake, Gontran noticed that the asteroidal current englobed the giant planet entirely, along with its rings and its constellation of satellites. Saturn filled half the sky now with its blue-tinted disk, and the young Comte could not help admiring the multiple and varied evolutions of the eight satellites, which passed repeatedly over the Saturnian horizon, their routes becoming confused, as a juggler's balls do to the great bewilderment of idlers. Flammermont's admiration was so profound that he forgot about the *Eclair* and the mission entrusted to him.

Suddenly, without him noticing it, the sky darkened—or, rather, took on a milky appearance that it had not had before. A rain of fire striped the Saturnian atmosphere, at the same time as the cosmic current seemed to double its compactness. The Sun had shrunk further, and its rays gave no more than a feeble light in competition with the planet's own irradiation. Totally absorbed in his study of the Saturnian satellites, Gontran did not notice any of these surprising changes; in spite of his ignorance, however, he had a presentiment that something abnormal was about to happen.

"Already?" he said, on hearing Fricoulet come into the engine-room to replace him.

"Is it very interesting, then?" asked the engineer.

"You can judge for yourself," the young Comte replied, regretfully abandoning his telescope.

"And nothing new?" said Ficoulet, coming closer to put his eye to the ocular lens.

"Absolutely nothing."

He had scarcely finished this reply when the engineer, uttering an exclamation of amazement, leapt backwards. A single glance had sufficed for him to observe the abrupt transformation of the sidereal horizon. "The rings!" he cried, shaking Flammermont. "Where are the rings?"

Utterly confused by this abrupt and brutal interrogation, the young Comte replied: "You're boring me with your rings! Was that what you gave me to guard?"

"No," the engineer replied in a firm voice, "but I gave you our own lives to guard."

"So?"

"So, God knows that, by virtue of your culpable negligence, they've been seriously compromised."

Gontran went pale. "What do you mean?"

"That you've nodded off, and while you were asleep, the vehicle has gone astray."

"I swear by all that I hold sacred," Gontran retorted, gravely, "that my eye has not left the eyepiece of the telescope for a single instant."

"Didn't you notice, then, what was happening around us?"

The young Comte shook his head negatively.

Fricoulet folded his arms. "Do you know where we are?"

"Word of honor, I don't know anything!"

"Well, quite simply, you've allowed to *Eclair* to deviate from the route that it ought to be following."

"Which is to say?"

"That we're no longer in the cosmic current."

Gontran uttered a cry of fright. "Great God!" he said. "Where are we, then?"

"In the rings of Saturn!" cried the engineer, in a furious voice.

Just as he pronounced these words, Ossipoff appeared on the threshold of the engine-room. His face was very pale, and utterly distraught; his eyes were shining with a strange fire and his tremulous lips were stammering incomprehensible exclamations.

"Oh, my friends!" he said. "My children!"

The two young men went to the old scientist, not understanding his words. He seized Fricoulet's arms and squeezed them hard, saying: "What a favor you've done me!"

"Me?" replied the bewildered engineer.

"Didn't you just say that we were in the rings of Saturn?" the old man asked.

"Indeed—but I don't understand..."

"What! You don't understand that by that means we'll be able to study the configuration of the planet in its entirety, even better than we would have been able to do by staying in the asteroidal current?"

The engineer gave Gontran a knowing look. "Well, Monsieur Ossipoff," he said, "it's not me that you have to thank." He pointed to Gontran. "It's him... Yes, he was the one who, during the night watch, had that excellent idea."

Ossipoff ran forward, took the young man in his arms, and hugged him to his breast, saying: "Yes...my son, my son! Only a scientist like you could have had that sublime inspiration, and the audacity necessary to execute it..."

Totally confused, Gontran slipped away from the old man's warm thanks.

The latter, wildly enthused, cried: "Don't you think that it would be a crime to pass within range of this marvelous world and not land there?"

Gontran gave Fricoulet a look that meant: *Aha! My blunder is no longer so culpable, since it's resulted in the old madman changing his opinion.* Understanding, however, that to encourage the old scientist along that path, the best thing to do was to put up a little opposition, the young Comte replied: "Certainly, my dear Monsieur Ossipoff, that would be my most ardent desire, but how are we going to get from the rings to the planet to the Saturnian surface?"

"There's an atmosphere through which we can navigate at will," the old man replied, triumphantly, "so nothing stands in the way of our putting such a fine plan into execution."

"Nothing, indeed," retorted Fricoulet, "except your own word..."

The scientist stepped back. "My own word!" he said.

"Yes," replied the engineer. "Have you forgotten our last discussion on the subject of our voyage already?—a discussion that was ended by a formal promise, made by you, not to stop at any further new world and to return to our native planet following the cosmic current..."[55]

"Unless," said Flammermont, "you preferred to make a stop on Saturn and return to Earth immediately afterwards..."

"Without having seen Uranus or Neptune?" moaned the old man.

Fricoulet raised his arms in the air. "Those were the exact terms of your promise," he replied.

"But since we've abandoned the cosmic current..."

"Bah!" said the engineer. "Don't torment yourself overmuch...at the rate at which we're traveling, we'll have circled around the planet in five hours—which is to say that in 20 minutes, we'll arrive at the point of intersection of the rings and the cosmic river..." He added: "Instead of moaning, you'd do better to employ your time in studying the configuration of the planet."

"Unfortunately," said Gontran, who was looking through a porthole, "the clouds are so thick that it's impossible to distinguish anything."

Ossipoff, prey to a profound despair, was literally tearing his hair.

"Father, I beg you," implored Selena, "don't get so upset."

"Eh?" groaned the old man. "You can't possible understand...to pass so close..." He turned to Gontran and looked at him, his gaze full of reproach. "But you—a scientist! Oh, it's a crime!"

Flammermont took Selena's hand. "It's now nearly four years that I've given up for astronomy. I think it's just that astronomy should now give way to love."

Ossipoff hung his head.

"Come on, Monsieur Ossipoff," said Fricoulet, who was scanning space with his eye to the lookout telescope. "You must make a decision: to overshoot Saturn and continue our voyage on the cosmic river...or to land on Saturn and return directly to Earth." He consulted his watch and added: "You've got five minutes to decide."

The old scientist hesitated; then, in a low and regretful voice, he replied: "Let's continue the voyage!"[56]

---

[55] This improvisation is an obvious breach in the narrative's continuity, which rapidly opens up into a yawning gap.

[56] This makes no sense at all, either in terms of the narrative's internal logical or its ostensible ambitions; the vital necessity of landing on Saturn has already

Chapter XLVIII
Fedor Sharp in sight

"So it's decided?" said the engineer, rotating his gaze around the people surrounding him. "We're overshooting Saturn?"

"Yes," said Gontran, firmly.

"Yes," Selena repeated, in a softer but no less assured voice.

"Yes," said Ossipoff, in his turn, releasing a profound sigh. And he ran to shut himself in his cabin to hide his range and despair.

"Poor Father," murmured the young woman, following him with an affectionate gaze.

Flammermont shrugged his shoulders significantly.

"There's still time," Fricoulet said, "to revert to our own decision."

"And retrace our steps," muttered Gontran.

"That's what I meant."

Selena shook her head. "No, Monsieur Fricoulet," she said. "Let's pursue our course, since it's the majority decision." She sighed and sat down, very sadly, in a corner of the engine-room.

"All right—it's done," declared the engineer, pressing down on the commutators with all his strength.

The vehicle's entire framework shuddered, and it seemed to leap forward.

"You're not worried about blowing everything up?" said the young Comte, a trifle alarmed by the terrible trepidation that was agitating the *Eclair*.

"Bah!" the engineer retorted, carelessly. "We've seen worse, when it was a matter of getting out of the Jovian atmosphere." His eyes were on the compass, while he held the tiller in a firm hand. "We're leaving the rings," he declared, after a quarter of an hour of silence.

"Everything's going well, then?" asked the young Comte. "We're on the right path?"

Fricoulet did not reply. Bending over the accumulators, he was studying them carefully, furrowing his brows and pursing his lips as he usually did when some incomprehensible incident occurred. "Gontran!" he said, curtly.

The young Comte came nearer.

---

been established, on pain of certain death for the voyagers, and the whole point of a cosmic tour story is to visit the other worlds in the Solar System. What on Earth is the point of bringing the voyagers all the way to Saturn only to let them fly past, having offered the reader nothing but a few sketchy speculations regarding its inhabitants? I shall reserve further comment on this puzzling issue until the afterword.

"Take the tiller for a moment."

The engineer went rapidly to the rear, put his face to a porthole and remained there for a few minutes, attentively examining the functioning of the helix. Then he came back and pressed down on the accumulator levers again.

"What are you doing?" asked Flammermont.

"I'm trying to compensate for the consequences of the error you made yesterday," the engineer replied, dryly.

"And what are these consequences?"

"While we were circling Saturn, the bulk of the battalion of asteroids continued with its customary velocity—with the effect that the corpuscles that serve us as a point of support have become more rarefied. If we'd been delayed by only a few hours, we'd have found ourselves in the void."

"So?"

"So, as you see, I'm increasing the electric force to make up for lost time and rejoin, if possible, the center of the cosmic river in which we've so far been sailing." Seeing that his friend was having difficulty concealing an urgent desire to sleep, he said: "It pains me to look at you," he said. "Go to bed."

"But it's my turn on watch."

In spite of his anxiety, Fricoulet burst out laughing. "Thanks very much," he said. "So that you can make another mistake or go to sleep with your nose on the tiller—no, I prefer to stay up all night, if necessary. That way, I'll be certain of the *Eclair*'s progress."

"If that's your preference," grumbled the young Comte, in a slightly piqued tone, "it's mine too." Without shaking his friend's hand, he turned on his heel and went to lie down in his hammock, where sleep was not long in taking possession of him.

When Gontran de Flammermont woke up the next day, his chronometer marked 10 a.m. He ran out of the cabin, ashamed of his laziness, but hoping that the emotions and fatigues of the previous day had prolonged his friends' slumbers to the same degree.

When he went into the engine-room, he found Ossipoff and Fricoulet standing in front of one of the portholes, engaged in animated discussion.

"I tell you that it is," said the old man.

"I'm not denying it," the engineer retorted, "but I can't, in all conscience, tell you that I see it when I don't."

At this reply, the old scientist stamped his foot impatiently. On perceiving Gontran, he cried: "Ah! Monsieur de Flammermont—you couldn't have arrived at a better time!" He held out the telescope that he had in his hand. "Look carefully at the constellation Cassiopeia!"

A slight grimace creased the young Comte's lips. "You want me to..." He stammered.

"To verify which of us is right—Monsieur Fricoulet or me."

The engineer protested. "Wait a minute! I'm not claiming that you're wrong; I only say that I can't see..." He turned to the young Comte, and said: "Monsieur Ossipoff claims that he can see a new star in the constellation Cassiopeia, not marked on the celestial maps, whose nature he doesn't know."

"I don't claim, Monsieur," growled the old man, red with anger, "I affirm..."

"In that case," murmured Gontran, "there's no need for me to check that your affirmation is well-founded."

He returned the telescope to Ossipoff—who pushed it away, saying. "Please. From one scientist to another, it often happens, especially in astronomy, that one falls victim to optical illusions."

The young man was obliged to obey the old scientist's injunction. He took the telescope and, absolutely ignorant of the position occupied in the sky by Cassiopeia, aimed the instrument out into space.

"I don't see anything," he declared, boldly, after a few seconds of examination.

Ossipoff sneered. "That doesn't astonish me," he said. "I was talking about Cassiopeia and you're looking at Orion's belt."

Gontran slapped his forehead. "I really don't know where my head is," he murmured. Immediately, he added: "Besides, the ocular's not focused for me, and I can only make things out vaguely."

Fricoulet came to the rescue yet again. "If you had the big telescope from Nice Observatory," he said, laughing, "it wouldn't get you much further. Where there's nothing to see, the most powerful instruments can't make anything out."

Ossipoff looked at the young engineer furiously. Snatching the instrument from the Comte's hands, he muttered: "We'll see in a few hours." And he resumed his place at the porthole, through which he was able to contemplate the famous constellation entirely at his ease.

Fricoulet returned to his tiller. "Well, where are we?" Gontran asked him, in a low voice, "where are we?"

"We've been going hell for leather all night, and we've rejoined the great asteroidal tide. So, as you can see, the *Eclair* has resumed its normal speed."

The young Comte leaned closer to his friend's ear. "What about this new star that he claims to have discovered? Is there any truth in it?"

Fricoulet shook his head. "I don't know," he replied. "There are such singular surprises in these diabolical stars."

"If you scientists are taken by surprise, how can you expect a layman like me...?"

Fricoulet laughed. "There's one simple thing you can do," he said. "Ask Ossipoff."

"And he'll reply, as in *The Italian Straw Hat*: 'Take back your myrtle, my son-in-law; it's all off!' "[57]

The engineer looked at his friend oddly. "Frankly," he said, "would it pain you greatly if he gave you back your myrtle?"

Gontran darted a rapid glance at Selena; then leaning even closer to his friend's ear, he murmured: "It's human nature. If you'd asked me that question a few months ago, I'd have grabbed your throat by way of reply."

"While today..." said the engineer, with a little smile.

"While today, without being affirmative..."

"You're having doubts, aren't you?" Fricoulet went on. Placing his hand on his friend's shoulder, he added: "Don't worry. In a few weeks you'll no longer have any doubts on the matter, and you'll take back your myrtle of your own accord, if that's possible..."

Gontran took offence. "Alcide," he declared, "that's one thing I'll never do; I've given my word, and unless it's given back to me...I'm a gentleman, old chap..."

"You'd better be an astronomer, old chap," riposte the engineer. "If I'm not mistaken, here's Ossipoff coming to fall upon you again."

The old man—who had been giving every evidence of extreme agitation for some time—had, indeed, abruptly quit the porthole at which he had been installed. Brandishing his telescope, he cried in a vibrant voice; "Victory! Victory! I have it!"

"What's that?" asked Fricoulet.

"Why, my star, of course! My new planet! The one I perceived just now, in the constellation of Cassiopeia, whose existence you denied."

"In fact," said the engineer, "I denied nothing. I simply declared that I couldn't see..." Taking possession of the telescope that the old scientist was offering to Flammermont, he aimed it into space. "What's its location?" he asked.

"12 hours right ascension, 30 degrees northern inclination," the astronomer replied.

Fricoulet got his bearings right away. After a few seconds of observation, though, he straightened up abruptly and murmured; "There's certainly something very curious."

He left the porthole and ran to a celestial map hanging on the engine-room wall. After consulting it attentively, he went back to the porthole and examined the sky again.

"Well, was I right?" asked Ossipoff, folding his arms and looking at the engineer disdainfully.

---

[57] *Un Chapeau de paille d'Italie* [The Italian Straw Hat] (1851) by Eugène Labiche and Marc Michel was one of the most famous stage comedies of the 19th century, and played a key role in helping to launch the rich tradition of French farce.

"Assuredly," Fricoulet replied. "There's something there—but what?"

"Eh? What do you think it might be, if not a star?"

"It could be a planet," declared Gontran, who thought it prudent to make a contribution to the conversation.

The old man shook his head. "That's doubtful," he murmured.

"Because?"

"Because it seems to me that no planet can exist in the region of space where we are, in such close proximity to Saturn." Ossipoff looked hard at Flammermont.

The latter thought the best thing to do was to appear not to share the old scientist's opinion, in order to make him suppose that he had one of his own. He pushed out his lips in a dubious moue. "Pooh!" he said, laconically.

"You may think what you wish," the old man replied, in the slightly dry tone he adopted whenever he was contradicted. "For myself, I persist in believing that Saturn would have prevented the formation of such a world. Besides, even assuming that nothing was opposed to it, astronomers would have discovered it a long time ago."

"In that case, what do you think?"

Ossipoff raised his arms toward the ceiling. "Thus far, I don't think anything…I'm waiting…"

"Waiting for what?"

"For us to get close enough to the body to be able to study it in more detail.

"That's a wise course," declared Fricoulet. "And if all the scientists on Earth reasoned thus, there'd be a lot less time wasted in silly discussions."

"In a few hours, we'll know what we need to know."

"Perhaps we should devote ourselves to baptizing the new star," Gontran proposed.

"That's a good idea," Selena put in.

"Well," said Fricoulet, "since it's your idea, the honor belongs to you of selecting the name with which the newborn shall be adorned."

"Shouldn't the name be that of the scientist who discovered it?"

Osssipoff shook the young man's hand excitedly. "Thank you, my dear Gontran," he stammered, "but I can't accept the great honor that you offer me…" With a smile, he added: "There are already more than enough names on maps of the sky that are difficult to write and remember, without adding another one. Until we're more amply informed, let's simply designate this star by a letter of the Greek alphabet."

"So be it," said Gontran. "Go for Omicron."

"Or Omega," said Fricoulet.

The old scientist shook his head. "That's not possible," he said. "You're forgetting that stars in the same constellation of Cassiopeia already bear those names on astronomical maps."

"That's true," observed the engineer.

"But nothing proves that this shining body belongs to the constellation of Cassiopeia," observed Gontran, coming back to his earlier idea.

Ossipoff shrugged his shoulders and went back to his porthole. Fricoulet went back to his levers. As for Gontran, he went to lie down in a corner and started day-dreaming, with his eyes half-closed, while whistling a refrain from the last operetta he had seen before his departure from Earth.

An exclamation uttered by Ossipoff snatched him from the delights of his idleness; he leapt to his feet and ran to the scientist.

The latter's face was utterly distraught. "You were right," he said, hoarsely, to the young Comte.

"Right? Me! About what?"

"About the new body I discovered in the constellation of Cassiopeia."

"It doesn't exist? An optical illusion?"

"It definitely exists. Only..."

"Only?"

"It doesn't belong to the constellation."

The young Comte smiled victoriously. "What did I tell you?" he cried. "It's a planet!"

"Definitely not."

"What, then?"

"It's a bolide."

Fricoulet and Selena ran up, simultaneously shouting: "A bolide!"

"Traveling through space and heading for the Sun."

"Well," said Flammermont, "I don't see anything in that to cause so much excitement."

"But this is the first time, in our successive voyages, that we've had a chance to study one of these strange bodies."

Gontran felt that too great an indifference on his part might awaken the suspicions of his future father-in-law, so he reached out for the telescope, saying: "May I see too?"

Ossipoff changed the instrument's eyepiece. "Look," he said, when he had finished.

The former diplomat was beginning to get used to such instruments. He therefore adjusted its focus to his eye and increased the magnification of the objective lens until he could make out contours distinctly. Then, interested in spite of himself by the spectacle offered to his view, he uttered a cry of surprise. "Indeed," he murmured, "it's not a star...and no more a planet. It's a fragment of debris...hold on...let's see..."

He was ready to withdraw to let Fricoulet take his place, but Ossipoff's hand came down on his shoulder, holding him still. "Wait a little while longer," said the old scientist.

The rocky block, which was sparkling like a star against the black background of the sky, was rotating rapidly about an axis that appeared to be sharply inclined, and the young man was easily able to distinguish the irregularities of the polyhedron launched into space like an arrow.

"If I saw correctly," said Ossipoff, "that asteroid must by nearly a kilometer and a half wide about its major axis, and a kilometer in its smallest dimension. Don't you think so?"

"That depends on its rotation," Gontran replied.

"It's an hour and a half—I calculated it, thanks to an extremely luminous patch that's visible near the north pole."

"A luminous patch?" murmured Flammermont, widening his eyes in vain.

"Don't bother searching for it," Ossipoff went on. "It's on the face that's presently invisible."

"Have you noticed the rapidity with which the corpuscle is moving?" Gontran asked, after a few minutes.

"I calculated that we're heading toward one another with a speed of 130,000 meters a second."

"130,000 meters a second!" exclaimed Selena.

"Yes. The calculation's simply to make, my dear child. Our velocity is 85,000 meters per second, its own is 45,000...that gives us more than 40,000 leagues an hour."[58]

Flammermont stood aside; Fricoulet took his place at the telescope's eyepiece so that he too could examine the strange world. Suddenly, he uttered a stifled exclamation.

Ossipoff, who was recording his observations, raised his head and said, mockingly: "Have you, by chance, made some interesting observation?"

The engineer did not reply immediately; he was plunged in attentive contemplation. Finally, with some slight emotion in his voice, he said: "Could be."

"And what's your opinion?" said Ossipoff, still jeering. "Are we in the presence of a star, a planet or a bolide?"

"A bolide, assuredly."

"Ah! I'm delighted to be in agreement with you. And have you an opinion as to the nature of the bolide?"

The engineer, pretending not to notice the bantering tone that the old man was employing in talking to him, replied very calmly: "It's of a cometary nature."

The old man burst out laughing. "Really? Can you be more precise, please?"

"What do you man by *more precise*?"

"Why...indicate, for example, to what comet the fragment belongs, in your opinion."

---

[58] Actually, scrupulous arithmetic gives a combined velocity of about 117,000 leagues per hour—but the authors seem to intend to cite their own mistaken figure again when they subsequently misrender it by adding an extra zero.

"To Tuttle's Comet," the engineer replied, unhesitatingly.

Ossipoff shrugged his shoulders.

"What's impossible about that?" retorted Fricoulet. "Isn't it the first example we've had of cometary fragmentation? Didn't something similar happen, in 1846, to Biela's Comet? The comet broke into two parts, which sailed on in convoy for some time, but which have never returned to perihelion since the time of the catastrophe. There wouldn't be anything extraordinary in some similar accident happening to Tuttle's Comet."

The old scientist stamped his foot impatiently. "Your imagination's carrying you away, my dear Monsieur Fricoulet," he said. "Assuming that your supposition were correct, how would you explain our encountering a fragment of Tuttle here?"

"In the simplest fashion in the world, my dear Monsieur Ossipoff! Isn't Tuttle's aphelion beyond Saturn, at the exact point in space that we have presently reached?"

"Agreed—but you're forgetting that the comet won't arrive here for several years, the duration of its revolution being 13 years. It won't reach its aphelion until 1890; this can't, therefore, be that one."

And, certain of having crushed the engineer with this incontrovertible argument, Ossipoff fixed Fricoulet with a triumphant gaze.[59]

Fricoulet straightened up, and looked the old man full in the face. "As for me," he said, "without having any pretension to explain to you how it happened, nor at what point in space the fragmentation took place, I can assure you that it really is a fragment of Tuttle's Comet that we have before our eyes."

Ossipoff laughed skeptically. "An assurance from you and nothing," he said, "is very nearly the same thing."

"What if I were to give you proof?"

"Porrof?" said the old scientist, widening his eyes. "What proof?"

"That shining point you used to establish the duration of the worldlet's rotation—do you know what it is?"

"Doubtless some snowy peak."

Fricoulet shook his head. "Wrong," Monsieur Ossipoff, wrong," he replied. "It's the shell that Sharp stole from us on the Moon."

"The shell!" cried several voices.

"Yes," the engineer confirmed, "the shell that served us as a habitation during the long months that we spent on the planet."

---

[59] The argument is, indeed, incontrovertible—but the authors seem content to ignore the fact. The point might also be made that if, as may be presumed, Tuttle's Comet and the asteroidal current are both orbiting the Sun in the same direction, the comet's return course could not intersect with the current's outward course.

Ossipoff had hurled himself upon the telescope and had aimed it at the bolide. For a long time he stood still, as if petrified, his face glued to the eyepiece, his limbs agitated by a nervous tremor. Finally, he murmured: "It's true." Then, after a further pause, he said: "But how did it get there?"

Fricoulet raised his arms toward the ceiling, signifying his complete ignorance. "It's sufficient that it is there," he replied.

Gontran uttered an exclamation. "But if the shell is there," he said, "it's not impossible that Fedor Sharp is there too."

Ossipoff shrugged his shoulders significantly. "He must be long dead," he replied.

The engineer had taken his notebook out of his pocket and jotted down a few calculations on a blank page. "I don't know," he said to Ossipoff, "whether you're right about the admittedly-probable decease of Fedor Sharp—but your calculations are exact, at any rate."

"Were they in need of verification then?" the old man asked, mockingly.

"I don't think so. In any case, I've thought of one thing that you haven't."

"What?"

"That the bolide will cut across our course at an angle."

"So what?"

"So what? What would you say if it collided with us in passing?"

"Pooh! It's improbable."

"So far from improbable, my dear Monsieur, that we are, at this moment, 600,000 leagues away from it—and, as we're traveling towards one another at a rate of 460,000 leagues an hour, the impact will take place in one hour 20 minutes."

Gontran stifled a curse. Selena uttered an exclamation. Ossipoff paled slightly.

"But we'll be smashed to bits!" murmured Flammermont.

The engineer shook his had. "I think, in fact," he replied, with imperturbable self-composure, that we'll simply go up in smoke." He rubbed his hands together and added, with admirably-simulated satisfaction: "Motion abruptly annihilated and transformed into heat will make a tiny sun of us."

Gontran turned to Ossipoff, whose face had resumed its customary placidity. "Did you hear that, Monsieur?" he asked.

"Monsieur Fricoulet is absolutely right," the old man replied, "but he's forgetting that we have a very simple means of avoiding death."

"And that means," said the Comte, "is...?"

"Is not going to meet it," the engineer replied. "We have only to stop and let the express train that would inflict so much damage pass by in front of us."

"We could even increase the electricity-supply and get ahead of the asteroid," suggested Ossipoff.

"That would be dangerous," the engineer declared. "The accumulators are extracting the maximum amount of electricity, and we can't go any faster. The propeller is going at top speed; we're covering 80 kilometers a second—which is the width of the Atlantic in a minute, 72,000 leagues an hour."

"In that case," Gontran exclaimed, "We have to do what we said just now—which is to say, to stop."

"Let's stop, then," said Ossipoff, in a resigned manner. "Although, it would give me considerable pleasure to get as close to that bolide as possible."

"At the risk of breaking our heads, like a bat flattening itself on a wall."

"Or transforming ourselves into a sun again," Fricoulet added, gaily.

"I don't know whether Mademoiselle Selena has any aspiration to the role of a star," said the Comte, "but for myself, I've no appetite for what another meeting with Fedor Sharp would bring."

"Then it's decided?" said the engineer. "We're stopping." He looked around to interrogate his companions. "Once...twice...three times," he added. "No more bids? Right—we're stopping."

And while Ossipoff, followed by Selena and Gontran, left the engine-room and went back to the common room, Fricoulet headed for the motor.

"It's a pity," he said, softly. "I would have greatly enjoyed seeing that rogue Sharp again...simply to know how he's been getting along..."

Leaning over the apparatus, the young engineer did not notice that a door behind him had opened by a crack. The door was that of the cabin in which Jonathan Farenheit had been locked.

Chapter XLIX
A collision in space

For more than a month—which is to say, since his crazy and criminal attempt to blow up the *Eclair* and everyone aboard—the American had been locked in a rear cabin, where his companions regularly brought him doses of the liquid nutrient indispensable to his miserable existence. The man's life was, indeed, miserable, thus caged like a wild beast, breathing with difficulty, and condemned never to see the light of the Sun and the starry sky again before he died. Was he suffering? It was scarcely probable. He had fallen into a quasi-comatose physical state, and it seemed that his intelligence had faded into complete annihilation, in which only the instincts of a brute survived. Most of the time, he crouched in a corner—the darkest in his cell; he spent entire days there without making a movement, as if he were dead. Then, abruptly, he suddenly got up and strode back and forth, marching without pause for long hours, uttering hoarse cries and groans. Afterwards, exhausted by the fatigue of this unaccustomed exercise, he threw himself into his hammock, where he remained for several days on the trot, without making a gesture or saying a word.

On the eve of the day on which Ossipoff thought he had discovered a new star in the constellation Cassiopeia, Farenheit had taken a long walk around his room that had sent him to his hammock exhausted after several hours. He was drowsing when, all of a sudden, the name of Fedor Sharp, pronounced a few paces away behind the door of his cell, made him shudder. It was as if the name of his enemy, suddenly striking his ears, had galvanized his intelligence.

He passed his hand over his forehead distractedly. "Sharp!" he stammered. "Sharp!" The name evoked a whole world of memories in his brain; gradually, his face lost the expression of bestiality that it had worn for several weeks; his gaze became more purposive and less bleak; his mouth, continually twisted by a nervous tic, resumed its original immobility.

He sat up on his elbow and pricked up his ears. For the first time in a long time, he listened and understood. "By God!" he muttered. "What's happened, then? I seem to be awakening from a long sleep. If I haven't been mad, I can't have been far from it."

The voices in the next cabin became a little louder, and the sound of the conversation now reached the American distinctly. Suddenly, he slid out of his hammock and crept over the floor, then glued his ear to the door.

"Yes," he murmured, after a short while, "I wasn't mistaken. They're talking about Sharp—but in what context?" Suddenly, a mute laugh widened his mouth. "Ha ha!" he said. "They've seen him—he's close by!" And he rubbed his hands together with evident satisfaction.

Almost immediately, though, his face darkened abruptly and his eyebrows furrowed. "By God!" he muttered. "They're letting him pass in front of us! We're stopping. These people of the Old World definitely don't have blood in their veins." His cheeks trembled with wrath, and a dark fire burned in the depths of his pupils. "Ah, by God!" he added, shaking his head furiously. "They're afraid of dying! As if the life we've been leading for several months were a life. As if death weren't a thousand times preferable to this idiotizing reclusion! And to die in avenging oneself...that's to live in a few moments everything that remains of life. Ah, by God! No, he won't escape, and if we must..." He began sniggering again.

"Yes, yes," he continued, in a hiss, "stop as much as you like for fear of bumping into that honorable rogue! You'll bump into him anyway, and whether you like it or not, I'll avenge all my tribulations and all my disappointments on the wretch's hide..." He cocked an ear and his cheeks, hollow and emaciated, were colored by a rush of blood. "Into a sun," he murmured. "That Fricoulet said that we might be transformed into a sun." He snapped his fingers impatiently and growled: "It would ensure my election to the presidency of the Eccentric Club if they knew in New York that Jonathan Farenheit was one of the stars before which the scientists of Earth swoon in admiration!"

At that moment, the voyagers' conversation ceased; Ossipoff left the engine-room with Selena and Gontran, and silence fell. It was then that the American opened his door slightly—a door that they had neglected to lock since he had fallen into the comatose state that rendered him harmless.

Without the engineer being aware of it, Farenheit watched all his movements. He saw him approach the apparatus producing the electricity and the system that composed the motor, then attentively consult the indicators of the generator's output, calculate the speed of the propeller and examine various instruments of precision.

Afterwards, Fricoulet headed for the motor. A series of handles was disposed on the consoles, moving in the fashion of ordinary levers. The engineer pushed one of these handles back and lowered a horizontal lever that controlled the distribution of the motive force. Immediately, the continuous vibration of the propeller in its housing diminished in intensity. Then Fricoulet pushed back all the handles one by one, and the motor slowed down progressively, until it stopped entirely. After that, the engineer gave the whole of the apparatus one last glance of inspection and left the engine-room.

Up above, Ossipoff—with his eye glued to his telescope once again—was examining the asteroid, which was advancing through space with vertiginous rapidity.

"Well, my dear Monsieur," said Fricoulet, "have you made any interesting discoveries?"

"My father's looking for Sharp," said Selena.

The engineer was smiling slightly. "That research might be premature," he replied. "Remember that we're 400,000 leagues away..."

"Moreover," said Gontran, in his turn, "the presence of our shell on the pebble doesn't necessarily imply the presence of that villain!"

"In any case," Fricoulet observed, "that asteroid, whose equator measures scarcely three-quarters of a league around, must be a very singular abode." He added: "If I've calculated correctly, the meridians can't be more than five kilometers from one pole to the other."

"A pebble, what?" said Flammermont, disdainfully.

"Ha ha!" riposted Ossipoff, turning toward them. "A pebble that has a surface area of 20 square kilometers and a volume of several 100,000 cubic meters is a very respectable pebble."

"Pooh!" replied the young Comte, with a heavily emphasized moue. "A tenth the size of Phobos."

"A millionth of the Moon," Fricoulet added.

"For one lone man, that appears to me sufficient," the old man replied—and he resumed his observations.

"One thing it would interest me to know," said Selena "is what means Sharp has employed to prolong his miserable existence."

"At the moment when we abandoned the comet," Fricoulet went on, "the vehicle's stores were very nearly empty. As for reserves of breathable air, it didn't need much to exhaust them."

"Sharp isn't an imbecile," the Comte replied, "and if he's over there, he must certainly have found a means to subsist there."

Fricoulet burst out laughing. "That, if I'm not mistaken, is a La Palisse verity.[60] If Sharp isn't dead, it's because he's succeeded in staying alive." The hilarity became general. The engineer added: "As regards Sharp, I'm entirely of Gontran's opinion. I'll go even further and declare that he's a superior man. Unfortunately, if his intelligence is vast, his conscience is non-existent—and his scruples are, for that reason, in absolutely inverse proportion to his abilities. So, if he didn't perish in the cataclysm that engendered the fragmentation of Comet Tuttle, I'll bet my head that he's still alive. He's an energetic fellow, unparalleled in his obstinacy, as we've previously been able to observe. If he's intent on returning to Earth and depositing an account of his voyages in the office of the

---

[60] Jacques La Palisse or La Palice (1470-1525) was a highly successful military leader. After his death, his men composed a song in his honor which contained the line "*S'il n'était pas mort, il serait encore envié*" [If he were not dead, he would still be envied]. "*Envie*" is, however, phonetically identical to "*en vie*" [alive], and the misinterpreted line was established proverbially as a "verité de La Palisse"—i.e., a tautology, or, at least, a statement far too obvious to be worth making.

St. Petersburg Academy of Science before Monsieur Ossipoff, nothing will stop him…"

As the engineer pronounced these final words, the old scientist stood up straight and, making an abrupt about-turn, showed his companions his utterly pale and distraught face. "I didn't think of that," he said, hoarsely.

"What didn't you think of, Father?" asked Selena, who was the first to be struck by the alteration in the old man's features.

"That the bolide that we can see, which will cut across our path in less than an hour, will reach the Earth's atmosphere in five months, so that if Fedor Sharp has found a means to escape death…he'll be the first to gather the glory of this marvelous voyage, of which I thought, and whose means of execution he stole from me…"

Fricoulet shrugged his shoulders. "For which there's only one remedy," he said.

"What?"

"To risk everything in order to gain everything, and continue in our course; we'll collide with the bolide, it's true, and even run the risk of being volatilized, but we'd also have a chance of breaking up the worldlet on which we suppose our enemy to be—and perhaps Providence will permit justice to triumph…."

Gontran shook his head. "That's a good one!" he murmured. "I value my life a little more than vain terrestrial glory, and I wouldn't give the end of my little finger for the report of a secretary, however permanent he might be…"

"However…" murmured Selena, with an imploring glance in the young Comte's direction.

Ossipoff grabbed his daughter's hand. "Brave girl," he said. "You'd be ready to make the sacrifice…but I'd be a monster of ingratitude if I were to accept." He released a profound sigh and, turning round, put his eye to the telescope's ocular lens.

"Filial devotion and paternal obligation, entirely Platonic," murmured Fricoulet, sarcastically. "Whatever one might wish, it's now too late to attempt to run into the Tuittle fragment." And he added, after a moment's silence: "There's only one thing to wish for now."

"What?"

"That Sharp has rendered his villainous soul to the Devil."

"Amen," said Gontran.

"Besides," the engineer went on, "the bolide will pass by at a close enough distance for nothing on its surface to escape Monsieur Ossipoff's investigations." He took out his watch. "In four hours and 20 minutes exactly, it'll cut across our path."

"How many kilometers away will be it be then?" asked Selena.

"About 800, Mademoiselle—which is 200 leagues. Your father's telescope will reduce that distance to less than two kilometers."

"Do you think that, if Sharp's alive, he'll be able to see us?" asked Mademoiselle Ossipoff.

The engineer stretched his lips into a dubious moue. "That's less than certain," he replied. "We're traveling away from the Sun and getting further away, while the bolide is approaching it, following a diametrically opposite course. If we can make it out so perfectly, it's because it's fully lit by the solar light; for him, on the contrary, our apparatus would be confused with the darkness of space, since its illuminated face isn't turned toward him. If Sharp's over there, it's probable—perhaps even certain—that he has no inkling of the presence of our vehicle."

"It makes no difference," Gontran put in. "I'd have great difficulty admitting that a human being might exist on the surface of a body so microscopic."

"It's certain," said the engineer, that it must be one of the most singular abodes for a human being, and that life on so small a world could not exist without some strange particularities. The surface gravity must be infinitely weaker than on the satellites of Mars, and you know that it can hardly be felt there. Sharp wouldn't weigh more than a few grams over there, and he'd have to abstain from the slightest overly abrupt movement, which could launch him outside his planet's zone of attraction. If need be, and if the whim took him, he could juggle with the shell-vehicle that serves as his habitation...."

"But to live, he must breathe, and a morsel of rock like that one must be totally lacking in atmosphere."

"Totally, no—but it must have very little. If he ventures outside the shell, though, can't he put on the helmet of a respirol?"

"Of course," said Selena. "One thing that I wouldn't be able to get used to is the short duration of the days and nights."

"Indeed, their duration is nearly ten times less than that on Earth—but if Sharp wants to give himself the luxury of terrestrial days and nights, nothing is easier."

"Bah! How?"

"By living near to the pole, and moving around as the rotation is completed. He even has the great advantage of being able to regulate the length of his days and nights, according to his whim."

During this conversation, Ossipoff had maintained the profoundest silence. "Well, Gontran suddenly asked him. "Do you see any vestige of human presence?"

The old man shook his head negatively.

"You're too impatient," said Fricoulet. "We aren't close enough yet. At this distance, remember, the bolide measures no more than 15 or 20 seconds of arc."

As if these words had recalled him to reality, the old scientist cried: "You're wrong, Monsieur Fricoulet. The arc subtended measures at least twice that."

"That's not possible."

"If you care to, you can convince yourself," the old man murmured, a trifle piqued that anyone should take the liberty of doubting one of his affirmations—and he stood aside from the telescope to let the young engineer take his place.

Scarcely had the latter applied his eye to the ocular lens than he leapt backwards, releasing an exclamation of surprise. "Damn!" he said. "That's very odd."

"As odd as all that?" asked Gontran.

"Yes! Unless I'm seeing things...and Monsieur Ossipoff too." He rummaged in his pocket and took out a micrometer, which he fitted to the instrument. To Gontran, he said: "Put yourself there, aim at the bolide, and bring the screw of the micrometer into play."

After a few minutes, Gontran stood aside and said: "It's done."

Fricoulet examined the micrometer and his face already anxious, became even darker. "33 minutes," he said.

"Well?" demanded his companions.

"I don't understand it. I put the machine in reverse, and the force of the motor is neutralizing the force of the current, maintaining us stationary in space, so that the bolide, moving at normal speed, should still be 200 kilometers away from us. Now, if the micrometer marks 31 seconds, it's necessary to conclude that we're only separated by half the distance we should be." He reflected for a few seconds, then murmured: "It's just as if the motor were functioning at top speed."

"Perhaps your calculations are wrong," suggested Mademoiselle Ossipoff.

"What do you mean by that, Mademoiselle?"

"I mean that perhaps the bolide's moving more rapidly than you calculated initially."

The old scientist shook his head. "If the calculations had been made by Monsieur Fricoulet alone," he said, "one might well doubt their exactitude..."

"But from the moment that you checked them," added the engineer, "no error could have crept in. *Errare humanum est* doesn't apply to you."

Gontran, who had applied his eye to the ocular lens again, then exclaimed: "If the calculations are correct, and if the machine's really been put in reverse, something inexplicable is happening." And he added, in an alarmed tone: "The bolide's grown prodigiously in five minutes—we seem to be falling upon it."

A glint of joy came into Ossipoff's eyes. "If that were true," he murmured, between his teeth, "we'd at least have a chance of preventing that wretch Sharp from arriving on Earth before us and deflowering the glory that awaits us..." He shook his head. "Alas!" he added, in a regretful tone, "we're surely victims of an optical illusion."

"You are, in truth, ferociously egotistical, my dear Monsieur Ossippoff," muttered Gontran. "To satisfy your futile scientific self-respect, you'd prefer that we break our bones!"

Selena, who had moved to a porthole, put her hands together in a gesture of terror. "Messieurs," she pleaded, "it's frightful! Monsieur Fricoulet, Father, I beg you...save us...save me!" Precipitating herself upon her father, she wrapped her arms around him, trembling and moaning. "I'm frightened...I'm afraid of dying!"

Flammermont, moved by his fiancée's desperate appeal, ran out of the cabin, hurtled down the little ladder that connected the vehicle's two floors, and arrived at the door of the engine-room. He tried to open it. It resisted. "Damn it!" he groaned. "What's happening?"

He made a further effort, which encountered the same resistance. Then, as rapid as a lightning-flash, an idea suddenly came into the young man's head. "It's that damned American!" he murmured. Then, hurling himself against the door with all the violence of desperation, he tried to break it down—but the lithium panel did not budge. Gontran only bruised himself in vain. "Farenheit!" he roared. "Farenheit!"

From the other side of the door, a calm voice asked. "What do you want?"

"Open up! In God's name, open up without losing a moment."

Farenheit wore a mocking smile. "In truth," he said, "are you in as much of a hurry as that?"

"Mr. Farenheit, I beg you, listen to me! Understand me, your life is at stake...all our lives. Open up! Open up! You don't realize that every minute's delay is bringing us closer to death."

"I realize one thing—which is that every minute's brings us closer to that scoundrel Sharp!"

Gontran uttered a cry of despair. "Ah!" he groaned. "We're doomed! He's still mad!"

"I beg your pardon," Farenheit replied, phlegmatically, "but I'm no longer mad. I understand perfectly that the wretch who, after stealing from me, attempted to murder me—the scoundrel Sharp—is close by, and I want to join him."

"But you can't think that...if you heard that, you must also have heard that we'll be smashed if the *Eclair* collides with that bolide. Besides, there's no proof that Sharp is there. So you're risking your life—and ours—for a chimerical vengeance. Besides, you have no right to exercise that vengeance; we've forgiven..."

"You, perhaps," Farenheit replied, "but me—no."

Gontran no longer knew what argument to invoke. "Mr. Farenheit," he implored, "Mr. Farenheit! Open up, I beg you. The bolide's less than 40,000 leagues away. Every minute that goes by brings us 2000 leagues closer. In the name of Heaven, open up..."

"I wouldn't open up in the name of the Devil," replied the American.

At that moment, Fricoulet and Ossipoff, astonished by Flammermont's long absence, appeared at the top of the stairway. "Help me, Fricoulet! Help me!" cried Gontran. "Farenheit's locked the door of the engine-room."

"He's the one who's moved the levers!" howled the engineer. In two bounds, he was next to his friend. "We have to break down the door," he said.

"I've tried that," said Gontran.

The engineer looked round, seemingly searching for some instrument, or tool...but there was nothing. Suddenly, he let out a cry of joy, took out his revolver and, having taken off the safety-catch, fired three shots.

"Us, now!" he cried. And he hurled himself at the door, at the same time as Gontran. Yielding to the impact, it was flung back into the room's interior.

Farenheit had leapt backwards and was standing in front of the motor, crouching down, fists forward, ready to repel anyone who dared to advance.

"Gontran! Monsieur Fricoulet!" shouted Mademoiselle Ossipoff, left alone in the upper room. "Hurry up! Hurry up! The bolide's hurtling upon us!" Veritably mad with fear, she cried out in a strangled voice: "Help! Help!"

There are certain critical moments in life in which speech is unnecessary for communicating thought; a glance suffices. That glance Fricoulet darted at Gontran and Ossipoff. Then he hurled himself on the American.

The latter was waiting for him, and while his left hand grabbed the engineer by the collar of his jacket, he lifted up his right, as terrible as a mallet, and brought it down. Fricoulet, however, among his other physical qualities, possessed a singular suppleness. With a movement of his torso, he avoided the blow that was about to fracture his skull, and immediately, before the fist could be raised again, he grabbed it with both hands.

At that moment, Ossipoff came to the rescue and suspended himself from Farenheit's left arm, while Gonran, moving nimbly behind the American, threw his leather belt around his neck and applied the "coup de Père François"[61] so familiar to pickpockets—which is to say that he hung on to the improvised halter with his entire weight.

The effect was instantaneous. A surge of blood reddened Farenheit's face; his eyes seemed to pop out of their orbits, and his mouth twisted, foaming. With a superhuman effort, he sent Ossipoff and Fricoulet spinning to the far side of the room. Strangled and half asphyxiated, however he lifted his arms above his head, beat the air desperately, as if seeking some handhold on which to get a grip—then his knees gave way beneath him and he fell backwards, gurgling.

Fricoulet, who had got up, stepped over the American's body, reached the motor and pushed down the levers. All trepidation stopped immediately.

"Just in time," he said.

---

[61] The origins of this phrase are mysterious, but it pertains to a maneuver favored by pairs of footpads, whereby one of the two would seize the victim in a stranglehold while the other rifled his pockets.

Gontran and Ossipoff had laid Farenheit in his hammock. After taking off the belt that was strangling him, they busied themselves bringing him round.

"All my congratulations, my dear Gontran," said the engineer, smiling. "Your Père François stroke has saved us!"

At that moment, Selena arrived, almost fainting. "We're doomed!" she said. "The bolide's upon us!"

Gontran ran to a porthole. "Thunder!" he groaned.

At that moment, the light reflected by the asteroid flooded through the portholes into the engine-room, generating bluish plumes: a sublime but sinister effect. The rock seemed to be falling with vertiginous rapidity on to the *Eclair*—whose entire framework, although its motor had stopped, was trembling as if it were being sucked in by a giant's breath.

Fricoulet did not lose his head. He leapt to the motor and threw the control-levers into reverse, forcing the electricity in order that the vehicle could hold its own momentarily against the asteroidal current that was carrying it.

"If we can just remain motionless for two minutes," he shouted, "we're saved!"

Rooted to the spot, the Terrans waited anxiously, looking at one another with terrified expressions.

But the speed of the vehicle was too great for the engineer's desperate maneuver to be able to slow it down. Like those moths that fly through open windows on summer evenings and fly in a hectic course to burn their wings in candle-flames and lamps, the *Eclair*, borne along at a vertiginous speed, hurtled through space toward the rocky mass that was attracting it.

"Doomed!" said Fricoulet, having darted a rapid glance outside.

At the same instant, a formidable crack was heard, shaking the lithium vehicle apart; the metal fittings of the walls splintered, pieces of the motor and the generator were hurled in all directions—and the Terrans, knocked over by the violence of the impact, were stretched out on the metal floor, motionless, and perhaps lifeless.

For a second, a strange light, totally different from the bolide's radiation, lit up the vehicle; then, abruptly, without transition—as if a curtain were coming down—intense, absolute darkness fell: the night of death and birth. At the same time, a strange odor permeated the engine-room.

For several minutes, a profound silence reigned in the cabin. Then an imperceptible noise was heard. It was like the scratch of a match struck against a hard body.

Finally, a feeble light interrupted the darkness, and Fricoulet appeared, lying on the ground, supporting his upper body on one hand, while the other was raised above his head, brandishing a magnesium rod. "Oh! Oh!" he stammered, in a thick voice, after directing a circular glance around him. "All these people seem to be badly injured!"

He made an effort, and succeeded in getting to his feet. "Just as long," he added, dragging himself along the wall, "as the *Eclair* was able to resist! But first of all, where are we?"

He went to a porthole, but no matter how he strained his eyes he could only see darkness...nothing but darkness...the most intense darkness he had ever seen.

"Strange," he murmured, laconically. He put his hands to his forehead, staggered, and supported himself against the wall. "It's stifling in here," he muttered. "There's no shortage of air...but it's as if I'm in a furnace..."

Intrigued, and driven by his natural curiosity, he returned to the porthole, struck another match, moved it right up to the glass—and stepped back, highly surprised by the observation of a sort of scintillation produced by the light outside, on a body seemingly belonging to the mineral or vegetable kingdom.

A few seconds of reflection sufficed for the engineer to get to the bottom of the mystery. "Of course!" he said. "The *Eclair*, driven by its prodigious velocity, must have run into the bolide head-on, and doubtless perforated its friable mass. just as a needle penetrates a pat of butter. Except..." He did not finish his sentence, but he uttered a singular "Brrrr!" that would certainly have communicated some apprehension to Flammermont if the latter had been able to hear any of what had been said.

The engineer shook his head. "Unfortunately," he murmured, "our force was insufficient to take us all the way through the bolide on which that villain Sharp is riding, and we're buried in its mass, just like some antediluvian fossil." He uttered a humorless laugh that had nothing human about it, and added: "This time, we're really doomed."

He collected himself, cast an eye over his companions, and went on: "When I say *we*, I'm wrong, for they appear to have completed their great voyage...I, therefore, am..." He interrupted himself, touched his forehead with his finger, and murmured; "But how is it that I haven't followed their example? Has some evil spirit condemned me to live here eternally, in company with these cadavers...? How stupid am I? Do spirits even exist...? No, there are no miracles—there are only natural consequences of facts..."

He broke off, dragged himself as far as Ossipoff, who happened to be the closest one to him, and put his hand on his chest.

The old scientist's heart was beating normally.

One by one, the engineer examined Gontran, Selena and Farenheit. Like the old man, all three seemed to be sleeping calmly and peacefully.

"That's too much!" exclaimed Fricoulet. "But how are they contriving to breathe?"

Only then did he notice the singular odor that permeated the engine-room. "Ah!" he said. "That's quite bizarre!" He struck a third match—his last—and inspected the cabin's wall minutely.

One of the partition walls—that of the bunker in which the supplies of the liquid nutrient brought from Mars were stored—had a large crack in the upper section, which had put the bunker in communication with the reservoir of breathable air. The engineer let slip a brief laugh. "Of course!" he said. "We're in a nutritive atmosphere, and we're supplying our needs, breathing and eating, through our skin, with the result that..." He stopped, grabbed his head in both hands and stammered: "Oh, what's got into me? One would think that I were choking. Am I going the same way as my brave friends. Is it...?"

His voice gave out, and he fell to his knees, his face slightly convulsed, his limbs agitated by a nervous tremor. Nevertheless, by virtue of the instinctive horror that the moribund have of darkness, his clenched fingers hung on to the magnesium match, whose vacillating light produced a sinister clarity.

Soon, though, Fricoulet did not even have enough strength to sustain him on his knees. He fell backwards and let go of the match, which continued to burn on the floor like a funerary candle, illuminating the *Eclair*'s engine-room like a tomb, bearing the bold explorers of planetary realms into the sidereal depths.

Chapter L
In which Fedor Sharp has more luck than he deserves

On the surface of the bolide, in the vague shadow that enveloped the worldlet, a strange being was moving, creeping slowly and painfully over the ground, which it was inspecting minutely.

Bent double, shapeless, swollen up like those balloon-men that that aeronauts release for the amusement of idlers at traveling fairs, the creature appeared to be humanoid in form. Its long legs were covered by rags; its equally long arms terminated in hands with bony fingers; one held a bizarre lamp—a little glass bulb in which shone a bright white spark, like a star—the other clutched a steel spike, which seemed to serve the function of ensuring the progress of this unnamable creature.

Was it a man? Was it part of that bizarre humankind with which the imagination of poets and philosophers was pleased to populate the sparkling worlds strewn amid the profound azure of the Heavens?

It moved, stopped, moved again, to stop again further on. It moved soundlessly and its feet, which hardly seemed to be touching the ground, awoke no echo in the cold silence of the night.

At intervals, it bent over, leaning down toward the ground as if to examine it more attentively with its enormous, monstrous head, made of wrinkled leather, within whose face the lamplight brightened two scintillating dots. It raised the spike it held in its hand, striking the ground forcefully, which splintered under the impact, crumbling into impalpable dust and shooting enormous pieces of stone into the air, which seemed as light as snowflakes.

The creature shook its head, and dragged itself further on, to halt again and recommence the same stratagem.

The asteroid that served as its abode was bare, deserted, bleak and desolate. No breath of wind moved through its rarefied atmosphere; no animal alleviated that solitude, darker and more disheartening than that of the lunar plains, with the sound of its footfalls or its fluttering wings.

From time to time, however, the creature traversed regions covered with a luxuriant vegetation, and in the midst of plains whose less arid ground was velveted by dark green moss, majestic trees of unknown species and bizarre appearance held up their bristling heads—from which flexible branches dangled—to the black sky.

Strangely and incomprehensibly, though, this appearance of life was even more dismal and terrifying than the desolate regions of a while before, for it seemed to have been stricken with death by the hand of some evil spirit. These trees, whose trunks seemed made of marble, extended icy shadows over the ground, and their immobile foliage had a metallic rigidity. A stream had traced its bed across the plain, but no susurrus rose from its banks; one might have thought that the waters had been suddenly petrified in mid-course.

Little by little, however, the Sun emerged from the horizon, dissipating the darkness of the night with its reddish rays. In a few minutes, dawn broke, and the entire surface of the asteroid became bathed in a soft luminous clarity.

The creature put out its lamp; the smallest details of its costume and person were now marvelously distinct. It seemed to be tall, but no proportion existed between the different parts of its body. The upper body, which was enormous, as if bloated, was mounted on legs that were admittedly long, but thin and gaunt. Arms were attached to the monstrous shoulders, which resembled in their thinness the legs of a gigantic crane-fly. What had seemed in the darkness to be its head now appeared as a leathern helmet with two transparent plates mounted in the facial section.

It was still moving forward, stopping at every protuberance of the ground, obstinately digging away—and resuming its course every time, with evident signs of discouragement. Its progress was getting slower, its pauses more frequent and longer; it seemed to be dragging itself along with increasing difficulty and, from time to time, it placed its hands on its breast, in a gesture of indescribable suffering.

Suddenly, something strange appeared at the summit of a sort of wooded hill, sparkling in the rays of the Sun, which had now risen into the sky. It was a metallic cone a few meters high, shining like silver. It was the luminous point of which Mikhail Ossipoff had made use to establish the bolide's coordinates, and on the presence of which Fricoulet had based his affirmation that the bolide had a cometary origin. This shining point, this metallic cone, was the shell that had transported Ossipoff and his companions from the Earth to the Moon—the same one that Fedor Sharp had stolen from them, and in which he had landed on Tuttle's Comet after his peregrinations around the Sun. On perceiving it, the creature made a seemingly joyous movement, raising its arms in the air, and its progress apparently accelerated.

It took five more steps; it was half way to the top of the hill—but it stopped abruptly, tottered, and fell to its knees. Then, using its feet and hands, it dragged itself further, stopping at almost every step, scratching the ground with its fingers—which became grazed and bloody—but drawing nearer to its goal with incredible resolve.

Suddenly, it fell on its side and remained lying there, without moving. In that struggle between life and death, had the latter carried the day? But no—the instinct of self-preservation, sustained by an indomitable will, triumphed. The creature crawled on—oh, slowly, very slowly!

The Sun had now described nearly its entire course; its disk was almost touching the horizon and, in a few minutes, night would be sole mistress of the worldlet. Ten meters still separated the creature from the shell, whose radiation was extinct and whose contours were already blurred by the evening mist. The creature coughed; it twisted in frightful convulsions; it uttered desperate moans—but it went on, it still went on. Death was already taking hold of it—but it went on again.

Finally, it touched the shell. Its fingers, in a supreme convulsion, clutched the lever that controlled the manhole that served as its entrance. The manhole opened. With a desperate surge, the creature precipitated itself into the interior, and shut the door with a violent kick.

It lay on the floor, writhing in agony, overwhelmed by asphyxia. Again, in its indomitable will, it found sufficient force for its tremulous fingers to unfasten the leather helmet that imprisoned its head.

The helmet rolled on the ground and Fedor Sharp appeared: pale—mortally pale—his eyes bloodshot and bulging, but breathing the benevolent oxygen of which the shell was full through lips that were already violet-tinted. Once again, the Terran was victorious; death had been vanquished!

In order to enable the reader to comprehend the exact accuracy of Alcide Fricoulet's deductions concerning the cometary bolide into which the *Eclair* had crashed, it is necessary that he consent to go back in time a few months—which is to say, to the moment when Farenheit, by unexpectedly cutting the cable that retained the metallic balloon to Comet Tuttle, had abandoned his enemy Fedor Sharp there.

The permanent secretary of the St. Petersburg Academy of Sciences had rolled like a ball as far as the Mercurian hill, where a tree-trunk had finally put an end to his tumble—a trifle rudely, for he remained there for some time, lying on his back with his eyelids closed and his mouth wide open. Fortunately for him, the Slav-Teuton hybrid had a robust constitution and, after a brief period of unconsciousness, he came round—badly bruised, no doubt, but with his limbs intact and his brain in complete equilibrium.

At first, he was quite astonished to find himself there, lying in the comet's carbonaceous dust. He looked around, searching for his companions in order to ask them for an explanation of that strange situation. Then, all of a sudden, his thoughts, a trifle befogged by the fall that he had suffered, were restored to order, and the memory of what had happened came back to him.

Then, overexcited by anger, he leapt to his feet and he climbed the gentle slope of the hill to the summit, crowned by the shell, at a run. He bounded up the steps of the little stairway leading to the vehicle's nose-cone and, once there, aimed the large telescope that Ossipoff had installed there into space. His heart beating precipitately, and his breast crushed by a profound anxiety, he searched the radiant immensity with an ardent eye, hoping to discover some trace of his companions—but there was nothing: absolutely nothing but the direly uniform blue of the celestial depths to which the Sun lent a magical glow. Out there, however, far away—thousands of leagues away already—there was a dot: a simple dot shining brightly white amid the gilded irradiation.

"It's them!" groaned Sharp. Mad with rage, he launched his clenched fist toward the sky, threateningly but also impotently—fortunately for our friends.

For nearly an hour, the ex-permanent secretary of the Academy of Sciences abandoned himself to his rage, moving back and forth and up and down within the shell, never ceasing to proffer the most horrible blasphemies and to utter the most terrible oaths. Oh, if ever Ossipoff and his friends fell into his hands!

A strange thing is human nature! This abandoned man, alone and resourceless on that vagabond world wandering through space—submissive to the perturbations of the large planets, not even following a regular route—for whom death was on the lookout during every minute of his existence, thought of only one thing: vengeance. The millions of leagues that separated him from Earth were of scant importance to him; the possibility that he would never see his native planet again did not preoccupy him at all. What his malevolent soul desired with all its innate force was that he might one day—in weeks, month or even years—in whatever part of infinity he happened to be, find himself face to face with the miserable traitors who had played with him disrespectfully and abandoned him pitilessly. And that wretch, whose existence had been, until that moment, nothing but a retinue of knavery and treason, found frightful epithets in his heart to qualify the conduct of others in that regard.

When he had sworn, raged and railed his utmost, however, nature reclaimed its rights and, exhausted by fatigue and emotion, he sat down on the circular divan that ran around the vehicle's interior. Little by little, calm returned to his mind and he understood the necessity of finding, as son as possible, means of subsistence on that parcel of Mercurian ground on to which hazard had thrown him. His first task was to make up an inventory of resources on which he could count.

It will be recalled that Gontran and Fricoulet had made a very exact census of the comestible humankind that had accompanied them from the planet Mercury on the comet; that humankind was of two sorts—or, at least—belonged to two species, one avian and one leporid. Sharp only had to cast a glance over a sort of register in which Selena had recorded every hecatomb of these interesting beings to take a head-count of 53 representatives of the hairy race and 29 of the feathered. It was not very many, but it still represented a few months of guaranteed food-supply, without taking into account the instances of reproduction that might have occurred, augmenting the Mercurian colony without the Terrans even being aware of it. To that, he had to add a whole carboy of the nutritive paste fabricated by Ossipoff before his departure from the Moon and a near-full storage-locker of distilled water.

The voyagers, as we know, had only taken with them what as strictly necessary in terms of clothing, weapons and instruments, for fear of overloading the metallic sphere that was transporting them. Sharp, therefore, had a very complete and varied wardrobe, and a laboratory very well equipped for physics and chemistry, but the items of astronomical significance had been taken away by Ossipoff, with the exception of the large telescope in the upper part of the vehicle—which was too heavy and too bulky to have been accommodated in the gondola of the balloon—a pair of marine binoculars, a sextant and all the books on astronomy that Mikhail Ossipoff knew by heart and would have weighed down the balloon needlessly.

Until that day, Fedor Sharp had lived without any great preoccupation with all these details; now, every new object he discovered drew a cry of joy from him; he took it, examined it as if he had never seen it before, and even felt a certain affection as he put it carefully away in a place where it could neither deteriorate nor be damaged.

"Come on! Come on!" he murmured, rubbing his hands together with satisfaction. "If no further incident occurs, I'll be able to live quite tolerably."

A sharp disappointment awaited him, however, at the reservoir of air, and he uttered an exclamation near to terror when, on consulting the barometric indicator, he observed that the reservoir was almost empty. He ran to the storage-lockers, hoping discover some of the little steel cylinders filled with liquid oxygen that Ossipoff had brought from Earth. Exactly half a dozen remained. That was a fortnight's supply, and he would have to be careful not to use it prodigally—which is to say, not to carry out any exhausting tasks requiring more abundant respiration, and hence an excess of oxygen.

Strictly speaking, Sharp would have been able to live for a month, perhaps six weeks, but on condition that he lay in his hammock and spent his time reading, avoiding any work that might tire the lungs and force them to extra consumption—but immobility did not suit a temperament like Sharp's. His mind always active, demanded a corporeal activity that dictated the minimum reserve of air he would require. He shook his head to expel even the thought of the monastic existence suggested by the six drums of liquid oxygen.

"I need to find something else," he murmured, in a firm voice. "For, if I want to live..."

Oh, yes, he wanted to live! He wanted it ardently, in order to satisfy the two passions that shared possession of his soul: vengeance and glory. To live long enough to get his hands on Ossipoff! To live long enough to return to Earth and be, if only for a few hours, the object of admiration of his contemporaries.

He lay down and slept profoundly, his mind as calm and orderly as if he had been in the little attic apartment in which he lived at the St. Petersburg Institute.

When he woke up the next day, his first thought was devoted to the question of air—which was, for him, a matter of life or death, and which had tormented him during his slumber. He equipped himself with test-tubes that he had evacuated, put on his respirol, and went down the Mercurian hill.

Having arrived on the ground of the comet itself, he knelt down, uncorked one of the test-tubes and immediately re-corked it. Then, getting up, he repeated the operation five times more as he climbed the side of the hill to different heights. After that, returning to the shell, he shut himself in the laboratory and analyzed the specimens of air he had collected with the utmost care. He thus established, as Ossipoff had done before him, that, from the ground level of the comet to an altitude of between four and five meters, there was a dense layer of unbreathable carbon dioxide. Above five meters, lighter pure oxygen floated on top of it. It was therefore a matter of storing that pure oxygen, in such a way as to provide a reserve and constitute an artificial atmosphere.

Fortunately, Sharp had a compression-pump at his disposal and all the equipment that had been used to fill the metallic sphere with gas. He took the long pipes that had connected the enormous barrels constructed by Gontran and Farenheit for the manufacture of the gas, and extended them to the layer of pure oxygen that was floating 20 meters below the vehicle. Their ends were connected to the lower storage-locker, in which he had decided to store the oxygen in s great a quantity as possible.

With the aid of the pump, he forced the compression as far as prudence permitted; he did not rest until his muscular force became insufficient to overcome the resistance of the compressed air. The most that he was able to obtain was a pressure of about 20 atmospheres, and he judged that he must have stored 100 cubic meters; that was a provision which might last several months if eked out parsimoniously.

Having established that reserve to ward off the most improbable eventualities, he established a conduit connecting the shell's nose-cone to the layer of pure oxygen, which—thanks to an elementary ventilation system—furnished the breathable air necessary to his existence. That pure air was, however, insufficient to ensure the good functioning of his lungs; he still needed to get rid of the pollutant residues of respiration and pulmonary combustion. Now, the vehicle was short of caustic soda; scarcely half a sack remained in the laboratory. Sharp therefore had to be content with that, and in order to do that, he had to resolve not to purify his air of the carbon dioxide it contained until the proportion became so great as to constitute a veritable mortal toxicity.

Gradually, he accustomed himself to respiring with impunity a mixture of 90 parts oxygen and ten of carbon dioxide instead of air composed, as on Earth, of 79 parts nitrogen and 21 of oxygen. When he had acclimatized himself to this singular regime, Fedor Sharp observed—not without a certain astonishment—that his health improved rather than deteriorating, as he had feared at first. He rapidly got fatter, even becoming plump, swollen by soft yellowish fat, having previously been hollow-cheeked and able to count his ribs. Oddly enough, though, only his face and trunk were subject to this transformation—his arms and legs conserved the skeletal thinness that was their natural state. Without explaining this difference in transformation between the parts of his body, Sharp attributed the plumpness of his face and trunk to his mode of respiration.

While the ex-secretary of the St. Petersburg Academy of Sciences dedicated himself to these works of installation, the comet carrying him continued its course toward aphelion, undeviatingly but with ever-decreasing velocity. Mars was lost in the depths of the Heavens and was longer, for the sole inhabitant of the cometary nucleus, anything but a beautiful morning star. Earth, Venus and Mercury no longer existed for him, drowned as they were in the solar radiance. As for the central star, the arc subtended by its disk was diminishing on a daily basis.

As Ossipoff and his companions were being carried towards the south pole of Mars by the frightful tempest that was ravaging the red planet, Fedor Sharp traversed the zone of the minor planets and headed for Jupiter, whose titanic mass deflected the court of Tuttle's Comet. Far from being frightened by the considerable deviation exerted on Tuttle's ellipse by the attraction of the giant planet, Sharp obtained, by contast, an intense satisfaction therefrom.

"Tee hee!" he said, rubbing his hands together, one evening when his micrometer measured a prodigious augmentation of the Jovian disk. "A few more days, and I'll know what mysteries of the titan of our universe has in store for me." And his contentment was redoubled by the thought that Ossipoff and his companions, had they been able to attain the objective of their voyage, were stranded on the surface of Mars without any hope of returning to their native planet. He, on the other hand, would shortly arrive at the comet's aphelion, make a turn around Saturn at a distance of only a few million leagues, and resume the road to the Sun—and the Earth—with ever-increasing velocity.

The Earth! To reach the Earth! That was the object of all his thoughts, the subject of all the dreams that troubled his sleep during the long nights.

What means could he employ to quit the cometary nucleus that served as his mount? That he did not know; everything depended on the circumstances and proximity in which his native planet would pass by—but he was henceforth resolved to try anything in order to enjoy, if only for a few months, or even a few hours, the great aureole of glory that was bound to surround the marvelous voyage he had undertaken.

Only one thing caused him any anxiety, and that was the time the comet would take to travel through the millions of league of space that separated him from the terrestrial orbit. Sharp would have to live in Tuttle's nucleus for nearly ten years before coming in sight of the Earth!

Ten years! Would he find the means to prolong his existence for so long? Would he have the patience to wait? Once, an insane plan had crossed his mind: to increase the rapidity of his journey by diminishing the body that carried him. It was risking everything to gain everything—but the means, admissible in theory, were impractical, given that Sharp did not have any explosive at his disposal capable of breaking up the cometary nucleus.

Ah! If only he had had his laboratory in St. Petersburg at his disposal, he would have had no difficulty in fabricating, within a few days, 100 kilograms of that powder whose formula he had stolen from Ossipoff and which had permitted him to carry out his celestial journey!

Despairing of the cause, he had abandoned the idea, putting off to a later date the work of seeking some other plan.

While he racked his brains thus, he did not suspect that Jupiter might take responsibility for putting into execution the project that he had deemed impossible.

Desiccated by the intense heat that he had received during its passage through the perihelion, stony to its very core, the nucleus of Tuttle's Comet was no more than a spheroid composed of elements that were merely juxtaposed, linked to one another by simple attraction to its center of gravity. Gradually, by virtue of a slowly-augmented continuous attraction, as Tuttle's Comet drew closer to it the giant planet exercised a dissociative action on its elements. It was like a general break-up, of which Sharp would certainly have been aware if he had not spent his time shut up in the shell's nose-cone, which served as his study. There he made his notes and observed the stars.

Soon, the attraction of Jupiter was such that Tuttle's different constitutive elements were only held together by a miracle of equilibrium—an equilibrium that would be destroyed by any approach, however, slight, to the giant planet.

One evening, while Sharp was resting tranquilly in his hammock, a catastrophe occurred similar to the one that had led, a few years earlier, to the disintegration of Biela's Comet. Suddenly, there was a frightful shearing in the external envelope, and strident cracking sounds shook the heavy atmospheric layers. The cometary nucleus, like the metallic envelope of a bomb bursting under the violent pressure of the enclosed explosive, split and shattered, disseminating its fragments in every direction. While a fraction of the debris fell with vertiginous rapidity upon the Jovian disk, the fragment carrying Sharp was driven away with unimaginable force towards the black profundities of space.

At the first shock of the comet's quaking, Fedor Sharp had been thrown out of his hammock on to the laboratory floor; once there, he rolled back and forth for a few seconds under the impulsion of a rocking movement similar to that of a ship battered by furious waves. He finally succeeded in getting a grip on a side wall, and remained in the same position for nearly a quarter of an hour, with his knees on the floor and his neck bent, bruised by the impact of items of furniture and instruments that were tumbling around him. His heart was filled with an indescribable fear, and he scarcely had enough presence of mind to appeal for help to Saint Sergius, his patron.

Eventually, everything calmed down; the convulsions agitating the ground ceased at the same time as the hissing noises filling the air, and Sharp gradually recovered his composure. Taking every precaution, he got to his feet and headed for one of the portholes at a prudent pace. Unfortunately, it was as black outside as the inside of an oven, and it was impossible for him to get any idea of what might have happened.

He took out his watch. It marked 3 a.m. "It'll be daylight in five minutes," he murmured. "Let's wait."

Suddenly, in fact, the Sun's rays penetrated the vehicle, and Sharp rushed to the porthole again. Nothing around him had changed; the shell still stood on the summit of the Mercurian hill, the wooded slope of which descended steeply to the surface of the comet itself.

Then, seized by curiosity, he put on his respirol and went out, having decided to go on a mission of discovery.

He had no sooner reached the foot of the hill, on the bank of the little stream in which black and carbonaceous waters were trickling, than he stopped. Amazed and terrified, with cold sweat on his brow and his hair standing on end.

The edge of the Mercurian forest had vanished. Where giant trees had once stood, a profound ravine was hollowed out. Sharp leaned over the edge and reeled back, struck by vertigo. His sharp and penetrating gaze had been unable to sound the depths of the abyss; it seemed that a giant's axe had cut through the cometary surface so completely that the fragment on which he was located was ready to be detached from the nucleus.

Although the crevasse measured nearly 50 meters across, Sharp leapt it in one bound, by a simple thrust of his foot, as lightly as a bird.

That lightness seemed surprising, and it provided him with an indication of the radical transformation of the world that carried him. In fact, when he had walked for less than an hour, observing at every step the changes produced on the surface of the planet by the nocturnal cataclysm, he stopped again and uttered a cry of terror. Mirroring the sunlight, a brilliant point appeared, and although it was too far away to be clearly made out, he had the presentiment nevertheless that it was the shell he was looking at: the shell that he had left an hour ago, and to which he had already returned! He had, therefore, taken an hour to circumnavigate the cometary nucleus—when, previously, he and his companions had taken nearly two days to go all the way around it!

What did that signify?

He went back to the vehicle at a run, rushed up the stairs to the laboratory and threw himself on the telescope, which he aimed at Jupiter. The micrometer measured a sensible diminution of the Jovian disk. The comet was, therefore, drawing away! Sharp was increasingly perplexed.

While he was staring into space, he perceived something like a rain of corpuscles falling on Jupiter, and immediately thought that they might be cometary fragments attracted to the planet. He then devoted himself to spectral analyses of several of these asteroids, which convinced him of the accuracy of his guess. Yes, the infinite atoms that were before his eyes were certainly fragments of Tuttle's Comet.

But then, what had become of the comet itself? Doubtless it had been broken up, pulverized and annihilated—but what would be the fate of the piece of wreckage that carried him, less than a league around and devoid of significant attractive force, which was rotating about its own axis with extraordinary rapidity? It was drawing way from Jupiter, as the micrometer demonstrated, but where would it be thrown? What route would it follow?

Several days passed—although, for the inhabitant of the shell, the days was only two hours long—while Sharp was prey to a terrible anguish. If he had not been cowardly and pusillanimous by nature, he would have renounced that existence full of uncertainty and peril, in which a frightful death threatened him at every moment—but he was too fearful of death to inflict it on himself.

He waited.

One evening, as he was scrutinizing the black profundity of space, a radiance suddenly appeared in the field of the telescope; to his great surprise the radiance appeared to be that of the comet. At first, he could not believe his eyes; in his mind, the piece of wreckage that bore him was all that remained of Tuttle's nucleus. He was, however forced to yield to the evidence once an attentive examination had made him recognize that the plumed head, followed by a luminous tail that striped the sky, occupied—at a right angle from the Sun—the location that Tuttle's comet should have occupied.

For several days and nights he stood there with his eye glued to his telescope, studying the wandering star with a profound attention, minutely measuring its progress through the heavens. He soon acquired the conviction that the block carrying him, hurled in advance of the comet with a vertiginous rapidity, was following the orbit it traced through celestial space with mathematical precision.[62]

When he had observed this circumstance and checked it several times over, Sharp was seized by a delirious fever and started dancing madly in the middle of his laboratory, shouting, singing, weeping and addressing the warmest and most extravagant thanks to his patron, Saint Sergius. Just think: the plan that his desire-maddened imagination had made to return to Earth had been put into execution by Jupiter; the cometary fragment carrying him was flying through space at a speed of 1,000,000 leagues a second, which would reduce to only six months the time it would take to reach Earth's orbit. Six months! But that was life assured; it was the prospect, in the short term, of reaping the glorious harvest that his extraordinary adventures promised him.

Yes, Sharp was ecstatic—and to give his joy a manifestation in harmony with a certain passion that he had not satisfied for a long time, he went to look among the provisions in the storage-locker for a bottle of rum, with which he made up a gigantic bowl of punch, which he drank.

When Sharp came to after several days spent sleeping off his drunkenness, his first impulse was to look for the comet.

It had disappeared.

---

[62] Had the fragment really acquired such a dramatic increase in velocity, of course, it would not continue to follow the same orbit as before.

He rubbed his hands together energetically; that disappearance was the best proof he could have of the rapidity with which the piece of wreckage that carried him was traveling through space. In a few weeks, the fragment would reach the orbit of Saturn. Sharp made ready then to examine, carefully and in every detail, the world that could, without exaggeration, be classified as a celestial marvel.

Unfortunately, he had doubtless forgotten to inform Saturn of the rendezvous. The planet was exactly 30,000,000 leagues from the person who wanted to observe it—with the effect that, even with the aid of his telescope, he was unable to distinguish anything more than terrestrial astronomers could see without leaving their observatories.

One thing occurred to provide a diversion for the scientist's ill-humor: the route followed by the cometary fragment rounded an invisible focal point while approaching Uranus, which now appeared as a bluish disk about a minute of arc in diameter.

The cold had become intense; outside, the Walferdin liquid-overflow thermometer[63] indicated ten Centigrade degrees below zero in the sunlight and 75 degrees below in the shade. The atmosphere seemed to condense, solidify and become turbid, as if invaded by milky vapors emerging from fissures in the ground.

Despite the excessive rigor of the temperature, Sharp forced himself to make an entire tour of the world the bore him every day; a certain amount of exercise seemed indispensable to maintain his health in a near-satisfactory state. He put on over his respirol all the furs that he had found in the vehicle's wardrobe and, walking slowly, one step at a time, he maintained sufficient elasticity in his limbs to spare them ankylosis. In the same way, gripped by a terrible dread of becoming mute by virtue of living in solitude, he compelled himself to read aloud every day.

A sad existence, in sum, was that of the unfortunate castaway. It was impossible for him to keep warm in his laboratory; the torrid atmosphere no longer contained anything but carbon dioxide incapable of entertaining combustion. Soon, he even had to renounce his daily walks, which had the grave inconvenience of giving his lungs too much to do—and, in consequences, exhausting his provision of oxygen more rapidly.

For three weeks, therefore, he remained lying in his hammock, wrapped up in his furs, in a comatose state quite similar to that of Laplanders during the long boreal nights, looking forward to the moment when the asteroid carrying him resumed its route to its perihelion.

---

[63] The "hyperthermometer" invented by François Hippolyte Walferdin (1795-1880) was actually designed for measuring exceptionally high temperatures, but Jules Verne mistakenly cited it in *Autour de la lune* as a device for measuring very low temperatures; that is presumably the source from which the authors of the present text have borrowed the reference.

Finally, that moment arrived, and Sharp, forgetting about the intensity of the cold and rarefaction of the air in his joy, leapt down from his hammock to follow the cometary fragment's change of direction in space. In less than 100 hours, the bolide veered, described an accentuated curve, and resumed the road to the Sun.

For the second time since he had been abandoned by his companions, Fedor Sharp took a bottle of liquor from the food-supplies, with the aid of which he devoted himself to copious libations. He drank to the Sun, the source of light and life, to the Earth, the planet of his birth, which he would doubtless soon see again, to the glory that awaited him, and…he collapsed dead drunk on the floor.

Chapter LI
The Cometary Castaway

However joyful he was finally to resume the road to his cradle—which is to say, the planet of his birth—Fedor Sharp was inconsolable not to be able to devote himself to the profound study of the world of Saturn that he had contemplated. That was a profound lacuna in the series of observations that he had recorded of his intersidereal voyage, and he felt an anticipatory blush rising to his forehead as he thought that, in the book that he intended to publish, instead of a chapter relating to the celestial marvel, Saturn, he would have to put the simple words: *The author, having passed by at a distance of 30,000,000 leagues, was unable to distinguish anything.*

How shameful! And these regrets, pursuing him as he slept, occasioned him frightful nightmares, always the same, in which he saw himself, having returned to Earth, received triumphantly by a Congress of all he scientific glories of the world; he spoke, and each of his sentences generated thunderous applause. Suddenly, in front of him, a sort of specter loomed up, the form of which as initially indecisive, but which sharpened gradually, soon becoming Mikhail Ossipoff—and his enemy pronounced these simple words; "Fedor Sharp, shall we talk about Saturn?" Then he stammered, choked, became mute and left the Congress covered in shame, accompanied to the door by the audience's jeers.

Invariably, this was the moment at which the ex-permanent secretary of the Academy of Sciences awoke, his limbs trembling and covered in cold sweat. He sat up on his elbow, looked around him vaguely, his ears still buzzing with satirical laughter and mocking whistles; then, he recognized his vehicle and released a profound sigh of satisfaction, smiling at all the familiar objects, glad of the great silence that enveloped him.

To that hallucination another was soon added: after the regret of having been unable to study Saturn, the terror gripped him of not being able to study Uranus. Then, although several days would pass before the bolide carrying him crossed the orbit of the planet, Sharp devoted himself to fantastic calculations in order to determine, in advance, at what distance he would pass Uranus.[64]

He succeeded in estimating that distance at about 300,000,000 leagues—and, as his telescope magnified by a factor of 300, he therefore only had 1,000,000 leagues to make his studies. This result filled him with joy; after that, his nights became calm. It produced a singular transformation in him, however. Formerly so cold indifferent and impassive, he became enthusiastic, becoming

[64] This is inconsistent with the last chapter, in which we were told that the cometary fragment had already resumed its route towards perihelion; previous indications have also suggested that the comet's orbit did not extend as far as Uranus.

emotional at the memory of the great scientific discoveries of which past centuries had been so proud, and vibrant at the thought of the sublime items reserved for the generations that will come after us in future centuries.

One evening when he was passing the time by riffling through one of the philosophical treatises that were among the astronomy books in the library, he slammed the book shut and hurled it into a corner of the room, prey to a cold anger.

"The lunatics!" he cried, shrugging his shoulders furiously. "Claiming to assign limits to the Universe! Have then never read the history of science, then, that they posit as a principle that such and such a planet serves as a limit to the Solar System? A movable and preliminary limit, then, since every year that goes by bears away a quantity of the previous year's errors, extending the field of human knowledge even further!"

He sniggered stridently, got up and strode back and forth across the narrow laboratory in which he happened to be. Far from calming down, his fury grew, to the point at which, as he passed close to the unfortunate book, he gave it a kick that sent it flying up to the ceiling. "To write such things in 1880, at the end of the 19th century, which has seen such a large expanse of the veil that hides nature from the human mind torn away! The wretches! But if they had lived in the last century, they would have burned Herschel for having pushed back the limits of the Solar System by 320,000,000 leagues."

He stopped, folded his arms and addressed an invisible audience: "Yes, Messieurs, from antiquity to the end of the 19th century, Saturn remained to the astronomical world what the Pillars of Hercules were to the first navigators: the extreme limit of the celestial Universe. It was only a little way beyond that distance, already ten times superior to that separating the Earth from the Sun, that a few audacious minds dared to place the stars. Suddenly, that quietude, in the midst of which the scientific world lived, convinced of the impossibility of a *beyond*, was disturbed and overturned; astronomical routines were demolished. A new planet had just been discovered, 733,000,000 leagues from the Sun.

"Ah, do not imagine, Messieurs, that the first response of scientists was a surge of admiration and enthusiasm for the man whose persistent work and bold genius had thus revolutionized the world. Far from it; William Herschel had to fight, and to publish report after report concerning the little star that he had discovered and which, according to him, presented a perceptible planetary disk.

"For their part, all the astronomers sought and observed the new body. Strangely enough, all of them wanted the new body to be a comet, and in that capacity, wanted it to follow a very long orbit whose summit would be close to the Sun—but all the calculations made in that regard had to be started again; no one ever succeeded in representing the sequence of positions taken up by the body, although it moved very slowly. Each month's observations were always in flagrant contradiction to those of the previous month. It was maddening—and that situation lasted several months, during which no one suspected that they were dealing, not with a comet, but with a veritable planet.

"Finally, when it was determined that all the ellipsoid orbits that the alleged comet supposedly followed were as false as one another, when it was duly established that what they had before their eyes was a circular orbit far more distant from the Sun than Saturn's, it was necessary to yield to the evidence and consent—still temporarily, while awaiting something better—to regard the star as a true planet, turning, like the Earth, around the system's central focal point.

"On Earth, that which lasts longest is the temporary—that is why, Messieurs, more than a century after William Herschel's sublime discovery, the planet Uranus is still of this world."

Fedor Sharp stopped short, nervously passed his hand in front of his eyes, looked around, then looked at himself, apparently quite astonished to see himself standing there, leaning on the back of his armchair, perorating in a loud voice. He became conscious then of his aberration, uttered a little dry laugh, and continued his walk, murmuring; "The philosophers are right to call the imagination an innate folly. I thought I was already in St. Petersburg, giving the scientific world the preliminary lecture on the history of the planets that ought to precede the story of my voyages."

He stopped near his telescope, stuck his eye to the ocular lens and searched space anxiously, searching for the desired planet. "Oh, Uranus! Uranus!" he repeated. But the body, in quadrature, remained invisible. Then the ex-permanent secretary went back to his armchair. With his elbows on his desk and his head in his hands, he allowed himself to be borne away by the current of his memories.

He saw himself at the Observatory of Pulkova, spending days, weeks and months researching that incomprehensible planet, always on the point of attaining it and always missing it by a minute, or even a second. Finally, thanks to an equatorial magnifying by a factor of 90, he had been able to catch it, and he recalled, even now, the profound emotion that had taken possession of him while his soul, gliding along his line of sight, had flown through space to an extent of 700,000,000 leagues from the Sun, over the border of that infinity populated by twinkling stars, 1000 times larger and more resplendent still that those of our Solar System. And when he thought that he was going to see that marvelous planet, in a few days or perhaps a few hours, at close range, in all its mysterious splendor, it seemed to him—so great was his joy—that his heart ceased beating and the blood paused in his veins.

For several days, crouched in front of a porthole, his eye to the ocular lens of his telescope, he remained on watch, surveying space as a cat crouching in a corner watches out for the mouse that it know to be in the vicinity, and which its instinct informs it will pass within ranged of its claws. From time to time, in order to relax, he read books specifically dealing with Uranus and took notes with a view to the great lecture on the history of the celestial worlds that he intended to give as a prologue to the story of his own adventures and the revelation of new theories based on his personal observations. It was thus that he found, in leafing through a Hindu book on astronomy, mention of an eighth plant named Rahu, and established that this eighth planet, known in the remotest times, could not be any other than the one discovered by Herschel—except that, for the Hindu scientists, this Rahu was not a distant planet but a celestial monster whose mission was to produce eclipses.

He also noted the names of astronomers who, although repeating the mistakes of the Hindus concerning the planetary nature of Uranus in a much more recent era, had established its existence—and found that between 1690 and 1771, the interesting planet had occupied the attention of four astronomers. Little more would have been needed for the most recent, Le Monnier,[65] to steal the glory of its discovery from William Herschel; it would have happened if the astronomer had only had a more orderly character, and had transcribed his observations regularly—but he had such an odd fashion of writing things down that the discovery was made at the Observatory of one of his observations written on a paper bag that appeared to have contained powdered rice.

Sic transit gloria mundi!

One morning, Fedor Sharp, having followed his custom of jumping down from the divan that served as his bed to run to his telescope, uttered a cry of joy. Uranus was there, in the location that his calculations had assigned to it, offering its disk to the scientist's rapt eye—to which the micrometer attributed a diameter of 58 seconds—almost a full minute—of arc. Knowing the exact distance that separated him from the heavenly body, this diameter was sufficient for him to obtain the dimensions of the real diameter, and he recorded in his notebook the figure 53,000 kilometers—which was exactly the same as that measured by Herschel and his successors. To measure the distance of the cometary fragment from Uranus, it had been sufficient for him to establish a proportional relationship between the visible diameter of the Earth, which was four seconds, the distance of the planet from the Earth and the diameter of 58 seconds that the disk of Uranus now manifested to him. Nothing was more simple, as is evident—thus, a diameter of 53,000 kilometers.

Uranus, although the smallest of the outer planets, nevertheless has the right to be placed among the giant worlds, since it exceeds on its own the total obtained by adding together the diameters of the four inner planets, Venus Mars, Mercury and Earth. From the location he occupied in the sky, Sharp was unable to perceive Neptune; it was therefore impossible for him to determine the mass of Uranus by means of the perturbations it exercised on the former planet. One resource remained to him, however, and that was to study the rotational velocities imposed by the planet on its four satellites.

---

[65] Pierre Charles Le Monnier (1715-1799) had made no less than 12 separate observations of Uranus before Herschel's "discovery," but had not collated them so as to identify the object as a planet.

First of all, was four really the number of the Uranian satellites? Herschel had, in fact, discovered six, and more recently, in 1851, Lassell had discovered two more, closer to the planet than Herschel's—which thus made eight. Admittedly, however, Lassell, in spite of the most assiduous research, had only been able to discover two of Herschel's six—which, with his own two, made a total of four Uranian satellites.[66] That number had been confirmed in 1875 by astronomers in Washington, but even though the number had been subsequently adopted as the expression of the truth, Sharp, like Saint Thomas, only believed what he had seen with his own eyes.

After long hours of examination, however, he was obliged to yield to the evidence and recognize that the astronomers of Washington had seen correctly through their huge 66-centimeter equatorial. He therefore inscribe in his notebook the vital statistics of the four satellites, conserving the names given to them by terrestrial astronomers, and established their distances from the planet by taking as extreme points their centers and that of Uranus: Ariel 49,000 leagues; Umbriel 60,000; Titania 112,500; Oberon 150,000. Once that was done nothing was easier than to calculate the duration of their revolution around the planet, and these are the results that he obtained, in terrestrial 24-hour days: Ariel 2 days 12 hours 29 minutes 21 seconds; Umbriel 4 days 3 hours 28 minutes 7 seconds; Titania 8 days 16 hours 56 minutes 26 seconds; Oberon 13 days 11 hours 6 minutes 55 seconds.

One of the new and particularly interesting aspects presented by this study was the dimensions of the satellites. If Sharp had experienced real difficulties in catching the planet itself in the field of his telescope at Pulkova Observatory, the same reasons had made it effectively impossible for him to obtain any exact perception of the four mathematical points that the satellites represented. Only after months of painstaking and obstinate observation had he been able to establish the preceding data, checked and confirmed from his cometary fragment. An obsession had seized him thereafter: to augment those data with the dimensions and masses of the Uranian satellites—but in that mad mission he had wasted his time and exhausted his eyes in vain.

Close as he now was to the Uranian system, that work became mere child's play, and it only took him ten minutes to recognize that Ariel had a diameter of 500 kilometers. As for the last, which seemed to him to be the largest, it sub-

[66] William Lassell (1799-1880) discovered Ariel and Umbriel in 1851, which would surely not have escaped Herschel's notice had he actually seen any more satellites than Titania and Oberon, the only two of the six he claimed that were evident to other contemporary astronomers. Late 20th century space missions have increased the number of known satellites of Uranus to 21, but the rest are too small for Herschel to have glimpsed them.

tended an arc of 1200 kilometers.[67] Without being of phenomenal dimensions, these four globes were therefore larger than a considerable number of the minor planets orbiting between Mars and Jupiter. Either by virtue of its size or its specific composition, Oberon appeared to present a particular topography, strewn with luminous points whose nature he strove to determine. Four days he remained still, his eyes fixed on the Uranian satellite with intense curiosity, but the cometary fragment carrying him was moving with such rapidity that observation was more difficult, and Sharp was not able to ascertain whether he was looking at chains of mountains, or even oceans.

When Sharp had irrefutably established the data relating to the dimension, rotation and mass of the satellites of Uranus, he returned his attention to the planet itself to continue the study he had begun. Extrapolating from the known to the unknown, using as bases what he knew about the satellites, he was then able to establish the exact mass of the planet, which seemed to him to be five times larger than that of the Earth, which gave the materials making up its crust a density five times less than that of terrestrial materials.

After verifying the calculations of astronomers relative to the orbit traveled by Uranus and having recognized the exactitude of these calculations, he recorded the following figures: nearest distance to the Sun (perihelion) 675,000,000 leagues; mean distance 710,000,000; greatest distance (aphelion) 742,000,000. Although these recent observations did not teach him anything new, only confirming what he already knew about the planet, the figures plunged him into a profound astonishment. Uranus was, therefore, 67,000,000 leagues closer to the Sun at its perihelion than at its aphelion, which caused its distance from the Earth's orbit to vary from 638,000,000 to 705,000,000 leagues. A difference of 67,000,000 leagues! What a singular experience the life of Uranian humankind must me, assuming that Herschel's planet had arrived at a point sufficient for it to be the abode of any humankind!

The ex-permanent secretary computed, in long reveries, the bizarre conformation of these imaginary inhabitants of Uranus, constrained to pass through such terrible and profound changes in temperature, although these changes would not occur without transition, as on the Moon—quite the contrary.

Sharp calculated, with ever-increasing surprise—even though he already knew the detail in question—the slowness of Uranus' movement in its orbit. A few minutes of observation sufficed for him to establish that the planet's

[67] Some text is evidently omitted here, as the narrative voice seems to assume subsequently that it has recorded the dimensions of all four Uranian satellites rather than only two. Presumably, the missing text was located between "subtended an arc" and "of 1200 kilometers," as that sentence does not make sense, and was omitted by virtue of a transcription error. The estimates that do survive are less accurate than most of those featured in the text—understandably, given the difficulty of observing the satellites.

progress was effectuated at a rate of 7500 meters a second, or 144,700 leagues per day, with the result that, in order to complete its orbit—whose diameter was 1,500,000,000 leagues and its length 400,000,000 leagues—the planet took no less than 40,668 terrestrial days, or 84 of our years.[68]

In truth, the Uranians had plenty of time to acclimatize themselves to new seasons! Then again, did seasons really exist on Uranus? Or, at least, if they existed, was it really solar heat that produced them? What effect could solar heat have at such a distance?

The whim took Sharp to resolve this question, which was more interesting to his own curiosity than to science. It was, in any case, simple to resolve. Uranus was 19 times further away from the Sun than Earth; it followed logically that the diameter of the Sun, seen from Uranus, was 19 times smaller than that seen from Earth, so that the central star offered the former planet a disk 390 times smaller than the second.[69] The inevitable result is that solar heat is 390 times weaker.

Measured by Fedor Sharp's micrometer, the solar disk offered a diameter of one minute 40 seconds, and the ex-permanent secretary wrote in his notebook that the Uranians received light from the central star equal to that which 1584 Moons would have sent them. Was that heat sufficient to develop and support life on the planet's surface? That was the problem, simultaneously scientific and philosophical, that Sharp posed himself. Was it not more logical to admit that Uranus, like other celestial realms, obtained the heat necessary to its humanity internally?

To elucidate this point, the ex-permanent secretary of the Academy of Sciences devoted himself to a profound study of the Uranian atmosphere. He attempted to analyze the atmosphere by means of his spectroscope. At first, his observations went well. One by one, he found traces of certain constitutive elements he had identified in the atmosphere of Jupiter. Suddenly, however, when he thought he was within reach of his goal, he discovered rays that it was impossible for him to assimilate into those furnished by terrestrial astronomy. They were unknown nuances, resulting from new compounds that his knowledge of physics, though profound, could not elucidate.

---

68 The figures in this paragraph are badly scrambled; the arithmetical operations are mistaken as they stand, and the numbers contained therein defy simple correction—although the figure given as 40,668 should presumably be 30,668, which is not so very far removed from the actual duration of Uranus' year, or from 80 terrestrial years. I have cut a superfluous terminal sentence which makes no sense at all.

69 This calculation, too, appears to be mistaken, unless "19" is an approximation, so that the actual figure being squared in order to achieve 390 is a fraction higher.

At first he thought that the relentless study to which he had devoted himself for several days running had enfeebled his sight, and he prescribed himself absolute rest for a few hours. It would certainly cost him the casual loss of precious time, but he resigned himself to it, thinking how abundantly the sacrifice might be recompensed if he succeeded in elucidating a question of such interest to astronomy.

He let several days pass—several local days, that is; which, it will be recalled, only measured two hours and 26 minutes. Then, feeling that his mind was calmer and his eyes well rested, he recommenced his observations—but with no more success, alas, than before. The same disconcerting rays were still present in the Uranian spectrum. Five times, six times, 20 times over he began again, always with the same result. He renounced his spectroscopic studies then, and wrote in his notebook that the atmosphere of Uranus contained gases that do not exist on our planet.

The cometary fragment carrying him continued its rapid course through space, like a stone launched from some giant's sling; for its own part, Uranus followed its orbit in a direction contrary to that of the bolide, with the result that the micrometer measured a significant diminution of the plant's diameter every day. Before long, it was lost in the depths of the skies.

By virtue of patient tenacity and scrupulous attention, the ex-permanent secretary of the St. Petersburg Academy of Sciences had succeeded in discovering a few small patches on the Uranian disk. At first, he thought they were clouds floating in the atmosphere, but he was soon able to convince himself that what he was perceiving were features of the planet's actual surface—and his joy was great, for, thanks to that circumstance, it would be possible for him to establish the exact duration of the Uranian day. That calculation not having been made exactly by any terrestrial astronomer, he thought that, once he had returned to his native planet, he ought to be able to obtain great profit and glory therefrom.

Two days of uninterrupted observation permitted him to add to his notes that the duration of the Uranian day was exactly 10 hours 40 minutes 58 seconds.[70]

Have we said that, in the meantime, Sharp had checked the exactitude of the scientific data concerning the orbit of Uranus, relative to the plane of the ecliptic in which the Earth moves? The two great peculiarities of Uranus, which distinguish that planet from all its heavenly sisters, are the inclination of its rotational axis and the motion of its satellites.

The axis around which Uranus moves is inclined to the plane of the ecliptic by no less than 76 degrees, while that of the Earth is only inclined by 29 degrees and that of Venus 55. On one veritably inspired page, Fedor Sharp departed

---

[70] This guess proved wide off the mark; Uranus' actual period of rotation is 17.2 hours.

from that observation to launch into astronomical and philosophical considerations full of profundity, on the subject of what he called "an inverted world."

The reader will grant us leave us not to descend into the depths of Fedor Sharp's philosophy—he would get more benefit from descending into a mine-shaft without a lamp, and would certainly find himself more at home there than in the midst of the contorted and incomprehensible pathos of the ex-secretary of the Academy of Sciences. We who have the gift of ubiquity, however, can read over the scientist's shoulder and will choose from the lines with which he blackened his notebooks those whose scientific substance might interest the reader:

75 degrees of inclination! What strange things those few words contain! A singular sight, that of the Sun as seen from the planet! For Uranian humankind, the central star appears to turn from Occident to Orient instead of from Orient to Occident.

A few lines devoted to the moral consequences of such a state of things, then:

During the course of the long Uranian year, the Sun must draw away to the latitude of the 76th degree. What would Terrans say if the Sun suddenly abandoned Africa and the Tropics to go and melt the ices of Greenland? And you, Parisians, would you be astonished if the Sun, deserting your temperate regions, emigrated toward the pole in order to turn about it without ever setting during a 21-year summer, to remain invisible thereafter for a winter of the same duration?

Passing on to the satellites, Fedor Sharp wrote:

They rotate in the direction of the equator, but by reason of that equator's inclination to the plane of the orbit, they move in a plane almost perpendicular to that in which the planet moves—and, contrariwise to all the other satellites in the planetary system, turn from east to west.

Carried away by enthusiasm, Sharp added:

Oh, why do spirits—good or evil—no longer exist, who might lift me with their wings and take me to land on that strange world?

It was, to be sure, largely curiosity that moved him to this invocation. Sharp, as we have said, was a scientist, and his actions were motivated, in great part, by the purpose of lifting the mysterious veil enveloping the worlds of the heavens. While that curiosity was unmixed and purely scientific in Ossipoff's case, however—Selena's father would willingly have given his life to possess omniscience, if only for five minutes—in Sharp's case, by contrast, it had a practical end. He would not have cried, like his colleague in the Academy of Sciences: "To know, and to die afterwards, if necessary!" He thought it preferable to know, because profit and glory flow from science.

Thus, after having written the enthusiastic avowal mentioned above, he put down his pen, folded his arms, rested his head on the back of his armchair, and devoted himself to reflection.

His reflections did not last long, and their result was betrayed by a grimace. No, decidedly, a sojourn on Uranus would only be pleasant in parts: a calendar of 60,000 days, an almost invisible Sun moving backwards through the thick clouds of an unknown atmosphere, moons with strange and incorrect manners—no, all that would definitely not tend to make him happy. Better the Earth, with the triumph that awaited him there.

And under the empire of that thought, he got to his feet, took up his telescope, changed its position and aimed it into space to search for his native planet. He did that mechanically, then shrugged his shoulders and smiled at his forgetfulness. How could he possibly perceive the Earth, so tiny that it ought to be invisible, so close to the Sun as to be lost in its radiation? Similarly for Mercury, Venus and Mars—as for Jupiter, after searching hard for it, Sharp discovered it, but had trouble recognizing it, so small was its disk and so feeble its light. It was the same for Saturn, which he distinguished from other stars solely because of its pallor—for, presenting only a half-disk, the "celestial marvel" only sent the Uranians an eighth of the light that the Earth received therefrom. As for Neptune, if the astronomer had not contrived to establish its position mathematically by means of a series of calculations, nothing would have distinguished it from other stars scintillating in space.

When Sharp aimed his telescope at Uranus again, the planet had disappeared. He released a profound sigh then, thinking fearfully of the voyage full of monotony that remained for him to accomplish. From now on, he would streak through the sidereal desert without skirting the slightest stellar oasis at which he might rest and refresh his mind.

For him, the days went by with desperate slowness; he divided his time between reading volumes that he knew by heart, the collation of his travel notes, and walks, which the exiguity of the worldlet on which he was living necessarily rendered short. By night he slept little, and was even constrained to employ an opiate draught to force sleep to numb his limbs and his thoughts. With all his might he appealed for any event, however dangerous, that might draw him out of the sort of cerebral and moral catalepsy into which he intelligence threatened to sink.

As if God had heard his appeal, an issue of the *Revue astronomique* that he had neglected until then fell into the scientist's hands one evening and he began to leaf through it for lack of occupation. Suddenly, he uttered an exclamation and sat up straight, his face animated, his eyes vibrant and his cheeks enflamed. The journal contained a long article on he asteroidal current that traced an immense orbit through space between Neptune and the Earth.

The cometary fragment had to pass through this current in order to reach the Earth—and during that crossing, something might happen. It was a danger—perhaps a mortal one! At the same time, though, for Fedor Sharp, it was a motive for shaking off the lethargy into which he had lapsed, and, from that moment on, he plunged himself into fantastic calculations designed to anticipate the exact moment at which he would penetrate the current.

It was in the very midst of these calculations that a formidable shock had occurred, making the shell shudder on the summit of the Mercurian hill that served as its base.

For a moment, Sharp had thought that it was the final catastrophe, resulting from the encounter of the worldlet that carried him with one of the corpuscles of the asteroidal river; almost immediately, though, under the influenced of the reaction to the impact, he had been jerked out of his armchair and thrown on to the floor, where he had remained for several minutes, stunned.

When he came round, his first impulse was to run to the porthole to observe the disasters occasioned by that formidable collision. Nothing seemed to have changed. He consulted his instruments. The fragment of cometary wreckage had not deviated by an inch from its course toward the terrestrial orbit, which it was following faithfully.

That seemed prodigious to Fedor Sharp, who rubbed his eyes energetically to convince himself that he was not dreaming. His tipped-up armchair, his overturned table and his disordered bookcase were there to prove to him that he was not the victim of a hallucination. There had certainly been an impact—and perhaps, by taking a tour of the worldlet, he would obtain evident proof of it.

It was then that, although it was still dark, he had put on his respirol and departed in haste on a mission of discovery.

We have seen, in the preceding chapter, how absolutely negative the results of his search had been, and how Fedor Sharp, almost asphyxiated, had only been able to get back to his metallic habitation with the greatest difficulty.

When he had returned to his senses, the ex-permanent secretary of the Academy of Sciences fell into a profound meditation, absorbed by the initially-insoluble problem. An impact had taken place—that was undeniable—but how could it have happened without leaving any trace? Since he had been living on this minuscule piece of wreckage, he had made enough tours to know every one of its nooks and crannies, and if any change, however small it might be, had been produced on its surface, he would have noticed it right away. But there was nothing—absolutely nothing.

He paced up and down in his narrow laboratory, turning round repeatedly, just as he was turning the question around and around in his mind: how could it have happened?

Suddenly, he stopped short in mid-stride, uttered a dull exclamation, slapped his forehead and exclaimed: "Eureka!" He had just recalled the principle of physics according to which the instantaneous arrest of movement engenders heat.

He ran to his work-table and wrote a few lines in his notebook, traced in a feverish hand:

Today, February 5 on the terrestrial calendar, awakened by powerful shock resulting from a collision with one of the corpuscles of the asteroidal current. Search of item of wreckage completely fruitless. Presume that the bolide encountered has penetrated the fragment that bears me deeply enough for the cometary crust, vitrified by heat, to have closed over it again, like the glaze that coats aeroliths.

And he added these words, which proved how deeply-rooted in his soul was the hope of getting back to his native planet safe and sound:

To be verified on my return to Earth.

Chapter LII
Like Light [71]

"Ah!"

At that exclamation, uttered in an anxious and pathetic voice, Fricoulet sat up in his hammock and perceived the Comte de Flammermont sitting on the edge of his own, his eyes haggard, his face pale and bathed in sweat, and his limbs all a-tremble.

"What's the matter?" asked the engineer, anxiously, running to his friend's bedside. "Are you ill?"

The young Comte shook his head, and looked at Fricoulet as if he had not recognized him at first; then his gaze mad a tour of his surroundings, examining every object with increasing astonishment. Finally, he passed both hands over his forehead, as if to gather his memories, and burst into loud laughter. "God!" he said, jumping down to the floor. "What a beast of a dream I've just had!"

Fricoulet's careworn face cleared. "That cry, then...?" he said.

"Did I cry out?" asked Gontran. "It doesn't surprise me. I was frightened enough." And he added; "It's so stupid...dreaming..."

"I don't agree. There's much that's pleasant therein. So, while you were suffering nightmares, I was dreaming...in a fashion that wasn't at all disagreeable...and you interrupted me at a lovely moment..."

At this point, we ask permission to open a parenthesis indispensable to the comprehension of the present chapter.

What is dreaming?

It is a faculty the human mind possesses of, so to speak, duplicating itself and living a special life—a veritable spiritual life, disengaged from the fleshy envelope, free of the material ties that weigh it down.

During sleep, the mind continues the work begun in the waking state, or resumes a train of thought whose course has been momentarily interrupted by the somnolence of the body. Existence continues veritably, without any loss of continuity. The sleeper's brain is disengaged from all physical preoccupation, being, in a sense, refined—or, to put it better, having its strength and acuity pushed to the ultimate power—and sometimes finds solutions in the sleep-state to important questions insoluble in the waking state. It may also bring to fruition unrealizable projects conceived and declared impossible a few hours before.

---

[71] The title of this chapter—"*Comme la lumière*" in French—is a trifle gnomic, but if one were to Latinize the second term it would be translatable as "Like *Lumen,*" signifying that the narrative becomes, from this point on, like Camille Flammarion's *Lumen*, a visionary fantasy.

It was under the empire of the mysterious and magical phenomenon of dreaming that our heroes had fallen while they were lying side by side on the floor of their vehicle in a lethargic state akin to death. And while their cataleptically-afflicted flesh resumed the route to their native planet, along with the cometary fragment in which they were, so to speak, buried—without their having any consciousness of the fact—their minds, disengaged from the bonds of matter, continued the voyage that they would logically have accomplished without the accident that had so unexpectedly stopped the *Eclair* in its tracks.

Having firmly established that, we shall close the parenthesis opened a few lines above, and resume the dialogue of the two drowsy voyagers at the point at which we interrupted it.

"My word, my dear Alcide," said the Comte de Flammermont. "I owe you my apologies; the existence we lead in this lithium cage is so desperately dull and monotonous that, in truth, when Providence sends you a dream, however slightly enjoyable..."

"More than enjoyable, my dear chap—marvelous, truly marvelous..."

"And you didn't want me in it?"

"You're joking...but you gave me quite a fright when you cried out..."

"If you'd been in my place, you'd undoubtedly have cried out, just like me." Gontran's shoulders shook. "Brrr," he said. "I'm still shuddering, just thinking about it."

"What was happening, then?"

"Imagine that I was on watch and that, to distract myself, I was looking out of one of the portholes in the engine-room, when, all of a sudden, an enormous, monstrous body appeared in the depths of space, racing toward us with lightning rapidity. I hurled myself toward the tiller, and pressed down on it with all my strength...but I was wasting my time. The vehicle continued in a straight line, refusing to obey, flying toward the bolide like an arrow, as if it were attracted to it by an invisible magnet."

While telling this story, the young Comte was re-experiencing all the anguish of his frightful nightmare, for his features had contracted and a light sweat was forming on his forehead. "The most horrible thing," he continued, "was that, despite all my efforts, I couldn't get out of the engine-room. It was as if I were nailed down beside the machinery, incapable of taking a step. I tried to call for help...my lips opened, but my throat was so tightened by terror that no sound could get out...and we were moving forward, still moving forward. Suddenly, the impact took place, with a frightful noise. The apparatus was flattened against the bolide like a bug that has crashed into a tree in the course of its maddened flight...then everything went black...and it was doubtless then that I uttered the scream that woke you up."

Fricoulet started laughing, on seeing Flammermont feeling himself anxiously and murmuring: "I had such a strong impression of the catastrophe that I feel as if my entire body has been bent out of shape, and I'm amazed to find my limbs intact."

"Well, personally," said the engineer in his turn, "I dreamed the opposite: while you were witnessing the destruction of the *Eclair*, I found a means of accelerating its progress..."

"Technology, always technology!" said Gontran, jokingly.

"Technology, my dear chap, is the most beautiful conquest of humankind," Fricoulet said—and added, as the young Comte shrugged his shoulders: "In any case, if anyone should disdain it, it's not you."

With a sardonic laugh, Flammermont replied: "I doubt that Monsieur Ossipoff would agree with you about that—in his eyes, astronomy prevails over all other human knowledge."

"Monsieur Ossipoff's opinion is of little importance to me—but with respect to you, I will remark that your disdain for technology appears to me to result from a character inclined to ingratitude."

"Because?"

"Because it's technology that has got you out of all the tight spots into which, until now, astronomy has got you—and because it's technology, again, that will save you now..."

"How's that?"

"By permitting me, as I said just now, to increase the progress of our apparatus significantly."

"But, my poor friend," said Gontran, incredulously, "you're forgetting that you dreamed this marvelous system."

"My dear chap," the engineer replied. "Dreams contain more reality than you think, and the proof..." Fricoulet interrupted himself to jot down a few calculations in his notebook, which he then held out to his friend mockingly.

"What's that?" groaned Flammermont, pushing away the engineer's notebook with his hand.

"It's the proof," said the latter, "that the 80,000 meters a second we're traveling—which is 75,000 leagues an hour—could be transformed into 75,000 leagues...per second."

"But that's sheer madness!" cried a voice from behind Fricoulet.

The latter turned round and found himself face to face with Ossipoff, who had emerged from his cabin. "It's madness!" the old scientist repeated.

Fricoulet looked at him mockingly. "Are you quite certain of what you're saying?" he asked.

"It seems to me that we've obtained the maximum velocity that electricity can give us."

"It certainly seems so to you, my dear Monsieur," the engineer replied, "for two reasons. The first is that, as you just said, quite rightly, electricity has given us the maximum speed that it is capable of giving us. The second reason is...that our supply of electricity is exhausted."

These words were greeted with the same terrified exclamation, emerging at the same time, from the mouths of Ossipoff and Flammermont. "Then we're doomed!"

"You mean, we would be, if I hadn't found this means."

The old scientist looked at the engineer incredulously. "And this marvelous means permits you to do without electricity?"

"Absolutely."

"In that case, what force drives your motor?"

"I don't need the motor."

"But what about the helix?"

"I don't need the helix."

Ossipoff took a step back, uttering an "Oh!" of bewilderment. As for Gontran, he did not have eyes wide enough to stare at his friend.

"I was right," murmured the old man. "It's madness!"

"It is, indeed, madness," Flammermont could not help saying in his turn.

"If you let me explain," the engineer riposted, calmly, "You'll be able to categorize me in full knowledge of the cause. In brief, this is it: I put the central tube in which the helix presently revolves in communication with one of our reservoirs of compressed air, whose release will procure us a rapidity superior to that of lightning."

Gontran tugged at his moustache pensively and Ossipoff stroked his beard energetically—which was, in him, an indication of profound meditation. "Then," he murmured, softly, as if taking to himself, "we'd advance by the force of reaction."

"Precisely. Well, what do you think of my means?"

Before the old man had time to reply, Flammermont exclaimed: "Personally, I think it's impracticable."

"Because?"

"Because, before thinking of going forward, it's necessary to think of staying alive."

"Well?"

"Well, if we use our provision of air to power our vehicle, what will power our lungs?"

The engineer smiled triumphantly and put his hand on the young Comte's shoulder. "Fear not," he said. "Your lungs will, even so, have what they need to sustain them abundantly. I'm going much further. I intend that, once returned to Earth, we'll be able to enable all the curious listeners to whom we'll recount our adventures to breathe at a rate of one cubic meter per person."

Ossipoff had taken Fricoulet's notebook and buried himself in a long series of calculations, whose equations were piled up one on top of another. "If I'm not mistaken," he said, "we could reach Uranus in two hours."

"Of course! At a rate of 75 leagues a second..."

"And we'd be at Neptune in four hours."

Seeing that the old scientist was taking the engineer's impracticable project seriously, Flammermont opened his eyes wide. "In that case," he said, "how long would it take us, under these conditions, to return to Earth?"

Before Fricoulet could open his mouth, Ossipoff replied: "No more than seven hours."

Flammermont looked at the old man in bewilderment, wondering whether he had suddenly gone mad...or whether he was mocking him. At the sight of Ossipoff's serious expression, however, he was obliged to yield to the evidence and accept that the other was speaking seriously. "Seven hours," he murmured. "Seven hours!"

Fricoulet had taken his notebook from the old scientist's hands. After casting an eye over it, he said: "I think you've made an error, Monsieur Ossipoff."

"What's that?"

"It's only five hours that we need, for the distance from Neptune to Earth is no more than a billion leagues. Now, at a rate of 75,000 leagues a second…"

"Agreed—but in the seven hours I mentioned, I was including the time necessary to search for and study Hyperion."

At that name, Gontran opened his eyes wide. Involuntarily, he was about to utter an astonished exclamation when a voice whispered softly in his ear: "It's the outermost planet of the Solar System."

The outermost planet of the Solar System! When he heard these words, Gontran was on the point of protesting. From his rapid and distracted reading of *Les Continents célestes* he had retained the impression that the limits of the Solar System were traced by Neptune's orbit—and now they were talking to him about Hyperion! In truth, though, that was a matter of astronomy. To hell with Hyperion and all the rest! In 12 days, he would see the Earth again; in 12 days he would have the banns posted at the Town Hall of the eighth arrondissement, and two week after that…

Such an imminent prospect of a happiness that had, for such a long time, vanished as soon as he touched it with his fingertip, chased away from his thoughts all the discouragement, disappointment, frustration and bitterness of which his life had been so full for months. He was only thinking of one thing now: that the eternal engagement would come to an end, that the day of the marriage was not far off, that he loved Selena more than ever, and that Selena would finally become his wife. He turned round, seized the young woman's hands in his, and looked at her with a gaze full of affection. "Oh, my love!" he murmured. They were the only words that his emotion permitted him to pronounce, at first.

Mademoiselle Ossipoff, who had not heard Fricoulet's revelations, did not understand her fiancé's emotion at all, and looked at him with an astonishment all the greater because—as we have mentioned in the preceding chapters—the young Comte's humor had grown more embittered with every new delay caused by Ossipof's incessantly-unsatisfied curiosity. Irritated by the father, he had been gradually drawing apart from the daughter. She was, therefore, quite astonished—but, deep down, a great joy swelled her heart. It had been such a long time since her fiancé had squeezed her hands so tenderly, such a long time since his voice had had such an affectionate intonation. A teardrop even formed at the tips of her long lashes—a tear of happiness, the scintillation of which Flammermont caught, the cause of which he understood, and which gave birth in his soul to a cruel remorse with regard to his brusque and rancorous attitude of the last few weeks. "What's happened, then, Gontran?" Mademoiselle Ossipoff asked, with a smile that betrayed her joy and pardoned the ingrate.

He squeezed her hands more emotionally still, and murmured: "What's happened, my dear Selena, "is that happiness, which fled from us such a long time ago, is finally allowing itself to be attained."

"What do you mean?"

"I mean that you'll be the Comtesse de Flammermont within a month."

The young woman looked at her fiancé as if she were looking at a madman; then her eyes went to her father, to interrogate him. At that moment, however, Ossipoff was much too busy checking Fricoulet's calculations to pay attention to his daughter—so Selena addressed herself to the engineer himself, who was looking at the two fiancés with a mocking expression. "Gontran tells me," she said, "that we're going to return to Earth?"

"Gontran is right Mademoiselle," Fricoulet replied, mockingly. "Tonight, like Joan of Arc, I have had a vision...and that vision will save us."

Mademoiselle Ossipoff held her hand out to the engineer. "Monsieur Fricoulet," she said, "it's to you that we owe our happiness."

The young man frowned slightly. "If it's from that viewpoint that you're thanking me, Mademoiselle," he replied, in a sullen tone, "you're mistaken—for I'm afraid that you'll only reproach me later for having snatched you away from the sidereal desert to return you to your native planet."

"Your ideas on marriage again?" the Comte riposted.

Fricoulet shook his head. "Happiness, in conjugal matters," he pronounced, sententiously, "can only result from an absolute compatibility of spouses."

"Do we lack that, then?"

"My dear chap, astronomy and diplomacy can never march in step." And, leaning close to Gontran's ear, he pointed with a tragicomic gesture to Ossipoff, who was still scribbling. "Look at him, fool," he said. "Do you believe, frankly, that you can be the son-in-law that a man like that requires?"

Gontran laughed. "As a son-in-law," he replied, "I might perhaps have my faults, but I think I have within me the stuff of which admirable husbands are made."

Fricoulet shrugged. "Dangerous theories," he muttered. "A man is imprudent who plays the part of the unexpected in a lottery like that of marriage. If I were a true friend..." He stopped, and fixed the Comte with a singular stare.

"Well," said Gontran, "if you were a true friend, what would you do?"

"I'd demand, before putting my plan into action, that you make a vow of celibacy. That way, I wouldn't have to reproach myself later for being the cause of your unhappiness."

Flammermont shrugged his shoulders. "You're mad!" he said.

The engineer was doubtless about to reply when a frightful racket was heard in the cabin that served as Farenheit's cell.

"Oh, good!" groaned the young Comte. "There's that devil of a Yankee, up to his tricks again." And he went to the door in order to impose silence on the prisoner by the usual method—which is to say, kicking the door loudly.

To his great surprise, however, the racket suddenly ceased, and the American's voice was raised, politely asking: "Is that you, Monsieur Fricoulet?"

Gontran turned to his friend. "Do you hear?" he whispered. "He's talking to you."

The engineer came forward in his turn. "Is it me you want, Mr. Farenheit?" he said.

"Yes—I want to tell you something."

"Go on—I'm listening."

"No, I can't talk like this—open the door."

"Not in this lifetime," cried Flammermont. "You'd only resume your stupidities."

"I'm no longer ill," replied the American, in a soft voice. "I swear that I'll be reasonable."

Gontran whispered in Fricoulet's ear: "There are no madmen worse than those who pretend not to be."

"If he were cured, though," murmured Mademoiselle Ossipoff, moved to pity, "it's sad to be locked up in there, like a ferocious beast in its cage..."

"I don't say any different—but remember that our pity might cost us our lives..."

"Bah!" said the engineer. "When one's forewarned..." And, gesturing to the other two to stand aside, he opened the door.

Immediately, the prisoner launched himself out of his cabin and fell upon Fricoulet—who, surprised by the impact, fell over, dragging him down with him. Only heeding his courage, Flamermont leapt on the American and, with the aid of Fricoulet—who had leapt to his feet—held him captive.

They did not have any difficulty doing so; Farenheit did not make a movement, abandoning the wrists to which they were clinging to their care without resistance.

"That's what you call being reasonable!" Fricoulet complained.

"I didn't mean to do you any harm," the American replied, seemingly quite confused.

"On the contrary, I suppose?" riposted the engineer, skeptically.

"I wanted to embrace you."

Fricoulet started in surprise while Gontran, addressing Selena, put his index finger to his forehead to indicate that, in his opinion, the Yankee was still mentally unbalanced. With a wink, Fricoulet instructed the Comte, who was ready to shut the American up in his cabin again, to be gentle. "I'm certainly very touched by this manifestation of affection, my dear Mr. Farenheit," he said, "but for what reason did you want to embrace me?"

"Because you're a great man."

"A great man! Me!"

"Yes, a great man," cried Farenheit, excitedly. "The greatest I know, not only in the entire world but in the United States!"

"At least explain why."

"Because you've found the means to get me back to New York, when *he* wanted to make me drag my miserable bones through all his diabolical planets." With an expressive gesture of the head he indicated Ossipoff. Then, disengaging himself abruptly from Gontran's grip, he threw his arms around the engineer's neck and kissed him on both cheeks, before he had time to react. Afterwards, in a vibrant and tender voice, he said: "When I think that, thanks to you, I'm going to see the pavements of Fifth Avenue, and my shareholders, and he Eccentric Club, and—ah, I promise you that my first concern will be to raise of bronze statue to you in the main square on New York..."

"You're too kind, Mr. Farenheit. Such a slender service as this isn't worth the trouble of your going to the expense..."

"How unfortunate it is," the American went on, "that the Heavens have never blessed my union with Mrs. Farenheit!"

Fricoulet raised his eyebrows in amazement.

"If only I had a daughter," the Yankee added, "it's with the greatest joy that I'd give you her hand."

The engineer pulled a face. *And it's with the greatest joy that I'd refuse*, he thought. Aloud, he said: "So you heard our conversation just now?"

"At first, I could only hear it. For several days I've felt less ill. My head seemed to me to be more liberated, my thoughts clearer, linking up with more logic—and, at the same time, my memory came back. Then, suddenly, certain words in your conversation struck my ears in a singular fashion. The fog darkening my brain dissipated as if by magic, and I understood. You were talking about the possibility of returning to Earth in a few days, and complete lucidity returned." Then, seizing the engineer's hands again, he shook them forcefully, saying: "You're a great man!"

Fricoulet nodded his head. "That's good, that's good," he said, laughing. "You can tell me that in New York. For the moment, we have a lot to do." Going over to Ossipoff, who was still engaged in checking the engineer's calculations, he said: "Well? Is it all right?"

"In my opinion, yes. Would you like to see, my dear Gontran?"

He held out the notebook to the young Comte, who refused it with a dignified gesture, saying: "I certainly have no need to check it after you."

"In that case," said the engineer, "to work."

"What do we have to do?"

"Get rid of the helix and the motor, then install the conduits for the compressed air."

Ossipoff shook his head. "Get rid of the helix," he muttered. "That's easy to say, but how?"

"Very simply," replied the engineer. He went to the lever controlling the rudder. "Get ready," he said. "I'll maneuver in such a way as to make the apparatus stand up vertically; prepare to change position."

Gradually, he moved the lever, and the *Eclair*, quitting its horizontal position, rose up on its rear end like a horse rearing up.

"There," said the engineer, after a few seconds. "That's done. Now, by means of this other lever, which communicates with the central tube, I'll unfasten the pivots of the propeller shaft, and the helix will fall away in one piece into empty space. As for the motor, we only have to open the manhole a little to throw it out of the vehicle. We'll lose a few cubic meters of air, but we'll be broadly compensated by the lightness we'll acquire."

"And then?"

"Then we'll set up the pipes conducting the compressed air to the central tube." While speaking, Fricoulet maneuvered a lever set in a corner of the engine-room and the voyagers distinctly heard a sort of grating sound in the very center of the vehicle. Suddenly, the *Eclair*'s hull quivered, and seemed to launch into space with a formidable bound.

"By God!" muttered Farenheit, clinging to the wall. "What's happening?"

"Simply what happens to a de-ballasted balloon."

"What! The helix...?"

"The helix is already transformed into a new type of corpuscle; now let's go on to the motor."

Fricoulet, armed with a lever, was about to attack the apparatus when Gontran put a hand on his arm. "Have you thought of one thing?"

"What?"

"That the surprising velocity of which you speak must surely be impossible in the bosom of the corpuscular ring where we are. The asteroids will probably put up a considerable resistance...who knows whether that resistance might even be enough to nullify our impulsion?"

Fricoulet stuck out his lips in a dubious moue. "It's doubtful," he murmured.

"But if it were the case..."

"Well, if that happens, we'll be able to take care of it simply by abandoning the asteroidal current, which will become more of a hindrance than a help."

Gontran threw up his arms. "And navigate in the void! But that's not possible!"

"It's necessary, however, that it becomes...possible. Anyway, at so great a speed, space will be dense enough to furnish us with a point of support." Seeing that the young Comte did not appear to understand, he continued: "You know very well that the void of space is not an absolute vacuum—which, being impossible to produce, is, in any case, a meaningless phrase. Space is furrowed in every direction by a quantity of cosmic atoms, the debris of destroyed worlds, and these atoms might become an effective point of support...on condition that our speed is excessive...."

On hearing these words, Ossipoff shivered and moved closer to the engineer. "So," he said, with a certain anxiety in his voice, "you think that the *Eclair* might be able to fly rapidly enough to be able to quit the corpuscular river?"

"I don't think it—I'm certain of it."

The old man's face lit up. "Then I was speaking the truth just now, without knowing it, when I talked about going to visit Hyperion?"

Fricoulet sniggered. "Assuredly," he replied. "Nothing would be easier than going to see Hyperion—but, just as making jugged hare requires a hare, in order to visit a planet, it must exist."

A surge of blood reddened the old man's cheeks. Folding his arms across his chest, he asked indignantly: "Dare you claim that Neptune is the extreme point of the Solar System?"

"I make no claims," Fricoulet hastened to reply. "I'm an engineer, not an astronomer—but I've heard it said that Neptune is the outermost planet that man has been able to perceive."

"To what, then, do you attribute the perturbations observed in Neptune's motion, if not to another world, invisible to us, which advances or delays the planet's course according to whether it is in advance of or behind it, and its attraction exerted on one side or the other?"

"I repeat," said the engineer, "that I can't enter into a debate on this subject—but I'd be very obliged if you'd tell me which point of the sky to steer for in order to find this famous transneptunian planet."

The old man hesitated before replying. "The truth," he said, after a few seconds of silence, "is that—thus far—we only have very vague data relating to Hyperion."

The engineer hid a mocking smile. "That being so, when it comes to setting a course for Hyperion, I'll confide the tiller to you and you can direct the *Eclair* wherever seems best...one can't do any better than that."

Ossipoff did not reply, but he looked at the engineer with a furious expression.

Flammermont, who had remained silent until then, intervened. "It seems to me," he said, "that this discussion is entirely Platonic."

"Because?" Fricoulet interrogated.

"Because the corpuscular river whose current we're descending doesn't go beyond the orbit of Uranus."

"But since Monsieur Fricoulet claims that, by imparting a particular velocity to the vehicle, we'll be able to go beyond the river of asteroids and find a point of support in the void, nothing prevents us from going beyond the orbit of Neptune and trying to pierce the mysterious veil that envelops the transneptunian planet." He assumed a vibrant tone. "Think, my son, what glory will be ours if we succeed in resolving that great scientific problem—in replying to the enormous question mark that stands before all terrestrial astronomers!"

"I'm not saying no," stammered Flammermont, in a tone suggestive of the scant extent to which he shared the old scientist's enthusiasm.

The latter continued: "And beyond Hyperion, do you not sense the infinity that attracts you? Don't you want...?"

It was Selena who interrupted him. "But, Father dear, infinity isn't included in our itinerary...."

"Eh? What!" cried Ossipoff. "Can we remain indifferent in the face of all the marvels that fill infinity? What about the stars, the double and triple stellar systems, the nebulas...?"

Farenheit started in veritable alarm. Fricoulet's shoulders shook.

"But, Monsieur Ossipoff," Gontran replied, "your curiosity's thirst is making you forget the reality of things. My friend Alcide told you just now that it was possible to impart a velocity of 75,000 leagues a second to our vehicle—now that's exactly the interval of space covered in the same lapse of time by a ray of light..."

"I know that as well as you do, my dear boy," the old man replied, rather dryly. "What are you driving at?"

"Simply this: that the nearest star to us is situated as a distance 7400 times greater than that which separates Neptune from the Sun, and a ray of light departing from that same star and traveling with a velocity of 75,000 leagues a second..."

"Takes three years and six months to reach us," said Fricoulet, finishing his friend's sentence.

"As for the other stars, nebulas, etc., they're incomparably more distant still. In my opinion, therefore, it's folly to dream of reaching them."

Ossipoff's lips pursed in an ill-humored grimace. "It wouldn't be folly," he said, "if Monsieur Fricoulet could—as he boasted just now—give us infinite velocity."

"Infinite!" protested the engineer. "I'm sorry, but I never said that. I said that I thought we might reach 500,000 leagues per second in the void. With such a speed, it wouldn't take us any longer to go to Alpha Centauri than we took to go from Mars to Saturn."

"That would be prodigious!" murmured Ossipoff, sitting down in a corner, where it did not take him long to fall into profound meditation.

"Fine ideas you've put into his head, with your insane speeds," Gontran muttered in Fricoulet's ear. "He'll take us to the Devil, you'll see."

"Bah!" riposted the engineer. "We're not children, and he won't do anything we don't want."

"May Heaven hear you!" replied Flammermont, shaking his head in an unconvinced manner.

While talking and arguing, however, they had been working. Once the motor and its accessories had been launched into the void through the minimally-opened manhole, the pipes designed to convey compressed air to the central tube—which had originally served to enclose the helix—had been put in place. Then Fricoulet had replaced the vehicle in the horizontal position and had subsequently opened the tap of the compressed air reservoir. Like a racehorse whose jockey applies a crack of the whip, the *Eclair* launched ahead.

"Well?" asked Ossipoff, anxiously.

"Well, my anticipations were correct; we have our 75,000 leagues a second. If you ask me, everyone ought to get a little rest now."

Everyone, including Ossipoff, hastened to follow this advice. A few minutes later, each of them, extended on a hammock, was sound asleep and snoring—including Selena.

The next day, the voyagers were woken up by a cry of despair. Thinking that something was wrong, they leapt out of their hammocks and ran to the engine-room.

Standing in front of his telescope Ossipoff was tearing his hair.

"Father! Dear Father, what's the matter?" asked Selena, all anxiety.

"Uranus…" replied the old man.

"Well, what about Uranus?" said Farenheit.

"Disappeared," replied Ossipoff.

During the few hours that the Terrans had been lying in their hammocks, the planet's orbit has been crossed, and it was this observation that had plunged the old scientist into such profound grief. It was an irreparable misfortune, and the situation would not have changed one iota if Ossipoff had torn out all the hairs that were resisting him.

In any case, a significant incident provided a diversion from his desolation. The corpuscles of the great meteoric current were becoming rarer and more scattered as it progressed, slanting away at a considerable angle. Before long, either the *Eclair* would emerge from the current, or the exhausted flow would no longer be any more able to play the role of point of support than the ambient void.

"My friends," said Fricoulet, who had been monitoring the progress of the apparatus for some time, "the time has come to make a decision."

"What's happening, then?" asked the Terrans gathered around the engineer, in unison.

"The meteoric current has gaps…in a few moments, we'll have reached its aphelion."

Farenheit threw his cap in the air. "En route for Earth, then!" he cried.

Ossipoff's face darkened. "At the aphelion," he murmured.

"I can even add," said Fricoulet, who had moved to a porthole, through which he was looking into space, "that we've reached a dissolution of the continuity of the cosmic ring, and are on the edge of the stellar desert. What shall we do?"

"Let's go on," implored Ossipoff.

"Straight to Earth!" said Gontran and Farenheit, together.

"Hurry up!" insisted the engineer. "In our situation, seconds are worth years."

"My friends, my dear friends," said the old scientist in a suppliant voice. "Do you have the courage to return without having seen Neptune and Hyperion? Gontran, my friend, my son, make me one more sacrifice—and you, my dear Mr. Farenheit, would you like it to be aid, on your return, that an American retreated before the prospect of a journey through the void?"

"Retreated!" cried Farenheit, his self-respect cut to the quick.

"And you, Monsieur Fricoulet—don't you want to put the theory of the effect of your compressed air on space to the proof?"

"Hurry up! Hurry up!" was the engineer's only muttered reply.

"It's a delay," said Gontran.

"Oh, a few days only!"

"It's a detour," said the American in his turn.

"Of about 1,500,000,000 leagues," riposted the old man. "A mere nothing."

Fricoulet tapped his foot. "Well?" he demanded. "What have you decided?" He paraded his gaze in a circle around him, and saw indecision in every physiognomy except Ossipoff's, which bore traces of the greatest anxiety. He took pity on the old man, and cried: "Straight ahead!"

He pressed down on the tiller. The vehicle vibrated momentarily, then turned and exited the asteroidal current. One more second and it was flying through the void, en route for Neptune.

Chapter LIII
In which our voyagers, intending to return to Earth, depart for the infinite.

"Eh? For myself, I tell you again that this is no longer astronomy."

Fricoulet looked at his friend in amazement. "What do you call it, then?"

"By any name you please, other than that. Astronomy consists of examining the celestial universe, of studying the worlds with which it is full...and, if necessary, searching space to discover unknown worlds."

"Well, Le Verrier wasn't doing anything else."

"Never in his life! I don't know that he even put his eye to a telescope in seeking Neptune. Someone said that 'he found Neptune at the tip of his pen'—that's a very good way of putting it."

"He was no less meritorious for that," the engineer replied.

"As a mathematician, perhaps—but as an astronomer, that's different."

Fricoulet laughed. "According to you, then, no one is an astronomer but a man who spends his entire existence with his eye glued to the ocular lens of a meridian or an equatorial?"

"Of course! Unless, in the matter of researching the exact position of a planet on a piece of paper, you find anything to do with astronomy. That proves that Le Verrier was a remarkable force in mathematics, that he juggled figures in an astonishing manner..."

"It's very kind of you to concede him that," the engineer riposted, mockingly.

"But," Gontran went on, "there was no need for him to be an astronomer to devote himself to his prodigious mathematical educations. Any other scientist patient enough to spend 15 years on the trot balancing his columns of figures, as he did, would have done as much."

"For you, then, Le Verrier wasn't an astronomer?"

"I don't want to quarrel about it—nor to steal from the learned company to which Monsieur Ossipoff belongs a glory of which it is proud. In my opinion, the true discoverer of Neptune wasn't the man who assigned it a place in the sky but the one who confirmed its existence."

The engineer moved his shoulders slightly, demonstrating that, although he did not share that opinion, he did not find it unreasonable. "It's certain," he said, "That a good pat of the paternity of Neptune belongs to Bouvard,[72] who was the first to notice certain irregularities in the motion of Uranus in 1821."

"And, in the same way that Saturn's irregularities had led to the conclusion of the existence of Uranus, the singular movement of the latter planet led Bou-

[72] Alexis Bouvard (1767-1843).

vard to decree that beyond the 733,000,000 leagues of Uranus' orbit, there was still something else." These words had been pronounced by Ossipoff, who had left his cabin, attracted by the young men's discussion.

"Yes," declared Gontran, still following his train of thought. "This Bouvard was a great man, and I'm astonished that astronomers have done him the flagrant injustice of attributing the glory that belongs to him to Le Verrier."

Ossipoff pushed his spectacles up on to his forehead—a gesture which, in him, was indicative of great surprise. "A great man," he said, "for having deduced from Uranus's irregularities that Neptune must exist? Pooh!"

"But those irregularities could perfectly well have been produced by another cause than Neptune," Gontran relied.

The old scientist shook his head. "Impossible," he declared.

"Why?"

"You're forgetting Titius's law, my dear friend."

"Titius's law?" stammered Gontran. "Titius's law...."

Fricolet whispered in his ear: "You know—the theory of the minor planets, 4, 7, 10, 16, etc."

Flammermont stated. "Of course!" he continued, immediately, with marvelous self-composure. "The work of Le Verrier was, in this case, greatly simplified, since he only had to look for the planet around the region corresponding to the distance 36 in the progression."

"That's what he did," replied Fricoulet. "Even though his work might have been simplified by that circumstance, however, it was no less frightful—so frightful that, when he announced his results to the Academy of Sciences in Paris on August 31, 1846, the learned academicians hesitated at first to endorse the declaration."

"A month later," Ossipoff went on, "Dr. Galle of the Berlin Observatory, personally invited by Le Verrier to search for his famous planet, found a star in the place indicated that offered thc eye a detectable planetary disk and which was not marked on the map; it was Neptune."

"Will you permit me to make one slight correction to what you just said?" the engineer put in.

Ossipoff frowned. "What?"

"In taking as a basis for his calculations the distance 36 from Titius's law, Le Verrier was mistaken. That made him assign a place to the planet that was incorrect. Galle found that out to his cost; having searched for Neptune for a month on the 326th degree of longitude, he perceived it by the 327th—which put it, in reality, at a distance of 30.[73]

[73] Although the authors have previously been using the conventional notation of the Titius-Bode law which represents Earth's distance as 10, they have switched here to a representation in which Earth's distance equals 1. The figure given as 36 is, however, wrong; the Titius-Bode figure for the trans-Uranian planet being

"Pooh!" said Gontran, lifting his shoulders. "That's an error of scant importance."

Ossipoff's eyes widened behind the lenses of his spectacles. "My dear Gontran," he replied, in a slightly nervous tone, "I understand that the adventures you have undergone have gradually caused you to lose your sense of time and distance; even so, a difference of nearly 60 years in the period of a planet..."

"60 years!"

"Certainly. Le Verrier's calculations, based on the distance 36, gave Neptune an orbit that would have required 217 terrestrial years to complete. Being at the distance 30, the planet takes no more than 165 years to effect its revolution. That's still a fair while."

Farenheit, who was lying asleep on a divan, sat up on his elbow. "Neptune isn't a French planet but an English one."

Fricoulet straightened up. "Why not American, while you're at it?" he muttered.

"Because it's English, having been discovered by an Englishman."

"Which one, if you please?" asked the engineer.

Farenheit shrugged his shoulders. "You're asking too much of me," he replied.

Fricoulet laughed. "You don't even have the discoverer, you see!" he said.

"Mr. Farenheit's right," Ossipoff put in. "While Le Verrier was working on the search for Neptune, a student at Cambridge University on the other side of the Channel, Adams, was also working on a solution to the same problem. Eight months before the French astronomer made his declaration to the Academy of Sciences, the English student wrote to the director of the National Observatory in London to tell him of his discovery."[74]

---

388 or 38.8. The error is copied from p.735 of *Les Terres du ciel*, where it is misrendered in a quotation from Flammarion's own *Astronomie populaire*; presumably, it should have been given as 39. The "actual" figure is much closer, Neptune's mean distance corresponding to a Titius/Bode figure of 300.6 or 30.06.

[74] John Couch Adams (1819-1892) did indeed produce a calculation similar to Le Verrier's (but slightly less accurate)—as reported, in the trunctated version of the story reproduced here, in *Les Terres du ciel*. Adams showed his figures to James Challis, the director of Cambridge Observatory, and tried to show them to the Astronomer Royal, George Airy, but Airy was out when he called and communication between the two by mail broke down. Adams never tried to claim priority for the discovery, but others—moved by nationalistic pride—did so on his behalf, and the heated dispute still generates echoes of controversy today. As with Uranus, the planet had been sighted and its position recorded on previous

"Why, then," asked Fricoulet, "did the director of the National Observatory not hasten to announce such important news to the scientific world?"

Ossipoff raised his arms to the Heavens to declare that it was impossible for him to answer that question.

The engineer clicked his tongue significantly. "It seems to me," he said, "that the light can't have been very bright, to have been thus hidden under a bushel..."

The conversation we have just reported took place in the engine-room, where Fricoulet was on watch, his eye to the lookout telescope and his hand on the wheel controlling the rudder. The *Eclair* was still flying through space with vertiginous rapidity; with every hour that passed, the voyagers were able to observe an increase in the size of the Neptunian disk, whose enormous mass barred the celestial horizon.

It was now possible to perceive, albeit still vaguely, set against the blur of a milky and thick atmosphere, a considerable number of corpuscles moving around the planet in a retrograde sense, following a plane extremely inclined to the ecliptic, just like the satellites of Uranus. Ossipoff, who had noticed these corpuscles some time before thanks to his telescope—the most powerful one aboard—had declared that they were the satellites of Neptune.

"The satellites of Neptune!" exclaimed Fricoulet, to whom the old scientist imparted this discovery. "But I only know of one—the one that Lassell discovered,[75] and which appears on Earth as a star of the 14th magnitude."

"There would be no purpose in making such a voyage," the old man muttered, "if we weren't able, in gong forward, increasingly to lift the veil that hides the mysterious marvels of infinity from Terrestrial eyes. Remember that Neptune's distance from the Sun is 30 times that of the Earth—which is to say, 1,112,000,000 leagues. We're now less than 20,000,000 leagues from the planet, so..."

Fricoulet interrupted him. "Are you quite certain of that distance?" he asked.

Ossipoff took him by the arm and led him to a backward-directed telescope aimed at the Solar System that the voyagers had taken months to traverse. "I measured the Sun just now," he said, "and I found a diameter of 64 seconds. See if I'm mistaken—then you can check that my calculations are correct."

The young man put his eye to the ocular lens and perceived in the distance—the very remote distance, lost in the darkness of space—a star twinkling with a prodigious glare, eclipsing that of all the surrounding stars: that was the Sun. For a moment, he felt strangely moved by the appearance of that marvelous

---

occasions, including two sightings by Galileo in 1612-13, but had always been mistaken for a star

[75] Triton, discovered by Lassell in 1846, only 17 days after Galle's epoch-making sighting of Neptune itself.

star, which offered itself to him as a disk 30 times smaller than that which it simultaneously offered to his compatriots. He mentally sounded the titanic abyss that separated him from the planet of his birth, represented by that diminution.

Involuntarily, before drawing away, he darted a glance at the open notebook placed on a shelf beside the telescope and read these words: *Seen from Neptune, solar disk offers surface 900 times smaller than that apparent on Earth—light corresponding to the intensity of 687 full moons—or to that of 40,000,000 stars equal in magnitude to the brilliant Sirius.*

The engineer shrugged his shoulders imperceptibly. *What use are such calculations?* he thought—and went to join Gontran, who was sitting in a corner with a piece of paper in his hand, which he appeared to be blackening with calculations. "What are you doing?" Fricoulet asked.

The young Comte stifled a yawn. "I'm so bored," he said, "that I'm trying to distract myself."

"By juggling figures?" exclaimed the astonished engineer.

"I'm trying to solve a riddle that I've set myself."

"What riddle?"

"Given that the orbit of Neptune is 6,987,000,000 leagues and that it takes 165 years to complete that orbit, I'm trying to calculate the rapidity of its progress."

Fricoulet laughed. "That's a simple matter of division," he said.

"Yes," said the young Comte, "but a division that involves billions makes for a lot of numbers in the quotient."

"So?"

"So, I haven't finished yet."

"Well," said the engineer, "know right away that Neptune travels at a rate of 5370 meters a second, 322 kilometers a minute, 5000 leagues an hour, 115,000 a day—which means that after 60,151 of our days it has completed an entire revolution." And he added: "It's the slowest of the known worlds; it moves—or, rather, crawls—along its orbit like a colossal tortoise. On the other hand, it turns on its own axis with considerable rapidity."

"How do you know that?" asked Flammermont—and then, immediately, added: "It's true that its speed of rotation has probably been calculated by means of some observation made of its disk."

The engineer shook his head. "My dear chap, in the eyes of terrestrial astronomers who know where to find it, Neptune presents, at best, the appearance of an eighth magnitude star, whose slightly blue-tinted disk is no more than three seconds of arc in diameter. How the Devil do you expect observations to be made thereon?"

"What did they do, then, to measure that rotational speed?"

"The simplest thing in the world. Lassalle, after having discovered the Neptunian satellite, established that its mean distance from the satellite is 13 Neptunian radii, or about 100,000 leagues, and that its revolution is effectuated in five terrestrial days and 21 hours. The logical consequence of the rapidity of the satellite is the rapidity of the planet itself, which must be similar to that of Jupiter, Saturn and Uranus. Besides, that's not the only point of resemblance between Neptune and Uranus; in addition to the similarity of rotational speed, the inclination of their satellites and their retrograde movement, the outermost two of the known planets also have almost the same mass, the same density, and the same surface gravity. The chemical composition of their atmospheres is also similar, as spectral analysis demonstrates."

"They're twins, then?" Gontran said, sardonically.

"Without knowing it, you've given them the same name that several astronomers have used in describing them. Moreover—you can convince yourself of it by looking through the telescope for a moment—Neptune, like Uranus, has a strongly inclined axis and is markedly flattened at the poles."

At that moment, Selena-who had left the engine-room with her father—came back into the room. Her face seemed quite distraught, and her cheeks bore the traces of recent tears. Gontran went to her.

"What's the matter, my dear Selena?" he asked. "Why are you so sad?"

She bowed her head and replied in a whisper, as if ashamed. "I've just left my father!"

"So?"

The young woman stifled a large sigh. "If you had seen him weeping..." she stammered.

The Comte started in surprise. "Weeping?" he repeated. "Why?"

"Because it will be the same with Neptune as with Uranus; he won't be able to find out anything about it, and won't even be able to see anything."

Fricoulet shook his head. "We can't do anything about that," he replied, "And, in truth, Monsieur Ossipoff is being unreasonable."

Selena looked at the engineer reproachfully. "It's true," she said, "that Monsieur Ossipoff is nothing to you, Monsieur Fricoulet, but you really do have a very hard heart."

"Yes," Gontran repeated, mechanically, fascinated by the young woman's presence and not even knowing what he was saying. "Yes, you have a very hard heart."

The engineer looked from one to the other, with a bewildered gaze. "Eh?" he exclaimed. "What do you mean by that? Have I, or Gontran, or you, Mademoiselle, a means of making the opaque atmosphere of Neptune become suddenly transparent? No, we haven't. So?" And he looked at them, almost furious.

"I thought," Selena murmured, addressing Gontran, "that it might perhaps be possible to get closer to the planet."

Fricoulet shook his shoulders. "Eh? To distinguish anything on the Neptunian surface, getting closer would not be sufficient."

"In that case," said Flammermont, in his turn, moved by his fiancée's heart-broken attitude, "can't we try to land?"

"Oh, Gontran!"

These two words escaped Mademoiselle Ossipoff's lips with such a profound tone of gratitude that even Fricoulet could not help shivering. Even so, he cried: "But that would be folly!"

"Oh, my dear chap," riposted the Comte, "How many follies have we committed already?"

"I thought that the series was concluded," said the engineer.

There was doubtless something in Fricoulet's voice that betrayed his emotion, for Selena approached him and took his hand. "Monsieur Fricoulet!" she implored.

The engineer shrugged his shoulders. "So be it!" he muttered. And he headed for the levers controlling the rudder.

Selena ran to the engine-room door. "Father! Father!" she cried. "Come down, quickly—we're landing on Neptune."

The stairs creaked under Ossipoff's hasty footfalls; he hurtled into the room like a bomb. "Is it possible?" he stammered, unable to believe his ears.

"Look," said Fricoulet, simply.

The old man ran to a porthole. "We're arriving!" he cried. "Watch out for the shock!"

Farenheit ran to his hammock and lay down in it.

Gontran seized Selena around the waist.

As for Fricoulet, immobile at his post, his hands riveted to the levers, his muscles tensed to breaking-point, he waited for the moment when Neptune's attraction would make itself felt to veer sideways and soften the fall, by means of the inhibition of the compressed air.

Suddenly, however, the old scientist uttered a cry of distress. "We're drawing away!" he said, hoarsely.

"That's not possible," retorted the engineer.

"I swear to you that we're getting further away," the old man insisted.

Fricoulet consulted his watch, and his face expressed an indescribable astonishment. "Given the time we've been falling," he murmured, "the contact should have taken place."

"Ah!" said Ossipoff, whose eyes never left the planet's disk. "Now we're getting closer again." A few seconds later, he said: "We're moving away again."

With his brow furrowed, his features violently contracted and his arms folded across his chest, the scientist sought to solve this stupefying problem. One might have thought that some phenomenon of repulsion was driving the metallic vehicle away from the planet and preventing it, in spite of its weight, from reaching the surface. Suddenly, he uttered an exclamation and shook his head. "Stop trying, Monsieur Fricoulet," he said, "it's useless."

"Why?"

"Because we're under the governance of the law that must determine the retrograde movement of satellites in this unknown world.[76]

"And that law is?"

"A law of electricity, which, acting by repulsion on the satellites of Neptune, maintains them in the orbits they occupy, counterbalancing the monstrous attractive force of the planet."

Farenheit rubbed his hands together.

"What have you got to be so satisfied about?" Flammermont asked him, in a low voice. "One would think that the impossibility of landing on Neptune pleases you."

"And one would not be mistaken. I am, indeed, quite content, for the time we would have spent on that uninteresting world would provably be more usefully employed in returning to Earth—don't you agree?"

"Do you doubt it?" replied the Comte.

"What shall we do now?" Fricoulet asked Ossipoff.

"By God!" exclaimed the American. "Do you have to ask? What we agreed—which is to set a course for New York, without any ports of call. Isn't that right, Papa Ossipoff?"

And, in the joy of the anticipated return, Farenheit forgot himself to the point of slapping the old scientist on the back. The latter, already plunged into reflection, shuddered like a suddenly-awakened sleeper. "Pardon me," he said, "I didn't hear."

"Monsieur Fricoulet asked you what we should do, and I told him there was only one thing *to* do—turn around."

Ossipoff released a profound sigh. "Alas," he said, dejectedly, "since you wish it...."

"Pardon me," Fricoulet riposted, dryly, "but it was agreed..."

"Yes...yes..." stammered the scientist. And, making a supreme effort of self-control, he addressed a smile to his daughter and added. "Then again, it's time for the father to replace the scientist, isn't it, darling?"

The young woman threw her arms around the old man's neck.

"*Et vous aurez bientôt des petit-fils ingambes/Pour vous tirer la barbe et vous grimper aux jambes*,"[77] quoted Fricoulet, mockingly.

---

[76] Triton does, indeed, have retrograde motion—i.e., it moves around Neptune in an opposite direction to the planet's own rotation—but no special law of nature is required to explain the phenomenon. Some of Jupiter's satellites also have retrograde motion, but they were all unknown in the 1880s and do not figure in the text. The authors' reference to other satellites is conjectural; Nereid had not yet been discovered at the time of writing, so they had no way of knowing that its movement is not retrograde.

[77] "*And you'll soon have lively grandsons, to tug your beard and climb up your legs*." From *Le roi s'amuse* (1832), a play by Victor Hugo depicting the adven-

"That animal Alcide knows everything," grumbled Flammeront. "The verses of Victor Hugo are as familiar to him as my famous namesake's *Les Continents célestes* or Monsieur X's treatises on mechanics."

Ossipoff's face suddenly became serious. "Gontran," he said, taking the young man's hands in his, "you must make me a promise."

"If it's in my power to do what you want me to promise," stammered the young man.

"Listen carefully, my dear boy," the old man went on. "I won't hide from you that it's the death of the soul to which I'm consenting in going back. As I've learned all these marvelous things that I didn't know before, a keen curiosity has taken hold of me to discover what I still don't know. Were I alone, I'd go forward, ever forward...the infinite attracts me and it's painful for me to tear myself away from it, in despair..."

"Father," murmured Selena, distressed by this speech.

A brief gesture from the old man imposed silence on the young woman. "Remember that, millions of leagues beyond the mysterious horizon that limits our view, another world undoubtedly orbits, invisible to terrestrial astronomers, but whose existence is indubitably affirmed by the perturbations observed in Neptune's motion..."

"We're back to the famous Hyperion," Fricoulet put in, "about which we were talking the other day."

The scientist directed a pitying gaze at the engineer. "Yes," he continued, "it's Hyperion I mean—Hyperion, regarding which I wanted to bring certain information back to Earth...but what human instruments can't do, human genius can accomplish. Witness Le Verrier, who, by simple calculation and the force of reason, succeeded in finding the location in the sky of an invisible planet. Well, I've devoted long years of my life to preliminary studies regarding Hyperion...but the little time I have left to live will not suffice for me to carry forward that great and important work."

"But my dear Monsieur," Gontran hastened to say, "you're in good health, and God will conserve you for a long time yet in the affection of your family."

The old man shook his head. "If I were to live to be 100," he replied, "that wouldn't suffice; remember that the movement of Hyperion through space must be so slow that it takes no less than three or four centuries to complete its orbit."

Flamermont's eyebrows were prodigiously raised.

"I therefore leave to you, my dear boy," the old man went on, emotionally, "the studies that I've made during my life on the subject of this planet; you'll continue them throughout your life."

"Oh, Father!" Selena interrupted, tearfully. "Are you afraid of dying, then?"

---

tures of King Francis I, banned because it was deemed to be a veiled caricature of current King Louis-Philippe.

"No, my child," the old scientist replied, "but at this solemn moment—a moment when, having arrived at the terminus of our voyage, we're about to head for our native planet—I expect that your fiancé's promise will be even more solemn. And that promise, my dear Gontran, is to leave to your own son, who will also be an astronomer, like his father and grandfather—good blood never lies—the duty of completing the work on Hyperion: work begun by me, continued by you, and to which he, the third in line, will attach his name as you and I will have attached ours. It's not asking too much of three human lives to succeed in lifting the veil behind which the Unknown is hiding."

After pronouncing these final words in a vibrant voice full of emotion, the old man fell silent, awaiting the reply for which he had asked.

Flammermont hesitated for two or three seconds. The role that he had been playing for such a long time was beginning to weigh heavily upon him and he wondered whether it might not be better to discard the mask and make a frank confession to the old man as to what he was. That would have broken the dream of happiness he had formed forever, but, in addition to the fact that the incessantly-postponed realization of that dream had diminished its value, now that he was more self-composed, the young man was beginning to find that his affection for Selena had perhaps drawn him beyond the licensed bounds of honesty and loyalty.

He would doubtless have spoken, and confessed everything, but his gaze went to Selena—and the young woman's face seemed so graceful, so charming and so adorable that Gontran, forgetting all his disappointments and torments, put the impulse to frankness that he had just experienced completely out of his mind. Entirely reconquered by his love, he exclaimed: "I promise you!" At the same time he made an imperceptible movement of his head, which Fricoulet interpreted as: *Bah! What am I risking?*

The hands of the future son-in-law and father-in-law came together in a cordial handshake—after which Selena threw herself into her father's arms and embraced him effusively.

"And now," Fricoulet declared, "I propose that everyone goes to take a nap. After so much emotion, we need rest. Besides, Mr. Farenheit has set us an example."

The American, a practical man, seeing a scene of tenderness appearing on his horizon, had furtively left the engine-room; his sonorous snoring could be heard in the cabin next door, making the lithium walls tremble.

The engineer's advice was judged good, and they hastened to follow it; less than five minutes had elapsed when Fricoulet and Gontran, having retired to their cabin, were sound asleep, and slumber had closed Selena's eyelids as she lay on her bed.

Only Ossipoff was still awake. Alone in the cabin that served as his laboratory, his face glued to a porthole, his eyes were fixed on the unfathomable infinity that he had dreamed of exploring and which it was necessary for him to abandon. His fingers scratched nervously against the wall of the vehicle, his nails becoming bloody, and the traces of the frightful combat ranging inside him were evident in his distraught face.

To abandon that dream—that insane, but sublime, dream! Certainly, he had acted in good faith just now when he had resigned himself to it, sacrificing his mad curiosity to his love for his daughter. But now...

Oh, no, now that he was alone, liberated from all emotion and all influence, his passion for the Unknown carried him away and he sensed that it would be useless to resist it; he was defeated in advance.

For a long time, he resisted; in the end, though, he could not hold out.

To reach the stairway leading to the engine-room he had to pass through the room where his daughter was asleep. He stopped momentarily, contemplating her in her calm and smiling sleep. Then a tear formed beneath his eyelid and he bent down to brush the young woman's forehead with his lips.

"Forgive me!" he murmured. Then, without making any noise, he slipped out of the room, went down the steps as lightly as a shadow, and went into the engine-room. If he had been able to see himself at that moment, the old man would have recoiled; his face was livid, his lips twisted into a dolorous grimace, and within his convulsed mask his eyes were shining with a feverish and diabolical gleam.

As if in a fit of somnambulism, Ossipoff marched straight to the levers controlling the rudder, seized them, and pushed them abruptly down.

Docile to this instruction, the *Eclair* turned around and headed in the other direction. Mikhail Ossipoff and his companions were en route for Infinity.

Chapter LIV
The Intersidereal Desert

For a long while, Mikhail Ossipoff remained motionless, his immeasurably-wide eyes fixed upon the levers that his hands had abandoned. He was prey to a sort of hallucination, wondering whether it was really true that he had done what he had just done, refusing to believe that he had really rendered himself guilty of the infamous treason that he had committed in regard to his traveling companions.

Only a short while before he had sworn to his daughter, the man who was to be his son and his friends that his astronomical folly was at an end—that, since nature was against him, he would renounce further struggle! His ears were still ringing with Selena's emotional thanks; she had finally recovered the father that she believed she had lost forever. On his cheeks he seemed to feel the soft brush of the young woman's lips. And in spite of all that, in spite of his oath and Gontran's promises, he had been abruptly repossessed by the passion of space, by the ardent curiosity that had been drawing him on for months, always further than he had declared.

And now...

In a man like him, though, in whom the desire for knowledge outweighed all other sentiments and all other passions, that initial dejection could not last. Almost immediately, he was repossessed by the fever that had been consuming him for so long; the scientist imposed himself yet again upon the father, Selena's tearful silhouette vanished, and all his mental energy was focused on the acute problem created in the scientific world by the hypothetical existence of Hyperion.

Yes, he sensed it, that star whose existence, orbiting in region where he now was, Babinet and Forbes[78] had affirmed. He was sure of it! What immortal glory would shower the first man who, placing his finger on a celestial globe, would unhesitatingly assign a certain location to the outermost world of the Solar System.

He did not wonder whether, in anticipating the glory for the sake of which he had just committed an insane action, he had lost his reason. Even if the scientific predictions of Babinet and Forbes were exact, and he could, so to speak, put his finger on that mysterious planet and study its route through space, would he ever be able to return from the profundities of that infinity, into which he was now launched, to say to the people of Earth: *I wanted to see; I have seen; it is*

[78] George Forbes (1849-1936) became far better known as an electrical engineer than a dabbler in astronomy.

thus? His reflection did not extend that far. For him, at that moment, there was but one thing, and one inadmissible thing—which was that he should not discover with his own eyes that which others had discovered solely by the power of logic and calculation.

He knew perfectly well—better than anyone else—how divided the scientific world was with regard to the problematic existence of the planet that certain audacious astronomers had not hesitated to baptize with the name of Hyperion, even though there was no proof that it existed. The reader, however, has already had the opportunity to be convinced of the fact that Ossipoff had been carried away by space and hallucinated by infinity; as Fricoulet had said on one occasion in speaking of the old man's exaggerated theories with regard to planets: "With him, when it's not a matter of *more*, it's a matter of *again*..."

So he believed in Hyperion. He believed in it with all the power of his imagination and all the force of his science. As he had said to Gontran, he had prepared a long work on the mysterious planet, designed to prove peremptorily the existence of the hypothetical world, and the preface of that work contained an energetic declaration of war against those in the scientific world who took leave to ridicule the audacity of the godfathers of Hyperion.

It ill becomes you, it proclaimed, *to mock the genius of Babinet and Forbes, having had the shame of ridiculing the audacious genius of Le Verrier! Was it not by science alone, based on Bode's Law, that Le Verrier, deducing the existence of an unknown planet from perturbations observed in the motion of Uranus, sought and found Neptune at distance 36? Despite your sarcasms and jokes, it was necessary for you to bow down before the facts and recognize the truth of the theories thanks to which Le Verrier has so enormously extended the dimensions of the solar world. Why, then, refuse Babinet the authorization to proceed in an analogous manner to affirm the existence beyond Neptune of a sphere that our optical instruments, as yet imperfect, do not permit us to discover? Have not serious perturbations been observed in the motion of Neptune, just as Le Verrier did for Uranus? And cannot these perturbations be attributed to the influence, sometimes retardative and sometimes accelerative, of an exterior sphere?*

Departing from there, the old scientist went on to examine scientific principles different from those of Babinet, on which other astronomers, including Dr. Forbes, based their declarations that Hyperion existed. The latter, following in the footsteps of Le Verrier, rose up forcefully against Babinet's suppositions; to them, the motion of Neptune and its irregularities were of scant importance. The principle of their research was founded on the theory that introduced comets into our Solar System as permanent members, considered as bodies with a particular composition and characteristics that move though the stellar spaces, subject to the laws of gravity.

If a comet approaches a planet with an accelerated velocity, it will describe a hyperbolic orbit and never return toward the Sun, but if the action of the planet reduces the body's velocity of translation, it will draw it into an elliptical orbit with the Sun at its focal point. In cataloguing the aphelion distances of all the known elliptical orbits, Dr. Forbes had found that they could be grouped in such a way that they corresponded to the distances of certain planets, and that beyond Neptune, it was only at distances of 100 and 300 times the radius of Earth's orbit that numerous groups formed; from that he concluded that planets exist at these distances.

Had not Ossipoff, based on these theories—which, for his part, he adopted with a fervor of belief—made all the necessary calculations many times over to determine the status of Hyperion in as scrupulous a fashion as if he had it within the field of the large equatorial at Pulkova? It was, according to him, a planet of the same size as Neptune, orbiting at distance 47—still according to Bode's Law[79]—following an orbit inclined by five degrees to the ecliptic, rotating around the Sun in 138,481 days, or 379 terrestrial years.

Understandably, having arrived by the power of reasoning and calculation at the acquisition of such precise information regarding Hyperion, the old scientist had been unable to resist the folly of convincing himself, with his own eyes, of the exactitude of his suppositions. Would he not have been in much the same situation as a provincial who failed to take advantage of his passage through Paris to visit the marvels that the capital contains?

Now that—without having been conscious, no to speak, of what he was doing—he had diverted the *Eclair* from the agreed route to launch it into the infinite, he told himself that, in truth, he would have been mad to neglect such an extraordinary opportunity to lift nature's veil.

As we said at the beginning of the chapter, the sort of hallucination to which he had fallen prey after having touched the levers only lasted for a few moments; almost immediately, he regained possession of himself and rapidly succeeded in establishing the precise position of the world he was seeking, if it really existed. Given the situation of the *Eclair*, the position of Hyperion in the sky could only be, relative to the Earth, at 174 degrees of longitude and 11 hours 40 minutes of right ascension. Having, therefore, set the aerial vessel's course

---

[79] The Titius-Bode sequence would locate a transneptunian planet at a distance of 77.2 astronomical units; 47 might be a simple misprint, but it is the evident basis of the subsequent calculation of Hyperon's distance from the Sun as 1780 million leagues. It might, however, be derived—slightly ineptly—from *Les Terres du ciel*, although most of this passage is derived from another source; Flammarion there employs a comet-grouping hypothesis similar to the one here credited to Forbes to support the conjecture that there might be a transneptunian planet at 48 or 49 A.U. Forbes' figures of 100 and 300 AU are, of course, larger than the figures generated by the Titius-Bode sequence for hypothetical ninth and tenth planets. Pluto, when it was eventually discovered, did not fit the Titius-Bode sequence or either of the comet-grouping conjectures.

for that point of the sky, Ossipoff went back to his cabin and aimed his telescope on the immutably black space that it was traversing at the speed of light.

It seemed that there was a gulf into which the apparatus was falling, without ever reaching the bottom; there was no point of reference to indicate the distance covered, only the distant—very distant—scintillating stars, like steel nails on a mortuary cloth. They were far too distant for Ossipoff to be able to judge their progressive approach, even at the velocity at which he was flying.

For six hours the lithium vehicle flew in this manner, heading straight for infinity, without the scientist seeing any body with the appearance of a planet enter the field of his telescope. Millions of leagues were added to millions of leagues, and the old man, absorbed in his research, had no consciousness of elapsed time, nor of the distance traveled.

A moment came, however, when Ossipoff—his brain enfevered, his eyes anxious, his limbs stiffened by such long immobility—cried out, and pointed his bony finger into the starry space that was visible through the porthole. "And yet it's there! I know it! I feel it!" He added, in a tone of consternation, as if he were taking account of the incredible figure that his lips were babbling: "1,780,000,000 leagues from the Sun!" That was the distance at which, according to his calculations, Hyperion ought to be following its sidereal course.

Then, waving his clenched fists in a gesture of rage against the infinity whose mysteries seemed to be escaping him, he uttered another cry, which exhaled a confession of his impotence: "And yet," he repeated, "Babinet, Forbes and Todd[80] can't all three be mistaken! Nothing...still nothing!"

A sudden idea crossed his mind and, abruptly downcast, he let himself slump down on a stool, where he remained, as if exhausted, with his elbows on his knees and his head between his hands, furiously raking his grey hair with his fingers. The possibility had struck him that he might not encounter the world of whose existence he was certain, to the discovery of which he was hurrying, dragging his companions—unconscious of his treason—with him.

Hyperion was not at the place to which he had directed the *Eclair.* There was no doubt, since Babinet and the others had decided it, that the orbit of the problematic planet really was at 174 degrees of longitude—but for the moment, Hyperion was perhaps, or even must be, at another point in its orbit. Perhaps, given the bad luck that had pursued him for such a long time, Ossipoff had turned in a direction diametrically opposite to that of the planet toward which he was trying to steer. If that were the case, what good would it do to do what he had done? He had broken his word, he had endangered the lives of all the voyagers contained within the lithium vessel's hull, and he had shattered his daugh-

---

[80] David Peck Todd (1855-1939) had an unsullied reputation as an astronomer, but is nowadays primarily famous because his wife had an affair that led to coming into possession of Emily Dickinson's poetry, thus becoming her "discoverer" and editor.

ter's happiness—for Gontran de Flammermont certainly would not forgive his intended father-in-law the treason of which he was guilty. And all that to know no more than he knew on his departure from Earth! Was it not enough to madden a brain better equilibrated than the old man's?

A hand placed on his shoulder snatched him out of this painful meditation. He got up abruptly and instinctively took a step back, on seeing Fricoulet in front of him, looking at him sardonically.

"Well, Papa Ossipoff," the engineer said, mockingly, "did the watch pass without incident?"

"Oh, it's you, Monsieur Fricoulet!" stammered the scientist.

"Yes, it's me. But is there, by chance, something abnormal about my face, that you should look at me with such a bewildered expression?" Emitting a burst of laughter, he added: "I see what it is—instead of standing your watch, you've taken a nap, and I've probably interrupted a very pleasant dream."

Ossipoff's first impulse was to protest energetically against a supposition that was, for a hardened scientist like him, almost an insult. Asleep, him! While nature was there, with its insoluble mysteries that had provoked such an ardent curiosity in him for such a long time! Obedient to his instinct, though, without reflecting on the fact that his lie could only delay for a brief interval the moment when the truth would become manifest, he turned his head away, lowered his eyes and stammered in an embarrassed tone: "What time is it, then?"

In response to that question, which replied to his suggestion in a more peremptory fashion than any all the confessions in the world could have done, Fricoulet gave free rein to his hilarity. Father Ossipoff caught *in flagrante delicto* in astronomical inattention! Father Ossipoff asleep next to his telescope while stellar marvels offered themselves to his observation! That was verging on the incredible! For several seconds, he stood there as if petrified, his mouth open and his eyes wide.

"But it's 7 a.m. on Earth, my dear Monsieur Ossipoff—if I can trust the indications of the ship's chronometer, at least."

7 a.m.! On hearing these words, the old scientist calculated thereby the truly vertiginous distance that they had traveled, in eight hours, since the moment when the *Eclair*, coming about, had abandoned the cosmic current carrying it toward Earth to launch forth into infinity. The old scientist's head hung down even more, and his shoulders seemed to be crushed by the weight of a load that had suddenly descended upon him. That attitude provided further confirmation of Fricoulet's initial impression.

Meanwhile, the engineer's outbursts of laughter, echoing sonorously from the metallic walls of the lithium vessel, had woken up the others. While Selena appeared to one side, Gontran and Farenheit came in through another door, one behind the other.

"By God!" exclaimed the latter, advancing toward the engineer with his arms extended. "That cheerfulness is a good omen!" He took out his watch, consulted the dial and added, addressing Gontran, while a joyful glint appeared in his grey irises: "If your calculations are correct, my dear scientist, it won't be long now before I set foot on the pavement of Fifth Avenue."

"Is there any reason," riposted Flammermont, who sensed Ossipoff's eyes upon him, "that my calculations should not be correct? I said that the *Eclair* would reach the terrestrial zone of attraction in 23 hours and, barring unforeseeable accidents, we should be getting home at the predicted time." He had pronounced these words in a curt and dry tone, affecting more indignation because Ossipoff was listening, and he did not want to appear, in his eyes, to be tolerating any doubt as to his scientific knowledge. While speaking, he darted a tender glance at Selena, who blushed slightly, while Fricoulet had the greatest difficulty keeping his face straight.

Things became even worse when, to add more force to the reply he had just given the American, Gontran moved Ossipoff gently aside in order to take his place at the telescope. The travelers gathered behind him, Fricoulet imperfectly dissimulating the smile that his friend's comedy had brought to his lips, Farenheit anxious to know whether the consultation of the stars would confirm Flammermont's optimistic prognosis, and Selena radiant at the prospect of finally seeing an end to the amorous romance whose denouement had been so long delayed. As for Ossipoff, who had retreated into a corner, he watched the transformations that passed over the face of his future son-in-law, not without anxiety.

The latter, without quitting the eyepiece, suddenly said: "Well, my dear Monsieur Farenheit, I can now assure you that my calculations were correct...or, at least...no, they were false..."

"By God!" swore the American, starting in alarm.

"Yes, false," the young man repeated, "for my predictions fall well short of the truth."

"What are you talking about?" Fricoulet asked, in a whisper, leaning toward his friend and trying to move him aside in order to take his place and see the astronomical phenomenon on which Gontran had based his remark.

It seemed, though, that the young diplomat was much too interested in the spectacle that presented itself to him to give way to Fricoulet's pressure. His eye still glued to the ocular lens, he continued speaking slowly, his attention attracted by a fixed point out there in space. "Yes, since yesterday it seems to me that we've been traveling like the Devil, and if we continue at this rate..." He stopped, and remained silent for a few seconds. Without seeming to be aware of it, he reflected aloud: "Let's see...that's not Uranus, nor Saturn, nor Jupiter—they're far behind us. Mars? Hmm—to the best of my recollection, its disk doesn't shine as brightly. Yes...yes, it's surely Venus...it can't be anything but Venus. But what I'd like to know is what happened to the Earth?"

At these words, Fricoulet straightened up abruptly and put his lips close to his friend's ear because of Ossipoff, who was still motionless in his corner.

"Venus!" he murmured. "You're mad! If it were, it would be necessary to admit that the *Eclair* was traveling at least ten times as fast as light. Come on, move away from there..." So saying, he pushed Gontran away in an amicable fashion, and sat down in front of the telescope, without noticing the sudden pallor that had overtaken Ossipoff's face.

Meanwhile, Selena, radiant with happiness, had to submit to a vigorous handshake on the part of Fareneheit—who, on hearing that Venus, the penultimate step of their homeward journey was in sight, had been unable to resist the desire to manifest his joy in a vertiginous entrechat.

"Hip, hip, Hurrah! Flammermont forever!" Abandoning the young woman's hands, the American threw himself on Gontran's, shaking them with frantic energy. Then he was overtaken by a sudden sentimentality at the thought that he was about to see New York again, soon than he had expected, along with the Eccentric Club and the shareholders in the Selene Co. Ltd.[81] Before his interlocutor was able to extract himself from his grip, he took him in his arms and hugged him to his bosom, squeezing the breath out of him and stammering: "You're our savior, my young and worthy friend! May all of Heaven's blessings pour down upon your head!"

When the young man had escaped the American's embrace, it was to submit to the gentle pressure of Selena's hands. Gazing at him with a tender expression, in which the intoxication of the new imminence of an oft-delayed happiness was legible, she said: "Oh, Gontran! My dear Gontran!"

The young woman's sentimentality, Gontran's satisfaction and Farenheit's enthusiastic excitement vanished as if by magic, however, and their radiant faces darkened within a split second.

"Damnation!" Fricoulet had just shouted, bounding prodigiously on the stool that served him as a seat. And on his suddenly-contracted features there was such amazement, and simultaneously such anxiety, that all three understood that some disastrous news was about to emerge from the engineer's lips. "That, Venus!" he finally contrived to say, seeking in vain to disguise the anguish that was choking him with his eternal mocking tone. "The Devil may take me if that has ever resembled Venus!"

This declaration was answered by a triple exclamation, which betrayed Gontran's surprise, Selena's anguish and Farenheit's anger. The three of them surrounded Fricoulet and leaned over him, trying to divine from the expression on his face how to translate the words he had just pronounced. They were so absorbed that none of them noticed the silent disappearance of Ossipoff.

---

[81] Farenheit's company has not previously been designated by this title, which appears to have been borrowed from the commercial enterprise featured in the extravagant Vernian romance *Les Exilés de la terre, Séléné Company Ltd.* (1887; tr. as *The Conquest of the Moon*) by Verne's sometime collaborator André Laurie [Paschal Grousset].

As soon as Fricoulet had pronounced his exclamation, the scientist had felt a cold sweat forming on his brow, while it seemed that his tremulous legs were about to give way beneath him. The moment of explanation had arrived—an explanation all the more redoubtable and painful because he would have to admit not only his treason but his error. He did not know which he feared most—the American's fury or the scornful sarcasm of Gontran and Fricoulet—so, profiting from the fixation of general attention on the engineer, he took himself away quietly and went into his cabin, which he locked.

"Not Venus!" cried the American, grabbing Fricoulet by the collar of his jacket and shaking him forcefully. "But Monsieur de Flammermont has declared...."

"Eh? Gontran is mistaken, that's all."

Farenheit then turned on the young Comte. "You've deceived me!" he roared. "You've deceived me!"

Fricoulet, however, was in no mood to let himself be distracted by his traveling companion's explosions of anger. "Give us some peace!" he declared. "We've got other things to do, at present, than shout and scream."

The American's fury immediately reached its climax. "By God! That's rich! I don't know where I'm going, you don't know where you're taking me, and probably don't know where we are...and I don't have the right to complain!"

Fricoulet leapt to the rear, applied his eye to the telescope permanently set up at the porthole, and looked out for a long time. Far away, in the remote distance of the stellar night, luminous points were pricking space, and with his profound knowledge of the celestial map, it did not take him long to get his bearings, in spite of the implausibility with which the truth presented itself to him. "Oh, the wretch, the wretch!" he muttered between his teeth, while he raised his clenched fist above his head to menace an invisible enemy, "He's the one who's done this!" These words were pronounced too indistinctly to be understood by the people surrounding him; they, moreover, had only one thing on their minds at that moment: finding out where they were.

Fortunately, Fricoulet was not the sort of fellow to fall apart, even in the face of the gravest events. Moved to pity by Selena's fearful expression, as well as Gontran's contrite attitude, he succeeded in recovering his self-composure and said to his friend in a good-humored tone: "I believe, damn it, that you won't find the Earth by looking in front of the vehicle. The Earth is in that direction, my old friend." And he pointed at the aft porthole.

"The Earth! In that direction!" growled Farenheit, in whose eyes a mad gleam had suddenly appeared.

"Yes, my dear Monsieur, whether we like it or not, the Earth is in that direction...and so is our entire Solar System."

"But who? Who did this?"

"Monsieur Ossipoff, of course," replied the engineer. "He was in charge of the engine-room last night..."

"Oh, Monsieur Fricoulet!" cried Selena, putting her hands together. "Why accuse my father, rather than attributing what has happened to us to some incident independent of his will?"

"Indeed," said Gontran, in his turn, moved by the imploring gaze that the young woman fixed upon him, "doesn't it happen frequently on Earth that transatlantic ships go astray in mid-ocean? Isn't it more likely that the *Eclair* deviated from its true path without the person on watch being aware of it?"

The engineer shrugged his shoulders skeptically and replied, confidently; "Inadmissible. Would you believe that a transatlantic liner heading for New York could, between one moment and the next, redirect its course to Le Havre? Well, that's what's happened to us. The Sun, which was on our bow yesterday, is now astern. The *Eclair* has turned through 180 degrees, which could not have happened if no hand had touched the rudder, and the hand in question can only have been that of Monsieur Ossipoff—who, despite his promise, was unable to resist the temptation to lift the mysterious veil enveloping the existence of Hyperion."

This speech, which Fricoulet had pronounced in a clear and calm voice, as if he were absolutely disinterested in the matter, was initially greeted with a profound silence. Selena had hidden her face in her hands, and it was easy to deduce from the little nervous tremors that shook her that she was weeping. As for Gontran, his head reeling, he had slumped into a chair, in which amazement and despair immobilized him; the delightful hope that he had had of finally seeing, in the imminent future, Selena's hand fall into his own, had vanished. It was the end of all the dreams of happiness that he had had, and which, during the years that had just gone by, had been alternately broken and reformed, in tune with the more or less problematic prospect of returning to his native planet.[82]

The American's fury, contained for a few seconds, suddenly burst forth. At first it took the form of a torrent of oaths that escaped his contracted lips; then, parading a terrible gaze around him, he cried: "Where is he? I'll strangle him!"

Selena uttered a desperate shriek. She knew from experience to what extremes Farenheit's violent character might carry him, and she threw herself in front of him, using her frail body to bar the stairway leading to the cabin in which the old man had taken refuge.

---

[82] The reader might be puzzled by all this distress, given that the *Eclair* seems to be capable of making sharp turns at light speed, and that the travelers have, as yet, no reason to believe that they cannot simply retrace their steps in a matter of hours. They are, however, locked in a collective hallucination, and doubtless have some subconscious inkling of the fact that their course, as reset by Ossipoff, is now beyond their control.

"Let me through! Let me through!" roared Farenheit, seizing the young woman by the wrists to force her to let him pass. With one bound, however, Flammermont was upon him; with the aid of Fricoulet, who also interposed himself, he pushed him back.

"Oh, these Europeans!" moaned the American, held firm by his two adversaries. "It's not blood they have in their veins but carrot juice! There's an old madman who, not content to have raged us into the most incredible adventures, breaks his promises and endangers our lives at the very moment we were saved..." He folded his arms and howled: "But wouldn't it give you some satisfaction of breaking his back before dying!"

Selena groaned, but Fricoulet replied serenely: "To tell you the truth, my dear Monsieur Farenheit, no—that wouldn't give me any satisfaction. I don't know whether you've noticed, but I'm a practical man, myself, and I try not to do anything that can't have any useful or pleasurable consequence. Now, I ask you—what use could Monsieur Ossipoff's bones be, in the present circumstances?"

"What about vengeance?"

"Yes, I know that it's been clamed that it's the pleasure of the gods—personally, I claim that Platonic pleasures are only worthy of imbeciles."

Farenheit started.

"And I'll prove it," the engineer added, imperturbably. He took out his watch and consulted the dial, which he shoved under the Amrican's nose mockingly. "It's now nearly a quarter of an hour—13 minutes, to be exact—that we've lost to your fury and rage," he said. "Now, do you know what each second of that quarter of an hour represents? No? Oh, my God, almost nothing—a mere bagatelle of 500,000 leagues. You see how far, thanks to you, we have advanced further into the intersidereal desert into which Monsieur Ossipoff's folly has launched us."

Although the American was not strong in the matter of calculation, he immediately saw a long column of figures dancing before his eyes, representing the distance that Fricoulet had mentioned, and a wild gleam lit up in his gaze. "After all," he stammered, after a few seconds, "to die here or to die further away..."

"But why are you talking like that?" protested the engineer. "We're lost, but that's no reason to say that we're dead. Isn't that so, Gontran?"

The latter, who had now reconciled himself to the situation, replied jokingly, if a trifle bitterly: "If only Monsieur Ossipoff had taken inspiration from the example of Petit Poucet and strewn pebbles along the route followed by the *Eclair*."

Fricoiulet extended his arm toward the porthole, pointing at the brilliant dots scintillating in the black sky. "But there are the pebbles that will help us find our way!" he cried. "Luminous pebbles, too. What more do we need?"

"Do you really think it's possible to repair the damage done by Monsieur Ossipoff's madness?" asked Gontran.

At that moment the engineer looked at Farenheit, who had been scribbling hastily in a notebook taken from his pocket, and was now tearing his hair in despair. "What's the matter, my dear sir?" he asked.

"I've...I've...hang on—look at this..." The American showed Fricoulet the page in his notebook, covered from top to bottom in figures, and added desolately: "And I haven't finished..."

They were calculations intended to establish what the quarter of an hour's delay he had caused represented, at a rate of 500,000 leagues a second.

Fricoulet slapped him on the shoulder amicably and said: "Bah—don't distress yourself so; the distance covered isn't lost. We've been moving forward for a quarter of a hour, and it's necessary that we continue in that fashion, in a straight line, for 12 hours."

Amazement showed in the American's face, as in Gontran's and Selena's. 12 hours at a rate of 500,000 leagues a second! But that represented an incredible distance! Had Fricoulet too been struck by insanity?

"What?" exclaimed Gontran. "You claim that the Sun, toward which we want to head, is behind us, and you're talking about drawing several million leagues further away?"

"Hold on," declared Farenheit, "while I run to the rudder and change direction."

Flammermont looked at his friend; the latter, shaking his head, smiled mockingly. "Take it easy," he said. "You must know that one of the elementary principles of navigation is that the pilot sets his ship's course for a point determined in advance. Now, without being indiscreet, I'd like to know exactly what point you're going to steer toward?"

"Eh? By God! The Sun! Didn't you declare just now that the exceedingly bright star behind the vehicle was the Sun!"

"Oh! Pardon me—I declared that it seemed so to me...but I wasn't as affirmative as that, especially as circumstances prohibited it."

These few words, pronounced coldly, produced the same effect on Farenheit's excitement as a bucket of cold water thrown on a fire. "In that case," he said, "admit frankly that we're lost."

"Damn it!" said Fricoulet. "I've been killing myself trying to tell you that for half an hour. Yes—we...are...lost...but I hope that we wont be, any longer, if you allow me to establish the parallax of the star that Gontran mistook for Venus. That will also tell me the identity of the star that is behind us, in which I thought I recognized the center of our planetary system."

"The parallax!" repeated Farenheit, whose eyes were wide open, testifying to the bewilderment generated by this expression, which was entirely new to him.

"Yes," said the engineer. "That's what the mathematical operation is called by means of which astronomers attempt to determine the distances of stars."

Preoccupied as he was by the critical situation, the American could not retain a Homeric outburst of laughter. "You want me to believe," he declared, "that it's possible to measure the vast distances that separate the worlds of stellar space?"

"Take note," Fricoulet replied, "that I said *attempt*—which signifies that the scientists do not pretend to give measurements as exact as those a surveyor can give by means of his chain."

"As proved," Gontran put in, "by the different results obtained from the observation of the same star by several astronomers."

"Very true," said Fricoulet. "To cite but two, first there's Sirius, the brightest star that Terrans are able to admire, to which Henderson credits 34 hundredths of a second, Maclear 16 hundredths, Gylden 19 hundredths and Abbe 27 hundredths."[83]

Selena, whose spirits had revived now that Farenheit's wrath had calmed down, added, in a slightly malicious tone: "You're forgetting to mention, Monsieur Fricoulet, that when Henderson and Maclear observed Sirius together they found 23 hundredths of a second—then, when they observed it separately, one got 34 and the other 16. I recall that every time the conversation turned to this subject among the gentlemen of the Observatory in St. Petersburg, my poor father came home in a state of inconceivable irritation."

Farenheit laughed. "That's typical of the worthy Monsieur Ossipoff—getting angry over a few hundredths of a second! He ought to emulate the cashiers of our great banks, who reckon time at its true value, and instead of spending hours searching for a few cents, as you do, write them down purely and simply as profits and losses."

"This isn't accountancy!" said the engineer, sarcastically. Without knowing it, you've just uttered the greatest enormity that has ever fallen from the lips of a serious man. Look—it's exactly as if you'd advised one of those cashiers you mentioned to pass of an error of several million as profits and losses."

The American started, looking at his interlocutor in alarm, and stammered; "Several million?"

"Indeed," said Fricoulet. "Do you know what the second that astronomers use as a basis for measuring the distance of stars represents? Quite simply, a distance equal to 200,000 times that of the Sun from the Earth." Further augmenting the bewilderment into which that revelation had plunged the American, he

[83] Thomas James Henderson (1798-1844) and Thomas Maclear (1794-1879) were in the forefront of the race to establish stellar parallaxes in the late 1830s and 1840s. Hugo Gylden (1841-1896) and Cleveland Abbe (1838-1916) joined the game at a much later stage.

added: "Which represents the distance light travels in three years and three months.

Farenheit scratched the end of his nose in perplexity, while Gontran said, jokingly: "I'll wager a louis to a sou that that there are people who enjoy sufficient leisure to calculate the distance traveled by light in a year!"

"And you'd win your bet: two French physicians, Fizeau and Cornu[84] devoted themselves to that little task, with the result that, the distance traveled by light in a second being 300,400 kilometers, or 75,000 leagues, for a year—composed so far as I can recall, of 32,266,000 seconds[85]—that gives a total of 2,420,000,000,000 leagues.

The American put his head in his hands in a genuinely fearful gesture, and Fricoulet heard him murmur: "Immeasurable..."

"It is, therefore, three times that distance on two trillion, etc., etc. that a second represents. You see now that even a hundredth of a second represents an appreciable distance, and that astronomers are entitled to get excited when their respective efforts produce even minimal differences."

"And it's an operation as delicate as that one that you have to carry out to determine where we are?" queried the American, with some anxiety.

"My God, yes—for I don't know any other means."

At that moment, Gontran took his friend by the arm, took him a little way to one side, and whispered: "You've told us the meaning of the word parallax, which is very nice, but what I want to know is what the operation consists of. I don't recall having read anything about it in *Les Continents célestes*, and it might well be that Father Ossipoff will quiz me on the subject."

Fricoulet smiled. "Suppose," he said, "that I represent the orbit of Neptune, the outermost known planet of the Solar System, by the fortifications of Paris. The Earth's orbit would occupy, in the center of that space, and area approximately equal to that of the Place de la Concorde. Now, on that comparative scale, it would be necessary, to reach the nearest star to the Solar System, to travel a further 30,000 kilometers—which is to say, the distance to China, going via Cape Horn."

"To travel!" repeated Gontran, utterly bewildered. "To do what?"

"To establish the parallax, fool." Fricoulet folded his arms and looked at his friend with an expression of scornful pity. "Great God! What do you learn in the Diplomatic Service, then, if you don't know that establishing a parallax consists of taking two sightings of the point under consideration from the extremities of a line of determinate length, so as to form a triangle..."

---

[84] Hippolyte Louis Fizeau (1819-1896) re-measured the speed of light—first estimated in the 17th century—in 1849; Marie Alfred Cornu (1841-1902) repeated his work with better apparatus in 1878 and obtained a more accurate result.

[85] Fricoulet's memory appears to be at fault; the actual number of seconds in a year is approximately 31,558,000.

Gontran interrupted, laughing. "I remember now," he said. "We learned that at school. If one side of a triangle and two adjacent angles are known, it's easy to calculate the other elements, including the bisection…"

"Whose height represents the distance of the point sighted. Q.E.D. Except that you must bear in mind, the orbit of Earth being represented by the Place de la Concorde, the smallness of the angles obtained by aiming a telescope from two of its corners at a beacon situated in China."

"Especially," added the young diplomat, "if, in order to arrive in China, the line of sight must go via Cape Horn! A feat of ocular gymnastics whose nature is absolutely refractory!" Then, slapping his friend on the shoulder, he added: "Understood, old chap—and if, by chance, it takes old Ossipoff's fancy to interrogate me on this, I'll be able to dazzle his eyes with a veritable firework-display of erudition."

Farenheit, meanwhile, had been showing visible signs of irritation for some time. He was staring into space with his face glued to the porthole, while his hands, folded behind his back, were repeatedly clenched by nervous contractions. Abruptly turning round, he said: "So we're going to proceed like this for 12 hours?"

"My God, yes. A little while ago, without your noticing, I measured the position of the so-called Venus noticed by Monsieur de Flammermont. After 12 hours, I'll make a new measurement; thus having a triangle of which I know the base and two angles, it will be easy for me to determine the distance that separates us from the star in question, and thus its identity. Then, knowing where we are and having that star for a reference-point, we'll be able to get back on our route."

The American's eyebrows contracted. "But that will take us to the Devil!" he complained. "It's a strange method that gets us more lost in order to find our way more easily thereafter."

"Have you an alternative method, then?" the engineer asked, mockingly. "For my part, I'm ready to use it if it's better than mine?"

"Yes, I have one!" Farenheit declared.

Fricoulet and Gontran started in surprise. "Bah!" said the engineer, utterly amazed. "And this method…?"

"Consists simply of asking that wretch Ossipoff what he did while we were asleep."

Selena intervened. "Oh, Monsieur Farenheit," she exclaimed, "do you really believe that my father…?"

With a circular movement of his arm, the American indicated the engine-room. "Isn't his disappearance," he replied, with a snigger, "the best proof of the infamous treason of which he's guilty, relative to us?" He leapt to the stairway, whose steps he scales in a few strides, and set about thumping his fists on the lithium partition that served as the old man's cabin door, like a madman.

"His method is, in fact, the simpler one," Gontran murmured in Fricoulet's ear, "And I'm astonished that none of us..."

"It's the story of Christopher Columbus and the egg," replied the engineer, shrugging his shoulders. "It was necessary to think of it." With a skeptical smile, he added: "All that remains now is to find out how old Ossipoff will welcome Farenheit's interview." He pointed at the staircase, from which emerged the echo of an infernal racket, and said: "Thus far, the result is rather negative. Listen to that!"

The entire framework of the *Eclair* was shaking, as the American's powerful fists battered the door like missiles from a catapult. In the corner, Selena, her hands pressed together, never ceased repeating: "My God! My God!"

Gontran, moved by his fiancée's pitiful expression, said to Fricoulet: "We ought to go up there—that madman's capable of striking Ossipoff down."

Up above, on the landing, they found Farenheit, his face red and streaming with sweat, his eyes bulging, still pounding vainly on the metal door. His fists were bleeding, but he had not succeeded in loosening either of the hinges, seemingly so fragile. "By God!" he roared, on seeing them. "He's hiding in there like a snail in its shell, and if we can't take the cabin by force, we'll have to starve him out."

"You're mad!" Fricoulet riposted. "That means will take longer than mine. A man can resist hunger for three days. There have been examples of individuals capable of prolonging their endurance much longer. You can imagine how far that will take us, at 500,000 leagues a second."

"Not to mention," said Gontran, striking an aggressive pose in front of the American, "that so long as I'm alive, I'll never permit anything to happen to Monsieur Ossipoff."

"Leave it to me—I'll try to negotiate." So saying, Fricoulet went to the door and knocked on it gently with his finger. "Monsieur Ossipoff," he said, with an engaging softness, "Will you let me in, please? I have a simple question to ask you." He waited a few seconds for a reply; then, hearing none, he put his ear to the door and listened.

Nothing: no sound at all. It was as if the cabin were empty.

"You see!" proclaimed the American. "The old hypocrite isn't going to say anything. Come on, let's break it down!" And he prepared to hurl himself at the door again.

Fricoulet stopped him, and said: "You're becoming annoying, with all your violence! Given all the good it's done thus far, I advise you to give it a rest. Calm down, I beg you." Once again he knocked on the door. "Monsieur Ossipoff, I promise that no one will do you any harm. We simply want to know the point in space toward which you've steered the *Eclair*, and our approximate position in the Heavens."

A few seconds went by, then a few minutes—but no more response was forthcoming than before.

Fricoulet stuck out his lips in a significant moue. "Hmm!" he murmured. "Father Ossipoff's not very chatty this morning." To Farenheit, he said: "I'm beginning to think that we'll be obliged to revert to my parallax idea."

Farenheit roared, and took out his watch. "Three quarters of an hour already! At 500,000 leagues a second. Another 11 and a quarter hours of that sort of progress? Never! Never! Let's try to break down the door. If we succeed in making the old man talk, we'll still save millions of leagues." Without waiting for his companions' reply, he picked up a stool, with which he set about striking the lithium partition as if it were a battering-ram.

Fricoulet and Gonrtran shook their heads. "That's no good at all," said the engineer. "Lithium is so elastic that blows rebound from its surface without being able to break it. We'd exhaust our muscles in vain, impotent to make the door budge by an inch."

"You know," Gontran said to Fricoulet, "I'm starting to get anxious. This silence on Ossipoff's part seems inexplicable to me. I know him well enough to be unable to believe that he's intimidated by Farenheit's threats—and anyway, he knows the two of us well enough to know that we won't let him come to any harm."

"What do you think has happened, then?"

"Damn! If what you think is true, and he really has turned the *Eclair* around in order to launch us into infinity, in a fit of scientific madness, perhaps, on reflection, he's been gripped by a fit of remorse, and he's..."

"Suicide!" exclaimed the engineer.

A dolorous groan caused them to turn round, and they saw Selena, pale and on the brink of fainting. Having heard the last words pronounced, she was leaning on the wall for support and murmuring: "My father...my poor father..."

The two young men ran to her and tried to reassure her. "No, Mademoiselle," said Fricoulet. "Gontran's suggestion is idiotic! Father Ossipoff, kill himself at the moment when Nature was about to unveil her profoundest mysteries for him? Oh, that's not a scientist's way!"

This argument had no influence on Selena's terror, though. The young woman had seized her fiancé's arm and repeated incessantly, through convulsively tremulous lips; "I'm afraid, Gontran...I'm afraid..."

Then, moved to pity, the young man looked at his friend with an expression that seemed to be begging him to find a means of reassuring Selena.

"My children," said the engineer, "only dynamite can reckon with that door. Gontran, go to the engine-room and fetch me what's needed."

In a few minutes the young man came back carrying a cartridge, the dimensions of which were soon reduced by Fricoulet in such a manner that the explosive, while being able to take care of the obstacle that had to be removed, would not do any damage to the structure of the vehicle itself. This cartridge, thus reduced, was placed by the engineer between the door and the frame, next to the lock, and he fixed a fuse to it, which he unreeled to the head of the stairway. Then, having obliged his companions to retreat down the steps, he lit the fuse.

A flicker of flame ran along the floor like a will-o'-the-wisp, reaching the charge in les than a second, and set it off. A formidable detonation resounded; the lock shattered into 1000 pieces and the door, impelled by the force of the explosion, flew open violently.

Chapter LV
In the Milky Way

With one bound, Fricoulet was in the cabin, with Farenheit and Gontran hot on his heels, followed by Selena. All of them, however, stopped abruptly, as the engineer had done almost immediately after crossing the threshold. The spectacle they beheld was, in truth, calculated to strike them with amazement.

Ossipoff was calmly sitting in his customary place within the cabin—which is to say, in front of the porthole—with his eye stuck to the ocular lens of his telescope and his body leaning forward in an attitude of ardent curiosity, searching space with a calmness that seemed to indicate that he had heard neither the frightful racket that Farenheit had been making for a quarter of an hour nor the loud noise of the explosion.

The engineer, confronted by this impassivity, was inclined to compare Ossipoff with the celebrated Archimedes—who, surprised by the enemies of his fatherland while occupied in solving a problem, not only disdained any attempt to flee but would not interrupt his calculation, stoically allowing himself to be killed.

It is probable that if the engineer had been able to read the old man's thoughts, it would have diminished is admiration considerably, for the truth was that Ossipoff knew perfectly well that he had nothing to fear from his traveling companions. Although Farenheit would have cursed and raged, Fricoulet would have joked, and Gontran, further restrained by his love for Selena, would, according to his custom, have protested with diplomatic dignity, things would not have gone any further. What was certain, though, was that as soon as they perceived his treason, Fricoulet and the others would have demanded that the machine be turned around, and the scientist had calculated that he could not stand them off alone. That was why, in order to gain time, he had turned a deaf ear to Farenheit's threats and Fricoulet's questions, telling himself that every second that went by brought him 500,000 leagues closer to the mystery he wished to penetrate.

Evidently, it was the purest egotism that was dictating his conduct yet again.

The stupor into which the old man's unexpected attitude had plunged the travelers only lasted for a few seconds, however. Farenheit, gripped once again by a wrath that was exasperated even further by that immobility, leapt upon Ossipoff, grabbed him by the collar of his jacket and lifted him off the ground as easily as if he had weighed no more than a feather. "Now will you answer, you old rogue?" he howled. "What did you do last night? And where are we?"

The old man tried in vain to free himself, but he was as powerless as a puppet in the American's muscular fingers. "Monsieur Farenheit," he implored, "let me look...every minute...every second wasted on me...I'll answer you, I swear, while consulting space."

Farenheit's reply was an outburst of loud laughter. "None of that, my brave Monsieur. Answer, or I swear to God I'll strangle you..."

Gontran and Fricoulet intervened then, saying to Farenheit: "Let him go. He's a maniac; we won't be able to get anything out of him by intimidation. Since he's promised to reply if we let him use his dear telescope, let him go."

The American's hands abandoned their prey, and within a second, Ossipoff was seated again, his eye riveted to the ocular lens, his gaze searching the immensity. "Yes," he said, in a curt tone, clipping his sentences, "I turned the *Eclair* around in its course. I understand your discontentment, but it was stronger than me. There is something in that infinity akin to a magnetic power, which attracts me and which I cannot resist."

"In any case," said Fricoulet, sardonically, "you won't talk to us about the magnet of Hyperion, for you can hardly have found any trace of it?"

A furtive blush passed over the astronomer's disconcerted face. He murmured: "And yet, my dear Gontran, the exact position of Hyperion in space, when the apparatus quit the asteroidal current in which it was sailing was definitely, with respect to the Earth, 174 degrees of longitude and 11 hours 40 minutes right ascension, was it not?"

Fricoulet shivered. A gleam appeared in his eyes, and he whispered in Flammermont's ear: "That's the information I needed."

Receiving no reply from his future son-in-law, however, Ossipoff turned round swiftly and looked him in the face. "What do you think?"

The embarrassment this question caused the young man is easily imaginable. In spite of the numerous "oral examinations" to which Ossipoff had subjected him in the three years of their acquaintance, and in spite of beginning to read *Les Continents célestes* several times over—the unfortunate almost knew them by heart—he was absolutely ignorant of what 174 degrees of longitude and 11 hours 40 minutes right ascension might signify. As he had no lack of aplomb, though, he adopted a concerned expression and muttered the reply: "That depends, my dear Monsieur, on the time at which the *Eclair* was brought about."

"It was exactly 35 minutes and 25 seconds past midnight."

Gontran shook his head several times, moving his lips silently, as one does when plunged into profound reflection. "It could well be that your calculations were exact," he eventually said, not wanting to commit himself too much.

During this time, Fricoulet—who had furtively written down the information furnished by Ossipoff in his notebook—was rapidly calculating the distance already traveled by the apparatus and the situation in space of the problematic point for which the old scientist had set a course. The result he obtained did not appear to satisfy him, though. He clicked his tongue impatiently, nervously ran his hand through his hair, and was soon heard to murmur in an irritated tone: "And yet, at a rate of two billion leagues an hour..."

The old man started, but did not abandon his telescope. "Two billion!" he riposted. "You're wide of the mark, my dear Monsieur Fricoulet. I measured our speed during the night, and was able to determine that it's considerably superior to your expectation. The *Eclair* is certainly covering two billion leagues, but per minute, not per hour."

Fricoulet inclined his head very coolly, as if the enormous figure that had just been communicated to him were not at all surprising, and contented himself with saying: "Of course. That's where my error comes from." And he calmly set about redoing his calculations.

Neither Gontran nor Farenheit, however—especially the latter—was endowed with a sufficient dose of philosophy to greet such news without protest. Just as they would have applauded that vertiginous rapidity if, by virtue of it, the *Eclair* had been able to transport them to their native planet in a shorter time than that previously anticipated, so they cursed the rapidity that was hurling them into infinity, depriving them of any hope of ever returning home.

"Two billion!" cried the American, literally terrified. "Two billion! But that makes..."

"That makes, my dear Monsieur," said Fricoulet, quite placidly, having completed his calculations, "exactly a trillion leagues, or four billon kilometers, in a little more than 30 hours."

"But where are we?" Gontran groaned. "Where are we?"

"Something like 1,200 billion leagues from our own Sun," the engineer replied. "For I'm certain now that the exceptionally bright star visible behind the vehicle is the center of our planetary system."

Farenheit waved his clenched fists in Ossipoff's direction. "Ah, bandit!" he proclaimed. "Ah, brigand!"

Impassively, the old man replied: "It's that inconceivable rapidity which drove me to do what I did. I saw the hand of Providence therein, which did not wish to leave my work unfinished and even sent me to explore the principal stellar regions, without it causing us any appreciable delay."

"Eh?" cried Gontran, who had finally lost his patience. "At the rate we're traveling, who knows whether we'll ever be able to return to Earth?"

"Just think," the old man went on, imperturbably, "that in less than a week..."

"We'll be on our way home," Farenheit put in.

"We'll be in another universe, different from the one we're leaving, and in which we'll be called to reap an inexhaustible crop of discoveries."

While the old man was speaking, the American's face had passed successively through al the colors of the rainbow, but when Ossipoff fell silent his wrath burst forth. After launching a torrent of curses of such force that modesty forbids us to reproduce them, he cried: "Never! If we allow ourselves to be led by a madman any longer, we'll be madder than him! If the rest of you, by virtue of some imbecilic weakness, encourage his folly, I'll save you in spite of yourselves!" He ran to the door, saying: "In a second, the *Eclair* will be heading for New York."

Fricoulet extended his hand. "Will you listen to me for a moment? When you've heard me you can do as you wish. Although the suet trade, which has made you rich, can have done little to open your mind on navigational matters, you'll easily understand that, in order to set a course for any port when one can't see it, it's necessary to have a compass or a beacon. Now, our beacon is the Sun that illuminates the Earth, and it happens that, by virtue of our distance therefrom, the Sun that must serve as a point of direction has fallen to the rank of a star. I shall, in consequence ask you toward what point of that sky swarming with sparks—which are as many Suns—you will direct the apparatus?"

The former Chicago businessman was immobilized, his feet nailed to the floor, dumbstruck by the justice of this reasoning.

"There's no longer any hope, then," said Gontran, truly downcast, "of ever seeing the Earth again, and we'll have to get used to the fact that the *Eclair* will be our tomb!" Then, exasperated by the words he had just spoken, he exclaimed: "No, no! It's not possible. Come on, Fricoulet, there must be a means of retracing our steps."

Ossipoff pivoted on his stool, and in a tone that betrayed a veritable pain, said: "What! Is it you, my son, who speaks thus? Were you not, in the beginning, the most ardent of collaborators?"

"Monsieur Ossipoff," the young man replied, visibly nervous, "I'm no longer a collaborator, friend or son; I'm only a man weary of all these evasions, all these delays, all these betrayals of good faith—and, were it not for your age, I'd add *all these lies*."

"Oh, Gontran," sighed Selena, reproachfully.

"He's hit the nail on the head, Mademoiselle," said Fricoulet, mockingly. "He's right!"

"We're not immortal, damn it! In addition to my patience having run out, our supplies aren't far from being exhausted—and I say, like Monsieur Farenheit: let's go back!"

From all that the young man had just said, the old man had retained but one thing: that which concerned the material impossibility of continuing the voyage. "It's you who's mistaken," he relied. "We still have breathable air, water and food for three months. Come on—give me those three months. Is a few weeks' delay too much to pay for the ineffable joy we'll experience in contemplating such marvelous worlds?"

Gontran made a forceful gesture, and had opened his mouth to reply with a categorical refusal of the old man's request, when Fricoulet leaned toward him and murmured rapidly in his ear: "Don't contradict him. Accept—there's no means of doing otherwise."

"What?" said the young man, with a start.

"It's impossible to turn round," the engineer added, in a whisper.

Low as his tone was, though, Farenheit had heard him. He stood up very straight, as if his legs had been moved by a spring, and raised his long arms toward the ceiling. "Impossible!" he shouted, in a Stentorian voice. "Impossible! I thought that word wasn't French."

Fricoulet shrugged his shoulders. "I assure you," he declared, "that if Napoleon had been in our shoes he'd never have dared to make such a statement. I'd have been curious to see what he would have done to turn round at the frightful velocity at which we're traveling."

The American roared wordlessly. "But then," he shouted, "there's no reason why we shouldn't continue in this fashion to the very end of all the worlds!"

"I don't know any more about that than you do, my dear Mr. Farenheit," Fricoulet retorted. "All that I can tell you is what I've established—and what I've established, unfortunately, is that we're traveling with a rapidity that, for some reason that escapes me, is still increasing."

"And there's nothing we can do? Nothing we can try?"

"For the moment, nothing. A miserable corpuscle, the *Eclair* is subject to stellar influences unknown to us, and against which, in consequence, it's difficult to struggle."

The American was dumbfounded, looking in turn at all the people who were there as if he expected one of them to speak up to give the lie to the engineer and affirm that all hope was not lost. Unfortunately, neither Selena nor Gontran, much less Ossipoff, was capable of reassuring his mind on that subject.

Just then, Flammermont—obedient to the advice that Fricoulet had given him—winked in Ossipoff's direction and said to the old man: "All right, then—we'll do as you wish. Let's continue on our insane course and hope that the responsibility you've taken, in acting as you did last night, won't come to weigh too heavily on your shoulders."

The old man, his mind full of scientific preoccupations, did not want to see anything in Gontran's words but a generous pardon granted to his treason. To thank him, he offered him his hand—but the young man was not inclined, for the moment, to match the old man's amicable gesture; pretending not to see it, he turned on his heel and went after Fricoulet, who was going down to the engine-room.

"I'm a man, old chap," he said, seriously. "I have the strength to hear, without trembling, the fate that's reserved for us—so I demand that you be absolutely frank."

"Well, frankly, I don't know. As I told Farenheit just now, we're presently subject to attractive forces that I can't explain. We're heading into the complete unknown. I doubt that even Father Ossipoff has any understanding of it, even though he's spent nearly all his life glued to the eyepiece of a telescope..."

This time, Gontran seemed genuinely overwhelmed, for he had absolute faith in Fricoulet's ingenuity—which had extracted them from the desperate situations that Ossipoff's mad ideas had got them into so many times since the commencement of the voyage. From the moment that the engineer told him that he could do nothing, there was only one thing to be done: await death stoically.

He went out of the engine-room without adding another word, went to his cabin and lay down in his hammock, where he was not long delayed in going to sleep, in spite of the perfectly natural anguish that his friend's frank reply had instilled in him.

He woke up on hearing his name pronounced close to his ear, and his eyes, opening suddenly, saw Fricoulet standing at his bedside, leaning over him.

"Well, you deserved a nap," said the engineer, lightly.

"Have I been asleep for long?" asked Flammermont, propping himself up on his elbow.

"Pooh! Something like six hours."

"Not possible!" exclaimed Gontran, jumping down to the floor.

The engineer's only response was to take out his watch and stick it under his friend's nose.

"My word—it's true," the latter murmured. Then the memory of the reality, which had vanished during sleep, suddenly came back to him. "Anything new?" he asked.

"Yes, one thing...something very important."

"You've succeeded in turning us around?"

"Not exactly—we're still going forward with ever-increasing speed."

"Ah!" said Flammermont, bleakly. "Then what's new, and so important?"

"My parallax, of course. You know...I've determined it."

"So what?"

"So, we know where we're going. That's something, isn't it?"

"I don't care where we're going, since it isn't where I want to go."

Fricoulet shrugged his shoulders insouciantly. "Bah!" he said. "All roads lead to Rome..." He slapped Gontran on the shoulder amicably and added: "And also to the Town Hall of the eighth arrondissement, old chap."

Flammermont released a sigh, which said a great deal about the state of lassitude he had reached. Lowering his eyes to avoid the engineer's inquisitive gaze, he replied: "Oh, my dear Alcide, if you only knew how little I care, at this moment, about the Town Hall of the eighth...and, if you want to know the truth, I'm not even thinking about it at all. I'm afraid that the further I go, and the less I think about it..."

Fricoulet burst out laughing, and slapped the apprentice diplomat on the shoulder again. "Go on, joker!" he said. "That's at least ten times since the beginning of the voyage that you've told me the same thing. You don't mean a word of what you say..."

"I swear to you..."

"No false oaths! It brings bad luck."

"Alcide..."

"Go on! Who could believe that a love great enough to drag you to the Moon in the wake of your beloved could then go up in smoke without leaving at least a portion…?"

"I'm not claiming that there's nothing left."

"In that case, you know that in incendiary matters, a fire isn't considered extinct while a single spark subsists; otherwise, it only requires a slightest breath of air to reignite the whole lot…"

Gontran bowed his head, slightly perturbed by his friend's perspicacity, although he wondered privately whether that perspicacity was capable of accurately disentangling that which he could not disentangle himself—which is to say, did he or did he not love Selena? That he had experienced a genuine and profound passion for the young woman could not be put in doubt; as Fricoulet had just said, quite rightly, one does not launch oneself forth, as he had done, into such extraordinary adventures without a powerful bond attaching you to the young woman who is drawing you in her wake. And although, disheartened by the successive delays in their return to Earth, wearied by the continual discussions raised by Ossipoff, he had indeed decided on many occasions to renouncing his love, that love had been stronger than his will and triumphed effortlessly over his irritations and bad moods.

Certainly, as he had said to Fricoulet, he still loved Selena—yes, he was sure of it; he loved her enough to marry her and to find, in that marriage, the happiness of which he had been dreaming for such a long time. But did he love her enough to continue to play, once she had become his wife, the role that he had been playing for months? That was the question he was asking himself—a question to which, even outside his moments of irritation, he thought he had to respond negatively. He had had enough of planets, bolides, comets, stars and suns! He had fully saturated himself in the reading of *Les Continents célestes*; his mind had proved itself to be absolutely insubordinate to the calculation of orbits, aphelions and all the scientific apparatus with which Fricoulet juggled as easily as if he had never done anything else in his whole life. He was powerfully indisposed to get his teeth into astronomy, and the mere sight of Ossipoff put him into a state of irritation that it was difficult to hide. Besides, the promise that he had made a few days earlier to dedicate his life to the continuation of the old scientist's studies of Hyperion and to leave his eldest son the duty of continuing his own studies—that promise made so lightly under the influence of Selena's tender smile—frightened him now that he reflected upon it coldly. What! It was not sufficient to Ossipoff's insane curiosity that he should sacrifice the few years he still had to live to the search for problematic worlds; it was also necessary that he should pursue the curiosity in question himself, and hand it on to the next generation! Had he been mad the other day when he had sworn to conform to the old man's desire?

It was under the influence of these thoughts that he raised his head and said to Fricoulet: "I swear to you that you're worse than me if it think you can affirm anything regarding what I'm going through. Certainly, Selena is a charming girl, who would make a no-less-charming companion, but astronomy....no, there's definitely too much astronomy at stake..."

"Bah! You've succeeded in hoodwinking Ossipoff for three years. For the short time that the voyage still has to go, you won't be stupid enough to take off your mask..."

Gontran folded his arms. "You imagine, then, that the old man will lay down his arms on the day of my marriage? I swear that one would think you didn't know him. But afterwards, my dear chap, it will be even worse; he'll have me within reach all the time, and he won't let a day pass without turning me over and over on his astronomical grill."

Fricoulet could not help smiling at the bitter animation his friend put into the pronunciation of these words. "You might well not be mistaken," he was obliged to reply.

"Then, as you can't be continually there to serve as my prompter, I'll be obliged to admit the truth, and he's not man enough to understand what sublimity there is, from the viewpoint of love, in a lie like mine, sustained for three years running without fail. You see now the existence I'll be forced to lead until it pleases God to call me back to Him..."

"And this love that has given you the strength to play your role of false scientist so marvelously—has it not given you the ability really to learn what you didn't know? That's what would have saved the situation..."

Gontran's frightened eyes widened. "Astronomy! Me?" he proclaimed. "Oh, you're going mad too! Oh, no, I'd far rather renounce..."

Fricoulet's face took on a singular expression. "Do you mean that seriously? Have you thought about the grief it would cause that child?"

"Certainly," Flammermont replied, with an ingenuous fatuity that brought a smile to his friend's lips, "I can't hide from myself the fact that Selena loves me dearly and that it will be a cruel blow for her to enounce the hope she had cherished for so long of being my wife—on the other hand, though, I can't soften my brain with all that scientific rubbish that idiotizes me...." After a pause, he added; "Oh, if only Ossipoff could disappear!"

"Shut up—you're being cruel."

"My dear chap, it's my happiness that I'm defending."

They fell silent briefly; then Fricoulet said to his friend: "It'll do no good to precipitate matters and, as long as you have me here, like a faithful dog, to save difficult situations, you can continue to play your role. Let's get back to Earth first. Afterwards, you can reconsider..."

"Get back to Earth! We're not taking that road, since you told me just now that we're flying through space in the opposite direction."

"That's true—except that we now know one thing that we didn't know when we first noticed that the *Eclair* had deviated from its course."

"Oh yes—that important thing. What of it?"

"What of it? The star that you mistook for Venus is merely Alpha Centauri."

Gontran's eyes widened. "Alpha Centauri!" he repeated, in a tone that so clearly revealed his ignorance that Fricoulet could not help bursting into laughter.

"Do you happen to know, perchance, what the Milky Way is?"

"Of course—I know what everyone knows about it: it's an agglomeration of stars so dense that it forms a long whitish streak in the sky, the appearance of which must have given rise to the mythological legend that represents it as a milky stain produced by the she-goat that nourished some god or other...."

"Indeed," said the engineer, with a slight shake of the head full of condescension, "That's what everyone knows—but as you're not everyone..."

"What do you mean?"

"No, the future son-in-law of Mikhail Ossipoff isn't everyone; in consequence, the Milky Way must be, for you, something other than what you've just told me..."

Gontran made a vague gesture of indifference. "If you knew how little that matters to me..." he replied. "I think my scientific baggage is adequate as it is, and I don't feel any need to increase it."

Fricoulet's face took on a tragicomic expression. "Imprudent!" he exclaimed. "You don't know that the question of the Milky Way is a palpitating, exciting actuality...and that, at any moment, Ossipoff might bring it into the conversation..."

"Well, I'll let him talk...which will be proof, on my part, of the deference due to his great age and knowledge. Then again, I have *Les Continents célestes...*"

"There's nothing in *Les Continents célestes*," the engineer replied, shaking his head, "so listen and be sure to remember..."

"I'm listening and I'll try to remember," Flammermont replied, in a resigned tone.

"It won't take long. First of all, you know, don't you, that our Solar System, with its eight planets orbiting around it, is only one island in the celestial Ocean, and that every star is a Sun like ours, the center of a planetary collection in the same way."

"I've known that since early childhood. Continue."

"First it's necessary that you know that the Milky Way surrounds the Earth and, in consequence, the entire Solar System, completely. Then, remember that Herschel has estimated the number of stars composing the Milky Way as 18,000,000, and, in addition, that these stars, seemingly so close to one another are, on the contrary, separated from one another by intervals of several million leagues—which permits the supposition that the agglomeration of Suns possesses a fabulous immensity—and, finally, that our Sun, our native planet and almost all the stars visible therefrom are part of the Milky Way. Have you understood and retained that?"

"Yes, yes—I don't know why you're telling me all this and why the question of the Milky Way is such a burning issue."

"That's true!" exclaimed Fricoulet. "I haven't told you: we're in the Milky Way at this moment and the point toward which we're headed in a straight line is situated in the region where the density of Suns is greatest: that point is Alpha Centauri. Well, when one's lost, I find that it's always a great advantage to have a means of finding oneself..."

Gontran tapped his foot impatiently. "Oh, at the end of the day, your optimism is boring. I ask you, what importance can there be in a beacon that tells you that the only road to follow is exactly the one it's impossible for you to take? Then again, you've just said yourself that we're heading for the most compact section of the Milky Way. Once we're adrift in the midst of that inextricable crowd of stars, all of which resemble one another, can you tell me, please, how we're ever going to know which one we need to steer for?"

This question was too full of common sense for the engineer to disdain to reply to it. On the other hand, though, he had obviously not anticipated it, for he was silent for a few seconds. Then Gontran exclaimed, in a tragic tone: "Here we are, condemned to wander through all the planetary systems of Infinity, veritable Wandering Jews of space, until we've found our native Earth...which is to say, until the end of time...or until our provisions..."

"No, no." said the engineer, smiling with the fine self-assurance that never abandoned him, "we aren't lost like that...and however immense the Universe might be, by going straight ahead we'll end up reaching its limit eventually."

At that moment, Selena came into the engine-room, advanced toward Flammermont and said to him, timidly: "Gontran, my father would like to know whether you'd be kind enough to join him; he dare not quit his telescope, but, at the same time, he wants to consult you..."

The young man's face fell. "Consult me, damn it!" he murmured, while he gazed anxiously at the scientist's daughter. "Do you know what the consultation is to be about?"

Selena gestured vaguely. "I can't tell you much," she replied, "except that you'll need to know something about the regions we're traveling through."

Fricoulet looked at his friend triumphantly. "What did I tell you?" he exclaimed. "Is the question of the Milky Way burning or not?"

"But I don't know anything about it," stammered Gontran, in the pitiful tone of a schoolboy from whom the teacher is demanding a repetition of his lesson.

Ossipoff's voice was audible in the stairwell. "Gontran!" he called. "Gontran...!"

The young man's gaze alternated between Fricoulet and Selena, as if asking for their advice.

"Come on, remember," said the engineer, pushing him toward the stairway. "Milky Way…mass of Suns…themselves centers of planetary systems…"

"But what about the constellations, Monsieur Fricoulet," said Selena, stopping the group in its tracks. "Have you told him about the constellations we'll pass through?"

"No, I didn't have the time. I was just about to tell him about that when you arrived."

"Quickly—tell me quickly…" begged the young Comte, anxiously.

"Well, here goes: the Milky Way extends across, starting from the north—remember that I'm talking about observations made from Earth—Aquila, where it divides into two branches, Antinous, Scutum Sobieski and Sagittarius. The two branches of the Way come together again in the southern hemisphere in the constellation of Scorpius; after that it crosses Centaurus, Triangulum Australe, Crux Australis…"[86]

Gontran put his head in his hands in a gesture of absolute desperation. "I'll never remember all that…"

"We'll prompt you, Mademoiselle Selena and I," Fricoulet affirmed. "I'll continue: we then find Canis Major, Monoceros, Taurus, Gemini, Auriga, Perseus, Cassipoeia and finally Cygnus, where it arrives, after circling the entire sky. Now, let's go…"

And he dragged Gontran away, the latter repeating in a low voice: "Antinous, Scorpius, Canis Major, Cygnus….no, I'll never remember…" He stopped and exclaimed: "Hold on—I don't even remember the name of the Sun we're heading for."

"Centaurus—three trillion leagues from the Sun. Don't forget that its light takes three and a half years to reach us."

They resumed their progress, while Selena, to comfort her fiancé, said to him softly: "Don't worry. I'm here, and I'll help you."

"I'll get it wrong for sure..."

"Bah!" jeered Fricoulet. "Think of the Town Hall of the eighth, and you won't go wrong."

Ossipoff, his eye still glued to his telescope, did not move when he heard the noise of footsteps entering his cabin. He contented himself with saying: "Ah,

---

[86] Translation of the names of the constellations poses a problem from this point on; Le Faure and Graffigny use the familiar French names, but only a few of the equivalent English names have ever enjoyed much common usage, the Latin names usually being far better known (partly by virtue of their routine use with respect to the constellations of the Zodiac). I have, therefore, decided to substitute the Latin names when the descriptions being issued are more technical than familiar. I thought it best to retain Antinous, here and elsewhere, in spite of the fact the constellation in question had already been declared obsolete in the 1880s and relegated to the status of a star-cluster in Aquila.

it's you, my dear friend. I've been waiting for you impatiently." His speech demonstrated that the old man, entirely recaptured by his scientific preoccupations, had completely forgotten the grievances held against him by his traveling companions, especially Gontran.

The latter drew near, saying: "What do you want, Monsieur Ossipoff?"

"To have your opinion on the situation. I've been observing for nearly 24 hours, and my ideas are no longer as clear as they were, but you must have been thinking on your own account. Where do you think we are at present?"

"In the Milky Way," replied he young man, confidently. "Isn't that so, Fricoulet?"

"It's not Monsieur Fricoulet I'm asking, but you, my dear friend," Ossipoff remarked, clicking his tongue impatiently. Pursing his lips to indicate the mediocre esteem in which he held the engineer's scientific knowledge, he added: "Why don't you ask Mr. Farenheit's advice while you're at it?"

The latter came in at exactly that moment and exclaimed: "My advice! You never followed it. Oh, if only you'd always followed my advice, we'd have committed fewer stupidities than we have. For a start, we wouldn't be here..."

The American had pronounced these words in a single breath, with a volubility that they tried in vain to interrupt—but when he had finished, Ossipoff said to him, disdainfully: "You don't know what you're talking about, my dear Monsieur—you're not up to date with the conversation." To Gontran, he said: "According to you, then, we're in the Milky Way?"

"There not a shadow of doubt." The young Comte made this reply in a much less confident tone, for the scientist had addressed him in the tone he normally adopted when he seemed to have surprised Gontran in flagrant ignorance or in an opinion divergent from his own.

"Ah, the Milky Way!" Ossipoff repeated, having considered him briefly through his spectacles. "Well, I'm sorry to have to give you the lie, my dear friend."

The word "lie" got under the young man's already-irritated skin, like the point of a needle. He went read and cried out: "Lie! Me!"

"These things are of no importance between scientists, joker," Fricoulet murmured in his ear.

"That's true," Gontran observed. Addressing Ossipoff, he said: "Without indiscretion, might one know why? For one of two things is happening: either you're asking for my opinion or setting me an examination..."

"Allow me..."

"Nothing, until I've finished. If you wanted to amuse yourself by setting me an oral exam, I tell you straight away that it's a bad time and that I think it in bad taste..."

"Oh, far be it from me..."

"If, on the contrary, you want to know my opinion, it's that you don't have any right, and that I have every right, to be astonished by your giving me the lie so forcefully…" The brave Gontran had genuinely lost his temper—for no good reason, it must be admitted—and the engineer, like the American, was looking at him in veritable amazement.

"Now that you've finished, I'll answer you," the old man said, quite placidly. He got up and pointed Gontran to the telescope, saying only one word: "Look."

The young man sat down, put his eye to the ocular lens and—slightly disconcerted, it must be admitted—said: "Well?"

"Have you looked hard?"

"Yes."

"The brightest star that we have ahead of us—what is it, according to you?"

"Alpha Centauri," replied Flammermont, boldly, after having glanced up at Fricoulet. Then, seeing Ossipoff raise his splayed fingers toward the ceiling, with all the most obvious signs of horror, he asked: "What do you think it is?"

Ossipoff bounded to the box that enclosed his most precious objects, which he had saved from the various catastrophes in which he had lost the greater part of his scientific materials. He came back brandishing a celestial map, which he unrolled before Gontran's eyes.

"Do you see any point of resemblance," he said, "between what is on this map and what is there in space? Here's Centaurus—there, under my finger. If what you claim to be Alpha really were, that assembly of stars would present itself to us with a similar appearance…"

After looking at the map, the young Comte put his eye to the ocular lens again. He had already opened his mouth to agree that the points of resemblance between what was and what ought to be were hardly numerous when Fricoulet—who was trying hard to get closer to his friend but could not do it because Ossipoff would not take his eyes off him—decided to intervene. "My God, Monsieur Ossipoff," he stammered, forcing himself to adopt an ingenuous manner, "excuse me if I'm being stupid—I'm scarcely up to date in such matters, as you know—but it seems to me that perspective must have something to do with that difference of appearance."

"Perspective!" exclaimed the old man, with a start.

"Indeed," the engineer went on. "Don't you think that a distance of three trillion leagues is liable to change the angle from which one perceives things slightly? It's quite natural for the forms of constellations not to be the same. The stars, which seem so close to one another when seen from Earth, have drawn apart. What do you think, Gontran?"

"I think," the latter replied, boldly, while thanking his friend with a wink for holding out a lifeline yet again, "that your logic has seen more accurately than Monsieur Ossipoff's science, and that you have just formulated the opinion that I was about to make known when you began to speak."

The engineer turned away slightly to conceal the smile provoked by his friend's effrontery, while Ossipoff almost elbowed Gontran aside in order to take his place at the telescope, murmuring in a voice trembling with emotion: "Alpha! Alpha!"

Farenheit leaned close to Fricoulet's ear and indicated the scientist with a nod of his head: "There he goes," he murmured, disdainfully.

Abruptly, without moving, Ossipoff said: "Gontran, didn't you tell me that you'd established the parallax of that star?"

Fricoulet hastily passed his friend a page from his notebook, on which he had made his calculations.

"Indeed, Monsieur Ossipoff."

"And that gave you?"

"Results confirming the exactitude of the parallax obtained by terrestrial astronomers—which is to say, 0.92, nearly a second." For the edification of Farenheit and Selena, he added: "Which corresponds to 222,000 times the distance from the Earth to the Sun."

"Or eight trillion leagues," said Fricoulet, in his turn, "which means that light from Alpha Centauri takes three years and three months to arrive on Earth, and that an express train traveling at 60 kilometers an hour would cover that distance of 32,000,000,000 kilometers in something like 60,000,000 years."

Ossipoff was not listening; he was plunged in admiration of the star, which he had never been able to observe from Pulkova Observatory, having not been lucky enough to be chosen by his colleagues to go to the globe's southern hemisphere—the only place from which it is visible—to study it in detail. Prey to an inexpressible anxiety, he was still repeating: "Alpha! Alpha!"

"Look out," murmured Fricoulet, leaning toward Gontran. "The devil may devour me if Alpha doesn't fall on your head like a roof-tile before much longer. So, star of first magnitude…light equal to the 27,000th part of the full Moon."

"That's not much."

"And yet, it's been concluded that Alpha is much brighter and more luminous than our Sun."

"I don't understand."

"It's easy, though. You mustn't forget that, although it would require 22,000,000 stars as bright as Alpha to give us the same light as the Sun, Alpha is 32,000,000,000 kilometers away, and, in consequence…."

"Understood—but people like you seem to find it amusing to juggle with figures; what interest is there, I ask you, in knowing that a train traveling at…etc., etc? One could prolong such examples indefinitely and, having established a train's record for speed, could establish a tortoise's record for slowness."

Without making any reply, the engineer went on: "Until 1689, Alpha passed for a simple star; it was Richaud,[87] at Pondicherry, who doubled it for the first time..."

"Doubled?" repeated Gontran, startled by the expression.

"Which is to say that Alpha has a companion, of an orange yellow color, 16 seconds distant from it—about 723,000,000 leagues..."

"And you call that being accompanied?"

"My dear chap, given the infinity in which the stars move, that distance is minimal. In any case, whether the expression is accurate or not, the facts are the same. The revolution of these two Suns about their center of gravity is effectuated in 84 years—a duration exactly similar to that of Uranus about the Sun. Can you remember that?"

"Yes, yes," Gontran replied, as irritated as ever by these mysterious repetitions of astronomy, which seemed to him to be even more irritating in the present circumstances. "Is that all?"

"No, it's not all. There's one more thing you have to remember, for it's one of the most important points concerning the stars: Alpha Centauri is animated by a very rapid proper motion."

"What! By a proper motion?"

"Which is to say that, not content to rotate about their own axes and around one another, the two Suns are moving through space from 0.477 seconds right ascension westwards and 0.776 declination northwards—which gives as a result, moving northwestwards, an arc of 3.463 seconds per year, six minutes per century, or a degree every ten centuries, relative to the Solar System."

"The constellations are moving, then?"

"Exactly."

"In that case, the celestial maps established by the astronomers of antiquity..."

"Are not identical to ours...any more than ours will be identical to those of your grandchildren," said Fricoulet, making allusion to the solemn promise that Gontran had made.

The latter muttered between his teeth: "If there's only my heirs to occupy themselves with Centaurus and Co., science stands a good chance of coming to a standstill."

Farenheit—who, having nothing else to do, had been listening to the engineer's explanation—said: "These eternal displacements must end up turning the sky upside down—and I thought that it was only humankind that changed!"

"Everything changes in Nature, Monsieur Farenheit," Fricoulet retorted. "In 12,000 years, Alpha Centauri will be part of the constellation of the South-

---

[87] Père Jean Richaud (1633-1693) was one of several notable Jesuit astronomers of the period.

ern Cross, the shape of which will be dislocated as the centuries pass and it continues to head toward Sirius…"

"But in 12,000 years, the Southern Cross itself might no longer exist."

"Yes, that's quite possible."

Gontran shrugged his shoulders. "What's the point, then, in taking so much trouble studying things that will no longer exist tomorrow?"

At that moment, Ossipoff released an exclamation that gathered his traveling companions around him. "Gontran! Fricoulet! Selena!" he said, in an admiring voice. "Oh, my friends, my child! I can see it…I can see it! There it is! There's no possible error—how beautiful it is! How beautiful!"

"My God, Monsieur Ossipoff," said Fricoulet, sardonically, "if you won't let us see, at least tell us what you're looking at."

"Omega,[88] my dear Fricoulet—it's Omega that I have here in the field of the telescope…" And the old man, gripped by his admiration, fell silent again, totally absorbed by the contemplation of the object.

"Omega?" repeated Farenheit, who had had no need to devote himself to the study of dead languages to make a fortune in the animal fat trade.

"A letter of the Greek alphabet, my dear sir," Fricoulet replied, "by means of which the astronomical catalogues designate one of the finest masses of stars in the celestial universe."

"A mass?"

"The wonderstruck eye of an observer named Sir John Herschel perceived a veritable swarm of several thousand stars, prodigiously grouped in a spherical form, measuring more than 20 seconds in diameter—which is to say, nearly two thirds the size of the disk of the full Moon."

Gontran nodded his head in the direction of the aged scientist. "In that case," he murmured, "Ossipoff must be in seventh heaven!"

He fell silent when the old man, whose lips had been moving silently, began to speak as if in ecstasy. "Yes, yes…Flammarion was right when he concluded from the clarity of those little luminous points and the considerable extent of the mass entirely resolvable into stars, that this is one of the nearest celestial universes to ours.[89] Oh, what a marvel! Oh, a truly sublime spectacle! And

[88] Ossipoff is referring to Omega Centauri, a globular cluster some 17,000 light years from Earth, which was first identified as such by John Herschel (1792-1871) in the 1830s.

[89] In fact, Flammarion was not entirely correct with respect to Omega Centauri being "another celestial universe" (the term "galaxy" had not yet come into use); it is one of many globular clusters lying around the edge of our own galaxy. The fundamental hypothesis that the Milky Way was merely one "celestial universe" among many, and that many nebulas were actually similar aggregations of stars, was still reckoned daring, however—but was, in essence, correct.

how good God is to have let me live long enough to admire Him in one of the most marvelous of his creations.

Farenheit muttered between his teeth: "That depends how you look at things—God would have done better if he'd permitted me to admire Fifth Avenue!"

"And me the Town Hall of the eighth," murmured Flammermont.

Selena took the young man's hand in hers, indicated the old man with an affectionate gesture, and said in a gentle voice; "Oh, Gontran, he's so happy!"

"You're forgetting, Mademoiselle," Fricoulet objected, "that his happiness is founded in the misfortune of others—but the fact is that his happiness seems to be at its peak..."

Ossipoff raised himself up on his seat, his hands gripping the telescope against which his face was stuck, his body agitated by a convulsive tremor, seeming to tense himself for a leap into space, so drawn was he to the spectacle that presented itself to him. Suddenly, though, he was heard to ask in a low voice: "Are we making progress? Is it the worlds that are moving? Are they, like us, obeying a movement of general translation?"

"What is he saying?" Gontran whispered to Fricoulet.

The latter smiled and, signaling to his friend to follow him, went out of the cabin on tiptoe.

"Given the ferocious manner in which Ossipoff is incessantly interrogating you," the engineer explained when they were alone in the engine-room, "it's best to avoid being in range as much as possible when you're not obliged to be. It's a matter of elementary prudence—especially when you're at risk of being dragged on to unfamiliar terrain."

"But what did he mean?" asked Flammermont, again.

"Oh, it's quite simple, but it's necessary to be up to date. The stars, in whatever part of the sky they might be, appear at first sight to be moving in all directions with all possible velocities. Attentive study, however, has established that all these movements, seemingly so diverse, are submissive to a law, and that law is regulated by our own Sun."

"Not very clear," murmured the young Comte.

"But yes, quite clear—have you ever stuck your nose out of the side window of a railway carriage?"

"What a question!"

"Then you must have noticed that in looking at the telegraph poles arranged along the track, the posts seem to be running away from the train with a speed greater than that of the train!"

"Perfectly true."

"Well, some astronomers claim that it's the same for the movement that seems to animate the stars. Our Solar System is traveling through space along a determinate line and with a velocity that has been successfully measured. Now, the stellar worlds toward which our Sun is moving seem, on the contrary, to be hurrying away from it, drawing further apart from one another the further it advances, while the contrary phenomenon is produced for those it has passed by. The result is a sort of current, which seems to be bearing the stars from the Sun's point of destination towards its point of departure. Do you understand now?"

"It's quite simple."

"Except that the theory of the apparent movement of stars is not admitted by everyone, and even gives rise to passionate debate. From the few words that Ossipoff pronounced just now, I infer that he does not have firmly fixed ideas on the subject..." There was a pause, at the end of which the engineer added: "You might, I think, go and suggest to Ossipoff that he let's you take his watch."

"It's Farenheit's turn to do it," Gontran retorted, vainly hiding a sonorous yawn behind his hand.

As he finished these words, the sound of soft footfalls was heard on the staircase; almost immediately, Selena's graceful face appeared in the doorway. "My father's asleep, Monsieur Fricoulet," she said, in a low voice. "I came to warn you that Mr. Farenheit has said that he'll take the watch."

"A marvel. For all the good it will do, he might as well sleep too. The speed at which we're traveling makes any maneuver impossible."

Within five minutes, everyone aboard was plunged into deep sleep, save for the American, whose heavy boots were making the lithium floor vibrate rhythmically.

How long would they sleep thus?

Suddenly, a frightful scream, waking them up abruptly, brought Ossipoff, Fricoulet, Gontran and Selena running from their cabins at he same time. A terrifying spectacle awaited them.

Farenheit was roaming like a madman through the cabin, which was afire with an intense light entering through the portholes, formed of all the colors of the prism. Hiding his face in his clenched hands, he was running, jumping and bumping his lowered head rudely into walls. Ossipoff, grabbing the tails of his jacket, tried in vain to bring him to a halt. The American was emitting veritable howls, like those of a wounded animal, shaking his head, as if he could not hear the objurgations of the old scientist he was dragging in his wake, unable even to perceive his weight.

"What's happening, Monsieur Ossipoff?" asked Fricoulet, immobile on the threshold.

"How do I know? I was drowsy, my eyes fatigued by the sparkling light coming from space, when screams woke me with a start. I don't know any more than that."

"Perhaps it's another fit of madness," murmured Selena, sympathetically.

"We need to lock him in his cabin again," Gontran proposed.

It seemed, however, that these words brought the American's overexcitement to its climax. His screams became shriller, his gestures more disordered, and he stammered: "My eyes! My eyes! Blind!"

This was like a flash of enlightenment for Fricoulet. "Oh, the poor chap!" he cried. "Quickly, quickly! Gontran, cover up the portholes! You, Monsieur Ossipoff, don't go near the telescope."

Briskly, with Selena's aid, Gontran blocked the portholes with anything that came to hand—blankets, cushions and tablecloths—and the voyagers immediately felt relieved in the relative obscurity that then descended.

"My dear Monsieur Farenheit," the engineer said then, in a firm voice, advancing toward the madman, "will you let me examine your eyes?" As he spoke, he extended his arm to stop the American in his tracks—but the other bounded away to the far side of the room, continuing to utter frightful squeals. The engineer made a sign to Gontran and Ossipoff and, in response to a mute signal, all three of them hurled themselves on the unfortunate. They succeeded in tying him up and maintaining him motionless on a chair.

"Hold his hands firmly behind his back," Fricoulet instructed Ossipoff. "Gontran, you prevent him from moving his head."

While the old man held the American's arms, the other seized his head—and Fricoulet, skillfully pinching the upper and lower eyelids of one eye between his fingers, drew them apart. "Oh, the poor devil!" he murmured, while his eyebrows contracted in annoyance. In reply to the interrogative gazes that his companions fixed on him, he said: "The retina is badly damaged."

"But how?"

"That accursed telescope, of course. Being on watch, to relieve the boredom somewhat, Mr. Farenheit decided to look at Alpha Centauri, and the heat, concentrated at the focal point of the ocular lens, must have seared his retina. Is that right?"

The American released a formidable sigh. "Alas, yes," he moaned. "Am I blind, then?"

"Let's hope not. How you go on! The other eye probably isn't as sore as this one."

"But what about this one?" cried Farenheit, shaking with rage at the thought that he had lost the sight of the eye.

Fricoulet stamped his foot impatiently. "Hold still, damn it! I can't tell you anything for the moment. Let's see the other..." He seized the lids of the left eye, drew them apart, and examined the retina attentively for a few seconds. Then his face cleared and he murmured, in tone of genuine relief: "With care, we'll save this one."

"But what about the other?" the American persisted.

"I don't know. In any case, whatever happens, you can count yourself lucky still to have one eye, when there was every chance you'd be blind."

Farenheit started violently, shrugging off those who were holding him.

“Mademoiselle Selena,” the engineer said to Ossipoff’s daughter, “please will you bring me my medical kit immediately.”

These words had the effect of putting the American into a fury again.

Ossipoff, who had been looking worried for some little time, said the young engineer in a whisper: “But in these conditions, it’s impossible to use the telescope!”

“Indeed!” the other replied, laughing. “You’ll have to deprive yourself of your cherished studies until further notice.”

The old man uttered a dolorous groan, to which Fricoulet replied with mocking laughter. Clapping the old man on the shoulder, he said: “Don’t worry—your beloved telescope will be all right. I give you my word that, if it weren’t indispensable to determine our route, I’d let it rest for a while.”

“True! But how are you going to make us of it?”

“What’s smoked glass for, damn it?” While talking, the multitalented Fricoulet spread a rapidly-compounded mixture on a scarf, with which he covered the eyes of the groaning and cursing American.

“Oh, what a fine spectacle!” Gontran suddenly cried, having just lifted up the blanket masking one if the portholes.

A vertiginously intense and variegated light filled space, and it seemed that the *Eclair* was flying through fiery dust.

Chapter LVI
At the South Pole of the world

"All the same—and you can say what you like—I'm beginning to feel that I've had enough of astronomy."

There was a brief silence, suddenly broken by Fricoulet's mocking laugh, and Gontran added: "If I knew who first thought up that accursed science, I'd consign his name to the execration..."

"Of generations to come?"

"Merely of generations of lovers—but *in saecula saeculorum*."[90]

This was said with such profound conviction, and at the same time so manifestly dejected, that the engineer could not help giving free rein to his hilarity. "You'll admit, however," he said, when his outbursts of laughter permitted him to formulate his thoughts, "that all you lovers would find it singularly inconvenient if no one had ever thought of examining the Heavens! What would become then of the entire vocabulary you use, in which it is always a question of the radiance of the skies, the twinkling of stars, moonlight, etc, etc.—in sum, the entire heap of silly nonsense by means of which you hypnotize the person you're addressing..."

The diplomat replied to this argument with a simple shrug of the shoulders—while Farenheit, who appeared to be drowsing in a corner, exclaimed: "You'll permit me to say, however, Monsieur Fricoulet, that lovers have existed since the creation of the world."

"Or very nearly," aid the engineer. "For you'll similarly concede that, in order for Adam to be amorous, it was at least indispensable for Eve to be created."

The American replied to this joke with an indistinct groan—for he did not much like being contradicted—and went on: "Now, when God created man, I never heard it said that he created at the same time, for his amusement, telescopes, meridionals and equatorials—in sum, all that ironmongery that gives such great joy to Monsieur Ossipoff."

Leaning slightly forwards, with his fists firmly set upon his knees, in an attitude of victory, the American fixed his eye upon the engineer, waiting defiantly for his response. We say "his eye" rather than "his eyes" because Fricoulet had not yet authorized the removal of the bandage that cut diagonally across his face since the accident that he had suffered.

"Of course!" riposted Fricoulet. "I had no intention of claiming that astronomy goes back to Adam and Eve; furthermore, one might suppose that in that era—which is to say, before the serpent had invited Eve to bite into the ap-

---

90 "*For centuries upon centuries*"—i.e., indefinitely.

ple—life on Earth was so delightful that the thoughts of our first ancestors had no need to rise above the crowns of the trees of Paradise."

Gontran laughed sardonically. "Do you think you can persuade me that Adam only invented astronomy to distract himself from the misfortunes that were suddenly heaped upon him?"

"As the newspapers of the time say nothing about it," the engineer said, "you'll permit me to remain equally mute on the subject. What is proven, though, is that astronomy is certainly the most ancient science there is..."

"A long-service medal doesn't make it any more interesting!" Gontran complained.

Farenheit started in surprise. "Then why did you take it up?" he asked.

"What! Why? Because..." The young man stopped short, noticing the singular gaze that the engineer had fixed on him, and a second's reflection showed him the stupidity he was about to commit by revealing to Farenheit the secret of the comedy that love had led him to play for such a long time. In a penetrating tone, he replied: "Because I was irresistibly drawn to it."

"Good for you," said Farenheit. "You'll understand that for myself, being a suet merchant, there's nothing in the stars that could attract me..."

"Nothing at all," jeered Fricoulet. "Well then, why did you go to the Moon?"

In response to this question, which reminded him of the origin of all his misadventures, the American's face suddenly flushed. He stood bolt upright and waved his fist in the air. "By God! You ask me that! It was Sharp—that scoundrel Sharp—who got me into it. Oh, the diamonds of the Moon! A fine joke...and we claim that we're practical men! But that Russian...that wretched Russian..."

"Pardon me, but Sharp isn't a true Russian; he's a hybrid in which the German element is dominant..." Having said that, Fricoulet—whose lively tongue could not stay silent for long—continued, addressing Gontran: "Did you know that Aryan shepherds spent their nights contemplating the stars, that the Chinese—and after them, the Egyptians of the first dynasty—left records of a large number of highly valuable astronomical observations?"

"No, I didn't..."

"Progressively, century after century, the science of the universe was perfected by the improvement of optical apparatus..."

Farenheit laughed loudly. "And what's the practical consequence of all that?" he asked. "You tell us that generations of eyes, for thousands of years, wore themselves out against the ocular lenses of telescopes...what fine progress..."

The engineer pursed his lips, while a brief gleam lit up in his malicious eyes. "Tell me, my dear Mr. Farenheit," he asked, slyly, "do you like coffee?"

The American jumped slightly in response to this question and licked his lips appreciatively. "Have you, by chance, a cup to offer me?" he replied. "No, you haven't. So what connection is there between mocha and stars?"

A thin smile illuminated Fricoulet's face. "What connection is there!" he exclaimed. "Listen to me and you'll see that, in the absence of astronomical science, we inhabitants of the Old World wouldn't be able to drink coffee. Was it not from the exact knowledge of the movement of the stars that the division of time was deduced, the estimation of duration, the establishment of longitudes and their calculation in mid-ocean. Take away all that and tell me how long-distance voyages could be undertaken? Now, without the crossings to which astronomy assured a relative security, how would the importation into countries now arrived at maturity of the products of equatorial regions be achieved?" He concluded triumphantly with the classic formula: "Q.E.D."

"Pardon me," said Flamermont, laughing, "but *that which was to be demonstrated* was not only that astronomical science is favorable to important business conducted between Le Havre and Rio or Martinique, but favorable in itself."

Fricoulet opened his eyes wide. "In itself?" he repeated, interrogatively.

"I mean that the more advanced astronomical science becomes, the less one is advanced. It's the perfect example of chameleon science, which demolishes the day after what it discovered the day before, preventing you from recognizing anything in the work of your forebears—or so little that it's hardly worth talking about—and I confess quite frankly that astronomers require a pretty deep-rooted faith to continue working in such conditions..."

"I don't understand."

"It's easy, though," Gontran retorted. "Take, if you wish, Monsieur Ossipoff; there's a man who has, so to speak, exhausted himself in the search for Hyperion. The planet doesn't exist, I know, but suppose it did—he assigns it a location in the sky, traces its orbit, establishes the laws of its rotation, calculates its mass, its volume, its density. Ossipoff is a great man—and *bang!* In 100 years from now, or 200, the astronomers seek Hyperion and Hyperion has disappeared...or changed location, orbit, mass, density, etc. Now Ossipoff is treated as a victim of illusion, if he isn't simply written off as a donkey..." The young man turned to Farenheit. "Is that true?" he asked. "Is that fair?"

"I didn't understand any of it," replied the American, imperturbably, "but it seems quite logical to me."

Fricoulet shrugged. "For myself," he said, "I assure you that the Heavens are just as well-known, even better-known, than the entire Earth. Very precise maps have been drawn up of all its regions by numerous astronomers, and before long, a photographic map of all the stars, obtained directly, will give the exact positions of the stars that astronomers, to facilitate their research, have associated into constellations..."

This conversation was taking place in the engine-room, where Gontran was finishing his watch, having been accompanied throughout by Fricoulet—who was interested, in spite of himself, in the intersidereal desert through which the vehicle was flying—and Farenheit, who could not sleep, annoyed by the thought that they were flying away from the Earth instead of heading toward it.

Ossipoff, shut up in his cabin, had been taking a well-earned rest after nearly 30 hours of continual wakefulness, and Selena—as was her custom—was making a fair copy of the notes the scientist had made in the course of his observations.

Fricoulet had just pronounced the words reported above when the American, who was looking distractedly through one of the portholes, next to which he was sitting—a porthole blackened by smoke as a precaution—exclaimed in an admiring tone: "That's truly superb! Come and look at this, Monsieur de Flammermont."

Gontran, long blasé about the various surprises reserved for him by the celestial immensity, nonchalantly joined Farenheit and put his face beside the American's, the latter being too interested to surrender his place. Despite his skepticism, the young man could not help crying out too: "Wonderful!"

The spectacle that offered itself to the voyagers was indeed enchanting and magical. The profound blackness of space was packed with multicolored stars. Here were entirely white globes that radiated milky tints of extraordinary delicacy into space; there were mysterious worlds brightening the depths of space with a glow that passed through all the shades of red, from scarlet to the finest orange-yellow; a little further on there was an assemblage of stars of different hues, resembling the colors of an extraordinary palette. Some of these worlds seemed blurred by a luminous mist, like Venetian lanterns whose flames flicker as the festivals they illuminate come to an end, ready to go out. A large number, on the other hand, sent rays into space as raw and ardent as the brightest electric lamps, and all these rays intersected with one another, becoming confused, and ended up forming an atmosphere around the lithium vehicle so strangely multicolored that the Terrans' eyes, full of surprise, could not comprehend its composition.

"Damn!" murmured Gontran. "If the organizers of the Festival of Flowers held annually in the Bois de Boulogne could see this, they'd hand in their resignation lest they die of shame."

Farenheit, for his part, added: "Since its foundation, the Eccentric Club has held many parties and dances that would have surprised the people of the Old World, but this is something that far surpasses the luxury of our settings..." Then, after a few moments spent contemplating the marvelous spectacle, the American asked: "Are all those stars?"

"Certainly," said Fricoulet. "Why does that surprise you?"

"Simply because I thought all stars were subject to a continual scintillation, while all the lights we see at present are steady."

"It was the same when we looked at them on Mars," Gontran added. Almost immediately, he added in a diffident tone: "An optical illusion, no doubt."

"What!" exclaimed Fricoulet. "No doubt—that's certainly the case. And do you know to what that optical illusion is due? Simply to the thickness of Earth's layer of atmosphere, which produces the phenomenon of stellar scintillation. Here, we're afloat in the void and the light of the stars appears to us as it really is—which is to say, steady, or very nearly so…"

Gontran, who was listening to his friend distractedly, all his attention being drawn to the marvelous spectacle in space, objected: "But the light of Mars, Venus and even the Moon, doesn't scintillate, and yet, in reaching us, its light traverses the Earth's atmosphere just like that of the stars."

"That's how the planets are distinguished," Fricoulet replied. As he spoke he drew nearer to Flammermont, into whose ear he whispered: "Now, if ever Ossipoff interrogates you on this subject, you'll be able to tell him that it's the white stars that scintillate most and the red and orange stars that scintillate least."

"In the spectra of the former we find all the colors of the prism, with the black lines characteristic of hydrogen; in the latter, the spectra are traversed by large nebulous dark bands forming a sort of colonnade." It was Ossipoff who had pronounced these words from the bottom step of the stairway, from which he had only heard the engineer's last few words. Persuaded as he was of the scientific knowledge of his future son-in-law, the quite natural idea that presented itself to his mind was that Fricoulet was replying to an "oral examination" set by his friend. Smiling sarcastically, he added: "Do you at least know the number per second of the variations in color for all the stars observed and assembled at a similar height of 30 degrees above the horizon?"

Fricoulet winked knowingly at his friend and replied, with imperturbable assurance: "I wouldn't have the great privilege of answering you, my dear Monsieur Ossipoff, if Gontran hadn't just told me. The number is 86 for the white stars and 56 for the red." Then deliberately assuming a naïve expression to deceive the old man, he said: "In France, peasants claim that a more pronounced scintillation of the stars presages rain—and in general, they're not mistaken."

"Which isn't astonishing, since the presence of water vapor in the atmosphere, in a more-or-less considerable quantity, has a marked effect on the scintillation."

That said, Ossipoff's face underwent a complete transformation. A deep wrinkle appeared between his abruptly furrowed eyebrows and his lips pursed in an anxious moue. He took Gontran by the arm. "My dear boy," he said, in a low voice, as if he were ashamed, "I'd like to talk to you about a serious matter…"

The young man darted an anxious glance at Fricoulet—who made a hand gesture whose clear significance was *By the grace of God*—and followed the old scientist up the stairway, bleakly and silently, with his head lowered like that of a victim.

Once on the landing, Ossipoff opened the door of his cabin, stood aside to let his companion pass, leaned over to make sure that neither Fricoulet nor the

American would be able to listen in, and, having entered in his turn, carefully closed the door behind him.

Damn! Flammermont said to himself, mentally, looking at his future father-in-law surreptitiously. *What can he want with me?* His anxiety increased further when, having carefully closed the door, the old man came to stand directly in front of him and examined him through his spectacles in a singular manner, while passing his hand distractedly over his long white beard. One might have thought that he was somewhat apprehensive about speaking, and that before resolving to do it he was trying to discover in advance how his interlocutor might react to the communication he had to make to him.

Finally, making up his mind, Ossipoff coughed two or three times, and put his hand on the young man's arm in a paternal gesture. "My dear boy," he stammered, in an embarrassed manner, with an intonation of humility in his voice. "My dear boy, I have a painful confession to make to you."

Gontran felt a cold sweat suddenly forming on his brow. His upper body moved abruptly backwards, and he exclaimed, indignantly: "Again!" He thought that the old scientist had given way to some new fit of scientific madness, complicating the voyagers' situation even further.

"My dear boy," the old man went on, without getting upset, "I'm appealing to all your science and your memory..."

This time, Gontran felt a small frisson run over his entire body, making his skin prickle; Ossipoff's few words had forewarned him of the direction that the conversation was about to take.

"I asked you to come up," the old man explained, "for a reason that you, as a scientist, will understand. I didn't want to make you party to the strange mental weakness of which I am presently the victim in front of Farenheit and Fricoulet, who don't understand..."

"Oh, but Fricoulet's too modest a chap not to be indulgent," Gontran protested.

The last word was ill-chosen; it almost set fire to the powder, and the lenses of Ossipoff's spectacles suddenly sparkled, while he replied in a curt, dry and cutting manner: "I have no use for Monsieur Fricoulet's indulgence."

"What does it matter, anyway?" said Gontran. "What is this about?"

The old man hesitated again. What he had to say obviously seemed to him to be an enormity, and he was not certain that his trust was well-placed. On the other hand, though, driven by imperious necessity, he made his decision, releasing a little sigh. "Let's see—I have no need to ask you, have I, whether your calculations are exact?"

"What calculations?"

"Those which enabled you to establish the route followed by the *Eclair*."

Gontran started violently, as if the mere idea that anyone could doubt the authenticity of his calculations were sufficient to offend him. "Are you joking?" he contented himself with replying, with perfectly simulated dignity.

"Don't be offended, my dear friend," said Ossipoff, hastily. "Far be it from me to doubt your science—but what's happening is so extraordinary, so unbelievable that when I've told you...you'll find my question excusable."

The young man's anxiety was still growing. For an old scientist of Ossipoff's worth to lose his composure, it must indeed be a tough problem, for the solution of which all his cunning would be useless. "Speak, Monsieur Ossipoff," he said, in a voice that he tried to keep firm, "and if my modest intelligence can be of any use to you..."

"So, your calculations being accurate, and your observations exact, we've reached the Milky Way and have passed the star nearest to our Solar System."

"Alpha Centauri—that's correct."

"The majority of the suns that astronomers attribute to that constellation are to our right, and we're in the vicinity of Crux Australis?"

The final words were not as assured as the beginning of the sentence, but were pronounced in an interrogative tone that could only leave the young man somewhat perplexed. Nevertheless, as it as impossible for him to remain silent, he replied forcefully in the affirmative. "That's correct."

Ossipoff released a profound sigh, as if an enormous weight had been lifted from his bosom. "Ah, my dear boy," he stammered. "You don't know how happy I am to find you in agreement with me on that point—except that I'd like you to explain this phenomenon to me." He took the young Comte by the hand, led him to the telescope and, by applying a gentle pressure to his shoulders, constrained him to sit down before the instrument, saying: "Look!"

Utterly bewildered, Gontran put his eye to the lens. Looked, and, thinking that the old man was disconcerted by the strange coloration of the worlds distributed in space, was about to launch into a variation of the explanations that Fricoulet had just given him regarding the different hues observed in the radiation of stars, when Ossipoff exclaimed: "Well? You're looking for it, like me—but you can wear out your eyes and search every corner of the sky, and you won't find it..."

Gontran said to himself, privately: *I'd give a lot to know what he's talking about.* But he searched in vain to discover what the old man might have been looking for in that celestial Venetian fête.

"It's hopeless," Ossipoff finally said. For five hours I've searched all the constellations—there's no more Crux Australis than there is in my hand..."

It's the Southern Cross he wants, thought the young Comte. *I'm damned if I'd ever have found it. I wouldn't recognize it...* He straightened up and said, in the most natural tone in the world: "Just as you've been searching for it, my dear Monsieur Ossipoff, so have I. And then?"

"What? And then? But where is Crux Australis? Where is the group of stars that ought to be on our right? Where's Alpha, in fact?" He clutched his head in both hands in a veritable gesture of desperation and added: "I'm losing my head, my boy. I can no longer recognize the appearance of the sky. I, who knew—or, at least, believed that I knew—the celestial universe like the back of my hand, am obliged to confess to you that I feel like a Kurd or a Kirghiz transported to the Nevsky Prospect...that's why I've had recourse to you to assure me that we really are on the right course, and then to explain to me by what phenomenon..."

While Ossipoff was speaking the young man had regained possession of himself, so it was with that fine assurance of which he had already given so many proofs in the course of the adventurous voyage that he replied: "Calm yourself, my dear father; we really are in the Milky Way; it really is Omega Centauri that is visible to our right, just as we can still perceive Alpha Centauri behind us."

"But what about Crux Australis, my poor Gontran? What about the Southern Cross?"

"It's quite simple. It's the same here as in other instances. By virtue of getting nearer to these worlds, their appearance has changed; their position had altered relative to our viewpoint, and the dislocation of the Southern Cross must be attributable to the different angle from which we're presently viewing."

Although he had no scientific knowledge, Gontran was endowed with a strong dose of logic and common sense. That is why, in this instance, as in many others just as difficult, he might have succeeded in tricking the old man even if the Providence that was watching over him had not sent his eternal savior to him, just in time to spare him any embarrassment.

Ossipoff had, in fact, opened his mouth to protest against the explanation the young man had just furnished—a rather vague explanation that did not appear to him, and with reason, to be applicable to the situation, when someone knocked rudely on the door and Fricoulet's voice rang out. "Monsieur Ossipoff," the young man called, "it's your turn to stand watch."

Before the old man could stop him, Gontran had opened the door. Followed by Farenheit, the engineer irrupted into the cabin.

"Not a word in front of him," Ossipoff whispered hastily in his future son-in-law's ear.

"Don't worry," Gontran replied, in the same fashion.

In his other ear, Fricoulet whispered: "I'm just in time—you were about to commit an enormity that would have ruined everything."

"How do you know?"

"I was listening at the door—for the sake of prudence..."

Meanwhile, Ossipoff, his brows furrowed and his manner stiff, said to Fricoulet: "Thank you for your promptness—but I'd like to finish a conversation before going down to the engine-room..."

Without giving him time to finish, Gontran said to Fricoulet, with the imperturbable seriousness that as his strong suit: "We'll see if you remember the explanations I gave you yesterday regarding the changes we had to expect on the appearance of the sky..."

Controlling himself so as not to laugh, the engineer replied immediately, in the manner of a schoolboy repeating a lesson: "There are two reasons for the changes. The first is the difference in distance between two observation-points—which is to say, the Earth and the vehicle in which we're presently situated. There's an optical rule, to which the stars are subject. The second reason is due to the rapidity with which light crosses the distances separating Earth from the constellations in whose vicinity we find ourselves—including, among others, the Southern Cross."

Ossipoff squinted, trying to guess what the young engineer was driving at, and murmured cantankerously: "I don't understand."

"Let him finish," said Gontran, with a reassuring smile, and you'll understand.

"It's quite simple: the radiation of the Southern Cross takes about five years to reach terrestrial telescopes. Now, given the motion to which these constellations are subject, it's quite natural that we'll no longer find them either so close to one another, in the same places they seem to be to the eyes of our astronomers."

The old scientist touched his forehead with his index finger. "My word—that's true," he murmured. He added, with a pitying smile: "Nothing was simpler than to think of that—where was my head?"

Gontran tried to speak, but Fricoulet used an imperceptible blink of the eyelids to signal that he should be allowed to continue. "That's not all," he said. "Didn't you tell me that the precession of the equinoxes had something to do with it?"

The young diplomat judged it appropriate to play his part. "Something to do with it!" he repeated. "How you go on! It's of capital importance." He turned to Ossipoff, shrugging his shoulders. "Oh, these laymen!" he exclaimed. "It's just like Mr. Farenheit, who, the other easy, spoke of passing off as profits or losses the seconds that serve to measure the parallax of the stars."

"Well," muttered Farenheit, who had said nothing thus far, "what's this procession of the equinoxes?"

"*Pre*cession, Mr. Farenheit," Fricoulet corrected, ironically. "It's the name we give to the oscillation of the Earth on its axis…an oscillation that makes the world's pole shift slowly relative to the constellations."

Ossipoff, who had been listening for some while with increasing signs of impatience, exclaimed: "Shift! Shift! It's hardly worth talking about—a circle 23 degrees in radius, which requires no less than 23,765 years to complete. Is that appreciable?"

Fricoulet, cut to the quick, retorted: "What! Is that appreciable? To the extent that 14,000 years ago, Vega was the Earthly pole star, and in 12,000 years it will be again."

"There are celestial maps from that era which tell us so!" the American exclaimed, slyly.

"No, Mr. Farenheit, but my simple common sense—or rather, that of my friend Gontran—permits me to give you a glimpse of what the sky was like 64 centuries ago, which is to say, in the days of the Pharaohs and the first Chinese civilizations. Almost all the constellations of the southern sky—Centaurus, Crux Australis, Canopus, Achernar, Tucana, Indus—were visible from the northern hemisphere at the latitude of Paris, while Sirius, Orion and Eridanus remained invisible, hidden by the Earth. Search now for the southern constellations. Disappeared! Vanished beneath the horizon, while we can see Ursa Major, Eridanus, Rigel and others perfectly well."

Farenheit folded his arms and exclaimed: "Why, then, did you protest so energetically a little while ago when Monsieur de Flammeront told you that astronomy was the least of the sciences?"

"Gontran!" exclaimed Osipoff, choking. In a tone that testified to a profound and sincere grievance, he repeated: "Oh, Gontran…"

"You misunderstood me, Monsieur Farenheit," Fricoulet protested.

"Didn't Monsieur de Flammermont say that?" cried the American, beside himself, thinking that he detected a lie in those words.

"He said it, but not in the sense that Monsieur Ossipoff has understood it. In his opinion, astronomy is definitely the foremost of the sciences, from the viewpoint of interest—since he had devoted his life to it—but he also deems it the least, in terms of the results it has yielded. Everyone is entitled to his opinion, isn't he?"

Literally dumbfounded, the old scientist listened uncomprehendingly, while the engineer directed a sly wink at his friend in a fashion that meant: "Over to you now—and be bold."

Gontran understood, and with perfectly feigned ill-humor, he said: "Frankly, my dear father, can you deny that what has happened to you is one more proof in support of my reasoning? Here you are, one of the princes of modern astronomy, whose entire life, without a moment's interruption, has been dedicated to the study of stars, having arrived, so to speak, at the limit of life, and just as embarrassed, at this moment, as a child who has never put his eye to a telescope!"

A furtive blush colored Ossipoff's cheek. "Gontran," he stammered. "You promised…"

"Bah!" replied the young man, shrugging his shoulders. "Given what Fricoulet has just told you, don't you think he knows as well as you and me the material impossibility you find in recognizing the condition of the sky? Besides the proper motion of the stars, which displaces them, besides the oscillation of the Earth on its axis, which tell you that the Southern Cross, or at least the worlds that comprise it, have long gone to join the old moons…"

"Oh!" exclaimed Ossipoff, flabbergasted by such an audacious theory. "I saw it from Pulkova Observatory three years ago…"

"Are you quite sure that you weren't only seeing a ray of light, en route for five years—perhaps the last flicker of that dying constellation?"

Ossipoff lowered his head and remained silent, in a meditative posture—but that mediation did not last long before Farenheit interrupted it with a thunderous curse. "What I can see most clearly," he proclaimed, "is that we're well and truly lost, billions of leagues from our fatherland, and that our return home is getting more and more problematic."

"Eh?" retorted the old man "Home, home—that's the only word you have in your mouth. Frankly, haven't all our travels given you a taste...?"

"For my hearth!" the American said, interrupting. "Oh very much so—more than ever."

"Besides, my dear Monsieur Ossipoff," said Flammermont, in his turn, in a firm voice, "our return to Earth is no longer in question. The point has been settled for a long time, and we can't admit a new debate on the subject."

"Then why does Mr. Farenheit keep coming back to it?" grumbled the scientist.

"Why? Why?" cried the American. "Because the further we go the less you seem to me to be in agreement, and I wonder whether, as we go deeper and deeper into infinity with each passing second..."

"Were getting closer to Fifth Avenue?" said Fricoulet, laughing. "Don't worry, my dear Farenheit, for it's the only means we have of returning to or point of departure. As for being lost, as you say, it's a vain fear. Although the constellations are disappearing, calculation easily permits us to recover the positions that they occupied in the sky... Say something, Gontran—you're standing there mute, as if you were taking a malign delight in increasing our friend's anguish! Repeat what you told me only a moment ago—we're in the very heart of the Southern Cross."

Without noticing Gontran's bewildered expression, Ossipoff raised his head again and looked at Fricoulet, while the incredulous Farenheit went to the telescope, saying: "In that case, show me the four stars that comprise it."

The old scientist laughed, in a tone full of pity. "Four stars! But there are more than four stars visible from the point in space at which we're located. Then again, from the Earth it has been observed that it's not four but eight stars that make up the Cross—four of the first magnitude, and four less bright."

"Not to mention," Fricoulet added, that some of them, such as Alpha and Beta Crucis, might be double stars."[91]

"How do you know that?"

"Here's my scientific *vade mecum*," said the engineer, with an imperturbable aplomb, pointing to Flammermont. Seemingly interrogating his friend with his gaze, as if to confirm his apparently-fallible memory, he added: "I even

[91] Delta Crucis is also a double star; Beta Crucis is also known as Mimosa.

know that out of those eight stars, two are a bright ruby red, one marine blue, two emerald green and three pale green. Is that right, Gontran?"

The young Comte inclined his head, murmuring: "You're a marvelous pupil."

Ossipoff seized his future son-in-law's hands affectionately. "Oh, my dear boy," he cried, "what glory awaits you on your return to Earth! And how I thank Providence for having given me a collaborator like you to complete and continue my work!"

Gontran pulled a slight face—which, if the scientist had glimpsed it, would have proved to him that the young man's joy did not equal his own.

It was Ossipoff's turn to stand watch and Fricoulet—who was primarily responsible for the delimitation of time—having declared that it must be six o'clock in the evening on Earth, everyone else went to his hammock, where it did not take long for them to fall asleep.

Scarcely had sleep taken possession of him when Gontran fell prey to a nightmare which did not let him go all night and only ended when Fricoulet's hand woke him up by shaking him rather roughly. Under the impression of the scientific explanations furnished by Fricoulet regarding the different colors of the unknown worlds through which the *Eclair* was carrying them, Gontran dreamed that he had returned to Earth, but that, during his absence, an inexplicable revolution had taken place in the illumination of his native planet. The Sun's rays, instead of being white, had suddenly become blue, and this transformation of light produced effects as stupefying as they were terrifying.

Things and creatures changed their appearance and quotidian life was completely overturned by that fact. Then, abruptly, the rays of the blue sun were mingled with those of a scarlet sun, which suddenly rose over the horizon, and those two suns were soon augmented by a third, then a fourth, each of which added a different shade to those of its predecessors. Alternately, the Earth received azure blue golden yellow and blood red daylight, but the yellow soon invaded the blue and married with it to produce a vivid green, with which the atmosphere was bathed, until the moment when the green was transformed into violet by virtue of the appearance of a new sun that irradiated space with a ruby color.

It was a chameleon world that Gontran now inhabited; at every second there was a transformation that broke the monotony of existence strangely and populated it with multiple surprises and uninterrupted astonishments. In time, a day awaited for so many long years finally arrived: a blue day, but a very pure blue, very soft and very clear, during which Selena, his fiancée, appeared to him in her nuptial veil, entirely bathed in golden vapor, resembling those saints that one sees in old missals, with their heads aureoled with rays of light.

The procession of relatives and friends extended through the streets in long multicolored rings, while Selena and he slowly climbed the marble staircase of the Town Hall of the eighth arrondissement. Bizarrely enough, due to a capricious trick of the light that he did not even try to explain, the young woman's face was bathed by a ruby ray that seemed to be the reflection of her virginal modesty, while he himself was radiantly scarlet, as a sign of the joy that was transporting him. By contrast, Monsieur Ossipoff, whose beloved work that feast-day had interrupted, betrayed a concentrated anger in his violent yellow features, and Fricoulet, suddenly somber since the marriage had been irrevocably decided, could not conceal a sharp jealousy beneath a pale green mask.

Then, suddenly, by virtue of an incomprehensible hallucination, it seemed to him that he heard the harmonious sounds of an organ announcing his arrival at the church, which reached him as very soft echoes. These sounds were insensibly transformed while the traditional "I do" was pronounced and he came back down the town hall steps to go to the church; now it was no longer sacred music that he heard but a joyful orchestra playing a waltz whose movements, sometimes rapid and sometimes slow, permitted the waltzers to launch themselves into rapid spins or to surrender themselves to delightful swaying.

As he turned his eyes, very surprised, to Selena to tell her what he could hear and ask her if she too could hear the same thing, his white suit suddenly became colored with different hues which made it pass, either successively or simultaneously, through all the colors of the prism, as if it were subject to the radiation of multicolored electric lights. At the same time, she quit his arm and ran her fingertips over his suit, which seemed so light and flexible that it seemed to be made of impalpable cloth or, rather, of the luminous radiance itself. She began to dance, following the rhythm of the orchestra, whose echoes reached her, borne on the wings of the breeze.

It was at that moment that Fricoulet's hand snatched him back from sleep.

"Eh? What! What's the matter?" exclaimed the young man. Then, rubbing his eyes, he looked round, and asked: "Where is she?"

"Who?" asked the bewildered engineer. "Selena?"

Gontran burst out laughing. "No—Loie Fuller."[92] And as his friend's eyes widened, the young Comte added: "All these stories of multicolored worlds

---

[92] Loie [Marie Louise] Fuller (1862-1928) was the dancer who pioneered the form of freely-improvised expressive dancing that was later taken up by Isadora Duncan and Maud White; American-born, she took up residence in France after her first Parisian stage show caused a sensation in 1892 by virtue of its exotic lighting effects, which included lights placed beneath a translucent stage; she held several patents for stage lighting and was also a member of the French Astronomical Society. She is featured in numerous *fin-de-siècle* literary works. It is, however, quite impossible that Gontran could have seen or heard of her before taking off on his interplanetary adventures in 1882, so the reference is blatantly anachronistic. It proves that the final draft of the fourth volume of the

went to my head to the extent that I was dreaming about them, you know. With the effect that, in conformity with that theory of the transformation of coloration, I seemed to be marrying Loie Fuller...and it was her that I looked for on waking up."

"Poor Selena," murmured Fricoulet, comically.

"Proof," said Gontran, in a tone that was half jocular and half serious, "that I really don't have a head sufficiently solid to take up science."

At that moment Farenheit came into the cabin precipitately; he seemed very agitated and his face was very flushed. His fiery gaze betrayed one of those furious fits of anger of which he had already provided many examples in the course of the voyage.

"Come on," said Flammermont. "What's up now?"

"That damned Ossipoff," moaned the American, "has played us another of his tricks."

"What's happened?"

"You said, didn't you, that the most certain mean of returning to Earth was to go forward, and keep going forward?"

"Certainly—for the very good reason that the velocity at which we're traveling makes it materially impossible to turn round."

"Well, Ossipoff must have found a means of turning round—for we're no longer going forward."

"Impossible."

"It's just as I say!" cried the American, who could no bear anyone doubting his affirmations. "I'm not a child, I think, and I know what I'm saying, don't I?"

Fricoulet ran to the engine room, drawing Gontran and Farenheit in his wake, and put his eye to the telescope."

"Well, so what?" he asked, after a brief interval of observation.

"That star," replied the American. "Do you see the star that's inundating the vehicle with such bright light?"

"Of course—one would have to be blind not to. It's Eta Carinae.[93] So what?"

"So what?" Farenheit repeated. "Not being able to sleep, I left my hammock and came to lie down here, thinking that the change of location might be favorable. Well, sleep still didn't want me...then, to pass the time, I sat down at

---

Aventures was not written until some years after the publication of the third, not long before its own publication.

[93] Eta Carinae became one of the most famous variable stars when it underwent a sudden flare-up in 1843, and then flared up again, less spectacularly, in 1870. By the time this passage was published it had undergone another minor flare in 1889—a frequency that evidently seemed to the authors to be sufficient to warrant this casual observation by Farenheit.

the telescope. Immediately, my attention was drawn to that star shining with an extraordinary brightness."

"Not surprising," murmured Fricoulet. "It's one of the most important in the southern sky, after Alpha Centauri."

"As the minutes went by," the other continued, "its dimensions increased in truly stupefying proportions—proof that we were following our course—when suddenly, in scarcely a quarter of an hour, it began to diminish with no less rapidity...proof..."

"That we're going backwards, of course!" said Gontran, with assurance. He too was beginning to get excited.

"Proof that you know nothing about astronomical matters, Monsieur Farenheit," declared the engineer, ironically. "Otherwise, you'd know that Eta Carinae is a variable star—the most variable there is—for, since 1677, the era in which the English astronomer Halley perceived its variability for the first time, until recent times, when Gould[94] has studied it, it has not ceased to vary in brightness, falling from the first to the eighth magnitude and then resuming its former rank." Addressing himself to Gontran, whose shoulder he slapped, he added, sardonically: "Which is neither here nor there, nothing to get excited about...making a mountain out of a molehill. So don't worry, my dear Monsieur Farenheit—Ossipoff has nothing to do with the phenomenon that frightened you so much, and the *Eclair* is still continuing its course towards infinity."

A voice behind them—that of the old scientist—then said: "Since you're such an expert on the subject, Monsieur Fricoulet, you might have added, for the complete edification of Mr. Farenheit, that all the stars in the sky are variable, for, in conformity with the laws that regulate the universe, new-born suns shine with increasing brightness until the moment when, after having stabilized, they begin to decrease, and finish up forming a crust and going out."

One might say the same of scientists, the American thought, privately, darting a hostile glance at Ossipoff.

"But human life is too short," the old man continued, professorially, "for men to be able to observe that sort of change, and I think that Monsieur Fricoulet only intended to talk about stars with periodic variations in brightness, caused either by the passage of a planet or a dark ring in front of the star's disk, or by an phenomenon analogous to that periodicity of sunspots. Isn't that so, my dear Gontran?"

Put on the spot, the young man made haste to reply. "Certainly, certainly—that's the sense in which I explained matters to Fricoulet, yesterday evening. When one isn't used to such things, though, it sometimes happens that the memory is hazy and makes mistakes, you know..." He had said this with such amazing aplomb that the engineer could not help but admire him.

---

[94] Benjamin Apthorp Gould (1824-1896).

"In addition to that," added Ossipoff, delighted to have an audience in the presence of which he could perform what Farenheit referred to irreverently as his astronomical acrobatics, "there are stars that shine at certain moments and become more or less completely extinct, as well as those whose brightness varies periodically..."

"Such as the star that shone so brightly in 1572 that Sirius, Vega and even Jupiter paled by comparison, which was seen in broad daylight, enthroned in the constellation of Cassiopeia." It was Fricoulet who spoke thus, hastening his response in anticipation of the inevitable question that was about to fall like a roof-tile on poor Gontran's head. He asked the latter: "Wasn't it Tycho Brahe who gave details on this subject?"

The young Comte inclined his head affirmatively, and added: "One finds many other examples of similar phenomena in Hipparchus' catalogue and the Chinese Encyclopedia of Man-Tuan-Lin, which was translated by Edouard Biot.[95]

Fricoulet put his hands together admiringly. "What erudition!" he exclaimed.

"With the aid of my namesake's book *Les Etoiles*,"[96] the young Comte whispered. What he forgot to mention—for his memory did not always serve him as well as it might—was the universal emotion produced by the appearance

[95] There is some exaggeration in this account of the discovery of accounts of ancient supernovas (as Tycho's "new star" of 1572 was ultimately deemed to have been). No actual copies of the star catalogue compiled by Hipparchus in c.135 B.C. or the star catalogues compiled in China by Shi Shen and Gan De in the Warring States period (between the 5th and 2nd centuries B.C.) survive, although the data was copied more-or-less wholesale into later catalogues like Ptolemy's *Almagest* and the catalogue compiled by Zhang Heng (78-139 A.D.). Hipparchus was said by Pliny the Elder to have become interested in the fixed stars after observing a nova, but the "evidence" for such events contained in these works requires a certain leap of the imagination to become perceptible. Edouard Constant Biot (1803-1850) was a renowned sinologist who published a long series of "*mémoires*"—actually essays in pamphlet form—including at least two on ancient Chinese astronomy; the encyclopedia named here is one of the sources from which he quotes.

[96] The equivalent of Camille Flammarion's *Les Etoiles et les curiosités du ciel* (1882), a popular guide to heavenly objects visible to the naked eye, intended as a supplement to *L'Astronomie populaire.* The tour of the stars undertaken by the voyagers follows the text of that book chapter by chapter, but in reverse order; almost all of the expository lumps deposited in the text being paraphrased therefrom. Like *Les Terres du ciel*, it is a heavy quarto volume entirely unsuited to use as a *vade mecum*, but the authors soon forget that they have provided Gontran with a copy.

of that extraordinary star. The astrologer Cardan declared that the star was none other than the one that had guided the Mage Kings to Jesus' cradle, and de Bèze, in pursuit of the same hypothesis, proclaimed that its appearance announced the Messiah's second coming; the Antichrist must have been born, affirmed Leovitius, the end of the world was nigh, and the stars were about to fall from the sky.[97] Fortunately, this excitement did not take long to calm down; the star had surged forth on November 11, and less than 15 months later it had vanished completely. As astronomical telescopes had not yet been invented—they would not be in use until 37 years later—no one could determine what had become of the famous star.

"And are there many examples of similar apparitions?" Fricoulet asked Ossipoff.

"About 50, between the origin of time and our own day. The most recent dates from only a few years ago, and was situated in the constellation of Andromeda..."[98] He would have continued, but he was interrupted by a sonorous noise coming from a corner of the cabin. Farenheit, seated on a stool with his back against the wall of the vehicle, was sound asleep and snoring. The scientist could not restrain a scornful gesture, and muttered: "That suet merchant will never be anything but a suet merchant, and it's scarcely worth the trouble of unveiling the mysteries of nature to him."

Gontran relied, tolerantly: "Each to his own; the stars are no more interesting to him than pigs are to you..."

Ossipoff pursed his lips indignantly. "A singular comparison!" he murmured.

"It's to such a case," Fricoulet added, laughing, "that one might apply the Latin words *margaritas ante porcos...*"[99]

Ossipoff extended his arm toward the porthole in a gesture full of enthusiasm. "I merely ask you," he cried, "whether any terrestrial jeweler could ever have made so marvelous a string..."

---

[97] Jerome Cardan (1501-1576) was one of the most celebrated post-Renaissance popularizers of astrology. Theodore de Bèze, or Beza (1519-1605) was a prominent Protestant theologian who was John Calvin's successor in Geneva. Leovitius was the Latinized signature of the Bohemian astronomer Cyprien Leowitz (?-1574), who was sufficiently prestigious in his lifetime to be consulted by Tycho Brahe and sufficiently notorious for his astrological predictions to be taken seriously; the cited text, first published in 1564, predicted that the world would end in 1584, but was still being reprinted and translated in 1610.

[98] The reference is presumably to the supernova observed in the Andromeda nebula in 1885—in which case it is anachronistic with respect to the narrative's time-frame.

[99] *Pearls before swine.*

In fact, the celestial region that the apparatus was passing through at that moment offered the most admirable spectacle imaginable to the voyagers' eyes. No scene-painter would have dared to imagine anything similar for the most extravagant of fairy plays. There was such a concentration of stars that it seemed that an impalpable but radiant curtain of light was drawn across space; it was the exact point at which Herschel had counted as many as 250 stars circumscribed by a single telescopic field 15 seconds in diameter—the equivalent of more than 5000 stars per square degree. Over an extent of 47 square degrees, the observer had seen nearly 150,000 multicolored stars pass before his eyes; imagine the appearance that formidable army of stars must present at such a relatively close distance that the assembly constituted a radiant palette formed of every possible color...

The variable star that Farenheit had pointed out sparkled with a vertiginous glare in the midst of that variegated agglomeration, behind which a vast nebula extended its meanders, revealing a lacy network set against the blackness of space, strangely jagged and spangled by suns, like as many rutilant gems, as distant from the voyagers as they were from their native planet.

"And to think that no one will ever know..." sighed the old man, who had fallen into a profound reverie at the sight of that incomprehensible and vertiginous spectacle.

"What?" demanded Fricoulet. "What is it that no one will ever know?"

"How these worlds were formed," stammered Ossipoff.

"Are you talking about the nebulas?"

"What else, if not that substance disseminated in space according to no apparent law, and not offering the slightest appearance of resolution into stars in any part of their extent? How many centuries does their light take to reach us? A mystery. At what point are we seeing them—as themselves, or simply the last rays projected into space in the course of their final agony? Another mystery." Putting his head in his hands, he added: "Why has God given human beings a brain whose scope is powerless to embrace all the marvels with which the universe is filled? Why has He only given us an intelligence that is impotent to sound all the mysteries with which nature is filled?"

Dropping his arms and joining his hands together, the old man remained immobile, his eyes riveted to the multicolored scintillation that the nebula scattered across space, far beyond the stars that glittered in the foreground.

Taking advantage of the meditation into which Ossipoff had fallen, Fricoulet took Gontran by the arm and silently drew him out of the cabin. Once they were in the engine-room he said to him: "My dear friend, at the present moment, I think I can assure you that we shall see the Earth again, unless some unforeseen accident overtakes us."

"And on what do you base such an assurance?"

"On the fact that I no longer have any uncertainty concerning the route we're following. The *Eclair* is presently at the South Pole of the world and we're flying through all the constellations of that region. The Earth's South Pole terminates between the Great Nebula, toward which we're heading, and the stars of Octans. We've left Crux Australis and Centaurus to our right and you'll soon see Canopus increasing on our south-eastern horizon..."

That name seemed to wake some distant memory in Gontran. "Canopus, Canopus," he repeated. "Just wait a minute..." He scratched the end of his nose lightly; then his face cleared somewhat, and he said: "I've got it! Wasn't Canopus Menelaus's pilot?"

"From the viewpoint of ancient history, yes. From the astronomical viewpoint, it's a star of the first magnitude, the second brightest in the entire celestial universe. It also belongs to the constellation Carina, whose prow it forms."[100]

"In that case," Gontran said, "I wasn't being so stupid in talking about Menelaus's pilot?"

"Certainly not, since he served as the godfather of the star in question."

There was a pause, at the end of which the young Comte asked; "Then you think we have some chance of getting back?"

"Definitely. We're no longer lost now, and we're following an itinerary that will necessarily bring us back into the terrestrial zone. We're leaving the Milky Way at top speed, you understand, heading back toward the northern hemisphere, straight toward Sirius, and..."[101]

Smiling, Gontran put his hand on Fricoulet's arm. The latter stopped. "Father Ossipoff isn't here, you know, Gontran said, "so there's no need to batter my ears with petty explanations. You assure me that we're back on course, and that's enough for me, without the need for more ample explanations. I'll go tell Selena the good news."

As he finished these words, the young woman appeared in the doorway. "What's that, my friend?" she asked.

"Great news! Good news!" exclaimed Gontran, comically. "We're leaving for Sirius..." As these words did not appear to communicate very much to Ossi-

---

[100] The authors render the name of the constellation here and elsewhere as *le Navire* [the ship], although that ancient constellation, named for the *Argo*, had long ago been broken up into three more convenient subunits, Carina [the keel], Puppis [the poop] and Velorum [the sails]. As the text's specific references are to stars in Carina (Canopus is Alpha Carinae), I have substituted that name, although it causes a problem here, where the references to the prow and the pilot refer to the entire ship.

[101] It becomes obvious here that the *Eclair* is now following a circular course through the firmament, with the solar system at its center, although we have previously been told that it was traveling away from the Sun in a straight line—but we must remember that this whole sequence is no less a dream than Gontran's vision of a multicolored Earth in which the true object of his vacillating affections is Loie Fuller.

poff's daughter, the young Comte added: "Passengers change there for the Sun, the Moon and Earth..."

The two young people's hands came together in a gentle grip, while Fricoulet, looking at his friend with an expression full of pity and commiseration, murmured to himself: "Come on...save that for the Town Hall of the eighth!"

Chapter LVII
In which things become confused

As Fricoulet had announced so joyfully to his friend, the region that the *Eclair* was passing though was situated exactly at six hours of ascension and 50 degrees southern declination, through the confines of the zone of attraction of Canopus, from which it was drawing away with vertiginous rapidity.

It was the celestial point at which the axis around which our world turns would end, were it indefinitely prolonged—in a word, the South Pole of the universe. At this point there was the constellation of Octans. On consulting the celestial map that they had aboard—a precious item of wreckage saved by Ossipoff from various catastrophes to which the voyagers had fallen victim since their departure from Earth—Gontran saw that the most remarkable neighboring constellations were the Lesser Cloud, Tucana, Phoenix, Hydrus, Horologium, Reticulum, Dorado, Pictor Carina, Chameleon, Apus, Crux Australis, Volans, Triangulum, Circinus, Ara, Pavo, Indus and Grus.

"Natural history has furnished the greater part of astronomical vocabulary," the young man said to Fricoulet, with a mocking laugh.

Making no reply, the latter pointed to a region of space to the left of the vehicle. "Over there, beside the Magellanic Clouds and Table Mountain, is the Greater Cloud."[102]

"Ah!" said Gontran, indifferently. "And what's special about your Greater Cloud?"

"Oh, nothing much; only this: at the distance that separates us from the Solar System—a distance that naturally brings us close to them—these nebulas have scarcely increased in size. From that I conclude that they must be vertiginously far away."

"My God, the universe is very large..."

These words were pronounced in a tone that betrayed such a lack of interest in the question that the engineer could not help laughing. "I'm not talking about the dimensions of the universe," he replied, "but simple the distance of a world—or, rather, an aggregation of worlds, for Herschel counted no less than 284 nebulas, 66 groups of stars and 582 isolated stars within the Greater Cloud, in the same way that in the Lesser Cloud he revealed the existence of 52 nebulas, six groups of stars and 200 individual stars..."

"God, that's interesting!" stammered Gontran, having difficulty trying to stifle a mighty yawn with his hand.

---

[102] The separate reference here to the "*Nuées de Magellan*" [Magellanic Clouds] is puzzling, because the references to the "*Grand Nuage*" [Greater Cloud] and "*Petit Nuage*" [Lesser Cloud] are certainly to the same two compound objects.

Selena's face became sadder. "My poor Gontran," she said, "you'll never be able to..."

"Oh, never," declared the young man, forcefully.

"You have no need to affirm it," said Fricoulet. "It's obvious, Permit me to say, though—and this in Mademoiselle's presence—that you appear to me to be in a very poor condition to brave marriage..."

"Monsieur Fricoulet!" Selena protested.

"Apologies—it wasn't to you that I was alluding, but rather to Monsieur Ossipoff. You'll presumably be living together, and every evening, instead of the traditional game of piquet or yellow dwarf, Gontran will be compelled to play stars with his father-in-law. Isn't that so?"

With an embarrassed smile, the young woman relied: "Perhaps you're right—but Gontran has nothing to fear. I'm good enough at that game; I'll try to stay behind him and prompt him."

"As when I executed my lessons at school—it will be charming."

This was said with a bitterness too ill-concealed bitterness for Selena not to notice it. Saddened, she murmured, "Alas, Gontran, there's still time for you to retract and renounce the plans we've made."

Without replying directly, Flammermont sighed: "From now until we reach the Earth again—if we ever do reach it—we have plenty of time to unmake and remake our plans."

Ossipoff's voice became audible in the stairwell, very excited: "Gontran! Gontran! Can you see it?"

"What? What are you talking about?" cried the young man, without budging from his place and will an ill-humored frown.

"Eh? The Coal Sack, of course!"

Gontran looked at Fricoulet and Selena in turn, with a fearful expression, stammering: "The Coal Sack?"

"Answer: *yes—very curious*," Fricoulet whispered in his ear.

Meekly, without understanding, the young man relied: "Yes—very curious."

Satisfied by these words, the old man called out: "Selena...come here for a moment..."

The young woman left the two friends, who heard her climb the steps of the staircase as lightly as a bird.

"And now?" asked Flammermont.

The engineer went to the telescope aimed through the engine-room porthole, put his eye to it, and turned it on its pivot until the moment when he said: "Come and see..."

Gontran, having replaced his friend, uttered a slight exclamation, and could not help saying: "That's quite bizarre!"

There was a sort of rip in the Milky Way, seemingly produced by a total absence of stars. While in certain places there were swarms that illuminated space, here there was a vast solitude, dark and dismal, making a deep black hole in the marvelous scintillation of the stars, into which the astonished gaze might plunge for inconceivable distances into the infinity of the heavens. To what cause could these desert regions be attributed? Were they once, like their neighbors, fecund with stars, and was their present solitude due to some incomprehensible sidereal catastrophe? Was it, on the other hand, indispensable to the equilibrium of the universe that immense steppes should remain deserted in the midst of exactly those constellations that were the most densely populated and shone most brightly? That is a dilemma in which the human mind is lost, and will probably be lost for centuries to come. As if to form a contrast with these solitudes, the eye discovered in their midst the constellation Tucana, an aggregation of stars forming a kind of island of light.

"There's something to prove to you—if you were in the business—how prodigiously far away we are from our own system," Fricoulet said, looking over his friend's shoulder. "From the Earth, Tucana appears to the naked eye as a tiny milky stain, while presently, for us, it's a veritable casket of diamonds whose beauty and gleam are only comparable to the beauty of Centaurus."

For a few moments, the two young people remained motionless and silent, captivated by the strangeness of the spectacle.

"And that's what astronomers cal the Coal Sack," Gontran murmured, eventually. "I no longer recognize their habitual vocabulary…so full of poetry."

There was a hint of mockery in these words, which Fricoulet caught immediately, and with which he was the first to sympathize.

"Monsieur Fricoulet!" It was Selena who was calling to him in a stage whisper. He went to the threshold of the engine-room and, on looking up, saw the young woman's charming face framed up above, in the stairwell.

"I'd like to ask a favor of you, Monsieur Fricoulet," she said, with a polite smile.

"At your disposal, Mademoiselle," the engineer exclaimed, hurrying up the stairs.

Gontran started to follow him, muttering between his teeth, irritated and—let us admit it—slightly jealous on seeing that his fiancée, having need of a service, had asked someone other than himself. He arrived in Ossipoff's cabin at almost the same time as Fricoulet, and the first thing he saw was the old man lying in his hammock, sound asleep. Near the telescope, Selena and the engineer were chatting beside a little table, on which were various objects whose forms were unfamiliar to Gontran—and whose purpose, in consequence, escaped him.

"You understand," Selena said, "that I'm sufficiently familiar with the observations, but I no longer recall how to set this up." Noticing from the expression on Flammermont's face that he was discontented, she added: "You don't have to look at me like that, Gontran—it's a small matter, with which you couldn't help, of setting up a spectroscope." With a hint of malice, she added:

"Then again, my father's been tormenting you quite enough when he's awake for you to be able to take a little rest while he's asleep."

The young man shrugged his shoulders imperceptibly. Without saying a word, he remained standing by the table while the engineer busied himself assembling the various parts of the spectroscope with remarkable dexterity.

It is well known that the apparatus in question comprises four essential parts: a dispersion system formed by one or more prisms; a collimator disposed so as to send a pencil of parallel rays to the prism, formed by the tube of a telescope, closed at one end and open at the other, and a lens; an eyepiece whose axis is directed in such a manner as to receive the rays emerging from the prism; and a micrometer to measure the deviations and determine the positions of the various spectral rays.

The spectroscope was invented by Messieurs Kirchhoff and Bunsen and significantly improved by Monsieur Duboscq and Monsieur Pellin, but the one that Ossipoff used, and whose assembly Fricoulet was working on, was of a very special manufacture invented by Monsieur Thollon to facilitate the analysis of stars.[103] Direct in its vision, it was sufficient to point it at a star to decompose its light and reveal the rays that characterized the body's spectrum. It included a "composite prism"—which is to say, formed partly of crystal- or crown-glass and partly of liquid carbon sulfide, which gave it such power and precision that if one were to examine the spectrum of the Sun with the instrument, it would give a spectrum of an apparent length of 15 meters, in which no less than 4000 dark bands could be counted.

"What are you going to do with that?" Gontran finally asked, strongly intrigued, deep down, by the bizarre instrument.

"With this, my dear Gontran," Selena said, speaking in a low voice so as not to wake the still-sleeping Ossipoff, "the nature of stars is characterized. You know, don't you, that when a ray of solar light passes through a prism, the light is decomposed into its elements and it become evident that it's constituted by seven different colors whose superimposition produces white light."[104]

---

[103] The references are to Gustav Kirchhoff (1824-1887), Robert Bunsen (1811-1899), Louis-Jules Duboscq (1817-1886), Philippe Pellin (1847-1923) and Luois Thollon (1829-1887); the last-named developed the first direct vision spectroscope in 1875.

[104] In fact, only five colors are properly manifest in the spectrum of white light (red, yellow, green, blue and violet), which are readily reducible to three (red, green and violet) in modern color-producing processes, which produce the other two by combination, but Isaac Newton thought seven was a sacred number, so he added in an extra two fringe effects to make up that number, and loyal physicists have never gone back on his decision.

The young Comte nodded his head affirmatively, murmuring: "Violet, indigo, blue, green, yellow, orange, red...yes, I remember that from my schooldays—a verse by Newton, overly rich because it has one foot too many."

"One foot too many!" said the engineer, straightening up.

"Certainly: violet has three syllables...but it doesn't matter." Addressing Selena, he said: "So what?"

"When it was realized that the spectrum emitted by the incandescent vapor of a metal was formed of bright rays, and that these rays, constant for the same metal, differed from one metal to another, it was concluded that by examining the spectra of heavenly bodies one could determine, so to speak, their geological constitution. The solar spectrum was therefore compared with those of metals, and it was determined that the Sun contained sodium, magnesium, calcium, iron, nickel, and many other elements..."

"How knowledgeable you are!" exclaimed Fricoulet.

"I've no great merit in that respect," the young woman replied, modestly. "In St. Petersburg, I assisted my father in his spectroscopic studies, and by virtue of hearing the same things repeated..."

"Is that what you're doing now?" Gontran asked.

"My father, being tired, asked me to set up the spectroscope while he got a few minutes' rest and to begin to examine the rays of Crux Australis."

"Curious, is it, the Southern Cross?" the young Comte asked.

Selena understood the spirit of his question perfectly well, and replied with a guarded smile on her lips: "Oh, Monsier Gontran, you know that, personally, I'm not as fervent about astronomy as my occupations might lead a random observer to believe—but you're not a random observer; you know very well what has made me forsake the customary feminine occupations to busy myself with science and optical instruments. I love my father more than anything; I love him with all the strength of my filial heart and all the strength of my gratitude for the way in which he has brought me up, my mother having died." She added, in a firmer tone: "And there's nothing I'm not ready to do to save him trouble and procure him some satisfaction."

During this stark declaration, Gontran seemed embarrassed, for the young woman's words contained a scarcely-dissimulated accusation aimed at him; nevertheless, when she had finished, he replied in a slightly piqued tone: "There's nothing wrong with loving your father, Selena, and no one would ever think of blaming you for it—but I hope that you would no more deny the affection that I have for you...an affection that has caused me to abandon the Earth and to engage myself on a path of duplicity and dissimulation that is scarcely in rapport with the frankness of my character."

"Reproaches!" said the young woman, with a slightly bitter smile.

Gontant protested sharply "That's not fair, Selena," he said, "but at the end of the day, human nature is human nature, and you'll forgive me if I sometimes let slip some word or gesture that betrays, perhaps a little too clearly, the irritation I feel in seeing the moment of happiness to which I have so long aspired perennially delayed."

The final words brought a radiance to Selena's face. She offered her hand to the young man, murmuring in a genuinely sympathetic tone: "Poor Gontran!"

The young Comte retained the tips of Mademoiselle Ossipoff's slender fingers between his hands and said to her, in an utterly charming tone of submission: "Well, to give you pleasure, would you like to initiate me into the beauties of spectroscopic studies? Speak—I'm listening..."

"Seriously?" asked the young woman.

"Seriously."

She enveloped her fiancé with an affectionate gaze full of gratitude, and then, adopting a serious expression, said in a professorial tone: "The star Gamma Crucis, which, as you have already been able to observe, presents a clear orange coloration, has a very characteristic spectrum; it belongs to the third category, remarkable for its ribbed appearance, and is analogous to that of Betelgeuse or Alpha Herculae. The lines produced by the presence of magnesium and iron are recognizable therein, but its great originality is constituted by the absorption lines that indubitably indicate the presence in the star of water vapor."

"I will make the observation to you, Mademoiselle," said Fricoulet, "that Monsieur Ossipoff has discovered nothing new in that, for an astronomer from New Zealand, Monsieur Pope,[105] pointed out those lines long ago, whose presence has also been affirmed in our own Sun."

"Certainly! But what distinguishes my father's studies is the conclusion he draws from them. For him, the star in Crux Australis is much more advanced in its lifespan than the Earth's Sun, and from the fact that water vapor is presently dominant in its atmosphere, he deduces that hydrogen has been combined with oxygen in enormous quantities." Smiling, she added: "Can you remember all that?"

"Easily, I think, and I'll appear to be as wise as you, one you've explained an expression of which you made use just now."

"Which one?"

"You said that the star in question belongs to the third category."

"The young woman was about to embark on further explanations when Fricoulet showed his friend a page in his notebook on which he had rapidly scribbled a few lines while listening to Selena.

"Here," he said, "read that—learn it by heart, if necessary. I've summarized as succinctly as possible what it's indispensable to know."

This is what was written in the engineer's notebook:

Stars divided into four categories, from the spectroscopic viewpoint:

[105] Little seems to be known about the New Zealand astronomer J. H. Pope except that he was a schoolteacher in Otago.

White stars, such as Sirius, Vega, Procyon, Altair—spectra almost continuous with lines of hydrogen, sodium, magnesium—temperature extremely high, very dense hydrogen atmosphere—the most numerous category, comprising more than half of known stars.

Yellow stars, such as Aldebaran, Capella, Arcturus, whose lines, similar to those of our own Sun, betray the presence of hydrogen, iron and magnesium.

Orange or reddish stars: Antares, Miraceti, etc.—spectra composed of strong dark lines and brilliant points, giving them the appearance of ribbed columns seen in perspective, from which the supposition arises that two distinct patterns of light are superimposed—atmosphere very absorbent. Hydrogen almost absent, carbon abundant.

Red stars—colonnade-like spectra, demonstrating the existence of carbon compounds, probably gaseous oxides, which indicate a very low temperature.

Fricoulet added, as a note:

One can therefore suppose, with some plausibility, that the white stars are the youngest, given the violence of their combustion, that the yellow are in a stable state, and that, finally, the red suns are oxidizing and almost extinct.

Since the *Eclair* had been launched into the infinite, however, the engineer had—according to the popular expression—been sleeping with one eye open. He was exhausted—so, imitating Ossipoff's wisdom, he went back to his cabin, leaving Selena to her spectroscopic studies and Gontran to the study of stellar categories. The apparatus was being carried along at a vertiginous velocity, obedient to the attraction of the stars for which it was headed, and there was no need to keep watch on a progress that no human agency was capable of slowing or steering. He therefore slept soundly, without knowing that Gontran, after conscientiously reading the note about the stars twice over, had ended up falling asleep with his head tilted back.

Selena too had no suspicion of the soporific effect produced on her fiancé by the engineer's laconic prose; absorbed by her work, she had no thought but to satisfy, to the extent that she was able, her father's desires, and her attention was entirely concentrated on the stars.

Sirius was now displayed in the infinity of the heavens, in the midst of a host of worlds, an immense disk presenting a surface nearly four times as large as the full Moon, inundating the engine-room with a pallid light that would have been blinding but for the blinds with which Fricoulet's ingenuity had prudently provided the portholes.

Although located about 39 trillion leagues from Earth—as had been established by the various parallax measurements taken by Maclear in 1837 and Gylden in 1870—Sirius nevertheless appears to the inhabitants of our planet as a Sun, so intense is its light. The heat that this formidable disk radiated could be felt, now that the lithium vehicle was less that half that distance away. Selena, while pursuing her observations, was veritably amazed by the results she obtained; they gave, compared to our Sun, a surface 144 times greater, a volume

1700 times larger, and a diameter 12 times as wide. Mentally, she compared the dimensions of this colossus of space and those of her native sphere, the latter being 108 times smaller and 1280 times less voluminous than the Sun lighting it, and she was appalled by the "infinite smallness" of the terrestrial globe.

As her analysis advanced further, the young woman was subjugated by ever-increasing curiosity obedient to a sort of enthusiasm that impelled her to more difficult and demanding researches, but which led her to an even more profound knowledge of that marvelous sun. She lit a candle and superimposed the spectrum of Sirius on the solar spectrum obtained from the flame, which permitted her to observe that it was displaced toward the red end of the fixed spectrum—proof that the star was moving away from the Solar System. As for the velocity with which that distancing was effected, it was easy for her to calculate; it was only slightly less than 35 kilometers a second—nearly 75,000 leagues per day, approximately 268,000,000 a year! It was vertiginous!

She could not retain an exclamation that made Gontran start. His eyes wide and his eyelids red with sleep, he exclaimed: "Eh? What? What's happening?"

In an exclamatory tone, the young woman—who had not noticed anything—replied: "Oh! Sirius! Gontran...Sirius!"

Still half-awake, the Comte leapt down, thinking that some cataclysm had occurred. "Someone up to his old tricks again!" he muttered. At the first step he took, however, he stopped, blinded by the sparkling light with which the cabin was filled, in spite of Fricoulet's prudent precautions. He put one of his hands in front of his eyes to preserve them from the unexpected dazzle that had caused him a sharp pain, while he wiped sweat from his brow with the other hand, simultaneously murmuring: "God, it's hot!"

Selena, who had gradually grown accustomed to the light and heat due to the proximity of the star—which was increasing by the second—burst out laughing. "It's Sirius," she said. "There's no need to get upset."

For a few moments she rapidly wrote down her observations, while the young man, who had come closer to her, read over her shoulder.

"268,000,000 leagues!" he exclaimed, in order to seem interested in his fiancée's work. I'd never have thought that a star could move as quickly!"

Selena started. "Don't speak so loudly," she said. "If my father heard you..."

"So what? What would he say? I'm not obliged to know results of which he is presently ignorant himself, since you've only just obtained them."

"Undoubtedly," replied the young woman, laughing, "but what an astronomer like you ought to know is that all the stars are animated by extremely rapid motions, many of which have long been calculated with extreme precision. The one which, thus far, is know to have the greatest velocity in star 1830 in the Groombridge catalogue, which attains 5.78 seconds southward declination and 0.344 degrees eastward right ascension, totaling 7.03 seconds southeastwards, per year..."

Gontran listened to the young woman talk with mouth agape; the expression on his face was superabundant proof of the fact that everything she said was a closed book to him. "7.03 seconds southeastwards per year," he repeated.

He seemed so bewildered that Selena could not help laughing. Taking his hands, she said to him tenderly: "My poor Gontran, you must love me very much, in order to resist the aridity of all these things that are so awkward for you."

"How I love you!" he cried, ardently. In a slightly sad tone, he added: "And yet, there are moments when I'm afraid that my love, however strong it might be, can't help me to play the role of fake scientist, which is so contrary to my nature and my character..."

A hand placed on his shoulder made him turn around, and he found himself face to face with Fricoulet, who said to him: "Eros is the strongest of the gods. He can do whatever he wishes. Of all the masters of Olympus, he's certainly the one that works the most miracles."

"In the meantime," said Selena, whose face had fallen in response to Flammermont's words, "you still don't know what 7.03 seconds a year represents?"

"You're talking about Groombridge 1830!" Fricoulet exclaimed. Addressing Gontran, he said: "That represents the mere bagatelle of 2,600,000,000 leagues, or 300 kilometers a second."

Flamermont, however, was getting bored with the enthusiasm that gripped his friend and his fiancée, and he adopted a mocking tone to pose the essentially logical question: "So what?"

"What do you mean, so what?"

"Well, you know that this star moves at a velocity of 300 kilometers a second—that's something, but not everything. The interesting thing would be to know where this colossal sun has come from, where it's going, with what purpose it was created, what role it plays in the Universe and what influence it might have on the progress of humankind and celestial civilization."

Fricoulet tightened his lips in order to retain a strong desire to laugh. "Oh!" he said. "Celestial humankind!"

Gontran started and pointed at the porthole. "You aren't insinuating that that Universe is dead, and that it was created with the sole purpose of brightening our terrestrial nights?"

"Certainly not."

"Well, then I'm right to ask you whether such a colossus is not equipped by nature to have a prodigious influence on humankinds that live on the surfaces of worlds whose shores it brushes in its progress...."

The engineer raised his arms toward the ceiling, in a strangely comical gesture. "Oh, poet!" he exclaimed. "Would you like me to tell you something? In your lyrical flight of fancy you remind me of your scientific namesake, the author of *Les Etoiles*: 'What is the origin of such vehemence? Who launched it thus into the ethereal spheres? Into what abysm will it fall? So many questions! So many mysteries! And when one thinks that, if no external influence modifies its progress, this prodigious cannonball will continue to move in a straight line with that same constant velocity for millions and millions of years—for all of eternity—without ever approaching any terminus, without being able to reach the horizon of infinity! The mind hesitates in terror before such a contemplation; the imagination suspends its flight and falls in a faint before the splendor of the absolute!' "

The engineer had pronounced these words in a somewhat emphatic and overly bombastic tone, deliberately making the sentences resonate, their emotional quality masking their meaning somewhat. Gontran was enthusiastic to make a riposte, and not slow in doing so. "Very good—go on," he said mockingly, "but all that doesn't tell me anything new. My namesake proceeds by questions, which he is careful not to answer, and his imagination, instead of 'falling in a faint' before the mysteries of nature, would do better to try to explain them. If an astronomer is content to ask questions, should he therefore count on a layman like me to tell him what he does not know?"

The engineer's only response was to purse his lips in an expression which seemed to indicate that, deep down, he was not far distant from sharing his friend's opinion—but it was Selena who exclaimed: "If my father heard you talking like that! Daring to challenge the scientist for whom he has such a profound admiration..."

"But I admire him too," the young man replied, "except that I find that he puts too much poetry in his inkwell and I'm disappointed when, instead of finding a figure or a scientific explanation, I only find a flight of fancy, which soothes my reason without satisfying it completely."

The conversation would doubtless have continued further in this vein, but, on hearing the floor of Ossipoff's cabin creaking overhead, Gontran anticipated that the scientist was about to rejoin his daughter; fearful that he might not pass an examination on the subject of Sirius, he drew away on tiptoe and silently climbed back into his hammock.

Not far away, Farenheit was sleeping like a brute, his fists closed, exhaling a powerful breath through his half-open lips that filled the room with a noise like the buzzing of an enormous mosquito.

There's a man who isn't much tormented by astronomical laws, the young Comte thought, darting an envious glance at his neighbor. *How right he is!* He added, with a sigh that—if she had been able to hear it—would have given Selena considerable insight into her fiancé's state of mind: *Eros, Eros, when you get hold of us...* He did not finish the sentence. From a nearby shelf he took his copy of *Les Continents célestes,* a few pages of which he always read before going to sleep—a habit he had adopted since the beginning of the voyage, not so much to complete his education as to distract his mind momentarily from the myriad anxieties tormenting it.

Whether because the astronomical explanations had wearied his mind, however, or because the extraordinary heat due to the proximity of Sirius had overwhelmed him, Flammermont let his head fall back on his pillow. He went to sleep, still clutching the book in his fingers, having scanned less than ten pages. Then, in consequence of a perfectly understandable hallucination, the philosophical suppositions of the wise author of *Les Continents célestes* were animated in a sort of dream, bringing the descriptions contained in the pages he had just read to life before his very eyes.

Miraculously, without his seeking to explain how such transformations might take place, his sight, surpassing the limits of telescopic vision, had acquired a supernatural power, so that his sense of duration and time permitted him to grasp and comprehend the vastest intervals of time. Then, as if by magic, the apparent immobility in which the azure vault of the heavens is fixed disappeared; the innumerable stars, like those eddies of dust that are raised on our roads in summer by gusts of wind that presage great storms, flew off in all directions, scattered to all the corners of infinity; the nebulas, torn apart, dismantled and lacerated, were no more than formless shreds that disappeared, whirling into the depths of the sky, like gigantic birds plucked and borne away by the violence of the tempest; rolled up into themselves—condensed, so to speak—they changed appearance, devouring worlds; like all the others, the Milky Way came apart and, deformed and disseminated, became unrecognizable.

In sum, there was an agitation, a movement, a life in space, similar to those of which the Earth provides examples, but in such colossal proportions that Gontran was terrified. One might have thought that giants' hands were furiously chasing the stars, catching them and throwing them to the winds of Infinity, where they vanished beneath a colossal breath.

Miraculously, the sleeper's mind was separated from the fleshy envelope that constrained it, hindering the expansion of its strength, binding it to one Earth or another, and it was therefore able to comprehend infinity in space and time. It was no longer the silent night of a dismal, immobile, seemingly dead sky that it beheld, but a frightful immensity in which myriads of scintillating and disorbited Suns moved, no longer obedient to any law of gravitation but launched according to the caprice of an unknown will, strewing space with the multiple forms of an inextinguishable and universal vitality. With every passing moment, Flammermont's fearful gaze, endowed with an incomprehensible acuity, plunged further forward into the unsoundable depths of space. It seemed as if there were an infinite number of superimposed veils, which were withdrawn one after another, still masking the depths of the celestial gulf in which Gontran thought he could perceive the truth of everything—but the stars, the suns and the planets were being carried away by a storm wind and the appearance of the sky did not remain stable for a single minute, or a single second, and in the face of these uninterrupted metamorphoses, the young man never ceased to be in ecstasy. Finally, there came a moment in which the vertigo occasioned by that saraband of stars caused him an anguish so terrible that he awoke with a start, releasing a cry.

Sitting up on his elbow, his face soaked with sweat, he saw all his traveling companions grouped around his hammock, looking at him anxiously. He understood then that he had simply been prey to a nightmare, and remained silent, slightly ashamed of his weakness, although it was independent of his will.

"Well, what's up then?" said Fricoulet, mockingly. "Were you dreaming about Loie Fuller?"

Gontran blushed slightly, and murmured ill-humoredly: "A few more weeks of this existence and I'll go mad..." Mechanically, he felt his skull, as if he wanted to convince himself that there was no crack therein.

"A nightmare?" Farenheit asked.

As Ossipoff was also there, though, the young man was ashamed to confess the astronomical vision that had disturbed his sleep and, immediately recovering his presence of mind, replied: "Yes, a nightmare, and a nightmare caused by that accursed Sirius. I was unable to admit that, although Sirius has been drawing away from the Earth for an immeasurable interval of time at a rate of 35 kilometers a second, its light is not only still visible, but undiminished in intensity."

Ossipoff smiled indulgently and murmured: "The special state into which dreams put a lucid and scientific mind is very singular. Here you are, an astronomer whose knowledge no one, not even me, dares dispute, excited by an objection that a child's reasoning is sufficient to refute. If you had been in your normal state, would you not have understood that what appears to you phenomenal is simply due to the enormous distance that separates us from the Earth? The distance covered in 4000 years is not the 1/50th part of the distance that separates Sirius from Earth; in such conditions..."

Gontran nodded his head affirmatively.

"If your nightmare hasn't left you too tired," the old man added, "I'd be very obliged if you'd come to help me with certain studies I'd like to make..."

A shadow crossed Flammermont's face; in a weary tone he murmured: "Give me time to splash a little water on my face, and I'm yours...."

"Hurry up—for, at the rate the *Eclair* is traveling, we'll be out of range before long..." While speaking, the scientist had taken a few steps toward the door, but he came back and slapped the young man on the shoulder. In a low voice, in the tone in which a gourmet speaks of a delicious dish that makes his mouth water, he said: "Perhaps we'll know what we're dealing with, this time...and whether it's a matter of a planet or a sun..." Without noticing the bewilderment that these words produced in Flammermont, he went out.

"Whether it's a planet or a sun..." Gontran repeated. His alarmed, questioning eyes went from Farenheit to Fricoulet. "This time," he declared, "I really believe I'm lost."

The engineer spread his arms in a gesture of complete ignorance. "If anyone knew what he meant..."

All three of them were still and silent, looking at one another, when someone knocked gently on the door and Selena's voice was heard. "Monsieur Gontran," she said. "My father's asking whether you'll be joining him soon?"

"Let him go to the Devil!" muttered the young Comte.

"Him, by all means—but not her," said Fricoulet—and he went to the door to let Ossipoff's daughter in. "We're rather perplexed, you know," he said. "Perhaps, as you're up to date with your father's work, you can save us from embarrassment. This is what it's about..."

Having heard the explanation rapidly given by the engineer, Selena smiled. "I believe that my father was alluding to the satellite of Sirius..."

Fricoulet clapped his hands together joyfully. "Of course!" he cried. "I get it now."

Gontran, however, murmured wearily: "Oh, if the stars are going to have satellites now..."

Fricoulet did not have the leisure to sympathize; time was pressing, Father Ossipoff was waiting and the engineer did not want to expose Gontran to the astronomical tournament to which the old man had invited him without having larded him in advance with scientific notions. "In brief, this is it: the proper movement of Sirius, instead of proceeding uniformly, being subject to certain alterations, an astronomer named Bessel[106] has not hesitated to attribute them to the action of an invisible body of considerable mass—a dark body, the debris of a dead word, circulating in space. In 1854, Le Verrier commended that theory, supporting it with the periodic inequalities presented by Procyon, of which no one had ever been able to discover a satellite.[107] That did not prevent Monsieur Peters, in 1851, from crediting an orbit to the unknown and invisible body, in the form of a very elongated ellipse through which it moves in a period 50 years..."

Farenheit could not retain an outburst of loud laughter. "No one knows what the body is, no one has ever seen it, and no one even knows whether it exists—but that doesn't prevent astronomers from advertising the circumstances of its motion."

"If they only advertised that," Fricoulet continued. "However, in 1862, Messieurs Auwers and Safford[108] credited the problematic satellite with a positional angle of 85.4 degrees and an angular distance of 10.6 seconds."

---

[106] Friedrich Wilhelm Bessel (1784-1846).

[107] Procyon did, indeed, eventually turn out to have a dark companion similar to Sirius B—which is actually a white dwarf star, and really is, therefore, "the debris of a dead world."

[108] Arthur von Auwers (1838-1915) and Truman Henry Safford (1836-1901). Safford had been something of a child prodigy, renowned as a "lightning calcu-

The American raised his arms into the air, exclaiming ironically: "Incredible!"

"Laugh as much as you wish, Monsieur Farenheit," Selena declared. "That takes nothing away from the fact that on January 31, 1862, Mr. Alvan Clark, Jr.,[109] using an 18-inch telescope, perceived a luminous point to the left of Sirius, at an angle exactly equal to 84.6 degrees—which is to say, differing by only one degree from the calculation made by Messieurs Auwers and Safford."

"And that's the full extent of what's known about this satellite?" asked Gontran, ironically.

"Not at all. Its brightness is almost equal to that of a star of the ninth magnitude and its mass is about half that of Sirius—which is to say, seven times that of the Sun—although its luminosity is about 5000 times less than that of the principal star. Now that you're informed..." So saying, the engineer pushed Gontran toward the door, for he could hear Monsieur Ossipoff calling loudly to his young "colleague."

Before going out, however, the latter, who never went into that sort of conversation without apprehension, asked: "Then, the question at issue is whether this famous satellite is a planet or a sun?"

"Yes, according to what Ossipoff said."

"And...do you have a personal opinion on the matter?"

"None, seeing as, until now, the subject has left me quite indifferent—but if you ask me, given the uncertainty, you should let him do the talking; if he asks you, you can boldly propose any theory that suits you..."

In his cabin, the old man was stamping his feet impatiently while waiting for Gontran, simultaneously searching space to extract the secret of the mysterious world that intrigued him so much. Was there, in fact, a sun there, shining with its own light, or was it only a matter of an enormous planet of that distant system?

Ossipoff favored the latter hypothesis, and Flammermont had scarcely crossed the threshold when he cried: "You know, my dear chap, for me there's no longer the shadow of a doubt—it's a planet!"

"Really?"

"And you'll understand my reasons: here's a world of great volume, to which nothing prevents us from attributing a very white surface, illuminated by a sun twice as intense per unit of surface area and having a surface 40 times more extensive than Earth's Sun. What's impossible about such a planet, even at

---

lator;" he delighted in applying his talent to astronomical calculations like the one in question.

[109] Alvan Graham Clark (1832-1897) was the son of the famous astronomer and optical instrument-maker Alvan Clark (1804-1887); he discovered Sirius B on the indicated date while testing one of his father's instruments.

a distance of more than 1,000,000 leagues from its central torch, being perceptible at a distance of 39 trillion leagues?"

In order not to compromise himself, Gontran thought he ought to approve the theory—which was no more important to him, fundamentally, than its contrary—with a nod of the head, which had the advantage of permitting him to maintain an absolute silence. Besides, the scientist seemed to have forgotten his companion's presence, entirely gripped by the increasing interest of his study, which was growing in extent by the second. Having minutely examined Sirius and its satellite, he succeeded in distinguishing other luminous points, one at 114 degrees and 72 minutes, the other at 159 degrees 104—which he did not hesitate to identify as also belonging to the Sirian system.

The exclamations of triumph uttered by the old man brought Fricoulet and Selena running. When Ossipoff had explained the reason for his joy, the engineer said: "My God, my dear Monsieur, I certainly don't want to contradict your assertions, but, besides the fact that your theory regarding the famous satellite's whiter surface seems highly debatable to me, I also think that you're augmenting the Sirius system in a blithe fashion that's slightly childish..."

The old scientist stiffened prodigiously and his face abruptly went red. He abandoned the telescope, swiveled on his heels like a top, and looked daggers through the lenses of his spectacles. "And what basis do you have, my young friend," he hissed, "for permitting yourself to contradict me so categorically?"

"I don't permit myself to do that," protested Fricoulet, "as I said at the outset. But it's permissible to wonder whether these luminous points are really dependents of the Sirius system, or whether they're simply situated beyond that star, appearing to be in its neighborhood simply by virtue of the hazards of celestial perspective."

The old man was obliged, privately, to recognize the logic of this observation—but he did not like contradiction and, while containing his irritation, he retorted in a bitter tone: "I would be curious, in that case, to know what orbit you would assign to the satellite of Sirius—assuming that, for you, it's not a planet but a sun..."

"My God, I don't have any strong personal opinion on that subject, you know, but Gontran—who was taking to me about it only yesterday—has given me some very interesting information."

"You!" exclaimed the old man, in an indignant tone.

"Me!" cried Flammermont, in his turn. "I talked to you about that?"

Indifferent to his friend's indignant surprise, Fricoulet continued: "Let's see, didn't you tell me that, in a binary system, several cases might pertain—either each component can have planets rotating in circles around their respective suns, or planets might describe triple spirals, symmetrical formed, before returning to their point of departure...?"

Ossipoff burst out laughing, and said to the young Comte: "Ah! It's not imagination you lack! Unfortunately, there's a wide margin between the products of imaginations and scientific studies. So, have you formed a near-exact idea of the singular years and the bizarre seasons that similar revolutions might produce? No? Well, I assure you…" He interrupted himself abruptly, remembering the acquiescence that the young man had given to his theory concerning the satellite of Sirius a few moments before. "Why didn't you contradict me just now," he asked, "and reply *sun* when I said *planet* to you?"

Taken aback by this question, the young man replied with a shrug of the shoulders testifying to the unimportance of the matter. "My God, Monsieur Ossipoff, all opinions are respectable; besides I'm not much given to contradiction, especially when addressing people older than myself…"

Ossipoff lost his temper. "There's no age," he cried, "when science is at stake! On numerous occasions since the start of this voyage I've bowed my white head to your knowledge, and nothing could humiliate me more than such condescension to my old age…" He fell silent for a few moments, mumbling unintelligible words between his teeth. Then, abruptly dismissing Gontran with a hand gesture, he said "Go away. If that's the way it is, I have no need of you." And without paying any further heed to the people who were there, he applied his eye to the ocular lens, entirely gripped once again by his ardent curiosity.

Once they were on the landing, with the door carefully closed behind them, Gontran asked Fricoulet, in an irritated tone: "What's got into you? Where did you get the idea of telling Ossipoff things that aren't so?"

"It wouldn't be the first time," said the engineer, mockingly.

"True—but on the previous occasions, we were in agreement."

"Wasn't it necessary to find a means of avoiding the questions he would surely have asked you?" Then, ill-humored in his turn, as if Flammermont's reproach appeared to him to be unjustified, the engineer complained; "That's all right—from now on, I'll let you get yourself out of it on your own." And while Gontran went back into his cabin, he went slowly down the steps that led to the engine-room, murmuring with a singular smile: "Who knows? Stranger things have been seen…"

Chapter LVIII
In which Gontran and Fricoulet are seriously at odds

It was already two days—or, rather, two periods of 24 hours—since the *Eclair*, sailing through the Milky Way, had left Sirius and the constellation of Canis Major, to which that star belonged, far behind. Borne away by an immeasurable force, obedient to the invincible attraction exerted upon it by the worlds of Infinity, the apparatus flew straight ahead, like the hyperbolic cannonball of which the author of *Les Continents célestes* speaks in his works, but without apparently being able to reach the goal it was pursuing, the limits of the space through which it was moving retreating the further it advanced.

Inside the vehicle, a certain constraint had reigned since the scene we reported at the end of the preceding chapter.

Between the more-than-heterogeneous elements of which the little company of travelers was composed, Fricoulet served as a unifying link, his natural good humor calming Farenheit's anger, dissipating Ossipoff's suspicions and soothing the wounds unintentionally inflicted on Gontran's self-respect. It is needless to add, once more, that without his friend's scientific knowledge, the former diplomat would have been incapable of sustaining a conversation with Ossipoff, however short it might be. Like an actor who, to replace an absent colleague, is pushed into the scene by the director without knowing a word of the role that he must play, Flammermont would have broken down at any moment if he had not had a prompter as skilled as Fricoulet.

Now, since the incident—seemingly very slight—to which the discussion of the satellite of Sirius had given rise, the two friends seemed to be avoiding one another. Perhaps it would have been admissible, or at least comprehensible, that Gontran had taken against the engineer, for he might have considered it a bad joke on his part to have adopted an opinion diametrically opposed to that old the old man, without any need, for Flammermont could not suppose that the engineer took any pleasure in starting arguments between the old man and himself—all the more so as, since leaving Earth, he had given proof of an inexhaustible complaisance in his regard. Was it not, therefore, out of pure caprice, with the sole desire of doing him a bad turn and amusing himself at his expense that Fricoulet had put words into his mouth that he had never spoken? As for the explanations that the engineer had given after leaving Ossipoff's cabin, he only put a very mediocre trust in them. Indeed, he assumed that the engineer had only furnished his friend with the explanations he judged indispensable concerning Sirius, while keeping others to himself.

Gontran's ignorance in astronomical matters already rendered his attitude very difficult, if not impossible; existence would become untenable if Fricoulet often got such whims into his head. Headstrong as he was, accustomed never to keep to himself his opinion concerning anyone or anything, a believer in frank and prompt explanations, Gontran had immediately thought of asking Fricoulet why he had acted in that fashion, but some instinct that he could not quite fathom had made him keep silent—and, as happens in such circumstances, the ill humor that a few minutes of conversation might perhaps have dissipated was transformed into a sulk.

Strangely enough, as the hours ran by, the young Comte had felt himself becoming increasingly determined not to go back to the incident. He felt vaguely—but, we repeat, without being able to form even an indistinct opinion on the subject—that, to act as he had done, the engineer must have had a reason, but he also had a presentiment that he would not be told what that reason was. In such circumstances, why provoke a confrontation that could not do otherwise than degenerate into an argument, all the more painful and all the more perilous because circumstances forced the two friends to live in such close proximity? Gontran had, therefore, started to avoid Fricoulet and as, while avoiding Fricoulet, he did not want and could not risk encountering Ossipoff on the scientific ground on which he always dreaded a dangerous slip, he pretended to be ill and did not budge from his hammock.

Fricoulet, for his part, also seemed to be sulking. We say "seemed," for the engineer's playful and jovial character was absolutely averse to sulking; no less frank than Flammermont, he did not like things to drag on and liked situations to be swiftly clarified. In this circumstance, however, he experienced a singular inhibition, not to say a sort of repugnance, with respect to the prospect of addressing a word to his friend. The truth is that, if he was annoyed—as it seemed—his annoyance was not directed against Gontran but against himself. Yes, against himself. He was discontented with what he had done—even though, in doing it, he had, so to speak, been acting without his own consent, obedient to some unfathomable sentiment, driven by an instinct that he could not explain.

Undoubtedly, in attributing to Gontran an opinion contrary to that manifested by Ossipoff, he had had no intention of confusing matter and provoking an unexpected denouement in the comedy that he had been playing for such along time, unknown to the old man, which did not conform to the desires of the principal actors. It seemed to him, though, that such a denouement would not be as displeasing to him as it would be to Flammermont and Selena. Why not? Ah...he did not know. If he had wanted to know, perhaps it would not have been very difficult for him to figure it out—in order to do that he, a highly skilled chemist, would only have had to analyze the troubled and slightly bizarre mixture that his own sentiments formed deep inside him.

If he had wanted to—but he did not want to; a secret instinct warned him that, in his own and everyone else's interest, it was better not to probe the question deeply. In that, he obeyed the same instinct that pressed Gontran to shun an explanation—and, imprisoned in his mutism, he remained confined to the engine-room.

Ossipoff, annoyed by Gontran's indisposition—which deprived him of the scientific partner who was presently indispensable to his existence—absorbed himself even further in the contemplation of the stars. Meanwhile, Selena, who was utterly disconcerted, not knowing what the abrupt change that had overtaken the two friends' relationship signified and sensing a vague anxiety invading her soul, began writing to her father's dictation, as she had in St. Petersburg, to pass the time.

We shall not say anything about Farenheit, for and for good reason; it made no difference to him that Fricoulet and Gontran were at odds and that the old man's scientific conversations had been interrupted. Only one thing interested him: the progress of the *Eclair*. Every second that went by brought him closer to Fifth Avenue, and that had sufficed, for 48 hours, to maintain his face in a state of serenity that his traveling companions had not seen for a very long time. Besides, he spent almost all his time in his hammock, where he lay sound asleep; when hunger pangs woke him up, he went to the storage unit, drank a few mouthfuls of nutritive liquid and then, to facilitate digestion, he spent a quarter of an hour or a little more—depending on how interesting the sky was—at a porthole...except when he recommenced, for at least the twentieth time, the calculation of the sum that might accrue to him for his share in the sale of the lithium vehicle once they returned to Earth. If new excavations made since his departure had discovered new deposits, and if, in consequence, the value of the precious metal had diminished...

If...if...

These anxieties sufficed to break the monotony of existence for a man whose brain did not possess very ambitious appetites.

It is understandable that, in these conditions, life aboard lacked gaiety and that, for Gontran, Fricoulet and Selena, the minutes were as long as hours and the hours as long as centuries. That did not prevent hundreds of thousands of leagues being added to the millions of kilometers behind the *Eclair*, which maintained its course impassively. Its prow directed toward Orion, it flew toward the constellation of Monoceros, which forms, along with the celestial province in which it is situated, one of the most bizarre—and, at the same time, one of the most interesting—corners of space.

Already, with the aid of his telescope, Ossipoff could examine, much more minutely than he had been able to do from the Pulkova Observatory, the famous star number 11,[110] or, rather, the ternary system whose three dazzling white

---

[110] The text has thus far employed the more familiar system of star classification that identifies the stars within each constellation by means of Greek letters; the occasional switch here and hereafter to the numerical system based on the catalogue compiled by John Flamsteed (1646-1719), posthumously published in 1723, presumably echoes the sources from which the authors are quoting. Although the other two stars cited here could have been identified by Greek letters,

components looked like three incandescent lamps that a divine hand had lit in front of the variegated curtain of space. Afterwards, number 15, or S, appeared, with its two yellow components and a third azure blue in color—and the old scientist was able, in a few minutes, given the rapidity with which the apparatus was moving—to enjoy the amazing spectacle of the variability that takes 3 days, 10 hours and 498 minutes to reveal itself to the eyes of terrestrial astronomers.

The intensity of the light emitted by the ternary system alternately rises from the sixth to the fourth magnitude, then falls back to the sixth, with the result that it produced a flickering quality that Ossipoff's eyes found extremely tiring. It was so uncomfortable that he had to ask Selena to relieve him at the telescope for want of Gontran, who judged it wise to remain deaf to the old scientist's invitations.

It was, therefore, through the eyes of his daughter that Ossipoff was able to take approximate account of a bizarre phenomenon produced by that multiple assemblage of variable stars: star no. 8, a double star very curious by virtue of its components, one yellow and the other blue, animated by a common proper movement, although remaining fixed with respect to one another for the 100 years that they have been studied. Not far away, a nebula of cometary appearance was pointed out by the young woman. Then, so numerous that it was futile to attempt to count them, a mass of little stars of various colors, and may nebulas of a very curious form.

Despite the pain caused to his eyes by the glare of all these stars, Ossipoff, gripped by curiosity, could not be long content to admire all these marvels through the intermediary of Selena, and he swiftly resumed his place at the ocular lens. It was, in any case, a rather inconvenient manner of doing astronomy—and he had become anxiously impatient with the young woman several times over, notably in the matter of Procyon...

"Don't you see a first magnitude star to our north-west?" he had demanded.

"I see several of them," Selena had replied, looking in the direction indicated.

"Several, of course-but not like this one—the one I'm talking about shines like an electric light—it has a brightness similar to that of Sirius. Do you see it? Come on, damn it, you must see it!"

"Yes...it seems to me...to the north-west, you say..."

It was then that, stamping his foot impatiently, the old man had pushed his daughter away. Yes, it was definitely Alpha Canis Minoris—a star so curious by virtue of its proper motion—and the old man experienced an unalloyed joy after having verified the parallax established by Auwers in 1862—a parallax equal to

---

star 15 had been set aside from the Greek letter system because it is a variable star within a nebula (now known to be a galaxy, NGC 2264) and was therefore alternatively identified, as the text indicates in passing, as S Monocerotis.

0.123 seconds—and determining the velocity of the star, which until now, he had only been able to examine imperfectly by reason of the 62 trillion leagues that separated it from Earth.

While examining it, Ossipoff was occasionally prey to an illusion that can impose itself on a traveler in a moving railway carriage. Assuming that the train is traveling at a speed of 60 kilometers and hour and that, parallel to it, a second train is moving at a similar speed, the carriages of the second train can appear to the traveler contained in the first to be motionless, just as, considering himself as motionless, he seems to see the telegraph poles, stations and various buildings bordering the track moving backwards at a speed of 60 kilometers an hour. Finally, if he is traveling in the opposite direction to a train on the other track moving at an equal speed, he might, if he has the illusion that he is motionless, think that the other train is twice as fast, traveling at a rate of 120 kilometers per hour. Well, although the old scientist was used to the sorts of illusions by which novice astronomers can be caught out, but which the veterans of the science defy, because he was so close to the star it occasionally seemed to him that Procyon was animated by a velocity twice as great, by reason of his traveling through space in the opposite direction to that in which the Solar System was moving.

In a curt voice, which caught in his throat, he dictated notes to Selena in chopped sentences—notes incomprehensible to anyone but him, figures to which it was necessary to have a key to make any sense of them whatsoever. From time to time, when there was nothing bizarre or interesting to note down, he said in a commanding tone, in which no trace of paternal affection was discernible: "Add...divide...multiply..." And finally, he demanded: "Have you done that?" Then, the young woman gave him the results of these operations; if they concurred with those obtained by Ossipoff during his sojourn on Earth, he would express his satisfaction with a little snigger; if not, he clicked his tongue, mumbling incoherent words that invariably terminated in a dry: "Start again."

Fortunately, the old man's calculations relating to Procyon proved to be correct, and he estimated the rapidity with which the star was moving through space at 43 kilometers per second, or 2580 a minute, 154,000 per hour, 3,715,000 per day—which, for the year, gave the fine figure of 1,357,000,000 kilometers. Ossipoff experienced an indefinable joy at these calculations, which ended up giving almost unimaginable results, before which any other mind than his own would have been stupefied—but which, on the contrary, transported his own well beyond the limits of human comprehension, opening up to him, so to speak, the profundities of Infinity.

"Do you realize," he said to Selena, in a voice vibrant with enthusiasm, "what the combined motions of Procyon and our Sun add up to? 1,409,000,000 leagues per year!" And he added, in the tone of a gladiator entering the arena with the firm determination to fell his opponent: "It's the turn of the other now."

"The other?" Selena queried.

"Yes—the satellite of Procyon." From that moment on he did not say a word. His body leaned forward, quivering with impatience, his dilated pupil glued to the telescope, while his hand traced figures and geometric symbols feverishly on the notepad set in front of him. He was there for about six minutes, motionless, without his taut lips relaxing once, oblivious to the presence of Selena—who, saddened by the abandonment to which Gontran had left her for two days, was still sitting, resignedly, in a corner of the cabin when Fricoulet came in on tiptoe.

The young woman was putting a finger to her lips to instruct the engineer to be silent when, at that very moment, Ossipoff's discouraged voice was heard. "nothing...I can't see anything...and yet Struve was quite definite..."

"Too definite, Monsieiur Ossipoff, much too definite," Fricoulet could not help saying, "for, when verification was attempted with the aid of telescopes more powerful than those at Pulkova Observatory, his affirmation was deemed erroneous..."

The old man stood up straight, as if moved by a spring, and looked daggers at Fricoulet. "Erroneous!" he exclaimed. "Otto Struve observed Procyon's companion for more than two years..."[111]

"An astronomical hallucination, Monsieur Ossipoff. Take note that I'm not denying the good faith of the Imperial Observatory..."

"That can be taken for granted..."

"...But in the final analysis, it's well-established that the satellite in question only existed in Monsieur Struve's mind." To calm the old man's anger, he hastened to add: "I couldn't ask for better proof of it than the lack of success of your present research; if Procyon had a companion, it would certainly be visible to the naked eye from our present location."

This argument stemmed the flood of words ready to spill from Ossipoff's lips, but almost immediately, he said: "I'd very much like to know, in that case, to what Monsieur de Flammermont attributes the irregular movement of Procyon and the oscillations observed in its trajectory. I say Monsieur de Flammermont, for I imagine that what you've just said was inspired by him..."

Selena put her hands together, seemingly begging the young man not to poison the discussion and not to make the situation any worse than it was.

Albeit with a slight grimace that betrayed a concentrated ill humor, the engineer nodded his head to reassure her, and replied: "You're not mistaken on that point—but without being able to go into all the explanations that Gontran has given me, I remember that he told me that he didn't share the opinion of Auwers..."

---

[111] Whether or not Otto Struve really did catch glimpses of Procyon's white dwarf companion while serving as director of Pulkova Observatory is impossible to determine, but the first visual confirmation of its existence is nowadays dated to 1896.

"Damn!" exclaimed the old man, ironically. "Dear Gontran is rather disdainful. Auwers is, however, rather definite, since he has gone so far as to say that the satellite in question rotates in a plane perpendicular to the visual ray, not around Procyon itself but a common center of gravity. He has even established that its revolution is accomplished in a period of 40 years..."

Fricoulet pursed his lips. "Pooh! I think you're making the worthy Auwers more definite than he was himself. He said: 'it could be that...' and that 'he would not be at all astonished if...' But his very phraseology proves that between his hypotheses and the declarations of your compatriot Struve..."

This reply seemed too peremptory to the old man for him to deem it useful to prolong the debate—a debate that his own observations proved futile, and in which he had only been pushed so far by patriotism and respect for Otto Struve, under whose direction he had worked at Pulkova Observatory. Changing the topic, he said to Fricoulet: "You ought to alert Monsieur de Flammermont to the fact that we'll soon be level with star 60 in Orion."

The engineer's face was illuminated by an ironic smile, and without really thinking about what he was saying, he replied: "Why—what do you expect him to do about it?"

The old man went very stiff, as much in amazement as indignation. "What?" he cried. "What I expect him to do..." He interrupted himself, uttered a small mocking laugh full of pity, and added: "I understand...you're speaking for yourself...to you, of course, it matters little that we're leaving the southern hemisphere to enter the northern hemisphere—but with respect to him, I have no fear of being too forward in declaring that it will interest him to know that the *Eclair* will soon cross the equator and that we shall shortly be able to contemplate at close range the stars that we perceive from Europe and America..."

An exclamation rang out at the same time, and it seemed that a storm-wind rushed into the cabin through the open door. At the same time, before he was able to react, Ossipoff felt himself lifted from the ground. After having received a resounding accolade on each cheek, he found himself back on his feet, while Farenheit executed a mad dance in front of him, shouting, singing and waving his exceedingly long arms in the air—in brief, giving all the signs on the most insensate joy.

The old man glanced at Fricoulet, with an expression that clearly revealed his thoughts. *Right!* said his gaze. *There's the madness taking hold of him again!*

But the American guessed what the glance meant, and proclaimed in a penetrating voice: "Yes, I'm mad! But mad with joy. The Earth, finally...the Earth..." And, as he saw the eyes of everyone there fixed upon him in amazement, he added: "Didn't you just mention the equator? A change of hemisphere...the stars we perceive from Europe and America...oh, especially America...?"

"Yes. So what?"

"So what? It's a sign that we're getting close, isn't it? That we'll soon see our planet again...that we'll soon...?" He stopped, suffocated by emotion, sponging his sweat-covered brown with a colored handkerchief while, with his free hand, he shook hands energetically, one by one, with Fricoulet, Selena, and Gontran—who had been attracted by the noise.

The others looked at one another, rather embarrassed, not knowing quite what to do to dissuade the brave American and explain to him that his joy was premature. They knew from experience how deceptions manifested themselves in that sanguine and violent man, and hesitated to speak. So, without exchanging a word, they fell into tacit agreement to let Farenheit remain in error, at least for the moment—except that Fricoulet said to him: "Yes, it's now a matter of a few 48-hour intervals."

"As much as that! I thought that our velocity..."

"Our velocity will diminish slightly by reason of the change of hemisphere. Then again, it's necessary to allow for the unforeseen..."

Farenheit's brown furrowed. "We Americans," he replied, rudely, "never allow for the unforeseen; we head straight for the goal we've set ourselves, in spite of any obstacles that might arise on the way..."

"That's what we've always done, thus far, and will continue to do," said Fricoulet. "What I'm saying is simply to let you know that you have time to pack your bags..." Laughing, he added: "The train isn't in the station yet..."

The American sighed. "It's very annoying," he said, by way of conclusion, "that the stores aren't better furnished with liquids—we'd be able to celebrate crossing the line with a few bottles of champagne."

This was said in a tone that testified to such sincere regret that everyone burst out laughing except Ossipoff; the old man was already sitting in front of the porthole with his eye glued to the telescope. Seeing that, Fricoulet went out of the cabin, followed by Gontran and the American.

"It's my turn on watch, isn't it?" asked Flammermont.

"Very nearly," replied the engineer, "but if it won't inconvenience you, we can stand it together—I need to talk to you."

The young Comte nodded his had mutely and they both went down to the engine-room.

"Old chap," said Fricoulet, when they had both taken their places beside one another in front of the levers, "you and I are behaving as stupidly as little boys. We're grown up, though, and at present we're risking compromising a friendship of many years..."

Gontran kept silent for several seconds, after which he said, quite sincerely: "I agree with you."

"We've been avoiding one another for two days, instead of explaining ourselves frankly," the engineer continued.

"It's been very hard for me," the other attempted to suggest.

Fricoulet slapped the Comte's shoulder amicably, and said: "Not as hard as it's been for me, but you started it..."

"And didn't I have reason?" Gontran retorted, with a hint of bitterness. "You did me a bad turn..."

"Not deliberately," declared the engineer. "I was obedient to an impulse of which I wasn't initially the master—but I've been thinking about it for 48 hours; I've analyzed my feelings, and I've arrived at a conclusion that frankness obliges me to confess to you..."

At these words, Gontran shivered slightly; he understood that the vague matter about which his instinct had been warning him since the day before last, without his being capable of defining it, was about to be revealed. Suddenly interested, he listened.

"I'll begin by giving you my word of honor," Fricoulet said, "and you know me well enough to know that I'm incapable of breaking a promise, that I'm entirely on your side, with as much devotion as ever, and that every time you have need of me, you'll find me there, as you have in the past."

Flammermont's surprise was increasing; at the same time, though, he felt himself invaded by a certain malaise caused by the serious tone in which this declaration had been made.

"That said," the engineer continued, lowering his voice, "this is what it's about: I fear that the communal life we've led since the beginning of the voyage has not left me as insensible as I ought to have been to the charms of Mademoiselle Ossipoff..."

Gontran started. "You're in love with Selena!" he exclaimed.

"I wouldn't go that far," Fricoulet replied, reassuring him with a gesture, "but I feel that I'm beginning to fall in love with her..."

A rush of blood reddened the young Comte's face, which had been very pale to begin with. "And you're telling that to me!" he said.

"To whom do you want me to tell it, if not to you, who has the greatest interest in it? Lovers, who are said to be blind, are clairvoyant on certain occasions, especially when jealousy comes into play, and I preferred to put you squarely in the picture rather than have you realize it yourself..."

A silence followed this confession.

"So...what now?" asked Gontran.

"Now!" repeated Fricoulet. "Well, nothing. I began by telling you that you could count on me, so I'll continue to sustain with all my might the role that you've begun to play—except that, if it happens that you end up tiring of the role, and renounce the hand of Mademoiselle Ossipoff of your own accord..."

Here the engineer stopped for a few seconds, waiting for an indignant protest from his friend—but instead of the forceful "Never!" that these words ought to have provoked, Gontran simply asked: "In that case?"

"You won't think it unseemly, will you, if I throw my hat into the ring?"

The young Comte was touched by a similar delicacy; he took his friend's hands in his own and shook them firmly, saying, in an emotional voice: "My brave Alcide!"

"You're not offended, then?"

"Offended? That is to say, I thank you for your frankness, my dear friend; I'm touched and grateful..." Then, wagging his finger threateningly, while smiling, he added: "But it's agreed that you won't go behind my back!"

"Alliance as before—until the day when you set me at liberty yourself." Again, the engineer anticipated a protest that did not come—and, without quite knowing why, he felt something inside himself that gave him pleasure. He added: "The best proof that nothing has changed is that I shall immediately warn you about a danger."

"A danger?"

Which will present itself in the form of the giant of the Heavens, by the name of Orion."

From Gontran's wide eyes the engineer divined that what he had just said meant nothing to his friend. Rummaging in one of his pockets, which were still stuffed with a host of disparate objects, he pulled out a piece of chalk, with which he rapidly drew a sketch on the engine-room wall.

"What are you doing?" asked Flammermont, gaily. "That's not a celestial map—it's a nude portrait!"

"Exactly. Well, this nude represents one of the oldest known constellations, since it has constituted the calendar of mariners and laborers since the time of Hesiod, and it is represented on the most ancient maps in the form of a giant pursuing Taurus the Bull or the Pleiades with club in hand..."

"Taurus the Bull!" Gontran joked. "Somewhat akin to a torero, then—here's a constellation that the 'aficionados' ought to put on their coats-of-arms..."

Fricoulet remained phlegmatic. "Let's talk seriously, if you will," he said, "for I doubt that Father Ossipoff has a taste for such fantastic astronomy."

"I'm all ears," Flammermont replied, with a yawn.

"To the astronomer's eye, Orion simply presents the appearance of a vast quadrilateral, of which the stars I've marked here, Alpha and Gamma form the giant's shoulders, Beta and Chi the legs, Lambda the head and, finally, Sigma, Epsilon and Delta—or the Three Kings—the belt."

Gontran shook his head. "It's necessary to be endowed with a certain dose of imagination to find any trace of a nude in those seven points...even a sketchy one."

"That's left to the appreciation of the individual," the engineer continued, imperturbably, "but as that's relatively unimportant, let's go on."

And, underlining each of his explanations with the chalk, he taught his listener all that he knew himself about the marvelous constellation. In less than a quarter of an hour, Gontran knew as much as his teacher. He knew that Beta

Orionis, or Rigel, situated at the lower right extremity of the quadrilateral, is as white as Sirius but is vastly more distant from the Solar System, for all attempts made to measure its parallax and establish its proper movement had remained fruitless. Although trillions of leagues distant from the Earth, and although its light takes thousands of years to reach us, one is entitled to suppose that this sun is 1000 times more voluminous, more ardent and more formidable than ours, since it sends us so much light over such a distance. Furthermore, the spectroscope demonstrates a predominance of hydrogen in the light of that star, from which it is concluded that Rigel is a nascent star, while Alpha Orionis, or Betelgeuse, with its orange-yellow tint and its spectrum of fundamental columns in which carbon dioxide is predominant, is considered to be senescent.

"I'd give a lot," murmured Gontran, at that moment, "to know in what calendar astronomers have gone in search of such names. Betelgeuse! Rigel! They don't exist!"

"In a calendar, no—but it is explicable otherwise. In the Arabic language, *ridj-al-jauza*, or Rigel, signifies *giant's leg*, and *ibt-al-jauza*, from which Betelgeuse comes, *giant's shoulder...*" Still continuing his demonstration with the chalk, Fricoulet added: "Now here, among the most interesting stars in the constellation of Orion, is number 31, orange in color—a very rare type, by reason of the special characteristics of the yellow, green and blue bands in its spectrum, near-certain indications of a very cold world. In the vicinity, among others of variable brightness and almost all red in hue, I draw your particular attention to one I've marked here, to the south of Rigel, in the constellation Lepus, which resembles a veritable drop of blood. It was discovered by Hind[112] in 1845—a variable star, going from the eighth to the sixth magnitude in a period of 438 days. We also have star Zeta, a double, whose satellite is such a strange color that in order to describe it, Wilhelm Struve invented a special term: *olivaceasubrubicunda*."[113]

"Not bad," Gontran quipped. "Not easy to pronounce, but of considerable descriptive power."

"We also have, as number 14, an item no less remarkable for its rapidity, for, since 1842—the epoch of its first observation—its angle had turned through 50 degrees. In addition, it's the only one of Rigel's companions whose motion has been demonstrated, for none of the rest, recently discovered, form any system with these stars."

"In that case, why associate them in the same constellation?"

---

[112] The discovery of R Leporis by John Russell Hind (1823-1895) was considered sufficiently remarkable for the star to become known as "Hind's Crimson Star."

[113] Zeta Orionis, for which Wilhelm Struve (1793-1864)—the father of the previously-mentioned Otto—invented this descriptive term, meaning "slightly reddish orange," is also known as Alnitak.

"Because they appear to be linked together by a simply effect of perspective—but in reality, they're far beyond them..."

Gontran shrugged his shoulders. "I don't really understand. I thought that astronomy was an exact science, but you're telling me that appearances play a considerable role."

"Don't be finicky—inasmuch as it doesn't change anything in the inexorable laws of the Universe. Anyway, if it had pleased the ancients to see in the stars comprising Orion the silhouette of a horse instead of that of a man, the devil may take me if that would modify the motion of Rigel and Betelgeuse in the slightest. It's necessary to take scientists as they are, and astronomy as it is..."

"Which is to say, in the form of a pill that's very bitter to swallow!" murmured the young Comte, with a significant grimace. Then, getting to his feet, he added in a mock-enthusiastic tone: "And now I'm larded with science from head to toe, I'll go summon Ossipoff to the dueling-ground." He launched himself out of the engine-room, followed by Fricoulet's anxious gaze.

The latter, seeing him so vibrant and so full of ardor, thought that it was probably not the old scientist that Gontran was in a hurry to see again, but his daughter. He sighed deeply. "It's stupid, anyway," he thought aloud, when he had heard his friend's footsteps die away on the stairs. "Me, Alcide Fricoulet, in love! And in such circumstances! Practically no hope at all...or, at least, so little that it's hardly worth mentioning..." He interrupted himself, shook his head, and added: "So little...what do I know about it? Perhaps the worthy Gontran's patience has reached its final limit, and Ossipoff, between now and the end of the voyage, has enough time to saturate and supersaturate him with astronomy, to disgust him completely." He began laughing very softly, comforted by that prospect. "Yes...that might come about...then again, shouldn't we, in the interests of everyone, wish that it works out that way? Poor Gontran is certainly no more fitted to be Ossipoff's son-in-law than I am to be a diplomat...Selena will be unhappy...and him too...whereas, if he renounces his project, I doubt that Ossipoff could ever find a son in law who fits his bill better than me." Shaken by an increasingly forceful hilarity, he added, comically: "May it please the gods that Ossipoff be crushed beneath a rain of stars, comets and nebulas, so that he never gets up again..." Then he shrugged his shoulders and said: "Is it really living to have a star of Damocles suspended continuously above one's head?"

Nevertheless, and whatever one might think of Fricoulet's sentiments toward his friend after what has just been recorded, we ought to say that he was as firmly resolved as before to keep the promise he had made. So it was not only by virtue of curiosity but of interest that he left the engine-room to go and see how things were going in Ossipoff's cabin.

When he came in there was a profound silence. Selena and her fiancé, sitting next to one another holding hands, indicated Ossipoff to the newcomer by simultaneous nods of the head. The latter was sitting up straight on his stool, sounding space with a fever of which he had rarely set an example until now.

Armed with a pencil, his fingers were sketching a strange figure on a piece of paper in front of him; its contours were imprecise, but in the middle were two groups of points—presumably stars—one of four and the other of three. All around it, on the white margin of the paper, there was a hectic and dizzying accumulation of algebraic formulas and geometric designs.

As Fricoulet made as if to move forward the floor creaked slightly beneath his eight; the old man made a slight movement, curt and authoritarian, to instruct him to stay where he was, the slightest noise being capable of disturbing his calculations. In addition to the various qualities of which the reader has seen examples in the course of these adventures, however, the engineer was endowed with a certain amount of obstinacy—with the effect that, instead of staying still, he continued on his way until he was immediately behind the old man's back. Then he stopped, leaned over his shoulder, and examined the sketch attentively for several seconds.

When he straightened up again, he had traces of an evident perplexity on his face, which he expressed even more clearly by nervously twisting the downy hair ornamenting his chin.

"Well?" whispered Gontran. "What is it?"

The engineer's lips pursed into a dubious moue.

"Another star for me, I suppose?" murmured the Comte.

"I'm afraid so," Fricoulet replied, in the same fashion.

His friend's features contracted, and he said in a slightly anxious tone: "You know what you promised me..."

"That's agreed—but it's still necessary for me to know myself what subject the next examination might be on...and since my own knowledge isn't universal...."

Gontran stared at him. "Alcide," he said, "you're abandoning me..."

"Me!" exclaimed Fricoulet. "You don't know me."

This conversation between the two young men had taken place in whispers, the engineer having gone to join his friend; Selena looked at them, her eyes wide, not understanding what they were talking about.

The engineer shrugged his shoulders slightly—a gesture full of pity. "Abandoning you!" he repeated. "If I were going to do that, I'd have done it a long time ago, my poor friend." Having said that he returned to Ossipoff, still making no sound, resumed his place behind him, bent down and, having tried for several moments, succeeded in getting a line of slight along the axis of the telescope. He started abruptly and murmured: "It really is!" But he remained where he was, suddenly immobilized and silent, his eyes dilated and his lips pinched, his face imprinted with a strangely indefinable expression, overwhelmed by the marvelous and mysterious spectacle confronting him, his mind seized by vertigo as it was crossed by the multiple considerations suggested by what his eyes beheld.

There was something like an immense cloud invading almost the entire horizon—or, rather, a gaseous mass without precise contours, which appeared to be melting into space itself and which, without having precise limits, gave that impression. Fricoulet sensed the incandescent fire burning behind that veil of gas, whose very fabric appeared to be composed of luminous points—a fabric so light that behind it, in spite of its interior incandescence, other luminous points situated in the utmost depths of infinity were visible. He understood that, this time, he was not the victim of an illusion showing him an agglomeration of patches forming a sort of curtain extended across the heavens; this gaseous mass was a body in itself, a bizarre and mysterious body whose components did not appear to have any system of connections between them, and yet were linked together by hidden bonds.

This extraordinary world was none other than the famous Orion Nebula, and the light of the stars comprising that constellation that were situated far beyond it, on the horizon of space, lent a very singular green tint, with a hint of red, to the gaseous mass through which it was passing. These were the stars that Ossipoff had represented in his sketch by the little black dots situated in the middle of the sketch. Seen from the Earth, the Orion Nebula seems as distant—although in reality it is much nearer—than Rigel.[114] Its apparent grandeur being five degrees, this licenses belief in an extent of more than ten trillion leagues of phosphorescent gas or incandescent cosmic matter. An express train traveling at 60 kilometers and hour would take more than 100,000,000 years to go from one end of that strange and mysterious fog to the other.

Given the close approach of the *Eclair*, the prodigious effect that the great nebula had on the Terrans is easily imaginable—which is to say that Fricoulet, skeptical as he was in astronomical matters, was astounded by it. He reflected mentally on those worlds that drift through space, so strange that human reason can comprehend neither their genesis nor their purpose, simultaneously enveloped by such great mystery that humankind must give up hope over ever having its curious appetites satisfied. A world so vast that it would require millions of years to cross its surface! A world so distant that its light takes millions of years to reach us! And what could prove to him that, at the very moment at which he was contemplating it, that nebula still existed? Was it not possible that the body of which it was a part had changed not merely its appearance but also its constitution, several million years before? Might it not, at the present moment, be resolved into stars? Might it, rather, be a solar embryo or a planetary system in formation?

---

[114] The reverse is actually true; although it is impossible to measure Rigel's parallax, it is nowadays estimated to be approximately 800 light years away, whereas the Orion Nebula is estimated to be nearly 1300 light years away. The nebula's size is, in consequence, even larger than the text's estimate; it is some 24 light years across.

He was plunged in these reflections when a discreet appeal from Gontran distracted his attention; he then saw his friend's finger beckoning him to rejoin him.

"Well?" asked the Comte.

"Monsieur Ossipoff is examining the Great Nebula in Orion."

"The one perceived by Cysatus?"[115] asked Selena.

"In 1618? Yes, Mademoiselle—except that I should observe that it was a Frenchman, Picard,[116] to whom we owe the first drawings of the nebula."

"Bah!" replied the young woman, laughing. "That's of no great importance, since none of the drawings made thus far bear the slightest resemblance to one another. It required the improvements of photography to succeed in determining the silhouette of that strange world."

Fricoulet shrugged. "It is, as you say, relatively unimportant, Mademoiselle—all the more so as what you see is merely an illusion, a pure illusion, and not the reality of things. In thousands of years, the appearance of worlds changes. For example, if there is a humankind on the worlds that comprise the constellation of Orion, do you think that humankind perceives the Earth as we know it? Not on your life! The inhabitants of Orion perceive the gaseous incandescent mass that our native planet was on the day after its creation..."

"And the Ossipoffs of Orion ask themselves, on seeing the Earth, 'will it be a god, a table or a basin?' "[117] Gontran sniggered.

"One of their colleagues is doubtless wondering some such thing," Fricoulet replied.

At that moment, the old man abandoned the telescope and started pacing back and forth in the cabin, gesticulating and talking to himself as if he were alone. His face flushed, his eyes bulging and shining feverishly, he waved his arms around, clenching his gnarled fingers, as if he wanted to grasp some invisible body in mid-air. At intervals he stopped, put his head into his hands and uttered a dolorous groan; then he resumed his promenade, going back and forth in front of Selena and the two friends without seeing them. They watched him, quite bewildered, having no understanding of his exaltation, which was increasing by the minute.

Suddenly, he came to a halt in front of the porthole at which the telescope was aimed and stood up straight, threatening space with his closed fist. "Oh,

---

[115] Johann Baptist Cysat, aka Cysatus of Lucerne (1587-1618) is generally credited with being the first person to record the existence of the nebula, although his note, in a study of comets, is ambiguous.

[116] Abbé Jean Picard (1620-1682)

[117] "*Sera-t-il dieu, table ou cuvette?*" [Will it be a god, a table or a basin?] was the caption of a famous cartoon by Honoré Daumier in the *Charivari*, first published in April 1869. The drawing shows a sculptor about to go to work on a block of stone.

mad interrogation!" he exclaimed, in a ringing voice. "Oh, unfathomable mystery! Oh, Universe too vast for my overly narrow brain! Who will lift the veils that envelop it for me? Who will tell me the why of things? Who will educate me as to the end of everything?"

Anxiously, Selena went to him, placed her slender hand on is shoulder without his offering the least resistance, and drew him away from the porthole. "Father," she said, with that angelic sweetness that had the power to calm the old man's fits of wrath and appease his exaltations, "you're very tired, and a few hours rest would do you good!"

"Rest!" he repeated. "Rest! But that's time lost—precious time that I'll never be able to recover..."

"And you'll fall ill!"

"God will give me the strength to resist. I want to know...yes to know...." He trembled as he spoke, his legs buckling under him and his eyelids fluttering feverishly, masking and unmasking his eyes, whose gleaming pupils revealed an intense fever.

"Monsieur Fricoulet! Gontran!" appealed the young woman, who was afraid.

Scarcely had Selena made her appeal when the old man's arms were supported by the two young men, who carried him to his hammock, in which he lay in a coma-like state.

"Is it dangerous?" Selena asked.

Fricoulet, who was holding the old man's wrist between his fingers with the index finger on the pulse, shook his head negatively. "A fairly strong fever induced by a superabundance of effort...overwork, as we say in scholarly language. A little rest will take care of it." Then, turning to look at Gontran, who had taken the old man's place at the telescope, he said to Selena: "There's a man getting is teeth into astronomy."

She uttered a little sigh. "If only that were true," she murmured. "Personally, I doubt it..."

"Eros is a great conjuror," the engineer replied. "You give him a diplomat, and he transforms him into a scientist."

"I don't think so..."

Fricoulet clicked his tongue and replied, in a strange tone: "Eros is capable of many other miracles; thus, as for myself..." He stopped, biting his lip and blushing slightly.

"You?" the young woman asked, curiously.

"Nothing," the engineer replied, with a brusqueness intended to mask his anxiety. He turned on his heel, went over to Flammermont, and said, mockingly: "What are you doing there?"

"I'm looking for the gentlemen you drew for me down below...but I can't see anything at all."

"If you're searching for a gentleman, you'll certainly have trouble finding him."

Gontran turned around, annoyed. "Do you take me for an imbecile? Although not having the honor of belonging to the learned company of astronomers, I'm not to be counted as an idiot—and one would have to be an idiot, in my opinion, to see cartoon characters in the sky..."

Fricoulet burst out laughing. "You're very hard on me! A cartoon character—a nude that a pupil at the School of Fine Arts might have signed! You're searching for the stars of Orion, then?"

"Yes—the famous quadrilateral. Where is it? Rigel and Betelgeuse...the shoulders and the legs...one side apiece. One might think that the giant is quartered. As for the three stars forming the belt...unknown..." Then, slapping his forehead, he went on: "How stupid I am! Perspective of course! Isn't that what's causing the deformation of the constellation?"

The engineer shook his head dubiously. "Perhaps it is," he said, "but what's more important is that you're looking at Orion as it actually is, while from Earth we only see it as it was thousands of years ago—which is to say, when the luminous ray that we observe was emitted. Our vehicle is moving in the opposite direction to the light, with a much greater speed, and that's what explains the phenomenon..."

"But then," said the young Comte, "the further forward we go..."

"The more the appearance of the sky will change—which is to say, the better sense we'll have of the celestial truth." Laughing, he added: "Keeping things in proportion, Monsieur Ossipoff's Terran colleagues remind me of those provincial coquettes who astonish the good citizens of sub-prefectures with fashions that were in vogue in Paris four or five years previously. From the astronomical viewpoint, it's the same thing, and your worthy namesake is so far behind the times that he would blush, if he were aware of it..."

This comparison excited the hilarity of both the engineer's companions, but Gontran soon got back to the point. "Has a nebula any connection with the other stars?" he asked. "From the constitutional point of view, I mean."

Fricoulet raised his arms in the air, satirically. "Fool!" he exclaimed. "If Ossipoff could hear you...I think you'd be able to say goodbye forever to the Town Hall of the eighth."

Selena paled slightly, while Gontran, for whom the mere mention of the arrondissement in which his marriage was to take place was enough to put him in a bad temper, grumbled: "Instead of making fun, you'd do better to keep your promises."

"Fun! My promises!" repeated the engineer, slightly bewildered. "What do you mean?"

The young Comte took him by the arm, drew him into a corner and nodded furiously in the direction of the hammock in which Ossipoff lay. "Do you think that I can't see through your game, you cunning devil? You're pretending to be interested in my conjugal bliss, and you're doing everything you can to wake him up so that he'll hear you."

Fricoulet, amused by his friend's tragic attitude, burst out laughing. "My poor fellow," he replied, "if it were really my intention that Ossipoff should perceive your worthlessness..."

"Alcide!" Gontran interrupted, taking offence.

"Of your scientific worthlessness, of course," the engineer rectified. "I'd only have to let you flounder the first time he subjected you to an oral."

"What about your promise?" said the young Comte.

At the same time, Selena, who had overheard, came over to Fricoulet. "Oh, you wouldn't do such a thing, Monsieur Alcide," she said, pleading in her soft voice and fixing him with her lovely, tear-moistened eyes.

The engineer struck a dignified pose. "You don't know me very well, Mademoiselle, if you think me capable of such a thing. I may be no more than a mechanical engineer, but in that profession, our hearts are as well-situated as they are in diplomacy." Slapping Gontran slyly on the shoulder, he added: "Don't worry; I'll keep my promise until the end—but the rupture won't come from Ossipoff; it's you that will provoke it!"

"The rupture!" exclaimed the young woman. "What rupture?"

"Pay no attention to what he says, my dear Selena," Flammermont hastened to reply. "He's mad!" To Fricoulet, he said: "If you're counting on that, you'll have to be ready to change your tune, old chap. Now I know what to expect from you, I'll play it tight. I'll be a scientist, an astronomer, everything that one might wish, rather than let you take my place..." He had spoken in a tone low enough for Ossipoff's daughter to have perceived no more than a vague whisper. Fricoulet, for his part, pursed his lips and said nothing, while beneath his narrowed eyelids he fixed his friend with a piercing, inquisitorial gaze.

"That said," Gontran went on. "Tell me about nebulas."

The engineer passed his hand over his forehead, as if to chase away the evil thoughts darkening his consciousness. "You asked me a moment ago if nebulas had any connection with other stars; my reply is that there's none. Huggins[118] has established in the spectra of nebulas—including that of the nebula in Draco, of which he has made a particular study—three bright bands that prove their gaseous state and the presence of nitrogen as the principal constituent element, the second being hydrogen; as for the third, it hasn't been identified with that of any known substance."

"Probably a substance that only exists in that star," observed Gontran. "But is a nebula, in fact, a star?"

Fricoulet raised his eyebrows. "You've touched there on one of the most controversial problems in astronomy, without a doubt. Some claim that the ne-

---

[118] William Huggins (1824-1910) also analyzed the spectrum of the Orion Nebula, establishing its gaseous nature.

bulosities observed around certain stars, instead of constituting bodies with them, are masses of matter traveling through space with a proper motion, which happen to be interposed temporarily between the stars and us. Others, such as Herschel and Kant, see nebulas as types of successive states through which cosmic matter passes in order to form, by condensation, stars similar to ours own. Is that all you wanted to know?"

Gontran shrugged his shoulders. "How do I know? You're the one telling me what's necessary. So, regarding their form…well?"

"Oh, their forms…very variable and quite different; some have the appearance of rounded or elliptical disks, uniformly lit, sometimes solid and sometimes pierced like sieves; others have a nucleus in the middle or some other point of the disk in which the light is concentrated; others appear to be similar to true stars, with spectra similar to the Sun, while the luminous nimbus projects a fairly simple light."

"Is that all?"

"It's certainly more than you'll need to answer Monsieur Ossipoff successfully." Then, lowering his voice, he added, mockingly: "But I repeat, it's all futile, because, when you're overstuffed with the memory of stars, suns, comets and nebulas, you'll get such an indigestion that you'll be the first to beg for mercy…"

Gontran looked at his friend furiously, and replied, in a forceful voice, with the single significant monosyllable: "*Zut!*"

Chapter LIX
The relationships between the passengers become increasingly strained

"And I assure you that there's no doubt about the matter..."

"For you, perhaps, but for everyone else..."

"I have on my side the work done by all those of whom science is justly proud, all of whom have declared that the Egyptians possessed very extensive knowledge in the various branches of science, most especially in astronomy."

"But I think that I have men no less knowledgeable and no less eminent than yours to support my opinion."

"What about the zodiacs of Esneh and Denderah?[119] In your opinion, they don't count, then?"

"I don't claim that..."

"Find me others as old! Do you know that in the Esneh zodiac, the solstice is in the sign of Leo, and in the Denderah zodiac, it's in Cancer."

"So what does that prove? Hasn't Biot calculated that the Denderah zodiac dates from no earlier than 716 B.C., while India has something better than that to offer you...?"

Old Ossipoff burst into Homeric laughter. "Yes, I know...the famous zodiac found in the ruins of the pagoda of Cape Comorin,[120] which some say dates from 30,000 B.C., others only from 10,000..." He assumed an expression of condescension, filled with pity. "Eh? Don't you see, my poor Monsieur de Flammermont, that the exaggeration of those figures is precisely what demonstrates their inanity. 30,000 years before our era? Do you imagine that humans of that era were occupied with astronomy? That's insane, I tell you, insane! And I'm astonished that a serious mind like yours..."

Gontran, ill-prepared for so bitter a controversy, thought that he ought to feign offended dignity in order to mask an indispensable and prudent retreat. He headed for the door, saying in the cold tone of a man who is having difficulty

---

[119] I have retained the text's spellings of the names that are usually rendered nowadays as Esna and Dendera. The zodiac in the latter temple complex, discovered by the French during the Napoleonic campaign, was removed in 1820 and transported to the Louvre, where Graffigny presumably saw it. Both temples are Graeco-Roman and the zodiacs therefore belong to the tradition that culminated in the work of Ptolemy (Claudius Ptolemaius, 83-168 A.D.), so Biot was probably overestimating their antiquity.

[120] The pagoda in question is at Vendapettah, near Cape Comorin (nowadays known as Kanyakumari) in Southern India. The set of signs comprising the alleged zodiac was discovered in 1746; the estimates of antiquity suggested here are, as Ossipoff rightly observes, utterly ludicrous.

restraining himself: "In these circumstances, my dear father-in-law, it's preferable to leave it there, for I judge that, in order to debate a point, it's necessary, as a matter of principle, to have some common ground, and we're so far apart..."

Ossipoff turned on his heel and went back to his telescope sulkily. "Agreed, agreed" he murmured. "The further we go, the less we have...I, who thought I was attaching myself by ties of blood to a collaborator with whose ideas I was in perfect harmony..."

"A collaborator isn't a slave!" said Gontran, indignantly, as he crossed the threshold. And he went down the stairway that led to the common room, where he found Fricoulet sitting in his hammock, rubbing his sleep-swollen eyes and yawning.

"It must be time for my watch?" the engineer said, interrogatively.

"I believe so," Flamermont replied, dryly, going to sit down morosely to one side.

The engineer looked at his friend for a moment. "Come on," he said. "What's the matter now?"

Gontran waited a few seconds before replying, then suddenly leapt up from his seat. "The matter?" he groaned. "The matter is that life's becoming increasingly impossible. New arguments all the time...I swear, if things go on like this..."

"Well?" Fricoulet put on, leaning toward him.

Suddenly, though, as if the glint in the engineer's eye had produced the effect of a deluge of cold water on his irritation, Gontran calmed down and replied with extraordinary tranquility: "Well, if things go on like this, I'll have to arm myself with even more patience than at present...and with love to assist me, I'll succeed."

Fricoulet's eyelids fluttered feverishly, while his lips creased in an involuntary grimace. He paused for a moment, then asked: "Have you had another squabble with Father Ossipoff? I heard raised voices..."

"Yes-on the subject of the relative antiquity of astronomy in Egypt and India. He plumped for Egypt, me for India..."

"Why not say the same as him?"

Flammermont folded his arms. "That's a bit strong, you know! Wasn't it you who told me this morning that in the pagoda of Cap Comorin..."

"Certainly, I said that, and many other scientists have said it before me—but as soon as the poor chap plumped for Egypt, you shouldn't have contradicted him..."

"Certainly—if I wanted to look like a schoolboy, or an imbecile..."

"You'll end up alienating his favorable disposition, you'll see."

"And he'll see that I'll send him packing..."

"Except that you're forgetting one thing—which is that, in that case, Ossipoff won't go alone." Fricoulet added, sarcastically: "Besides, whether you like it or not, things are bound to end up like that. Are you the stuff of which astronomers are made? Come on, yield to the evidence…"

Perhaps because the young man was indeed privately yielding to the evidence, however, he only became more irritated when the engineer raised the issue. "If that were as evident as you claim," he replied, "I'd have renounced my plans a long time ago."

The engineer shrugged his shoulders mildly. "Stubborn," he murmured. In a very particular tone, he added: "It's true that you have an excuse—Mademoiselle Ossipoff's charms."

Flammermont stood in front of him. "Alcide," he declared, "you're annoying me considerably, and if you want us to continue to be good friends, never bring the conversation round to that topic again. Think what you will—that's your right—but keep your thoughts to yourself."

Scarcely had this forceful declaration been made when they heard Farenheit's voice emerging from the engine-room. "Monsieur de Flammermont! If you've nothing better to do, you might be good enough to come here for a moment…"

Delighted to have a pretext for parting company with Fricoulet, Gontran went out of the cabin. As he went into the engine-room, however, he stopped short on the threshold, taken by surprise. Farenheit was leaning forward, his hands clutching the telescope and his nose scraping the eyepiece. Farenheit studying the heavens! That was what had, of course, cased the young man such profound astonishment.

"Are you looking for something, Mr. Farenheit?" Gontran asked, with unconcealed irony.

"Yes—the Zodiac."

"And you can't find it?"

"No—although, as I'm very curious to see it…"

Somewhat embarrassed, Gontran scratched the end of his nose, not knowing how to respond to his traveling companion's curiosity without confessing his own complete ignorance in the matter. He knew no more about the Zodiac than what Fricoulet had told him that morning, and that rather briefly—which is to say that the Zodiac is the name given to a hypothetical celestial zone about 18 degrees wide, which forms a circle in the sky and is divided by the ecliptic, the name Zodiac coming from the fact that the majority of the constellations occupying it bear the names of animals. The argument with which the chapter began demonstrated the remote antiquity of the Zodiac's origin; that comprised, along with the nomenclature of the dozen signs or sections into which the zone is divided, all that Fricoulet had had time to teach the young man.

"My God, my dear Mr. Farenheit," he said, eventually, "Without being indiscreet, I'd like to know what can have excited your curiosity in this manner."

"Oh, my word, it's quite simple. I confess to you that since the beginning of the voyage, the contemplation of all your faces has become exhausting in its monotony—so seeing the animals would make a slight change."

"Only slight! How kind you are!"

"I mean…but you know what I meant…"

"Yes...but what I don't understand is how you expect to see animals."

Farehenheit turned round, so astonishing did Flammermont's question seem to him, and he looked at him briefly, as if he doubted that he was in his right mind.

"Animals! Why…in the Zodiac, of course!"

"In the Zodiac?"

"Aries the Ram, Taurus the Bull, Cancer the Crab and Leo the Lion! Aren't they animals?"

"Certainly—but…"

"And Scorpio…Capricorn…Aquarius…Pisces…aren't they animals too?"

Gntran understood then how enormous and incredible the American's error was, and he had all the difficulty in the world not hooting with laughter. "But then, you ought to derive some pleasure in contemplating the features of Virgo, the Gemini and Sagittarius, which, along with Libra, make up the 12 signs of the Zodiac?" he asked, not without irony.

Farenheit clenched his large fists, while his bushy eyebrows bristled. "Tell me, Monsieur de Flammermont," he complained, "whether I'm mistaken in thinking that you're mocking me?"

"I'm not mocking you, Mr. Farenheit—but your mistake is so amusing…" This time, the laughter burst forth, all the louder for having been restrained for so long.

The riposte was unexpected; his face reddened by a rush of blood, Farenheit extended his arm and his fist struck Flammermont full in the chest; the latter tottered, and ended up falling backwards on to the floor—where he remained seated, having difficulty getting his breath back.

The noise brought Fricoulet running. Seeing his friend almost knocked out, he ran forward, saying: "Gontran! Mr. Farenheit! What's happening?"

Poor Flammermont, still winded, could make no reply, and the American, already ashamed of his violence, stammered: "A disagreement, my dear sir—a simple disagreement."

"You hit him?" the engineer continued. "It's you who knocked him down?"

"Monsieur de Flammermont took the liberty of mocking me, and we Americans never allow that…never…"

Fricoulet looked at Gontran, as if to demand confirmation of these words; the young man, still incapable of talking, shook his head.

"I'm lying, then?" shouted the suet merchant, his anger taking hold of him again.

Gontran shook his head negatively.

"Explain yourself, then!"

"That's right—explain yourself."

Flammermont, who had finally succeeded in getting his breath back, stammered painfully: "Damn it! To explain, one has to be able to talk! I mean that Mr. Farenheit was mistaken in thinking that I was mocking him, when I simply laughed because what he said to me seemed funny."

"That's very subtle," groaned the American.

Gontran, who had regained full possession of himself, got to his feet and said in a clear voice: "Take it any way you please, then..."

"Thanks for the invitation," retorted the American, sarcastically. "I've already taken it...badly, as you were able to observe."

This allusion to his brutality, in rather bad taste, brought a slight red flush to the young Comte's face. "I assume, Mr. Farenheit, that you don't intend this affair to stop here," he said, mastering himself.

"Of course not." Farenheit rubbed his hands. "A duel!" he exclaimed, suddenly joyful. "Very well! That will break the tedium. A little duel in the American style, eh? Is that all right by you? A rifle apiece, and off we go..."

He was still rubbing his hands when Fricoulet cried: "What? You're out of your mind!"

Farenheit's radiant face darkened. "That's true! I forgot that the armaments locker was thrown overboard, to lighten the selenium sphere when we left Mercury..." He features cleared again, however. "No need for rifles...knives will do..."

Gontran replied, impassively: "Knives it is!"

Fricoulet got carried away. "What! You're both out of your minds! Do you think that we'll authorize such butchery?"

"Butchery!" repeated Farenheit, indignantly. "In the United States..."

"We're not in the United States!" the engineer said, interrupting brutally. "We're aboard the *Eclair*, which Monsieur Ossipoff commands. A captain is master of his vessel, and Monsieur Ossipoff will refuse to authorize any such thing..."

"I've been struck, and I demand reparation," said Gontran.

"I'll be the first to offer it to you," declared Farenheit, impassively.

"That's understood—it's agreed," said the engineer, "but it's not up to you to set the ground-rules."

"Nevertheless..." the American began to say.

"I'm only allowing you one thing, and that's to listen to me. Customs in France are not the same as in the United States; there, we fight with swords or pistols, with seconds. Do you have any swords? Pistols? No. Seconds? Nor them..."

"What about Monsieur Ossipoff? Yourself?"

Fricoulet started. "Are you mad? So, as present circumstances lack these impossibilities, you have a duty to postpone the settlement of this affair. Each of us has an obligation to his companions to cooperate, within the limit of his means, for the general safety..." Addressing himself more specifically to Farenheit, he went on: "Suppose that Monsieur Ossipoff and I lent our support to such a duel, that chance favored you, and that you killed Monsieur de Flammermont. It would be necessary for you to renounce ever seeing Earth, New York and Fifth Avenue again, for he alone knows how to ally pure science with a sufficiently practical mind to get us out of the hole that Ossipoff's folly has got us into."

As one might imagine, this argument had a considerable impact on the American, and although it cost him dear to be obliged to owe his life to the man he wanted to kill, he murmured: "So be it, Monsieur Fricoulet." To Gontran, he said: "Don't forget, Monsieur de Flammermont, that I'm at your disposal whenever and wherever you please." He bowed very correctly and left the engine-room—but as he was going, the engineer heard him sigh: "It would have been nice to break the monotony of the voyage, though."

When the two friends were alone, Fricoulet asked: "Now tell me, briefly, what happened."

"Nothing very serious. Farenheit expected to see a whole menagerie in the sky, composed of the signs of the Zodiac, and the idea seemed so nonsensical to me that I couldn't help laughing. Then, like the veritable brute he is, he gave me a mighty thump with his fist, which knocked me down..." And the young Comte muttered between his teeth: "Oh, I've definitely had my fill of astronomy, you know..."

"You've only just begun!" Fricoulet quipped.

"Ossipoff's examinations...arguments with you...fisticuffs with the other one..."

"And with all that in the balance, Selena's charms don't outweigh it?"

Gontran frowned, and murmured: "Oh, if it weren't for that..."

"If it weren't for that! You'd still be attached to the embassy in St. Petersburg, you poor chap! It's true that you have your relatives—you might find an equivalent position on your return..."

The other folded his arms. "By then I'll have been rolling around in space for years, undergoing the most incredible adventures, traveling through the most incredible countries, supporting Ossipoff's astronomical monomania with angelic patience, swallowing concoctions of scientific quintessence until they made me sick—and all to have the pleasure of writing a memoir of the voyage that some editor would probably refuse to publish! Oh no! A thousand times no! I want at least to have legitimate compensation for all my fatigue, all my rancor, all my yawning...."

"You're claiming your bonus, eh?"

"Exactly. And the proof is that I'm waiting for your lecture on the Zodiac, which will probably be the topic of Ossipoff's next exam." So saying, the young Comte sat down, adopting an attitude of such perfect resignation that Fricoulet could not help laughing.

"You're sticking to it?" he asked.

"What! Am I sticking to it? Of course! You'd like nothing better than for Ossipoff to sniff out the secret and send me back to my diplomacy, but me, that's another thing. I've invested too much in this to lose the benefits of the acquired capital. So, to the Zodiac..."

The engineer looked at him silently for a moment with a slightly vexed expression, because he expected his rival—for Gontran was his rival now—to renounce his project at any moment. Fortunately for him, though, once he got an idea into his head, Fricoulet never let go of it easily; besides, he was wise enough to know that everything comes to him who waits, and he knew that time and Ossipoff were on his side. "What's agreed is agreed," he said. "I promised you my help and I'll keep my promise. You want to know about the Zodiac...as you wish. First, though, how did that argument with Ossipoff come about?"

"As all arguments of that sort have come about thus far," Gontran complained. "I wanted to show off what you'd said to me and as Ossipoff, on waking up, asked me what route the *Eclair* was following, I told him that we were passing through the constellation Aries. One thing let to another and—there you go."

Fricoulet shook his head. "That was rather imprudent," he said, "for I'd forgotten to warn you that, by virtue of the precession of the equinoxes, the positions of the signs no longer correspond to the constellations of the same name. Thus, in the time of Hipparchus, the primary points of Aries and Libra corresponded to the spring and autumn equinoxes, and those of Cancer and Capricorn to the summer and winter solstices. That's another thing, and a very important one, that it's imperative you remember."

"But what about the names given to the constellations?"

"Oh, they have no relationship with the constellations themselves. The Chaldeans, the Egyptians and the Greeks baptized them thus, either because of a vague resemblance to the objects in question or to perpetuate the memory of some hero...but, with respect to that..." He stopped, his attention suddenly attracted to the porthole, which had just been penetrated by the first ray of a singular light, which seemed to combine all the colors of the rainbow. "Aldebaran!" he said, getting up and going to apply his eye to the telescope.

"Aldebaran!" repeated Flammermont.

"A first magnitude star that serves as the eye of Taurus; the head is formed by an assemblage of stars known since the remotest antiquity under the name of the Hyades, and the tail by the Pleiades." While giving this explanation, the engineer continued to look into space, keenly interested in spite of his skepticism by the sight of the star in question, whose reddish tint formed a mysterious nimbus all around it. "Sodium, magnesium, hydrogen, calcium, iron, tellurium, bismuth, mercury, antimony," he murmured, recalling the composition of the spectrum of the star, so distant from the Earth that it had always been impossible to determine its parallax. Then he started smiling, shrugging his shoulders. "It's very pretty," he went on. "Not the slightest trace of the satellite discovered by Herschel—which is to say that he was quite simply fooled by an effect of perspective!"[121]

Gontran, however, to whom Fricoulet's specialist studies were of scant interest, came to take him by the arm. "Come on," he said, "let's get back to the Zodiac. You're forgetting that Ossipoff might descend upon me at any moment..."

The engineer regretfully abandoned the telescope and came back to sit beside his friend. "There's no point going into much detail about the Pleiades; for 3400 years before the Christian Era, all astronomers have studied them—Ptolemy, Sufi, Ulugh Beigh,[122] Copernicus, Tycho Brahe and many others—without any of their drawings agreeing with one another..."

"Let's get on, let's get on..." said Gontran.

"In Taurus, again, I should draw your attention to the Crab Nebula, discovered in 1788 by Messier[123] and thus baptized by the English by reason of the fringes and curious appendages that give it a vague resemblance to the crustacean whose name it bears."

Fricoulet was about to go on when Gontran exclaimed: "You don't say! But if there's as much in all the signs of the Zodiac, I'll never get all that into my head!"

"Calm down—I began with the most interesting constellation..."

"What must the others be like, then?" murmured Flammermont, stifling a yawn.

"...And, in consequence, the one most heavily charged with information," Fricoulet went on, smiling. "In Aries, there's nothing much to point out—a few systems of double stars and the triple star number 14, white, blue and lilac. In

---

[121] Aldebaran did eventually turn out to have a companion star, albeit a rather distant one, much less obtrusive than Sirius B or Procyon B by virtue of being a red dwarf rather than a white one, so it is improbable in the extreme that Herschel could have glimpsed it. A supergiant planet of Aldebaran was detected by the Hubble Space Telescope in 1997, but Herschel cannot possibly have seen that either.

[122] Sufi (Abd Al-Rahman Al Sufi, 903-986, also known as Azophi) and Ulugh Beigh, or Beg (c.1393-1449) were Persian astronomers.

[123] Charles Messier (1730-1817) was the first person to make an extensive study of nebulas, including most of the other galaxies visible to the naked eye, which are still routinely identified by the catalogue numbers he gave them, prefaced by the initial M.

Pisces, there are a certain number of variable stars, couples in rapid orbital motion, such as numbers 55 and 51, one orange and sapphire blue, the other pearly whiter and pale lilac. In Aquarius, which comprises a multitude of fifth magnitude stars, there's Zeta, a double star of the third magnitude, observed for the first time in 1777 by Christian Mayer,[124] whose orbital motion is effected in 1000 years, plus a host of stars first taken for a nebula by Messier in 1746 and subsequently resolved by Herschel, and, finally, a nebula of planetary appearance composed of incandescent gas, a world in formation that's estimated to be 264 billion times larger than the Sun."

This figure seemed enormous to Gontran, who could not suppress an exclamation. "But the Sun is itself 1,283,700 times more voluminous than the Earth..."

"You see what that represents, approximately. About Capricorn there's little to say; it contains very few stars...at present, for it might be that with the ever-increasing power of optical instruments, new ones might be discovered. In Sagittarius, composed of five stars distributed along a curved line, which reminded the ancients of a bow held by a centaur, there are a great many red stars of varying brightness; according to Julius Schmidt of Athens they'll be covered in sunspots, beginning to oxydize; take note of one double star and several triple and quadruple systems. Now we get to Scorpius..."

Flammermont took his forehead in both hands, with such marked anguish that the engineer stopped. "Are you in pain?" he asked.

"My head's aching, yes—badly—for everything you're telling me is going through my brain like water through a sieve. I won't remember anything of your lecture..."

"The fact is that the nomenclature is rather dry," Fricoulet observed, "and for someone who isn't interested..."

"You've been talking for a quarter of an hour, and you're only up to Scorpius," observed the young Comte, dispiritedly.

"Do you want to suspend the session?"

"No, go on...better to swallow the medicine all in one go...it seems less bitter then..."

"As you wish. Scorpius, of which you'll be able take account with your own eyes in a few hours is, out of all the signs of the Zodiac, the one most exactly reminiscent of the form of the animal after which it's named. It's the one that possesses, at its heart, the famous star Antares, whose component parts are orange red and emerald green—both of them suns in the process of cooling, as indicated by their spectra, in which carbon dioxide is dominant. Frequent variations in light and heat; proper motion not very rapid. What's particularly notable about Scorpius is the fashion in which the components of various ternary sys-

[124] Christian Mayer (1719-1783) was an enthusiastic observer of double stars, who published a significant catalogue of them in 1787.

tems to be seen there relate to one another; while the first two, very close together, rotate around one another in 98 years in elliptical orbits, the third has a retrograde motion relative to the other two, How does that come about? How can such a strange motion, so contrary to the laws of nature, be explained? No one knows! They're content to observe the phenomenon without explaining it."

"Which is simplest and most convenient," Gontran murmured.

"Take note also of several temporary stars[125] and a nebula in the form of a cometary ray, situated not far from the star Alpha, and finally, among the multiple systems, Nu, which is quadruple and whose components, aggregated two by two, are animated by a rather rapid movement.

"So one finds everything in Scorpius!" exclaimed Flammermont. "It's the bazaar of astronomy."

"Now we pass on to Libra, fabricated in the third century or thereabouts with the scorpion's claws—little to say, for it includes only 21 stars visible to telescopes and only eight to the naked eye. Virgo contains the famous star Spica, which shines in the due south in the month of May—it enjoys great notoriety, because it's thanks to Spica and Regulus that, 127 years before our era, Hipparchus discovered the law of the precession of the equinoxes. It's one of the constellations in which the greatest changes have taken place in 3000 years, as attested by a simple glance at ancient maps; in this celestial district more than 500 nebulas have been discovered, many of which are double, moving around one another—notably that which bears the identification M99, which looks like a Catherine Wheel of suns. It includes thousands of stars. Finally, I'll have said everything about Virgo when I've added to the list of its curiosities the interesting double star Gamma, one of the first discovered with the aid of a telescope, whose period of rotation is 175 years; it has been established that the two suns comprising it rate around one another and their common center of gravity. They're too far away to offer a measurable parallax, and..."

Fricoulet stopped short and looked at Gontran. The young man, lulled by his friend's voice, had dozed off; it was the regular, slightly heavy breathing, similar to a hum, emerging from his slightly-parted lips that had attracted the engineer's attention. He started laughing, shrugged his shoulders, and rose to his feet. "If that's the effect the Zodiac produces," he murmured, "I'm damned if he'll be able to keep up with Ossipoff. So much the worse for him; I'm in order with respect to my promises and, if he goes astray he'll have no one to blame but himself." That said, he left the engine-room, went to the cabin in which Farenheit was sleeping, lay down in his hammock, and was doubtless about to fol-

---

[125] I have translated "étoiles temporaires" [temporary stars] literally rather than substitute the more familiar "novas," partly because the text antedates the common usage of the latter term but mainly because (as will soon become clear) the authors give credence to a false theory regarding their origin, and the use of the latter term would therefore give the wrong impression.

low the American's example when he was gripped by remorse. Had he not a duty to wake the young Comte up and force him to listen to the rest of his lecture?"

In any other circumstances, he would have surrendered himself peacefully to the delights of sleep—but when he woke up, wouldn't Gontran have the right to reproach him for what, strictly speaking, might be considered a treason on his part? Wasn't it, in fact, in the engineer's interest to leave him defenseless against Ossipooff's interrogations? Certainly—and for the sake of his honor, Fricoulet was obliged to act in such a manner that his friend could not formulate any such reproach. On the other hand, Gontran tended to wake up grumpy, and there was nothing to suggest that Fricoulet would be greeted in an amiable fashion, in spite of his good intentions…

The young man remained briefly perplexed; a secret presentiment told him that Providence was supporting his projects—but precisely because of that presentiment, he didn't want his conscience or Gontran to have anything with which to reproach him…

Eventually, he took a middle course; instead of lying down, he sat on the edge of his hammock and, taking up his notebook, set about hastily writing a few notes in which he summarized as succinctly as possible that which it seemed to him to be necessary to get into his friend's skull, in order to allow him to reply successfully to the old scientist in case the fancy took him to discuss the Zodiac with his young "colleague."

These were the notes:

Leo. The chief star of this constellation is Regulus, whose radiance is magnificent; distance from the Solar System about 100 trillion leagues, in view of the light it emits; gigantic volume—moving away from us at 37 kilometers a second, escorted by a double star of the eighth magnitude, only known for 100 years. Take note: several nebulas of bizarre appearance, notably M65, an elliptical spiral, and M56, oval in form.

Cancer. The smallest and poorest of the signs of the Zodiac; only one pale milky nebulosity perceptible to the naked eye; an agglomeration of faint stars, described by the ancients as "the manger."

Gemini. Remarkable for Castor and Pollux, two stars considered for a long time to be linked—a theory demonstrated to be false by the spectroscope. While Pollux is traveling toward the Earth at a velocity of 64 kilometers a second, Castor is drawing away at 45 kilometers a second. Since the time of Hipparchus, these two suns have drawn apart from one another by more than 2.5 trillion leagues, and the intensity of their light has not varied in those 20 centuries. Castor and Pollux are followed in their course by another, more distant star, which suggests that one is dealing not with a double system but a triple one—according to the studies of Herschel, the revolution of Castor and Pollux about one another takes no less than 1000 years. Gemini includes several colored double stars, a certain number of variable stars and several nebulas.

Perseus. The principal star is Algol, which marks the position in the heavens of Medusa's head—a variable star, descending from the second to the fourth magnitude every 2 days 20 hours 40 minutes 53 seconds, and that sort of eclipse only lasts six minutes, doubtless because of the passage of a dark body in front of the disk. A large number of double stars and two small nebulas.

Auriga. Particularly evident at the return of spring, which has associated it since the remotest antiquity with agricultural labor. Capella, a first magnitude star, almost as white as Vega, 170 trillion leagues away, the principal of the group, positioned at the zenith of Paris in December and January. Nothing interesting to note except, not far from the group, the constellation Lynx, which includes a large number of interesting double stars, particularly numbers 38, 15, 12, 19 and 20, ternary systems of very slow revolution.

Fricoulet had reached this point in his notes when Ossipoff's thunderously loud voice became audible in the stairwell. "Gontran! Gontran!" he called.

The engineer shivered. At the same time, Farenheit, woken up with a start, leapt down from his hammock. "By God!" he muttered, looking at his neighbor in alarm.

"Don't worry," Fricoulet said to him, smiling. "It's Monsieur Ossipoff calling Monsieur de Flammermont, nothing more..."

At that moment the young Comte came in, rubbing his eyes. "You heard," he said.

"That question..."

"Yet another dissertation in preparation!" Gontran moaned.

"Probably."

The old man called again: "Gontran! Gontran!"

Flammermont folded his arms. "Oh, you're a clever one, you!" he said. "You let me sleep..."

"Because I had better things to do..."

The young Comte motioned with his head toward the ceiling, where the scientist could be heard stamping his feet impatiently. "What am I going to say to him?" he murmured, in a desolate tone.

"Here!" said the engineer, giving him the notes that he had just scribbled in haste. "Read that. I'll go calm him down..." And he ran toward the stairs.

On hearing the sound of his footsteps, the old scientist, bent over the telescope , asked without turning round: "Come here quickly, Gontran...were you asleep?"

"Monsieur de Flammermont isn't asleep, Monsieur Ossipoff," Fricoulet replied, "but he has Andromeda at the end of his telescope at present, and he sent me to tell you that he can't be disturbed for the time being..."

A frisson ran over the old man's entire body. "It's on the exact subject of Andromeda that I wanted to interrogate him, for I also am occupied with it, and I have uncertainties that I'd like to clarify by chatting to him..."

Selena, who was standing next to her father, turned to the engineer, her face clouded by anxiety. In the gaze that she fixed upon him, there was a clearly comprehensible question: "Is he ready?"

Fricoulet shook his head negatively. At the same time, though, he made a reassuring gesture with his hand, for an idea had just crossed his mind. "It will, indeed, be very reassuring," he said to Ossipoff, "to check your observations against his; but there's a simple means of doing that without disturbing either of you." Addressing Selena, he added: "Mademoiselle, would you be good enough to go find Monsieur de Flammermont and ask him to dictate to you what he's already observed in Andromeda, then give the note to Mr. Farenheit and ask him to bring it to us."

"Not a bad idea," murmured Ossipoff, in a satisfied tone, while his daughter, having thanked the engineer with a charming smile, fled from the cabin as lightly as a bird.

Fricoulet lost no time himself and wrote a few lines on a page ripped out of his notebook. He had finished by the time Farenheit arrived with a piece of paper that he handed over.

"Here," said the engineer, handing Ossipoff the page from his notebook instead of the one Gontran had sent.

"Read it," said Ossipoff, who was not about to interrupt his observation for anything in the world.

"Gamma, with its orange sun and its two emerald and sapphire satellites—what a marvel! Eyes dazzled...brain weary..."

"Pass on!" exclaimed the old man. "Poor Gontran's caught up in considerations of no interest. That's been known since 1777—Gontran forgets that Bradley[126] has doubled Gamma before him..." Then, in a keenly curious tone; he added: "What about the nebula? Doesn't he say anything about Simon Marius of Franconia's nebula?"[127]

"My word, no, but..." To Farenheit, he said: "Quickly—run and tell Monsieur de Flammermont that we're waiting for his observations on the nebula."

The American went out, protesting against the commissionaire's role that Fricoulet had given him, and Fricoulet said to the scientist: "If, in the meantime,

[126] James Bradley (1693-1762) succeeded Halley as astronomer royal, but does not seem to have been responsible for identifying Gamma Andromedae (Almaak) as a double star; the credit is usually given to Christian Mayer, but the date of 1777, which was cited a few pages ago in respect of Mayer's identification of a different double star, might be mistaken. Wilhelm Struve discovered in 1842 that Gamma Andromedae B was itself a double star, so Ossipoff would surely have known that the star had been "tripled."

[127] Simon Marius (1573-1624) was the first person to sight the nebula in Andromeda now known as M31.

you record your observations, Monsieur de Flammermont can check them while you check his…"

"Write, then," murmured the old man, feverishly. "From here, as from Pulkova, the nebula has the appearance of an immense gaseous lens, seen side-on, its silhouette being elliptical in consequence. I notice a central focus of condensation and two secondary foci, one round, the other oval, along with two black longitudinal fissures…"

Farenheit came back at that moment and handed a piece of paper to Fricoulet, who exclaimed: Wait…wait, Monsieur Ossipoff, dear Gontran has sent you something very interesting…"

"Really?"

"He's studied the nebula's spectrum...no trace of stars...not the slightest trace of any band characterizing a gaseous mass…"

"That's right…that's right!" said the old man, prey to an extraordinary agitation. "A continuous spectrum, without transverse bands…"

"In sum," Fricoulet went on, still pretending that he was reading Gontran's notes, "Monsieur de Flammermont is no further forward than on Earth. He counts more than 1500 stars in the neighborhood of the nebula, but despite all his efforts, he can't be sure whether their proximity is real or only due to perspective."

Ossipoff uttered a heart-rending sigh. "I hoped that he'd be more fortunate than me…"

"He has succeeded in measuring the surface area of that strange world, of course; he finds its length to be a minimum of 300 billion leagues, which makes it approximately 300 times as large as the entire Solar System…"

Although Ossipoff had established al these details with his own eyes, he raised his arms in the air in a random gesture, stammering: "Fabulous, fabulous!"

"Assuming," the engineer said then, "that the nebula is no more distant from us than the nearest stars—which is in no way proven…"

Ossipoff let his head fall into the palms of his hands, profoundly exhausted, while his lips murmured: "What good is it, then? What good…?"

For many hours already—33, to be exact—the *Eclair* had been traveling through the zodiac; the ruse devised by Fricoulet to permit Flammermont to avoid Ossipoff's interrogation on the Andromeda Nebula had brought a measure of cordiality back to the relationship between the two young men. As for the altercation between Gontran and Farenheit, it had been decided, by common accord, that no one would breathe a word of it, in order not to make Selena anxious. The question would be settled on Earth, if fortune desired that the voyagers ever saw their native planet again; until then, it would be as if nothing had happened.

The engineer, who had finished his watch, had just pointed out the constellation Canes Venatici, whose stars were brightly visible ahead of the vehicle, when Flammermont, who came to take his friend's place in the engine-room, noticed a strange drawing beside the engineer. He was opening his mouth to ask for an explanation when Fricoulet got in first. "You were born in 1863, weren't you?"

"Yes—why?"

"On September 28, if I'm not mistaken?"[128]

"Again, yes. Are you intending to wish me happy birthday?"

Fricoulet's only response was to burst out laughing, while looking at the drawing that had caught the young Comte's attention as he entered the cabin. His hilarity was such that it brought Selena and Farenheit running.

"Would it be indiscreet, Monsieur Fricoulet," said the young woman, "to ask for permission to laugh along with you?"

The engineer seemed slightly disconcerted, and attempted to hide the piece of paper he had in his hand behind his back, but Selena's keen eye had spotted his movement. "Oh—what's that?" she exclaimed.

"Nothing…just something I was drawing to keep me awake."

"May we see?"

It would have been impolite for Fricoulet to conceal it any longer; he handed the piece of paper to Mademoiselle Ossipoff, telling himself that, after all, he was running no great risk in setting before their eyes something they would undoubtedly not understand. His amazement and disappointment were, therefore, considerable when he heard Selena exclaim: "But it's a birth-chart!"

"It must be mine, then!" exclaimed Gontran, in his turn.

The engineer seemed embarrassed, and held out his hand to take the paper back, stammering: "A joke, I assure you…a mere joke…"

Selena, however, who was examining the diagram closely, exclaimed: "You were born under the influence of Mercury, which was then at an exponent of 17 degrees in Pisces, Venus being in Libra, Mars in Gemini and Saturn in Cancer."

"You're very good!" stammered Fricoulet, with a forced smile.

"You know something about it, then?" Gontran asked, incredulously.

"Indeed! Here—these 12 triangles represent the 12 Heavenly Houses, with their positions in space at the moment of your birth…"

Farenheit, who had remained silent thus far, hoisting himself up on tiptoe to look over the young woman's shoulder, then said: "One can foretell the future by this method, then?"

---

[128] This birth-date is flagrantly incompatible with data the text has previously provided relating to Gontran's age but it is the actual birth-date of Raoul Marquis, alias Henry de Graffigny, and that presumably explains its intrusion.

"Accurately," replied the engineer, without turning a hair. "You've heard mention of astrology, haven't you—well, this is it!"

"There was once—in the last century, I believe—a very wise man named Cagliostro, who read in the stars..."

Gontran burst out laughing and exclaimed: "No, Mr. Farenheit, no! Don't believe everything that Fricoulet tells you. Once, yes, people believed—because certain cunning folk created the belief—in the favorable or unfavorable influence of the stars on human existence, according to where they were, in respect of one another, at one time or another. It was pleasant nonsense from which the ancestors of our modern card-sharps and somnambulists made a good living..."

The engineer looked at his friend with a mocking expression while he spoke, and a slight satirical smile ran over his lips when he had finished—a smile that clearly signified: *We'll soon see, my fine friend, whether your skepticism is as resistant as it seems...*

Selena intervened then. "Permit me to tell you, though, my dear Gontran, that a host of predictions based on the knowledge of the stars have been realized in every detail. Consider the story..."

"The young man shrugged his shoulders. Of course! Do you imagine that those who made a profession of astrology were imbeciles? Far from it. They brought to it a considerable finesse, a profound insight and a very extensive knowledge of human beings and the human heart....not to mention that they had spies in political circles who kept them up to date with what's being said, even in the utmost secrecy—with the result that it was scarcely difficult for them, knowing what such and such a person was considering, or what preparations were being made for such and such an event, to predict the future with almost complete accuracy...while appearing to base their predictions on their charlatanesque operations..."

"If you'll permit me..." Fricoulet tried to say—but the other was in full flow, and cut him off.

"The best proof that I have of the truth is that the clientele of astrologers was only recruited from among important persons, those on whose account it was easy to find 'sources.' That was what caused Voltaire to say that only the great have stars, the rest being the rabble with whom the stars don't mix."

"We must believe that you're an important person, then," Fricoulet replied, ironically, "for there's a birth-chart such as the great men of Earth have never had."

Gontran undoubtedly had a suspicion, however, that the chart concealed some new trick on his friend's part, for he hastened to add: "And Voltaire isn't the only one who has affirmed, not merely his incredulity, but his scorn, with regard to the manner in which astrologers juggle with the stars. Long before, him, Shakespeare said..."

"Shakespeare!" observed Fricoulet, slyly. "Are you sure?"

"What? Am I sure? When I was an attaché in the Italian embassy, we put on a performance of *King Lear* for the English Ambassador..."

"In English?"

"Of course! Can you see us performing Shakespeare in French in the English embassy?"

"Strictly speaking, I could see you...but no matter. So?"

"So, I often remember declaiming the tirade: 'When we are sick in fortune—often the surfeit of our own behavior—we make guilty of our own disasters the Sun, the Moon, and the stars; as if we were villains by necessity, fools by heavenly compulsion, knaves, thieves and treachers by spherical predominance, drunkards, liars and adulterers by an enforce obedience of planetary influence; and all that we are evil in, by a divine thrusting on: an admirable evasion of whoremaster man, to lay his goatish disposition to the charge of a star! My father compounded with my mother under the dragon's tail, and my nativity was under *Ursa Major*, so that it follows I am rough and lecherous. 'Sfoot! I should have been that I am had the maidenliest star in the firmament twinkled on my bastardizing.' "[129] Carried away by his subject, the young man had delivered this tirade in a single breath, as if he were on stage, with the fire and apparent conviction that a true actor would have put into it.

"Thank you for having delivered that in French!" said Fricoulet, sardonically. "I'd have been incapable of appreciating the great English dramaturge in his native language..." Then, taking the piece of paper, which Selena had never ceased examining closely, he said: "This is of no importance, anyway—although, without believing in astrology, I have an opinion diametrically opposed to that of the late Shakespeare regarding the laws that preside over human destiny..."

"Yes, yes...the new theory...human irresponsibility—which permits advocates in the assize courts to defend the heads of clients arrested with bloody knives in their hands by saying that, if they killed, it was because they were born with a criminal instinct..." And he burst out laughing.

"You believe, however," Farenheit objected, "that one can be born with some particular faculty or other...as witness yourself, who, although having embraced a diplomatic career, came into the world with the astronomical bump..."

At these words, pronounced in a tone of admiring conviction, the young man could not help blushing slightly, all the more so because he felt the mocking and slightly malicious gazes of Fricoulet and Selena weighing upon him.

The latter, moving closer to the engineer, then said: "You'll be kind enough to translate for me what you've got there..."

---

[129] Act II; the speaker is the villain, Edmund. I have of course, used Shakespeare's original words rather than back-translating the text's somewhat less colorful French.

"But I assure you that it's not serious—and since you don't believe in astrology anyway..."

"What does it matter? Then again, one always believes in these things...without believing in them. It depends..."

"What? It depends...on what?"

"On what the stars predict for us..."

The engineer could not help laughing. "Exactly—one is much more credulous with respect to predictions that are in accord with our secret desires than others..."

Selena, knowing that he had seen through her, lowered her eyes and blushed.

"In those circumstances," Fricoulet went on, "it's better that I don't translate Gontran's horoscope for you."

"Why not?"

"Because the stars and you aren't in accord."

"Go on!" exclaimed Flammermont, his brown furrowing.

"Do it anyway," the young woman insisted.

Fricoulet sighed, and declared; "You'll remember, at any rate, if you're not content, that it was you who demanded it..." Taking the piece of paper the young woman held out to him, he said: "Monsieur de Flammermont, being born under the influence of Mercury, has a marked propensity for the exact sciences, Mercury being the god of mathematicians..."

Had it not been for the presence of Farenehit, Gontran would have given free rein to his hilarity; he contented himself with smiling, while a glint of amusement appeared in Mademoiselle Ossipoff's pupils.

"In compensation," the engineer went on, "he has a fickle and capricious character, and is not apt to constitute what is called on Earth 'a good family man, a good citizen and a good soldier.' "

"So you say...so you say," Gontran protested, with a taut smile. "It seems to me that the stars are going a bit far in their appreciation."

"Monsieur de Flammermont has an adventurous temperament..."

"That's not very clever," sneered the young Comte. "What I did several years ago isn't evidence of stay-at home habits..."

The engineer went on, imperturbably. "As for the future, it follows from the grouping of the various relevant constellations that you'll one day occupy a senior position..."

"Director of an Observatory," declared Farenheit, boldly.

"No—the stars speak of a political position."

"Politics!" cried Selena. "But my father..."

"The stars also say that your family will perish with you..."

"And that's all?" Gontran complained, furiously, while Selena left the room, sulkily.

"My God, yes—that's all..."

“Well,” cried Flammermont, wrathfully, “I’ll believe in your astrology when it predicts that you’ll be rich and married one day.”

“It might,” Fricoulet replied, impassively.

Chapter LX
Ossipoff's nightmare

Meanwhile, the *Eclair* continued on its route through space, imperturbably following a line conforming to its own propulsive force and the power of the attraction that constrained it to go onwards, ever onwards, just as a projectile expelled from the barrel of a cannon traces a mathematical trajectory through the air until the moment when the forces to which it is obedient abandon it and it finally returns, inert, to the ground from which it departed.

The Pole Star had already been sighted, and in the depths of the Milky Way, in the vicinity of the imaginary point at which the extrapolation of the Earth's axis ended, a singular constellation appeared, forming an obvious gigantic W in scintillating stars. This was Cassiopeia, and that name awoke mythological memories in Gontran, left over from his student days on the school benches, when he had not had the slightest suspicion in the world that a day would dawn when he would be able to admire the namesake of Andromeda's unfortunate mother at such close range.

One by one, he recalled the charming verses in which Ovid, in his *Metamorphoses*, had recounted the misfortunes of the Ethiopian princess who, a victim of her mother's presumption—she had been audacious enough to compare her beauty to that of the Nereids, daughters of Neptune—had been attached to a rock in order to be devoured by a sea-monster. The audacity of Perseus, the magical Pegasus, the details of the duel between the hero and the monster, and the victory of the ancient knight all reappeared before Flammermont's eyes, as clear and bright as if a magic wand had taken him 20 years back in time, to that misunderstood Golden Age known as one's 'schooldays.'

Lulled by his memories, he listened with a distracted ear to the explanations that Fricoulet was giving him, finding the commentary with which the teacher had once accompanied Ovid's poetry much more captivating than the other's astronomical demonstrations.

The engineer had declared, with an air of conviction, that of the 30 stars enclosed by Casiopeia, there were many of great interest, including the triple variable star Psi, golden yellow, azure blue and pale pink. Gontran, closing his eyes, saw Perseus mounting Pegasus and racing to rescue Andromeda. *Since Nature is all-powerful*, he thought, *why should she not trace these charming and heroic figures in the heavens? It would give astronomy a charm that it lacks…*

Fricoulet continued, though, wanting to keep the promise he had made his friend, to maintain his image in Ossipoff's eyes, to the last. Although he did not believe in astrology, he believed in destiny, and if his own destiny really was to become Selena's husband, he did not want his conscience to have anything with which to reproach him. So he continued his course, speaking successively of Eta, a fourth magnitude double, golden yellow and red, rotating around one another in 200 years, perceive for the first time by Herschel in 1779, about 15 trillion leagues away from the Solar System, a distance that takes light 21 years to travel; then star 3082 in Struve's catalogue, which forms a very close pair and whose resolution is one of the most rapid known, accomplished in 140 terrestrial years; then the triple Iota, golden yellow, purple and lilac, forming a ternary system in motion; Mu, remarkable for the velocity of its proper motion, which rises to 1,700,000,000 leagues a year; and finally, a magnificent mass of stars discovered in 1783 by Miss Caroline Herschel...

"The astronomer's daughter, no doubt," murmured Gontrran, suddenly snatched from his reverie.

"Exactly."

"How delightful family life must be," Flammermont exclaimed, ironically, "for those who spend their time glued to a telescope!"

"One can't say, at any rate, that it's a down-to-earth existence."

"Not sufficiently, in my opinion, for while the mistress of the house is away in the stars, the house goes to rack and ruin...but continue..."

There was a pause, during which Fricoulet examined his friend curiously, reading what was passing through his mind as clearly as an open book. Then, in a resigned tone, he said: "Next we pass on to Cepheus, a neighbor of Ursa Minor, which, among other curiosities, includes Sigma, a double star of the fifth magnitude, orange-yellow and turquoise-blue in color, and Mu, which Herschel described by the name of Garnet Sidus,[130] a deep red star, by virtue of a radiance like that projected by a ruby struck by electric light. Also in Cepheus we have Delta, a variable, Beta, double, white and blue..."

The engineer paused momentarily, got to his feet, and after having darted a glance through the telescope, said to Flammermont: "Here! If you want to see a pretty spectacle, look..."

As he spoke, he pushed Gontran by the shoulders, forcing him to abandon his mythological daydreams, bidding farewell to Perseus and Pegasus, in order to apply his eye to the optical apparatus.

"Well?" he asked, after a few seconds.

"The Cross of Cygnus," the engineer explained. And after giving his friend time to admire it at his leisure, he went on: "You see, don't you, the disposition of the stars comprising that constellation, to which it owes its name...the one shining there, directly in front of you, with a golden-yellow light, is Albireo, which is doubled with the other one slightly to its right, which is sapphire blue. If we had a spectroscope here, I'd show you the enormous difference that exists

[130] Strictly speaking, it was Giuseppe Piazzi who described the red supergiant Mu Cephei as "Garnet Sidus" in his catalogue, although he was merely translating its common designation as "[Herschel's] Garnet Star."

in the constitution of those two worlds; while the former presents a spectrum of the second type, the latter, by contrast, allows perception of a fine network of tightly-arranged lines confining the red and the yellow, from which one concludes that its temperature is lower; its volume being smaller, there's a chance that it's cooling more rapidly and that, in a few centuries, it will solidify into a planet orbiting Albireo. Are you listening to me?"

"That's all I'm doing," Gontran stammered.

"I call your attention particularly to number 61; it's the first star whose distance was calculated, and it was by reason of its very rapid proper motion that the idea arose of measuring its parallax—which, determined by Bessel in 1840, is 0.511 minutes, giving an approximate distance of 15,000,000 leagues. It moves at a rate of 1,000,000 leagues a day, at a minimum. I pass over several double stars and point out a group designated by the name of Vulpecula, in which one finds a nebula discovered in 1764 by Messier, which presents the silhouette of a gymnastic dumb-bell. The English..."

At that moment, an exclamation escaped Gontran's lips, cutting off the engineer, who asked: "What's the matter?"

"An eclipse! A stellar eclipse!"

"What are you making a song and dance about?" said Fricoulet, shrugging his shoulders.

"The truth, no less," replied Flammermont, who had not quit the telescope. "A moment ago, there was a very bright white star, and it suddenly disappeared—or rather went out, like a snuffed candle..."

"Unbelievable! Stars aren't snuffed out like candles!"

"That's why I called it an eclipse," retorted Gontran, stung by his friend's mockery. "Besides, it's just reappeared again..."

As the young man finished speaking, Ossipoff's voice was heard. "Gontran! Are you looking in the direction of Lyra down there?"

"Yes, yes...an eclipse...doubtless a planet passing in front of the star that it orbits...."

The old man was heard hurtling down the stairs like an avalanche, and he came into the engine-room like a hurricane.

"No, no," he cried, "it's not that! There's no double star in that direction! We're in the presence of some celestial phenomenon that it's up to us to examine in depth."

The young Comte looked at his friend anxiously. *What new folly is he meditating?* he thought.

Doubtless Fricoulet had the same thought, for he exclaimed: "Oh no! No stupidities, you know, Monsieur Ossipoff."

"A slight twitch of a lever, my dear Fricoulet," implored the old man. "A mere twitch, to divert us slightly to the right, so as to get closer to the point in question. It won't take us off course at all, and I think we'll witness an interesting spectacle."

The engineer shrugged his shoulders and replied: "My God! If that's all it takes to make you happy..." He seized a lever, lowered it a notch or two, and added: "There—it's done!"

Without thanking him, Ossipoff turned on his heel, and they heard him running back to his cabin.

"What do you suppose it might be?" asked Flammermont, after the old man's departure.

Fricoulet pushed out his lips in a dubious moue. "I've no idea. I can see no other explanation than the occultation of the star by a planet that serves as its satellite. Anyway, there's no point racking our brains, since we'll find out soon enough. So, let's not think about it any more, and, as they say in the theater, let's get back to the script."

"Back to the script," Gontran repeated, in a melancholy tone full of resignation.

"The constellation Lyra, in the vicinity of which the phenomenon in question occurred, owes its reputation to Vega, whose parallax was established by Brünnow in 1870,[131] its figure of 0.18 seconds corresponding to a distance of 42,000,000 leagues. Vega is one of the brightest stars in the celestial universe, but its temperature is not in proportion to the intensity of its light. Its spectrum reveals the presence of hydrogen, sodium and magnesium in its photosphere. Vega is approaching the Solar System at a velocity of 71 kilometers per second and, in 12,000 years, will return to the place it occupied at the world's North Pole 14,000 years ago."

"Yes, I know," murmured Gontran with a sigh. "The precession of the equinoxes."

"Although Lyra is one of the smallest constellations, it includes several sidereal curiosities, notably a magnificent quadruple system; the first pair rotates in 1800 years, the second in 3700 years, and the duration of the revolution of the two couples around their common center of gravity is estimated at 10,000 centuries. Also notable is what Herschel called a perforated nebula,[132] the surface area of which is at least equal to that of the entire Solar System. In the neighborhood of Lyra we have various astronomical small fry: Sagitta, Scutum Sobieski and Aquila, about which there's little to say, except that the constellations are in a

---

[131] Franz Brünnow (1821-1891) did indeed measure Vega's parallax in 1870, but it is curious that Ossipoff does not see fit to mention that Wilhelm Struve had obtained very nearly the same result in the 1830s—unfortunately, he was persuaded that it was incorrect by Bessel, who had obtained a very different and badly mistaken figure shortly thereafter.

[132] William Herschel did indeed call the toroidal M57 "a perforated nebula, or ring of stars," although it is nowadays regarded as a key example of a "planetary nebula"—a term that Herschel also coined, but did not apply to that particular object.

region very rich in stars, since Herschel counted 330,000 of them within a five-degree span."

"What patience!"

There was a loud noise overhead, produced by several stools falling over on to the floor, and Ossipoff's footsteps made the stairs tremble once again. When he appeared he was pale, his eyes were shining with an extraordinary gleam, and he was waving his hands feverishly above his head. The two friends thought that some unknown danger was threatening the apparatus, and they ran to meet him anxiously.

"It's pretty, your eclipse!" exclaimed the old man, folding his arms and looking both of them up and down, disdainfully. The role of planet is filled by an enormous dark globe moving at tremendous velocity—for I've seen it successively occulting several stars…"

Fricoulet opened his mouth to reply, but Ossipoff did not give him time to utter a syllable. "And do you know what's happening? Well, that globe is heading straight for another dark body, whose motion is slower, but whose mass is irresistibly attracting the first, whose velocity is accelerating with every passing second…."

"We're going to witness a collision, then!" cried the engineer.

The old man rubbed his hands together energetically. "I certainly hope so."

A shadow of anxiety passed over Gontran's face. "Shouldn't we be fearful," he murmured, "that the *Eclair* will be subject to the attraction of these two masses, and that some peril…"

"We're too far away," replied the old man.

While they were talking, Fricoulet had sat down at the telescope. "There's a spectacle that won't be banal," he declared. "The impact of two worlds hurtling toward one another with a velocity of several 100 kilometers a second…no railway accident can give an idea of that…" He shouted at the top of his voice: "Mr. Farenheit! Mr. Farenheit!"

The American came in, rubbing his eyes, and the smiling engineer, alluding to his altercation with Gontran, said: "You like duels—there's one about to take place such as you've never seen, which swill certainly break the monotony of the voyage…" While speaking, he was scribbling in his notebook. "Monsieur Ossipoff," he declared, "if you want to return to your telescope, the event will occur in about ten minutes…"

The scientist fled with a rapidity of which one would not have believed his old legs capable—and the engineer, still calculating, added: "A final velocity of 500 kilometers a second! What a cataclysm! That, my friends, will produce a little firework compared with which Ruggieri's are no more than child's toys..."[133]

Farenheit, Gontran and Selena took up positions at the portholes, while Fricoulet, his chronometer in his hand, counted the minutes out loud as they went by. Finally, in a voice that was slightly tremulous, he said: "One more second." After that, he put the chronometer back in his pocket and put his face to the telescope.

He was just in time; the two bodies, whose masses had grown to the extent of filing the entire horizon, were crashing into one another; instantaneously, from the two dark spheroids, surged an immense sun, a gigantic, incandescent nebula, at the center of which a whirlpool of exceedingly luminous stars emerged, more blinding than the most powerful electric arc-light, rising up progressively, filling space with radiant flashes dispersed in every direction. As Fricoulet had predicted, it was like a sheaf of fireworks, raised to the 1/100,000th power, with an intensity such that the human brain could not conceive it.

In the blink of an eye, space was illuminated, and such heat emerged from that nucleus of incandescence that the Terrans had to retreat from the portholes, which were masked again to avoid accidents similar to the one that had struck Farenheit.

"And that's how old moons are made into new suns!" Fricoulet exclaimed, in jest.

"The terrestrial astronomers must be delighted!" exclaimed the American.

The engineer shook his head. "Not as much as you think," he relied, "for the good reason that they won't find out about it for some years."

"Some years!"

"Yes—you're forgetting that we're traveling faster than light, and that a luminous ray projected by that new light will only arrive on Earth in 25 or 26 years' time..."

This explanation seemed to cheer Farenheit up. "In that case," he said, "we'll be able to watch it happen all over again..."

"In every detail, no—but we'll be able to predict, to the day, hour and almost the minute, the moment when, at an exact spot that we'll be able to identify in advance, a new star will appear in the sky." Jokingly, Fricoulet added: "That should make certain of your election to the presidency of the Eccentric Club." Turning to Gontran, he said: "That will convince those who don't believe in astrology! Imagine yourself predicting at a scientific conference, several years in advance, the birth of a world! That would be enough to get you appointed to all possible and imaginable academies on the spot!"

---

[133] The reference is to the 18th century Italian pyrotechnist Gaetano Ruggieri, who put on the display for which Handel composed his "Music for the Royal Fireworks."

"Thanks a lot," replied the young Comte, sardonically. As the spectacle he had just witnessed had made a considerable impact on him, however—although he did not want to admit it—he asked: "And what will the outcome of the phenomenon be?"

"Quite simple, as you'll see. You know that heat is merely an aspect of movement, like light and sound—except that the waves are different and act differently. Moreover, there's a perfect equivalence between the heat expended to produce mechanical work and the work necessary to produce heat; thus, the heat necessary to raise the temperature of a kilogram of water by one degree corresponds to the work required by the elevation of a weight of 424 kilograms to a height of one meter, and vice versa..."

"Advocate, let's get to the Deluge,"[134] said Gontran, satirically.

"Extrapolating from this principle, it's easily understandable that the result of the abrupt stopping of the two dark bodies will be a fantastic rise in temperature. The motion with which they were animated has been transformed into heat and from two stony, worn-out worlds, Nature has fabricated a nebula, an embryo of future worlds, which will one day give birth to a sun, then to planets—and so on, *in saecula saeculorum*."

"It's an eternal recurrence."

"You said it."

"That's the method of creation employed by Nature, then?" murmured Selena.

"Or, at least, one of the methods, Mademoiselle—for we must suppose that the arsenal of procedures employed by the supernatural power that rules the Suns is inexhaustible. In any case, it's certain that it's always a nebula, formed at a point in space for whatever reason—and there's no lack of them—that gives rise to suns, stars and worlds. Nothing is lost; nothing is created!"

Flammermont started laughing. "That's a nice turn of phrase!"

"Which isn't mine—I picked it up from some old book or other; in any case, wherever it comes from, it's true."

Fricoulet thought that he was done with explanations, but he had reckoned without the American, in whose ear what he had said a few moments before about the Eccentric Club had struck a chord. Certainly, it would be an originality fit to ensure his election to the presidency to convene a conference on his return to New York at which he would predict the birth of a world. Him—Jonathan Farenheit of Chicago, pig-merchant, and none other, taking up astronomy! That would definitely not be banal! But it was necessary not to be stupid, and to plan his effects with the greatest number of possible chances; for that, the collaboration of the engineer was indispensable to him.

[134] See Volume 1, Note 50.

So, when Fricoulet went back to his cabin, the American followed him, and as the young man lay down in his hammock, said "One moment, Monsieur Fricoulet—I'd like a few words with you...just a few..."

The engineer looked at him questioningly, and the American went on: "It's with regard to what just happened..."

Fricoulet was 100 leagues away from suspecting that his interlocutor might still be thinking about the birth of the nebula that they had just witnessed, so he asked, ingenuously: "And what just happened, my dear Mr. Farenheit?"

"But...the nebula!"

"That interests you, does it?" exclaimed Fricoulet, surprised.

"By God! Of course it interests me—because of the Eccentric Club!"

This time, the engineer understood straight away, and said: "You'd like more precise information?"

"Indeed! You understand that I can't limit myself to make a prediction. I want, as far as possible, to give a few details, a few explanations. They'll ask me questions, you see; they'll want explanations. I should be ready! So, if you'd like..."

"To explain it to you...I'd like nothing better."

"I'd prefer you to write me a little note—I have a hard head, and I fear that it might not retain your explanations."

"I'll tell you orally anyway—afterwards, I'll write you a little note. To begin with, then, know that attraction is a force inherent in every atom of matter. In that gaseous cloud produced by the impact of two dead worlds there are parts that are more or less dense, which will attract other portions of the nebula to themselves, and in the slow fall of distant particles toward that more attractive region, a general rotational movement will be produced, which will affect the entire mass. Have you got that?"

"When it's written down I'll understand it, and remember it better."

"Eventually, its form will become spherical, the natural form of all substance, gaseous or liquid, left to its own devices. The laws of mechanics determine that the gaseous sphere, as it condenses and shrinks, will rotate with increasing rapidity, flattening out at the poles; the centrifugal force developed by that rotational movement can then surpass the force of central attraction, and detach a gaseous ring from the equator—an inevitable consequence of the rupture of equilibrium. That ring condenses into sphere itself, while the nebula continues to rotate faster and faster. Do you understand?"

"It isn't difficult to understand...but to remember..."

"It's convenient that I put it in writing for you..."

The American tugged at his long beard with an attitude of such evident perplexity, however, that Fricoulet could not help asking him: "What's the matter now?"

"It's...it's that someone might ask me, when I've repeated like a parrot what you've just told me, how long it will be before Terran astronomers can study the new planets whose birth we witnesses just now...and then..."

The engineer raised his arms toward the ceiling in a gesture of bewilderment. "Oh, God alone knows! Perhaps millions of years...maybe longer..."

"As much as that!"

Fricoulet folded his arms, mockingly. "Oh, Mr. Farenheit!" he exclaimed. "Do you imagine that worlds are like your Chicago pigs, whose melted fat only takes a day to solidify? Do you think it's the same for nebulas?"

"But..."

"Millions of years! I underestimated! It will undoubtedly take millions of years for nothing to remain of the primitive nebula but solidified planets..."

The America scratched the end of his nose energetically, in a fashion that betrayed a profound perplexity. "You think so?" he murmured. "But in the final analysis, assuming that you're not exaggerating, can you specify the duration?"

This time, Farenheit's pretensions went too far, and the engineer was driven to cry out: "Mad! You'r mad! Where do you think I could obtain the elements necessary for the basis of such an estimate? Do I know the mass or the surface area of the nebula? I know that, according to Helmholtz and Tyndall,[135] supposing that the specific heat of the condensing mass to be that of water, the heat of the condensation would be sufficient to produce a temperature of more than 28,000,000 degrees Centigrade...but then...and then again, that's not right...you're confusing me with your preposterous questions!"

Farenheit was contrite. "I assure you, my dear Monsieur Fricoulet, "that I'm extremely sorry..."

"Then again," added the engineer, "of what interest could it be to your audience to know the date of a phenomenon that will not happen for millions of centuries! The Earth will have joined the old moons a long time ago by then—unless the Earth's encounter with some other world has given rise to a new nebula!"

Instinctively, Farenheit's face became fearful. "By God!" he exclaimed.

The engineer shrugged his shoulders. "Bah!" he said. "That a man might be interested in his grandchildren, or even his grandchildren, is all well and good—that one might be concerned, when one belongs to history, with what might happen a century or two hence is also permissible—but what can it matter to you, a Chicago suet merchant, whether terrestrial humanity will or will not exist millions of centuries hence?"

---

[135] The physicists Heinrich Helmholtz (1821-1894) and John Tyndall (1820-1893), who both made significant contributions to the fledgling science of thermodynamics—but the most famous attempt to apply the insights of that discipline to cosmic calculations was an essay by Lord Kelvin, with which Fricoulet does not appear to be familiar.

It was with these fundamentally reasonable words that Fricoulet concluded his little lecture. He turned on his heel and went to lie down in his hammock, without seeming to pay any heed to the bewildered attitude of his listener, who appeared to be expecting something more. *Uh oh*, he thought, privately, *I can do without the American starting to want lessons in astronomy too; I wouldn't have enough time, and I'd do better to open a free public course.* The last remark brought a smile to his lips and he went to sleep, while the charming silhouette of Selena was vaguely sketched on his eyelids.

While these conversations had been taking place, the *Eclair* had passed through Ursa Minor, whose seven component stars—including the Pole Star—were now shining in its wake. Given the parallax of that star, calculated by Peters in 1842 and estimated at 0.076 seconds, it was then about 100 trillion leagues from the Solar System—a fantastic distance that an express train traveling at 60 kilometers an hour would take more than 720,000,000 years to cross.

If Farenheit had had any suspicion of this detail, he would doubtless have suffered a new fit of madness, but he was profoundly asleep for the time being, his brain overtired by the explanations that Fricoulet had given him.

The latter rested too, while Gontran, on watch, chatted with Selena and the truly indefatigable Ossipoff continued his studies. On the little table set next to him the pieces of paper piled up, covered with hastily-scribbled notes that would serve the great work telling the story of the fantastic voyage that has lasted nearly three years.

As they passed through Draco, the old man noted that Alpha, the one-time Pole Star that, by reason of the precession of the equinoxes, had formed the extremity of the world's arc 2700 years before our era, shone with a brightness much less considerable appeared to the eyes of terrestrial astronomers. Although it was too far away to determine the cause visually, he did not hesitate to note that this was, without any doubt, evidence of a sun going out.

He searched in vain to penetrate the mystery enveloping the double system Nu, of which the companion has remained fixed relative to the other for 200 years even though they are moving through the heavens at a rather rapid rate. He was too far away, and he was obliged to conclude that, as for the Pole Star, the duration of revolution must be between 6000 and 7000 years. Oh, if he had dared, he would certainly have redirected the route of the apparatus to get closer, but he could hear the faint buzz that the voices of Gontran and Selena made as they chatted in the engine-room, so he stayed at his telescope…

Besides, the panorama that offered itself to him was so captivating that he had scanned twice over without moving a muscle. To begin with, there was Omicron, which formed a charming couple, golden-yellow and lilac, then the components of Psi, immutable since 1755, the year in which it had been studied for the first time, and then the famous elliptical planetary nebula, at the center of which shone a little star that seemed to be the heart of the world in formation. Ossipoff examined the nebula spectroscopically with extreme care, and the examination confirmed the studies that he had made at Pulkova; its constitution was essentially gaseous, and it represented one of the phases of planetary transformation.

What interested him more than anything else was, however, Ursa Major, the Great Bear—the most popular and most recognizable celestial constellation of all, thanks to the seven bright stars composing it, whose assembly was more commonly known in France as "David's Chariot."[136] It was with an extreme joy that, being so close to the constellation, he was able to penetrate the secret of the physical system of Mizar and Alcor, the orbital movement of which Earthly astronomers had been unable to detect. He attributed that impossibility to the slowness of their movement—so slow that it would probably take centuries to measure it—but he did not get sufficiently carried away to take a closer look. Perhaps, deep down, he told himself that he was not risking much in being so affirmative, since no one would be able to check the accuracy of his contention.

Besides, that was a matter of little importance by comparison with an event that suddenly turned his poor brain upside-down. In the field of the telescope, at the moment when he least expected it, a star appeared, flying through space with an inconceivable rapidity, its radiant streak turning space blue.

In the first instant of admiring amazement he put his hands together, exclaiming: "That's it!" It was no one other than the star marked in the Groombridge catalogue as number 1830, one of the curiosities of Ursa Major, to which it belonged—or seemed to belong. He had examined it many times, during his nights of observation at Pulkova, trying to discover the secret of this enigmatic star, whose lightning speed defied all calculation and frustrated all hypotheses…

"Ah, you won't escape this time!" the muttered between his teeth, once his initial surprise had passed, in the tone of a fighter whose opponent has been avoiding him for a long time, but who finally finds himself face to face with him. "300 kilometers a second! With such a speed, is it possible to admit that 1830 Groombridge belongs to our universe? That's madness! Such a supposition is in flagrant opposition to all known scientific principles!

"Among these principles, notably, is one according to which a body arriving on Earth from space would strike the surface of that planet with a final velocity of 11.3 kilometers per second!

"If one knew exactly the masses of all the stars and their arrangement in space, one would even be able to calculate the maximum speed that a body would acquire in falling fro an infinite distance to any point of the stellar system whatsoever!

"Well, if we find that a star is moving faster than that velocity, we must conclude—must we not?—that the star does not belong to the visible Universe, that it is a simple voyager, arriving from Infinity and incapable of being stopped

---

[136] The same formation is better known in England as the Plough, or Charles's Wain.

by the combined attraction of all the known stars! Is this not the case with the star 1830 Groombridge? According to Newcomb, a body falling from Infinity to the heart of our Solar System would only be animated by a terminal velocity of 40 kilometers per second. Now, that is only an eighth of the proper speed of the star in question.

"On the other hand, Flammarion establishes that, by supposing that there are 100,000,000 stars in our Universe, each one being, on average, twice as massive as ours, and that the diameter of our Universe is the distance traveled by light in 30,000 years...well, gentlemen, to obtain the figure of 300 kilometers a second, the speed at which the star in question is traveling, it would be necessary to suppose an attractive mass 64 times stronger than that supposed above...

"Thus, either the stars that comprise our visible Universe are more numerous and more massive than the telescope seems to indicate, or 1830 Groombridge does not belong to our Universe—that star in passing through it without the combined attraction of all our stars being able to stop it..."

Ossipoff had pronounced these final words in a ringing, triumphant tone, while menacing an imaginary audience with his extended arm, his face flushed and his eyes flashing.

Abruptly, the hallucination to which he had been subject for some minutes died away; he seemed to hear mocking laughter behind him and turned round. He was alone, but the movement was enough to break the charm. He looked around, bewildered, passed his hand over his sweat-soaked brow as if to collected his momentarily-scattered thoughts, and seemed very surprised to find himself there, standing up and gesticulating.

"I could have sworn that someone laughed," he murmured.

Rather crestfallen, he sat down at the telescope again. Scarcely had he put his eye to the lens, though, than he jumped. There, in space, was a strange shining face: a sort of human head, which seemed to be looking at him with two unequal, squinting eyes, while its mouth opened widely as if to mock him.

He burst out laughing himself, though; this time, he had regained his self-possession; he was merely the victim of some hallucination, and what he was looking at was nothing more than the little nebula that bears the number 97 in Messier's catalogue.

Without paying any great attention, partly because he was still slightly fatigued by what had just happened and partly because the celestial regions were really only of relative interest, he saw, successively arrayed before him, Leo Minor, Canes Venatici and Comas Berenices. He recovered all his presence of mind, though, and shook off the sort of cerebral torpor that had numbed him, when the beautiful nebula discovered by Messier in 1772 appeared in the telescopic field, the admirable spiral form of which had only been recognized three-quarters of a century later by Lord Rosse.[137]

It was an unalloyed joy for Ossipoff to be able to admire, even more clearly than from Pulkova Observatory, the truly surprising details of that star. The spirals presented two very bright branches formed of several threads; the intervals between these branches were filled with light, and an almost-continuous nebulosity linked the two nuclei together, while the nucleus at the center of the great spirals shone like an incandescent lamp.

What was most interesting of all was to be able to compare the appearance the star presented to him now—which is to say, as it would appear to his colleagues on Earth in several centuries—with the one it had presented some years before, not only in the era when Lord Rosse had studied it, but more recently, when it had been drawn by Charcornac in 1862.[138]

In those drawings, the two branches identified by Lord Rosse still exist, but more condensed; the intervals are less luminous, the two nuclei are almost identical in brightness, the central nucleus is detached and the spiral structure of the threads surrounding it is clearly distinct. In 1876, new observations by Wolf[139] and further changes: the spirals are condensed and reduced by a factor of three, the intervals are almost completely ark, the secondary threads no longer exist and the gap between the nuclei is absolutely black; the second nucleus has been transformed into a brilliant star, of superior brightness to that of the first.

In addition to the interest offered by this aspect of his study, the old scientist found a truly unique opportunity to assure himself of the ancient existence of matter; those spirals of bright stars, falling towards a common center, permitted him to take account of the most immense period of duration that human intelligence had ever been able to conceive. Had he, in fact, to imagine a Milky Way that had begun to pivot and form spirals of stars all heading toward a future foc-

---

[137] William Parsons, 3rd Earl of Rosse (1800-1867) built the 72-inch "Leviathan of Parsonstown," then the largest telescope in the world, in 1840. He made a special study of nebulas, engaging in a fierce controversy with John Herschel regarding their nature. Having observed its spiral form Rosse christened M51 the Whirlpool Nebula, correctly arguing that it was composed of stars rather that being gaseous, but failed to make the additional imaginative leap necessary to identify it as an "island universe" (in Kant's then-existing terminology), a "celestial universe" (the term more familiar in the 1880s) or, in modern terms, a galaxy.

[138] Jean Charcornac (1823-1873) produced his drawing of the Whirlpool Nebula in April 1862.

[139] This name is rendered Wolff in the text, but the reference is far more likely to be to Charles Joseph Etienne Wolf (1827-1918) than any of several other astronomers who had similar names.

al point? How many millions of centuries would be required for these gigantic spirals to rotate?

The imagination becomes confused when one thinks that every one of these myriads of suns, separated from us by immeasurable distances—lost in infinity, so to speak—might be the center of a planetary system. What lowly rank in the universal assembly would then by taken by our Sun, whose grandeur, with its cortege of worlds and satellites, nevertheless overwhelms us. It is only with great difficulty that one can allow oneself to measure it and compare it to those colossal creations that gravitate imperturbably in the sidereal desert.

That is what Ossipoff said to himself, genuinely overwhelmed by these philosophical thoughts, to which excessively prolonged contemplation of celestial marvels had given birth. His fingers had dropped the pencil that he had been using to take notes; sitting slightly apart from the telescope, with his elbow on his knee and his chin in the palm of his hand, he fell into a profound reverie that transformed itself imperceptibly into drowsiness, and then into sleep.

Then, a bizarre dream—or, rather, a dolorous nightmare—came to torment him, a counterpart of the unforgettable spectacle to which he had been witness, or the collision of two worlds, suddenly transformed into nebulas. Nature had revealed to him the secret of creation, and now, before his frightened eyes, the mystery of destruction was revealed!

By a miracle that his brain neglected to penetrate—for he was content to observe the facts without wishing to research their causes—he had the sensation of living, in less than a few minutes, through centuries: the last centuries of terrestrial humankind...[140]

The atmosphere surrounding the Earth as a gaseous envelope, after having diminished every year, suddenly disappeared entirely, leaving the planet defenseless against the ardent rays of the Sun, drying up the seas, rivers and streams. Then the Earth's desiccated crust began to absorb in its turn, every trace of humidity remaining, not only on its surface but in space; then the waters combined chemically with the rocks, and the absorption continued as the cooling increased. Gradually, the nitrogen, oxygen and water vapor were also absorbed and soon, the surface was exposed, without protection, to the glacial cold of space, 273 degrees below zero.

Then death, which had, until that moment, been largely content to mow down humankind, covered the entire surface of the planet with its vast wings,

---

[140] In between the publication of the third and fourth volumes of the present text, Camille Flammarion had published *La Fin du monde* (1894; tr. as *Omega: The Last Days of the World*), whose second part describes the ultimate fate of the world—a vision that has much in common with this one, although both echo, to some extent, the final phases of Poe's *Eureka*. The author of this part of the text had certainly read Flammarion's work, from whose first part he borrows extensively in a later passage.

and life ceased. Only one creature was alive, not on the surface itself, but in space, where his spirit floated, and that creature was Ossipoff.

As soon as the last human soul was extinct, a complete transformation overtook the Earth; there had been nothing to that soul, or hardly anything—the soul of a new-born infant frozen upon the body of its dead mother—and yet, for as long as the heart in that minuscule body had beaten, it had seemed that life had not yet retreated from the planet. The slight breath emerging from the blue lips had scarcely been audible to the ear, and yet, it appeared that that manifestation of life had been sufficient to make a difference to the very existence of that dying world—but when the last heartbeat in that infantile breast had sounded, a frightful silence suddenly reigned over the surface and in space.

The Earth was dead!

Ossipoff immediately felt overwhelmed by a mortal cold: the cold that radiated from his native planet; a cold that froze the blood in his veins and cracked his skin, which had instantaneously dried out, like the bark of a tree struck by frost.

Oh, that cold! What frightful torture! In the midst of his nightmare, the old scientist's teeth chattered and all his limbs shivered. And yet, although he could have fled, he stayed there, invisibly immobilized by his curiosity.

The Earth was dead, and the last human family lay rigid beneath a shroud of ice.

What was going to happen?

Was Nature not going to unveil its mysteries for him? What would He who created everything and destroyed everything going to do with that which had existed a little while ago, but now no longer existed?

Desiccated, solidified, stony all the way to its center, the terrestrial planet continued to rotate through space, only conserving in juxtaposition by a miracle of equilibrium the materials comprising it, which would henceforth no longer be welded together by any aggregation.

Then, a stupefying spectacle was offered to Ossipoff's gaze: the Moon, attracting the planet to which it had previously served as a satellite to itself, provoked a gigantic tide; but it was no longer waves of liquid on which it exerted its attraction but waves of rocks and earth. Then the attraction of the Moon was combined with that of Mars, Venus and other neighboring planets and, little by little, still rotating on its axis, the Earth continued its route through space, disintegrating completely, strewing fragments of itself along its orbit.

Then, the Earth having been destroyed, Ossipoff witnessed the destruction of the Sun; for centuries, already, the center of our Solar System had been cooling, abandoning its extraordinary heat to space, and a moment came when, worn out in its turn, as its planet had been, the star disintegrated and scattered itself in the void as cosmic dust...

Breathless and terrified, Ossipoff, to whom this spectacle caused frightful suffering, could not, however, make a decision to withdraw from it, even though that only required an act of will. The Worlds had been destroyed! Would their nature die too, then—or would they not rather, as he had foreseen philosophically, be transformed? That was what he wanted to know, and that is why, still floating, he followed the terrestrial and solar molecules moving through the void with an anxious gaze.

Suddenly, without him being able to figure out why, a sort of hurricane was manifest in space: a sort of aerial tornado into which all the terrestrial and solar debris was drawn, gradually attracted towards an invisible center that was abruptly transformed into an incandescent nucleus. A new nebula had just been born, from which future solar systems would emerge.

At that moment, Ossipoff woke up. He was bathed in sweat and all his limbs were twisted, as if he had been beaten unmercifully.

His eyes wide open, he saw Selena, Gontran, Fricoulet and Farenheit gathered around his hammock, looking at him anxiously. He tried to prop himself up on his elbow to see them better, but Selena and Gontran immediately reached out, placing their hands gently on his shoulders to hold him still. He tried to speak, but Fricoulet immediately put a finger on his lips, instructing him to be silent. At the same time, the old man felt a cold damp cloth cover his forehead.

"That'll bring him round," he heard Farenheit murmur.

"I think so," replied the engineer. "Look—his eyes are clearer, the pupils are no longer dilated, his breathing's less labored."

"Do you think so, Monsieur Fricoulet?" asked Selena, her hands clasped, as she looked at the engineer anxiously.

The latter shrugged his shoulders, took the old man's wrist between his fingers, and replied: "Of course. The pulse is normal; the fever has disappeared. In two days, he'll be back on his feet..."

Ossipoff asked, in a low, seemingly-fearful voice: "What's happened to me, then?"

His companions looked at one another interrogatively.

"Hmm," Gontran murmured.

"Oh, my God, we can tell him the truth now," the engineer opined. Addressing the old man, he said: "What's happened to you, Monsieur Ossipoff? Very little, in sum—just a little cerebral crisis..."

Ossipoff tried to laugh, incredulously, but he immediately felt such a pain in his head that his mouth remained open, his lips distended in a cruelly fixed smile. "A cerebral crisis!" he stammered. "But I was just having a nightmare...a horrible nightmare, it's true, but..."

"To such an extent that it took three of us—Mr. Farenheit, Gontran and myself—to keep you in your hammock! You wanted to run down to the engine-room, unscrew a porthole and hurl yourself into space to see what was happening on Earth..."

The old man was bewildered. "Me?" he murmured.

"Yes, you. A nightmare! You mean a fine bout of fever. Oh, you said such things...the Earth...the Sun...Pulkova Observatory...your instruments...the cold...the ice...the nebulas..."

"A true Russian salad, what!" exclaimed Flammermont.

"Yes...yes, I remember now..." And while his face suddenly lit up, as if inspired, Ossipoff cried: "Oh, I wouldn't give up the nightmare that's just tormented me for my entire life. It's God who sent it to me, to allow me to lift the mysterious veil with which Nature is enveloped....I've had foreknowledge of the end of worlds...I..."

Selena grasped the engineer's hand. "Calm him down, Monsieur Fricoulet," she begged. "The fever's taking hold again..."

"Let his speak. Trying to stop him would make him worse..."

Sitting up, his index-finger raised in a prophetic attitude, the old man stated talking. "No, nothing dies, but nothing is created...in universal Nature, matter and energy are indestructible. Since the creation of Worlds, not an atom of matter has been destroyed, not a parcel of potential energy has been lost. If, once planets were dead and Suns extinct, their dust remained inert and inactive, could the Universe have the appearance it presents to us...?" He paused, uttered a little sardonic laugh in response to the objections that his feverish imagination set ringing in his ears, and continued: "If that were the case, would the stars not have had sufficient time, since the epoch of their formation, to go out, leaving only the most recent, relative to the centuries elapsed, to shine? No, no...we aren't heading for the annihilation or the universal death of everything that we know! Creation is the law of Nature. What is the Creator's purpose? It's not given to our infinitesimal intelligence to perceive it, but Infinity is eternal!"

These final words had been shouted rather than spoken, in a hoarse voice; at the same time, exhausted by that supreme effort, he fell backwards, his head immobilized on the bolster, his face flushed, his eyes bulging, and his gaze wandering in space...

Selena leapt forward, but Fricoulet, gently pushing her to one side, calmly said: "Don't worry. The overexcitement will fade, and in a few hours, you'll be able to see him calm and smiling, as before. Go get a little rest. I can look after him for the time being."

"But you haven't slept for four days!" exclaimed the young woman.

Without saying a word, the engineer pushed her toward the door along with his two companions and then came back to take his place by the invalid's bedside.

Chapter LXI
The End of Everything

"Berenice, the daughter of King Ptolemy Philadelphius, had just married her own brother, Ptolemy Evergetes, when a war suddenly declared upon Seleucus, King of Syria, led to the separation of the two young spouses. In her distress, the princess promised to make a sacrifice of her hair to Venus if her husband returned victorious—and having made this vow to the goddess, Berenice cut off the most beautiful tresses that had ever graced a female head, with her own scissors, the day after Ptolemy's return, and took them to the temple of Venus. A few days later, though, that votive offering of an entirely new species had disappeared, doubtless stolen by some lover of the princess—unless the tresses had caught the eye of some wig-maker of the period, who saw it as material for the fabrication of superb hairpieces.

"Whatever had happened, it provoked an enormous scandal; Berenice's distress redoubled the fury that the theft occasioned in her husband, who was beside himself. To calm the royal couple slightly, it required an astronomer of the time named Conon, whose knowledge was greatly respected, to declare that the author of the larceny was none other than Venus herself—who, in order to honor the conjugal fidelity of which Berenice had given proof in sacrificing her hair, had carried the tresses into the heavens, where they shone in the form of stars.

"And in support of what he said, the astronomer showed the young spouses a new constellation—which, he affirmed, had just appeared. The result was that everyone was content and the spouses' self-regard was flattered. The thief was able to enjoy the fruits of the larceny in peace, and the astronomer received a nice gift by virtue of that pleasant deceit—and even the astronomers of the future were spared the trouble of choosing a name for that beautiful constellation, since they found it ready-traced and ready-baptized in the celestial globe by the Observatory of Alexandria."[141]

---

[141] Fricoulet has confused two Berenices, although it is not entirely his fault, the beginning of his story being quoted word-for word from chapter V of *Les Etoiles*. The daughter of Ptolemy Philadelphius was, indeed, called Berenice, but she married the Seleucid king Antiochus II Theos. The Berenice who married Ptolemy III Evergetes in the 3rd century B.C. was the daughter of Magas, King of Cyrene, so Ptolemy was not her brother. It was the latter Berenice who allegedly dedicated her hair to Venus and placed it in the temple in Zephyrium, from which it was stolen, causing Conon of Samos to improvise the relevant fantasy. The apocryphal story is derived from second-hand accounts of a narrative poem by Callimachus, of which only a few actual lines survive.

Having finished this story, in his characteristic satirical and skeptical tone, Fricoulet paused briefly and looked at Gontran. The latter, with his face to the telescope, seemed to be examining the constellation in question attentively—but in reality, his eyelids were shut.

"Are you asleep?" asked the engineer, in the most natural tone possible.

"Me?" exclaimed the young Comte, as if any such suggestion were offensive. "Not at all! I just closed me eyes for a moment in order to fix what you were telling me more firmly in my memory."

Fricoulet laughed. "And what was it, damn it? Would you care to forage in your memory for what it's necessary to see? You'll never become an astronomer by playing the blind man. What if Ossipoff takes it into his head to ask you for the results of your observations?"

"I'll tell him that Coma Berenices is situated below Canes Venatici, that it's formed by combining several stars that Tycho Brahe combined into a constellation in 1790...but that Tycho hadn't invented anything new, since...and I'll tell him the pretty story of conjugal fidelity that you've just told me..."

Gontran had recited all this in a single breath, in a monotonous tone of voice, like a child reciting a lesson learned parrot-fashion.

"All right—but if he asks you about the coloration of number 24 in Flamsteed's catalogue, will you be capable of answering?"

"Yes, since you've just showed it to me."

The engineer gave the telescope a slight push; it pivoted toward him and was then aimed in the direction of the constellation in question.

"Look now," he said. "What do you see?"

"Two stars, one projecting orange fire and the other radiating a lilac color."

"That's number 24. I draw your attention to number 42 not far away, similarly double, whose orbital motion is so rapid that the rotation of the two suns about their center of gravity only requires 25 years to complete. As a matter of detail, that revolution takes place exactly in the plane of our line of sight, so the motion is only visible in profile, with the effect that the two components hardly appear to be separate from one another. A little to the right, you can see number 35, a triple system which is only visible from Earth with the aid of powerful optical instruments..."

"Yes, I can see three stars. So what?"

"Nothing worth mentioning, except that they've rotated through 45 degrees in 70 years, which allows the duration of their complete revolution to be calculated as between 400 and 500 years..."

Hearing a noise of soft footsteps behind him, the engineer turned round and saw Selena, who was coming into the engine-room on tiptoe. "Well," he said, "how is he?"

"Better—he's woken up and wants to talk to Gontran."

The young Comte turned round, displaying a face so discontented that Mademoiselle Ossipoff was profoundly affected by it. "What's the mater now?" he could not help muttering between his clenched teeth.

"Don't worry," the young woman replied, sadly. "My poor father's coming to terms with his condition, and I don't think the conversation he wanted to have with you will revolve around astronomical questions."

Gontran became veritably anxious then, and said solicitously: "Is he falling ill again?"

"On the contrary; his mind is somewhat detached, the oppression in his chest has diminished, and he seems to be thinking quite clearly." At that moment, a sort of plaintive moan was heard coming from the stairwell, and Selena added: "My father's getting impatient. Are you coming, Monsieur Gontran?"

The latter looked at Fricoulet. "It won't augment or aggravate his illness?"

"I don't think so. In any case, it would be more dangerous still to annoy him. Go with Mademoiselle...I'm yours, and if Ossipoff wants to launch into scientific discussions, call a halt! As his doctor, I'll intervene."

Alas, Gontran's fears were chimerical; as Selena had told him, the old man, although better, was still suffering the effects of the cerebral crisis that had laid him low three days before, like an old tree felled by the woodcutter's axe. His eyes had, to be sure, recovery their lucidity, and an intelligent gleam had reappeared in his eyes, but his face was white, with hardly any more color than the white pillow on which his head was resting. His mouth was taut, his lips still blue, and his extraordinarily thin hands were immobile upon the bedspread.

At the sight of Flammermont, however, it seemed that the invalid's cheeks took on a hint of color—oh, very slightly—and his bony fingers sketched out a faint gesture of welcome. "Gontran...my son," the sick man stammered, in a voice as light as a breath, as the young man came closer. "Don't worry...I'm feeling better...much better. I'd like to ask you a favor."

"Go on, go on," said Flammermont, hastily.

The old man remained silent for a few moments, as if gathering his strength, then finally asked: "First of all, where are we?"

"On the fringes of Coma Berenices," said the Comte.

"Good...good," the old man murmured. "Then we can't be far from Bootes."

"We're approaching it rapidly, Monsieur Ossipoff," Fricoulet said, having remained on the threshold of the cabin until then. "But you shouldn't worry about such things for the moment, or it will slow down your recovery."

Ossipoff nodded his head weakly. "I know, I know," he stammered, "but while I'm here, we're going forward and I'm losing the opportunity to be able to study at close range the marvelous stars that one sees so imperfectly from Earth..." The old man had become animated, a vivid fire being displayed his cheeks and his eyes suddenly shining with an extraordinary brilliance.

“Monsieur Ossipoff,” Fricoulet said, authoritatively, “I absolutely forbid you to speak about these things, or even to think about them, and if I had known that you had asked to talk to Gontran for that…”

“No, no!” the old man exclaimed, desperately, like a littler boy forbidden to play with his favorite toy. He extended his trembling hands toward the young man, and stammered: “Gontran, my boy, my son…I only wanted to ask you to take notes in my stead.” His head suddenly falling backwards and his eyes vague, he began to speak as if in a fit of delirium: “Bootes, Corona Borealis, Serpens…”

Gontran hurriedly leaned over the bed.

“My dear Monsieur Ossipoff,” he said, “I promise to study the constellations we find on our route at close range, so well that, when you're better, you'll be able to imagine that you saw it all yourself…”

Already, though, the old man was incapable of listening; the fever had gripped him again and, while Fricoulet and Selena huddled around him—one bearing smelling salts and the other applying a cloth dampened with cold water continuously to his forehead—the old man started speaking again, very loudly, prey to an extraordinary state of exaltation. “Arcturus! Arcturus!” he exclaimed, while his index-finger, raised toward the ceiling, seemed to be pointing out in space the star that he saw his imagination, in default of his sight.

Mentally, Flammermont remembered two lines from Virgil, evoked by that name: *At sit non fuerit tellus fecunda, sub ipsam/Arcturum teniut sat eriot suspendere sulco.*”[142]

By some strange phenomenon of the association of ideas, he seemed to hear the voice of the professor of rhetoric commenting on these lines, explaining that in the time of Hesiod and Homer, Arcturus was consulted as an oracle of rural life, Virgil advised waiting for Bootes—in which Arcturus is the brightest star—to set before planting lentils and laboring, at times when Arcturus shone directly overhead. The astronomers of that remote era associated stars with agriculture and Arcturus was especially feared because its return often coincided with the storm season.

Gradually, however, Ossipoff's excitement declined and, thanks to his daughter's urgent care, a relative calm overtook him, to the extent that he closed his eyes and became drowsy. Then, at a sign from Fricoulet, Gontran went out of the cabin silently and went down to the engine-room, where the engineer soon joined him, bearing the various parts of the spectroscope, which he had dismantled.

“What's bad for some is good for others, you see,” Fricoulet said, fitting the pieces together again, “and Ossipoff's indisposition could not have happened

[142] The quote is from the *Georgics*; it translates roughly as “Should the land not be fruitful, it will suffice to plough it lightly on the eve of Arcturus' rising.”

at a more appropriate time to allow you to play your little role of bedroom astronomer without danger…"

"How odd it is," Gontran grumbled, "that the author of *Les Continents célestes* didn't say anything about the stars."

"Odd—no; on the contrary, perfectly logical. The stars are nothing to do with the planets. Besides, what does it matter, since you have me at hand and can riffle through my pages at your leisure…"

As Gontran greeted these words with a shake if the head, he engineer added, with a mocking laugh: "Yes, yes…I know how disagreeable it is for you to ask me, your rival, for the elements necessary to compete with me. But what can you do about it? That's the situation, and neither you nor I can change anything."

He had succeeded in setting up the spectroscope and, which busying himself getting it into position at the telescope, he continued: "First of all, you need to know that Bootes, one of the most ancient constellations in the heavens, has changed its name several times over the centuries. It has been called Arctophylon, or the Bear-keeper—by reason of its proximity to Ursa Major—Guardian of the North and the Crier. The Arabs, who saw the four stars of David's Chariot as the corners of a coffin, called it the Gravedigger, because it seemed to be marching behind a hearse."

"That's what they call gay astronomy!" Gontran quipped.[143]

"Arcturus—which is, with Vega, one of he most magnificent stars of the northern hemisphere, passed for a long time as one of the stars closest to the Earth, by virtue of its brightness—but when the astronomer Peters succeeded in determining its parallax in 1842, it turned out, on the contrary, to be very distant from our planet: about 60 trillion leagues…"

At that moment, Flammermont took off his cap, displaying his sweat-stained brow to the engineer. "God, it's hot," he murmured.

Fricoulet smiled and gently set aside the veil masking the porthole; immediately, a blinding light streamed through the opening, which inundated the engine-room. The two Terrans were dazzled for some seconds, even after the curtain—having fallen back into place—had restored the gloom.

"Arcturus!" said the engineer. "Without your perceiving it, I nudged the lever slightly, and we've been heading straight for the Gravedigger for a quarter of an hour. Now you can observe for yourself that its spectrum is identical to that of our own Sun, for here are the lines that betray the presence in that star of the very same metals." The engineer compelled his friend to lean over the apparatus. Underlining his explanations with demonstrations given with his finger, he

---

[143] The Occitan phrase "*le gai saber*" [the gay science] was once used in the south of France to refer to the art of the troubadours, whose songs were often devoted to mythological themes in a spirit of sly sarcasm and general skepticism.

went on: “Can you imagine the rapidity with which Arcturus is moving through space? You know that its displacement reaches 0.078 seconds in westward right ascension and southward declination and 1.97 in southern declination, which gives 2.26 seconds a year following a south-western arc of the circle. Well, can you grasp the logical consequences of that rapidity? Simply this: that in 800 years, Arcturus will have traveled a distance across the celestial analogous to the full Moon seen from Earth, and in several centuries, it will no longer belong to the constellations of the northern hemisphere. It will have crossed the equator and will be incorporated into the groups of the southern hemisphere.”

Gontran listen to all this with an attitude of absolute indifference; what did it matter to him, in fact, that Arcturus would some day belong to the southern hemisphere? In his eyes, it would be a thousand times better if it did not exist at all; that would have been one less torture to inflict on his memory.

“Arcturus,” Fricoulet continued, impassively, “is moving in the direction of an Earthly observer’s line of sight with a velocity of 66 kilometers a second; by adding that velocity to that of its displacement within the celestial vault, equal to 83 kilometers a second, we arrive at the jolly total of 149 kilometers per second, 8490 per minute…”

The young Comte shrugged his shoulders, muttering: “And how do you expect people to recognize it, with the stars continually in motion? The ancients’ constellations are no longer the same as ours…or, at least, are no longer in the same places. So what proves that they’re the same ones?”

Without paying any heed to his friend’s sally, the engineer took him by the arm and obliged him to put his eye to the lens, saying; “Instead of grumbling, admire Pulcherrima.”[144]

“What’s that?” asked the other, bewildered.

“The double star that you can presently see, with one of its two components bright golden-yellow and the other sea blue. That’s Epsilon, which Struve baptized with the name Pulcherrima. While you’re there, you can see Delta, half golden-yellow and clear lilac. Their originality lies in being fixed in relation to one another, although a rapid motion is drawing them both through space. It’s necessary to remember, among the curiosities of Bootes, star Ksi, formed by two orange-colored stars—a rather rare occurrence, for in nearly all doubles in which the principal Sun is yellow, the satellite is white, green or blue—star 44, Iota, curious for its inclination of 70 degrees to its orbital plane in the line of sight; and the fourth-magnitude star Mu, which is first doubled into two stars, of which the smaller is itself double. Then…”

This time, Gontran’s patience had run out; he stood up, folded his arms and exclaimed, angrily: “Do you imagine that I’m going to remember all that?

---

[144] Pulcherrima means “loveliest;” the Struve who thus “baptized” Epsilon Bootis, or Izar, was Wilhelm.

You've been talking for at least an hour, and we're still in the same constellation! Personally, I don't have any desire to go mad!"

"Do you want me to stop?" Fricoulet asked, quite calmly. "Personally, I don't have any vocation for the teaching profession…"

"Perhaps not—but you now have that of marriage," Flammermont riposted, slyly, calmed by these words as if by enchantment. He took his place again with angelic meekness. "Continue, my good Alcide," he said. "I'm all ears."

The engineer made a slight grimace, which betrayed the disappointment occasioned by his friend's sudden resignation. Then he took up his role and continued in a professorial tone: "Do you recall Ovid's verses, in which he tells the story of Bacchus hurling Ariadne's crown into the stars? No? Well, pretend that you do recall them, and remember that it's to that legend that the constellation Corona Borealis owes its name. Now, you might ask me why the Arabs gave that same constellation the name of the Pauper's Bowl…"

"No," said Gontran, "I won't ask you that, because I know."

"You know!" exclaimed Fricoulet, amazed.

"Perhaps I'm only a donkey in astronomical matters, but on the Quai d'Orsay it's generously recognized that I don't lack logic. That's why I imagine that there's a kind of beauty and virtue in these constellations relative to which every people has particular ideas, different from those of its neighbors. The Arabs see a bowl where the ancient Greeks saw a crown and the astronomers of the future will see some other figure."

The engineer nodded his head in approval and, after aiming the telescope, said to his friend: "Look now. The crown is formed by the five stars that you'll see in the field of the telescope."

"Not very big, the stars…" Gontran murmured.

"One of them, however…the one furthest to the right…is a tenth magnitude star which, on May 12, 1866—I'm being precise, as you see—increased to the second magnitude and then, in less than three weeks, reverted to its original insignificance."

"And since then?"

"Since then, it's remained stable. Anyway, the five stars I'm showing you are periodic variables."

"And how is that temporary brightness explained?"

"In the simplest possible manner. The flare is due to a mass of hydrogen suddenly exploding in the heart of the star, and it lasts for as long as the combustion of the hydrogen. But what's particularly curious is that, examined by a spectroscope, the ephemeral sun exhibited a kind of fog—a vaporous atmosphere that dissipated as the brightness faded. Similarly, two superimposed spectra were observed, one formed of a network of tightly-arranged black bands, the other of luminous bands—which proves that the light of the star comes from two different sources. A liquid or solid photosphere will be one of the sources, emitting light through absorbent vapors as in our Sun; the other source must be an incandescent gas—hydrogen, for example…"

"Do I need to remember that?" Gontran asked, finding the explanation a trifle confusing.

"As much as possible, because of the influence a similar conflagration might have on the humankinds of the worlds illuminated by our Sun. Imagine what would become of the Earth if, from one day to the next, the Sun's intensity increased to ten times that of a bright midday in July."

"All right," muttered the young Comte. "I'll do my best to remember…"

"Corona Borealis," Fricoulet continued, includes some fine specimens of double stars: Zeta, of the fourth magnitude, white and green; Sigma, white and blue; Eta…I'll skip that and better ones to get on to Hercules."

Flammermont took his friend's hands in his own and squeezed them effusively, exclaiming comically: "You're skipping! Oh, how good you are!"

Shrugging his shoulders, the engineer busied himself aiming the spectroscope at a star, and remained silent for several seconds, absorbed in his task. Afterwards, he summoned Gontran and said: "Let's see if you remember what I've taught you. Read a little of that spectrum for me."

The young man was silent for some time. "Secchi's third type, typical of red or orange stars…ribbed appearance; hydrogen bands inverted, luminous, with those of magnesium, sodium and iron very pronounced…"

"Very good; you've just established the characteristics of one of the most curious stars in Hercules, Alpha—a very strange Sun whose instability must, by virtue of its variations of heat and light, make life very difficult on the planets dependent on it. Let's not waste time searching for its satellite; just remember that it's very close and that its color is emerald green."

As Fricoulet paused at this point in his explanation, Flammermont asked, with a little smile of relief: "That's all, for Hercules?"

"You're in too much of a hurry. I haven't said anything yet about Kappa, a double that resembles Mizar and Alcor; number 95, golden yellow and bright blue; Delta, sky blue and violet; or Zeta, whose components gravitate around their common center in 34-1/2 years. Oh! One thing I forgot, which is very important, is that the constellation Hercules marks the point toward which the Sun and its planetary system are heading." He paused again, orientated the telescope, and simply said: "Look!"

In spite of his strong skepticism, Gontran could not retain and admiring gesture. A magnificent stellar mass had just appeared in the field of the instrument, which reminded him of the one in Centaurus: a myriad of luminous points that protected a sheaf of rays toward the vehicle, by which the young Comte was almost blinded.

"Well?" said Fricoulet, who had noticed his friend's gesture. "That's rather nice, isn't it? When you think that more than 5000 suns there, every one of which might be more voluminous than our own, you can get an idea of the distance that separates them from us." The engineer stifled a yawn, rubbed his eyes and, after a pause, got to his feet, adding: "Do you know what you ought to do? You ought to study Ophiuchus, Serpens and Ursa Major by yourself. I haven't slept for nearly 18 hours, and I feel an irresistible need..."

Gontran, who saw this simply as an excellent opportunity to "cut" his astronomy class, hastened to reply: "Go on, then, old chap. While you're asleep, I'll make use of the telescope..."

Fricoulet rummaged in his coat pocket and took out a small book with a badly worn and smudged cover, which he handed to his friend. "There! With that book, like a Joanne guide, you'll be able to circulate at your ease in the starry lands. But above all, don't simply amuse yourself by reading—check by means of the telescope. If not, you risk making enormous gaffes."

"Understood."

When the engineer had left the engine-room, Gontran set to work conscientiously. Supplementing his reading with the aid of the telescope, he succeeded, without too much difficulty, in writing brief notes which gave quite a good impression of true science.

After having remembered that Ophiuchus—which the cartographers personified as a fighter clutching a serpent—comprised all the stars scattered in the region of the sky situated to the south of Hercules, he reviewed the curiosities of the constellation: first, the variable stars, then Alpha, with its four suns, one of which belonged to Scorpius. On that subject, he established that the companion of the principal star took 840 years to complete its orbit; with respect to the orbital movements of two other groups, he estimated that it would require no less that several 100,000,000 years to complete them.

Thanks to the *vade mecum* Fricoulet had given to him, he confirmed Herschel's studies of group nmber 70, composed of two reddish stars revolving around one another with a period of 92 years 9 months, and observed that the orbit—which appears elliptical from Earth, deformed as it was by perspective—is circular. By means of the parallax that he found in Fricoulet's book, Gontran established that the distance of this star was 45 trillion leagues, and that its two components were about 1,100,000,000 leagues apart. The young man went even further in his observations and posited—based on the duration of its satellite's revolution—that the Sun weighs three times as much as the one illuminating the Earth, which is as much as 25,000 terrestrial globes put together. Passing on to the other curiosities of Ophiuchus, the book mentioned Lambda, whose very rapid orbital motion is completed in 233 years; Tau, which takes 218 years to trace its orbit; number 67, an orange couple; Rho and number 39, two couples colored yellow and blue.

With respect to Serpens, which Ophiuchus clutches, Flammermont noted several variable stars, a few binary systems and several stellar aggregations of which he found descriptions in the famous little book. "Ah!" he sighed, while writing, "Why didn't that imbecile Fricoulet give me this astronomical catechism sooner? It would have avoided a great many discussions…" He found the catechism so comfortable that, in order to terminate the duty imposed on him by Ossipoff's desire more rapidly, he contented himself with copying almost word-for-word what it said about Ursa Major, neglecting the recommendation made by the engineer that he make use of the telescope to check the accuracy of his reading. By way of compensation, however, he added a sketch to his notes traced from an illustration in the volume, which clearly depicted the details of Ursa Major.

"Oof!" he exclaimed, with an enormous sigh of relief, as he closed the book. "That's the homework done." And he threw his soft cap at the ceiling like a real schoolboy, a joyful manifestation entirely out of keeping with the habits of his diplomatic service. After that, he crept up the stairway, went into Ossipoff's cabin, gave the notes he had written to Selena—who was still sitting by her father's bedside—and then went to lie down in his hammock, where he was not long delayed in enjoying the sleep of a man whose conscience is clear.

When he woke up, he observed that Fricoulet's hammock was empty.

"I must have been asleep for a long time!" he murmured. He glanced at his chronometer and observed that the hour-hand had made a complete circle of the dial since he had gone to bed. "12 hours sleep! Astronomy must have a soporific effect on me!" Rubbing his hands together, however, he added in a satisfied tone: "Which doesn't alter the fact that the pill has been swallowed! And if Ossipoff isn't content…"

He had scarcely finished these words when the old man came into the cabin.

"You're up!" cried the young man, leaping down from his hammock and running toward the scientist. "What imprudence!"

"I'm feeling better," Ossipoff retorted, dryly. "Much better, even…but tell me…" He showed the creased papers he was holding in his hand to Gontran, who recognized them as his famous notes. "Is this really the result of the observations that I begged you to make?" asked the old scientist, aggressively.

"Yes," Gontran replied, gripped by a vague unease as he looked at his interlocutor's contracted features. "Aren't they satisfactory?"

"Yes and no. Certain parts are accurate, while others…"

"*Errare humanum est…*" the young man stammered.

Ossipoff leafed through the papers with a nervous hand and showed his interlocutor the drawing of Ursa Major.

"So what?" said the Comte. "It's Ursa Major."

"I can see that," retorted the other, a trifle sharply. "But it's not the constellation as you're able to see it from here."

Seeing himself caught *in flagrante delicto* in his ruse, Gontran preferred to say nothing, and contented himself with nervously caressing his moustache.

"Given our proximity in space, the perspective has changed and the disposition of the starts composing the constellation is no longer the same as it is when viewed from the Earth."

The young man maintained the same prudent mutism; one wrong word on the subject might have got him into even deeper trouble, so he elected to let Ossipoff continue his little lecture.

"Actually," dceclared the old man, haughtily, "the assemblage of suns that terrestrial astronomers see in face-on in the form of a quadrilateral, we perceive almost in profile, following a broken line. From our present position, moving faster than light, we see Ursa Major in the form of a gigantic cross..." Thinking, by virtue of a movement by Flammermont, that the latter wanted to check what he said with his own eyes, he exclaimed: "Oh, there's no need. If I tell you this it's because I know it, and if I know it, it's because I've established it visually...which you haven't done..."

The tone in which these last few words had been pronounced was imprinted with such sharpness that Gontran was tempted to dig his heels in. "If you'll permit me to say so, my dear Monsieur Ossipoff, it seems to me that you might proffer your explanations in a different manner. I'm not a schoolboy, damn it!"

"You're certainly not a schoolboy," riposted the old man. "If you were, I'd shrug my shoulders and tear up your drawing without attributing any more importance to the incident than it would then warrant—but you're a scientist, my collaborator, the continuer of my work, the man to whom I must entrust the care of my reputation..."

Vibrant with impatience, and containing himself with difficulty, the young man cried: "I'm very flattered, to be sure, by the honor you do me in confiding your reputation to me—if, however, you think it's in the wrong hands, you're free to go in search of others..." He pivoted on his heels, leaving the old man completely nonplussed by the reply, which he did not understand at all. On the threshold of the cabin, though, he was almost bowled over by Fricoulet, who was arriving in haste.

"You're going," said the engineer. "Stay..." His voice was trembling slightly and his face was pale. "Oh, Monsieur Ossipoff," he added, heading for the old man. "You're up—so much the better! I have something to ask you..."

The silhouette of Farenheit appeared in the doorway. His face was anxious and his eyes wandering.

"Speak, young man," said Ossipoff, with a dignity full of condescension, "and if I can be of any use to you..."

"You can be useful to everyone at the same time, for if I'm not mistaken..." Catching sight Selena, however, who was looking at him in an anguished fashion, trying to guess the news he was bringing, he took the old man by the arm, drew him into a corner of the cabin and leaned toward him, whispering in his ear: "If I'm not mistaken, we're in great danger..."

"Oh!"

"The greatest danger we've run since the beginning of our voyage..."

"What do you mean?"

"This—last night, while on watch, I observed perturbations in the *Eclair*'s progress."

The old man started. "Perturbations!" he repeated. "The *Eclair*'s no longer on course?"

"No, I tell you—and I tried in vain to bring it back into line. It's obedient to a force I can't explain...I even bent a lever."

Ossipoff's face darkened. "That's serious," he murmured.

"So I wanted to ask you what our exact position is—for it might well be that, without being aware of it, we're in proximity to some world whose influence is making itself felt on the *Eclair*.

Ossipoff reflected momentarily. "We're exactly on Earth's equator," he said, "between the small constellations Scutum Sobieski and Antinous; as for the nearest star whose mass might disturb our progress, I can't think of any except for the Sun situated in the center of the Great Nebula in Scutum."

Fricoult was perplexed. "That's exactly what I observed—but we're more than a trillion leagues away from the Nebula, and I don't think the danger can come from there..."

Although the old man had a certain fondness for the engineer, because of the care he had given him, he only considered him an apprentice in science, especially in astronomy; it was, therefore, with a slightly incredulous smile that he asked: "Are you quite certain that we've gone astray?"

"We haven't gone astray, Monsieur Ossipoff—we're falling. We're falling with lightning rapidity."

The old man turned to his telescope and said: "I'll verify what you've told me—for if what you've told me is true, there's only the Nebula in Scutum that might be capable..."

"Despite its enormous distance?"

"Yes, despite its enormous distance." And having said that, as placidly as if he were installed in Pulkova Observatory, Ossipoff sat down and began his observations.

Meanwhile, seeing the engineer alone, his companions came over to him.

"What's happening now?" Farenheit complained.

"Come on, talk," said Gontran, in his turn. "We're men, damn it! We've suffered so many injuries in the last three years that one more or less..."

Catching sight of the glance by which Fricoulet directed his interlocutors' attention to her, however, Selena exclaimed: "Oh, don't worry about me, Monsieur Fricoulet. I hope I've given you enough proof of courage for you not to hesitate to tell me the truth."

Then, making a forceful effort to hide the emotion that took hold of him in spite of everything, the engineer said: "My God! My good friends, what is happening to us at present is what happens to moths that have the imprudence, on summer evenings, to fly around lighted candles. We're in dire danger of being burned."

"Burned!" exclaimed the Americanm. "By God! By what?"

"By a star toward which we've been diverted, several hours ago, with an incredible velocity..."

"That's no reason to be burned," Flammermont retorted. "The only risk we're running is that of being forced to land on a new world. Well, it'll be one more port of call, that's all."

"That's all," repeated Farenheit, for whom Gontran still possessed a scientific halo.

This fine confidence cheered the engineer up. "I'd like to know how we'd have landed on the Sun," he said, sarcastically. "We would, I think, have been roasted twice over. What am I saying? Roasted! Volatilized, I meant to say..."

"There's no proof that the star in question is a sun."

"You're right. There's no proof that it's a sun—it might be several suns!" He put his hands in his coat pockets and added: "For my part, I tell you frankly that we're in the worst situation we've been in since our departure from Earth. If, in spite of its velocity, the *Eclair* can't fight the force that's attracting it, the mass of the star must be colossal." He consulted his watch and said, in the most natural tone in the world: "Anyway, there's no point in racking our brains, or even arguing; within ten hours, our fate will be decided..."

"Because?"

"Because, at the rate at which we're traveling, that's when we'll penetrate the planetary system that the sun in question serves as a center." At that moment, seeing Osipoff get up from his stool as if his legs contained springs that had suddenly been released, he went over to him, his lips opening to interrogate him.

Before he had pronounced a syllable, though, the old man had seized his hands and said, in a tremulous voice: "You were right. Monsieur Fricoulet."

"In that case, what do you think?"

Ossipoff's gaze turned to Selena; large tears rolled down his wrinkled cheeks, and the engineer heard him murmur: "She's doomed..." Then, without saying anything else, he extracted himself from the clasp that joined his hands to Fricoulet's and returned to his telescope. His insatiable curiosity was more powerful than the anguish caused by the death that was lying in wait for the person dearest to him in all the world.

"Well?" asked Gontran and Farenheit, simultaneously.

Fricoulet's lips creased into a moue that implied many things. He looked for Selena, but the young woman had quietly slipped away, as if she already knew what her father had said to the engineer, and was now on her knees on the floor in a corner of the cabin, her hands joined together, her eyes fixed on a soiled, creased and faded holy image that she had succeeded in saving from all the catastrophes that had overtaken them since the commencement of their voyage.

"Poor mite," the engineer said, in a low voice, full of sincere pity. "That's the best thing for her to do."

"Is there truly no more hope?" asked Farenheit.

With a gesture of his head, the engineer signaled to his two companions to follow him and went down to the engine-room.

"You want to know the truth, don't you?" he said. "Anyway, you're men and I don't see why you should display any less stoicism than that young woman. Well, yes, we're doomed."

The other two remained silent, as if crushed by this declaration.

"Bah!" Fricoulet exclaimed, then, his insouciant character gaining the upper hand again. "There's nothing to prove, at this moment, that we won't be saved again in a little while! It wouldn't be the first time that some such surprise had cropped up. Natural phenomena are so strange that one never knows..."

"That's true," stammered Farenheit, clinging to hope.

"Besides," the engineer went on, shrugging his shoulders philosophically, "if we have to die—and everyone has to do it, don't they—it's better to be roasted, or rather volatilized, than to suffer the torments of hunger and thirst..."

"Charming," muttered the American. "That's not the question—and we don't have that alternative..."

"I beg your pardon. In a week, we'd no longer have a drop of nutritive liquid, or a molecule of compressed air. Thus, we'd be condemned to die of starvation and asphyxia...two chances instead of one of never coming back..."

"But in a week, we could have been back home!" Gontran suggested.

Fricoulet looked at his friend and burst out laughing. Then he clapped him on the shoulder, saying: "Unfortunately, old chap, the attractive force of the Town Hall of the eighth arrondissement can't compete with that of the sun toward which we're heading..."

Flammermont pulled a face. "Ah, the Town Hall of the eighth..." he murmured.

"You've had enough!" exclaimed the engineer, joyfully. "You're passing the hand..."

The other looked at him furiously. "What reason is there for you to say that?" he complained. "Whether I've had enough or not hardly matters, since it will all be over in ten hours..."

The engineer raised his index finger. "Unless," he said, "a miracle..."

"Unfortunately, we're not in the time of Christ, nor that of the fairies..." Gontran made a nervous movement of the head and added: "And after all," he said, "perhaps there's a bright side..."

"What do you mean?" asked the surprised engineer

"I mean that Selena is very charming, even adorable, but that father of hers..." He raised his arms despairingly, waving his clenched fists in the air. "Oh, that father!" he growled.

"If one could only make two lots, eh?" sniggered Fricoulet. "Take the daughter and leave the father...unfortunately, it's necessary to take on the whole..."

"Or nothing," Gontran let slip, his friend's jokes beginning to annoy him somewhat. Suddenly, Flammermont leaned toward his friend, looked him straight in the eyes, and said "Zut!" full in his face—and after that energetic declaration, he went to sit down in a corner, and stayed still.

Not at all offended by this manifestation of ill humor, Fricoulet was still smiling, secretly satisfied and thinking: It's coming, it's coming...if only luck permits us to return to Earth, I don't think my friend Gontran will be making the acquaintance of the tricolor sash of the Mayor of the eighth."

It was at that moment that Farenheit, tugging on his sleeve, asked him: "Do you really think that we might be able to get out of this?"

Fricoulet, annoyed at being interrupted in the midst of such pleasant thoughts, cried "*Zut!*" in his turn—and then went to take his place at he telescope installed at the back of the engine-room.

As the hours went by, as brief for the voyagers as if they lasted no longer than quarter-hours—the apparent disk of the star identified by Fricoulet grew, so to speak, visibly. Its light and heat increased at the same time, with the result that the travelers inside the vehicle endured frightful suffering, constrained to close their eyes in spite of the fabric masking the portholes, which was powerless to tame the penetrating glare of the blinding rays.

Only Ossipoff and Fricoulet, with incredible persistence, remained steadfast at their observation-posts, wanting to look the danger in the face—and that danger became increasingly inevitable with every passing second; the fiery globe now presented the dimensions of the full Moon as seen from Earth, and a blood red light inundated the *Eclair*'s interior. The thermometer, which had marked ten degrees Centigrade only two hours earlier, now stood close to 45! What would that become, when the apparatus had entered the photosphere?

In spite of themselves, the Terrans had shaken off their torpor; with their faces stuck to the portholes, they considered the incandescent maw of the frightful furnace that was opening as if to swallow them. In the meantime, the vehicle's speed continued to increase, and before the voyagers were able to take account of it, the *Eclair* was borne away in a veritable whirlwind of flame.

But then, just as they though they were lost, the scene suddenly changed. A thick blue cloud interposed itself between the gulf and the apparatus, which was bathed in violet light; they had just penetrated the Great Nebula of Scutum, and were passing through it with hurricane speed, falling vertiginously toward the center of gravity, while the phosphorescent nebula radiated livid blue electric sparks—a grandiose and sinister spectacle, away from which the fascinated Terrans could not tear their eyes.

An eruption of flames 100,000 kilometers high was launched from the solar furnace, which now occupied the entire horizon. A rain of fire fell back upon the incandescent disk, which was agitated by tumultuous movements like an ocean in fusion, hollowed out in certain spots by maelstroms of liquefied matter vaporized by the ambient atmosphere.

The vehicle was surrounded by sparks, flaming like a beacon.

This time, it was really death: absolute and final annihilation! The superhuman adventures of these audacious explorers of the eternal void were about to end in the photosphere of an as-yet-unknown star, which would consume the *Eclair* and its passengers in less than a second—and the terrestrial astronomers who would perceive that new world in the field of their telescopes, 50,000 years hence, would never suspect that the nimbus of radiant light with which it was surrounded was the tomb of those glorious souls!

Chapter LXII
In which the scientific world rejoices—and Fedor Sharp too.

No other meteoric phenomenon has ever frightened humankind as much as bolides and comets.

It has to be admitted that, at first sight, the uniformity of the heavens seems to be disturbed by the unexpected arrival of these bodies, and that is why the ancients regarded comets as frightful monsters, precursors of the most frightful cataclysms—the death of some great man, a bloody war, or even the end of the world. With respect to the last named scourge, at least a dozen predictions of this sort can be cited, most notably in 1456, 1538, 1577, 1680, 1770, 1833, 1857, and even in 1872.

In 1456, three years after the Turks had taken the city of Constantinople, putting everything to fire and the sword, sowing dread that the last days of Christianity were nigh, an immense comet suddenly appeared—a certain indication, in everyone's eyes, of divine wrath. To avert the danger and implore the Lord's mercy, Pope Callixtus III ordered that all the bells in Christendom should be rung at midday, in order that the faithful, gathering at the same hour, should pray to God with one voice. That, it is said, was the origin of the Angelus.

Can one have any idea now of the impact made by the comet of 1538 on minds that were certainly not among the most vulgar? This is what Ambroise Paré—one of the most intelligent men of the era, from the scientific viewpoint—said:

"This comet was so terrifying and engendered such great panic in the vulgar that some died of fright and others fell ill. It appeared to be exceedingly long, and the color of blood. At its head, the figure of a curved arm was seen, holding a large sword in its hand, as if it were about to strike. At its tip there were three stars; on both sides of the comet's tail were seen a great number of axes, daggers and bloody swords, among which were perceived hideous human faces with beards and bristling hair."

One may judge, on the basis of this description due to an enlightened mind, the effect that must have been produced on the naturally credulous imagination of laymen by the sudden appearance in the sky of an unknown star.

In the last century, once again, a general panic shook minds in the wake of the publication by the observer Lalande of a pamphlet in which the scientist announced the probability of a collision of a comet with the Earth. Humankind, misunderstanding the import of this work, thought that the astronomer was predicting the end of the world, and Lalande, by order of the king, was obliged to publish a second pamphlet designed for lay readers, in which he forcefully refuted the prediction attributed to him.[145]

Even in the course of the present century, did not a profound emotion take possession of people in 1833, in the wake of a communication made to the scientific world by a well-known astronomer, Monsieur Damoiseau?[146] He had calculated that Biela's comet would intersect the Earth's orbit at midnight on October 29, and the public had concluded therefrom that the end of the world was nigh, because the Earth was bound to be pulverized by the collision. The scientist's calculations were correct, but Monsieur Damoiseau had forgotten to mention—a scientist cannot think of everything—that on October 29 the Earth would not be at the point through which the comet would pass, and would not arrive there until the thirtieth of November, which would leave a fairly respectable distance of more than 20,000,000 leagues between the two worlds.

Although the general level of education has been considerably raised, especially in the second half of the century, fear of the world ending due to the impact of a comet has been manifest several more times, notably in 1857. A hoaxer had advertised the return of the great comet of Charles V[147] and its impact with the Earth for June 13 of that year; rural populations were plunged into genuine alarm, and even in Paris there was terrified talk of the imminent cataclysm. Some people, mistaking Venus for the body in question—which did not deign to show itself, in spite of the predictions—even maintained that they had seen the comet's tail.

Today, thanks to the ever-increasing popularization of scientific knowledge, scarcely anyone worries any longer about the possibility of a cometary impact, even though—rationally speaking—there would be nothing impossible in one of these long-haired wandering bodies colliding with our globe in its passage, staving it in, pulverizing it or, at the very least, poisoning all humankind with the injurious exhalations of its caudal atmosphere.[148] If that is the situation

---

[145] As with almost all of the information in this passage, the account of the panic accidentally provoked by Jérôme Lalande (1732-1807) in his comments on the return of Halley's comet in 1759 is paraphrased from the first part of Flammarion's *La Fin du monde.*

[146] Marie-Charles Damoiseau (1768-1846).

[147] The "*grand comète de Charles-Quint*" was so-called because it appeared in the year of that king's abdication, 1556. The reference to a hoaxer is a trifle unfair; the comet's return had been predicted on the basis of its presumably-erroneous but not entirely unreasonable speculative identification with a 13th century comet.

[148] This is rather disingenuous; many popularizers of science—especially Camille Flammarion—loved to play up the melodramatic implications of scientific discovery, and frequently celebrated the awful possibility of cometary collision, just as the authors do here, in frank contradiction of their own assertion.

here, though—if our rural populations, even those furthest away from great centers, are more worried about black clouds presaging rain at harvest-time than about more-or-less long-haired comets identified by our powerful observational instruments—there are countries in Europe that the exact notions of science have not yet penetrated and where the popular mind is no more advanced than ours was in the Middle Ages. Thus, one can imagine the emotion that the emotion that took hold of the central and eastern provinces of Russia when the presence in the sky of a new star was suddenly noticed, shining with an unsustainable glare, followed by a vaporous appendage, apparently heading for the Sun.

It was a parish priest in Orenburg, a man of considerable education who had some notion of astronomical science, who discovered the brilliant dot on chancing to lift his eyes toward the celestial vault, in the direction of Bootes. The observation might not have had any scientific result, if chance had not dictated that the Imperial College of Orenburg had an intelligent man for its rector, who was a passionate admirer of heavenly things and was therefore the possessor of a small telescope, with the aid of which he loved to study the worlds of Infinity.

Thanks to his telescope, the worthy Ivan Zarichkine observed that the body identified by the parish priest was a rapidly-moving planetary globe apparently belonging to the cometary species...unless it was simply a bolide passing across the sky. Whatever it was, he thought it his duty to call the attention of the scientific world to the event, all the more so because it could only assist his advancement; without delay, he telegraphed the results of his summary observation to St. Petersburg.

It was about 10 p.m., and the worthy Streiloff, the director of Pulkova Observatory, coming back from a soirée, was exchanging his black suit for the work clothes in which he spent part of every night, when the telegram from the rector of Orenburg was handed to him. Imagine his emotion! A new comet had risen over the horizon of the Empire of the Tsars! What news! And what consequences might the news have, for him, first of all—for the Emperor would doubtless compensate him handsomely for such a discovery—and then for science. His first impulse was to summon his personnel, astronomers and pupils, and having announced the fact to them, to order them to verify it. His second impulse, however—in conformity with a perfectly natural and understandable egotism—was not to say anything to anyone. Quite the contrary; he went to the cupola, benevolently told the pupils gathered there to go to bed, and then, left alone, took possession of the great equatorial, which he aimed in the direction indicated.

The first part of *La Fin du monde*, which describes a hypothetical scientific conference urgently convened to assess the likely consequences of exactly such an impending impact, initially appeared in a popular periodical and was rapidly translated for similar publication in the USA.

He had been observing for scarcely a quarter of an hour, with the aid of his great experience, when he found it; the supposed comet was heading directly for the Earth and it seemed to have accelerated considerably—but it was only a bolide, whose nucleus seemed to measure no more than half a kilometer in diameter, presenting a very irregular form, surrounded by a vague nebulosity. Continuing his study, he established the body's trajectory through space and observed that it was parabolic, terminating in the Sun, due to intersect the Earth's orbit at about one o'clock in the morning. At the moment when the rector of Orenburg College had telegraphed, the bolide's distance certainly could not have been less than several thousand leagues, in the direction of Persia, but it was diminishing incessantly, and there might come a moment…

An unpleasant frisson ran down the astronomer's spine at the thought of a possible collision between that errant world and his native planet, but he was a true scientist and, immediately detaching his mind from internal preoccupations, he continued his work. The trajectory extending from south-east to north-west, the respectable Streiloff estimated that the bolide in question had passed 2200 leagues over the zenith of Orenburg at about 8:30 p.m., 1380 leagues above Simbirsk at 9515 leagues above Nizhny-Novgorod at 9:30 p.m., and 310 leagues over Kostroma at 10:10 p.m. The scientist glanced at the clock; the hands stood at exactly 11 p.m., and he wrote that that body was passing over Vologda at that very moment, at a height of less than 40 leagues.

This observation of rapidly-diminishing distance nearly plunged the worthy man yet again into a state akin to terror; it would be 12:45 a.m. when the bolide passed over Olonetz, from which it would be no more than 60,000 meters distant—but he released a sigh of satisfaction when his calculations established that the vertical distance of the body would then begun to increase progressively. Escaping at a tangent, by eight o'clock in the morning it would be 1500 leagues above the North Pole, and from there it would resume its route into space. The scientist now knew enough to have acquired the uncontested priority of the discovery, and he immediately pushed the buttons connected to the electric bells established in the rooms in which the observatory's scientific personnel were lodged.

A quarter of an hour later, he announced the great news to the professors and pupils gathered around him and, having read them the succinct notes he had made in the course of his rapid observation, he invited them one by one to cast a glance over the new star, adding: "Its velocity is at least 20,000 meters a second, but as its motion is directly toward the Earth, it will seem very slow relative to the ground."

In a very short time however, the bolide had grown to extraordinary dimensions, and its glare had simultaneously acquired an incredible intensity. At the moment when it appeared to the rare individuals who were going home after spending part of the night dancing, it must have seemed to be falling vertically upon the capital of all the Russias. That gave rise to an emotion that spread throughout the city well before dawn, gluing the faces of the most curious to their widows and causing the majority of the fearful and superstitious population to kneel before icons.

As for the worthy Streiloff and the other astronomers of Pulkova, they had emerged from the cupola. Leaning on the rampart of the balcony that circled the summit of the observatory, they were following the progress of the strange body through the silent heavens with increasing interest.

Suddenly, it seemed that a cataclysm occurred on the surface of that mysterious world; one might have thought that it came apart, jets of greenish light springing from the central nucleus along with twisting orange flames enveloped by the black spirals produced by a sort of murky smoke. Abruptly, like a candle going out, the luminous trail following the body was extinguished.

They all stood still, looking up, open-mouthed and wide-eyed, stupefied and disappointed. "The comet! Evaporated! Dissolved!" murmured a pupil, searching the part of the sky that the bolide had occupied only a few seconds before in vain. At the same moment, the people gathered there perceived something like the feeble echo of a distant cannonade, and a handful of shooting stars streaked the dark curtain of the night with jets of flame.

"There's the firework display!" concluded Professor Streiloff—and as those surrounding him looked at him, seemingly inquiring about his sentiments regarding the strange, seemingly-inexplicable event, he added, speaking professorially: "The shooting stars? Pooh—fragments torn from the bolide's principal mass by the Earth's gravity and brought to incandescence by the friction of the atmospheric layers. They'll doubtless fall not far from here, and we'll undoubtedly hear talk of them tomorrow. As for that sort of cannonade, it was certainly due to the fragmentation of the bolide—and that's it! On that note, gentlemen, you can go to bed." And having wished them goodnight, he went back to his own apartment—where he went to bed forthwith, to sleep the sleep of a man who has not been wasting his time.

Perhaps that sleep would have taken a little longer to arrive if the scientist had been able to suspect what had really happened to the star that had just taken up a part of his evening—especially if he had been able to anticipate the strange events that the following day had in store for him.

More fortunate than Monsieur Streiloff, our readers will have no need to wait 24 hours before satisfying their curiosity; however, in order to understand the bizarre events that were soon to revolutionize the world of science, it is necessary for them to return with us, going back in time and into space to rejoin the cometary fragment on which we left Fedor Sharp riding through the celestial worlds.

It will be remembered that the last time we had occasion to occupy ourselves with the former permanent secretary of the Institute of Sciences was the moment of the *Eclair*'s impact with the item of comet wreckage carrying him. He had searched the entire surface of the Mercurian hill of which the shell—

Osipoff's famous shell—formed the summit for the slightest trace of the body whose impact had upset everything within his habitation, but in vain, and he had concluded from the negative result of his research that the foreign bolide had penetrated deeply enough into the Tuttle fragment for the crust, vitrified by heat, to have closed over it again. He might have tried to dig down to it, but, apart from the fact that he lacked the necessary tools, his strength was diminishing every day, and he preferred to conserve his remaining supplies of breathable air in order to eke it out until the moment when he might be able to return to Earth. It was with terror that he observed that he only had a few kilos of nutritive pills in his stores and 50 cubic meters of oxygen in the reservoirs.

Once the bolide had crossed the orbit of Jupiter, however, Fedor Sharp extracted himself with an extraordinary energy from the coma-like state in which he had been immobilized for several moments; he recovered all his strength and all his presence of mind and began to think about the mechanism of salvation that he needed in case Providence gave him an opportunity to return to his native soil.

He set about calculating—with the most rigorous precision—the perturbations of every sort that the various planets into whose proximity he was bound to pass might cause to the progress of his asteroid, and he succeeded in establishing, with absolute precision, the exact moment when he would have to abandon the Tuttle fragment on which he had lived for so long, by one means or another, no matter what the cost.

The calculations to which he had devoted himself had demonstrated to him that *Russia*—as he had baptized his bolide—would not strike the Earth, and that, in consequence, he had nothing to fear from any collision between the two bodies; they would pass one another at a distance of more than 60 kilometers; after that, *Russia* would resume its flight through space forever. It was, therefore, necessary for him to find a means of separating himself from it at the precise moment when that minimum distance was attained, and it was the discovery of that means to which the inventive mind of the former permanent secretary applied itself for many days.

Finally he arrived at the conclusion that only a parachute could get him out of trouble—a parachute from which he could suspend himself at the opportune moment, in order to return to the surface of his native planet. A descent of 60 kilometers was certainly considerable, and there was a strong probability that Fedor Sharp might break something, but between two evils, wisdom recommends choosing the lesser, and as he had no choice but to attempt that bold means or continue on into space again....

Having taken everything into account and examined the situation from every angle, Sharp realized that the best way was to separate himself entirely from the cometary fragment and land alone; otherwise, the initial rapidity with which the parcel to which he was attached would fall, and the consequent violence of the impact would be fatal. He did not want to return to his native soil only to be buried in it, but to harvest the glory due to his long and perilous endeavors.

It was, therefore, on the idea of a parachute that he settled: a parachute from which he would suspend himself at the desired moment—which is to say, when *Russia* had attained the point nearest to the Earth. We have already said that this point, according to the scientist's calculations, would be 60 kilometers from the planet. A descent of 60 kilometers would be quite something, and in any other circumstances...but first of all, it was necessary for him to think of a means of detaching himself from the attraction of the bolide, whose velocity would be no less than 20 kilometers a second, and which would keep him stuck to its surface forever if he could not withdraw himself brutally from its gravitational influence.

Having calculated the force of resistance of he very thin gaseous layer that surrounded the asteroid, he estimated that it was nevertheless sufficient to serve as a point of support for rockets that would permit him to rise into space.

Once this decision was irrevocably taken, Sharp got to work without delay; he emptied the shell's storage lockers of all the fabrics they contained, whatever their nature—blankets, sheets, coats, skirts and so on—and had stitched it all together, perhaps less elegantly than a Parisian seamstress but with sufficiently solidity to defy any competition. It formed a variegated assemblage vaguely comparable to a Harlequin costume, into which he then stitched spindle-like bands, which he joined together, giving him a multicolored orb vaguely reminiscent of a vast umbrella some eight meters in diameter. This became the principal element of his parachute, to the center of which he firmly attached a circle of wood made from a supple branch stripped from one of the trees on the Mercurian hill. To this circle he fixed four cords about a dozen meters long, designed to sustain a simple and slender wooden plank to serve as a seat. 24 other cords, connected to the seams of the fabric spindles, came together at the plank to prevent the parachute turning over in the course of its descent by virtue of the effects of air resistance and turbulence.

Once the parachute was finished, Sharp went on to the improvisation of the rockets designed to lift him up and free him from the weak gravitational attraction of the worldlet that carried him. All the paper and cardboard contained in Ossipoff's shell—except, of course, for the voluminous notebooks forming the scientific journal compiled by the astronomer—were employed in the fabrication of a monstrous cartridge measuring nearly a meter and a half in height and 30 centimeters in diameter, similar in every respect, save for its dimensions, to those that serve pyrotechnicians as firework-display rockets.

Once the envelope was fabricated—which took more than a week—it was necessary to fill it, and it was no easy matter for the scientist to compile the explosive mixture of 16 parts potassium nitrate, ten parts pure charcoal and four parts powdered sulfur.

The potassium nitrate he was able to extract easily enough; the shell's stores contained a certain provision of selenite, the explosive Ossipoff had invented in order to reach the Moon, and as potassium nitrate was one of the components of selenite, Sharp was able to leach it out, after which he crystallized it.

The fabrication of charcoal was more difficult, and cost him the greater part of the oxygen that he had been conserving so parsimoniously for many weeks, scarcely breathing in order to make his stock last as long as possible. He broke up all of the vehicle's items of interior furniture that he had not yet used to feed his stove and tore out the floors and the partition walls. He stacked up all of this material and set a fire, following the procedure of the charcoal-burners of Morvan, and, having lit it, alimented it with pure oxygen from the reservoir. In less than ten hours Fedor Sharp obtained about two bushels of very pure charcoal, in the form of bluish-black broken crystals, which he then crushed between two stones until he had reduced it to a thick powder.

With these two elements, which he mixed with four kilograms of powder forgotten at the bottom of a barrel,[149] the scientist compounded his explosive mixture; that done, he proceeded to pack his cartridge. He began by placing an iron rod inside, along the axis of the rocket, around which he heaped his mixture of powder, saltpeter and charcoal; after that, he replaced the metal rod with a long cotton wick improvised from the unraveled threads of his last shirt and impregnated with powder. The role of this wick was to set fire to the mixture instantaneously, along its entire length.

When this last operation was concluded, the amateur firework-maker wrapped his cartridge in cord and attached it thereby to the "stick" indispenable to ensure the perfectly vertical direction of the pyrotechnic device. Sharp fabricated this "stick" from one of Comet Tuttle's young trees; it measured no less than 20 centimeters in diameter and ten meters in length. The ring of the parachute was suspended from its extremity, by means of an iron hook.

At one of the corners of the polyhedron that constituted the voyager's entire domain stood the thin and leafless skeleton of another tree desiccated by solar heat and burned by the cold of space. It was the trunk of this tree, as straight as a mast, that Sharp used as a guide and support for his gigantic rocket; it was sufficient for this purpose to embed an iron spike in the end of the trunk, to which he fixed his rocket, with the fuse extending down to the ground. It would only require a spark for that fuse to catch fire and transmit the combustion almost instantaneously to the heart of the explosive mixture with which the cartridge was packed.

---

[149] *Poudre* [powder] would normally refer to gunpowder, which is what Sharp is trying to fabricate, so the reference here is presumably to the powdered sulfur identified in the initial recipe and necessary to the explosive mixture as a primer—although it seems far more likely that the shell's supplies would include ready-made gunpowder than a barrel of powdered sulfur.

These things, apparently so simple, which we have taken only a few lines to describe, took Fedor Sharp almost two months to accomplish. In addition to his lack of experience and the extreme awkwardness of his fingers, he did not possess any of the tools necessary to such specialized manufacture, and he could only proceed in a fumbling manner. Thus, when the parachute was rigged up and set in place, he could not help uttering a profound sigh of relief.

He was veritably exhausted, not being used to manual labor, even without taking into account the fact he only made use of his respirol with the greatest parsimony and only ate as a last resort. It was with veritable terror that he took out of the stores every morning what he would need during the day by way of air and nourishment, asking himself with ever-increasing anxiety whether a moment might arrive when his lungs and his stomach would both run out of sustenance. If that moment were to arrive before the point fixed for his departure from the asteroid was reached, he was doomed, and his cadaver would go on into space forever—so he lived in squalid avarice, breathing little and, so to speak, not eating at all.

When everything was ready and he returned to the shell, he fell rather than sat down on the floor, where he remained semiconscious for long hours, trying in vain to get a grip of himself, to tame his flesh in order to be able to continue the fight to the last possible second. He sought in vain to examine his instruments and make the calculations necessary to set himself on the path that still remained for him to travel; his cerebral anemia was such that he could not contrive to do it for several hours. When, by sheer will-power, he succeeded in finding sufficient lucidity to hold a pencil, he uttered a veritable cry of despair on determining that he still had a week to wait.

A week—and even by exercising the greatest possible parsimony, he only had supplies for four days! This was the ruination of his hopes, then—it was a sentence of death!

He reduced his rations of food and air by half; he condemned himself, in order to breathe less, to absolute inactivity. In order not to have to move, he placed the infinitesimal quantity of aliments that remained to him within arm's reach. He had to have the courage—even though an intolerable hunger was tormenting his entrails—not to devour them all in one go. He wanted to live, though, and in spite of the hunger, in spite of the thirst that was desiccating his throat, and in spite of the slow asphyxia to which he was subjected by the absorption of increasingly rarefied and increasingly polluted air, he lived.

Finally, the moment arrived when the terrestrial planet filled the entire horizon with its disk, like an enormous cannonball, and Sharp, whose dull eyes were following the march of the hands of his chronometer, suddenly felt a frisson of joy run through all his limbs. In 45 minutes, *Russia* would attain the point that Sharp's calculations had fixed as the closest to the Earth. Even though the attempt he was about to make might perhaps prove fatal, he waited for the moment of departure with ever-increasing impatience.

Suddenly, miraculously, it was as if his strength were galvanized; hunger, thirst and the tortures of asphyxia were forgotten! This was not a moment to allow himself to fall prey to discouragement or weakness. He needed to be strong, and he would be. Having put all the breathable air that remained to him into the rubber reservoir with which his respirol was equipped, he carefully fastened the straps of the apparatus over his shoulders and slipped outside the shell.

The sky was an absolute inky black, the Earth hiding the Sun—except that a vague luminosity floated in space: the reflection of the soft light of the Moon, then in its first quarter, bathing the surface of the asteroid. It was a strange spectacle, full of poetry. In any other circumstances, it would certainly have caught and held the astronomer's gaze; for the moment, though, he had too many preoccupations in his head even to think of sending an amicable salute to the lunar world that he had visited in such strange circumstances three years before.

He crept slowly toward the tree to which his rocket was attached, guiding himself with the aid of a lantern, which was consuming the last remnant of the shell's oil supply. It was with the flame of that lantern that he had to light the fuse whose ignition would set fie to the explosive mixture in the cartridge. The fuse had been designed to burn for exactly two minutes, so that the scientist would have time to moor himself securely to the parachute's board.

With his chronometer in his hand, he waited for the minute-hand to mark the time fixed by his calculations; in 20 seconds, *Russia* would resume its course into space. It was time to act. With a firm hand, Sharp brought the flickering lantern-flame to the end of the wick, which began to consume itself as the scientist sat down on the board, to which he fixed himself by means of a series of ingenious thongs.

The asteroid, as we have already had occasion to say elsewhere, was animated by a slow movement of rotation about its major axis, which supplied its sole inhabitant with days and nights of four hours duration. Now, at the precise moment when the former secretary brought the lantern to the extremity of the wick, the famous tree to which the parachute was attached was situated on the face of the asteroid facing the Earth, which formed a sort of vast dark ceiling above Sharp's head.

Suddenly, a bright flame sprang forth from the opening to the interior of the vast rocket. A sheaf of sparks was scattered in the air, while the apparatus, shuddering violently, rose obliquely into space, which seemed to catch fire. While it shot away with an incredible velocity, Sharp gazed in amazement as an enormous blaze was ignited below him by the conflagration of the rocket. It was, without any doubt, the latter's influence that had caused the hydrogen trapped in the flanks of the asteroid to catch fire and burst forth, for cosmic reasons that were as yet incomprehensible to him.[150] What was certain, though, was

[150] Given the shortage of atmospheric oxygen on the bolide and the rarefaction of the Earth's atmosphere at the relevant altitude, it is not clear how this

that the flames were ravaging the surface of the last fragment of Tuttle's Comet. The air was too rarefied at this height to transmit sound, and it was the eye alone that could be impressed by that unleashing of the forces of nature.

Broken into enormous pieces by the explosion of the gas contained in its flanks, the asteroid continued its progress through space, in the midst of a hectic red light radiated by its conflagration; radiant fragments were rising and falling in the midst of a whirlwind of incandescent sparks.

It was the end of the world.

Sharp would undoubtedly have been interested in the sublimity of the spectacle if he had not been disturbed to see that he was being followed—or rather escorted—through space by items of debris, some of them monstrous, which seemed to be gravitating around him, the smallest of which would have sufficed to smash him to bits and hurl the torn and quivering fragments of his limbs to the four corners of the celestial universe. On the other hand, he found time to wonder what would happen in a few seconds, when he would pass into the terrestrial zone of attraction; would the fabrics of which his parachute was composed be strong enough to contend successfully with the air resistance?

The flame of the rocket was abruptly extinguished; the explosive mixture had exhausted all of its propulsive power and Sharp, clinging convulsively to the cords of his parachute, felt himself precipitated into empty space with unexpected force, like a projectile expelled from the muzzle of a gun. But the space that, until now, had been striped by a rain of fire to the limits of the celestial horizon, suddenly changed its appearance—or rather, it seemed to the voyager that a veil had been drawn over the landscape. The apparatus had just flipped over and now, on lowering his eyes, Sharp saw the Earth less than 50 kilometers beneath him, extending its moonlight-silvered panorama indefinitely.

An immense joy swelled the heart of the former permanent secretary; after three years of absence, a prodigal son, he was about to touch the soil of his native planet. Still unknown today, an obscure soldier in the great army of science, tomorrow his forehead would be crowned with glory, and his name would be inscribed in letters of gold in the register of the feats and actions of heroes.

The parachute deployed, spreading out like an immense veil above the scientist's head; instantly, the fall, which had lasted for nearly 20 minutes, slowed and was transformed into a descent. In the wake of the apparatus, cometary fragments were also descending, and the question Sharp asked himself was whether those rocks would reach the ground before or after him. If before, he was safe; if afterwards, he might be crushed and killed.

Fortunately, the anguish Sharp felt as a result of being unable to answer that question came to an abrupt end. It was not in the possibility of being crushed that death was threatening him but in the form of asphyxia; the air-tank

---

"trapped hydrogen" could "catch fire"—or, for that matter, how Sharp's oil-lantern could contrive to ignite the fuse and the rocket itself.

of his respirol was empty. After a few convulsive coughs, the scientist, whose fingers were desperately clutching the apparatus, let his head slump forward on to his breast, unconscious and motionless.

Dawn was breaking when he came to again. To begin with, when he raised his eyelids, weighed down by the commencement of the asphyxia that had almost put an end to him, he had no clear idea of what he saw. He thought, in fact, that he was the victim of one of the hallucinations to which he had so often fallen prey in the course of his travels.

That hallucination scarcely varied; it was always, or nearly always, a terrestrial landscape in which he appeared to find himself. Sometimes there were vast and desolate snow-covered steppes illuminated by the dismal light of a cold sun, rounded like a globe of fire, and sleighs going by at a rapid pace, punctuating the great silence with the tintinnabulation of their harness-bells, carrying men muffled in fur garments that left nothing perceptible of their faces but long black beards. Sometimes the sun was high in the sky, pouring torrents of fire down upon fields yellowed by ripe crops, while peasants in red blouses, with rolled-up sleeves and bare heads and necks, plied their sickles ardently, singing strange melodies that recalled the refrains of his native land. And whenever Sharp woke, after having spent several hours of his nights living an artificial life in those landscapes that his imagination created, it took him several hours to convince himself that he had only been dreaming, and that it was not, in fact, the interior of the shell that was the fiction.

He had been too often disillusioned in that fashion to let himself be taken in this time; meanwhile, with his limbs still numb and inert, his intelligence emerged to some extent from the comatose state in which it had been plunged a little while before. He kept his eyes, wide open but still vitreous and dull, on the landscape that unfolded in front of him, or rather beneath him, for, by means of a phenomenon that he could not understand, he found himself—or seemed to find himself, in the dream he thought he was experiencing—on the summit of a sort of hillock elevated a few meters above the ground level of a verdant plain, with trees whose leaves, still moist with nocturnal dew, glistened in the first light of dawn. Flocks of sheep were grazing the grass and there were indecisive silhouettes of house in the distance, still shrouded in light mist. At the same time, human forms were gathered around him, standing up, bending over or kneeling down, staring at him curiously. He had the feeling that they were speaking to him, for he could see their lips moving, but he could not hear anything, and it seemed to him that he was being gently touched.

All that, though—the countryside, the animals, the people, the sensations—was nothing to him but a nightmare, whose like he had had many times before, more tortuous than its precedents.

However, as one of the people around him introduced the neck of a bottle gently between his lips, he felt something cool moisten his palate, which went down his throat and suddenly arrived in his empty stomach, there producing the sensation of a rivulet of fire. The pain was so sharp that his limbs quivered, and a dull exclamation escaped his lips.

Then words suddenly boomed in his ear: "He's alive, you see..."

Sharp was suddenly able to comprehend these words clearly—so clearly, in fact, that he doubted that any nightmare could have such clarity, and instinctively, in order to understand better, he stretched our his lips gluttonously toward the bottle.

A second mouthful, and then a third, produced the same sensation in his entrails as the first, but less intense; at the same time, the congealed blood in his veins began to circulated again and his brain, emerging from the mortal limbo into which his intelligence had sunk, regained its self-possession.

He tried to speak, but in the three years that he had been living alone, in his own intimate company, he had, so to speak, forgotten the mechanism of lips and tongue, so he could only utter a few guttural and inarticulate barking sounds to begin with. Nevertheless, he clearly heard people murmuring all around him: "He's alive! He's alive!"

Then he began to speak with all the recently-resuscitated force of which he was capable, and stammered, in Russian—for the words pronounced by the people surrounding him had been in his native tongue—"Where am I?"

"In Priajenskoy." And the person who had answered extended his arm toward the isbas whose roofs were now more distinctly visible in the distance.

That meant nothing to Sharp, whose faculties were not yet fully awake, and, in spite of the very real sensations he was experiencing, he still had the lingering feeling that he was dreaming. "Priajenskoy?" he repeated, effortfully.

"Province of Planetz," someone answered him again.

Planetz! That word, resonating in his ear, seemed suddenly to snatch away the veil enveloping his comprehension. At the same time, his limbs seemed to recover their strength and agility in response to a cerebral whiplash. Planetz! He knew that—it was a large town of 3000 or 4000 souls, serving as the capital of a province situated 200 *versts* from St. Petersburg.

Then the memory returned to him, quite clearly, of everything that had happened: his departure from the fragment of Tuttle, the explosion of the bradyte,[151] his descent by parachute and his fall into unconsciousness.

Yes...yes, he really was on his native world! God had permitted that great miracle, allowing him to see his compatriots again and to terminate a life of labor and privation in a glorious apotheosis.

---

[151] The term "bradyte", improvised from the Greek *bradys* [slow], was coined by Edmond Halley to refer to a meteor whose unusually slow movement he attributed to its exceptionally close approach to the surface. The term fell into disuse thereafter until it was revived by Camille Flammarion, in one of whose works the authors presumably found it.

Yes...yes, he really was alive and awake! This time, it was not the mirage of a nightmare that he had before him; his eyes were seeing, his ears hearing, his hands feeling. Besides, there, a few paces away, he had just noticed the shreds of fabric that had constituted his parachute, and his clenched fingers still held the threads that had attached the board on which he was seated to the apparatus. He even recognized the stony mass on which he was set as one of the pieces of Tuttle's Comet that had accompanied him in his fall.

How had it come about that he was here, precisely, and not somewhere else? That was certainly an interesting question, from a scientific viewpoint, which he reserved for subsequent elucidation; for the moment, though, could there be anything more interesting to observe than the fact of his existence?

He made a violent effort to get to his feet. To his great surprise, though, he seemed at first to be so heavy that it was impossible for him to raise himself from the ground. Almost immediately, he began to smile, understanding that the effort he had made was insufficient to bring about the desired result. Deprived of weight for nearly three years, his limbs had inevitably become unaccustomed to force, and now that he had instantaneously recovered his original weight of 70 kilos, his body needed to be, so to speak, re-educated or re-trained in order for him to move as before. But that was a mere detail; the main thing was that he should get himself to St. Petersburg without delay. He was in a hurry to enjoy the triumph that awaited him.

Is it necessary to describe here the details of his return to the capital? Fortunately for his plans, the former permanent secretary found a few paper roubles in an old wallet, by means of which he would be able to purchase a third-class ticket to St. Petersburg and, once there, get a room in a cheap hotel—for he did not doubt that the lodgings in which he had once lived would be occupied. He could certainly have employed the few roubles that comprised his entire fortune to telegraph the president of the Academy of Sciences from Olonetz, to tell him of his presence and ask for him help, but he judged it preferable to get there by other means. He was too starved of glory, and had been for too long, not to want to witness the initial surprise that his presence would provoke.

He took care to have a statement written by the parish priest of Priajenskoy establishing the circumstances in which the inhabitants of the village had found him, and on the same piece of paper the priest had described, as best he could—but not very well—the cometary fragment on which he had been found. With this paper in his pocket, carrying the voluminous packet containing his travel notes under his arm, on the day after his arrival in St. Petersburg—which was a Thursday, the day of the general meeting of the Academy of Sciences—Sharp headed for the monument that served as a haven for the intellectual quintessence of Russia.

While he was going through the narrow streets of the quarter in which he had spent the night, everything was normal, but when he set foot in a slightly more crowded quarter, his thin, fleshless frame, his unkempt beard and hair—

which fell to his shoulders in long greasy wisps—and his tattered clothing attracted such curiosity that several thousand curiosity-seekers were soon following in his footsteps, thinking that he as a madman.

Naturally, the police intervened and discussed taking the individual who was causing a scandal in the street to the station—but when they saw him walking quite calmly, with the tread of a man going about his business, having nothing against him but his wretched appearance, they did not think they had sufficient reason to incarcerate him and contented themselves with inviting the crowd to disperse. That was in vain, the crowd seeing this invitation, perversely, as one more reason not to abandon the individual. It was, therefore, with an entire army of curiosity-seekers dogging his heels that Fedor Sharp arrived at the Academy of Sciences.

The people following him were compelled to let him go in on his own, but they continued to stand outside the entrance, forming a numerous and silent group, waiting for...what, exactly? They did not know, but they had a sort of presentiment that something quite extraordinary was about to happen, which they would regret not having witnessed all their lives.

As for Sharp, he had boldly crossed the threshold of the monument, gone past the porter's lodge impassively, without paying any heed to the exclamations of the redoubtable functionary—who ran after him in order to turn him away—and climbed the steps of the great staircase leading to the session hall, imperturbable still.

The ushers tried in vain to stop him; he shook them off with a nervous twitch of his arm. Before they were able to grab him again, he pushed open the double door with muffled hinges and went into the sacrosanct refuge where the leading scientific lights of the Empire of the Tsars were deliberating.

At the sight of this creature with the strange face and pitiful appearance, the immortal who was speaking stopped dead, while the entire assembly turned to follow the direction of his gaze. There was an exclamation of stupefaction and horror, at the same time as the president, pointing out the intruder with a nervous finger, instructed the porter to throw him out—but Sharp, continuing to advance at the same tranquil and, so to speak, mechanical pace, thrust the porter aside and marched to the podium at which the speaker was standing. The latter, somewhat disquieted, thinking he was dealing with a madman, judged it prudent to return to his seat.

Imperturbably, Fedor Sharp climbed the three steps of the podium, drew himself up to his full height—which his emaciated thinness caused to appear immeasurable—and paraded his confident gaze over the assembly for several seconds, while bewildered and slightly frightened gazes converged upon him. Then he took hold of the notes left on the lectern by the scientist he had chased away, and a smile of triumph illuminated his face, rendering it even more sinister.

"Gentlemen, and dear colleagues," he said, finally, in a voice whose metallic accent made a frisson run down the spine of everyone there, "permit me to congratulate myself on arriving just in time to be able to bring a shining light into the discussion I have interrupted..." Here Sharp paused, and was able to observe the amazement into which the words *dear colleagues* had thrown the members of the Academy. "I see that you are occupied with the bolide that crossed the skies of Russia the night before last, and I permit myself to tell you that you are utterly mistaken." A vague murmur rose up, cut short by the orator's strident voice. "I might even dare to say," he declared, in a voice that revealed the superiority he was adopting with regard to the assembled company, "that you are floundering."

This expression made the scientists angry and raised voices were raised on every side: "Away with him! Out the door!"

Imperturbably, however, Fedor Sharp clutched the edge of the lectern with his bony fingers, defying the efforts of the porter suspended from the tails of his dilapidated frock-coat. "Gentlemen and dear colleagues, the bolide that you have seen is a fragment of Tuttle's Comet, and I have the honor of depositing on your podium a statement signed by the parish priest of Priajenskoy, countersigned by the authorities in Olonetz, establishing that on the night before last, at about three o'clock in the morning, the inhabitants observed in the neighborhood of the village the presence of a rocky mass. Now, this rocky mass was nothing other than a piece of the debris of the aforementioned body, whose appearance you had noticed at about 6 p.m...."

This confident statement had an impact on the scientists and the president, having consulted his colleagues with a glance, asked: "But what basis do you have, Monsieur, for affirming that the bolide in question originates from Tuttle's Comet?"

This question caused Sharp to draw himself up haughtily and reply, in a ringing voice: "No one can know that better than me! I've been living on it for 15 months."

There was a general stupor, and at that moment the entire audience was convinced that it was dealing with a madman.

"I similarly have the honor of depositing on the lectern," the other continued, "this book of notes written day by day during the voyage that I have made, during the last three years, through interplanetary space..."

The general bewilderment reached its peak.

"I ask the Academy, once the session has concluded, to appoint those of its members forming the astronomy section to an extraordinary committee, in order to examine these notes in collaboration with me, and to draw up a report to Monsieur the President."

Then, rising to their feet with a single movement, the Academicians, annoyed by what they considered to be a practical joke, shouted: "Who are you? Who are you?"

“I’m your former permanent secretary! I’m Fedor Sharp!”

Having said this, the voyager got down from the podium and ran to his bewildered colleagues. He took them successively by the hands, calling them by name, and making allusion to various details of their lives or their work. Then the suspicion changed into delirium; an incredible enthusiasm took hold of the previously-hostile individuals, and a clamor filled the vast hall.

“Hurrah for Fedor Sharp!”

Meanwhile the president, after deliberating in a low voice with his assistants, tapped his desk lightly with his paper-knife. Having obtained a momentary silence, he said, in a tremulous voice: “Gentlemen and colleagues, I propose that we continue the session, and that we give the floor to our colleague Fedor Sharp, for the recitation of his adventures and his work.”

Chapter LXIII
Sharp's triumph continues

For three weeks, Fedor Sharp had led an utterly extraordinary existence. It was an uninterrupted sequence of scientific receptions and society gatherings, of which he was inevitably the hero.

It had begun with the newspapers, which had all wanted the privilege, each one exclusively, of an interview with the famous explorer, to which they invited a small group of specially-selected friends. Then the officials, who had not wanted to be in debt to the Emperor, had insisted on receiving in their drawing rooms the man whom His Imperial Majesty had honored with a private audience. Finally, the chic society people who wanted to be "in the swim"—according to an expression picked up on the Boulevard des Italiens in Paris—had insisted on exhibiting "the man of the day" incessantly in their homes.

It was a truly curious spectacle to see these elegant folk in irreproachably-cut black suits and these worldly women in delightful gowns surrounding—almost fawning upon—an old man with the scowling face and withered limbs, whose black garments, ridiculous in form and hardly proper in appearance, gave him an unattractive and grotesque silhouette.

This existence, however—so unusual for a man who had lived alone for three years, withdrawn into himself—could not last long. It was, therefore, not without a real sense of relief that he had seen the craze whose "victim"—as he expressed it—he had been diminish somewhat once his ears had been battered by ovations and his throat desiccated by lectures.

These days, he only had to contend with the occasional scientific meeting convened in his honor in the afternoon or be constrained in the evening to show his face in a drawing-room between a waltz and a cotillion, rapidly passing through vaporous groups of dancers like the dark swallow passing through a swarm of gilded mosquitoes of which Bernardin de Saint Pierre speaks. Now that the intoxication of the first days had passed, though, and the admirers and the curiosity-seekers left him time for reflection, he began to regret not having had dealings with people who were less enthusiastic but more practical. There had been talk—he could not remember at which meeting—of erecting a silver statue of him; had he dared, he would gladly have imitated Philippe-Auguste,[152] who, when one of his seneschals told him of a similar project, extended his hand in a highly significant fashion and said: "Here is the statue's pedestal."

Oh, how he regretted that Lady Luck, in stead of causing him to fall in Russia, had not set him down in America. There, at least, people have an absolutely accurate sense of life, and, when they experience admiration for an indi-

[152] Philippe II (1165-1227) was king of France from 1180 until his death

vidual, they translate that admiration in other ways than acclamations, and even bouquets of flowers.

From the honorific point of view, it is certain that the scientist had nothing to desire; his desk was piled high with newspapers in which nearly all the columns were devoted to him, and scientific journals whose editorials strive to be more eulogistic and flattering than the rest. If he had been obliged to attend all the sessions of all the scientific and other societies that had been held "in his honor" to receive him into their ranks, he would have needed to be divided into ten or 15 different individuals. In the same way, if he had had to take seriously the title of "correspondent" that all the societies in the entire Universe had awarded him, he would have had to command an army of secretaries—who would, moreover, have been obliged to use typewriters. When he had dispensed hundreds of visiting cards to offer thanks for all the honors he had been awarded and all the meals to which he had been invited, however, and found himself alone, at a loose end, in the presence of the first sheet of blank paper on which he had to begin to write the story of his voyage, he was gripped by a sort of disgust for human beings, whom he accused of ingratitude.

If the worldly Gontran de Flammermont had been called upon to translate old Sharp's intimate sentiments into his boulevardier's language, he would certainly not have failed to invoke the memory of the actor Baron incarnating the legendary character of Calchas in *La Belle Helène* and saying, on viewing the offerings: "Too many flowers! Too many flowers!"[153]

Oh yes, too many flowers! Too many speeches! Too many meals! How much better the least grain of millet—as the fabulist[154] puts it—would have suited him...for the moment, at least, for, in the days immediately following his return, he had swollen up like the jackdaw in borrowed peacock feathers,[155] breathing in the intoxicating incense of flattery.

But now...

He had been promised that, immediately after the death of the present director of Pulkova Observatory, he would be given the post, to which he had more right than anyone else. On the other hand, a great nobleman, the owner of several hundred villages and a quantity of mines in Siberia, had undertaken to put at his disposal the millions necessary for the construction of the largest observatory in the entire world. But while he waited for the director of Pulkova to die and for the new observatory to be constructed, what was he to do?

---

[153] The actor who played the character of Calchas (the high priest) in the 1864 production of *La Belle Hélène* was Pierre-Eugène Grenier, but it has already been established that Gontran must have seen a later version. The reference is to Vincent-Alfred Baron (born 1820).

[154] Jean de La Fontaine, in the brief poem "Le coq et la perle."

[155] Again, the reference is to La Fontaine, citing the title of "Le Geai paré des plumes du paon."

Fits of rage caused his fingers to clench at his desk when he thought that so much fatigue, privations and peril had only brought him a small measure of glory—and ephemeral glory besides, since the newspapers were already ceasing to talk about him and games of charades and monologues were recovering their previous fashionability at soirées. At this rate, he would be forgotten in a week, and would have no means left of making money.

In the first days of excitement he had made a gift to the Museum of St. Petersburg of what remained of the apparatus that had transported Mikhail Ossipoff and his companions from the crater of Cotopaxi to the Moon, so, when a German circus-owner had recently come to offer him a relatively large sum to acquire the old shell—now famous by virtue of his intersidereal peregrinations—in order to exhibit it all over Europe, Sharp had bitterly regretted having so carelessly squandered the small fortune it represented.

Another circus-owner—this one a American—had come to propose a magnificent plan to him, which would inevitably give rise to extravagant results; it was a matter of nothing less than engaging him, Fedor Sharp, at a rate of 250 roubles a day, to exhibit the aerolith on which he had traveled, just as an animal-tamer shows off a ferocious beast. "We'll be in the money," the circus-owner had declared, "and, if you wish, I'll give you 25% of the receipts." Unfortunately, this individual had made his proposition prematurely; Sharp was still in the intoxication of his triumph, and the thought of exhibiting himself like an acrobat had made his hair stand on end. He had sent the man away, scornfully, and had renounced any property-rights he might have in the bradyte to Pulkova Observatory.

The day after this act of generosity, he had received a visit from one of the richest jewelers in St. Petersburg, who came to submit an idea of genius to him, which might be a source of considerable profit. The jeweler in question wanted to break up the bradyte to make paperweights, to each one of which would be added a certificate of provenance signed by Fedor Sharp. The scientist would only have got one rouble per signature, but the jeweler, who had made his measurements, affirmed that the bradyte would yield no less than 100,000 paperweights. That was, indeed, a tidy sum for Fedor Sharp, but, apart from the fact that the aerolith no longer belonged to him, he was still in the period of intoxication, and the proposition had inevitably met the same fate as its predecessors.

Thus, not only had there been no practical result of his extraordinary excursion, but even the glory that he had harvested was already vanishing like smoke!

Fedor Sharp was, therefore, sitting in his study, with his back supported by his armchair, and his half-closed eyelids filtering a hateful gaze directed at the immaculate piece of paper on which his penholder rested.

Suddenly, the voice of a newsvendor reached him, bringing a few confused words that the scientist's ear could only grasp imperfectly, but in which there seemed to him to be syllables that excited his curiosity considerably. He leapt to his feet, seized his hat on the run, opened the door and precipitated himself down the staircase.

Once in the street, indifferent to the recriminations of the people he jostled, Sharp ran after the merchant, from whom he tore one of the sheets he held in his hand, giving him ten times the price of the paper without demanding any change, so excited was he.

A coaching entrance happened to be nearby, and he plunged into it without regaining possession of himself, backing himself up against the wall because his legs were giving way beneath him. Scarcely had he cast his eyes upon the newspaper, in fact, than he saw, set below the title, in what technical parlance calls a "headline", these words printed in enormous letters: A NEW BRADYTE. FEDOR SHARP IN BRAZIL.

Rapidly, he read the article to which these words referred. The article, which was quite short, comprised a dispatch sent from Rio de Janeiro by the newspaper's correspondent, announcing that "an enormous aerolith has fallen 20 kilometers from Rio: an aerolith of colossal dimensions, measuring about 15 cubic meters," that "in the presence of this scientific phenomenon, the emperor Dom Pedro[156] has decided to convene, as rapidly as possible, a scientific congress composed of delegates from all the astronomical academies in the entire world," and that "it is proposed that the celebrated Fedor Sharp will be invited to come to Rio himself, in order to discover whether there is any relationship between this aerolith and his own bradyte."

Following this dispatch, the journal added that the Brazilian *chargé d'affaires* in St. Petersburg had asked the president of the Academies to convene his members immediately in order to listen to a message that his master the Emperor had cabled to him that morning.

Almost immediately, Sharp collected himself, and recovered the usage of his limbs as a great joy filled his heart. Obviously, he had been wrong to despair; Lady Luck had not abandoned him—quite the contrary; she appeared to be greater and more fortunate than ever, in the form of this short dispatch.

America, the land of practical men! Brazil, a country of people of swift enthusiasms! This was glory! This was fortune!

His first impulse was the race to the monument where the session of the Academies was taking place, but on reflection, he decided that it would demonstrate a slightly excessive haste. It would be more becoming to wait for the Brazilian minister to come to him, in an official capacity, to confirm the news given by the newspaper correspondent. He mastered his impatience, therefore, and

---

[156] Pedro II (1825-1891) had been forced into exile in Paris in 1889—when Brazil became a Republic—long before publication of this final part of the novel, but he was still in power in 1885, when this scene is set. Although the novel could be considered an episode of secret history prior to this chapter, it now becomes a manifest alternative history.

went home, forcing himself to walk slowly in order to not excite the curiosity of passers-by—and also to make the time pass, for he strongly suspected that once he was back indoors he would be gripped by a furious curiosity.

When he saw his house from a distance, though, he was tempted to start running; a considerable crowd had invaded the street and he suspected that something was happening that concerned him. He was not mistaken; as soon as he was recognized, cheers burst forth. Enthusiastic but respectful, the people gathered there cleared a passage to his door. Even the front steps were full of people: officials, notable scientists and reputable journalists were huddled on the steps in a confused mass, which he had difficulty penetrating in order to get to his modest lodgings. The Brazilian minister was waiting for him, surrounded by representatives of the various academies, in order to communicate to the interested party with all possible urgency the cablegram sent by Dom Pedro.

When the scientist had expressed his gratitude will admirably well-feigned emotion, for the great honor that was being done to him, an attaché of the Emperor's household informed Fedor Sharp that, following the Tsar's orders, the Minister of Marine had telegraphed Odessa to the effect that a ship should be ready to depart for Brazil within a week. At the same time, the Minister of Foreign Affairs had telegraphed instructions to the ambassadors to inform the governments by which they were accredited that Russia was offering free transportation to the delegations of all scientific societies. That done, the President of the Academies informed Sharp that urgent votes had been held to appoint the delegates charged with accompanying him to Rio, and that these delegates were at his disposal to receive his orders as to what measures to take.

For six days, the receptions and dinners recommenced, with the accompaniment of ovations of flowers. Again, Fedor Sharp became the hero of the day—but he only listened to the flattering compliments distractedly now, and the perfumes of the flowers left his nostrils insensible. He was dreaming of Brazil, that land whose every face legend delighted in gilding and decking with diamonds, and he told himself that honors might lead to fortune out there.

The fate of man is to live in hope, and hope helped to bring about a radical revolution in Sharp's manner; amiable and smiling, he showed himself full of enthusiasm during the preparations for departure.

First, he took care to cut away a sizeable portion of his own bolide, in order to have a point of comparison in studying the one whose characteristics he was crossing the seas to establish. That was no petty matter, for he had to proceed like a gem-cutter, the scientific body not wanting to hear any mention of hammers or pickaxes, and even less of mines. Afterwards, there was the matter of careful packaging, for it was necessary that the "specimen," as Sharp called it, should arrive unbroken. It was particularly important to shield the various constituent elements of the precious bradyte from the corrosive agents of the marine wind, and that required wrapping of a special and costly kind. Then it was necessary to transport this awkward parcel from St. Petersburg to Odessa; four trucks coupled by a gangway system were necessary to contain it. These trucks were hitched to a special train that the Minister of Highways and Communications put at the disposal of Sharp and his companions. Once at Odessa, where they arrived on the eve of their departure, the celestial explorer had to divide his time between the receptions he was required to attend and the care necessary to the transshipment of the specimen from the train to the deck of the ship.

Finally, they were ready to sail, and it was a truly fine spectacle that the steamer made as it left the jetty, decorated with the multicolored flags of all the nations whose representatives were aboard, to the cheers of a delirious crowd, which only ceased to applaud and cry out in order to listen, with heads bowed, to all the fanfares of the town performing the *Boje Tsara Krani* in unison.[157] A multitude of small boats escorted the ship for a long time, only abandoning it when it was far out in the open sea, because night was falling, forcing them to return to port.

From that moment on, Sharp led a relatively tranquil existence. Even though it was necessary for him drink champagne every evening—perhaps more than befit his scientific character and dignity—as the delegates of each nation received their colleagues in turn, he still had sufficient time to collect himself, alone in his cabin with his hopes and dreams.

The more he thought about it, the more convinced he became that it was Providence that had written the magical script in which he was presently playing the central role. From time to time, admittedly, there passed before his eyes—but so vaguely and so indistinctly that with a little will-power he would not have recognized them—the silhouettes of Mikhail Ossipoff and his traveling companions, but the crimes of which he was guilty in their regard now seemed to him so distant that he could scarcely retain the memory of a few details of them.

Doubtless it would have been more correct not to have sent Ossipoff to the mines and, having found him again in the lunar solitudes, not to have stolen the metallic engine in which he counted on continuing his voyage, but, besides the fact that he was the kind of person who only ever sees the end to be attained, without preoccupying himself with the means employed to achieve it, Sharp told himself, to lighten his conscience—which was, one may believe, not overloaded—that he had not acted in the interests of personal glory of fortune.

That had been true at first; exactly like his colleague at Pulkova Observatory, he too had been subject to scientific madness, an enthusiasm for the stars, and only the desire to make a contribution to astronomy had driven him to get rid of Ossipoff. It might be argued, logically, that it would have been better to combine his efforts with those of his colleague; to that he would have replied

---

[157] The quoted phrase translates as "God Save the Tsar;" there is no Russian hymn of praise with that title—which is, of course, constructed by analogy with the English national anthem—but it crops up frequently in French jokes and popular literature, with a variety of spellings.

that Mikhail Ossipoff was more of a dreamer than a man of action and that years were passing by before passing from theory to practice. Besides, Selena's father was a loner, jealous of his own knowledge, and no accommodation would have been possible with him.

Such had been the initial sentiment that had planted in Sharp's skull the idea of getting rid of his colleague; then, very rapidly, his general interest in science had been grasped by the claw of his own interest, his glory, his fortune—and by the time he had succeeded in convincing Jonathan Farenheit, Sharp was utterly determined to make a fortune, thanks to the contributions granted to him at the formation of the Selene Co. Ltd. Then, it had become necessary for him to revert to his initial hopes, the Moon's diamond mines being a chimera, as was the possibility of ever recommencing the bold voyage that he had just concluded.

Like a silly fool, for three weeks he had allowed himself to be lulled by congratulations, flowers and Platonic honors—but now that, at the exact moment at which he had despaired, the hope had been born of finding an occasion to make money out of his glory, he did not intend to let the opportunity slip away, no matter how it presented itself. A showman might now offer him an engagement to exhibit the bolide in question to the Old and New Worlds, and give idlers more-or-less scientific explanations, and he would rise to the occasion, even if it were necessary to replace his austere black frock-coat and official white cravat with the baroque costume of a clown.

Yes, more than ever, Fedor Sharp was ashamed of his poverty; he wanted to be rich and he intended to be—and whenever he happened to think about Mikhail Ossipoff, he congratulated himself for the trick he had played on him in leaving him in the lurch on Mercury.[158] If he had followed the old scientist in the selenium sphere on which they were counting to continue their voyage he would in all probability, have shared their fate—which is to say that his being, like theirs, would have returned to the great All—while, as things were, not only was he alone in harvesting a glory of which a good part (the better, he confessed in secret) belonged to Mikhail Ossipoff, but Providence had also arranged things so well that it had got rid of an inconvenient victim for him.

That was the state of mind in which Fedor Sharp found himself when the vessel transporting him, his traveling companions and the famous specimen arrived in sight of Rio. At the same time as the pilot, who came aboard to steer them through the channels, a crowd of boat arrived in haste, full of officials, scientists and literary men anxious to pay homage to the hero of the day—and Fedor Sharp began to get intoxicated all over again by the capital perfume of flattery and ovations. Before even disembarking, it was necessary for him, in

---

[158] It is not obvious here whether it is the authors' memories that are at fault or whether Sharp is deliberately falsifying his own past, so I have left the misstatement uncorrected.

order to satisfy the curiosity of the newcomers without delay, to make a speech in which he summarized the various phases of his voyage as succinctly as possible.

On disembarkation, one of the Emperor's carriages was waiting at the far end of the gangplank to take him to the palace, where His Majesty gave him the most cordial welcome he could ever have imagined. On taking leave of him, Dom Pedro even took the trouble to tell him that he would have kept him in his presence longer, but that he did not want to deprive his citizens of the pleasure of presenting their homage.

In the courtyard of the palace another carriage, bearing the city's coat-of-arms, was waiting to take the hero to a grand plaza, in the center of which stood a tall granite pedestal, which must have supported the bronze effigy of some Brazilian general a few days earlier. For the present, the Brazilian general was lying on the ground covered with a canvas sheet, and a wooden stairway had been set up beside the pedestal, covered with a scarlet cloth.

Then the president of the municipality explained to Fedor Sharp that the city, to honor the scientist more specifically, had given him the title of "citizen of Rio" and that, to help him to find his feet publicly, the city to which he now belonged had decided to hold a parade of scientific societies and workingmen's organizations from every corner of Brazil and from abroad as well, for him to witness from the top of the pedestal.

Even a head stronger than Sharp's might well have been slightly disequilibrated by such honors, so he had to stiffen himself somewhat in order to climb the steps of the stairway without vacillating—and while climbing the steps, he asked himself conscientiously what attitude he ought to strike on the platform. It was an awkward problem. He needed something that gave a good impression of the astronomical science incarnate in his person and, at the same time, allowed the perception of a certain modesty that was always incumbent on a true scientist.

Mechanically, once he had reached the top, he thrust out his hips, bearing his entire weight on his left leg with the right slightly flexed. His head was stiff, his gaze looking downwards. One of his hands, closed, was set behind his back, the other half-hidden in the aperture of his waistcoat, whose top button was undone. Without his being aware of it, his limbs had conserved a reminiscence of the favorite posture of a great man; as the city's newspapers remarked the following day—without any hint of criticism—Fedor Sharp had posed as the Napoleon of astronomy.

The president of the municipality stayed on the top step of the staircase, slightly below the level of the platform, while the members of the city council formed a group at the foot of the pedestal. Then the instruments of a brass band, hidden in the foliage, blasted forth. Four artillery pieces, positioned at each corner of the plaza, thundered simultaneously. Immediately, a procession emerged from the mouth of a street in which it had gathered, marching slowly, circling around the pedestal on which the motionless Fedor Sharp would have seemed to be veritably cast in bronze if he had not inclined his head periodically to salute the delegations that the president of the municipality named for him in a whisper as they filed past.

It lasted an hour—a long hour, during which, in spite of the strongly glaring Sun, Sharp gave no sign of weariness, although it ought to be mentioned that, following the instructions given by the municipal chief, a gold-unformed domestic came to stand behind the hero in order to hold an immense parasol over his head, in the colors of Russia and Brazil.

The end of the procession was made up of an innumerable host of individuals of both sexes—although the majority belonged to the masculine sex—dressed, for the most part, in gaudy traveling costumes and coiffed with cloth caps or soft felt hats (on the male side), or in badly-cut dresses disappearing beneath ample ulsters and coiffed with hats in extraordinarily bad taste (on the female side). Each of these individuals, without exception, was holding an umbrella and a rolled-up blanket, with a leather bag and a set of opera-glasses slung over the shoulder; the opera-glasses were all momentarily focused on Fedor Sharp, with the rudeness that characterizes the English abroad.

Surprised and slightly shocked, the hero abandoned the bronze-like immobility in which he had be fixed for nearly an hour to lean toward the president of the municipality and ask him who these people were. The other explained to him that since news had spread through the entire world of the scientific solemnities of which Rio would be the theater, Cook's and similar agencies had organized excursions to Brazil from all points of the globe at reduced price. For a week, bands of tourists with long teeth and yellow side-whiskers had been landing in the country, avid to contemplate the features of the man of the day and to see the fragment of celestial rock with which Providence had blessed Brazilian territory.

"It's the city's good fortune," said the president of the municipality, smiling, by way of conclusion.

"It's also the ruination of the museums," replied Sharp, alluding to the well-known recklessness with which the children of Albion do everything possible to carry away "little souvenirs."

Despite these mistrustful words, our hero could not do other than salute, as graciously as possible, these people who had come so far solely to contemplate his features.

Once the procession was over Sharp was taken to his hotel with great pomp. There he had just enough time to change his dusty clothes for a black suit before going to a great banquet held by the government for the scientific delegations. The banquet was like all official banquets—which is to say that it was an uninterrupted sequence of cold dishes, in which disguised pieces of meat floated in unidentifiable peppery sauces, generously washed down with so-called vintage wines which had only cost their proprietors the effort of naming them. A series of toasts began with the dessert and Sharp had already risen to his feet in response to the deluge of compliments with which 15 orators had been drowning him for an hour when a servant brought the president of the Council of Ministers, to whose right the hero was seated, a sealed envelope.

"Urgent," said the servant.

The minister tore the letter open with nervous fingers. "Damn!" he murmured, after reading the three or four lines comprising the missive. He reflected for a few seconds, the tore a page out of his notebook, on which he hurriedly scribbled a few words.

"Take this to the Minister of War, with all possible haste," he commanded. Then, leaning toward his neighbor, he smiled and said: "You'll never guess the order that I've just given, my dear scientist."

Sharp sketched a vague gesture. "It would be difficult for me, Excellency," he stammered, "to guess..."

"I've just given the order to send half a line-regiment and a squadron of cavalry by special train to Las Pueblas."

The astronomer sat up straight. "Las Pueblas!" he said. "But isn't that the village near which the famous bradyte fell?"

"Precisely."

Assuming, given the ceremony with which he had been received, that these troops had only been sent to confirm in striking fashion the honor in which the Brazilian government held him, Fedor Sharp stammered, with admirably feigned confusion: "It's too much, Excellency...in truth...too much..."

The minister shook his head, while his lips extended in a significant moue. "I rather fear," he murmured, "that it might not be enough—these English devils are legion..."

Sharp understood, hearing these few words, that he had been mistaken, and had a vague presentiment of danger. "Would Your Excellency deign to explain?" he said. "I don't quite understand..."

"It's quite simple. The mayor of Las Pueblas has telegraphed me that flocks of tourists have arrive, with no more urgent intention than attacking the bradyte with walking-sticks and umbrellas. Some of them even have pick-axes hidden under their clothing."

Sharp got to his feet, very pale. "Oh, my God!" he exclaimed.

"The Mayor goes on to say that if order is not restored before tomorrow, the tourists will have sliced up—that's the expression he used—the entire bradyte...and that's why I've sent the troops."

His interlocutor seized his hands and said, in an emotional voice: "Oh, thank you, Excellency! Thank you in the name of science..."

"But where are you going? You're leaving? What about your speech...?"

"This is no time for speeches," the scientist replied, prey to an inexpressible emotion. "I ask your permission to leave with the train carrying the troops. My place is out there...the interests at stake are too considerable...by staying here I'd be deserting my post, which is where the danger is..."

He had pronounced these final words in a loud voice, with the result that, in the midst of the general silence provoked by his surprising attitude, everyone heard them. Promptly updated by the few words that the minister judged it appropriate to say to excuse Sharp, the delegates of the scientific societies rose as one man to declare that they were accompanying their leader and that the English would have to pass over their dead bodies before laying their sacrilegious hands on the bradyte. Only the representatives of the Academies of London abstained, explaining in very sensible language full of moderation that, while condemning the attitude of their compatriots in the name of science, they nevertheless could not risk getting mixed up in acts of hostility against them.

Two hours later, the special train, heaving with troops and scientists, came to a halt in Las Pueblas station, and the scientists, following on the heels of the infantrymen by the light of torches, headed toward the spot where the precious block lay. The cavalry had taken the lead in order to sweep the terrain clear, by means of a few peaceful charges, and to prevent any bloodshed. Sharp had pleaded so fervently with the officer commanding the detachment that he had obtained the favor of riding behind one of the cavaliers. It was a sight both strange and grotesque to see that tall, thin man in a black suit and white cravat with his arms around the soldier's waist, while his trousers, riding up to his calves, allowed a glimpse of bare leg, imperfectly imprisoned by crumpled white socks.

The mayor had offered to serve in person as guide; mounted on a small but spirited horse, he trotted at the head of the detachment, holding up a lantern to indicate the route to be followed. They were soon going across open country, and the pace became less rapid, until the moment when the guide stopped, extended his arm in front of him and said: "There it is!"

In the misty darkness of the night, lit by a full Moon like a huge silver plate, a dark mass appeared about 500 meters away, somewhat reminiscent of a small hill rising up from the countryside. Its silhouette was blurred, preventing perception of its exact conformation. Moving human forms, also very vague, were visible, some surrounding the mass in question, others clambering up is flanks, and yet others perched of its crest.

"Charge! Charge!" cried Sharp. At the same time, he gave the rump of the horse carrying him a smack with a large umbrella, with the result that the beast bounded forward, dragging the entire detachment in its wake, the men believing that their commander had given a command.

It was a stampede; the human forms perceived from a distance fled in all directions, terrified by the arrival of these cavalrymen, whose uniforms could not be distinguished and to whom the darkness lent a fantastic aspect. When the first ranks came to a halt—with the cavalier bearing Sharp behind him at least 20 meters ahead, of course—the place was empty. Here and there, objects abandoned by the runaways lay on the ground: opera-glasses, blankets, hats and cloth caps.

With an agility of which one would not have thought him capable, Sharp leapt to the ground and started running like a madman, circling the base of the bolide, pausing occasionally to pass his hands over the rocky walls like a miser fondling his treasure. When he arrived back at his point of departure, he began to scale the rock, using his umbrella like an alpenstock to help him, grabbing the slightest handhold whenever the ascent was too steep. Finally having failed to break his neck at least 20 times over, he reached the crest, and, when the scientific delegates arrived behind the infantry detachment, they saw the huge silhouette of Fedor Sharp, silvered by a ray of moonlight that struck him full on, standing out like some fantastic apparition against the dark background of the night.

He raised his umbrella above his head then, its shadow seeming to stretch as far as the shiny disk of the Moon, and he cried at the top of his voice: "Long live science!"

Down below, amid a formidable hurrah uttered in all the languages of the world, he heard the words: "Long live Fedor Sharp!"

He bowed solemnly. Then, while the officer under whose command the troops had been placed made the necessary arrangements to protect the integrity of the bolide—which is to say that he placed a series of guard-posts all around it, at a distance of 100 meters, each with forward sentries, then sent patrols of cavalry and infantry to beat the surrounding countryside and prevent any further offensive on the part of the Cook Agency's tourists—the scientists made what arrangements they could to set up camp on the battlefield.

No doubt some among them—perhaps even a large number—thought, privately, that it was a trifle excessive to compromise the health of the cream of the world's scientists in this manner; passing the night under the stars after a heavy meal, with their heads heated up by wine and their stomachs overloaded with spiced meat, there was a good chance of contracting a serious congestion. Some of those present, therefore, left to their own devices, would have hastened to return to the village and to find what accommodation they could in the only hotel to be found there. Human respect, however, forced those who had the strongest inclination to retreat pretend to be the bravest, however, and no one wanted to be the first to take the initiative.

In any case, a bad night is soon passed, so, the soldiers having lent their capes to the scientists, the latter rolled themselves up therein and lay down on the ground, their feet warmed by the fires lit at intervals, and were not long delayed in going to sleep, while the officers smoked strong cigars and drank large glasses of *aguardiente*.[159]

---

[159] *Aguardiente* [firewater] is a slang term used, with slight variations of spelling, throughout the Spanish- and Portuguese-speaking world to refer to strong liquor.

At the first light of dawn, clarions and trumpets sounded. That campaign reveille frightened all the little birds that were still asleep in the cornfields and coffee-bushes. When the scientists had stretched their arms and flexed their jaws, their backs aching somewhat from the hardness of the ground and their heads a trifle heavy due to the previous evening's libations, they looked around and were veritably amazed.

The Brazilian government had certainly not exaggerated matters when it had announced to the scientific world, through the voice of its official representatives, that the most extraordinary specimen of celestial rock that had ever been seen had fallen on its territory. Those who had made the voyage on the strength of that affirmation were quite unable to regret their displacement.

Imagine a block that presents, on each face, a surface area of about 1300 square meters, measuring no less than 40 meters in breadth by 30 meters in height: a gigantic pebble fallen to Earth from space, and which, in its fall, has embedded itself in the ground to a depth of at least half a dozen meters.

Around it there was a veritable devastation, as if a gigantic fire had passed over the fields and through the woods; there was nothing but charred tree-trunks and obliterated crops; it was as if the flames had even penetrated the soil to destroy the roots, which could be seen in crevices, twisted and blackened. There was a thick layer of fine, impalpable ash on the ground, which rose in eddies into the air at the slightest breath of wind, obscuring the blue sky and making the atmosphere reek.

As soon as their eyes were open wide enough to stare, and their brains sufficiently unclouded to understand, the company of scientists rushed to assault the bolide, in order to examine it, touch it and set stethoscopes to all its nooks and crannies. While some took photographs of its various faces, others surveyed those same faces, measuring its dimensions, engaging in endless arguments over discrepancies of a few centimeters in their different measurements. Others still climbed up it to measure its height.

Soon, a moment arrived when everyone was gathered on a sort of plateau that formed, so to speak, the summit of the minuscule mountain. Then, under the supervision of Fedor Sharp, the detailed study of the bolide began. The scientist seemed to be reveling in the experience, and with the same frenetic passion that had sustained him in the midst of terrible ordeals, he led his invited guests through all the sinuosities of the rocky mass for several hours, stopping at almost every step to invite them to admire some detail, observe some particularity or interest themselves in some curiosity.

Climbing up, coming down and climbing up again, going to the right and going to the left and then coming back again, Fedor Sharp was indefatigable, seemingly careless of the visible exhaustion of the colleagues he dragged in his wake, sweating and breathing heavily, mopping their foreheads and gagging with thirst.

"It's the proprietor's tour," joked one of the French delegates, a member of the Academy of Sciences and a man of considerable wit.

Every moment was an opportunity for Sharp to deliver another lecture, now on mineralogy, now on geology, now on astronomy, and all with an assurance that dazed his interlocutors. Joking apart, this devil of a man knew everything! A moment arrived, however, when the "proprietor's tour" was complete—and more than complete, for it had gone over the same ground several times—and the president of the Council, who had remained by the scientist's side throughout, timidly whispered the suggestion in his ear that it might perhaps be time to take a break. One may interrupt the order and progress of a congress to eat.

A very agreeable surprise awaited the audience; while Fedor Sharp had been making the society visit every nook and cranny of the famous bolide, the troopers had erected an immense tent on the crest, under which tables were set up, and it was around these tables that the famished company was invited to sit down to recover somewhat.

To tell the truth, for almost the entire duration of the meal science was set aside, and although Sharp continued his lectures unabated, the others only listened very distractedly, a hungry belly having no ears. In any case, by courtesy of the mayor of Las Pueblas, the village band had come to add the elevating blast of its instruments to the ceremony, and their fanfares drowned out the voice of the orator. At dessert, however, he was able to take his revenge; it was the appointed hour of toasts, and the musicians, whose throats were completely dry, went to refresh them—which permitted Sharp to make his slightly hoarse voice audible once again to his audience.

He began by affirming that the stony fragment that had fallen in the vicinity of St. Petersburg and the one on which he presently found himself in such eminent company both belonged to the bradyte detached from Tuttle's Comet, on which he had traveled through a considerable distance of space for several months. No further proof of that was needed than the constitutive elements of each one being exactly the same as those of the other. From the mineralogical point of view, there was a similar identity, and also from the geological perspective, as proven by the fact that the same strata were observable in both. Finally, what proved beyond any doubt that the fragment from which he had emerged had been detached from the enormous mass presently in question was the collection of photographic prints he had made of all the faces of his bolide, one of which seemed to fit exactly into the right-hand face of the Brazilian bradyte.

"All this, gentlemen and dear colleagues," he added, by way of conclusion, "has to be verified in detail, for we are in the presence of one of the most important problems that has ever presented itself to men of science, and I do not intend to state anything that has not been checked and rechecked by the eminently competent men that you are. I am only permitting myself—being, so to speak, a member of the household"—he smiled complacently as he pronounced these words—"to give you a few nudges in the right direction. You are free, now, to decide what it is that you are dealing with."

As might be imagined, this apparent modesty on the part of the hero of the day produced a considerable effect on these jealous and self-infatuated men of science; they applauded wholeheartedly and one of them, spontaneously taking the floor, thanked the eminent scientist for the confidence he had in the modest enlightenment of his colleagues, who would call upon all their knowledge and all their good will to justify the confidence that His Majesty the Emperor had been so kind as to place in them...

"The first thing to do, it seems to me," said the minister, President of the Council of His Majesty Dom Pedro, "is to bring together this bradyte and the specimen that you have brought from St. Petersburg. The comparative studies will be greatly facilitated, I think, by this procedure."

There was general applause.

Sharp then made the observation that it would be quite difficult to transport the stony parcel brought from Odessa. He added that it would also involve considerable expense, of which he begged His Excellency to take account before engaging in the operation. With great dignity, the minister replied that in a question of such scientific importance, he thought it inappropriate to talk about expense; furthermore, he knew the Emperor's intentions, and could affirm that in case of any budgetary insufficiency, Dom Pedro would open his own coffers.

There was more general applause.

Then a member of the congress—let us say right away that he was old, and could only walk with the aid of a stick—made the observation that the location where the bradyte had fallen might perhaps increase the difficulty of the multiple and arduous operations to which it would certainly be necessary for them to carry out. Between where they were and Las Pueblas—assuming that they could adopt the village as a domicile—there was a distance that would have to be covered on foot, by virtue of the total lack of means of transport. Would that not be very tiring for the members of the congress, who were no longer young, knowledge generally only coming with age?

A murmur of approval greeted these words—but then Sharp got up, frowning, and asked in a booming voice: "How does my honorable colleague intend to resolve this question? For I assume that he does not want to propose that we return without having done everything possible to attain the goal that we accepted in coming to Brazil."

Thus sharply questioned, the "honorable colleague" hastened to reply that it was an insult to imply that he had any such intention; the truth was that, in his view, it would be more practical and favorable both to the health of his colleagues, eminent scientists, and to the result to be obtained, to establish their operational base in Rio.

There was a general outcry. To live in Rio, when the pivot of the operation was here! What a waste of time! And how wearisome! It was irrational...

The orator stuck to his guns, though. "You misunderstand me, gentlemen and dear colleagues," he replied, very calmly. "If I make the proposition to make Rio the base of our operations, it's because I see nothing impossible in transporting..."

"The bradyte, perhaps?" exclaimed several voices.

Undisconcerted, the other replied: "Exactly!"

The laughter and jokes provoked in the entire audience by that *exactly* can be imagined—but the scientist, who had served in his country's Parliament for a long time before taking refuge in the Academy of Sciences, was, in consequence, accustomed to paying no heed to noise, mockery and even insults. Imperturbable, he remained standing, waiting for the fit of mad hilarity that had greeted his words to subside. Then he went on: "All modesty aside, gentlemen and dear colleagues, can I not say that my name is honorably regarded by all of you as that of a man to whom questions of mechanics are familiar?"

This was so undeniable the unanimous response was a murmur of approval.

"You will, therefore, believe me when I affirm that I believe the transport I have proposed to you to be possible..."

"But even assuming that you succeed in finding a means of extracting the bradyte from the hole that it hollowed out in falling," came the cry from every direction, "what system of traction would you use to carry it 20 kilometers from here?"

The scientist shook his head. "That's one of the least aspects of the question," he replied, with a scornful smile. "Permit me to say, firstly, that His Excellency the President of the Council would not refuse to have a connecting railway track constructed from here to Las Pueblas, or requisition a locomotive—two, or even three, if necessary—to draw the pebble..."

The last wounded Sharp's vanity; he got up, white faced and eyes glinting, and retorted in a hostile tone: "I regret that our honorable colleague has thought it appropriate to apply such an expression to this fragment of celestial rock that will serve as the platform for profound study by the intellectual elite of the human species..."

The orator was interrupted here by a murmur of great approval; the words "intellectual elite" had made their impact. Sharp bowed to the right and left condescendingly, and went on: "But at the end of the day, since a 'pebble' is what it is, and our honorable colleague thinks it practical to transport such a mass 20 kilometers from here, I think, myself, that the attempt is sufficiently interesting from every point of view for us to ask His Excellency"—so saying, he turned to the President of the Council of Ministers—"to put everyone to work in order that such a result might be obtained."

The minister got up in his turn and declared that His Majesty the Emperor would be only to glad to cooperate in an operation of such interest to the limit of his means, but that his private purse was unfortunately nor inexhaustible; as for the national budget, it was in such a state of disequilibrium that he could not see any means of taking the smallest sum from public funds that would permit the government to lend an efficacious collaboration to so bold a project...but that he would, however, talk to his colleagues, examine the matter in collaboration with them in a very profound manner, and, if the government were to find the means to impose a new tax that put new resources at his disposition, the scientists could count on him.

As he finished this speech, there was an unexpected commotion at the foot of the bolide. The soldiers were running to their weapons, the cavaliers leaping into the saddle and curt commands were being shouted.

Everyone got up from the table and went to the edge of the crest to get a better view of what was happening. Half a squadron departed, sabers draw, at a rapid trot. They all turned to the minister then, to find out whether or not the poor man was as ignorant as his guests.

"Look over there!" someone said, suddenly, pointing toward the far side of the plain.

A cloud of dust was floating at ground level, as if raised by the feet of a numerous troop on the march—but that cloud was soon confused with the one raised by the cavalrymen. The latter were galloping now, and their sword-blades were gleaming in the bright sunlight like streaks of lightning.

"One might think that they were charging!" observed one voice.

The scientists looked at one another, and their features expressed an astonishment in which a hint of anxiety was mingled. In the distance, however, the cavalry came to an abrupt halt. The dust dissipated slightly, and a numerous host of people became visible, who had been stopped by the soldiers, and with whom they appeared to be negotiating.

"What can it signify?" murmured the President of the Council of Ministers. He was already turning to a servant to give him orders to send for information when a few cavaliers were seen to turn their bridles and come back toward the camp as fast as their mounts could carry them. In less than ten minutes, they were close enough for an individual wearing a blindfold to be made out, perched on the rump of one of the horses, clutching the rider around the waist. As might be imagined, the general surprise could only increase further.

The little detachment finally reached the foot of the bolide and came to a halt. The officer in command leapt down from the saddle, helped down the individual with bandaged eyes and, taking him by the hand, began climbing the steep flank of the stony block.

"Excellency," he said, pausing in front of the minister, "this gentleman has been sent to you as a negotiator."

These words transformed surprise into stupefaction. A negotiator! This man dressed in a strangely checkered macfarlane, coiffed with a cloth cap and wearing a leather shoulder-strap bearing a set of opera-glasses!

"What is this joke, sir?" the minister asked him, severely.

The man with blindfolded eyes answered in bad Portuguese, with an English accent that could be perceived a mile away: "Excellency. I've been sent to you by my traveling companions to propose a compromise..."

"A compromise!"

"We're tourists—about 1000 of us—brought to Brazil by the Cook Agency to admire the great intersidereal voyager Fedor Sharp and contemplate the fragment of celestial rock that has fallen on your territory—and we hoped that each of us would be able to carry away a piece of that marvelous pebble as a souvenir..."

These words provoked a murmur of disapproval in the audience of scientists.

"Your soldiers chased us away last night—without weapons, we weren't crazy enough to try to fight them—so we thought we might be able to reach an understanding in another way. Each one of us is willing to pay the Brazilian government 25 pounds sterling in return for half a kilogram of this thing..." So saying, he tapped the bolide with the heel of his yellow shoe.

There was an explosion of wrath. Insults, in every language of the globe, rained down upon the head of the unfortunate negotiator. The scientists would gladly have taken other measures had the President of the Council of Ministers not protected him bodily. "Gentlemen, gentlemen," he declared, "the person of a negotiator is sacrosanct!"

Fedor Sharp came forward then, and said, in a voice trembling with indignation; "Go tell your companions that you are vandals! Before laying your sacrilegious hands on this rock, you'll have to pass over our dead bodies!"

Applause burst forth.

The Englishman inclined his head, quite phlegmatically, and replied: "I'll follow your instruction—but the treasury of Brazil isn't so rich that it can so easily refuse a sum of 25,000 pounds..." He turned on his heel and left, led by the officer who served as his guide.

"Excellency," said Sharp, "I beg you to be on your guard, for there's nothing as crazy as an Englishman, and the Cook Agency's tourists won't give up."

"Have no fear—but this proves the urgency of taking measures to make the bolide safe."

"And to devise a means of getting it away from here as soon as possible," said the gentleman who had proposed transporting the precious pebble to Rio.

The President of the Council called for silence then, and said: "Gentlemen, I shall immediately begin gathering the funds necessary to mount this gigantic operation; I leave it to you to find the practical means." With a smile brimming with politeness, he added: "And I don't doubt that you'll do that first..." He bowed all round and ran down the steep slope, secretly adding: *Glory's all very well, but it's very dear when one has to pay for it...* And as he headed for Las Pueblas station, he began racking his brains to find a way to get his hands on the 25,000 pounds offered by the English.

Chapter LXIV
The Surprise Package

For three weeks the village of Las Pueblas had seen a great deal of hard work done. The presence of the Congress members had brought an extraordinary animation to the neighborhood. Buildings had sprung up from the ground all around the bolide as if by magic: drinking dens and restaurants made of planks and tar-paper for the workmen, metallic sheds to serve as workrooms, canvas tents for the soldiers, and a hotel built in less than three days for the gentlemen scientists.

The troopers being insufficient in number, all the local people had been drafted to wield pick-axes and shovels and push wheelbarrows. Enticed by the promise of a fee, the peasants had temporarily abandoned field-work, leaving their families and ploughs on the plain. It would be no easy task to extract the stony block from the soil in which it was embedded and to raise it to a sufficient height to deposit it on the enormous platform on which it would then be taken to Rio de Janeiro.

The minister had anticipated correctly in telling the members of the Congress that they would find the mechanical means of transport before he had found the pecuniary means. The day after the famous dinner that had concluded with the Englishman's outrageous proposition, the promoter of the idea had begun making all his calculations, drawing up all his plans, and had called a meeting of all those of his colleagues belonging to the Committee for the Industrial Application of Mechanics and Mathematics.

The plan that he submitted to them was childishly simple: it was a mere matter of establishing steam-powered cranes around the bolide, arranged in threes to increase their force, and caused them to raise the enormous block, by means of chains passed underneath it, until its base was 50 centimeters above the ground. Once there, the cranes would go into action horizontally, in order to deposit their burden on a platform made of enormous oak beams mounted on steel truck furnished with crude but very large wheels. To this cart, which would measure no less than 30 meters in length by 12 in breadth, 400 oxen would be hitched in tens in front, while a system of electrical jacks would push from the rear. A few sharp prods applied to the oxen's rumps, a little current to the jacks, and away it would go…

By virtue of its very simplicity, this means had enthused all the inventor's colleagues—at first sight, at least, for it was then necessary to subject all the calculations on which the specialist had based his plan to scrupulous filtration: the cubic capacity of the bolide; its weight; the tensile strength of the chains; the traction exerted by the cranes; the elasticity of the platform's springs; the resistance of the combined efforts of the oxen and that of the wheels. All of this was scrupulously examined, weighed and verified. The President of the Council had been summoned and the results of the studies submitted to him, along with an approximate estimate of the necessary expenditure.

It added up to a pretty sum of 500,000 francs.

That was a lot! And the scientists, in the two days since they had established that figure, had become exceedingly anxious. The people of the village had been talking, and from their conversation had emerged, as clear as daylight, the confirmation of what the English tourists' delegate had said: the Brazilian budget was totally unbalanced, and, in spite of ordinary and extraordinary taxes, the State's coffers were filled with an ever-increasing and ever-more-intense void. Thus, there was no hope of seeing the money to furnish the needs of the enterprise, and even less hope that it might be raised by means of some new tax—that prospect was enough to throw the inhabitants into a frightful fury, and they talked of nothing but greeting the tax-collectors with weapons in hand.

Now, a revolution for the sake of transporting a pebble, even a celestial one…

Despite the Emperor's enthusiasm for astronomy, the scientists were obliged to doubt that he would take that enthusiasm so far as to want to cut his subjects' throats. There remained His Majesty's own purse—but His Majesty was known to be fundamentally good and generous, and, at that time of the year, it was feared that his own purse would be in almost exactly the same state as the government's coffers. The scientists, therefore, felt a sweet joy bathe their souls when, having cast an glance over the estimate—which was a preliminary one—the President of the Council of Ministers had smiled condescendingly and murmured: "Good…very good…the sum is reasonable, and the moment you can guarantee success…"

"So, Minister…?" Fedor Sharp had prompted, in a voice strangled by emotion.

"So, gentlemen, you can go ahead. The government will cover the expenses…"

There was an explosion of joy. The minister's hands were grabbed to be shaken; it would not have taken much for the scientists to kiss them…and they went ahead.

While the troopers, supported by the peasants recruited for that purpose, dug a large ditch around the bolide to clear its base, mechanics got busy setting up the steam-powered cranes and all the equipment necessary for the extraction, brought from Rio by special trains. At the same time, the gigantic platform was constructed in the rapidly-erected sheds, and the trucks and wheels designed to complete the astonishing carriage were forged. Compounds were hastily established to receive the oxen that livestock traders went, not to buy, but to hire from the surrounding country, and which would then be trained to bear the yoke and pull.

After three weeks, the base of the bolide was sufficiently clear for subterranean tunnels to be dug at intervals in order to pass through the steel chains—whose links had been carefully checked, one by one, in advance. By this time, the cranes had been set up, and the platform had been constructed and hoisted on to its trucks, ready to receive its formidable burden and to be towed away.

A great deal of work had undoubtedly been done, but it was nothing compared to what remained to be done. If the author of the project had made the tiniest error, if the thickness of the chains were insufficient to resist the treble tension to which they would be subject, if a beam split, or a spring snapped, or a wheel broke…it would make all that effort, all that trouble, all that expense….

As may be imagined, the members of the congress got little sleep that night; it was at daybreak that the steam cranes would begin to function, and the scientists were up and about long before dawn, prowling around the bolide, hauling on the chains, testing the beams of the platform, even going so far as to inspect the oxen that were sleeping peacefully, sprawled in the grass.

Finally, the trumpets sounded, sending the warning notes of the reveille to every corner of the camp; in the blink of an eye, an extraordinary animation reigned in the village and its surroundings. The mechanics lit the boilers, the herdsmen started hitching up the oxen to the complicated harness—so complicated that it would take several hours, at least—and the scientists set off in the direction of the bolide, escorting the President of the Council, who had understandably requested to witness the festival. He alone seemed cheerful; all around him there were none but white faces bearing all the traces of a profound anxiety. Many of those present were doubtless sufficiently enamored of science to be willing to sacrifice one of their members, if that could possibly have averted the risk of anything happening to their beloved "pebble". Unfortunately, that was a scheme impossible of realization, and they were forced to remain still, inactive and useless, in a compact group, a few paces behind the minister.

Fedor Sharp, meanwhile, went to enormous trouble, going from the mechanics to the herdsmen, from the soldiers to the laborers, activating a machine here, adjusting the yoke of an ox there, encouraging those who plied the picks and begging the soldiers to be on their guard. The bolide was his wealth, his obsession, and he supervised its departure as if it were a matter of a member of his own family…more, even.

The difficulty, in that bold operation, was to obtain perfect harmony on the part of the 18 cranes charged with plucking the enormous block from the ground; it would only require a difference in level of one centimeter for a supporting chain to be subject to a more considerable weight than its neighbor and break. That partial rupture might cause a general rupture and a fall that would inevitably result in the slitting of the precious pebble. Just thinking about it gave the assembly of scientists the shivers.

Meanwhile, the boilers were going full blast and the steam was circulating though the pipes, working the pistons at maximum pressure.

The moment had come.

Little by little, with meticulous prudence, the chains were tightened—but before giving the signal for the maximum effort to be exerted, Fedor Sharp, escorted by the special committee for "industrial applications of mechanics and mathematics," visited each of the cranes, striking every one of the chains with steel hammers, assuring themselves that they were all rendering the same sound in response to the shock. That was the only means by which it could be ensured that the tension was equal throughout. They were, in consequence, obliged to make a few trivial readjustments—which, strictly speaking, would not have been indispensable, but how can one be too meticulous in such circumstances?

Finally, everything was ready and Sharp, the commander-in-chief of the army of workmen, was just about to give the order to begin, when a loud noise was heard in the direction of the platform. The 200 pairs of oxen, coupled five by five—not without difficulty, undoubtedly—had been there for about an hour, as motionless as if the beasts were made of bronze, every one held by a herdsman, cattle-prod in hand. As the Sun had risen higher above the horizon, though and the heat had become more intense, the oxen had become impatient and, in spite of the rings passed through their nostrils, it had become increasingly difficult to prevent them from shaking their heads, consequently jerking the yokes that linked them, which were connected to the platform. Now, it was indispensable that the latter remained absolutely still in order to receive the enormous mass for which it was designed, without even the slightest bump.

Eventually, an incident that no one had foreseen had occurred, transforming such beautiful regularity into extreme disorder. A swarm of flies that had been dormant in the grass, with their wings weighed down by dew, had been gradually warmed up by the sunlight and they rose up from the ground, buzzing and whirling around the great herd of animals, whose strong scent attracted them. The oxen began giving signs of anxiety, furious as they were at being immobilized by the yokes and thuds, so to speak, left defenseless against the attacks of their enemies. At first, they attempted to beat their flanks with their tails, moving them with the regularity of a censer in order to put the winged pests to flight—but when the flies, with their insectile intelligence, understood that they would find defenseless spots on the ruminants' heads, they came to settle impudently on the moist muzzles, shamelessly penetrating the large nostrils, pricking the heavy eyelids with their stings and clinging to wattles covered in drool. Then a sort of enormous shudder ran through the beasts comprising the gigantic team, and the platform quivered.

The bewildered Sharp came running in response to the herdsmen's cries. If a means could not be found to re-establish the absolute immobility indispensable to the success of the operation, that would be it—but Sharp, with the genius of a great captain, found that means immediately. On his orders, the cavaliers cut off the tails of their horses at the rump, and the infantry soldiers ran up, armed with those new model weapons, by means of which they set about chasing away the accursed swarm, while the laborers, abandoning their picks, hastily scythed down the long grass and heaped it up in the form of little ricks, to which they set fire. Admittedly, the torrent of smoke, driven by a light breeze, blinded the scientists, but it conclusively chased away the flies, whose stings had brought them within an inch of losing the precious bolide.

That danger averted, the perfect horizontality of the platform was re-established, with the aid of chocks slipped under the wheels, and Sharp finally gave the signal.

The steam was released from all the boilers, with a sharp whistling sound that rent the morning air and set frightened birds flying full tilt into the blue sky. The chains stretched, and it seemed for a moment that they might break under the enormous weight they were supporting, but the steel was well-tempered and the links held. Then, however, instead of the cranes lifting the bolide towards them, they, on the contrary, appeared to lean over in its direction. Their jibs bent and, for several seconds, it seemed that they were about to break.

During those few seconds, the scientists' hearts stopped beating, the blood froze in their veins and their throats, choked by anguish, would not let air into their lungs.

The anxiety was in vain; the steel of the cranes' jibs was as fine as that of the chains' links; rediscovering their elasticity under the action of the steam that was like a generous blood circulating in their metal limbs, they stood up straight again, stiffening in a supreme effort.

"It moved!" exclaimed Fedor Sharp. And even though they had seen nothing, the others cried in their turn: "It moved!"

In their turn, though, the mechanics uttered cries of alarm: the boilers were in danger of bursting.

"Let them go!" said Fedor Sharp, in a voice that hissed like the steam within its cylinders.

The mechanics opened the taps very wide; the vapor escaped tumultuously. As if they were intelligent machines possessed of souls, the cranes seemed moved by human pride in their struggle against brute matter. Like athletes who are out of breath, but nevertheless put all their remaining energy into one last supreme effort, they seemed to brace their arms of steel; the links of the chains stretched, deforming under the incredible tension, but resistant to the weight—and this time the enormous mass, incapable of resistance, surrendered.

They saw it rise up very gradually, and rise…then come entirely clear of the hole in which the violence of its fall had embedded it—and Fedor Sharp, lying flat on his belly to judge the progress of the work more accurately, watched his cherished bolide emerge from the bowels of the Earth with an anxious eye. Finally, when he judged that the base had reached the level of the platform, he made a sign. The cranes stopped, breathing hoarsely, like exhausted laborers, and everyone—scientists, mechanics, soldiers—mopped their sweat-soaked brows in unison. Every one of them had striven, as if he were pulling the chains hauling the block with his own arms.

But that was only the first part of the task; the second was perhaps the more perilous, for, its successful completion was no longer a question of mechanical force, for which the science of mathematics had been able to furnish a few prognostications; it was now a question of dexterity, skill and eyesight. The cranes were set in motion along the rails that ended at the platform; it was a matter of making them move in parallel—all in step, so to speak—without any of them getting ahead, even by so much as five centimeters, of the one opposite, under threat of destroying the equilibrium of the entire apparatus.

The President of the Council, at Sharp's request, had summoned the military band of one of the regiments garrisoned in Rio, and it was to the sound of its brass instruments and drums that the metallic battalion had to march, the steel troopers regulating their step to the big drum and the fifes.

Before chaining up the bolide, they had, admittedly, practiced this maneuver several times, and had arrived at a perfect execution—but would not the immense weight that the cranes had to support inhibit such a perfect march?

Fedor Sharp only had to give the order to begin—but if a single false maneuver were to cast down his precious pebble…

Incapable of speech, he finally made a broad gesture with his arm, and the leader of the band raised his baton; then the big drum reverberated, the cymbals crashed, the brass thundered, and 150 strident whistle-blasts were released from the boilers.

In unison, as if a magic wand had been waved, the cranes began to glide along the rails in slow motion, almost insensibly. It was a truly extraordinary spectacle to see those enormous steel arms outlined against the blue sky, drawing the enormous mass of the bolide, suspended from the chains hanging down from them.

They had scarcely 200 meters to travel thus, but those 200 meters took five hours to cover, with the scientists marching to either side of the rails, forming little groups that escorted each machine with paternal solicitude. Some chatted with the mechanics, taking an interest in the play of the pistons and the circulation of the steam in the pipes, anxious whenever the arm seemed to flex or when they thought they heard something abnormal in the grinding of the wheels. Others went even further, addressing speeches to the machines themselves, encouraging them with kind words as they would have done with a horse.

Now the bolide was suspended above the platform, and it was necessary for the oxherds to use all their muscular energy to restrain the beasts, frightened by the hum of the wheels and the hissing of the steam.

"Halt!" cried Fedor Sharp.

The military music fell silent, the cranes became still—and very gently, in response to a further signal, the chains were lowered, until the moment when the base of the bolide made contact with the platform. Then, with wooden chocks covered in rubber, the form of which was exactly adapted to the contours of the rocky mass, it was brought into perfect equilibrium on the vehicle on which it was to make its triumphal journey.

As night had already fallen, they postponed the departure until the following morning, and the workmen, as a sign of victory, amused themselves by decorating the block with foliage and tree-branches gathered in the nearby forest. And while the scientists were banqueting to celebrate that triumph of human industry, under the presidency of Fedor Sharp—standing in for the first minister, supposedly retained in Rio by important business—the first minister, taking advantage of the darkness, arrived in Las Pueblas incognito, slipped into the only posada in the region and there, in a tightly sealed room, met with an individual who had arrived as secretly as him a few minutes earlier. This individual was none other than the English tourist whose companions had sent him, in the capacity of negotiator, to the proprietors of the bradyte in order to make them the strange offer that the reader has certainly not forgotten.

"Your Excellency has my infinite thanks for getting to the rendezvous on time," the negotiator began by saying.

"What's agreed is agreed," the other replied, in a dignified fashion.

"Besides," the Englishman observed, maliciously, "isn't it tomorrow that you're supposed to make an initial payment for the work done?"

The minister grimaced slightly and nodded his head; then, in a voice to which he tried in vain to give a detached tone, which betrayed a certain anxiety, he asked: "Do you have the money?"

The Englishman took a fat wallet from his jacket pocket, which he placed on the table, and said laconically: "There it is."

A gleam of satisfaction lit up in the minister's eyes; he reached out, but the other put his hand on the wallet. "Do you have the papers?" he enquired.

In his turn, the Brazilian statesman brought out a wad of papers bearing a government stamp. "Here are the bonds," he said—and he held one out to the Englishman, who read, in a low voice: "*Bond for half a kilogram of bolide, to be delivered to the bearer by the agency of the Brazilian government, at the end of the current month.*" The Englishman started. "The end of the month!" he exclaimed. "That's a pretty long way off…"

"Impossible to bring it forward by a single day," replied the minister, in a tone that admitted no reply. "The delegates won't embark for Europe until that date, and I don't want to bring down the censure of the science of the Old and New Worlds upon myself."

"But we agreed…"

"Take it or leave it," declared the President of the Council

The Englishman remained silent for a moment, seemingly reflective; then, making up his mind, he said: "We'll have to come to an understanding with the Cook Agency, for the end of the month is also the scheduled date of our return…" He opened his wallet and took out a quantity of bills which he passed to the minister, saying: "Here's your 25,000 pounds, payable on presentation at any bank in Rio." And while the minister took the precious pieces of paper, with visible satisfaction, the Englishman reached out for the wad of bonds, saying: "May I?"

"Of course!"

Meticulously, the son of Albion began counting the bonds as if they were banknotes, one by one. At the 1000th, he released a sigh of satisfaction, then put them all in his wallet, and the wallet in his pocket.

"Now that we have nothing further to say to one another," said the minister, "I ask you permission to return to Rio; I have to take the train at 1 a.m. tomorrow in order to come back here and witness the departure of the carriage, and I don't want to excite any suspicion..."

He headed for the door, but turned round on the threshold. "Above all," he instructed, "this deal shouldn't make any noise—that would cause me the greatest annoyance..."

The Englishman having reassured him with a smile, the statesmen bowed one last time, and disappeared.

At dawn, everything was ready for the departure. The oxen, which had been bedded down where they were, and which had spent the night ruminating, were put to the yoke and the oxherds, cattle-prods in hand, waited for the signal that would set the enormous machine in motion. At the rear, the electric jacks were set up, and the electricians, at their posts, were ready to send the current into the wires, which would give the carriage a sufficient boost to get it under way.

Sharp had spent part of the night on his feet, checking the route that the vehicle would follow with a crew of workmen, rectifying any defects that might hinder its forward progress. For three weeks they had been cutting down trees, filling in ditches and laying stones on cultivated ground, in order that the platform's wheels should not sink in hub-deep under the enormous burden that weighed upon them. It had been no easy task, and would, in normal circumstances, have cost a fortune; fortunately the fever induced in the scientists by the "celestial pebble" had infected the public, and the peasants had not only consented to their fields being turned upside-down, without receiving any indemnity, but had even offered the strength of their biceps for free.

Sharp went on horseback along the track that the monumental vehicle would follow until daybreak, and he did not return to camp until the first light of dawn. Everyone was at his post, waiting for the signal to depart—which the illustrious scientist had arrogated the right to give. Having inspected his staff with a single glance, to assure him that everyone was at his post and that everything was ready, Sharp stood up in his stirrups like a colonel about to give the command to charge, and suddenly brandished his old, patched and faded blue cotton umbrella above his head.

The big drum reverberated, the brass instruments burst forth, the cymbals thundered, and the oxen, their rumps larded at the same time by a thrust of the prod, stretched their necks, bracing their backs with all their strength to lift the heavy machine, while at the rear, the electric jacks pushed with the full force of the current.

Nothing budged; one would have thought that the wheels were riveted to the ground.

The big drum reverberated more loudly, the brass instruments, the cymbals and the pistons became furious, the spikes dug deeper into the flesh of the animals, whose hides were visibly distended by the frightful torsion of their muscles, and the electricians sent a current into the jacks of sufficient intensity to melt the wires.

Then a grinding sound was heard from the axles; the entire framework creaked in a sinister fashion, giving birth to the idea that the whole thing was about to collapse—but the wheels turned, and the ponderous machine, hauled by the 400 oxen and pushed by the jacks, began to move forward. Oh, so slowly! Very slowly, for it required a double set of jacks, which the workmen placed one after another, the second ready to continue the work of the first without the progress of the rig being suspended for a single second; the oxen would not have been capable of a new effort sufficient to get the celestial pebble under way again.

Besides, what did it matter how slowly it moved forward? The main thing—the only thing—was that it did move forward, and once it had begun to move forward, it was best that it did so as slowly as possible, in order to avoid any possibility of an accident.

It is understandable that, once the first few meters were completed, that result occasioned a triumph for the promoter of the idea of transporting the aerolith to Rio; he received unending congratulations—congratulations that Sharp was the first to offer, even though the was privately enraged, considering that this success lessened his own, and that his colleague had impudently stolen a portion of his glory.

Curiously enough, as the bolide advanced, Sharp—who had, for three weeks, dedicated all the strength of his body and his mind to the success of the enterprise, which has now become evident—began to pray for some accident to happen. At the very moment when the carriage broke down, his colleague's glory would evaporate, and Fedor Sharp would remain the only victor. Even if—although Sharp hardly dared admit it to himself—the bolide were to suffer some damage, that would be preferable to a complete success. He did not expect that Providence would be disposed to grant his wishes in so complete a fashion—otherwise, the madman would surely have preferred a divided glory to the annihilation that awaited him—but man is so made that he is often the artisan of his own misfortune; he begs God to intervene in his affairs, and God then regulates matters in the interests of justice and equity.

Fedor Sharp's fury only increased as the vehicle rolled forward on the road to Rio; it reached the point at which he wished, in the absence of a material accident, that the English might intervene to stop the convoy and prevent it from going any further. The troop of Cook Agency tourists was still visible on the horizon, kept back by the government cavalry that was escorting the convoy, and Sharp, who knew nothing of the secret agreement they had made with the first minister, did not suspect that they were following his precious bolide, not to try to take possession of it, as before, but to keep track of the deposit of 25,000 pounds given to the president of the council.

There had been a brief debate about calling a halt at midday to let the men and the beasts rest while eating, but the special committee for industrial applications of mechanics and mathematics, after examining the question in depth, had declared that once the vehicle had stopped there was no guarantee that it could be started again. Sine the initial thrust, the 400 oxen would have provided a quantity of traction that would have exhausted almost half of their strength, and would certainly be incapable of starting all over again if required. It would then be necessary to have recourse to a different team, which would require not only the time to find them, but also to put them in harness—and in that case, there was no reason why it should ever end. It had, therefore, been decided that the people and the animals would take refreshments while on the march; the oxherds attached muzzle-bags full of barley to the heads of their ruminants, while the scientific company tucked into slices of cold meat set between two slices of bread as they walked.

The vehicle had been rolling along for some six hours, and had covered no more than a kilometer—which, according to the committee for the industrial application of mechanics and mathematics, was already a marvelous result—when a sinister crack was suddenly heard; it was an axle that was about to break. The carriage immediately stopped, the oxen immobilized as if by magic, and everyone looked at his neighbor with a terrified expression. What was going to happen?

They did not have long to ask themselves this question, for events undertook to reply almost immediately.

A second crack, and then a third, followed the first at one-minute intervals, and the platform subsided on the right-hand side on its pulverized wheels. There was scarcely time to release a cry of alarm before the bradyte, sliding down the inclined plane, touched the ground. Then, by virtue of its mass and acquired momentum, it tipped over.

Misfortune dictated that the ground was slightly inclined at the place where this fall occurred, following a gentle slope for a distance of about 300 meters—and those 300 meters the enormous mass traveled, rolling over and over with ever-increasing speed, crushing everything in its path: crops, trees and houses. A flock of sheep was reduced to pulp, and a little hamlet was pulverized.

The scientific company followed the furious course of its beloved pebble in consternation, trembling at every jolt it made, dreading that an accident might overtake it—and the despairing committee for the industrial application of mechanics and mathematics, feeling dishonored, discussed nothing less than going to lie down in the bradyte's path, by way of expiation.

Sharp was inwardly jubilant; his glory would remain intact, while that of his colleague and competitor would vanish—but the proverb says that misfortunes never arrive singly. Once again, events undertook to demonstrate the exactitude of that proverb; after 300 meters, there was a hedge, enclosing the property in which the accident had occurred, and that hedge skirted the edge of an excavation formed by a stone quarry presently in exploitation. That excavation was about 50 meters deep. The bradyte leapt into empty space and disappeared from the sight of the fearful scientists. Then, almost immediately, there was a dull sound like the distant detonation of several artillery batteries firing at the same time, and an immense cloud of dust rose up from the excavation, masking the landscape.

Less than five minutes later, an enormous crowd had gathered at the bottom of the hole: scientists, herdsmen, soldiers and Cook Agency tourists—who had started running as soon as they had had a presentiment of catastrophe—were all there, considering the stony mass, whose sides had split, with dazed and confused expressions.

The English, being practical people, began to gather up the debris as soon as their initial astonishment had passed, while Sharp, brought out of his inertia by that sight, gave orders to the troopers to evacuate the location and form a tight cordon of sentinels that no troublemaker could cross.

Then the recriminations began among the members of the scientific congress, everyone attempting to attribute responsibility for the accident to his neighbor. Sharp had the perfect opportunity to crush the man who had nearly lessened his glory, and for more than an hour he heaped abuse on him and his colleagues on the committee for the industrial application of mechanics and mathematics. When he had finished speaking—after having declared, in the manner of a peroration, that the names of the wretches would be nailed forever to the pillory of 19th century scientific history—he asked what ought to be done now.

One of the members present said then that, while deploring what had happened from an aesthetic viewpoint, it was not necessary, from an astronomical viewpoint, to get overly upset about it. In its previous state, the block of celestial rock had only permitted the study of its surface; perhaps it was necessary to see the hand of Providence in this unfortunate accident, which would permit the scientists of planet Earth to plunge into the entrails of the mysterious fragment.

"What joy, gentlemen and colleagues," proclaimed the worthy man, warming to his own eloquence, "if we can discover in these stony flanks vestiges of the ancient humankind that might once have inhabited the surface of the world to which this bradyte belonged. Do we not discover every day, beneath the crust of our own globe, shells, weapons and coins that permit us to reconstruct the history of our ancestors? Who knows whether we might not find similar vestiges that will reveal to us the mysteries of infinity?"

Everyone applauded—and among those who applauded most loudly, surprisingly enough, were the members of the unfortunate committee charged with investigating the practical means of transporting the famous bolide to Rio. One of them even had the audacity to insinuate that, on mature reflection, they were owed a debt for having provoked an incident from which science would profit so greatly! Sharp darted a furious glance at that one, mumbled a few unintelligible words in response to the accusation implied by that perfidious insinuation, and sarcastically proposed that the assembly should offer its formal congratulations to those of its members whose mathematical errors had produced such a fine result. The President of the Council, however, after making a heartfelt speech intended to restore concord between the members of the congress, declared that the only thing to do was to take advantage of the accident and proceed to the nomination of a special committee of investigation.

Immediately, without taking time to rest, the committee members, gripped by a fine ardor, equipped themselves with spades, picks and lanterns, and descended into the cleft in the bradyte, while the others, gathered in an improvised tent, declared themselves in permanent session under the presidency of Fedor Sharp.

It was less than an hour after the "committee of investigation" has disappeared than its members suddenly re-emerged, pale and trembling, prey to an inexpressible emotion. Everyone pressed around them, overwhelming them with questions, but their distress was so great that they were incapable of pronouncing a syllable for some time. Finally, one of them, making a violent effort to pull himself together, succeeded in saying, in a scarcely-intelligible voice: "At the bottom of the crack, half buried in the rock, we've discovered a metallic block."

"Doubtless some ore-deposit," observed Sharp.

"No—it seems to bear the signs of human fabrication."

Mouths fell open in exclamations of amazement, but Sharp, who never got carried away, retorted in a mocking tone: "I must remind our colleague that this block is a fragment of Tuttle's Comet, which is uninhabited..."

The colleague thus chided pointed to the men who had accompanied him in his exploration and replied, not without a certain sharpness: "I must remind Monsieur Sharp, however, that I am not alone in having made this observation. These gentlemen remarked, as I did—and their word, it seems to me, provides support for mine—that the block in question bears no resemblance whatsoever to a natural mineral deposit; it bears the imprint of intelligent workmanship."

"Do you deny that Nature is the ultimate intelligent artisan?" Sharp cried, annoyed by the contradiction.

"Certainly not, but I don't think, all the same, that on the surface of Tuttle's Comet, as on the surface of our own world, Nature rivets plates of metal together or fabricates screws..."

Sharp became very pale, and stammered; "You've seen rivets...and screws?"

"In addition," the scientist continued, "we can declare that we are not dealing with a solid block, but a hollow one, which resonated when struck with our picks. It even seemed to us that we could make out a manhole."

"We must open it, and get inside!" cried the President of the Council of Ministers, prey to a great excitement.

"We attempted that, in vain. As I told you to begin with, the block, enclosed in the entrails of the bradyte, has emerged therefrom in response to the impact of the fall and is buried in the ground. It will require laborers armed with shovels to dig it out."

"Get soldiers, and hurry!" commanded the minister, fascinated in spite of himself by the mysterious aspect of the adventure.

The scientists ran to fetch the troopers. As for Fedor Sharp, he felt momentarily that his legs were about to give way beneath him; his tongue was dry and his tight throat would only let the air out of his lungs in a hiss. At the same time, a steel band was squeezing his temples, to the point that he thought his skull might burst, and an enormous weight upon his bosom was stifling him. Had he dared, he would have stayed there, feeling an enormous reluctance to follow his colleagues, but instinct, rather than any clear comprehension of the situation, drive him to do as the others did. Marching, so to speak, automatically, he joined the crowd forming a circle around the laborers.

Gripped by impatience, the scientists, including the minister himself, had grabbed picks and shovels, and were lending a hand to the troopers. Sharp alone stood aside, motionless, with his back against the side of the bolide and his fingernails digging into its cracks, while the strange malaise that had taken possession of him in response to his colleagues' surprising discovery increased from one minute to the next. His eyes were riveted to the metallic mass that the picks and shovels were gradually digging out of the ground.

As its form became more distinct, he felt the frightful presentiment that had taken hold of him at the outset become more substantial. What if his victims were to be found in that envelope of steel? What if the people he had robbed and betrayed—the people he had believed lost forever in the infinity of the heavens, whose glory he was, at this very moment, usurping—were about to appear before his eyes? It was not the torture of remorse that the wretch felt, but the apprehension of justice, of punishment.

Finally, with everyone helping, the picks and shovels having done their work, the *Eclair*—for that is what it was, as the reader will certainly have realized—was detached from the rocky envelope in which it had been resting ever since it had collided with the bolide carrying Sharp in the vicinity of Saturn.

With numerous precautions—and the scientists took charge of this delicate work themselves—the apparatus was transported a short distance away. After it had been examined, palpated and ausculated, it was decided that what appeared to be the entrance to this strange container should be forced open without delay.

Under the redoubled blows of the picks, the manhole—whose screws were locked internally—was opened; then there was a great deal of jostling, everyone wanting to go in first and everyone trying to get in. They had to draw lots to select five members of the congress, charged with exploring the interior of the apparatus—and the five scientists, although a trifle pale, boldly went in.

Fedor Sharp waited, his face bloodless and his eyes bulging, motionless and breathless.

A cry resounded from the interior of the *Eclair* and a scientist emerged, carrying an inert body in his arms; it was Selena. Then Farenheit, Gontran and Fricoulet appeared in succession, and, finally, Ossipoff.

At the sight of the last-named, Sharp uttered a loud screech and put his hands to his head, as if a blow had fractured his skull, and fell to the ground, stiff.

The scientists hastened to cluster around him.

He was dead!

Chapter LXV
In which everyone is content, except Jonathan Farenheit

A veritable regiment of doctors, summoned telegraphically, had arrived in Rio during the night by special train and, without pausing for rest, had decided to proceed immediately to an examination of the "subjects." Four by four, they had filed into the large hall of the Posada, now transformed into a dormitory, where each of the voyagers lay on a good bed, motionless and apparently not breathing.

For half an hour, the doctors examined, palpated and ausculated the "subjects"—then, gravely shaking their heads, their lips mute for fear of saying something stupid, they went out, surrendering their places to the next four, who did as their predecessors had done before rejoining them in a neighboring room.

Dawn was breaking when, the procession having reached its end, almost the entire medical corps of Rio found itself united, forming a very numerous assembly of imposing appearance. They whispered in corners, in little committees, each one attempting, before giving his own opinion, to discover what others thought, for fear of committing some enormous "gaffe"—but no one dared to say anything, for fear of compromising himself. Finally, as the situation threatened to be prolonged indefinitely, someone, ashamed by the thought of the unfortunates whose fate might perhaps depend on the decision taken by the wise assembly, hazarded a few timidly-pronounced words; "Perhaps we ought to enter into consultation..."

Immediately, everyone seemed to wake up, look at his neighbor, and say: "Yes, we should enter into consultation..."

But that course, seemingly so simple, presented enormous fundamental difficulties as soon as it became necessary to pass from theory to practice. A consultation between half a dozen colleagues is already an essentially uncomfortable affair, and they numbered exactly 122—no more, no less. To reach agreement between 122 members of the faculty of Rio...

As each one, however, taking account of this difficulty—not to say impossibility—darted an anxious glance at his neighbor, one of the members present suggested convening a conference. Everyone applauded. From then on, the impossibility was vanquished, the difficulties smoothed out; it only remained to nominate a committee—which took no more than an hour and a quarter, rivalries being considerable—and then to elect a president, which only took a further hour, the complications being considerable. After that, having a committee and a president, the Assembly declared itself properly constituted and ready for deliberation—and, as it was nearly eight o'clock, and they had spent the night on a railway train and were falling asleep, the president moved to suspend the session in order that the members present could obtain a little rest. The motion was passed. Before dispersing, however, the Congress adopted the following agenda for its labors: general rest until midday; get up at noon and proceed to table; dine until 2 p.m.; come back into session afterward.

There was loud applause—but it must be admitted that the applause was no less warm and prolonged when it was proposed that the Congress declare its own permanence, until a decision was taken.

Before separating in order that everyone might go in search of a niche in which to rest, the members of the Congress nominated one of their members to take the time necessary, in addition sleeping and eating, to write a report that would serve as the basis for discussion on the resumption of the session. The president having been charged in his turn to check with the innkeeper that the menu of the meal was worthy of the medical corps of Rio, everyone went his own way. Without a thought for those for whose salvation they had been convened, the worthy doctors attempted to forget their weariness in deep sleep, while the president and their host, sitting facing one another, scrupulously elaborated the menu for the meal, and the reporter, no less scrupulously, elaborated his report.

To be fair, it ought to be said that when 2 p.m. sounded, the Congress was in session, and the echo of the chimes had hardly died away when the president gave the floor to the reporter. Very skillfully, the latter began by eulogizing the Brazilian medical corps, naming the famous doctors who had not hesitated to abandon very interesting patients in order to bring the sum of their enlightenment to the resolution of the extraordinary problem set before them, and praising the devotion of humbler practitioners who had not been intimidated by the many kilometers they had to cover in order to attempt to bring the "subjects" discovered in the aerial block back from oblivion.

It was certainly not for him, the humblest of the humble, the most modest of the modest, to make any pronouncement on the veritably unprecedented case that had been submitted to them, but he did not think it too forward of him to declare that they were beings belonging to the present generation; no more proof was required of that than the garments—or, rather, the shreds of garments—they were wearing, which seemed to testify, on close examination, to modern fabrication.

He greatly regretted that the illustrious scientist whose recent voyage had turned the scientific world upside down had died so tragically, at the very moment when his expertise might have been so greatly and incontrovertibly useful, for if—as one might suppose—the bolide that had fallen a few weeks before in the vicinity of St. Petersburg had belonged to the bradyte in which the subjects in question had just been found, Fedor Sharp would undoubtedly have been able to offer precious information, from which it would have been possible to conclude, almost certainly, in what state the unfortunates found themselves, for the present.

It was certainly not for him to examine the scientific aspects of the question; others more competent than him would do that, with a greater authority than he could possibly bring to the task—but in the final analysis, before discussing whether the beings in question were or were not alive, it was, in his opinion, indispensable to be certain about the world from which they had come, and the exact composition of the bradyte in which they had been incrusted. These facts once acquired, it might be possible, knowing in what atmospheric and climatological conditions the subjects had lived, to determine whether it was possible to revive them. For that reason, he recommended the immediate convocation, by way of telegraphy, of a corps of chemists and astronomers to examine the bradyte and analyze its composition.

Although the first part of the report was, as one might imagine, applauded, the second was greeted with a significant coldness; it was thought, not without reason, that it was scarcely flattering to the medical corps of Rio to propose that they should allow themselves to be guided by astronomers and chemists. Demanding the floor, an orator climbed up to the podium to declare, on his own behalf and that of a large number of his colleagues, that they could not, to their great regret, adopt the conclusions of the reporter, because it was in their capacity as physicians that they had been convened in order to examine the inanimate bodies and to decide whether or not it was worth making an attempt to revive them. Every one of them had filed past the subjects, studied them—summarily, it is true, but sufficiently to from an opinion—and he asked the president to take a vote on the question of discovering the particular state that the subjects were in. A vote could then be held on the question of what solution it was appropriate to apply…

All of this was said in a curt, authoritarian voice that made a great impression, and the president, judging by the acclamation that greeted the orator on his descent from the podium, that the great majority shared his view. However, when he proposed a vote by raised hands, a certain number of attendees demanded that they proceed by secret ballot. The latter motion having been adopted, every one of the 122 doctors of the Faculty of Rio mounted the podium to deposit the ballot paper on which he had summarized his diagnosis in a soup tureen that had been provided by the innkeeper to play the role of urn and set before the president.

When the count had been made, it turned out that 33 of the 122 voters had plumped for a mummification of a unique sort, which, in producing death, nevertheless left the subject the appearance of life. 15 ballots suggested that they were in the presence of a case of incomprehensible catalepsy, which could only be brought to an end when its causes were discovered. 72 ballot papers were blank.

After announcing the result of the vote, the president suggested that it was regrettable that such a large number of colleagues had not thought it appropriate to venture an opinion, however absurd, because enlightenment sometimes emerged from absurdities. They then proceeded to a second round of voting, the objective of which was to formulate a decision relative to the action to take in respect of the subjects. On this point, there was unanimity; 122 ballot papers out of 122 demanded that the subjects should be transported to Rio and placed at the disposal of the School of Medicine, in order to be submitted to "serious anatomical observation."

"A certain number of our colleagues," said the president, then, in a serious tone, "have thought it incumbent on them to vote with the majority of the assembly, even though they are inclined to think that the subjects are merely in a state of catalepsy. I suppose that I am expressing the general sentiment in congratulating them on their stoicism, for they find themselves caught in a difficult case of conscience, with regard to the life that they believe to be latent in these individuals. Can true scientists hesitate, though, when the interest of science are at stake?"

In spite of its ferocity, this little harangue was applauded wildly.

Then, one of the members of the assembly asked to speak on a personal matter, and said: "I am one of those to whom our honorable president has just made allusion in such delicate and flattering terms, and if I have mounted the podium it is merely to say that, assuming that the subjects are in a cataleptic state, nothing but a miracle could bring them back to life, given our ignorance as to the causes of that state. Now, as God alone performs miracles and we are but men, I have deemed that it is necessary for science to take advantage of a unique opportunity to study a case of sidereal catalepsy in the flesh..." He added, in a vibrant voice: "So, to the dissecting theater!"

And they all rose to their feet, waving their arms in the air, to repeat, like an echo: "To the dissecting theater!"

At that moment, the door of the hall opened. Fricoulet appeared on the threshold, pale and weak, clutching the door-frame with both hands in order not to fall, and stammered, in a hoarse tone that caused a supernatural sensation: "Bravo, gentlemen! Except that you've forgotten to ask our permission!"

A sudden lightning-bolt could not have produced a more radical effect; for a second, the 122 scientists were immobilized, their features frozen as if gorgonized, their eyes bulging in fear, their mouths opened by cries of anguish that had choked in the throat on passing through. Then, suddenly, a cry emerged from all the throats at once, revealing the horror that this sudden apparition has caused, and the doctors ran in a mad stampede to the doors, the windows and anything else that might be susceptible to use as an exit, in order to put themselves beyond the revenant's reach.

In less than a minute, the hall was empty.

Fricoulet burst out laughing—but this laughter, the first he had uttered since his return to Earth, echoed so strangely in his ears that he shuddered, feeling a disagreeable frisson run through him from his feet to his head.

"Brrrr!" he said. Pivoting on his heels, he went back into the room in which his traveling companions, lying on their bunks, conserved the immobility that encouraged the belief that they were dead. "Poor friends," murmured the engineer. "They've had a narrow escape. But for me, they'd have been lying on the dissection table within 24 hours."

He looked around and saw a shelf above the counter, on which a respectable line of bottles was visible, containing liquids of various colors.

"There's more than enough there to bring a dead man back to life!" He hoisted himself up on the counter and consulted the labels. He took a bottle of rum, which he uncorked, and from which he swallowed a large mouthful. After that, slightly cheered up, he headed for the bunks.

He stood still for a moment, looking to the right and the left, seemingly indecisive with regard to the choice he had to make—but his indecision did not last long; he went to Selena and gently parted the young woman's lips in order to trickle a few drops of alcohol between her clenched teeth. Leaning over her, lifting her upper body with one arm while he used his free hand to dampen her forehead with a rum-soaked handkerchief, he followed the progress of Selena's resurrection in her features, with poignant anxiety.

To begin with, there was only an imperceptible quiver in the facial muscles; then the bosom swelled slightly, sending a slight breath through the pale lips—so slight that it would scarcely have lifted a bird's feather. Fricoulet felt that breath on his cheek, though, and it drew an exclamation of joy from him. "Selena…my dear Selena," he murmured.

Almost immediately, however, he blushed at his audacity and darted an anxious glance at Gontran, as if the latter were capable of hearing him. Then, brought back to reality by the sight of his friend, he released a sigh of regret and his radiant face darkened.

Beneath the young woman's dull skin, however, it seemed that the blood was circulating again; a light rosy tint soon appeared in her cheeks, rendering an appearance of life to that poor face, previously the color of wax. The bosom began to rise and fall more obviously under the regular action of the lungs, and the lips recovered their former redness. Finally, the eyelids, after fluttering several times, came half-open and her gaze, vague for several seconds, suddenly lit up as it focused on the engineer.

"Monsieur Fricoulet!" the young woman stammered.

Intoxicated by joy, Fricoulet seized her hand and covered it with kisses, stammering: "Mademoiselle…oh, Mademoiselle!"

Although she had recovered consciousness, Selena, as one may imagine, had no sense of reality—so, looking around in surprise, trying to take account of the new objects that surrounded her, without being able to do so, she murmured the classic phrase employed by everyone emerging from a faint: "Where am I?"

"On Earth, Mademoiselle," exclaimed Fricoulet. "We're on Earth…finally!"

Then the memory of beings who were dear to her returned to the young woman and, her throat choked by anguish, she cried: "Father! Gontran!" Perceiving the old man and her fiancé lying side by side, she let herself slump into the engineer's arms, half-fainting, and stammered: "Dead! Oh, my God!"

"No, no, don't worry—it's the same with them as with you...at least, I hope so..."

With a forceful effort, Selena had got up, finding in her filial affection the strength necessary to triumph over the weakness that threatened to render her unconscious. "Take care of Monsieur de Flammermont," she said. "I'll look after my father." And with an energy of which one would not have believed the poor child capable, having been numbed by a death-like catalepsy only a short while before, she set about rubbing the old man's limbs, as Fricoulet had done for her.

The engineer employed the same procedure with Gontran as he had with the young woman: rum introduced between the contracted lips, rubbing the face with an alcohol-soaked cloth and massaging the chest to re-establish the action of the lungs. As with Selena, his efforts were crowned with success.

The most curious thing was that Farenheit came back to life at the same time as the young Comte, without anyone's assistance. The odor of the alcohol had doubtless stimulated his olfactory nerves in a very particular fashion, for, obedient to a sort of instinct, as if he were in a somnambulistic state, he reached for a liter of rum positioned within arm's reach and swallowed almost all of its contents in a single draught. The rapid absorption of such a large quantity of alcohol produced in his stomach, deprived of alcohol for such a long time, the effect of a powerful reactive, which provoke an almost instantaneous resurrection—and that resurrection was initially manifest in a formidable sneeze, which burst forth like a cannon-shot, making the room's windows tremble.

"By God!" the American exclaimed, with a start, not having realized that he was the author of the explosion. "By God—the *Eclair*'s exploding!" With one bound he was out of his bunk, but the state of extreme weakness that had numbed him like death for several weeks made his limbs buckle so abruptly that he became motionless, quite amazed, looking around in bewilderment. "Monsieur de Flammermont!" he appealed. "Monsieur de Flammermont!" But he stopped short, passed his hand over his forehead, and started laughing, adding: "Damnable dream! For I'm surely dreaming...that window...that counter...those chairs...all this isn't the *Eclair*..."

He opened his eyes wide, looking at the groups formed by Selena beside Ossipoff and Fricoulet beside Gontran, unable to imagine that he was not the victim of a nightmare that was showing him his traveling companions in close proximity. However, as he still had the liter of rum in his hand, he lifted the mouth of the bottle to his nose, sniffed vigorously, and exclaimed: "By God, though...this is real...I'm not seeing things!" He extended his hand toward the engineer. "In the name of God, Monsieur Fricoulet," he begged, "I entreat you..."

As he spoke these words, Gontran came to—and, exactly like the American, began by doubting reality. Fortunately, a most opportune incident tore away the veil shrouding his brain and forced him to admit the truth. Outside, a buzz of voices was heard, increasing by the second, suddenly attaining a powerful intensity. At the same time, the shutters were suddenly flung open and a pyramid of human heads, heaped one atop another, appeared behind the windows. It was the entire population of the village, augmented by the inhabitants of the surrounding countryside—who, alerted by the flight of the terrified doctors, wanted to see with their own eyes what truth there might be in the alleged resurrection. When they had perceived the travelers standing up next to the bunks, on which some of them had previously seen them lying, the miracle was obvious to everyone's eyes, and a loud exclamation uttered by hundreds of throats proved to Farenheit's and Gontran's ears that, this time, they really were treading on the soil of their native planet.

The American did not so much run as fly to one of the windows, opened it wide and, brandishing his cap at the full extent of his arm, howled with all his might: "Hurrah! Hurrah!" And the enthused crowd, which had initially taken a prudent step backwards, repeated after him: "Hurrah! Hurrah!" Then a religious silence fell; they were waiting for him to make a speech.

Nature, however, momentarily numbed, suddenly reasserted her rights; the American's speech was very short, and was limited to this: "Food! Drink!"

Like a flock of sparrows put to flight by the detonation of a forearm, the villagers scattered in all directions; almost instantaneously, Farenheit found himself alone in the frame of the wide-open window. He went back to his companions then. The first effusions of joy having passed, Gontran and Fricoulet had joined forces with Selena to bring Ossipoff round.

The old man's resurrection was slow, though. In three years, the brain had slain the body, the plough had worn out the furrow, and now that the will had been numbed—perhaps killed—the limbs, having lost their master, were no longer obedient. By means of energetic friction, however, and by virtue of patient and skilful insufflations between the discolored lips, the bosom eventually rose up almost imperceptibly, and Selena, who was leaning over her father's livid face, suddenly straightened up with joy in her eyes.

"He's breathing!" she exclaimed.

"Shh!" said Fricoulet, putting a finger to his lips. "No excitement!" He continued to massage the old man's chest gently, while Gontran rubbed his temples with rum and Selena used her handkerchief as a fan to direct slightly fresher air on to his face.

Little by little, these efforts were compensated; the lungs resumed their natural action, the eyelids were raised, the gaze moved from one to another, and Ossipoff eventually asked, in a cavernous voice: "Who's looking after the engine-room?" Receiving no response, he added, trying to get up: "I'll set a course for Ursa Major…I want to see...I want to know…" He stopped, put his hands to his breast in a dolorous gesture, and stammered: "I'm in terrible pain…"

"Hunger, of course," said the American.

A gleam lit up in the old man's pupils. "Yes, yes…you're right, Farenheit…but the larder's empty…" Then a flood of tears sprang from his eyes. "Oh, my daughter…my friends…how guilty I feel! Forgive me, forgive me, for having thrown you into this mad adventure. The stars! They were too far away…and we're condemned to die of hunger."

As he finished these words, a loud noise became audible from the direction of the door, which eventually opened under a violent pressure, giving passage to a crowd of brave souls who had been looking at the travelers from outside a short while before. Under the guidance of the innkeeper, they had come back loaded with provisions; one bore a basketful of grapes on his head, another held bottles of wine in his arms, a third was paying homage with a leg of mutton, a fourth, somewhat poorer, had divided in two the loaf of bread intended for his family….

They paraded in front of the bewildered travelers, cheering, and deposited their gifts on the floor, which ended up as a heap of victuals formed into a rampart. Each of the voyagers had to shake the hand of each of the donors, and when the last one had gone out, the innkeeper stayed behind on his own to set the table. "Well," he said, while laying out the plates, "it's made quite a noise, your adventure—which is to say that I'll be able to make money out of you. There's talk of organizing pleasure trips out here…and as my inn is the only one in the vicinity…"

He was speaking Portuguese, and as Gontran had been attached to the French legation in Lisbon for several months while he was in the diplomatic corps, he asked: "Pardon me, my friend, but would you care to tell us where we are?"

The innkeeper looked at him with wide eyes; then he burst out laughing, exclaiming: "That's true! You can't possibly know. Well, you're in the establishment of Antonio Pajares, innkeeper in the village of Rocca, 25 kilometers from Rio…"

"Rio!" cried Gontran. "Rio de Janeiro?"

"The very same…"

Gontran turned to his companions and translated the Brazilian's reply into French.

Farenheit performed an entrechat. "America! We're in America!" He hurled himself on Gontran, shook his hand so frantically that the bones cracked, and said, in a tone he made every effort to render serious: "Thank you…thank you, my dear Monsieur de Flammermont, for that delicate attention—but while you were at it, you might as well have steered the *Eclair* to the United States…"

Fricoulet burst into loud laughter. "Why not to New York itself? Fifth Avenue…to your second-floor landing…?"

While joking, however, the engineer was thinking hard, racking his brains in vain to understand how he and his companions came to be in America, on Brazilian territory, a few kilometers from Rio. By what miracle had they crossed so rapidly, in order not to die of starvation, the trillions and trillions of leagues separating the regions of Ursa Major from their native planet? Even assuming that the velocity with which the *Eclair* had been animated during its journey through the sidereal desert had been multiplied tenfold, or even a hundredfold—he had no idea how—it would have taken them hundreds of years, and…

He looked at his traveling companions one after another; they appeared to him just as he had left them the previous evening, with the exception of Ossipoff, whose face bore traces of excessive mental strain…

Even admitting the inadmissible fact that the vehicle had been animated by a velocity that it was impossible for the human imagination to comprehend, however, by consequence of what circumstances, contrary to all the laws of physics and mechanics, had the *Eclair* not been first liquefied on penetrating the Earth's atmospheric zone and the smashed on colliding with the planet's surface?

That was what the engineer was thinking, with his head in his hands, while his companions—Gontran and Farenheit, at least—did full honor to the meal. Ossipoff, his expression vague and his hands slack upon his knees, maintained a dejected immobility, indifferent to the caresses that his daughter lavished on him.

"Aren't you hungry, Alcide?" said Flammermont, suddenly, having appeased his initial appetite and noticed his friend's thoughtful expression.

The engineer shivered, as if snatched abruptly from a dream, and replied, while throwing himself upon the plate set in front of him: "Yes…yes, of course…" And he set about eating, silently.

Suddenly, as the innkeeper came back in, Farenheit said to Gontran: "Would you be so kind as to ask that man to bring me a railway timetable?"

A few moments later, the American was leafing through the requested timetable, making notes in pencil, calculating the itinerary to be followed, noting down hours of departure and the connecting trains. "By God!" he ended up saying, in a discontented tone. "I can't leave before tomorrow morning…"

"Leave?" asked Fricoulet. "For where?"

"For New York, of course! You weren't thinking, by any chance, that I had any intention of staying in Brazil?" He scribbled a few hasty lines on a leaf torn from his notebook. "Would you care to oblige me again," he said to Gontran, "by asking the innkeeper whether there's a telegraph here?"

The man having replied in the negative, Farenheit added: "Does he know someone in the village who can take this dispatch on horseback to the telegraph in Rio?"

This time, the innkeeper extended his hand in a perfectly clear gesture, the embarrassed American stammered: "My dear Comte, would you happen to have any money on you?"

"Of course not—no more than you or Fricoulet."

Farenheit was rummaging in his pockets mechanically, although he knew very well that he would find nothing there, when his eyes suddenly lit up and his mouth formed a broad smile. At the same time, he took something from the breast pocket of his waistcoat, which he showed to Fricoulet, holding it between his fingertips.

"What?" said the engineer, interrogatively, putting out his hand.

The American opened his fingers to let the object he had been holding fall into his interlocutor's hand; it was simply a screw, as thick as his little finger and three centimeters long.

"So what?" asked Fricoulet, turning the screw over and back again.

"How much does that weigh, approximately?"

"My god." The engineer weighed the object in his hand. "I don't really know—in the 200...about 250 grams..."

The American took back the screw and deposited in the hand of the bewildered innkeeper, saying to Flammermont: "Explain to this man that it's for the delivery..."

Gontran studied Farenheit, then looked at Fricoulet, and murmured: "He's mad!"

"It's you who are mad!" retorted the American. "That screw comes from the *Eclair*'s engine-room...it's lithium. Now, on Earth, according to Monsieur Fricoulet, lithium is worth about 70,000 francs a kilogram, which gives that screw a value of almost 14,000 francs—to take a dispatch to Rio! I don't think the man is being robbed!"

Fricoulet shook his head. "The innkeeper wouldn't understand," he murmured. "Besides, it would be dangerous if he did understand, for that would set rumors going, and we'd risk being robbed."

These simple words sufficed to bring a frown back to the American's face; he took back the screw from the innkeeper's extended hand and put it in his pocket. He detached his watch, a superb gold chronometer, which he held out, while Gontran explained that the item was being entrusted to him as a guarantee of payment."

The man bowed deeply and was about to leave when Gontran—still serving as an interpreter, but this time on Fricoulet's behalf—asked him to bring some newspapers.

"What's in that dispatch that's so important," the engineer asked, "that you were ready to pay the commissionaire such a considerable sum?"

"I'm announcing my arrival in New York for the day after tomorrow and convening a general assembly of the shareholders of the Selene Company Limited."

"Why?"

"To render an account of my mandate and to declare that they'll be reimbursed to the last dollar, thank to a share in the profits from the sale of the *Eclair*."

Fricoulet lowered his head toward his plate. The *Eclair*! He dared not make poor Farenheit party to his anxieties, but he was exceedingly fearful that it had been liquefied or volatilized in passing through the atmosphere, or reduced to impalpable pieces on making contact with the ground.

Meanwhile, the innkeeper had brought the newspapers. There was a respectable quantity of them because the doctors, in the haste of their departure, had forgotten those they had brought with them to break the monotony of the journey from Rio. They were of every sort, format and language: large and small, political and scientific, dailies and illustrated weeklies, in Portuguese, English, French, Russian and so on—and all of them were almost exclusively occupied with the famous aerolith that had turned the entire scientific world upside down.

"Right!" said Fricoulet, his face radiant with a smile of satisfaction. "That's what I need!" He had just found a Rio newspaper printed in French, which gave the most elaborate details of the event.

Farenheit, for his part, had taken possession of all the English and American papers, leaving Gontran to read the Spanish and Italian ones. As for Ossipoff, he listened distractedly to Selena, who was reading to him in a low voice from a Russian scientific review.

"That's it!" Fricoulet suddenly exclaimed, giving the table a forceful thump with his fist. "I understand now!"

They all interrupted their reading and looked at the engineer

"What do you understand?" asked Farenheit.

"How we got here—when, logically, mathematically and scientifically, we should be millions of leagues from Earth."

At these words, a glint lit up in Ossipoff's dull eyes, and his gaze seemed to come to life.

Gontran, struck by the observation, exclaimed in his turn: "That's right! And then again, by what miracle weren't we volatilized in the nebula in Scutum Sobieski?"

Fricoulet looked at his friend, laughing—albeit sardonically—and replied: "By a very simple miracle, my dear Gontran, which you'll understand. We aren't still in Scutum Sobieski because we never went there."

It seemed that these words had produced the same effect on Ossipoff as a forceful whiplash applied to his calves; he stood up as if moved by a spring. Gripping the edge of the table with both hands, his upper body leaning forward as if he wanted to hurl himself upon the engineer, at whom he directed a fiery stare, he repeated: "Never went! You dare to say that..." He stopped short, shrugged his shoulders and turned to say to his daughter, Gontran and Farenheit: "He's mad, I swear!"

Fricoulet, however, contented himself with shaking his head, still smiling. "Eh? The maddest of you all is not the one you think."

"What do you mean?" exclaimed the old man, who appeared to have recovered all his vigor. "Do you dare to say that we haven't been to the Moon, or the planets, or..."

The engineer did not let him continue. "If you'll permit—don't put words into my mouth that I haven't said and that I had no intention of saying. I made no mention of the Moon, or the planets, small or large..."

"Ah!" sneered the old man. "You concede Jupiter, Saturn, Uranus..."

"No—there I stop you, Monsieur Ossipoff, for I don't concede Uranus..."

The old man folded his arms, in an attitude of profound indignation, and cried: "What! You dare to deny..."

"That we've been to Uranus? Exactly."

The others surrounded the engineer, very near to believing, as Ossipoff seriously believed, that the unfortunate fellow was mad.

For his own part, taking account of the sentiment that was moving them, Fricoulet could not help laughing. "Exactly," he repeated. "I deny Uranus and all the rest of our voyage."

"Oh, indeed!" Gontran protested, in his turn. "So you no longer remember..."

"Yes," the engineer replied, slyly, "I remember the treason of Monsieur Ossipoff, taking advantage of our sleep to take us out of the asteroidal current and launch us into infinity..." The old man lowered his head, somewhat ashamed "...And the accident to Monsieur Farenheit's eye..." The American searched for the bandage wrapped around his forehead, and seemed very surprise not to find it. "...And your dream about Loie Fuller, to whom you were married..." It was Gontran's turn to turn his head away to avoid Selena's reproachful gaze. "...And Monsieur Ossipoff's cerebral crisis," Fricoulet went on, "and the famous duel that Monsieur de Flammermont and Mr. Farenheit were to fight immediately after returning to Earth..."

Selena uttered a cry of terror, while the two adversaries suddenly drew apart, sensing the reawakening of the resentment that the vicissitudes of the voyage had put to sleep. "Oh," said Fricoulet, laughing, "you have nothing to fear, Mademoiselle, and you, my dear friends, can gladly shake hands...for your altercation only took place in a dream."

"In a dream!" they exclaimed, in unison.

"Assuredly, since it was in a dream that we accomplished our sidereal voyage..."

There was general astonishment.

"Come on," said the engineer. "Do you recall what happened as we passed close to Saturn? The question had been urgently raised as to whether we should continue our voyage in order to take advantage of the asteroidal current that was carrying us, or whether we should run the risk of landing on the planet, and coming back thereafter as best we could…"

"Perfectly," declared Farenheit. "I recall those details all the more clearly because you had locked me in my cabin and I was spending my time with my ear glued to the door in order to overhear what was said."

"It was then," Fricoulet continued, "that Monsieur Ossipoff discovered a new star in the constellation Cassiopeia, which Gontran declared, after careful observation, to be a bolide—and further specified by adding that the bright dot identified by Monsieur Ossipoff as a snowy mountain was nothing other than the vehicle serving as Sharp's habitation…"

A trifle humiliated, the old scientist muttered: "*Errare humanum est…*"

"That's precisely what I replied to you later, on the subject of my drawing of Ursa Major," said Gontran, delighted to have his revenge.

Ossipoff darted a covert suspicious glance at his intended future son-in-law, but said nothing more.

Then Farenheit, his memory completely refreshed by what the engineer had just said, exclaimed: "I remember very well! Since it was me who came out of my cabin, when everyone else was asleep, to put the *Eclair* back on track after it had been brought to a halt, in order to let the bolide in question pass…"

"Well," Fricoulet continued, "the *Eclair* ran head first into the bolide with such force that it ploughed right into it, but without sufficient force to go all the way through and come out on the other side." Addressing himself to Flammermont, he added: "Do you recall that frightful nightmare whose story you told me? It wasn't a nightmare at all, it was reality—and while our spirits were wandering through space, continuing the veritably incoherent voyage dreamed by Monsieur Ossipoff, our bodies, fallen into death-like coma and having the *Eclair* for a tomb, resumed the road to Earth, in the bolide that was carrying Sharp…" He added, with a slightly wry smile: "That's how it comes about that we're on our native planet today, when we were trillions of leagues away three days ago."

Ossipoff had seized his head in both hands, with the natural gesture of those who hear incredible things, and he stammered: "Impossible…impossible…impossible…"

"But what's impossible, my dear Monsieur," retorted Fricoulet, "is what we dreamed—that we really accomplished that fantastic voyage. Besides, you have only to read what Fedor Sharp said—you'll see that his story coincides absolutely with the events of which I've just reminded you…" And he stuck the newspaper he was holding—which gave as complete an account as possible of the events with which the scientific world had been occupied for several months—under the old man's nose.

Ossipoff was then forced to yield to the evidence and, struck in the heart by the demolition of the sublime dream that he had had, he uttered a groan and fell back on his chair, prey to a veritable collapse. His daughter hurried to his side, lavishing many caresses upon him and trying to find arguments to console him. It was in vain; his face remained distraught, and he maintained a desperate silence.

It was at that moment that the innkeeper came into the room. "Senhor," he said, addressing Gontran, "the Cook Company's tourists are asking if they might have the honor of paying homage to you as soon as possible."

The young man's eyes widened. "The Cook Company?" he repeated, in total surprise. "What's that?"

"Here, read this," said Fricoulet, holding out his newspaper, which devoted an entire column to the cut-price excursions organized by the famous Agency, known today throughout the world, to permit the curiosity-seekers of the Old World to come and see the monstrous bolide in which everyone in the world was so interested.

"We've been reduced to the status of curious animals!" cried the young Comte. To the innkeeper, he said: "Let them go look at the bolide—they can do that as much as they want, but they must leave us in peace..."

At that moment, Fricoulet burst into loud laughter and pointed at the window, behind which a mass of heads was visible, coiffed in the strangest and most various manner, whose round-eyed and open-mouthed faces expressed the most ardent curiosity and the most extreme surprise. "These gentlemen are getting a sneak preview," the engineer quipped. "For the moment, though, that's all we can allow them. Let them go look at the bolide...that will help them be patient."

"Unfortunately," replied the innkeeper, "even that consolation is not permissible, for the government has been obliged to post a double line of guards around the field in which the cart tipped over. Every one of the tourists wanted to carry off a fragment of the bolide as a souvenir..."

Fricoulet pretended to look frightened. "Quick, Monsieur Innkeeper," he said. "Close all the doors and windows! These gentlemen are capable of cutting us up into little pieces in order that they might also have a souvenir of the famous voyagers." Then, directing the man toward the door, he added: "Leave us in peace."

Feeling a tug on the sleeve of his coat, he turned around and found himself face-to-face with Farenheit. "You know, Monsieur Fricoulet," murmured the American, "I've a strong desire to take a turn around the *Eclair*. What if these brigands take it into their heads to sell it?"

"Pooh! Given that he's just told you that there are guards..."

"All the same, I'd prefer to watch over it myself."

The engineer shrugged his shoulders and said: "As you please, my dear chap—but if I were you, I'd wait until nightfall; otherwise, you'll be followed like a curious animal..."

The American displayed his fist. "That's for anyone who takes it into his head to look at me too closely..." That said, he put on his cap and took a billiard cue from the rack, which he twirled between his gnarled fingers with a skill that boded ill for the curiosity of the Cook's tourists, and went out.

Meanwhile, Ossipoff's dejection had finally yielded to his daughter's caresses and consolations. The latter, in order to cheer him up slightly, had also put an argument to him which, if not in scrupulous conformity with the truth, was nevertheless perfectly logical: since Sharp was dead, there was nothing to fear from any further lies on his part. The voyagers had only to reach an agreement to deny the story the scientist had told his colleagues and the newspapers. He had claimed that the bolide carrying him was a fragment of Tuttle's Comet. What proof was there that he had told the truth? What prevented Ossipoff from affirming, on the contrary, that the *Eclair* had encountered the bolide in the vicinity of Antinous or Scutum Sobieski?

That was a lie, evidently—but who would the lie hurt? No one—except Fedor Sharp's reputation, to which it would, in truth, do considerable damage. But was not Fedor Sharp the least of men? Was it not him who had condemned Ossipoff to the mines, in order to steal his glory? And had he hesitated to deceive him again on the Moon and steal the apparatus that would permit him to continue the sidereal voyage he had begun? And on his return to St. Petersburg, with what audacity had he played the charlatan, beating his own drum, attributing to himself the glory of having been the first to conceive such an adventurous project?

"No, Father dear," Selena said, by way of conclusion, "the more I think about it, the more convinced I am that you may use this innocent fraud. Who knows, even, whether Providence, by inspiring me, might be making use of us to punish that traitor Sharp posthumously?"

In pronouncing these words, the young woman had displayed an energy that she had previously employed on very few occasions, even in the moments when the numerous vicissitudes of the voyage had brought her and her companions to within inches of death. This was because poor Selena had a very good grasp of the situation. He filial love gave her an inkling of what was passing through her father's mind, and a terrible anguish gripped her at the thought that the annihilation of the marvelous dream that had lulled him for months might put him in his grave. While Fricoulet was explaining their presence on Earth so simply, she had seen the troubling transformation that had overtaken the old man very clearly; it was not so much the sudden pallor that had invaded his features that had struck her as the expression of sadness, discouragement and desperation that had suddenly taken possession the old man's gaze—and she had said to herself that if she could not find a means of drawing her father out of the comatose state into which he had plunged, one way or another, his brain might give way to that fit of despair. It was then that the idea of the fraud had come to mind, and she had employed all her eloquence in selling it to Ossipoff.

As docile as a child, the latter yielded to the arguments invoked by his daughter, although he murmured: "To what celestial world might that bolide belong?"

Delighted to see him submit to her reasoning, the young woman exclaimed: "Don't worry about that: it's an unimportant detail, which we can settle later." She turned to Flammermont, who was chatting with Fricoulet, and called: "Gontran!" Immediately, though, recalling the role that the young man was playing, she corrected herself. "No—not you—Monsieur Fricoulet..." Then, judging that the rectification might astonish Ossipoff, she added: "Oh! If both of you..."

Gontran pulled a face and came over, seemingly annoyed. Fricoulet, in response to the young woman's appeal, had covered the distance in a single bound.

"Messieurs," said Selena, then, "Sharp is dead and, if the newspaper can be believed, he would have sought to appropriate to his profit all the glory that belongs to my father. Do you think that it would do any great injury to that wretch to present as a real achievement the conclusion of the voyage that we only made in a dream?"

"Not in the least!" exclaimed Fricoulet. "He was a scoundrel! And then, as long as it might please you that Monsieur Ossipoff has penetrated Antinous, Ursa Major, Scorpius and so on, I see nothing inconvenient...we can all have gone there, if you wish..."

Smiling, the young woman stopped him with a hand gesture, while Gontran, surprise by such strange enthusiasm, looked at his friend, pursing his lips.

"A thousand thanks, Monsieur Fricoulet," said Selena, "but there's no need to exaggerate..."

"Oh, a little more, a little less..." Flammermont objected.

She glanced at him in surprise, and went on: "All the more so as we still have within us the sensations experienced during the long dream we had—and thus, it's almost the truth we'll be telling. Except..."

"Yes," the engineer put in, "Except that it's the bolide that brought us here, isn't it? That's what you're asking."

Mutely, Selena nodded her head.

"That can no longer be, as Sharp affirmed, a fragment of Tuttle's Comet; its orbit extends no further than the large planets, and we can't claim to have arrived on its back from the ultimate depths of space." As he pronounced these words, Fricoulet twisted the few wispy hairs ornamenting his chin enough to tear them out, seeing by that painful means to excite his cerebral matter. "Damn!" he murmured. "Damn!"

Both of them—he and the young woman, that is—were still standing there, looking one another in the whites of the eyes, with Gontran slightly to one side, playing distractedly with his monocle, when the door opened and the innkeeper came in.

"Gentlemen," said the latter, "there are some 50 people here asking for the honor of a private interview."

The two young men could not help bursting into laughter. "That's a request that seems to me to be difficult to grant in the circumstances," said Gontran. "50 people! That's no longer being received in private!"

"Your Lordship will excuse me," the innkeeper replied. "You haven't understood—or rather, I've expressed myself badly; these people are asking for private interviews one after another."

Fricoulet started. "But that'll take all day and part of the night!" he exclaimed. "And we aren't zoo animals!"

"Excuse me, Senhor—the gentlemen asked me to give you their cards." And the worthy fellow handed a small stack of printed cards to the engineer, who started in surprise.

"Aargh!" he murmured. "The press!" He continued in a low voice, rapidly reading out the names: "*El Correo del Brazil, South American Messenger, Der Brazil, Le Moniteur des Intérêts Français à Rio, Gazatta Brasiliana, Bresil Novosti...*" He stopped there, thoughtfully, playing mechanically with the little cards.

"You don't intend to grant an audience to all of them, I suppose?" Gontran sniggered.

"My father's in no state to receive them," said Selena in her turn.

"Possibly not," replied Fricoulet, shaking his head, "but given what you asked of me a moment ago, Mademoiselle, it might be that receiving these gentlemen would enable us to accredit the legend with which you desire us to glorify your father's name."

A gleam ignited in Selena's pupils. "In that case," she murmured, "if you think..."

"That's settled, then," said the engineer. "We'll get on with it right away." To Gontran, he said: "Come with me. You can come to the rescue if I flounder..."

"I'm not a very good liar," the young man replied, making a face.

The engineer looked at his friend with comical amazement. "No!" he said, after a moment's pause. "Are you saying that seriously?"

"Seriously..."

"In front of us!" Fricoulet burst out laughing, and put his hand on Gontran's shoulder. "Come on, old chap. You don't think that. You don't know how to lie! But that's what you've been doing for the last three years!"

The young Comte blushed, then went pale; his brows contracted and a nervous tremor—an indication of scarcely-controlled anger—made his lips quiver.

"Anyway," the engineer added, "I don't need you—if I asked for your help, it was more to give you a role to play in the little comedy than because I had any need of your specialist knowledge..."

"No, of course not!" Gontran complained. "I've had enough of role-playing. I've been on stage for three years..."

Selena looked at him, then murmured, softly: "If it weighs too much upon you, my friend..."

Fricoulet shrugged his shoulders, and said, in a sullen tone: "I'm going to receive my visitors." He went out, shutting the door carefully, so as not to awaken Ossipoff, who had dropped off.

Left alone, Selena and Gontran looked at one another silently for a few moments. She seemed sad; he appeared to be embarrassed. Both of them felt, in fact, that an explanation was necessary. There had been an unease between them for some months that they could not quite explain, but which now gave them a disquieting glimpse of the future of which they had dreamed.

Eventually, Flammermont uttered a sigh of resignation, as one does when, having deliberated carefully, one has made a decision. "Selena," he said, in a low voice, "I need to talk to you."

He took her hand and drew her gently to the far side of the room, into a window bay, where he sat her down in a chair. He sat down facing her, retaining her hands in his. "You don't doubt the sincerity of the affection that I had for you, do you?" he said.

"That you *had?*" she repeated, reproachfully

"That I still have," he corrected, hastily.

"I would be the most ungrateful of women, Monsieur de Flammermont," she replied, seriously, "if I forgot that, for me, you have abandoned your career and all those friends and relatives who were dear to you."

"When one loves truly, Selena, the woman beloved takes the first place in one's heart, and it is not upon the ostensible sacrifices I have made that I base my affirmation of the sincerity of my devotion to you."

Her eyes widened in astonishment.

"It's on the forgetfulness of my dignity."

"Your dignity!"

"Little by little, I let myself be drawn into playing a role incompatible with my character, and at length, in spite of myself, my self-esteem has diminished."

She put her hand together and exclaimed: "Oh, Gontran! Affection excuses everything."

He shook his head, and aid, in a firm voice: "The moment has come when it is necessary to crown an uninterrupted sequence of comedies and lies. Well, frankly, Selena, I don't think I have the courage to go any further along that road."

"You're sick of it?" she said, sadly.

"Sick of lying, yes. God knows, though, that after so long a course of instruction, my heart is as full of you as on the first day—and yet, the happiness that I have pursued beyond the extraordinary worlds of space, that happiness that I only have to reach out my hand to grasp, I must refuse, if, in order to have it, it is necessary for me to lie again."

The young woman lowered her head and maintained a silence full of affliction.

"Believe," he cried, "that I'm sincerely heartbroken by the pain I have caused you, but, before even my honor, which is at stake, before even my own happiness, it's your own happiness that I'm protecting."

She sighed, and stammered: "My happiness, alas!"

"This comedy that I have been playing for so long, with your affectionate complicity and the no less amicable collaboration of Fricoulet, excusable on the part of a man in love, would not be appropriate to the dignity of a spouse. I cannot see myself continuing, after our marriage, this deceptive existence via-à-vis the old man who will have given you to me. I cannot see myself obliged to blush before my children, if it pleased God to give me any." He took her hands again, and looked her full in the face. "Come on, be frank: am I right?"

"Very much so, alas."

"Oh, if, once the marriage was concluded, that would be the end of all these subterfuges, if I could become myself again, if it were never necessary to make any further allusion to the past..."

"You know that's impossible!" she replied, sharply. And, after a brief silence, she added, by way of explanation: "Everything you've just told me, Monsieur de Flammermont, I've been telling myself for some time. Perhaps I haven't examined the situation, as you have, from the viewpoint of your dignity...but I've thought about what life would be like once we were married. Many a time, without letting you see my sadness, I've noticed signs of impatience in you when my father, duped by both of us, was talking to you about things that were dear to him, and I ended up asking myself whether you would be able to continue making all the efforts that you were making to contain yourself, in order to have me for your wife, once I belonged to you."

As these words seemed to imply an interrogation, Gontran replied: "My God, a man is only human, you know...and that role had been weighing upon me for such a long time, in order that I might be engaged..."

"Oh, but I have nothing to ask of you...besides, I have told you several times, the love that I have for my father takes priority over any other sentiment, however strong it might be. I would sacrifice anything to the happiness of the years that still remain to him on Earth...and I've sworn to dedicate myself to his glory, so that when he is gone, his name will not die completely..."

Although emotional, the young woman had pronounced these words with a firmness that testified to an immutable resolve.

"It would be an insult to you, my dear Selena," Gontran said, "to address the slightest praise to you regarding such fine sentiments. You're a dutiful woman, just as I'm an honorable man. Let us part, therefore, bidding farewell to the future of happiness we glimpsed, and each go our own way."

He stood up, but without letting go of the young woman's hands, as if it seemed to him that the separation would not be truly definitive until that amicable grip was dissolved.

"What are you going to do?" she murmured.

He forced a smile, and replied: "Diplomacy awaits me..."

As he spoke, enthusiastic shouts burst forth outside, in the midst of which the name of Ossipoff resounded continually.

Waking up with a start, the old man stood up, straightened his legs, and—in spite of the weakness of his limbs—ran to the window.

In the courtyard, 50 individuals were shouting, in competition with one another, waving their hats and caps above their heads, while Fricoulet, standing at the top of the stone steps at the posada's entrance was also shouting at the top of his voice: "Long live Mikhail Ossipoff! Long live Mikhail Ossipoff!" Then he made a deep bow, which the individuals returned—after which he went back into the house, while the others went into the street, putting the notebooks and pencils wit which they were armed back in their pockets.

"Well, that's done!" exclaimed the engineer, arriving like a gust of wind in the room where Selena and Gontran were standing to either side of Ossipoff, holding him up as he seemed about to faint with joy. "What a success! Oh, you can sleep peacefully—there are 50 stout fellows charged with proving to the entire world that you've arrived from Scutum Sobieski—and even further away, if you like..."

The old man's tremulous hands extended toward Fricoulet. "Oh, young man, young man!" he stammered. "How can I ever thank you...?"

Gontran cut him off. "Monsieur Ossipoff," he said, "why not entrust my friend Fricoulet with the job of continuing what he had started so well? You'll be assailed by visitors, interviewers, letters...you won't be able to do everything, and, unfortunately, I'll be obliged to absent myself for some time—I have a family and friends in France that I have to reassure..."

"And doubtless also the Academy, to which you won't be displeased to communicate the result of our voyage," said the old man, suddenly smitten in the heart by jealousy.

"Have no fear, my dear Monsieur; I give you my word of honor not to open my mouth on that subject except to pronounce your name. To get back to Fricoulet, he'd be able to give you a great deal of help by replying to unwelcome requests and helping you write your memoirs."

"Hmm!" murmured Ossipoff, incredulously. "Will he be able to do it?"

The engineer pointed at the window. "Haven't you just seen how I handled that business?" he said. "Believe me, it won't be any more difficult to enthuse scientists than journalists."

The old man look at the engineer. "So you're beginning to love astronomy, Monsieur Fricoulet?" he asked, smiling.

"Oh, Monsieur," exclaimed the young man, enthusiastically, putting his hand on his heart and bowing to Selena, "how could anyone not love the stars?"

The young woman, embarrassed, turned her head away and led her weary father back to his bed—while Fricoulet, totally surprised, murmured in Gontran's ear: "What does that mean?"

Then, in a slightly sad voice, in spite of the smile playing upon his lips, Flammermont shook his head and said: "She's free."

"Really?" exclaimed the engineer, seizing his friend's hands.

At that moment, a loud noise became audible outside, like laughter mixed with jeers, but above which frightful oaths burst forth.

"That sounds like Farenheit's voice!" said Gontran, running to the window.

Fricoulet had only just joined him when a party of policemen came into the courtyard, in the midst of which Jonathan Farenheit was shouting and gesticulating, brandishing the billiard cue that he had taken on leaving to serve as a walking-stick, as if it were a truncheon.

The two young men ran out of the room and hurried into the courtyard, which was filling up with a company of villagers serving as an escort for the policemen.

"Farenheit!" cried Fricoulet, running toward the American—but he stopped a few paces away, frozen by the strange stare that his traveling companion fixed upon him.

"Oh, the poor wretch!" he said, taking a step back. And to Gontran, who interrogated him, he replied laconically: "Mad!"

The American had not recognized his name when it had been pronounced; even his eyes, although fixed upon the two young men, no longer recognized them, appearing not to have seen them. Suddenly, though, as if he had only just seen them, he flew into a frightful rage and hurled himself upon them, weapon in hand...

"Bandits! Thieves!" he howled, striking out at the policemen, who had seized him immediately. "One unfastens stars, sun, planets and nebulas for you...in order for you to take them..." And straining toward them, he spat in their faces: "Thieves! Thieves!" Then, his excitement fading, he began tearing his hair and weeping. "What about the shareholders in the Selene Company? What about the Eccentric Club?" But he began to laugh, singing and dancing. "I'm Ossipoff! It's me who's the scientist! Ah, you can take my lithium...I have the stars and the suns to sell on...I've a complete cargo of them...I'm rich...rich...!" He threw his cap into the air and caught it again, like a ball.

Fricoulet had seen correctly at first glance; Jonathan Farenheit had gone mad. But how had it happened?

Quite simply: the scientists, who had placed a cordon of troops around the bradyte to prevent anyone from stealing any of it, had completely neglected to protect the *Eclair* from the avid covetousness of the Englishmen—with the result that the latter had fallen greedily upon the lithium apparatus, which they had taken apart as rapidly as a column of ants strips the flesh from the corpse of an animal. When Farenheit, after leaving the posada, had reached the field where, according to the directions he had obtained on the way, he ought to have found the apparatus on whose value he had founded such great hopes lying on its side, he had seen a few metal fragments scattered on the ground, while the last Cook Agency tourists were disappearing in the distance.

It was as if he had received a violent hammer-blow on the skull; losing his head, he had run after the thieves and, having caught up with them, had knocked down half a dozen—but he had succumbed to the weight of numbers, and the policemen had arrived just in time to prevent a regular lynching.

That was why the shareholders in the Selene Company Limited, robbed for the first time by Sharp, never recovered their money, and why the Eccentric Club was deprived of the most extraordinary president of which its members could ever have dreamed.

THE END

Afterword

In the footnotes distributed through the text, I have attempted to clarify some of the numerous oddities contained in the original text of *Aventures extraordinaire d'un savant russe*, but a few supplementary remarks might usefully be made.

Most of the errors and confusions littering the original text undoubtedly arose from the mode of composition of the text, which appears to have been that commonplace among contemporary *feuilletonistes*—which is to say that the text was hurriedly dictated to an amanuensis by an author who frequently forgot what he had previously said, and whose reading of the proofs, if they were read at all, was cursory. There are, however, several other categories of errors and confusions that seem, for various reasons, to be more interestingly problematic.

Although there is no way to be sure, and the two credited authors might conceivably have taken turns to fulfill the office of dictator, the substance of the text suggests that the published draft may well have been entirely the work of Georges Le Faure, embellishing a rough draft provided by Henri de Graffigny. Had de Graffigny been in charge of producing even a part of the publication draft, he would surely have taken far more care with the scientific and mathematical data that are so horribly mangled in that version (to an extravagant extent that I have felt obliged to conceal to some degree in this translation). The evolution of the text also suggests that Le Faure might have become increasingly unsympathetic to the material provided by his collaborator, not only making progressively less effort to integrate it into his own melodramatized narrative, but increasingly using arguments between the characters to express his own opinions—for instance, the opinion that continual recitations of the number of double stars contained in each constellation of visible stars are as tedious as they are pointless. Whether this is true or not, however, there is no doubt that the text undergoes a drastic change of outlook in the course of its evolution, and that, by the time the story ends, it has come to embrace and embody ideas markedly different from those it embraced and embodied at the beginning—to the extent that it actually subverts and betrays its own initial prospectus.

To begin by considering errors of a relatively trivial sort, the most evident of the many continuity errors afflicting the text are those confusing the story's chronology. Although some of these flaws presumably result from mere memory lapses, others seem more deep-seated, and might well result from the two authors' divergent opinions regarding the appropriate pace of the narrative. For instance, if one counts back from the first explicit date recorded in the text—March 1882—it appears that the earlier action must all have taken place in 1881, although internal evidence of its earlier phases suggests 1880 as a likelier date. Had the plot really been unfolding in 1881, it is highly unlikely that no mention would have been made of Tsar Alexander's assassination in March of that year, which would have been highly relevant to Ossipoff's condemnation and imprisonment.

Considering the events of the plot objectively, it seems highly improbable that all the developments taking place between the crash-landing at Nice Observatory and the launch of the shell from Cotopaxi's crater could have been accomplished in the five months claimed by the text, in the run-up to March 1882. The likelihood is, therefore, that Le Faure simply skipped a year of the original time-frame in order to hurry the narrative along. A similar inclination to hurry through events on the Moon and Venus might then have got the characters too far in advance of the original time-scheme to facilitate their crucial encounter with Tuttle's Comet—whose return date was fixed, albeit somewhat inaccurately—with the consequence that the date in question seems far in advance of the pattern of events described.

Once 1884 becomes the reference-point for subsequent events, the overall chronology of the plot is primarily disturbed by incoherent observations relative to the ages of the characters, although the fragment of Tuttle's Comet carrying Fedor Sharp has to be given an arbitrary and highly improbable boost to its velocity and a tacit amendment to its course in order to fulfill its subsequent narrative functions, and estimates of the supplies of air and food remaining to the various voyagers have to be continually amended and fudged. The net result of these fudges is that the final sequence of the published text has to take place in 1885, although it is unlikely that the final sequence was planed in advance as a kind of alternative history. The likelihood is that the original scheme was planned to end in the near future of the novel's publication date—although any plan of that sort would, of course, have been brutally torpedoed by the folding of Edinger's publishing company and the long delay between the issuing of volumes three and four of the original version.

Given that the references to Loie Fuller prove that the final draft of the fourth volume had not been written when Edinger went out of business, it would not have been unduly surprising to find a shift in attitude between the third and fourth volumes, or an increase in continuity errors due to the long lapse in composition. It is, therefore, slightly surprising that the text's most abrupt and most crucial change of direction occurs long before that publication-gap, mid-way through volume three of the original text, in the chapter in which the voyagers, having survived a near-fatal close encounter with a turbulent Jupiter, approach Saturn.

In that chapter, after conscientiously laying narrative groundwork necessitating a landing on Saturn, the text takes a lurching sidestep, as the characters suddenly (and nonsensically) opt instead for a fly-past—whose consequence is a seemingly-arbitrary and direly implausible collision with the remnant of Tuttle's Comet, which has no possible business being in that vicinity at that time. At that point, the narrative appears to change its nature completely, suddenly becoming a very different sort of animal, in flagrant contradiction to its own initial ambitions. Whether or not this abrupt change of direction resulted from some kind of explicit quarrel between the two authors is impossible to determine, but it certainly resulted from a conflict, and a fundamental incompatibility, between the two agendas that the authors were presumably brought together to combine: the popularization of science and the concoction of an exciting narrative.

Most readers—both contemporary and modern—would undoubtedly have felt disappointed by the authors' decision not to allow the characters to determine whether their conjectures about life on Saturn were correct or not. They would have been equally disappointed by the extraordinarily tentative nature of Sharp's observations of Uranus and Ossipoff's observations of Neptune, which take great care not to give the reader any information that could not be obtained from Camille Flammarion's *Les Terres du ciel.* This new policy—in striking contrast to the passages describing natural conditions and life on the Moon, Venus, Mercury and Mars, all of which go far beyond the cautious warrant provided by *Les Terres du ciel*—is taken to a further extreme in the sequence describing the voyagers' excursion beyond the Solar System, whose informative content is crudely paraphrased from Flammarion's *Les Etoiles*, mostly decanted into the text in expository lumps, with hardly any attempt to make productive narrative use of it.

There is, of course, a sense in which this policy of expository dumping—however awkward and annoying it might be in narrative terms—is actually much more in keeping with the text's determination to conform to the limits of contemporary knowledge than the fanciful sections describing the humanoid inhabitants of the Moon, Venus and Mars. Although the data relating to Uranus and Neptune contained in the text has been shown to be slightly inaccurate by subsequent scientific inquiries, it was all in strict accordance with what was known at the time. That apparent determination to stick to the confines of the known does, however, appear to defeat the whole object of the hypothetical voyage. If the characters are not allowed to find out anything about the outer planets that is not already known to Earthly astronomers, what is the point of going there? Is it not exceedingly implausible, in fact, that an examination of those planets at relatively close range, even if no landings are attempted, would not produce a single new item of information? Hindsight informs us that, at the very least, Ossipoff and his fellows could not have failed to discover that all of the outer planets had more satellites than had so far been discovered, and that Uranus also has rings like Saturn's. The authors could not possibly have known that, however, and any guesses they made would have been far more likely to be wrong than right, just as the guesses they did make in respect of the inner planets—despite being extrapolations that seemed to them to be logical from data that seemed to them to be reliable—can now be seen, in the light of subsequent discovery, to be ludicrous.

The strange combination of the over-reaching speculation of the early chapters and the stubborn conservatism of the later ones provides, in sum, a striking illustration of the fact that would-be writers of hard speculative fiction always were and still are in a no-win situation. At a distance of 120 years, the modern reader can see with vivid clarity how impossible it was for de Graffigny and Le Faure to get *anything* right. By sending their characters to the surfaces Moon, Venus, Mercury and Mars, they committed themselves to describing conditions on the surfaces of those worlds, and even though their speculations—assisted but not limited by speculations that Camille Flammarion had already offered—were partly based on scientific data that were at least arguable, if not proven, the series of concrete guesses they made was wrong in every last detail. As diviners of reality and anticipators of discovery, they recorded a score of zero—exactly the same score, it should be noted, as almost all of their contemporaries.

Lest the slight modification of the last sentence should lead to undue inferences, it might be as well to include a note here about the exceptions. Most of the correct guesses regarding conditions on other worlds recorded in the relevant era were negative ones, such as the supposition that the Moon was, exactly as it appeared to be, an airless and lifeless world devoid. Such guesses are, inherently, not speculative but anti-speculative. Although, anti-speculative guessers are right far more often than speculative ones, in crude terms of the number of hits they score, they too fall down by throwing the baby out with the bathwater; the policy of denying all potential discoveries asserts, intrinsically, that the *status quo* will endure forever—which, of course, it never does, even on the most limited timescale. In this instance, a score of zero is more creditworthy than a positive score accumulated entirely by the denial of possibilities.

The authors' speculations were only partly based on scientific data because they were also partly based on the principles of narrative interest—but here, too, the reader is entitled to judge that they did not score much more than zero. Narrative interest assesses the inhabitants of other worlds in terms of their melodramatic potential: exoticism tending to frank monstrousness; challenge tending towards outright or insidious hostility; exemplification tending towards allegorical imputation. These priorities are, however, not merely different from those implicit in painstaking extrapolation from scientific data, but contradictory to them; scrupulous extrapolation and thrilling melodrama pull in opposite directions. As allegedly-conscientious would-be writers of hard science fiction, Le Faure and de Graffigny were, from the very outset, trying to serve two different masters, with little possibility of satisfying either.

Le Faure (assuming that the manufacture of narrative excitement was his responsibility) initially attempts to solve this problem in a fashion that many subsequent hard sf writers were to adopt; he refrains from making his other-worldly "humankinds" hostile, manufacturing melodrama entirely from conflicts between human beings and natural disasters—but that policy has an inevitable cost, in that it makes the otherworldly humankinds fade into the narrative background, becoming anodyne and unengaging, rather than remaining the focus of attention, as they surely ought to be. A further contribution to the same effect is that the characters cannot actually learn anything from the Selenites and the Martians that they do not already know, because the authors have no possible way of knowing what that "unknown knowledge" might amount to. Again, the reader is perfectly entitled to wonder what point there is in the characters meeting scientifically-advanced Martians if their own science is only augmented in ways that are unexplained to the reader—but that, alas, is yet another no-win situation for would-be writers of serious speculative fiction.

It seems likely that Le Faure and de Graffigny underestimated the extent of the problems they would face when they set out on their project, which they presumably did in a spirit of courage and optimism—but it is easy for the reader to see, as the text progresses, how badly dented and crushed that courage and optimism became. If the experience of reading the text is, in the end, frustrating and disappointing for the reader, how much more frustrating and disappointing must it have been for the authors? No one could have been more sharply aware of the evasions, compromises and adjustments to which the plot is continually subject than the person who actually had to compose the final draft—and the reader must bear in mind that the person in question was not only writing a longer text of this sort than had ever been attempted before, but a longer text than any that would ever be attempted for at least 100 years. (The very few sf novels longer than the *Aventures extraordinaires* that now exist are conspicuously lacking in hardness, using every trick in what was, by the time they were composed, a highly elaborate arsenal, to avoid the narrative pitfalls into which the present text falls time and time again.) It is hardly surprising, given that he had undertaken to run a marathon without ever having attempted it before, that Le Faure not only became exceedingly leg-weary but began openly cursing the unwisdom of ever having made the commitment.

Having said all that, though, it has to be admitted that de Graffigny and Le Faure did not entirely confine themselves to inevitable errors. If many of the false steps taken by the authors resulted from the imperfections of late 19th century science and the impossibility of extrapolating accurately therefrom, some significant ones also arose from the imperfections of their own understanding of what was accurately known, and from the essential stupidity of their extrapolation of their own misunderstandings. The most serious of these misunderstandings, from the viewpoint of a novel about space travel, is perhaps their misunderstanding of the principle of rocket propulsion—one of several unfortunate corollaries of a seemingly more fundamental incomprehension of Newton's laws of motion. De Graffigny and Le Faure think that, rather than being impelled by the force of reaction, a rocket needs something to "push against." Curiously enough, this mistake does not make them assume—as it caused some other speculators to assume—that a rocket-propelled craft would be utterly useless in space, but it does cause them to employ the rocket-powered *Eclair* in a very strange fashion that remains unique in the annals of speculative fiction.

In order to take the *Eclair* to the region of the outer planets, the authors borrow and amplify to an absurd extreme the notion that periodic meteor showers afflicting the Earth are caused by streams of particles following cometary orbits. In order to give the vessel something to "push against," they elaborate one such imaginary stream into a kind of "cosmic river" densely packed with tangible particles. When they have to expand the scale of their narrative by a further order of magnitude, however, they are forced to make another imaginative leap. In the first draft, this leap might have been taken by assuming, in all seriousness, that if the *Eclair* accelerates to a sufficiently high velocity, it can "push against" the etheric fabric of space itself—but in the published text that assertion is made manifestly ludicrous by the corollary notion that the propellant used to achieve the high velocity in question will be the vessel's supply of compressed air. That suggestion is passed over very quickly, the authors evidently being aware that it is simply too embarrassing for words, even in the context of the hallucinatory dream into which the narrative has recently been converted.

Because we only have the published version to study, we have no way of knowing exactly when the authors decided to convert the final phases of the narrative into a dream, but the move gives every evidence of being a belated improvisation—a desperate attempt to salvage some semblance of plausibility in a narrative that had become too obviously absurd. The decision is certainly half-hearted; the text makes no attempt to take advantage of the additional imaginative freedom tacitly granted by visionary fantasy, except for a few brief passages explicitly represented as dreams within the dream. Indeed, the reverse is the case; it is when the visionary fantasy begins that the authors' speculative imagination narrows dramatically, restricting itself to the mere ham-fisted exposition of data derived from telescopic observation. When they began, they must surely have intended the latter part of their characters' voyage to be as concrete as the earlier phases, and they must have been disappointed in themselves—if, in fact, they were both involved in the decision—when they decided that they simply could not support such a pretense. (Interestingly, the characters decide that they can and will maintain exactly that pretence, although the author of the final chapter is careful not to explain how they propose to do it.)

However belatedly it was made, and however absurd it might seem, the narrative move that turns a substantial part of the story into a mere dream inevitably demolishes any claim that might otherwise have been made on behalf of the *Aventures extraordinaires* to be the first significant account of faster-than-light travel authentically couched as "hard" scientific romance. (There had, of course, been previous accounts explicitly cast as fanciful thought-experiments, the most significant being included in Flammarion's *Lumen.*) The story does, however, conserve its status as a hopefully-coherent and developing narrative, maintaining the semblance of a plot around and alongside its expository dumplings. Although the characters have no further plausible engagement with the actual substance of the universe on the outskirts of and beyond the limits of the Solar System, they continue to engage in their private and personal battles, which retain a curious substantiality of their own, of a kind conspicuously absent from other cosmic visionary fantasies.

Even in the admission that it *was* a dream, the authors did make a significant attempt to rationalize their text—unlike Jules Verne in *Hector Servadac*, who was content to leave it to his readers to contend with the seemingly-paradoxical question of whether or not Servadac's entire adventure had been hallucinatory. Furthermore, the dream sequence that completes the voyage detailed in *Aventures extraordinaires* is, in some ways, more significant to the development of the novel's characters than any of the "actual" adventures preceding it, in a fashion that might be construed as a remarkable anticipation of Sigmund Freud's theory that dreams are expressions of wish-fulfilment. It is not until the dream sequence begins, in fact, that the five central characters begin to reveal themselves in their true colors, as previously-repressed desires burst through the restraints of the unconscious, emerging into positive thought and action. It is when the dream begins that Ossipoff's astronomical fascinations reveal the insanity and ugliness of their excess, while Gontran gradually discovers that he is not, after all, committed to the project of loving and marrying Selena; Fricoulet discovers that his opposition to that marriage is by no means as principled as he had contrived to convince himself that it was, and Selena slowly acquires both realizations. Intriguingly, Farenheit, who was quite mad before "reality" gave way to "fantasy," is restored by that transition to a state of relative mental stability—which can only endure, of course, until the dream ends.

Seen in this light, the novel's eventual decay into visionary fantasy is not quite the pusillanimous failure of nerve that it might seem at first glance. There is more honesty in it than mere cowardice—and more honesty, too, than there is in the apparent bravery that eventually made faster-than-light travel a staple of science fictional narrative and dishonestly brought the universe of stars within the apparent grasp of narrative "hardness." David Ketterer has pointed out that Edgar Allan Poe's "Unparalleled Adventure of Hans Pfaall" makes more sense if one regards it as a visionary fantasy rather than a failed attempt at verisimilitude, and that it is easily interpretable as a particular form of visionary fantasy that was still unidentified in Poe's day: a "posthumous fantasy," in which a character has a protracted fantasy experience at the point of death, not realizing until the fantasy reaches its climax that he is, in fact, dead. In Ketterer's reading, Pfaall's balloon blows up as it lifts off, and the rest of the story is a purer expression of the aeronaut's hopes and imaginative daring than any real journey could ever have provided. It is tempting to read both Verne's *Autour de la lune* and the *Aventures extraordinaires* in a similar fashion, given that we know perfectly well (as Verne and de Graffigny must have known too, had they been honest with themselves and their readers) that the inevitable consequence of being shot out of a giant cannon—or a volcano—would be instant death. Given what we now know about its speculative failures, in fact, can we any longer read the *Aventures extraordinaires* in any other way than as a beginning-to-end hallucination, interesting because rather than despite its visionary quality?

This kind of retrospective reinterpretation process, once started, need not and ought not to stop in the 19th century. Whatever the aficionados of hard science fiction might allege, the sad fact is that our current scientific knowledge assures us that faster-than-light travel is literally impossible, and that no amount of ingenious jargon can paper over that crack in its verisimilitude. There is a sense in which all accounts of travel to the outer limits of the Solar System and beyond are pure and irreducible fantasy, better regarded from a logical viewpoint as dreams—albeit dreams lavishly decorated, if only internally, with rational as well as psychological logic—than as hard-headed items of speculation. In that sense, *Aventures extraordinaires d'un savant russe* is not merely honest but prophetic, anticipating the entire spectrum and thrust of 20th century science fiction, with its determined but ultimately hopeless quest to add substance to the myth of a galactic Space Age.

In addition to mention of the errors produced by the authors' misunderstandings of current science, it might also be useful to say something more about the textual consequences of diplomatic omission. The clearest example in the text—footnoted at the time—is the omission of any mention of the possibility birth-control in the argument regarding the necessity of warfare on Mars, but this a specific example of a more general avoidance of unspeakable topics. Although a great deal of its speculation is cribbed directly from the pages of Camille Flammarion, one element of Flammarion's speculative thought that is not reproduced is his open championship of evolutionary theory. In *Lumen*, Flammarion's careful extrapolation of the notion that organisms evolve by adapting themselves to their physical circumstances enables him to offer a dazzling array of images of genuinely alien extraterrestrial life, just as Restif de la Bretonne had earlier done in the cosmic vision sequence of *Les Posthumes*, although he carefully moderated his penchant for reckless invention in *Les Terres du ciel.* There is, however, hardly any trace of any similar concretization in the *Aventures extraordinaires*.

Le Faure and de Graffigny do mention environmental adaptation, and they do make some effort to suggest that it would be a key principle in shaping life on other worlds, but they are very careful not to offend religious sensibilities by asserting that other worlds might harbor intelligent species not made in the same supposedly-divine image as terrestrial humankind. The sensitive reader might well take the inference from certain oblique hints that Alcide Fricoulet, at least, is an evolutionist and atheist, but there is no way the narrative voice is ever going to say so explicitly, or allow him to make any such formal declaration. The novel had, after all, been explicitly advertised as an educational work suitable for children. It is for that reason, rather than any strict adherence to theologically-based assumptions about the necessity of otherworldly life reproducing a progressive ladder that could only go beyond humans to produce angels, that the *Aventures extraordinaires* is so modest in its depictions of extraterrestrial life; even so, the modesty is there, and it did place a severe restriction on the adventurousness of the text.

There is one last oddity about story told in the *Aventures extraordinaires* that seems to me to be worthy of some afterthought, and that is the deliberately contradictory manner of its conclusion. It is something of a cliché, and only a slight overstatement, to say that 19th century novels typically end with a marriage and an enrichment (usually an inheritance or the discovery of a treasure); the *Aventures extraordinaires*, by contrast, ends with the definitive breaking of an engagement—in favor of a career in diplomacy—and a drastic impoverishment, by ironic courtesy of Thomas Cook's consumerization of travel. To some extent, the motive for this double violation of narrative norms is satirical, Le Faure (who was surely responsible for it) deciding to end the novel in a comical vein by mocking and slyly subverting what might well have been de Graffigny's initial pretensions, but there is a further propriety to it that is no less significant for the fact that he was probably blithely unconscious of it.

Marriage and enrichment qualify as "happy endings" providing "realistic" narratives with a satisfactory sense of closure precisely because they are the fundamental lures offered by everyday life—they are, in essence, ringing endorsements of the essentially satisfactory nature of the status quo. Speculative fiction is, however, logically and philosophically opposed to the satisfactoriness of the status quo; it is fundamentally committed to the necessity of change, the elaboration of knowledge, and the quest for new and further horizons of achievement. No matter what readers might expect or demand, it is an act of quintessential moral cowardice for a scientific romance or science fiction novel to end with a marriage and/or an enrichment—and Le Faure sensed that, even if he was probably not fully conscious of it. Whatever reason he actually had for choosing his ending, it was definitely the correct choice, in both moral and narrative terms. If only more science fiction novels had grasped that nettle as firmly as they grasped the nettle of domesticating such facilitating devices as faster-than-light travel and extrapolating the implications of evolutionary theory, the genre might have stood a slightly better chance of avoiding its gradual decay into a dispirited *fondu* of fear, cowardice, diplomacy and consumerism.

Whatever its faults—and they are admittedly legion—*Aventures extraordinaires d'un savant russe* did attempt to put up a measure of resistance to that eventuality, and is worthy of both attention and congratulation because of it.

Brian Stableford

BLACK COAT PRESS

M. Allain & P. Souvestre. *The Daughter of Fantômas*
Anicet-Bourgeois. *Rocambole*
Guy d'Armen. *Doc Ardan: The City of Gold and Lepers*
Aloysius Bertrand. *Gaspard de la Nuit*
A. Bisson & G. Livet. *Nick Carter vs. Fantômas*
Félix Bodin. *The Novel of the Future*
Lucien Dabril. *Rocambole*
V. Darlay & H. de Gorsse. *Lupin vs. Holmes: The Stage Play*
C.I. Defontenay. *Star (Psi Cassiopeia)*
Charles Derennes: *The People of the Pole*
Alexandre Dumas. *The Return of Lord Ruthven*
J.-C. Dunyach. *The Night Orchid: Conan Doyle in Toulouse*
J.-C. Dunyach. *The Thieves of Silence*
Paul Féval: *Anne of the Isles*
Paul Féval. *The Blackcoats: The Companions of the Treasure*
Paul Féval. *The Blackcoats: The Invisible Weapon*
Paul Féval. *The Blackcoats: The Parisian Jungle*
Paul Féval. *The Blackcoats: 'Salem Street*
Paul Féval. *Captain Phantom*
Paul Féval. *Gentlemen of the Night*
Paul Féval. *John Devil*
Paul Féval. *Knightshade*
Paul Féval. *Revenants*
Paul Féval. *Vampire City*
Paul Féval. *The Vampire Countess*
Paul Féval. *The Wandering Jew's Daughter*
Paul Féval, *fils*. *Felifax, the Tiger-Man*
Emile Gaboriau. *Monsieur Lecoq*
Arnould Galopin. *Doctor Omega*
V. Hugo, Foucher & Meurice. *The Hunchback of Notre-Dame*
O. Joncquel & Theo Varlet. *The Martian Epic*
Jean de La Hire. *The Nyctalope on Mars*
Jean de La Hire. *The Nyctalope vs. Lucifer*
Jean de La Hire. *Enter the Nyctalope*
Steve Leadley. *Sherlock Holmes - The Circle of Blood*
Maurice Leblanc. *Lupin vs. Holmes: The Hollow Needle*
Maurice Leblanc. *Lupin vs. Holmes: The Blonde Phantom*
Gustave Le Rouge. *The Vampires of Mars*
Jules Lermina. *Panic in Paris*
Gaston Leroux. *Chéri-Bibi*

Gaston Leroux. *The Phantom of the Opera*
Jean-Marc Lofficier. *The Katrina Protocol*
Jean-Marc & Randy Lofficier. *Edgar Allan Poe on Mars*
Jean-Marc & Randy Lofficier. *Robonocchio*
Lofficier. *Tales of the Shadowmen 1: The Modern Babylon*
Lofficier. *Tales of the Shadowmen 2: Gentlemen of the Night*
Lofficier. *Tales of the Shadowmen 3: Danse Macabre*
Lofficier. *Tales of the Shadowmen 4: Lords of Terror*
Lofficier. *Tales of the Shadowmen 5: The Vampires of Paris*
Xavier Mauméjean. *The League of Heroes*
William Patrick Maynard. *The Terror of Fu Manchu*
Frank J. Morlock. *Sherlock Holmes: The Grand Horizontals*
Marie Nizet. *Captain Vampire*
C. Nodier, Beraud & Toussaint-Merle. *Frankenstein*
Charles Nodier. *Lord Ruthven the Vampire*
G. de Pawlowski. *Journey to the Land of the 4th Dimension*
Henri de Parville. *An Inhabitant of the Planet Mars*
John William Polidori. *Lord Ruthven the Vampire*
P.-A. Ponson du Terrail. *The Vampire and the Devil's Son*
Albert Robida. *The Clock of the Centuries*
Eugène Scribe. *Lord Ruthven the Vampire*
Brian Stableford. *The Germans on Venus*
Brian Stableford. *News from the Moon*
Brian Stableford. *The New Faust at the Tragicomique*
Brian Stableford. *The Shadow of Frankenstein*
Brian Stableford. *Sherlock Holmes - The Vampires of Eternity*
Brian Stableford. *The Stones of Camelot*
Brian Stableford. *The Wayward Muse*
Villiers de l'Isle-Adam. *The Scaffold*
Villiers de l'Isle-Adam. *The Vampire Soul*
Philippe Ward. *Artahe: The Legacy of Jules de Grandin*
P. de Wattyne & Y. Walter. *Sherlock Holmes vs. Fantômas*
David White: *Fantômas in America*